(more)

Peter Straub

Ghost Story

PUBLISHED BY POCKET BOOKS NEW YORK

*For Valli Shaio
and Gregorio Kohon*

POCKET BOOKS, a Simon & Schuster division of
GULF & WESTERN CORPORATION
1230 Avenue of the Americas, New York, N.Y. 10020

Published by arrangement with Coward, McCann & Geoghegan, Inc.
Library of Congress Catalog Card Number: 78-27120

ISBN: 0-671-82685-9

First Pocket Books printing April, 1980

10 9 8 7

POCKET and colophon are trademarks of Simon & Schuster.

Printed in the U.S.A.

Contents

The chasm was merely one of the
orifices of that pit of blackness
that lies beneath us, everywhere.

—*The Marble Faun,*
    Nathaniel Hawthorne

Ghosts are always hungry.

—R. D. Jameson

Prologue

Driving South

1

What was the worst thing you've ever done?

I won't tell you that, but I'll tell you the worst thing that ever happened to me . . . the most dreadful thing . . .

2

Because he thought that he would have problems taking the child over the border into Canada, he drove south, skirting the cities whenever they came and taking the anonymous freeways which were like a separate country, as travel was itself like a separate country. The sameness both comforted and stimulated him, so that on the first day he was able to drive for twenty hours straight through. They ate at McDonald's and at root-beer stands: when he was hungry, he left the freeway and took a state highway parallel to it, knowing that a drive-in was never more than ten or twenty miles away. Then he woke up the child and they both gnawed at their hamburgers or chili dogs, the child never speaking more than to tell him what she wanted. Most of the time she slept. That first night, the man remembered the light bulbs illuminating his license plates, and

3

though this would later prove to be unnecessary swung off the freeway onto a dark country road long enough to unscrew the light bulbs and toss them into a field. Then he took handfuls of mud from beside the road and smeared them over the plates. Wiping his hands on his trousers, he went back around to the driver's side and opened the door. The child was sleeping with her back straight against the seat, her mouth closed. She appeared to be perfectly composed. He still did not know what he was going to have to do to her.

In West Virginia, he came awake with a jerk and realized that for some seconds he had been driving in his sleep. "We're going to pull up and take a nap." He left the freeway outside of Clarksburg and drove on a state road until he saw against the sky a red revolving sign with the words PIONEER VILLAGE on it in white. He was keeping his eyes open only by will power. His mind did not feel right: it seemed that tears were hanging just behind his eyes and that very soon he would involuntarily begin to weep. Once in the parking lot of the shopping center, he drove to the row farthest from the entrance and backed the car up against a wire fence. Behind him was a square brick factory which manufactured plastic animal replicas for display—for Golden Chicken trucks. The factory's asphalt yard was half-filled with giant plastic chickens and cows. In their midst stood a giant blue ox. The chickens were unfinished, larger than the cows and dully white.

Before him lay this nearly empty section of the lot, then a thick cluster of cars in rows, and then the series of low sandstone-colored buildings which was the shopping center.

"Can we look at the big chickens?" the girl asked.

He shook his head. "We're not getting out of the car, we're just going to sleep." He locked the doors and rolled up the windows. Under the child's steady unexpectant gaze he bent over, felt under the seat and drew out a length of rope. "Hold your hands out," he said.

Almost smiling, she held out her small hands, balled

into fists. He pulled them together and wound the rope twice about her wrists, knotted it, and then tied her ankles together. When he saw how much rope was left, he held out the surplus with one arm and roughly pulled the child to him with the other. Then he wound the rope about them both, looping them together, and made the final knot after he had stretched out across the front seat.

She was lying on top of him, her hands bunched in the middle of his stomach and her head on his chest. She breathed easily and regularly, as if she had expected no more than what he had done. The clock on the dashboard said that it was five-thirty, and the air was just beginning to turn cooler. He hitched his legs forward and leaned his head back against the headrest. To the noises of traffic, he fell asleep.

And awakened it seemed immediately, his face filmed with sweat, the faintly acrid, greasy odor of the child's hair in his nostrils. It was dark now; he must actually have slept for hours. They had gone undiscovered— imagine being found in a shopping center parking lot in Clarksburg, West Virginia, with a little girl tied to your sleeping body! He groaned, shifted himself to one side and woke the girl. Like him, she came immediately into wakefulness. She bent back her head and regarded him. There was no fear, only intensity in her gaze. He hurriedly untied the knots, dragged the rope from around them; his neck complained when he sat upright. "You want to go to the bathroom?" he asked.

She nodded. "Where?"

"Beside the car."

"Right here? In the parking lot?"

"You heard me."

He thought again that she nearly smiled. He looked at the girl's intense small face, framed in black hair. "You'll let me?"

"I'm going to be holding onto your hand."

"But you won't look?" For the first time, she showed concern.

He shook his head.

She moved her hand to the lock on her door, but he shook his head again and took her wrist and held it tightly. "Out on my side," he said and pulled up his own lock and got out, still clutching the girl's bony wrist. She began to edge sideways toward the door, a girl of seven or eight with short black hair, wearing a little dress of some thin pink material. On her otherwise bare feet were faded blue canvas sneakers, fraying at the tops of the heels. Childishly, she put one bare leg down first and then wiggled around to swing the other out of the car.

He pulled her around to the factory fence. The girl bent her head back and looked up. "You promised. You won't watch."

"I won't watch," he said.

And for a moment he did not watch, but let his head roll back as she stooped, forcing him to lean sideways. His eyes drifted over the grotesque plastic animals behind the fence. Then he heard some fabric—cotton—moving over skin, and looked down. Her left arm was extended so that she was as far from him as she could get. The cheap pink dress was pulled up over her waist. She too was looking at the plastic animals. When the girl was finished, he took his eyes from her, knowing that she would glance at him. She stood up and waited for him to tell her what to do next. He pulled her back toward the car.

"What do you do for a living?" she asked.

He laughed out loud with surprise: this cocktail-party question! "Nothing."

"Where are we going? Are you taking me someplace?"

He opened the door and stood aside as she climbed back into the car. "Someplace," he said. "Sure, I'm taking you someplace." He got in beside her, and she moved across the seat to the door.

"Where?"

"We'll see when we get there."

*   *   *

Again he drove all night, and again the girl slept most of the time, coming awake to stare out the windshield (she always slept sitting up, like a doll in her tennis shoes and pink dress) and to ask him odd questions. "Are you a policeman?" she asked him once, and then after seeing an exit sign, "What's Columbia?"

"It's a city."

"Like New York?"

"Yes."

"Like Clarksburg?"

He nodded.

"Are we always going to sleep in the car?"

"Not always."

"Can I play the radio?"

He said yes, and she leaned forward and twisted the knob. The car was invaded by static, two or three voices speaking at the same time. She punched another button and the same crowded hiss erupted from the speaker. "Twist the dial," he said. Frowning, her face concentrated, she began slowly to turn the selector. In a moment she had locked onto a clear signal, Dolly Parton. "I love this," she told him.

So for hours they drove south through the songs and rhythms of country music, the stations weakening and changing, the disk jockeys swapping names and accents, the sponsors succeeding each other in a revolving list of insurance companies, toothpaste, soap, Dr Pepper and Pepsi-Cola, acne preparations, funeral parlors, petroleum jelly, bargain wristwatches, aluminum siding, dandruff shampoos: but the music remained the same, a vast and self-conscious story, a sort of seamless repetitious epic in which women married truckers and no-good gamblers but stood by them until they got a divorce and the men sat in bars plotting seductions and how to get back home, and they came together hot as two-dollar pistols and parted in disgust and worried about the babies. Sometimes the car wouldn't start, sometimes the TV was busted; sometimes the bars closed down and threw you out onto the street, your pockets turned inside out. There was nothing that was not banal, there was no phrase that was not a cliché, but the child sat there satisfied and passive, dozing off to Willie Nelson and waking up to Loretta Lynn, and the man just drove, distracted by this endless soap opera of America's bottom dogs.

Once he asked her, "Have you ever heard of a man named Edward Wanderley?"

She did not reply but regarded him levelly.

"Have you?"

"Who's he?"

"He was my uncle," he said, and the girl smiled at him.

"How about a man named Sears James?"

She shook her head, still smiling.

"A man named Ricky Hawthorne?"

Again she shook her head. There was no point in continuing. He did not know why he had bothered to ask in the first place. It was even possible that she had never heard those names. Of course she had never heard them.

Still in South Carolina, he thought that a highway patrolman was following him: the police car was twenty yards behind, keeping the same distance whatever the man did. He thought he could see the state cop speaking into his radio; immediately he cut his speed by five miles an hour and changed lanes, but the police car would not pass. He felt a deep trembling in his chest and abdomen: he visualized the police car gaining on him, turning on its siren, forcing him to the side of the road. Then the questions would begin. It was about six in the afternoon, and the freeway was crowded: he felt himself being drawn helplessly along with the traffic, at the mercy of whoever was in the police car—helpless, trapped. He had to *think*. He was simply being drawn on toward Charleston, pulled by the traffic through miles of flat scrubby country: suburbs were always visible in the distance, miserable collections of little houses with frame garages. He could not remember the number of the freeway he was on. In the rear-view mirror, behind the long row of cars, behind the police car, an old truck sent out a tall column of black smoke through a chimneylike pipe beside the engine. He feared the patrolman cruising up beside him and shouting: "Get over!" And he could imagine the girl shouting, her high tinny voice shouting, "He made me come with him, he ties me onto him when he sleeps!" The southern sun seemed to assault his face, to grind at his pores. The state patrolman swung out into the next lane and began to draw up toward him.

—Asshole, that's not your girl, who is that girl?

Then they would put him in a cell and begin to beat him, working on him methodically with nightsticks, turning his skin purple . . .

But none of that happened.

3

Shortly after eight o'clock he pulled over to the side of the road. It was a narrow country road, loose red dirt piled on the shoulders, as if it had been only recently dug out of the earth. He was no longer sure of what state he was in, South Carolina or Georgia: it was as though these states were fluid, as if they—and all the rest of them—could leak over into one another, pushing forward like the highways. It all looked wrong. He was in the wrong place: no one could live here, no one could think here, in this brutal landscape. Unfamiliar vines, green and ropelike, struggled up the low bank beside his car. The fuel gauge had been on E for the past half hour. All of it was wrong, all of it. He looked at the girl, this girl he had kidnapped. She was sleeping in that doll-like way, her back straight against the seat and her feet in the ripped sneakers dangling above the floor. She slept too much. Suppose she was sick; suppose she was dying.

She woke as he was watching her. "I have to go to the bathroom again," she said.

"Are you okay? You're not sick, are you?"

"I have to go to the bathroom."

"Okay," he grunted and moved to open his door.

"Let me go by myself. I won't run away. I won't do anything. I promise."

He looked at her serious face, her black eyes set in olive skin.

"Where could I go, anyhow? I don't even know where I am."

"I don't either."

"So?"

It had to happen sometime: he couldn't hold on to her at every moment. "You promise?" he asked, knowing the question was foolish.

She nodded. He said, "All right."

"And you promise you won't drive away?"

"Yes."

She opened the door and left the car. It was all he could do not to watch her, but it was a test, not to watch her. A Test. He wished overwhelmingly that he had her hand trapped in his fist. She could be scrambling up the bank, running off, screaming . . . but no, she was not screaming. It often happened that the terrible things he imagined, the worst things, did not occur; the world gave a hitch and things went back to the way they had always been. When the girl climbed back into the car he was flooded with relief—it had happened again, no black hole had opened up for him.

He closed his eyes and saw an empty freeway, divided by white lines, unreeling before him.

"I have to find a motel," he said.

She leaned back into the seat, waiting for him to do whatever he wanted. The radio was turned low, and sounds from a station in Augusta, Georgia—a silky, lilting guitar—drifted out. For a moment, an image leaped to his mind—the girl dead, her tongue protruding, her eyes bulging. She gave him no resistance! Then for a moment he was standing—it was as if he were standing—on a street in New York, some street in the East Fifties, one of those streets where well-dressed women walk sheepdogs. Because there was one of those women, walking along. Tall, wearing beautifully faded jeans and an expensive shirt and a deep tan, walking along toward him with her sunglasses pushed to the top of her head. A huge sheepdog padded beside her, wagging its rump. He was nearly close enough to see the freckles exposed by the undone top buttons of the woman's shirt.

Ah.

But then he was right again, he heard the low guitar music, and before he switched on the ignition he patted the top of the girl's head. "Have to get us a motel," he said.

For an hour he just continued, protected by the cocoon of numbness, by the mechanics of driving: he was almost alone on the dark road.

"Are you going to hurt me?" the girl asked.

"How should I know?"

"You won't, I think. You're my friend."

Then it was not "as if" he were on the street in New York, he *was* on that street, watching the woman with the dog and the suntan come toward him. Again he saw the little random scattering of freckles below her collarbone—he knew how it would taste if he put his tongue there. As often in New York, he could not see the sun, but he could feel it—a heavy, aggressive sun. The woman was a stranger, unimportant . . . he was not supposed to know her, she was just a type . . . a taxi went by, he was aware of iron railings on his right side, the lettering on the windows of a French restaurant on the other side of the street. Through the soles of his boots, the pavement sent up heat. Somewhere above, a man was shouting one word over and over. He *was* there, he *was*: a portion of his emotion must have shown in his face, for the woman with the dog looked at him curiously and then hardened her face and moved to the outer edge of the sidewalk.

Could she speak? Could someone in whatever sort of experience this was utter sentences, audible ordinary human sentences? Could you talk to the people you met in hallucinations, and would they answer back?

He opened his mouth. "I have to"—*to get out,* he was
going to say, but he was already back in the stalled
car. A soggy lump that had once been two potato chips
lay on his tongue.

What was the worst thing you've ever done?

The maps seemed to show that he was only a few
miles from Valdosta. He drove unthinkingly on, not
daring to look at the child and therefore not knowing
if she were awake or sleeping, but feeling her eyes on
him nonetheless. Eventually he passed a sign which informed him that he was ten miles from the Friendliest
City in the South.

It looked like any southern town: a little industry on
the way in, machine shops and die-stampers, surreal
groups of corrugated metal huts under arc lights, yards
littered with cannibalized trucks; further in, wooden
houses in need of paint, groups of black men standing
on corners, their faces alike in the dark; new roads
went scarring through the land, then ended abruptly,
weeds already encroaching; in the town proper, the
teenagers patrolling endlessly, vacantly in their old
cars.

He passed a low building, incongruously new, a sign
of the New South, with a sign reading PALMETTO
MOTOR-IN; he reversed down the street back to the
building.

A girl with upswept lacquered hair and candy-pink
lipstick gave him a meaningless, dead smile and a room
with twin beds "for myself and my daughter." In the
register he wrote: Lamar Burgess, 155 Ridge Road,
Stonington, Conn. After he handed her a night's pay-
ment in cash, she gave him a key.

Their cubicle contained two single beds, an iron-
textured brown carpet and lime-green walls, two pictures—a kitten tilting its head, an Indian looking into
a leafy gorge from a clifftop—a television set, a door
into a blue-tiled bathroom. He sat on the toilet seat
while the girl undressed and got into bed.

When he peeked out to check on her, she was lying
beneath a sheet with her face to the wall. Her clothes

were scattered on the floor, a nearly empty bag of potato chips lay beside her. He ducked back into the bathroom, stripped and got into the shower. Which blessed him. For a moment he felt almost as though he were back in his old life, not "Lamar Burgess" but Don Wanderley, one-time resident of Bolinas, California, and author of two novels (one of which had made some money). Lover for a time of Alma Mobley, brother to defunct David Wanderley. And there it was. It was no good, he could not get away from it. The mind was a trap—it was a cage that slammed down over you. However he had got to where he was, he was there. Stuck there in the Palmetto Motor-In. He turned off the shower, all traces of the blessing departed.

In the little room, only the weak light over his bed to illuminate those ghostly surroundings, he pulled on his jeans and opened his suitcase. The hunting knife was wrapped in a shirt, and he unrolled it so the knife fell out on the bed.

Carrying it by the chunky bone handle, he crossed to the girl's bed. She slept with her mouth open; perspiration gleamed on her forehead.

For a long time he sat beside her, holding the knife in his right hand, ready to use it.

But this night he could not. Giving up, giving in, he shook her arm until her eyelids fluttered.

"Who are you?" he asked.

"I want to sleep."

"Who are you?"

"Go away. Please."

"Who are you? I'm asking, who are you?"

"You know."

"I know?"

"You know. I told you."

"What's your name?"

"Angie."

"Angie what?"

"Angie Maule. I told you before."

He held the knife behind his back so that she could not see it.

"I want to sleep," she said. "You woke me up." She turned her back to him again. Fascinated, he watched sleep settle over her: her fingertips twitched, her eyelids contracted, her breathing changed. It was as if, to exclude him, she had willed herself to sleep. Angie— Angela? Angela Maule. It did not sound like the name she had given him when he had first taken her into the car. Minoso? Minnorsi? Some name like that, an Italian name—not Maule.

He held the knife in both hands, the black bone handle jammed into his naked belly, his elbows out: all he had to do was thrust it forward and jerk it up, using all his strength . . .

In the end, sometime around three in the morning, he crossed over to his bed.

4

The next morning, before they checked out, she spoke to him while he was looking at the maps. "You shouldn't ask me those questions."

"What questions?" He had been keeping his back turned, at her request, as she got into the pink dress, and he suddenly had the feeling that he had to turn around, right now, to see her. He could see his knife in her hands (though it was back inside the rolled-up shirt), could feel it just beginning to prick his skin. "Can I turn around now?"

"Yeah, sure."

Slowly, still feeling the knife, his uncle's knife, beginning to enter his skin, he turned sideways on the chair. The girl was sitting on her unmade bed, watching him. Her intense unbeautiful face.

"What questions?"

"You know."

"Tell me."

She shook her head and would not say any more.

"Do you want to see where we're going?"

The girl came toward him, not slowly but measuredly, as if not wishing to display suspicion. "Here," he said, pointing to a spot on the map. "Panama City, in Florida."

"Will we be able to see the water?"

"Maybe."

"And we won't sleep in the car?"

"No."

"Is it far away?"

"We can get there tonight. We'll take this road—this one—see?"

"Uh huh." She was not interested: she hung a little to one side, bored and wary.

She said: "Do you think I'm pretty?"

What's the worst thing that ever happened to you? That you took off your clothes at night beside the bed of a nine-year-old girl? That you were holding a knife? That the knife wanted to kill her?

No. Other things were worse.

Not far over the state line and not on the highway he had shown Angie on the map but on a two-lane country road, they drew up before a white board building. *Buddy's Supplies.*

"You want to come in with me, Angie?"

She opened the door on her side and got out in that childish way, as if she were climbing down a ladder; he held the screen door open for her. A fat man in a white shirt sat like Humpty Dumpty on a counter. "You cheat on your income tax," he said. "And you're the first customer of the day. You believe that? Twelve-thirty and you're the first guy through the door. No," he said, bending forward and scrutinizing them. "Hell no. You don't cheat Uncle Sam, you do worse than that. You're the guy killed four-five people up in Tallahassee the other day."

"What—?" he said. "I just came in here for some food—my daughter—"

"Gotcha," the man said. "I used to be a cop. Allentown, Pennsylvania. Twenty years. Bought this place because the man told me I could turn over a hundred dollars' profit a week. There's a lot of crooks in this world. Anybody comes in, I can tell what kind of crook they are. And now I got *you* straight. You're not a killer. You're a kidnapper."

"No, I—" he felt sweat pouring down his sides. "My girl—"

"You can't shit me. Twenty years a cop."

He began to look frantically around the store for the girl. Finally he saw her staring gravely at a shelf stocked with jars of peanut butter. "Angie," he said. "Angie—come on—"

"Aw, hold on," the fat man said. "I was just tryin' to get a rise out of you. Don't flip out or nothin'. You want some of that peanut butter, little girl?"

Angie looked at him and nodded.

"Well, take one off the shelf and bring it up here. Anything else, mister? 'Course if you're Bruno Hauptmann, I'll have to bring you in. I still got my service revolver around somewhere. Knock *you* flat, I'll tell you that for free."

It was, he saw, all a weary mockery. Yet he could scarcely conceal his trembling. Wasn't that something an ex-cop would notice? He turned away toward the aisles and shelves.

"Hey, listen to this," the man said to his back. "If you're in that much trouble, you can just get the hell out of here right now."

"No, no," he said. "I need some things—"

"You don't look much like that girl."

Blindly, he began taking things off the shelves, anything. A jar of pickles, a box of apple turnovers, a canned ham, two or three other cans he didn't bother to look at. These he took to the counter.

The fat man, Buddy, was staring at him suspiciously. "You just shook me up a little bit," he said to him. "I haven't had much sleep, I've been driving for a couple of days . . ." Invention blessedly descended. "I have to take my little girl to her grandmother, she's in Tampa—" Angie swiveled around, clutching two jars of crunchy peanut butter, and gaped at him as he said this—"uh, Tampa, on account of her mother and me split up and I have to get a job, get things put together again, right, Angie?" The girl's mouth hung open.

"Your name Angie?" the fat man asked her.

She nodded.

"This man your daddy?"

He thought he would fall down.

"Now he is," she said.

The fat man laughed. " 'Now he is!' Just like a kid. Goddam. You figure out the brain of a kid, you got to be some kind of genius. All right, nervous, I guess I'll take your money." Still sitting on the counter, he rang up the purchases by bending to one side and punching the buttons of the register. "You better get some rest. You remind me of about a million guys I took into my old station."

Outside, Wanderley said to her, "Thanks for saying that."

"Saying what?": pertly, self-assuredly. Then again, almost mechanically, eerily, ticking her head from side to side: "Saying what? Saying what? Saying what?"

5

In Panama City he pulled into the Gulf Glimpse Motor Lodge, a series of shabby brick bungalows around a parking lot. The manager's lodge sat at the entrance, a separate square building like the others, with the exception of a large pane of plate glass behind which, in what must have been ovenlike heat, a stringy old man with gold-rimmed glasses and a mesh T-shirt was visible. He looked like Adolf Eichmann. The severe inflexible cast of the man's face made Wanderley remember what the ex-policeman had said about himself and the girl: he did not, with his blond hair and fair skin, look anything like the girl's father. He pulled up before the manager's lodge and left the car, his palms sweaty.

But inside, when he said that he wanted a room for himself and his daughter, the old man merely glanced incuriously at the dark-haired child in the car, and said, "Ten-fifty a day. Sign the register. You want food, try the Eat-Mor down the road apiece. There's no cooking in the bungalows. You planning on staying more than one night, Mr.—" He swung the register toward him. "Boswell?"

"Maybe as long as a week."

"Then you'll pay the first two nights in advance."

He counted out twenty-one dollars, and the manager gave him a key. "Number eleven, lucky eleven. Across the parking lot."

The room had whitewashed walls and smelled of lavatory cleaner. He gave it a perfunctory look around: the same iron carpet, two small beds with clean but worn sheets, a television with a twelve-inch screen, two awful pictures of flowers. The room appeared to have more shadows in it than could be accounted for. The girl was inspecting the bed against the side wall. "What's Magic Fingers? I want to try it. Can I? Please?"

"It probably won't work."

"Can I? I want to try it. Please?"

"All right. Lie down on it. I have to go out to do some things. Don't leave until I come back. I have to put a quarter in this slot, see? Like this? When I get back we can eat." The girl was lying on the bed, nodding with impatience, looking not at him but at the coin in his hand. "We'll eat when I get back. I'll try to get you some new clothes, too. You can't wear the same things all the time."

"Put in the quarter!"

He shrugged, pushed the quarter into the slot and immediately heard a humming noise. The child settled down onto the bed, her arms fully extended, her face tense. "Oh. It's nice."

"I'll be back pretty soon," he said, and went back out into the harsh sunlight and for the first time smelled water.

The Gulf was a long way off, but it was visible. On

the other side of the road he had taken into town the land abruptly fell off into a wasteland of weeds and rubble at its bottom bisected by a series of railroad tracks. After the tracks another disused weedy patch of land ended at a second road which veered off toward a group of warehouses and loading sheds. Beyond this second road was the Gulf of Mexico—gray lathery water.

He walked down the road in the direction of town.

On the edge of Panama City he went into a Treasure Island discount store and bought jeans and two T-shirts for the girl, fresh underwear, socks, two shirts, a pair of khaki trousers and Hush Puppies for himself.

Carrying two large shopping bags, he emerged from Treasure Island and turned in the direction that was downtown. Diesel fumes drifted toward him, cars with *Keep the Southland Great* bumper stickers rolled by. Men in short-sleeved shirts and short gray crewcuts moved along the sidewalks. When he saw a uniformed cop trying to eat an ice-cream cone while writing out a parking ticket, he dodged between a pickup truck and a Trailways van and crossed the street. A rivulet of sweat issued from his left eyebrow and ran into his eye; he was calm. Once again, disaster had not happened.

He discovered the bus station by accident. It took up half a block, a vast new-looking building with black glass slits for windows. He thought: *Alma Mobley, her mark.* Once through the revolving door, he saw a few aimless people on benches in a large empty space—the people always seen in bus stations, a few young-old men with lined faces and complex hairdos, some children racketing around, a sleeping bum, three or four teenage boys in cowboy boots and shoulder-length hair. Another cop was leaning against the wall by the magazine counter. Looking for him? Panic started in him again, but the cop barely glanced at him. He pretended to check the arrivals-and-departures board before moving, with exaggerated carelessness, to the men's room.

He locked himself into a toilet and stripped. After

dressing up to the waist in the new clothes, he left the toilet and washed at one of the sinks. So much grime came off that he washed himself again, splashing water onto the floor and working the green liquid soap deep into his armpits and around the back of his neck. Then he dried himself on the roller and put on one of the new short-sleeved shirts—a light blue shirt with thin red stripes. All of his old clothes went into the Treasure Island bag.

Outside, he noticed the odd grainy grayish blue of the sky. It was the sort of sky he imagined as hanging forever over the keys and swamps much further south in Florida, a sky that would hold the heat, doubling and redoubling it, forcing the weeds and plants into fantastic growth, making them send out grotesque and swollen tendrils . . . the sort of sky and hot disk of sun which should always, now that he thought of it, have hung over Alma Mobley. He stuffed the bag of old clothes in a trash barrel outside a gun shop.

In the new clothes his body felt young and capable, healthier than it had all through that terrible winter. Wanderley moved down the shabby southern street, a tall well-built man in his thirties, no longer quite aware of what he was doing. He rubbed his cheek and felt that blond man's feathery stubble—he could go two or three days without looking as though he needed a shave. A pickup driven by a sailor, five or six sailors in summer whites standing up in the rear of the truck, drove past him, and the sailors yelled something—something cheerful and private and derisory.

"They don't mean no harm," said a man who had appeared beside Wanderley. His head, with an enormous hair-sprouting wart dividing one eyebrow, came no higher than Wanderley's breastbone. "They's all good boys."

He smiled and uttered a meaningless agreement and moved away—he could not go back to the motel, could not deal with the girl; he felt as though he might faint. His feet seemed unreal in the Hush Puppies—too far down, too far from his eyes. He found that he was walking rapidly down a descending street, going toward an area of neon signs and movie theaters. In the grainy sky the sun hung high and motionless. Shadows of parking meters stood out, purely black, on the sidewalk: for a moment he was certain there were more shadows than parking meters. All the shadows hovering over the street were intensely black. He passed the entrance to a hotel and was aware of a vast brown empty space, a brown cool cave, beyond its glass doors.

Almost unwillingly, recognizing a dread familiar set of sensations, he went on in the terrific heat: consciously he kept himself from stepping over the shadows of the parking meters. Two years before the world had gathered itself in this ominous way, had been slick and full of intent—after the episode of Alma Mobley, after his brother had died. In some fashion, literally or not, she had killed David Wanderley: he knew that he had been lucky to escape whatever it was that took David through the Amsterdam hotel window. Only writing had brought him back up into the world; only writing about *it,* the horrid complicated mess of himself and Alma and David, writing about it as a ghost story, had released him from it. He had thought.

Panama City? Panama City, Florida? What was he doing there? And with that strange passive girl he had taken with him? Whom he had spirited down through the South?

He had always been the "erratic one," the "troubled one," the foil to David's strength, in the economy of family life his poverty the foil to David's success; his ambitions and pretensions ("You actually think you can support yourself as a *novelist?* Even your uncle wasn't that dumb": his father) the contrast to David's hard-working good sense, to David's steady progress through law school and into a good law firm. And when David had bumped into the daily stuff of his life, it had killed him.

That was the worst thing that had ever happened to him. Until last winter: until Milburn.

The shabby street seemed to open like a grave. He

felt as if one more step toward the bottom of the hill and the sleazy movie theaters would take him down, down, as if it would never stop but turn into an endless falling. Something which had not been there before appeared before him, and he squinted to see it more clearly.

Breathlessly he turned around in the piercing sunlight. His elbow caught someone's chest, and he heard himself murmuring *sorry, sorry* to an irritated woman in a white sunhat. He unconsciously began to move quickly back up the street. Back there, looking down to the intersection at the bottom of the hill, he had momentarily seen his brother's tombstone: it had been small, of purple marble, the words *David Webster Wanderley, 1939–1975* carved into it, sitting in the middle of the intersection. He fled.

Yes, he had seen David's tombstone, but David had none. He had been cremated in Holland, and his ashes flown back to their mother. David's tombstone, yes, with David's name, but what sent him rushing back up the hill was the feeling that it was for him. And that if he were to kneel in the middle of the intersection and dig up the coffin, within it he would find his own putrefying body.

He turned into the only cool, welcoming place he had seen, the hotel lobby. He had to sit down, to calm himself; beneath the disinterested regard of a desk clerk and a girl behind a magazine counter, he sank down onto a sofa. His face was clammy. The fabric of the sofa's upholstery rubbed uncomfortably into his back; he leaned forward, ran his fingers through his hair, looked at his watch. He had to appear normal, as if he were just waiting for someone; he had to stop trembling. Potted palm trees had been placed here and there about the lobby. A fan whirled overhead. A thin old man in a purple uniform stood by an open elevator and stared at him: caught, he looked away.

When noises came to him he realized that since seeing the tombstone in the middle of the intersection he had heard nothing. His own pulse had drowned all other sound. Now the efficient noises of hotel life floated in the humid air. A vacuum cleaner hummed on an invisible staircase, telephones dimly rang, the elevator doors closed with a soft whoosh. Around the lobby, small groups of people sat in conversation. He began to feel that he could face the street again.

6

"I'm hungry," she said.

"I got you some new clothes."

"I don't want new clothes, I want food."

He crossed the room to sit in the empty chair. "I thought you'd get tired of wearing the same dress all the time."

"I don't care what I wear."

"Okay." He tossed the bag onto her bed. "I just thought you might like them."

She did not respond.

"I'll feed you if you answer some questions."

She turned away from him and began picking at the sheets, wrinkling them and smoothing them out.

"What's your name?"

"I told you. Angie."

"Angie Maule?"

"No. Angie Mitchell."

He let it go. "Why haven't your parents sent the police out to find you? Why haven't we been found yet?"

"I don't have any parents."

"Everybody has parents."

"Everybody except orphans."

"Who takes cares of you?"

"You do."

"Before me."

"Shut up. Shut up." Her face became glossy and self-contained.

"Are you really an orphan?"

"Shut up shut up shut up!"

To stop her screaming he lifted the canned ham out

of the box of groceries. "All right," he said. "I'll get you some food. We'll have some of this."

"Okay." It was as if she had never screamed. "I want the peanut butter too."

While he was slicing the ham she said, "Do you have enough money to take care of us?"

She ate in her dedicated way: first she bit off a mouthful of ham, then dipped her fingers in the peanut butter and brought a wad of it home and chewed the two together. "Delicious," she managed to utter around the food.

"If I go to sleep, you won't leave, will you?"

She shook her head. "But I can take a walk, can't I?"

"I guess so."

He was drinking a can of beer from a six-pack he had picked up at the little store on his way back; the beer and the food together made him drowsy, and he knew that if he did not get to bed, he would fall asleep in the chair.

She said, "You don't have to tie me onto you. I'll come back. You believe me, don't you?"

He nodded.

"Because where could I go? I don't have anywhere to go."

"Okay!" he said. Once again, he could not talk to her as he wished: she was in control. "You can go out, but don't be gone too long." He was acting like a parent: he knew that she had put him in this role. It was ludicrous.

He watched her go out of the mean little room. Later, rolling over in bed, he dimly heard the door clicking shut and knew that she had, after all, come back. So she was his.

And that night he lay on his bed, fully dressed, watching her sleep. When his muscles began to ache from being held so long in the same position, he shifted his body on the bed; in this way, over a period of two hours, he went from lying on his side and supporting his head on his hand to sitting up with his knees raised and his hands crossed behind his head to leaning forward, elbows on knees, and finally back to lying on his side, cocked up on one elbow: as if all these postures were elements of a formal round. His eyes scarcely ever left the girl. She lay absolutely still—sleep had taken her somewhere else and left only her body behind. Simply lying there, both of them lying there, she had escaped him.

He rose, went to his suitcase and took out the rolled-up shirt and went back to stand beside his bed. He held the shirt by the collar and let gravity carry the hunting knife to the bed, unrolling the shirt as it fell. When it hit the bed it was too heavy to bounce. Wanderley picked it up and hefted it.

Holding the knife once again behind his back, he shook the girl's shoulder. Her features seemed to blur before she turned over and dug her face into the pillow. He grasped her shoulder again and felt the long thin bone, the prominent wing jutting out from her back. "Go 'way," she muttered into the pillow.

"No. We're going to talk."

"It's too late."

He shook her, and when she did not respond, tried to roll her over by force. Thin and small as she was, she was strong enough to resist. He could not make her face him.

Then she turned over by herself, as if in contempt. Lack of sleep showed in her face, but beneath the puffiness she looked adult.

"What's your name?"

"Angie." She smiled carelessly. "Angie Maule."

"Where do you come from?"

"You know."

He nodded.

"What were your parents' names?"

"I don't know."

"Who took care of you before I picked you up?"

"It doesn't matter."

"Why not?"

"They aren't important. They were just people."

"Was their name Maule?"

Her smile became more insolent. "Does it matter? You think you know everything anyhow."

"What do you mean, 'They were just people'?"

"They were just people named Mitchell. That's all."

"And you changed your name yourself?"

"So what?"

"I don't know." That was true.

So they looked at one another, he sitting on the edge of the bed, holding the knife behind him and knowing that whatever was going to happen, he would be unable to use it. He supposed that David too had been unable to take life—any life but his own, if he had done that. The girl probably knew he was holding the knife, he thought, and simply dismissed it as a threat. It was not a threat. He too was probably not a threat. She had never been even apprehensive of him.

"Okay, let's try again," he said. "What are you?"

For the first time since he had taken her into the car, she really smiled. It was a transformation, but not of a kind to make him feel easier: she did not look any less adult. "You know," she said.

He insisted. "What are you?"

She smiled all through her amazing response. "I am you."

"No. I am me. You are you."

"I am you."

"*What* are you?" It came out in despair, and it did not mean what he had meant the first time he asked it.

Then just for a second he was back on the street in New York, and the person before him was not the stylish suntanned anonymous woman, but his brother David, his face crumbled and his body dressed in the torn and rotting clothing of the grave.

. . . *the most dreadful thing* . . .

Part One

After Jaffrey's Party

Don't the moon look lonesome,
  shinin' through the trees?
Don't the moon look lonesome,
  shinin' through the trees?

—Blues

I

The Chowder Society:
The October Stories

America's first fictional heroes were old men.
— Robert Ferguson

Milburn Observed Through Nostalgia

One day early in October Frederick Hawthorne, a
seventy-year-old lawyer who had lost very little to the
years, left his house on Melrose Avenue in Milburn,
New York, to walk across town to his offices on Wheat
Row, just beside the square. The temperature was a
little colder than Milburn expected so early in its autumn, but Ricky wore his winter uniform of tweed topcoat, cashmere muffler and gray, no-nonsense hat. He
walked a little briskly down Melrose Avenue to warm
up his blood, moving beneath huge oaks and smaller
maples already colored heart-wrenching shades of
orange and red—another unseasonal touch. He was
susceptible to colds, and if the temperature dropped another five degrees, he'd have to drive.

29

But in the meantime, as long as he could keep the wind from his neck, he enjoyed the walk. After he had turned out of Melrose Avenue toward the square, he was warm enough to go at a more leisurely pace. Ricky had little reason to rush to his office: clients rarely appeared before noon. His partner and friend, Sears James, probably would not appear for another forty-five minutes, and that gave Ricky enough time to amble through Milburn, saying hello to people and observing the things he liked to observe.

What he chiefly liked to observe was Milburn itself—Milburn, the town in which all of his life except for his time in university, law school and the army had been spent. He had never wanted to live anywhere else, though in the early days of his marriage, his lovely and restless wife had often claimed that the town was boring. Stella had wanted New York—had wanted it resolutely. That had been one of the battles he had won. It was incomprehensible to Ricky that anyone could find Milburn boring: if you watched it closely for seventy years, you saw the century at work. Ricky imagined that if you watched New York for the same period, what you saw would be mainly New York at work. Buildings went up and down too fast there for Ricky's taste, everything moved too quickly, wrapped in a self-absorbed cocoon of energy, whirling too fast to notice anything west of the Hudson but the Jersey lights. Also, New York had a couple of hundred thousand lawyers; Milburn had only five or six that counted, and he and Sears had been for forty years the most prominent of these. (Not that Stella had ever cared a whit about Milburn's notions of prominence.)

He entered the business district which lay along two blocks west of the square and continued for two blocks along the other side, passed Clark Mulligan's Rialto theater, and paused to look at the marquee. What he saw there made him wrinkle his nose. The posters on the front of the Rialto showed the blood-streaked face of a girl. The kind of movies Ricky liked could now be seen only on television: for Ricky, the film industry had lost its bearings about the time William Powell had retired. (He thought that Clark Mulligan probably agreed with him.) Too many modern films were like his dreams, which had become particularly vivid during the last year.

Ricky turned dismissively away from the theater and faced a prospect far more pleasing. The original high frame houses of Milburn had endured, even if nearly all of them were now office buildings: even the trees were younger than the buildings. He walked, his polished black shoes kicking through crisp leaves, past buildings much like those on Wheat Row and accompanied memories of his boyhood self down these same streets. He was smiling, and if any of the people he greeted had asked him what he was thinking about, he might (if he allowed himself to be so pompous) have said: "Why, sidewalks. I've been thinking about sidewalks. One of my earliest memories is of the time they put in the sidewalks along the whole stretch of Candlemaker Street here, right down to the square. Hauling those big blocks up with horses. You know, sidewalks made a greater contribution to civilization than the piston engine. Spring and winter in the old days you had to wade through mud, and you couldn't enter a drawing room without tracking some of it in. Summers, the dust was everywhere!" Of course, he reflected, drawing-rooms had gone out just about the time the sidewalks had come in.

When he reached the square he found another unhappy surprise. Some of the trees lining the big grassy space were already completely bare, and most of the others had at least a few bare limbs—there was still plenty of the color he'd been anticipating, but during the night the balance had turned and now black skeletal arms and fingers, the bones of the trees, hung against the leaves like signposts to winter. Dead leaves carpeted the square.

"Hi, Mr. Hawthorne," someone beside him said.

He turned and saw Peter Barnes, a high school senior whose father, twenty years younger than Ricky, was in the second periphery of his friends. The first circle consisted of four men his own age—there had been five, but Edward Wanderley had died almost a year earlier. More somberness, when he was determined not to be somber. "Hello, Peter," he said, "you must be on your way to school."

"It starts an hour late today—the heaters broke again."

Peter Barnes stood beside him, a tall amiable-looking boy in a ski sweater and jeans. His black hair seemed almost girlishly long to Ricky, but the width of his shoulders promised that when he started to fill out, he would be a much bigger man than his father. Presumably his hair didn't look girlish to girls. "Just walking around?"

"That's right," Peter said. "Sometimes it's fun just to walk around town and look at things."

Ricky nearly beamed. "Why that's right! I feel exactly the same thing myself. I always enjoy my walks across town. The strangest things pop into my head. I was just thinking that sidewalks changed the world. They made everything much more civilized."

"Oh?" said Peter, looking at him curiously.

"I know, I know—I told you strange things occur to me. Heavens. How is Walter these days?"

"He's fine. He's at the bank now."

"And Christina, she's fine too?"

"Sure," Peter said, and there was a touch of coolness in his response to the question about his mother. A problem there? He remembered that Walter had complained to him some months before that Christina had become a little moody. But for Ricky, who could remember Peter's parents' generation as teenagers, their problems were always a little fictional—how could people with the world still in front of them have truly serious problems?

"You know," he said, "we haven't talked like this in ages. Is your father reconciled to your going to Cornell yet?"

Peter smiled wryly. "I guess so. I don't think he knows

how tough it is to get into Yale. It was a lot easier when he went."

"No doubt it was," said Ricky, who had just remembered the circumstances under which he had last had a conversation with Peter Barnes. John Jaffrey's party: the evening on which Edward Wanderley had died.

"Well, I guess I'll poke around in the department store for a while," Peter said.

"Yes," Ricky said, remembering against his will all the details of that evening. It seemed to him at times that life had darkened since that night: that a wheel had turned.

"I guess I'll go now," Peter said, and stepped backward.

"Oh, don't let me hold you up," Ricky said. "I was just thinking."

"About sidewalks?"

"No, you scamp." Peter turned away, smiling and saying goodbye, and strode easily up the side of the square.

Ricky spotted Sears James's Lincoln cruising past the Archer Hotel at the top of the square, going as usual ten miles an hour slower than anyone else, and hurried on his way to Wheat Row. Somberness had not been evaded: he saw again the skeletal branches thrusting through the brilliant leaves, the implacable bloodied face of the girl on the film poster, and remembered that it was his turn to tell the story at the Chowder Society meeting that night. He hastened on, wondering what had become of his high spirits. But he knew: Edward Wanderley. Even Sears had followed them, the other three members of the Chowder Society, into that gloom. He had twelve hours to think of something to talk about.

"Oh, Sears," he said on the steps of their building. His partner was just pushing himself out of the Lincoln. "Good morning. It's at your house tonight, isn't it?"

"Ricky," said Sears, "at this hour of the morning it is positively forbidden to *chirp*."

Sears lumbered forward, and Ricky followed him through the door leaving Milburn behind.

Frederick Hawthorne

1

Of all the rooms in which they habitually met, this was Ricky's favorite—the library in Sears James's house, with its worn leather chairs, tall indistinct glass-fronted bookcases, drinks on the little round tables, prints on the walls, the muted old Shiraz carpet beneath their feet and the rich memory of old cigars in the atmosphere. Having never committed himself to marriage, Sears James had never had to compromise his luxurious ideas of comfort. After so many years of meeting together, the other men were by now unconscious of the automatic pleasure and relaxation and envy they experienced in Sears's library, just as they were nearly unconscious of the equally automatic discomfort they felt in John Jaffrey's house, where the housekeeper, Milly Sheehan, forever bustled in, rearranging things. But they felt it: each of them, Ricky Hawthorne perhaps more so than the others, had wished to possess such a place for himself. But Sears had always had more money than the others, just as his father had had more money than theirs. It went back that way for five generations, until you reached the country grocer who had cold-bloodedly put together a fortune and turned the James family into gentry: by the time of Sears's grandfather, the women were thin, palpitating, decorative and useless, the men hunted and went to Harvard and they all went to Saratoga Springs in the summers. Sears's father had been a professor of ancient languages at Harvard, where he kept a third family house; Sears himself had become a lawyer because as a young man he had thought it immoral for a man not to have a profession. His year or so of schoolmastering had shown him that it could not be teaching. Of the rest, the cousins and brothers, most had succumbed to good living, hunting accidents, cirrhosis or breakdowns; but Sears, Ricky's old friend, had bluffed his way through until, if he was not the handsomest old man in Milburn—that was surely Lewis Benedikt—he was the most distinguished. But for the beard, he was his father's double, tall and bald and massive, with a round subtle face above his vested suits. His blue eyes were still very young.

Ricky supposed that he had to envy that too, the magisterial appearance. He himself had never been particularly prepossessing. He was too small and too trim for that. Only his mustache had improved with age, growing somehow more luxuriant as it turned gray. When he had developed little jowls, they had not made him more impressive: they had only made him look clever. He did not think that he was particularly clever. If he had been, he might have avoided a business arrangement in which he was unofficially to become a sort of permanent junior partner. But it had been his father, Harold Hawthorne, who had taken Sears into the firm. All those years ago, he had been pleased—even excited—that he would be joined by his old friend. Now, settled into an undeniably comfortable armchair, he supposed that he was still pleased; the years had married them as securely as he was married to Stella, and the business marriage had been far more peaceful than the domestic, even if clients in the same room with both partners invariably looked at Sears and not himself when they spoke. That was an arrangement which Stella would never have tolerated. (Not that anyone in his right mind, all through the years of their marriage, would have looked at Ricky when he could have looked at Stella.)

Yes, he admitted to himself for the thousandth time, he did like it here. It went against his principles and his politics and probably the puritanism of his long-vanished religion too, but Sears's library—Sears's whole splendid house—was a place where a man felt at ease.

Stella had no compunctions about demonstrating that it was also the sort of place where a woman too could feel at ease. She didn't mind now and then treating Sears's house as though it were her own. Thankfully, Sears tolerated it. It had been Stella, on one of those occasions (twelve years ago, coming into the library as if she led a platoon of architects), who had given them their name. "Well, there they are, by God," she had said, "The Chowder Society. Are you going to keep my husband away from me all night, Sears? Or aren't you boys through telling your lies yet?" Still, he supposed it was Stella's perpetual energy and constant needling which had kept him from succumbing to age as old John Jaffrey had. For their friend Jaffrey was "old" despite his being six months younger than Hawthorne himself and a year younger than Sears, and in fact only five years older than Lewis, their youngest member.

Lewis Benedikt, the one who was supposed to have killed his wife, was seated directly across from Ricky, an image of expansive good health. As time rolled through them all, subtracting things, it seemed only to add to Lewis. It hadn't been true when he was younger, but these days he bore a definite resemblance to Cary Grant. His chin would not sag, his hair would not fall. He had become almost absurdly handsome. This evening, Lewis's big placid humorous features wore—like all their faces—an expression of expectancy. It was generally true that the best stories were told here, in Sears's house.

"Who's on the griddle tonight?" asked Lewis. But it was only courtesy. They all knew. The group called the Chowder Society had only a few rules: they wore evening clothes (because thirty years ago, Sears had rather liked the idea), they never drank too much (and now they were too old for that anyhow), they never asked if any of the stories were true (since even the outright whoppers were in some sense true), and though the stories went around the group in rotation, they never pressured anyone who had temporarily dried up.

Hawthorne was about to confess when John Jaffrey interrupted. "I've been thinking," he said, and then responded to the others' inquisitive glances, "no, I know it's not me, and a good thing too. But I was just thinking that in two weeks it will be a year to the day since Edward died. He'd be here tonight if I hadn't insisted on that damned party."

"Please, John," said Ricky. He didn't like to look directly at Jaffrey's face when it showed his emotions so clearly. His skin looked like you could push a pencil straight through it and draw no blood. "All of us know that you were not to blame yourself."

"But it happened in my house," insisted Jaffrey.

"Calm down, doc," Lewis said. "You're not doing yourself any good."

"I'll decide that."

"Then you're not doing the rest of us any good," Lewis said with the same bland good humor. "We all remember the date. How could we forget?"

"Then what are you doing about it? Do you think you're acting as though it never happened—as though it was normal? Just some old poop kicking the bucket? Because if so, let me inform you that you're not."

He had shocked them into silence; even Ricky could think of nothing to say. Jaffrey's face was gray. "No," he said. "You're damned well not. You all know what's been happening to us. We sit around here and talk like a bunch of ghouls. Milly can hardly stand having us in my house anymore. We weren't always like this—we used to talk about all sorts of things. We used to have fun—there used to *be* fun. Now there isn't. We're all scared. But I don't know if some of you are admitting it. Well, it's been a year, and I don't mind saying that I am."

"I'm not so sure I'm scared," said Lewis. He took a sip of his whiskey and smiled at Jaffrey.

"You're not so sure you're not, either," snapped the doctor.

Sears James coughed into his fist, and everybody immediately looked at him. My God, thought Ricky: he can do that whenever he wants, just effortlessly capture our attention. I wonder why he ever thought he couldn't be a good teacher. And I wonder why I ever thought I could hold my own with him. "John," Sears said gently, "we're all familiar with the facts. All of you were kind enough to go through the cold to come here tonight, and none of us are young men anymore. Let's continue."

"But Edward didn't die at *your* house. And that Moore woman, that so-called actress, didn't—"

"Enough of that," Sears commanded.

"Well, I suppose you remember how we got on this kick," said Jaffrey.

Sears nodded, and so did Ricky Hawthorne. It had been at the first meeting after Edward Wanderley's odd death. The remaining four had been hesitant—they could not have been more conscious of Edward's absence had an empty chair been placed among them. Their conversation had stuttered and stalled through half a dozen false beginnings. All of them, Ricky had seen, were wondering if they could bear to continue to meet. Ricky knew that none of them could bear not to. And then he had had his inspiration: he had turned to John Jaffrey and said, "What's the worst thing you've ever done?"

Dr. Jaffrey had surprised him by going pink; and then had set the tone of all their subsequent meetings by saying, "I won't tell you that, but I'll tell you the worst thing that ever happened to me—the most dreadful thing . . ." and following it by telling what was in effect a ghost story. It was riveting, surprising, frightening . . . it took their minds off Edward. They had gone on like that ever since.

"Do you really think it's just coincidence?" asked Jaffrey.

"Don't follow," Sears grumped.

"You're dissembling, and it's beneath you. I mean that we started on this tack, me first, after Edward . . ."

His voice trailed off, and Ricky knew that he was caught between *died* and *was killed.*

"Went west," he put in, hoping for lightness of touch. Jaffrey's stony lizardlike eye, darting at him, told him he'd failed. Ricky leaned back in the opulent chair, hoping to vanish into the luxurious background and be no more conspicuous than a water stain on one of Sears's old maps.

"Where did you get that from?" Sears asked, and Ricky remembered. It was what his father had used to say when a client died. "Old Toby Pfaff went west last night . . . Mrs. Wintergreen went west this morning. There'll be the devil to pay in probate court." He shook his head. "Yes, that's right," Sears said. "But I don't know . . ."

"Exactly," said Jaffrey. "I think something pretty damn funny is going on."

"What do you advise? I take it that you're not just talking for the sake of interrupting the proceedings."

Ricky smiled over the tops of his joined fingers to show that he took no offense.

"Well, I do have a suggestion." He was doing his best, Ricky saw, to handle Sears carefully. "I think we should invite Edward's nephew to come here."

"And what would be the point of that?"

"Isn't he by way of being an expert in . . . in this sort of thing?"

"What is 'this sort of thing'?"

Pushed, Jaffrey did not back down. "Maybe just what's mysterious. I think he could—well, I think he could help us." Sears was looking impatient, but the doctor did not let him interrupt. "I think we need help. Or am I the only man here who has trouble getting a decent night's sleep? Am I the only one who has nightmares every night?" He scanned them all with his sunken face. "Ricky? You're an honest man."

"You're not the only one, John," Ricky said.

"No, I suppose not," said Sears, and Ricky looked at him in surprise. Sears had never indicated before that he too might have awful nights—certainly it never showed on that big smooth reflective face. "You have his book in mind, I imagine."

"Well, yes, of course. He must have done research—he must have had some experience."

"I thought his experience was of mental instability."

"Like us," Jaffrey said bravely. "Edward must have had some reason for willing his nephew his house. I think it was that he wanted Donald to come here, if anything should happen to him. I think he knew that something would happen. And I'll tell you what else I think. I think we ought to tell him about Eva Galli."

"Tell him an inconclusive story fifty years old? Ridiculous."

"The reason it's not ridiculous is that it is inconclusive," the doctor said.

Ricky saw that Lewis was as surprised, even shaken, as he that Jaffrey had brought up the story of Eva Galli. That episode lay, as Sears had said, fifty years in their past; none of them had mentioned it since.

"Do you think you know what happened to her?" the doctor challenged.

"Hey, come on," Lewis put in. "Do we really need that? What the hell is the point?"

"The point is trying to find out what really happened to Edward. I'm sorry if that wasn't clear."

Sears nodded, and Ricky thought he could detect in his longtime partner's face a sign of—what? Relief? Of course he would not admit to it; but that it could be seen at all was a revelation to Ricky. "I'm in a little doubt about the reasoning," Sears said, "but if it would make you happy I suppose we could write to Edward's nephew. We have his address in our files, don't we, Ricky?" Hawthorne nodded. "But to be democratic, I'd like to put it to a vote first. Shall we just verbally agree or disagree and vote like that? What do you say?" He sipped from his glass and looked them over. They all agreed. "We'll start with you, John."

"Of course I say yes. Send for him."

"Lewis?"

Lewis shrugged. "I don't care one way or the other. Send for him if you want."

"That's a yes?"

"Okay, it's a yes. But I say don't drag up the Eva Galli business."

"Ricky?"

Ricky looked at his partner and saw that Sears knew how he was going to vote. "No. Definitely no. I think it's a mistake."

"You'd rather have us go on as we have been going on for a year?"

"Change is always change for the worse."

Sears was amused. "Spoken like a true lawyer, though I think the sentiment ill becomes a former member of YPSL. But I say yes, and that makes it three to one. It's carried. We'll write to him. Since mine was the deciding vote, I'll handle it."

"I've just thought of something," Ricky said. "It's been a year now. Suppose he wants to sell the house? It's been sitting empty since Edward died."

"*Faw.* You're inventing problems. We'll get him here faster if he wants to sell."

"How can you be sure things won't get worse? Can you be sure?" Sitting as he had at least once a month for more than twenty years in a coveted chair in the best room he knew, Ricky fervently wished that nothing would change—that they would be allowed to continue, and that they would simply tease out their anxieties in bad dreams and stories. Looking at them all in the lowered light as a cold wind battered the trees outside Sears's windows, he wished for nothing more than that: to continue. They were his friends, he was in a way as married to them as a moment ago he had considered he was to Sears, and he gradually became aware that he feared for them. They seemed so terribly vulnerable, sitting there and regarding him quizzically, as if each of the others imagined that nothing could be worse than a few bad dreams and a bi-weekly spook story. They believed in the efficacy of knowledge. But he saw a plane of darkness, cast by a lampshade, cross

John Jaffrey's forehead and thought: John is dying already. There is a kind of knowledge they have never confronted, despite the stories they tell; and when that thought came into his well-groomed little head, it was as though whatever was implied in the knowledge he meant was out there somewhere, out in the first signs of winter, out there and gaining on them.

Sears said, "We've decided, Ricky. It's for the best. We can't just stew in our own juices. Now." He looked around the circle they made, metaphorically rubbing his hands, and said, "Now that's settled, who, as Lewis put it, is on the griddle tonight?"

Within Ricky Hawthorne the past suddenly shifted and delivered a moment so fresh and complete that he knew he had his story, although he'd had nothing planned and had thought he would have to pass; but eighteen hours from the year 1945 shone clearly in his mind, and he said, "Well, I guess it's me."

2

After the other two had left, Ricky stayed behind, telling them that he was in no hurry to get out into that cold. Lewis had said, "It'll put blood in your cheeks, Ricky," but Dr. Jaffrey had merely nodded—it really was unseasonably cold for October, cold enough for snow. Sitting alone in the library while Sears went off to freshen up their drinks, Ricky could hear the ignition of Lewis's car grinding away in the street. Lewis had a Morgan which he'd imported from England five years before, and it was the only sports car Ricky had really liked the looks of. But the canvas top wouldn't be much protection on a night like this; and Lewis seemed to be having a lot of trouble getting the car to start. *There*. He'd nearly got it. In these New York winters, you really needed something bigger than Lewis's little Morgan. Poor John would be frozen by the time Lewis got him home to Milly Sheehan and the big house on Montgomery Street, around the corner and seven blocks up. Milly'd be sitting in the semi-dark of the doctor's waiting rooms, keeping herself awake so that she could jump up as soon as she heard his key in the door, help him off with his coat and pour a little hot chocolate into him. As Ricky sat listening, the Morgan's engine coughed into life—he heard them drive away and pictured Lewis clapping a hat on his head, grinning at John and saying, "Didn't I *tell* you this little beauty would perform?" After he'd dropped John off, he'd leave town altogether, zipping along Route 17 until he was out in the woods, and go back to the place he'd bought when he had returned. Whatever else Lewis had done in Spain, he had earned a lot of money.

Ricky's own home was literally just around the corner, not a five-minute walk away; in the old days he and Sears had walked to their office in town every day. In warm weather they sometimes still did: "Mutt and Jeff," as Stella said. This was directed more at Sears than himself—Stella had never actually liked Sears. Of course she had never let this submerged dislike interfere with her attempts to dominate him a little. There was no question that Stella would be waiting up with hot chocolate: she'd have gone to sleep hours ago, leaving only a hall light burning upstairs. It was Stella's conviction that if he was going to indulge himself at his friends' houses and leave her behind, he could knock around in the dark when he got home, bumping his knees on the glass and chrome modern furniture she had made him buy.

Sears came back into the room with two drinks in his hands and a freshly fired-up cigar in his mouth. Ricky said, "Sears, you're probably the only person I know to whom I could admit that sometimes I wish I'd never got married."

"Don't waste your envy on me," Sears said. "I'm too old, too fat and too tired."

"You're none of those things," he answered, accepting the drink Sears gave him, "you just have the luxury of being able to pretend you are."

"Oh, but you pulled out the prize plum," Sears said. "The reason you wouldn't say what you've just said to anyone else is that they'd be stupefied. Stella is a famous beauty. And if you said it to her, she'd brain you." He sat back in the chair he'd occupied earlier, stretched his legs out and crossed them at the ankles. "She'd slap a box together, dump you in it, bury you in five seconds flat and then run off with an athletic forty-year-old smelling of salt water and bay rum. The reason you can tell me is that—" Sears paused, and Ricky feared that he'd say, *I sometimes wish you'd never married too.* "Is it that I am *hors de combat,* or is it *hors commerce?*"

Listening to his partner's voice, holding his drink, Ricky thought of John Jaffrey and Lewis Benedikt speeding away to their houses, of his own redecorated house waiting, and was aware of how settled their lives were; of how much they had found a comfortable routine. "Well, which is it?" Sears asked, and he replied, "Oh, in your case *hors de combat,* I'm sure," and smiled, stingingly aware of their closeness. He remembered what he had said before, *all change is change for the worse,* and thought: *that's true, God help us.* Ricky suddenly saw all of them, his old friends and himself, as on a fragile invisible plane suspended high up in dark air.

"Does Stella know you have nightmares?" Sears asked.

"Well, I didn't know that you did," Ricky answered, as though it were a joke.

"I saw no reason to discuss it."

"And you've been having them for—?"

Sears leaned further into his chair. "You've had yours for—?"

"A year."

"And I. For a year. So have the other two, apparently."

"Lewis doesn't seem ruffled."

"Nothing ruffles Lewis. When the Creator made Lewis, he said, 'I am going to give you a handsome face, a good constitution and an equable temperament, but because this is an imperfect world, I'll hold back a little on brains.' He got rich because he liked Spanish fishing villages, not because he knew what was going to happen to them."

Ricky ignored this—it was all part of the way Sears liked to characterize Lewis. "They started after Edward's death?"

Sears nodded his massive head.

"What *do* you think happened to Edward?"

Sears shrugged. They had all asked the question too many times. "As you are surely aware, I know no more than you."

"Do you think we'll be any happier if we find out?"

"Goodness, what a question! I can't answer that one either, Ricky."

"Well, I don't. I think something terrible will happen to us. I think you'll bring down disaster on us if you invite that young Wanderley."

"Superstition," Sears grumbled. "Nonsense. I think something terrible has already happened to us, and this young Wanderley might be the man who can clear it up."

"Did you read his book?"

"The second one? I looked at it."

This was an admission that he had read it.

"What did you think?"

"A nice exercise in genre writing. More literary than most. A few nice phrases, a reasonably well-constructed plot."

"But about his insights . . ."

"I think he won't immediately dismiss us as a bunch of old fools. That's the main thing."

"Oh, I wish he would," Ricky wailed. "I don't want anybody poking around in our lives. I want things just to keep on going."

"But it's possible that he will 'poke around,' as you say, and end by convincing us that we are just spooking ourselves. Then maybe Jaffrey will stop scourging himself for that blasted party. He only insisted on it because he wanted to meet that worthless little actress. That Moore girl."

"I think about that party a lot," Ricky said. "I've been trying to remember when I saw her that night."

"I saw her," said Sears. "She was talking to Stella."

"That's what everybody says. Everybody saw her talking to my wife. But where did she go afterward?"

"You're getting as bad as John. Let's wait for young Wanderley. We need a fresh eye."

"I think we'll be sorry," said Ricky, trying for one last time. "I think we'll be ruined. We'll be like some animal eating its own tail. We have to put it behind us."

"It's decided. Don't be melodramatic."

So that was that. Sears could not be swayed. Ricky asked him about another of the things on his mind. "On our evenings, do you always know what you're going to say in advance, when it's your turn?"

Sears's eyes met his, marvelously, cloudlessly blue. "Why?"

"Because I don't. Not most of the time. I just sit and wait, and then it comes to me, like tonight. Is it that way with you?"

"Often. Not that it proves anything."

"Is it like that for the others too?"

"I see no reason why it shouldn't be. Now, Ricky, I want to get some rest and you should go home. Stella must be waiting for you."

He couldn't tell if Sears were being ironic or not. He touched his bow tie. Bow ties were a part of his life, like the Chowder Society, that Stella barely tolerated. "Where do these stories come from?"

"From our memories," Sears said. "Or, if you prefer, from our doubtless Freudian unconsciouses. Come on. I want to be left alone. I have to wash all the glasses before I get to bed."

"May I ask you one more time—"

"What now?"

"—not to write to Edward's nephew." Ricky stood up, audacity making his heart speed.

"You can be persistent, can't you? Certainly you may

ask, but by the time we get together again, he will already have my letter. I think it's for the best."

Ricky made a wry face, and Sears said, "Persistent without being aggressive." It was very much like something Stella would have said. Then Sears startled him by adding, "It's a nice quality, Ricky."

At the door Sears held his coat while he slipped his arms into the sleeves. "I thought John looked worse than ever tonight," Ricky said. Sears opened the front door onto dark night illuminated by the street lamp before the house. Orange light fell on the short dead lawn and narrow sidewalk, both littered with fallen leaves. Massive dark clouds moved across the black sky; it felt like winter. "John is dying," Sears said unemotionally, giving back to Ricky his own thought. "See you at Wheat Row. Give my regards to Stella."

Then the door closed behind him, a spruce little man already beginning to shiver in the cold night air.

Sears James

1

They spent most days together at their office, but Ricky honored tradition by waiting until the meeting at Dr. Jaffrey's house to ask Sears the question that had been on his mind for two weeks. "Did you send the letter?"

"Of course. I told you I would."

"What did you say to him?"

"What was agreed. I also mentioned the house, and said that we hoped he would not decide to sell it without inspecting it first. All of Edward's things are still there, of course, including his tapes. If we haven't had the heart to go through them, perhaps he will."

They were standing apart from the other two, just inside the doorway to John Jaffrey's living rooms. John and Lewis were seated in Victorian chairs in a corner of the nearest room, talking to the doctor's housekeeper, Milly Sheehan, who sat on a stool before them, dangling a flowered tray which had held their drinks. Like Ricky's wife, Milly resented being excluded from the meetings of the Chowder Society; unlike Stella Hawthorne, she perpetually hovered at the edges, popping in with bowls of ice cubes and sandwiches and cups of coffee. She irritated Sears to almost exactly the same extent as a summer fly bumping against the window. In many ways Milly was preferable to Stella Hawthorne—less demanding, less driven. And she certainly took care of John: Sears approved of the women who helped his friends. For Sears, it was an open question whether or not Stella had taken care of Ricky.

Now Sears looked down at the person fate had put closer to him than anyone else in the world, and knew that Ricky was thinking that he had weasel-worded his way out of the last question. Ricky's sagacious little jowls were taut with impatience. "All right," he said. "I told him that we weren't satisfied with what we knew of his uncle's death. I did not mention Miss Galli."

"Well, thank God for that," Ricky said, and walked across the room to join the others. Milly stood up, but Ricky smiled and waved her back to the stool. A born gentleman, Ricky had always been charming to women. An armchair stood not four feet away, but he would not sit until Milly asked him to.

Sears took his eyes off Ricky and looked around at the familiar upstairs sitting room. John Jaffrey had turned the whole ground floor of his house into his office—waiting rooms, consulting rooms, a drug cabinet. The other two small rooms on the ground floor were Milly's apartment. John lived the rest of his life up here, where there had been only bedrooms in the old days. Sears had known the interior of John Jaffrey's home for at least sixty years: during his childhood, he had lived two houses down, on the other side of the street. That is, the building he had always thought of as "the family house" was there, to be returned to from boarding school, to be returned to from Cambridge. In those days, Jaffrey's house had been owned by a family named Frederickson, who had two children much younger than Sears. Mr. Frederickson had been a grain merchant, a crafty beer-swilling mountainous man with red hair and a redder face, sometimes mysteriously tinged blue; his wife had been the most desirable woman young Sears had ever seen. She was tall, with coiled long hair some color between brown and auburn, and had a kittenish exotic face and prominent breasts. It was with these that young Sears had been fascinated. Speaking to Viola Frederickson, he'd had to struggle to keep his eyes on her face.

In the summers, home from boarding school and between trips to the country, he was their baby-sitter. The Fredericksons could not afford a full-time nanny, though a girl from the Hollow lived in their house as cook and maid. Possibly it amused Frederickson to have Professor James's son baby-sit for his boys. Sears had his own amusements. He liked the boys and enjoyed their hero worship, which was so much like that of the younger boys at the Hill School; and once the boys were asleep, he enjoyed prowling through the house and seeing what he could find. He saw his first French letter in Abel Frederickson's dresser drawer. He had known he was doing wrong, entering the bedrooms where he now freely stood, but he could not keep himself from doing it. One night he had opened Viola Frederickson's desk and found a photograph of her—she looked impossibly inviting, exotic and warm, an icon of the other, unknowable half of the species. He looked at the way her breasts pushed out the fabric of her blouse, and his mind filled with sensations of their weight, their density. He was so hard that his penis felt like the trunk of a tree: it was the first time that his sexuality had hit him with such force. Groaning, clutching his trousers, he had turned away from the photograph and seen one of her blouses folded on top of the dresser. He could not help himself; he caressed it. He could see where the blouse would bulge, carrying her within it, her flesh seemed to be present beneath his hands, and he unbuttoned his trousers and took out his member. He placed it on the blouse, thinking with the part of his mind that could still think that *it* was making him do it; *it* was making him push its distended tip down where her breasts would cushion it. He groaned, bent double over the blouse, a convulsion went through him, and he exploded. His balls felt as if they'd been caught in a vise. Immediately after, shame struck him like a fist. He rolled the blouse up into his satchel of books and, going a roundabout way home, wrapped the once-flawless thing around a stone and tossed it into the river. Nobody had ever mentioned the stolen blouse to him, but it was the last time he'd been invited to baby-sit.

Through the windows behind Ricky Hawthorne's head, Sears could see a street lamp shining on the second floor of the house Eva Galli had bought when, on whatever whim or impulse, she had come to Milburn. Most of the time he could forget about Eva Galli and where she had lived: he supposed that he was conscious of it now—of her house shining at them through the window—because of some connection his mind made between her and the ridiculous scene he had just remembered.

Maybe I should have cleared out of Milburn when I could, he thought: the bedroom where Edward Wanderley had died exactly a year ago was just overhead. By unspoken common agreement, none of them had alluded to the coincidence of their meeting here again on the anniversary of their friend's death. A fraction of Ricky Hawthorne's sense of doom flickered in his mind, and then he thought: *you old fool, you still feel guilty about that blouse. Hah!*

2

"It's my turn tonight," Sears said, relaxing as well as he could into Jaffrey's largest armchair and making sure he was facing away from the old Galli house, "and I want to tell you about certain events that happened to me when I was a young man experimenting with the profession of teaching in the country around Elmira. I say experimenting because even then, at the beginning of my first year, I had no certainty that I was destined for that profession. I'd signed a two-year contract, but I didn't think they could hold me to it if I wanted to leave. Well, one of the most dreadful things in my life happened to me there, or it didn't happen and I imagined it all, but anyhow it scared the pants off me and eventually made it impossible for me to stay on. This is the worst story I know, and I've kept it locked up in my mind for fifty years.

You know what a schoolmaster's duties were in those days. This was no urban school, and it was no Hill School either—God knows that was where I should have applied, but I had a number of elaborate ideas in those days. I fancied myself as a real country Socrates, bringing the light of reason into the wilderness. Wilderness! In those days, the country around Elmira was nearly that, as I remember, but now there isn't even a suburb where the little town was. A freeway cloverleaf was put up right over the site of the school. The whole thing's under concrete. It used to be called Four Forks, and it's gone. But back then, during my sabbatical from Milburn, it was a typical little village, ten or twelve houses, a general store, a post office, a blacksmith, the schoolhouse. All of these buildings looked alike, in a general sort of way—they were all wooden, they hadn't been painted in years so they all looked a bit gray and dismal. The schoolhouse was one room, of course, one room for all eight grades. When I came up for my interview I was told that I'd be boarding with the Mathers—they'd put in the lowest bid, and I soon found out why—and that my day would start at six. I had to chop the wood for the schoolhouse stove, get a good fire going, sweep the place out and get the books in place, pump up the water, clean the boards—wash the windows, too, when they needed it.

Then at seven-thirty the students would come. And

my job was to teach all eight grades, reading, writing, arithmetic, music, geography, penmanship, history . . . the "works." Now I'd run a mile from any such prospect, but then I was full of Abraham Lincoln on one end of a log and Mark Hopkins on the other, and I was bursting to start. The whole idea simply enraptured me. I was besotted. I suppose even then the town was dying, but I couldn't see it. What I saw was splendor—freedom and splendor. A little tarnished perhaps, but splendor all the same.

You see, I didn't *know*. I couldn't guess what most of my pupils would be like. I didn't know that most country schoolteachers in these little hamlets were boys of about nineteen, with no more education than they'd be giving. I didn't know how muddy and unpleasant a place like Four Forks would be most of the year. I didn't know I'd be half-starved most of the time. Nor that it would be a condition of my job that I report for church every Sunday off in the next village, an eight-mile hike. I didn't know how rough it would be.

I began to find out when I went over to the Mathers with my suitcase that first night. Charlie Mather used to be the postmaster in town, but when the Republicans got into office they made Howard Hummell the postmaster, and Charlie Mather never got over his resentment. He was permanently sour. When he took me up to the room I was to use, I saw that it was unfinished—the floor was plain unsanded wood, and the ceiling consisted of just the roofing joists and tiles. "Was makin' this for our daughter," Mather told me. "She died. One less mouth to feed." The bed was a tired old mattress on the floor, with one old army blanket over it. In the winter, there wasn't enough warmth for an Eskimo in that room. But I saw that it had a desk and a kerosene lamp, and I was still seeing stars, and I said fine, I'll love it here, something to that effect. Mather grunted in disbelief, as well he might.

Supper that night was potatoes and creamed corn. "You'll eat no meat here," Mather said, "unless you save up and buy it yourself. I'm getting the allowance to keep you alive, not to fatten you up." I don't suppose I ate meat more than six times at the Mather table, and that was all at once, when somebody gave him a goose and we had goose every day until there was nothing left of it. Eventually some of my pupils began bringing me ham and beef sandwiches—their parents knew Mather was a mean-fisted man. Mather himself ate his big meal at noon, but he made it clear that it was my duty to spend the lunch hour in the schoolhouse— "offering extra help and giving punishments."

Because up there they believed in the birch. I'd taught my first day when I found out about that. I say, *taught,* but really all I'd managed to do was keep them quiet for a few hours and write down their names and ask a few questions. It was astonishing. Only two of the older girls could read, simple addition and subtraction was as far as their math went, and not only had a few of them not heard of foreign countries, one of them didn't even believe they existed. "Aw, there's nothin' like that," one scrawny ten-year-old told me. "A place where people ain't even American? Where they don't even talk American?" But he couldn't go further, he was laughing too hard at the absurdity of the idea, and I saw a mouthful of appalling, blackened teeth. "So what about the war, dopey?" another boy said. "Never heard tell of the Germans?" Before I could react, the first boy flew over the desk and started beating the second boy. It looked as though he was literally set on murdering him. I tried to separate the two boys—the girls were all shrieking—and I grabbed the assailant's arm. "He's right," I said. "He shouldn't have called you a name, but he is right. Germans are the people who live in Germany, and the world war . . ." I stopped short because the boy was growling at me. He was like a savage dog, and for the first time I realized that he was mentally disturbed, perhaps retarded. He was ready to bite me. "Now apologize to your friend," I said.

"Ain't no friend of mine."

"Apologize."

"He's queer, sir," the other boy said. His face was

pale, and his eyes were frightened, and he had the beginnings of a black eye. "I shouldn't never of said that to him."

I asked the first boy what his name was. "Fenny Bate," he managed to drool out. He was calming down. I sent the second boy back to his desk. "Fenny," I said, "the trouble is that you were wrong. America isn't the whole world, just as New York isn't the whole United States." This was too complicated, and I had lost him. So I brought him up to the front and made him sit down while I drew maps on the board. "Now this is the United States of America, and this is Mexico, and this is the Atlantic Ocean . . ."

Fenny was shaking his head darkly. "Lies," he said. "All that's lies. That stuff ain't there. It AIN'T!" When he shouted he pushed at his desk and it went crashing over.

I asked him to pick up his desk, and when he just shook his head, starting to slobber again, I picked it up myself. Some of the children gasped. "So you've seen or heard of maps and other countries?" I asked. He nodded. "But they're lies."

"Who told you that?"

He shook his head and refused to say. If he had shown any signs of embarrassment, I would have thought that he'd learned this misinformation from his parents; but he did not—he was just angry and sullen.

At noon all the children took their paper bags outside and ate their sandwiches in the lot around the school. It would be window-dressing to call it a playground, though there was a rickety set of swings in back of the school. I kept my eye on Fenny Bate. He was left alone by most of the other children. When he roused himself from his stupor and tried to join a group, the others pointedly walked away and left him standing alone, his hands in his pockets. From time to time a skinny girl with lank blond hair came up and spoke to him—she rather resembled him, and I imagined that she must have been his sister. I checked my lists: Constance Bate, in the fifth grade. She had been one of the quiet ones.

Then, when I looked back at Fenny, I saw an odd-looking man standing on the road outside the building, looking across the school grounds at him, just as I was doing. Fenny Bate was sitting unaware between us. For some reason, this man gave me a shock. It was not just that he was odd in appearance, though he was that, dressed in old disreputable working clothes, with wild black hair, ivory cheeks, a handsome face and extremely powerful looking arms and shoulders. It was the way he was looking at Fenny Bate. He looked feral. And with the wildness, there was a striking sort of freedom in the way he stood there, a freedom that went deeper than mere self-assurance. To me he seemed extremely dangerous; and it seemed that I had been transported into a region where men and boys were wild beasts in disguise. I looked away, almost frightened by the savagery in the man's face, and when I looked back he was gone.

My notions of the place were confirmed that evening, when I had forgotten all about the man outside on the road. I had gone upstairs to my drafty room to try to work out my lessons for the second day. I would have to introduce the multiplication tables to the upper grades, they all could use some extremely elementary geography . . . things of this sort were going through my mind when Sophronia Mather entered my room. The first thing she did was to turn down the kerosene lamp I had been using. "That's for full dark, not evening," she said. "We can't afford to have you using up all the kerosene. You'll learn to read your books by the light God gives you."

I was startled to see her in my room. During supper the previous evening she had been silent, and judging by her face, which was pinched and sallow and tight as a drumhead, you would say that silence was her natural mode. She made it very expressive, I can tell you. But I was to learn that apart from her husband, she had no fear of speech.

"I've come to quiz you, schoolteacher," she said. "There's been talk."

"Already?" I asked.

"You make your ending in your manner of beginning, and how you begin is how you'll go on. I've heard from Mariana Birdwood that you tolerate misbehavior in your classes."

"I don't believe I did," I said.

"Her Ethel claims you did."

I could not put a face to the name Ethel Birdwood, but I remembered calling it out—she was one of the older girls, the fifteen-year-olds, I thought. "And what does Ethel Birdwood claim I tolerated?"

"It's that Fenny Bate. Didn't he use fists on another boy? Right in front of your nose?"

"I spoke to him."

"*Spoke?* Speakin's no good. Why didn't you use your ferule?"

"I don't possess one," I said.

Now she really was shocked. "But you *must* beat them," she finally got out. "It's the only way. You must ferule one or two every day. And Fenny Bate more than the rest."

"Why particularly him?"

"Because he is bad."

"I saw that he is troubled, slow, disturbed," I said, "but I don't think that I saw that he was bad."

"He is. He is bad. And the other children expect him to be beaten. If your ideas are too uppity for us, then you'll have to leave the school. It's not only the children who expect you to use the ferule." She turned as if to go out. "I thought I would do you the kindness of speaking to you before my husband hears that you have been neglecting your duties. Mind you, you'll take my advice. There's no teaching without beating."

"But what makes Fenny Bate so notorious?" I asked, ignoring that horrific last remark. "It would be unjust to persecute a boy who needs help."

"The ferule's all the help he needs. He's not bad, he's badness itself. You should make him bleed and keep him quiet—keep him *down*. I'm only trying to help you, schoolmaster. We have use of the little extra money your allowance brings us." With that she left me. I did not even have time to ask her about the peculiar man I had seen that afternoon.

Well, I had no intention of doing further damage to the town scapegoat.

(Milly Sheehan, her face puckered with distaste, set down the ashtray she had been pretending to polish, glanced at the window to make sure the drapes were closed and edged around the door. Sears, pausing in his story, saw that she had left it open a crack.)

3

Sears James, pausing in his story and thinking with annoyance that Milly's eavesdropping was becoming less subtle every month, was unaware of an event which had occurred that afternoon in town and would affect all of their lives. This was unremarkable in itself, the arrival of a striking young woman on a Trailways bus— a young woman who stepped out of the bus on the corner of the bank and the library and looked around with an expression of confident satisfaction like that of a successful woman returning for a nostalgic look at her home town. That was what she suggested, holding a small suitcase in her hand and smiling slightly in a sudden fall of brilliant leaves, and you would have said, watching her, that her success was the measure of her revenge. She looked, with her long handsome coat and her abundance of dark hair, as if she had come back to rejoice discreetly over how far she had come—as if that were half the pleasure she felt. Milly Sheehan, out shopping for the doctor's groceries, saw her standing by the stop as the bus rolled away toward Binghamton and thought for a moment that she knew her; as did Stella Hawthorne, who was having a cup of coffee beside the window of the Village Pump restaurant. Still smiling, the dark-haired girl strode past the window, and Stella turned her head to watch her cross the town square and go up the steps of the Archer Hotel. Her companion, an associate professor of anthropology at the nearby SUNY college, named Harold Sims, said, "The scrutiny one beautiful woman gives another! But I've never seen you do it before, Stel."

She, who detested being called "Stel" said, "Did you think she was beautiful?"

"I'd be a liar if I said I didn't."

"Well, if you think I'm beautiful too, I guess it's all right." She smiled rather automatically at Sims, who was twenty years younger than herself and infatuated, and looked back at the Archer Hotel, where the tall young woman was just negotiating the door and disappearing within.

"If it's all right, why are you staring?"

"Oh, it's just—" Stella closed her mouth. "It's just nothing at all. That's the sort of woman you ought to be taking to lunch, not a battered old monument like me."

"Jesus, if you think that," Sims said and tried to take her hand beneath the table. She brushed his hand aside with a touch of her fingers. Stella Hawthorne had never appreciated being fondled in restaurants. She would have liked to have given his paw a good hard slap.

"Stella, give me a break."

She looked straight into his mild brown eyes and said, "Hadn't you better get back to all your nice little students?"

In the meantime the young woman was checking into the hotel. Mrs. Hardie, who had been running the Archer Hotel with her son since the death of her husband, emerged from her office and came up to the lovely young person on the other side of the desk. "May I help you?" she asked, and thought *how am I going to keep Jim from this one?*

"I'll need a room with a bath," the girl said. "I'd like to stay here until I can find a place to rent somewhere in town."

"Oh, how nice," said Mrs. Hardie. "You're moving

to Milburn? Well, I think that's real sweet. Most all the young people here nowadays just can't wait to get out. Like my Jim, he'll take your bags up, he thinks every day here is another day in jail. New York is where he wants to go. Would that be where you're from?"

"I've lived there. But some of my family lived here once."

"Well, here are our rates, and here's the register," said Mrs. Hardie, sliding a mimeographed sheet of paper and the big leather-bound register across the counter to her. "You'll find this a real nice quiet hotel, most of the folks here are residential, just like a board-inghouse really, but with the service of a hotel, and no loud parties at night." The young woman had nodded at the rates and was signing the register. "No discos, not on your life, and I have to tell you straight off, no men in your room past eleven."

"Fine," the girl said, turning the register back to Mrs. Hardie, who read the name written in a clear elegant handwriting: Anna Mostyn, with an address given in the West Eighties in New York.

"Oh, that's good," said Mrs. Hardie, "you never know how girls will take that these days, but"—she looked up at the new guest's face, and was stopped short by the indifference in the long blue eyes. Her first, almost unconscious thought was *she's a cold one,* and this was followed by the perfectly conscious reflection that this girl would have no trouble handling Jim. "Anna's such a nice old-fashioned name."

"Yes."

Mrs. Hardie, a little disconcerted, rang the bell for her son.

"I'm really a very old-fashioned sort of person," the girl said.

"Didn't you say you had family here in town?"

"I did, but it was a long time ago."

"It's just that I didn't recognize the name."

"No, you wouldn't. An aunt of mine lived here once.

Her name was Eva Galli. But you probably wouldn't have known her."

(Ricky's wife, sitting alone in the restaurant, suddenly snapped her fingers and exclaimed, "I'm getting old." She had remembered of whom the girl had reminded her. The waiter, a high-school dropout by the look of him, bent over the table, not quite sure how to give her the bill after the gentleman had stormed off, and uttered "Huh?" "Oh get away, you fool," she said, wondering why it was that while one half of high-school dropouts looked like thugs, the other half resembled physicists. "Oh, here, better give me the bill before you faint.")

Jim Hardie kept sneaking looks at her all the way up the stairs, and once he had opened her room and put her suitcase down offered, "I hope you're going to stick around a good long time."

"I thought your mother said you hated Milburn."

"I don't hate it so much anymore," he said, giving her the look which had melted Penny Draeger in the back seat of his car the previous night.

"Why?"

"Ah," he said, not knowing how to continue in the face of her total refusal to be melted. "Ah, you know."

"I do?"

"Look. I just mean you're a goddamn great-lookin' lady, that's all. You know what I mean. You got a lot of style." He decided to be bolder than he felt. "Ladies with style turn me on."

"Do they?"

"Yeah." He nodded. He couldn't figure her out. If she was a nonstarter, she would have told him to leave at the beginning. But though she let him hang around, she wasn't looking interested or flattered—she wasn't even looking amused. Then she surprised him by doing what he had been half hoping she would do, and took off her coat. She wasn't much in the chest department, but she had good legs. Then, entirely without warning, a total awareness of her body assaulted him—a blast of pure sensuality, nothing like the steamy posturing of

Penny Draeger or the other high-school girls he had bedded, a wave of pure and cold sensuality which dwindled him.

"Ah," he said, desperately hoping she would not send him away, "I bet you had some kind of great job in the city. What are you, in television or something?"

"No."

He fidgeted. "Well, it's not like I don't know your address or anything. Maybe I could drop in sometime, have a talk?"

"Maybe. Do you talk?"

"Hah. Yeah, well, guess I better get back downstairs. I mean, I gotta lot of storm windows to put up, this cold weather we got . . ."

She sat on the bed and held her hand out. Half reluctantly, he went toward her. When he touched her hand, she placed a neatly folded dollar bill in his palm. "I'll tell you what I think," she said. "I think bellboys shouldn't wear jeans. They look sloppy."

He accepted the dollar, too confused to thank her, and fled.

(It was Ann-Veronica Moore, thought Stella, that actress at John's house the night Edward died. Stella allowed the intimidated boy to hold her fur coat. Ann-Veronica Moore, why should I think of her? I only saw her for a few minutes, and that girl really didn't resemble her at all.)

4

No, Sears continued, I was resolved to help that poor creature, Fenny Bate. I didn't think there was such a thing as a bad boy, unless misunderstanding and cruelty were to make him bad. And that you could redress. So I began a little reclamation program. When Fenny tipped over his desk the next day, I righted it myself, much to the disgust of the older children; and at lunchtime I asked him to stay inside with me.

The other children filed out, buzzing with speculation—I'm sure they thought I was going to cane him once they were out of sight—and then I noticed that his sister was lurking in the dark rear corner. "I won't hurt him, Constance," I said. "You can stay behind too if you wish." Those poor children! I can still see both of them, with their bad teeth and tattered clothing, he full of suspicion and resentment and fear and she simply fearful—for him. She crept into a chair and I went to work to try to straighten out some of Fenny's misconceptions. I told him all the stories of explorers I knew, about Lewis and Clarke and Cortez and Nansen and Ponce de Leon, stuff I was going to use later in class, but it had no effect on Fenny. He *knew* that the world went only about forty or fifty miles out from Four Forks, and that the people within this radius were the world's population. He clung to this notion with the dogged stubbornness of the stupid. "Who in the world told you this, Fenny?" I asked. He shook his head. "Did you make it up yourself?" He shook his head again. "Was it your parents?"

Back in the dark corner, Constance giggled—giggled without any humor. That laugh of hers sent chills through me—it conjured up pictures of a nearly bestial life. Of course, that was what they had; and all the other children knew it. And as I found out later, it was much worse, much more unnatural, than anything I could have imagined.

Anyhow, I raised my hands in despair or impatience, and the wretched girl must have thought I was going to strike him, because she called out, "It was Gregory!"

Fenny looked back at her, and I swear that I've never seen anyone look so frightened. In the next instant he was off his chair and out of the schoolroom. I tried to call him back, but it was no good. He was running as if for life, off into the woods, sprinting in the jackrabbit country way. The girl hung in the doorway, watching him go. And now she looked frightened and dismayed—her whole being had turned pale. "Who is Gregory, Constance?" I asked her, and her face twisted. "Does he sometimes walk by the schoolhouse? Is his hair like this?" And I stuck my hands up over my head, my fingers spread wide—and then she was off too, running as fast as he had.

Well, that afternoon I was accepted by the other students. They'd assumed that I had beaten both of the Bate children, and so taken part in the natural order of things. And that night at dinner I got, if not an extra potato, at least a sort of congealed smile from Sophronia Mather. Evidently Ethel Birdwood had reported to her mother that the new schoolmaster had seen reason.

Fenny and Constance didn't come to school the next two days. I stewed about that, and thought that I'd acted so clumsily that they might never return. On the second day I was so restless that I paced around the schoolyard during lunchtime. The children regarded me as they would a dangerous lunatic—it was clear that teacher was supposed to stay indoors, preferably administering the ferule. Then I heard something that stopped me dead and made me whirl around toward a group of girls, who were sitting rather primly on the grass. They were the biggest girls and one of them was Ethel Birdwood. I was sure that I'd heard her mention the name Gregory. "Tell me about Gregory, Ethel," I said.

"What's Gregory?" she asked, simpering. "There's no one with that name here." She gave me a great coweyed look, and I was certain she was thinking of that rural tradition of the schoolmaster marrying his eldest female pupil. She was a confident girl, this Ethel Birdwood, and her father had the reputation of being prosperous.

I wasn't having it. "I just heard you mention his name."

"You must be mistaken, Mr. James," she said, dripping honey.

"I do not feel charitable to liars," I said. "Tell me about this Gregory person."

Of course they all assumed that I was threatening her with a caning. Another girl came to her rescue. "We were saying that Gregory fixed that gutter," she said, and pointed to the side of the school. One of the rain gutters was obviously new.

"Well, he'll never come around this school again if I can help it," I said, and left them to their infuriating giggling.

After school that day I thought I'd visit the lion's den, as it were, and walk up to the Bate home. I knew it was about as far out of town as Lewis's house is from Milburn. I set off on the most likely road, and walked quite a way, three or four miles, when I realized I'd probably gone too far. I hadn't passed any houses, so the Bate home had to be actually in the woods themselves, instead of on their edge as I had imagined. I took a likely-looking trail, and thought I would simply tack back and forth toward town until I found them.

Unfortunately, I got lost. I went into ravines and up hills and through scrub until I couldn't have told you where even the road was anymore. It all looked appallingly alike. Then, just at dusk, I was aware of being watched. It was a remarkably uncanny feeling—it was like knowing a tiger was behind me, about to pounce. I turned around and put my back against a big elm. And then I saw something. A man stepped into a clearing about thirty yards from me—the man I had seen before. Gregory, or so I thought. He said nothing, and neither did I. He just gazed at me, absolutely silent, with that wild hair and that ivory face. I felt hatred, absolute hatred, streaming from him. An air of utter unreasonable violence hung about him, along with that peculiar freedom I had sensed earlier—he was like a madman. He could have killed me off in those woods, and no one would have known. And trust me, what I saw in his face was murder, nothing else. Just as I expected him to come forward and attack me, he stepped behind a tree.

I went forward very slowly. "What do you want?" I called, simulating bravery. There was no answer. I went forward a bit more. Finally I got to the tree where I had seen him, and there wasn't a trace of him—he had just melted away.

I was still lost, and I still felt threatened. For that was the meaning of his appearance, I knew—it was a threat. I took a few steps off in a random direction, passed through another thick stand of trees, and stopped short. For a moment I was scared. Right before me, closer than that apparition had been, was a thin shabbily dressed girl with stringy blond hair: Constance Bate.

"Where's Fenny?" I asked.

She raised one bony arm and pointed off to the side. Then he too rose up like a—"like a snake from a basket," I must admit, is the metaphor that comes to mind. On his face, when he stood up in the tall weeds, was that characteristic Fenny Bate expression of sullen guilt.

"I was looking for your home," I said, and they both pointed at once in the same direction, again without speaking. Looking through a chink in the woods, I saw a tarpaper shack with one greasepaper window and a stingy little pipe of a chimney. You used to see a lot of tarpaper shacks here and there, though thank goodness they have disappeared now, but that one was the most sordid I ever did see. I know I have the reputation of being a conservative, but I've never equated virtue with money, nor poverty with vice, yet that mean stinking little shack—looking at it, you knew it stank—somehow for me appeared to breathe foulness. No, it was worse than that. It wasn't merely that the lives within would be brutalized by poverty, but that they would be twisted, malformed . . . my heart fell, I looked away and saw an emaciated black dog nosing at a dead cushion of feathers that must have been a chicken once. This surely, I thought, must be how Fenny got the reputation for being "bad"—the prim folks of Four Forks had taken one look at his home and condemned him for life.

Yet I didn't want to go in there. I didn't believe in evil, but evil was what I felt.

I turned back to the children, who had the oddest

frozen look in their eyes. "I want to see you in school tomorrow," I said.

Fenny shook his head.

"But I want to *help* you," I said. I was on the verge of making a speech: what I wanted to say to him was that it was my plan to change his life, to rescue him, in a sense I suppose to make him human . . . that obstinate, frozen look on his mug stopped me. There was something else in it too, and I realized with a shock that something about Fenny was reminding me of my last glimpse of the mysterious Gregory. "You must come back to school tomorrow," I said.

Constance said, "Gregory doesn't want us to. Gregory said we have to stay here."

"Well, what I say is he comes, and you come too."

"I'll ask Gregory."

"Oh, to hell with Gregory," I shouted, "you'll come," and walked away from the two of them. That queer sensation stayed with me until I found the road again —it was like walking away from damnation.

You can guess what the result was. They did not return. Things ticked on in their normal way for several days, Ethel Birdwood and some of the other girls giving me liquid glances whenever I called on them for an answer, me toiling over the next day's lessons in that frigid box of a room and rising extremely unlike Phoebus with the dawn to prepare the schoolhouse. Eventually Ethel began bringing me sandwiches for lunch, and soon my other admirers among the girls were bringing sandwiches too. I used to save one in my pocket to eat in my room after supper with the Mathers.

On Sundays I made the long hike to Footville for my required visit to the Lutheran church there. It was not as deadly as I had feared. The minister was an old German, Franz Gruber, who called himself Dr. Gruber. The doctorate was genuine—he was a much subtler man than his gross body or residence in Footville, New York, suggested. I thought his sermons were interesting, and I decided to speak to him.

When the Bate children finally appeared, they seemed worn and tired, like drinkers after a strenuous night. This became a pattern. They'd miss two days, come in, miss three, come in for two: and each time I saw them, they looked worse. Fenny in particular seemed in decline. It was as though he were aging prematurely: he grew even thinner, his skin seemed to crease on his forehead and at the corners of his eyes. And when I saw him, I could swear that he looked as though he were smirking at me—Fenny Bate smirking, though I would have sworn that he didn't possess the mental equipment for it. For him, it seemed corrupt—it frightened me.

Therefore, one Sunday after the service I spoke to Dr. Gruber at the church door. I waited to be last to shake his hand, and when everybody else had filed away down the road, I told him that I wanted his advice on a problem.

He must have thought that I was going to confess to an adultery, or some such. But he was very kind, and invited me into his home, across the street from the church.

Very graciously, he escorted me into his library. This was a large room, entirely book-lined—I hadn't seen a room like it since I'd left Harvard. It was obviously the room of a scholar: it was a room where a man comfortable with ideas worked with them. Most of the books were in German, but many were in Latin and Greek. He had the patristic writings in big soft leather folios, Bible commentaries, works of theology and the great aid to sermon-writers, a Bible concordance. On a shelf behind his desk I was surprised to see a little collection of Lully, Fludd, Bruno, what you could call the occult studies of the Renaissance. Also, even more surprisingly, a few antiquarian books about witchcraft and Satanism.

Dr. Gruber had been out of the room fetching beer, and when he came in he saw me looking at these books.

"What you see," he said in his guttural accent, "is

the reason you find me in Footville, Mr. James. I hope
you will not think me a cracked old fool on the evidence of those books." Without my prompting him,
he told me the story, and it's as you'd expect—he'd
been brilliant, approved of by his elders, he had written books himself, but when he had shown too much
interest in what he called "hermetic matters," he was
ordered to stop that line of study. He'd published one
further paper, and been banished to the most out-of-
the-way congregation the Lutheran establishment could
find. "Now," he said, "my cards are on the table, as
my new countrymen say. I never speak of these hermetic matters in my sermons, but I continue my studies
in them. You are free to go or to speak, as you please."
This sounded a little pompous to me, and I was a little
taken aback, but I saw no reason not to continue.

I told him the whole story, not stinting on the detail.
He listened with great attentiveness, and it was clear
that he had heard of Gregory and the Bate children.
More than that, he seemed to be very excited by the
story.

When I finished he said, "And all of this happened
just as you have explained?"

"Of course."

"You have spoken of it to no one else?"

"No."

"I am very happy you have come to me," he said,
and instead of saying anything further, pulled a gigantic
pipe out of a desk drawer, filled it and began to smoke,
all the while fixing me with his protuberant eyes. I began to feel uneasy, and half-regretted that I had taken
his earlier comments so lightly. "Your landlady never
gave you any idea of why she thought Fenny Bate was
'badness itself'?"

I shook my head, trying to rid myself of the negative
impression I'd just had of him. "Do you know why
she would?"

"It is a well-known story," he answered. "In these
two little towns, actually it is quite a famous story."

"*Is* Fenny bad?" I asked.

"He is not bad, but he is corrupt," said Dr. Gruber. "But from what you say—"

"It could be worse? I confess," I said, "it's entirely a mystery."

"More so than you imagine," he said calmly. "If I try to explain it to you, you will be tempted, on the basis of what you know about me, to think me insane." His eyes bulged even more.

"If Fenny is corrupt," I asked, "who corrupted him?"

"Oh, Gregory," he replied. "Gregory, without doubt. Gregory is in back of it all."

"But who is Gregory?" I had to ask.

"The man you saw. I'm positive of that. You have described him perfectly." He held his pudgy fingers up behind his head, imitating my own gesture to Constance Bate. "Perfectly, I assure you. Yet when you hear more, you will doubt my word."

"For the sake of heaven, why?"

He shook his head, and I saw that his free hand was trembling. For a second I wondered if I really had stumbled into intimate conversation with a madman.

"Fenny's parents had three children," he said, puffing out smoke. "Gregory Bate was the first."

"He is their brother!" I exclaimed. "One day I thought I saw a resemblance . . . yes, I see. But there's nothing unnatural in that."

"That depends, I think, on what passed between them."

I tried to take it in. "You mean something unnatural passed between them."

"And with the sister as well."

A feeling of horror went through me. I could see that cold handsome face, and that hateful careless manner—Gregory's air of being free of all restraint. "Between Gregory and the sister."

"And, as I said, between Gregory and Fenny."

"He corrupted both of them, then. Why isn't Constance as condemned by Four Forks as Fenny?"

"Remember, schoolteacher, that this is the hinterland. A touch of—unnaturalness—between brother and

sister among those wretched families in shacks is perhaps not so unnatural after all."

"But between brother and brother—" I might have
been back at Harvard, discussing a savage tribe with a
professor of anthropology.

"It is."

"By God, it is!" I exclaimed, seeing that crafty, prematurely aged expression on Fenny's face. "And now
he is trying to send me off—he sees me as an interference."

"Apparently he does. I hope you see why."

"Because I won't stand for it," I said. "He wants to
get rid of me."

"Ah," he said. "Gregory wants everything."

"You mean he wants them forever."

"Both of them forever—but from your story, perhaps
Fenny most of all."

"Can't their parents stop this?"

"The mother is dead. The father left when Gregory
grew old enough to beat him."

"They live alone in that appalling place?"

He nodded.

It was terrible: it meant the miasma, the sense of
the place as somehow damned, came from the children
themselves: from what happened between them and
Gregory.

"Well," I protested, "can't the children themselves
do something to protect themselves?"

"They did," he said.

"But what?" I had prayer in mind, I suppose, since
I was talking with a preacher, or boarding with another
family—but as to that, my own experience had shown
me how far charity went in Four Forks.

"You won't take my word for it," he said, "so I
must show you." He abruptly stood up, and gestured
for me to stand as well. "Outside," he ordered. Beneath
his excitement, he seemed very disturbed, and just for
a moment I thought that he found me as unpleasant as
I did him, with his showers of pipe tobacco and his
bulging eyes.

I left the room and on the way out of the house, passed a room with a table set for one. I smelled a roast cooking, and an open bottle of beer sat on the table, so it could be that all he disliked was being kept from his lunch.

He slammed the door behind us and set off back toward the church. This was mystifying indeed. When he had crossed the road, he called to me without turning his head. "You know that Gregory was the school handyman? That he used to do odd jobs around the school?"

"One of the girls said something about it," I replied, watching him continue on around the side of the church. What next, I wondered, a trip into the fields? And what would I have to be shown before I would believe it?

A little graveyard lay behind the church, and I had time, following waddling Dr. Gruber, to idly look at the names on the massive nineteenth-century tombstones—Josiah Foote, Sarah Foote, all of that clan which had founded the village, and other names which meant nothing to me. Dr. Gruber was now standing, with a decided air of impatience, by a little gate at the back of the graveyard.

"Here," he said.

Well, I thought, if you're too lazy to open it yourself, and bent down to lift the latch.

"Not that," he said sharply. "Look down. Look at the cross."

I looked where he was pointing. It was a crude hand-painted wooden cross, standing where a tombstone would, at the head of a grave. Someone had lettered the name Gregory Bate on the horizontal piece of the cross. I looked back up at Dr. Gruber, and there was no doubt this time, he was looking at me with distaste.

"It can't be," I said. "It's preposterous. I saw him."

"Believe me, schoolteacher, this is where your rival is buried," he said, and not for a long time after did I

notice his peculiar choice of words. "The mortal portion of him, at any rate."

I was numb; I repeated what I had said. "It can't be."

He ignored my remark. "One night a year ago,
Gregory Bate was doing some work in the schoolyard.
While doing it, he looked up and noticed—I imagine
this is what happened—that the rain gutter required
some attention, and he went around to the back of the
school and got the ladder and went up. Fenny and
Constance saw their chance to escape his tyranny, and
knocked the ladder out from under him. He fell, struck
his head on the corner of the building, and died."

"What were they doing there at night?"

He shrugged. "He always took them with him. They
had been sitting in the playground."

"I don't believe that they killed him on purpose," I
said.

"Howard Hummell, the postmaster, saw them running off. It was he who found Gregory's body."

"So nobody actually saw it happen."

"Nobody had to actually see it, Mr. James. What
happened was clear to all."

"It's not clear to me," I said, and he shrugged again.
"What did they do afterward?"

"They ran. It must have been obvious that they had
succeeded. The back of his head was crushed. Fenny
and his sister disappeared for three weeks—they hid out
in the woods. By the time they realized they had nowhere to go and returned home, we had buried Gregory.
Howard Hummell had told what he had seen, and
people assumed what they assumed. Hence, you see,
Fenny's 'badness.' "

"But now—" I said, looking down at the crudely
lettered grave. The children must have made and lettered the cross, I realized, and suddenly that seemed
the most gruesome detail of all.

"Oh yes, now. Now Gregory wants him back. From
what you tell me, he *has* him back—he has both of
them back. But I imagine that he will wish to remove

Fenny from your—influence." He pronounced this last word with a meticulous Germanic precision.

It chilled me. "To take him."

"To take him."

"Can't I save him?" I said, almost pleading.

"I suspect at least no one else can," he said, looking at me as from a great distance.

"Can't you help, for God's sake!"

"Not even for His. From what you say, it has gone too far. We do not believe in exorcisms, in my church."

"You just believe—" I was furious and scornful.

"In evil, yes. We do believe in that."

I turned away from him. He must have imagined that I was going to return and beg him for help, but when I kept on walking, he called out, "Take care, schoolteacher."

Walking home I was in a sort of daze—I could scarcely believe or accept what had seemed irrefutable while I talked with the preacher. Yet he had shown me the grave; and I had seen with my own eyes the transformation in Fenny—I had seen Gregory: it is not too much to say that I had felt him, the impression he made on me was that strong.

And then I stopped walking, about a mile from Four Forks, faced with proof that Gregory Bate knew exactly what I had discovered, and knew exactly what I had intended. One of the farmers' fields there formed a large wide bare hill visible from the road, and he was up on the hill staring down at me. He didn't move a muscle when I saw him, but his intensity quivered out of him, and I must have jumped a foot. He was looking at me as though he could read every thought in my head. Far up in the clouds above him, a hawk was circling aimlessly. Any trace of doubt left me. I knew that everything Gruber had told me was true.

It was all I could do not to run. But I would not show cowardice before him, no matter how cowardly I felt. He was waiting for me to run, I imagine, standing up there with his arms hanging straight and his pale face visible as only a white smudge and all that feeling arrowing toward me. I forced myself to continue home at a walk.

Dinner I could scarcely force myself to swallow—I had no more than a bite or two. Mather said, "If you'll starve yourself there's more for the rest of us. It's no matter to me."

I faced him directly. "Did Fenny Bate have a brother as well as a sister?"

He looked at me with as much curiosity as he possessed.

"Well, did he?"

"He did."

"What was the brother's name?"

"It was Gregory, but I'll thank you to refrain from speaking about him."

"Were you afraid of him?" I asked, because I saw fear on both his face and his wife's.

"Please, Mr. James," said Sophronia Mather. "This will do no good."

"Nobody speaks of that Gregory Bate," her husband said.

"What happened to him?" I asked.

He stopped chewing and put down his fork. "I don't know what you heard or who you heard it from, but I'll tell you this. If any man was damned, it was that Gregory Bate, and whatever happened to him was deserved. That's an end to talk of Gregory Bate." Then he pushed more food into his mouth, and the discussion was over. Mrs. Mather kept her eyes religiously on her plate for the rest of the meal.

I was in a stew. Neither of the two Bate children appeared in school for two or three days, and it was almost as though I had dreamed the whole affair. I went through the motions of teaching, but my mind was with them, especially poor Fenny, and the danger he was in.

What above all kept the horror before me was that I saw Gregory in town one day.

Because it was a Saturday, Four Forks was filled

with farmers and their wives who came in for their shopping. Every Saturday, the little town had almost a fairground look, at least in contrast to the way it looked normally. The sidewalks were crowded and the stores were busy. Dozens of horses stamped in the street, and everywhere you saw the eager faces of kids, all piled into the backs of wagons, their eyes wide open with being in town. I recognized many of my pupils and waved to some of them.

Then a big farmer I'd never met before tapped my shoulder and said that he knew I was his son's teacher and that he wanted to shake my hand. I thanked him and listened to him talk for a bit. Then I saw Gregory over his shoulder. Gregory was leaning against the side of the post office, indifferent to everything about him and staring at me—just intently staring, as he must have been doing from the hilltop. My mouth dried up, and something obviously showed in my face, because my pupil's father stopped talking and asked me if I felt all right.

"Oh yes," I said, but it must have looked as if I were being deliberately rude, because I kept looking over his shoulder. No one else could see Gregory: they just walked by him, carrying on in the normal way, looking right through him.

Now where I had seen that abandoned freedom I could see only depravity.

I made some excuse to the farmer—a headache, an abscessed tooth—and turned back to Gregory. He was gone. He had vanished during the few seconds I was saying good-bye to the farmer.

So I knew that the showdown was coming, and that he would pick the time and place.

The next time Fenny and Constance came to school I was determined that I would protect them. They were both pale and quiet, and enough of an aura of strangeness enveloped them for the other children to leave them alone. It was perhaps four days since my seeing their brother leaning against the Four Forks post office. I could not imagine what had been happening to them since I had last seen them, but it was as though a wasting disease had hold of them. They seemed so lost and apart, those ragged backward children. I was determined to keep them under my protection.

When the lessons for the day were over, I kept them back as the others raced for home. They sat uncomplaining at their desks, stricken and dumb.

"Why did he let you come to school?" I asked.

Fenny looked at me blankly and said, "Who?"

I was dumbfounded. "Gregory, of course."

Fenny shook his head as if to blow away fog. "Gregory? We ain't seen Gregory for a long time. No, not for a long time now."

Now I was shocked—they were wan from his absence!

"Then what do you do with yourselves?"

"We go over."

"Go over?"

Constance nodded, agreeing with Fenny. "We go over."

"Go over where? Go over what?"

Now they were both looking at me with their mouths open, as if I were very dense.

"Go over to meet Gregory?" It was horrible, but I could think of nothing else.

Fenny shook his head. "We don't never see Gregory."

"No," said Constance, and I was horrified to hear regret in her voice. "We just go over."

Fenny seemed to come to life for a moment. He said, "But I heard him once. He said this is all there is, and there ain't no more. There ain't nothin' but this. There ain't nothin' like you said—like on maps. It ain't there."

"Then what's out there instead?" I asked.

"It's like what we see," Fenny said.

"See?"

"When we go," he answered.

"What do you see?" I asked.

"It's nice," Constance said, and put her head on the desk. "It's real nice."

I didn't have the faintest idea of what they were talking about, but I didn't like the sound of it much, and I thought I'd have time later to talk about it further. "Well, nobody's going anywhere tonight," I said. "I want both of you to stay here with me tonight. I want to keep you safe."

Fenny nodded, but stupidly and halfheartedly, as if he didn't care much where he spent his nights, and when I looked to Constance for agreement I saw that she had fallen asleep.

"All right then," I said. "We can fix up places to sleep later, and tomorrow I'll try to find beds for you in the village. You two children can't stay out in the woods on your own anymore."

Fenny nodded slackly again, and I saw that he too was on the verge of falling asleep. "You can put your head down," I said.

In seconds both of them were sleeping with their heads on their desks. I could almost have agreed with Gregory's dreadful statement at that moment—it was really as though this was all there was, all there was anywhere, just myself and the two exhausted children in a cold barn of a schoolhouse—my sense of reality had had too many knocks. As we three sat in the schoolhouse, the day began to end and the whole area of the room, dim at the best of times, became dark and shadowy. I did not have the heart to turn on the lights, so we sat there as at the bottom of a well. I had promised them that I would find beds in the village, but that miserable little hamlet not fifty paces down the road seemed miles off. And even if I'd had the energy and confidence to leave them alone, I couldn't imagine who'd take them in. If it were a well, it was really a well of hopelessness, and I seemed to myself as lost as the children.

Finally I could stand it no longer, and I went over to Fenny and shook his arm. He came awake like a frightened animal, and I held him on his chair only by using all of my strength. I said, "I have to know the truth, Fenny. What happened to Gregory?"

"He went over," he said, sullen again.

"Do you mean he died?"

Fenny nodded, and his mouth dropped open, and again I saw those terrible rotting teeth.

"But he comes back?"

He nodded again.

"And you see him?"

"He sees *us*," Fenny said, very firmly. "He looks and looks. He wants to touch."

"To touch?"

"Like before."

I put my hand on my forehead—it was burning. Every word that Fenny spoke opened a new abyss. "But did you shake the ladder?"

Fenny just looked stupidly at his desk, and I repeated my question. "Did you shake the ladder, Fenny?"

"He looks and he looks," Fenny said, as if it were the largest fact in his consciousness.

I put my hands on his head to make him look up at me, and at that moment the face of his tormentor appeared in the window. That white terrible face—as if he wanted to stop Fenny answering my questions. I felt sick, dumped back into the pit, but I also felt as if the battle had come at last, and I pulled Fenny toward me, trying to protect him physically.

"Is he here?" Fenny shrieked, and at the sound of his voice Constance dropped to the floor and began to wail.

"What does that matter?" I yelled. "He won't get you—*I* have you! He knows he's lost you forever!"

"Where is he?" Fenny shrieked again, pushing at me. "Where is Gregory?"

"*There*," I said, and turned him around to face the window.

He was already jerking himself around, and we both stared then at an empty window—there was nothing out there but an empty dark sky. I felt triumphant—I had won. I gripped Fenny's arm with all the strength of my victory, and he gave a shout of pure despair. He toppled forward, and I caught him as if he were jumping into the pit of hell itself. Only a few seconds later did I realize what I *had* caught: his heart had stopped, and I was holding a dispossessed body. He had gone over for good.

"And that was it," Sears said, looking at the circle of his friends. "Gregory too was gone for good. I came down with a nearly fatal fever—that was what I'd felt on my forehead—and spent three weeks in the Mathers' attic room. When I had recovered and could move around again, Fenny was buried. He really had gone over for good. I wanted to quit my job and leave the village, but they held me to my contract and I went back to teaching. I was shattered, but I could go through the motions. By the end of it, I was even using the ferule. I'd lost all my liberal notions, and when I left I was regarded as a fine and satisfactory teacher.

"There is one other thing, though. On the day I left Four Forks I went for the first time to look at Fenny's grave. It was behind the church, next to his brother's. I looked at the two graves, and do you know what I felt? I felt nothing. I felt empty. As though I'd had nothing at all to do with it."

"What happened to the sister?" asked Lewis.

"Oh, she was no problem. She was a quiet girl, and people felt sorry for her. I'd overestimated the stinginess of the village. One of the families took her in. As far as I know, they treated her as their own daughter. It's my impression that she got pregnant, married the boy and left town. But that would have been years later."

Frederick Hawthorne

1

Ricky walked home, surprised to see snow in the air. *It's going to be a hell of a winter,* he thought, *all the seasons are going funny.* In the glow surrounding the street lamp at the end of Montgomery Street, snow-flakes whirled and fell and adhered to the ground for a time before melting. Cold air licked in beneath his tweed topcoat. He had a half hour walk before him, and he was sorry that he hadn't taken his car, the old Buick Stella happily refused to touch—on cold nights, he usually drove. But tonight he'd wanted time to think: he had been going to grill Sears on the contents of his letter to Donald Wanderley, and he had to work out a technique. This, he knew, he'd failed to do. Sears had told him just what he wanted to, and no more. Still, the damage, from Ricky's point of view, was done; what point was there in knowing how the letter was worded? He startled himself by sighing aloud, and saw his breath send a few big lazy flakes spinning off in a complicated pattern as they melted.

Lately, all the stories, his own included, had made him tense for hours afterward; but tonight he felt more than that. Tonight he felt especially anxious. Ricky's nights were now uniformly dreadful, the dreams of which he had spoken to Sears pursued him straight through until dawn, and he had no doubt that the stories he and his friends told gave them substance; still he thought that the anxiety was not due to his dreams. Nor was it due to the stories, though Sears's had been worse than most—all of their stories were getting worse. They frightened themselves each time they met, but they continued to meet because not to meet would have been more frightening yet. It was comforting to get together, to see that they were each bearing up. Even Lewis was frightened, or why would he have voted in favor of writing to Donald Wanderley? It was this, knowing that the letter was on its way, ticking away in a mailbag somewhere, that made Ricky more than usually anxious.

Maybe I really should have left this town ages ago, he considered, looking at the houses he passed. There was scarcely one he had not been inside at least once, on business or pleasure, to see a client or to eat a dinner. *Maybe I should have gone to New York, back when I got married, as Stella wanted to do:* it was, for Ricky, a thought of striking disloyalty. Only gradually, only imperfectly had he convinced Stella that his life was in Milburn, with Sears James and the law practice. Cold wind cut into his neck and pulled at his hat. Around the corner, ahead of him, he saw Sears's long black Lincoln parked at the curb; a light burned in Sears's library. Sears would not be able to sleep, not after telling a story like that. By now, they all knew the effects of reliving these past events.

But it's not just the stories, he thought; *no, and it's not just the letter either. Something is going to happen.* That was why they told the stories. Ricky was not given to premonitions, but the dread of the future he'd felt two weeks earlier while talking to Sears came thudding back into him again. That was why he had thought of moving out of town. He turned into Melrose Avenue: "avenue," presumably, because of the thick trees which lined either side. Their branches stood out gesturally, tinted orange by the lamps. During the day the last of the leaves had fallen. *Something's going to happen to the whole town.* A branch groaned above Ricky's head. A truck changed gears far behind him, off on Route 17: sound traveled a long way on these cold nights in Milburn. When he went forward, he could see the lighted windows of his own bedroom, up on the third floor of his house. His ears and nose ached with the cold. After such a long and reasonable life, he said to himself, you can't go mystic on me now, old friend. We'll need all the rationality we can muster up.

At that moment, near where he felt safest and with this self-given reassurance in his mind, it seemed to Ricky that someone was following him: that someone was standing back on the corner, glaring at him. He could feel cold eyes staring at him, and in his mind it seemed that they floated alone—just eyes following him. He knew how they would look, clear pale luminous and floating at the level of his own eyes. Their lack of feeling would be dreadful—they would be like eyes in a mask. He turned around, fully expecting to see them, so great was his sense of them. Abashed, he realized that he was trembling. Of course the street was empty. It was simply an empty street, even on a dark night as ordinary as a mongrel pup.

This time you really did it to yourself, he thought, you and that gruesome story Sears told. Eyes! It was something out of an old Peter Lorre film. *The Eyes of . . . of Gregory Bate?* Hell. *The Hands of Dr. Orlac.* It's very clear, Ricky told himself, nothing at all is going to happen, we're just four old coots going out of our minds. To imagine that I thought . . .

But he had not thought the eyes were behind him, he had known it. It had been knowledge.

Nonsense, he almost said aloud, but let himself in his front door a little more quickly than usual.

His house was dark, as it always was on Chowder Society nights. By running his fingers along the edge of the couch, Ricky skirted the coffee table which on other nights had given him a half dozen bruises; having successfully navigated past that obstacle, he groped around a corner into the dining room and went through into the kitchen. Here he could turn on a light without any possibility of disturbing Stella's sleep; the next time he could do that was at the top of the house, in the dressing room which along with the horrid sleek Italian coffee table had been his wife's latest brainstorm. As she had pointed out, their closets were too crowded, there was no place to store their unseasonal clothes,

and the small bedroom next to theirs wasn't likely to
be used ever again, now that Robert and Jane were
gone; so for a cost of eight hundred dollars, they'd
had it converted into a dressing room, with clothes
rails and mirrors and a thick new carpet. The dressing
room had proved one thing to Ricky: as Stella had
always said, he actually did own as many clothes as she
did. That had been rather a surprise to Ricky, who was
so without vanity that he was unconscious of his own
occasional dandyism.

A more immediate surprise was that his hands were
shaking. He had been going to make a cup of camomile tea, but when he saw how his hands trembled, he
took a bottle out of a cabinet and poured a small
amount of whiskey into a glass. Skittish old idiot. But
calling himself names did not help, and when he brought
the glass to his lips his hand still shook. It was this
damned anniversary. The whiskey, when he took it
into his mouth, tasted like diesel oil, and he spat it out
into the sink. Poor Edward. Ricky rinsed out his glass,
turned off the light and went up the stairs in the dark.

In his pajamas, he left the dressing room and crossed
the hall to his bedroom. Quietly he opened the door.
Stella lay, breathing softly and rhythmically, on her
side of the bed. If he could make it around to his side
without knocking into the chair or kicking over her
boots or brushing against the mirror and making it rattle he could get into bed without disturbing her.

He gained his side of the bed without waking her
and quietly slipped under the blankets. Very gently,
he stroked his wife's bare shoulder. It was quite likely
that she was having another affair, or at least one of her
serious flirtations, and Ricky thought that she had probably taken up again with the professor she'd met a year
ago—there was a breathy silence on the phone that
was peculiarly his; long ago Ricky had decided that
many things were worse than having your wife occasionally go to bed with someone else. She had her life,
and he was a large part of it. Despite what he some-

times felt and had said to Sears two weeks before, not being married would have been an impoverishment.

He stretched out, waiting for what he knew would happen. He remembered the sensation of having the eyes boring into his back; he wished that Stella could help, could comfort him in some way; but not wishing to alarm or distress her, thinking that they would end with every new day and thinking also that they were uniquely, privately his, he had never told her of his nightmares. This is Ricky Hawthorne preparing for sleep: lying on his back, his clever face showing no sign of the emotions behind it, his hands behind his head, his eyes open; tired, uneasy, jealous; fearful.

2

In her room at the Archer Hotel, Anna Mostyn stood at a window and watched individual snowflakes drift down toward the street. Though the overhead light was off and it was past twelve, she was fully dressed. The long coat was thrown over the bed, as if she had just come in or was just going out.

She stood at the window and smoked, a tall attractive woman with dark hair and long blue eyes. She could see down nearly the entire length of Main Street, the deserted square to one side with its empty benches and bare trees, the black fronts of shops and the Village Pump restaurant and a department store; two blocks on, a traffic light turned green over an empty street. Main Street continued for eight blocks, but the buildings were visible only as dark shopfronts or office buildings. On the opposite side of the square she could see the dark façades of two churches looming above the tops of the bare trees. In the square a bronze Revolutionary War general made a grandiose gesture with a musket.

Tonight or tomorrow? she wondered, smoking her cigarette and surveying the little town.

Tonight.

3

When sleep finally came to Ricky Hawthorne, it was as if he were not merely dreaming, but had in fact been lifted bodily and still awake into another room in another building. He was lying in bed in a strange room, waiting for something to happen. The room seemed deserted, part of an abandoned house. Its walls and floor were bare planks; the window was only an empty frame, sunlight leaked in through a dozen cracks. Dust particles swirled in these stark rays of light. He did not know how he knew it, but he knew that something was going to happen, and that he was afraid of it. He was unable to leave the bed; but even if his muscles were working, he knew with the same knowledge that he would not be able to escape whatever was coming. The room was on an upper floor of the building: through the window he saw only gray clouds and a pale blue sky. But whatever was coming was going to come from inside, not out there.

His body was covered with an old quilt so faded that some of its squares were white. Beneath it, his legs lay paralyzed, two raised lines of fabric. When Ricky looked up, he realized that he could see every detail of the wooden planks on the wall with a more than usual clarity: he saw how the grain flowed down each board, how the knotholes were formed, the way the nailheads stood out at the tops of certain boards. Breezes filled the room flicking the dust here and there.

From down at the bottom of the house, he heard a crash—it was the noise of a door being thrown open, a heavy cellar door banging against a wall. Even his upstairs room shook with it. As he listened, he heard some complex form dragging itself out of the cellar: it was a heavy form, animal-like, and it had to squeeze through the doorframe. Wood splintered, and Ricky heard the creature thud against a wall. Whatever it was began to investigate the ground floor, moving slowly

and heavily. Ricky could picture what it saw—a series
of bare rooms exactly like his. On the ground floor,
tall grass and weeds would be growing up through the
cracks in the floorboards. The sunlight would be touching the sides and back of whatever was moving heavily,
purposefully through these deserted rooms. The thing
downstairs made a sucking noise, then a high-pitched
squeal. It was looking for him. It was snuffling through
the house, knowing he was there.

Ricky tried again to force his legs to move, but the
two lumps of fabric did not even twitch. The thing
downstairs was brushing against walls as it passed
through the rooms, making a scratchy noise; the wood
creaked. He thought he heard it break through a rotten
floorboard.

Then he heard the noise he had been dreading: it
shouldered through another doorway. The noises from
downstairs were suddenly louder—he could hear the
thing breathing. It was at the bottom of the staircase.

He heard it hurl itself at the stairs.

It thumped up what sounded like a half dozen
stairs, and then slipped back down. Then it went more
slowly, whining with impatience, taking the stairs two
or three at a time.

Ricky's face was wet with perspiration. What most
frightened him was that he couldn't be sure if he were
dreaming or not: if he could be certain that this was
only a dream, then he had only to suffer through it, to
wait until whatever it was down there got up to the
top of the stairs and burst into the room—the scare
would wake him up. But it did not feel at all like a
dream. His senses were alert, his mind was clear, the
entire experience lacked the rather disembodied, disconnected atmosphere of a dream. In no dream had he
ever sweated. And if he was wide awake, then the thing
banging and thundering on the stairs was going to get
him, because he couldn't move.

The noises changed, and then Ricky realized that
he was indeed on the third floor of the abandoned
building, because the thing looking for him was on

the second. Its noises were much louder: the whining, the slithery sound as its body rubbed through doors and against walls. It was moving faster, as if it smelled him.

The dust still circled in the random beams of sun; the few clouds still drifted through a sky that looked like early spring. The floor rattled as the creature thrust impatiently back onto the landing.

Now he could hear its breathing very clearly. It threw itself at the last staircase, making a noise like a wrecking ball hitting the side of a building. Ricky's stomach seemed packed with ice; he was afraid he would vomit—vomit ice cubes. His throat tightened. He would have screamed, but he thought, even while knowing it was not true, that if he did not make any noise maybe the thing would not find him. It squealed and whined, banging its way up the staircase. A stair rod snapped.

When it reached the landing outside his bedroom door, he knew what it was. A spider: it was a giant spider. It thudded against the door of his room. He heard it begin to whine again. If spiders could whine, that was how they would do it. A multitude of legs scrabbled at the door as the whining grew louder. Ricky felt pure terror, a white elemental fear worse than he'd ever experienced.

But the door did not splinter. It quietly opened. A tall black form stood just beyond the doorframe. It was no spider, whatever it was, and Ricky's terror decreased by an unconscious fraction. The black thing in the doorway did not move for a moment, but stood as if looking at him. Ricky tried to swallow; he managed to use his arms to push himself upright. The rough planks rubbed against his back and he thought again: *this isn't a dream.*

The black form came through the door.

Ricky saw that it was not an animal at all, but a man. Then another plane of blackness separated off, then another, and he saw that it was three men. Beneath the cowls draped over their lifeless faces, he saw the familiar features. Sears James and John Jaffrey and Lewis Benedikt stood before him, and he knew that they were dead.

He woke up screaming. His eyes opened to the normal sights of morning on Melrose Avenue, the cream colored bedroom with the graphics Stella had bought on their last trip to London, the window looking out on the big back yard, a shirt draped over a chair. Stella's firm hand gripped his shoulder. The room seemed mysteriously absent of light. On a strong impulse he could not name, Ricky jumped out of bed—came as close to jumping out of bed as his seventy-year-old knees would permit—and went across to the window. Stella, behind him, said, "What?" He didn't know what he was looking for, but what he saw was unexpected: the entire back yard, all the roofs of the neighboring houses, were dusted with snow. The sky too was oddly without light. He didn't know what he was going to say, but when he opened his mouth he uttered: "It snowed all night, Stella. John Jaffrey should never have had that dadblasted party."

4

Stella sat up in bed and talked to him as if he had said something reasonable. "Wasn't John's party over a year ago, Ricky? I don't see what that has to do with last night's snow."

He rubbed his eyes and his dry cheekbones; he smoothed down his mustache. "It was a year ago last night." Then he heard what he had been saying. "No, of course not. There's no connection, I mean."

"Come back to bed and tell me what's wrong, baby."

"Oh, I'm okay," he said, but returned to the bed. When he was lifting the blankets to get back in, Stella said, "You're not okay, baby. You must have had a terrible dream. Do you want to tell me about it?"

"It doesn't make much sense."

"Tell me anyhow." She began to caress his back and

shoulders, and he twisted to look down at her head
on the dark blue pillow. As Sears had said, Stella was
a beauty: she had been a beauty when he met her,
and apparently she would be a beauty when she died.
It was not a plump chocolate-box prettiness, but a matter of strong cheekbones, straight facial planes and
definite black eyebrows. Stella's hair had gone an
uncompromising gray when she was in her early
thirties, and she had refused to dye it, seeing long before anyone else what a sexual asset an abundant head
of gray hair would be when combined with a youthful
face: now she still had the abundant gray hair, and
her face was not much less youthful. It would be more
truthful to say that her face had never been precisely
youthful, nor would it ever truly be old: in fact with
every year, up nearly to fifty, she had come more completely into her beauty, and then had pitched camp
there. She was ten years younger than Ricky, but on
good days she still looked only a blink over forty.

"Tell me, Ricky," she said. "What the hell is going
on?"

So he began to tell her his dream, and he saw concern, horror, love and fear cross her elegant face. She
continued to rub his back, and then moved her hand to
his chest. "Baby," she said when he was through, "do
you really have dreams like that every night?"

"No," he said, looking at her face and seeing beneath the superficial emotions of the moment the self-
absorption and amusement which were always present
in Stella and which were always joined, "that was the
worst one." Then, smiling a little because he saw where
she was going with all this rubbing, he said, "That
was the champ."

"You've been very tense lately." She lifted his hand
and touched it to her lips.

"I know."

"Do all of you have these bad dreams?"

"All who?"

"The Chowder Society." She placed his hand on her
cheek.

"I think so."

"Well," she said, and sat up and, crossing her arms elbows-out before her, began to work her nightdress over her head, "don't you old fools think you ought to do something about it?" The nightdress went off, and she tossed her head to flip her hair back into place. Their two children had left her breasts sagging and her nipples large and brown, but Stella's body had aged only a little more than her face.

"We don't know what to do," he confessed.

"Well, I know what to do," she said and went back down on the bed and opened her arms. If Ricky had ever wished that he had remained a bachelor like Sears, he did not wish it this morning.

"You old sexpot," Stella said when they were done, "you would have given this up a long time ago if it hadn't been for me. What a loss that would have been. If it weren't for me you'd be too dignified to ever take your clothes off."

"That's not true."

"Oh? What would you do, then? Chase after little girls like Lewis Benedikt?"

"Lewis doesn't chase after little girls."

"Girls in their twenties, then."

"No. I wouldn't."

"There. I'm right. You wouldn't have any sex life at all, like your precious partner Sears." She folded back the sheets and blankets on her side of the bed, and got out. "I'll shower first," she said. Stella demanded a long time by herself in the bathroom every morning. She put on her long white-gray robe and looked as if she were about to tell someone to sack Troy. "But I'll tell you what you should do. You should call Sears right now and tell him about that awful dream. You won't get anywhere if you won't at least talk about it. If I know you and Sears, you two can go for weeks at a time without saying anything personal to each other. That's dreadful. What in the world *do* you talk about, anyhow?"

"Talk about?" Ricky asked, a little taken aback. "We talk about law."

"Oh, law," Stella said, and marched off toward the bathroom.

When she returned nearly thirty minutes later he was sitting up in bed looking confused. The pouches beneath his eyes were larger than usual. "The paper isn't here yet," he said. "I went downstairs and looked."

"Of course it isn't here," Stella said, dropping a towel and a box of tissues on the bed, and turned away again to go into the dressing room. "What time do you think it is?"

"What time? Why, what time is it? My watch is on the table."

"It's just past seven."

"*Seven?*" They normally did not get up until eight, and Ricky usually dawdled around the house until nine-thirty before leaving for the office on Wheat Row. Though neither he nor Sears admitted it, there was no longer much work for them; old clients dropped in from time to time, there were a few complicated lawsuits which looked to drag on through the next decade, there was always a will or two or a tax problem to clarify, but they could have stayed home two days of every week without anybody noticing. Alone in his part of the office suite, Ricky lately had been rereading Donald Wanderley's second book, trying unsuccessfully to persuade himself that he wanted its author in Milburn. "What are we doing up?"

"You woke us up with your screaming, if I have to remind you," Stella called from the dressing room. "You were having problems with a monster that was trying to eat you, remember?"

"Um," Ricky said. "I thought it looked dark outside."

"Don't be evasive," Stella called, and in another minute or two was back beside the bed, fully dressed. "When you start to scream in your sleep, it's time to start taking whatever is happening to you seriously. I know you won't go to a doctor—"

"I won't go to a head doctor, anyhow," Ricky said. "My mind is in good working order."

"So I said. But since you won't consider that, you should at least talk to Sears about it. I don't like to see you eating yourself up." With that, she left for the downstairs.

Ricky lay back, considering. It had been, as he said to Stella, the worst of the nightmares. Simply thinking about it now was unsettling—simply having Stella go down the stairs was, at some level, unsettling. The dream had been extraordinarily vivid, with the detail and texture of wakefulness. He remembered the faces of his friends, bereft poor corpses, abandoned of life. That had been horrid; it had been somehow immoral, and the shock to his morality even more than the horror had made him open his mouth and scream. Maybe Stella was right. Without knowing how he would bring up the subject with Sears, he nevertheless picked up the receiver of the bedside phone. After Sears's phone had rung once, Ricky realized that he was acting very much out of character and that he didn't have the faintest idea why Stella thought Sears James would have anything worthwhile to say. But by then it was too late, and Sears had picked up the phone and said hello.

"It's Ricky, Sears."

Evidently it was the morning for demonstrating inconsistency of character; nothing less like Sears than his response could be imagined. "Ricky, thank God," he said. "You must have ESP. I was just going to call you. Can you come by and pick me up in five minutes?"

"Give me fifteen minutes," Ricky said. "What happened?" And then, thinking of his dream, "Did anybody die?"

"Why do you ask that?" Sears said in a different, sharper voice.

"No reason. I'll tell you later. I take it we're not going to Wheat Row."

"No. I just had a call from our Vergil. He wants us

out there—he wants to sue everybody in sight. Step on it, will you?"

"Elmer wants us both at his farm? What happened?"

Sears was impatient. "Something earthshaking, apparently. Pull the plug out, Ricky."

5

While Ricky hurried into a scalding shower, Lewis Benedikt was jogging on a path through the woods. He did this every morning, jogging a regular two miles before making breakfast for himself and whatever young lady might have spent the night at his house. Today, as always after Chowder Society nights and far oftener than his friends imagined, there was no young lady, and Lewis was pushing himself harder than usual. The night before he'd had the worst nightmare of his life; its effects still clung to him, and he thought that a good run would blow them away—where another man would write in a diary or confide in his mistress or have a drink, Lewis exercised. So now, in a blue running suit and Adidas shoes, he puffed his way along the path through his woods.

Lewis's property had included both woods and pasture along with the stone farmhouse he had cherished from the moment he had seen it. It was like a fortress with shutters, a huge building constructed at the start of the century by a rich gentleman farmer who liked the look of the castles in the illustrated novels by Sir Walter Scott admired by his wife. Lewis neither knew nor cared about Sir Walter, but years of living in a hotel had left him with a need for the sense of a multitude of rooms about him. He would have had claustrophobia in a cottage. When he had decided to sell his hotel to the chain which had been offering increasing amounts of money for it over the six preceding years, he had enough money left after taxes to buy the only house in or near Milburn which would truly have satisfied him, and enough to furnish it as he wished. The paneling, guns and pikestaffs did not always please his female guests. (Stella Hawthorne, who had spent three adventurous afternoons at Lewis's farm shortly after his return, had said she'd never been had in an officers' mess before.) He'd sold the pasture land as soon as he could, but kept the woods because he liked the idea of owning them.

Jogging through them, he always saw something new which quickened his sense of life: one day a pocket of snowdrops and monkshoods in a hollow beside the stream, the next a red-winged blackbird as big as a cat peering wild-eyed at him from the branches of a maple. But today he was not looking, he was simply running along the snowy path, wishing that whatever was going on would stop. Maybe this young Wanderley could set things right again: judging by his book, he had been to a few dark places himself. Maybe John was right, and Edward's nephew would at least be able to figure out what was happening to the four of them. It could not just be guilt, after all this time. The Eva Galli business had happened so long ago that it had concerned five different men in a different country: if you looked at the land and compared it to what it was in the twenties, you'd never think it was the same place. Even his woods were second growth, though he liked to pretend that they were not.

Lewis, running, liked to think of the huge climax forest that had once blanketed nearly all of North America: a vast belt of trees and vegetation, silent wealth through which moved only himself and Indians. And a few spirits. Yes, in an endless vault of forest you could believe in spirits. Indian mythology was full of them—they suited the landscape. But now, in a world of Burger Kings and Piggly Wiggly supermarkets and Pitch 'n Putt golf courses, all the old tyrannical ghosts must have been crowded out.

They aren't crowded out yet, Lewis. Not yet.

It was like another voice speaking in his mind. Like hell they aren't, he said to himself, passing one hand over his face.

Not here. Not yet.

Shit. He was spooking himself. He was still affected by that damned dream. Maybe it was time they really talked about these dreams to one another—described them. Now suppose they all had the same dream. What would that mean? Lewis's mind could not go so far. Well, it would mean something: and at least talking about it would help. He thought he had scared himself awake, this morning. His foot came down into slush, and he clearly saw the final image of his dream: the two men withdrawing their hoods to show their wasted faces.

Not yet.

God damn. He came to a halt, exactly halfway on his run, and wiped his forehead on the sleeve of the running jacket. He wished he had already completed the run and were back inside his kitchen, brewing up coffee or smelling bacon frying in the pan. You're tougher than this, you old buzzard, he counseled himself, you've had to be, ever since Linda killed herself. He leaned for a moment on the fence at the end of the path, where it circled back into the trees, and looked aimlessly out over the field he had sold. Now it was lightly covered with snow, a bumpy expanse from which hard light momentarily bounced and sang. All that too would have been forest. *Where the dark things hid.*

Oh hell. Well, if they did, they weren't anywhere in sight now. The air was leaden and empty, and you could see nearly all the way across the dip in the valley to where the trucks on Route 17 steamed on toward Binghamton and Elmira, or the other way toward Newburgh or Poughkeepsie. Only for a moment, the woods at his back made him feel uneasy. He turned around; saw only the path twisting back into the trees; heard only an angry squirrel complain that he was going to have a hungry winter.

Pal, we've all had hungry winters. He was thinking of the season after Linda had died. Nothing puts off guests like a public suicide. And is there a Mrs. Ben-

edikt? Oh yes, that's her bleeding all over the patio—
you know, the one with the funny bend in her neck.
They had cleared off one by one, leaving him with a
deteriorating two-million-dollar asset and no cash
inflow. He'd had to let three-fourths of the staff go, and
paid the rest out of his own pocket. It had been three
years before business had returned, and six years before
he had paid his debts.

Suddenly, what he wanted was not coffee and bacon,
but a bottle of O'Keefe's beer. A gallon of it. His throat
was dry and his chest ached.

Yes, we've all had hungry winters, pal. A gallon of
O'Keefe's? He could have swallowed a barrel. Remembering Linda's senseless, inexplicable death made him
yearn for drunkenness.

It was time to get back. Shaken by memory—Linda's
face had come back to him with utter clarity, claiming
him through the nine years since that moment—he
turned from the fence and inhaled deeply. Running,
not a gallon of ale, was his therapy now. The path
through the mile and a half of woods seemed narrower,
darker.

Your problem, Lewis, is that you're yellow.

It was the nightmare that had brought back the memories. Sears and John, in those cerements of the grave,
with those lifeless faces. Why not Ricky? If the other
two living members of the Chowder Society, why not
the third?

He was sweating even before he started the run back.

The return path took a long angle off to the left before turning back in the direction of the farmhouse:
normally this loafing misdirection was Lewis's favorite
part of his morning run. The woods closed in almost
immediately, and by the time you had gone fifteen paces
you forgot all about the open field at your back. More
than any other part of the path, it looked here like
the original climax forest: thick oaks and girlish birches
fought for root space, tall ferns crowded toward the
path. Today he ran it with as little pleasure in it as it
was possible for him to feel. All those trees, their

number and thickness, were obscurely threatening: running away from the house was like running away from safety. Going over the powdery snow in white air, he pushed himself hard toward the cut back home.

When the sensation first hit him, he ignored it, vowing not to allow himself to be whammied any more than he was already. What had come into his mind was that someone was standing back at the beginning of the return path, just where the first trees stood. He knew that no one could be there: it was impossible that anyone had walked across the field without his noticing. But the sensation persisted; it would not be argued away. His watcher's eyes seemed to follow him, going deeper into the crowded trees. A squadron of crows left the branches of an oak just ahead of him. Normally this would have delighted Lewis, but this time he jumped at their racket and almost fell.

Then the sensation shifted, and became more intense. The person back there was coming after him, staring at him with huge eyes. Frantic, despising himself, Lewis pelted for home without daring to look back. He could feel the eyes watching him until he reached the walkway leading across his back garden from the edge of the woods to his kitchen door.

He ran down the path, his chest raggedly hauling in air, twisted the doorknob, and jumped inside. He slammed the door behind him and went immediately to the window beside it. The path was empty and the only footprints were his. Still Lewis was frightened, looking out to the near edge of his woods. For a moment a traitorous synapse in his brain told him: maybe you should sell out and move into town. But there were no footprints. Nobody could possibly be out there, keeping out of sight in the shelter of the trees—he wouldn't be scared out of the house he needed, forced by his own weakness to trade his splendid comfortable isolation for a crowded discomfort. To this decision, made in a cold kitchen on the first day of snowfall, he would hold.

Lewis put a kettle on the stove, got his coffee pitcher

off a shelf, filled the grinder with Blue Mountain beans and held the switch down until they were powder. *Oh hell*. He opened the refrigerator, took out a bottle of O'Keefe's and after snapping off the cap drank most of it without tasting or swallowing. As the beer hit his stomach, a two-sided thought surprised him. *I wish Edward was still alive: I wish John hadn't pushed so hard for his godawful party.*

6

"Well, speak up," said Ricky. "What is it, trespassers again? We explained our position on that. He must know even if he won that he couldn't make enough on a trespassing suit to pay expenses."

They were just entering the foothills of the Cayuga Valley, and Ricky was handling the old Buick with great care. The roads were slippery, and though ordinarily he would have had his snow tires put on before making even the eight-mile drive to Elmer Scales's farm, this morning Sears had not given him time. Sears himself, huge in his black hat and black fur-collared winter coat, seemed as conscious of this as Ricky. "Keep your mind on your driving," he said. "There's supposed to be ice on the roads up around Damascus."

"We're not going to Damascus," Ricky pointed out.

"Even so."

"Why didn't you want to use your car?"

"I'm having the snow tires put on this morning."

Ricky grunted, amused. Sears was in one of his refractory moods, a frequent consequence of a conversation with Elmer Scales. He was one of their oldest and most difficult clients. (Elmer had come to them first at fifteen years of age, with a long and complex list of people he wished to sue. They had never managed to get rid of him, nor had he ever altered his perception of conflict as a situation best addressed by an immediate lawsuit.) A skinny, excitable man with jutting ears and a high-pitched voice, Scales was called "Our Vergil" by Sears because of his poetry, which he ritually sent off to Catholic magazines and local papers. Ricky understood that the magazines just as ritually sent them back—once Elmer had shown him a file stuffed with rejection slips—but the local newspapers had printed two or three. They were inspirational poems, their imagery drawn from Elmer's life as a farmer: *The cows do moo, the lambs do bleat. God's Glory walks in on thundering feet.* So did Elmer Scales. He had eight children and an undimmed passion for litigation.

Once or twice a year either partner was summoned out to the Scales farm and Elmer would direct him to a hole in a fence where a hunter or a teenager had cut through his fields: Elmer had often identified these trespassers with his binoculars, and he wanted to sue. They usually managed to talk him out of this, but he always had two or three litigations of other sorts under way. But this time, Ricky suspected, it was more serious than Scales's upsets were normally; he had never before asked—commanded—both partners to come out.

"As you know, Sears," he said, "I can drive and think at the same time. I'm doing a very sedate thirty miles an hour. I think you can trust me with whatever has Elmer worked up."

"Some of his animals died." Sears said this tight-lipped, implying that his speaking would be likely to result in their going off the road at any minute.

"So why are we going out there? We can't bring them back."

"He wants us to see them. He called Walter Hardesty too."

"They didn't just die, then."

"With Elmer, who knows? Now please concentrate on getting us there safely, Ricky. This experience will be grisly enough as it is."

Ricky glanced at his partner and for the first time that morning saw how pale Sears's face was. Beneath the smooth skin prominent blue veins swam at intervals into visibility; beneath the young eyes hung gray patches of webbed skin. "Keep your eyes on the road," said Sears.

"You look terrible."

"I don't think Elmer will notice."

Ricky's eyes were now safely on the narrow country road; this gave him license to speak. "Did you have a bad night?"

Sears said, "I think it's beginning to melt."

As this was a blatant lie, Ricky ignored it. "Did you?"

"Observant Ricky. Yes, I did."

"So did I. Stella thinks we should talk about it."

"Why? Does she have bad nights too?"

"She thinks that talking about it would help."

"That sounds like a woman. Talking just opens the wounds. Not talking helps to heal them."

"In that case, it was a mistake to invite Donald Wanderley here."

Sears grunted in exasperation.

"That was unfair of me," Ricky said, "and I'm sorry I said it. But I think we should talk about it for the same reason you think we should invite that boy."

"He's not a boy. He must be thirty-five. He might be forty."

"You know what I mean." Ricky took a deep breath. "Now I want your forgiveness in advance, because I am going to tell you the dream I had last night. Stella said I woke up screaming. In any case, it was the worst dream yet." By a shift in the car's inner weather, Ricky knew that Sears was immediately more interested. "I was in a vacant house, on an upper floor, and some mysterious beast was trying to find me. I'll skip the development, but the feeling of danger was overwhelming. At the end of the dream it came into the room where I was, but it wasn't a monster anymore. It was you and Lewis and John. All of you were dead." Glancing sideways toward his passenger, he saw the curve of Sears's mottled cheek, the curve of the hatbrim.

"You saw the three of us?"

Ricky nodded.

Sears cleared his throat, and then cranked the window down a quarter of the way. Freezing air rushed into the car. Sears's chest expanded beneath the black coat: individual spiky hairs of the furry collar flattened in the rush of air. "Extraordinary. You say there were the three of us?"

"Yes. Why?"

"Extraordinary. Because I had an identical dream. But when that dreadful thing burst into my room, I saw only two men. Lewis and John. You weren't there."

Ricky heard a tone in the other's voice it took him a moment to identify, and when he had named it, the recognition carried enough surprise to silence him until they turned into Elmer Scales's long driveway. It was envy.

"Our Vergil," Sears pronounced, to himself Ricky thought. As they went slowly up the drive toward the isolated two-story farmhouse, Ricky saw an obviously impatient Scales, dressed in a cap and a plaid jacket, waiting for them on the porch and saw also that the farmhouse resembled a building in an Andrew Wyeth painting. Scales himself looked like a Wyeth portrait; or, more accurately perhaps, a Norman Rockwell subject. His ears stuck redly out beneath the tied-up flaps of his cap. A gray Dodge sedan was pulled up in the cleared space beside the porch, and when Ricky parked next to it he saw the sheriff's seal on the door. "Walt's here," he said, and Sears nodded.

The two men got out of the car, pulling their coats in tightly around their necks. Scales, now flanked by two shivering children, did not move from the porch. He had the high hard look of excitement which accompanied his most passionate litigations. His reedy voice called to them. " 'Bout time you two lawyers got here. Walt Hardesty's been here ten minutes."

"He didn't have as far to come," Sears grumbled. The brim of his hat curled in the unobstructed breeze cutting across the fields.

"Sears James, I don't suppose any man alive ever

got in the last word with you. Hey, you kids! Get back
in the house, you'll freeze your butts off." He swatted
one with each hand, and the two boys scuttled back
inside the door. Scales stood above the two old men,
smiling grimly.

"What is it, Elmer?" Ricky asked, holding his coat
closed at his neck. His feet in his well-shined black
shoes were already chilled.

"You'll just have to see. You two town boys aren't
really dressed for a walk across the fields. Guess that's
your hard luck. Hang on a second, I'll get Hardesty."
He disappeared for a moment into the house and
emerged again with the sheriff, Walt Hardesty, who was
wearing a loose sheepskin-lined denim coat and a
Stetson. Alerted by Scales's remark, Ricky looked at
the sheriff's feet: he wore heavy leather hiking boots.
"Mr. James, Mr. Hawthorne." He nodded to them,
steam pluming out over his mustache, which was larger
and more ragged than Ricky's. In this cattleman's outfit, Hardesty looked fifteen years younger than his true
age. "Now that you're here, maybe Elmer will show
us what this mystery's all about."

"Damn right I will," said the farmer, and clumped
down the porch steps and began leading them away
from the house, walking on the path toward the snow-
dusted barn. "Just you come this way, gentlemen, and
see what I'm gonna show you."

Hardesty fell in beside Ricky. Sears was walking
alone, with immense dignity, behind them. "Colder 'n a
bitch," the sheriff said. "Looks like being a damn long
winter."

Ricky said, "I hope not. I'm too old for one of
those."

With exaggerated gestures and an expression like
glee on his skinny face, Elmer Scales was unhooking
a long rail fence which led into a side pasture. "Now
you pay attention, Walt," he called back. "You see if
you can spot any tracks." He pointed to a line of
splayed footprints. "Them's mine from this morning,
goin' and comin'." The prints returning were widely

spaced, as if Scales had been running. "Where's your notebook? Ain't you gonna take notes?"

"Calm down, Elmer," the sheriff said. "I want to see what the problem is first."

"You took notes fast enough when my oldest boy racked up his car."

"Come on, Elmer. Show us what you want us to see."

"You town boys gonna ruin your shoes," Elmer said. "Can't be helped. Follow me."

Hardesty did as commanded and set off beside Elmer; his broad back in the bulky coat made the farmer look like a capering boy. Ricky glanced back at Sears, just now approaching the gate and regarding the snowy field with disgust. "He might have told us we'd need snowshoes."

"He's enjoying himself," Ricky said wonderingly.

"He'll enjoy himself when I get walking pneumonia and fire a lawsuit at *him*," Sears muttered. "Since there's no alternative, let's go."

Gamely Sears put a well-shod foot down into the pasture, where it immediately sank into snow up to the laces. "Ugh." He retracted it; shook it. The others were already halfway across the field. "I'm not going," Sears said, jamming his hands into the pockets of his opulent coat. "Damn it, he can come to the office."

Ricky said, "Well then, I'd better go at least," and started after the other two. Walt Hardesty had turned around to look at them, stroking his ragged mustache, a frontier lawman translated to a snowy field in New York state. He appeared to be smiling. Elmer Scales plodded on oblivious. Ricky picked his way from one footprint to another. Behind him, he heard Sears emit enough air to fill a balloon and begin to follow.

Single file now, Elmer talking and gesticulating in front, they went across the field. With an odd air of triumphant glee, Elmer stopped at the top of a ridge. Beside him, half-covered by snow, were piles of dirty washing. When Hardesty reached the low gray piles, he knelt and prodded; then he grunted, pushing, and Ricky saw four neat black feet roll stiffly into the air.

His shoes soaked and his feet wet, Ricky came up to them. Sears, holding his arms out for balance, was still threading toward them, his hat brim flattened by the wind.

"I didn't know you still kept any sheep," he heard Hardesty say.

"I don't, now!" Scales yelled. "I just had those four, and now they're all gone. Somebody killed 'em. Just kept 'em around for the sake of the old days. My daddy had a couple hundred, but there's no money in the stupid dang things anymore. The kids liked 'em, that's all."

Ricky looked down at the four dead animals: flat on their sides, eyes glazed, snow in the matted wool. Innocent, he asked, "What killed them?"

"Yeah! That's it, ain't it!" Elmer was working himself up into a tantrum. "What! Well, you're the law around here, you tell me!"

Hardesty, kneeling beside the dirty-gray body of the sheep he had rolled over, looked up at Scales with distaste. "You mean you don't even know if these animals died naturally, Elmer?"

"I know! I know!" Scales lifted his arms dramatically: a bat in flight.

"How do you know?"

"Because nothing can kill a damn sheep, that's how I know! And what the hell would kill four at once? Heart attacks? Boy!"

Sears now joined them, his frame making the kneeling Hardesty look small. "Four dead sheep," he said, looking down. "I suppose you want to sue them."

"What? You find the lunatic who did this and sue his ass off!"

"And who would that be?"

"Dunno. But . . ."

"Yeah?" Hardesty looked up again from the sheep huddled at his knees.

"I'll tell you inside. Meantime, Mr. Sheriff, you look

'em over good and take notes and find out what he did to 'em."

"He?"

"Inside."

Hardesty, scowling, was probing the carcass. "You want the vet for this, Elmer, not me." His hands moved to the animal's neck. "Uh oh."

"What?" said Scales, almost leaping with anticipation.

Instead of answering, Hardesty crab-walked to the next nearest sheep and thrust his hands deep into the wool at its neck.

"You might have seen this for yourself," he said, and gripping its nose and mouth pulled back the sheep's head.

"Jesus," said Scales; the two lawyers were silent. Ricky looked down at the exposed wound: like a wide mouth, the long slash in the animal's neck.

"A neat job," Hardesty said. "A very neat job of work. Okay, Elmer. You proved your point. Let's get back inside." He wiped his fingers in the snow.

"Jesus," Elmer repeated. "Their throats are cut? All of 'em?"

Wearily Hardesty yanked back the heads of each remaining animal. "All of them."

Old voices spoke clearly in Ricky's mind. He and Sears looked at each other, looked away.

"I'll sue the heart out of whoever did this!" Elmer screeched. "Shit! I knew something was funny! I knew it! Shit!"

Hardesty was now looking around at the empty field. "You sure you went up here once, and then went straight back?"

"Uh *huh*."

"How did you know something was wrong?"

"Because I saw 'em up here this morning from the window. Normally when I'm washin' my face at my window them stupid animals is the first thing I see. See?" He pointed across the fields to his house. The shining pane of the kitchen window faced them. "There's

grass under here. They just walk around all day, stuffin'
themselves. When the snow gets real bad I pen 'em
up in the barn. I just looked out an' I saw 'em, like
they are now. Something sure was wrong, so I put on
my coat and my boots and came up. Then I called you
and my lawyers. I want to sue, and I want you to arrest
whoever done this."

"There aren't any tracks besides ours," Hardesty
said, smoothing his mustache.

"I know," said Scales. "He brushed 'em out."

"Could be. But you can usually tell, on unbroken
snow."

Jesus she moved she can't she's dead.

"And there's another thing," said Ricky, breaking
into the suspicious silence which had developed between
the two men and interrupting the lunatic voice in his
mind. "There's no blood."

For a moment all four men stared down at the sheep
and the fresh snow. It was true.

"Can we get off this steppe now?" Sears said.

Elmer was still staring down at the snow, swallowing.
Sears began to move across the field, and soon they
were all following.

"All right kids, out of the kitchen. Get upstairs,"
Scales shouted as they came into the house and removed their coats. "We gotta talk in private. Go on,
git." He shooed his hands at some of the children who
were clustered in the hallway, staring at Walter Hardesty's pistol. "Sarah! Mitchell! Upstairs, now." He led
them into the kitchen and a woman as thin as Elmer
shot up out of a chair, clasping her hands. "Mr. James,
Mr. Hawthorne," she said. "Could you use some coffee?"

"Kitchen towelling, if you please, Mrs. Scales," Sears
said. "Then coffee."

"Kitchen . . ."

"To wipe my shoes. Mr. Hawthorne undoubtedly re-
quires the same service."

The woman looked down in dismay at the lawyer's

shoes. "Oh, good heavens. Here, let me help you . . ." She took a roll of paper towelling from a cupboard, tore off a long section, and made as if to kneel at Sears's feet. "That won't be necessary," Sears said, taking the wadded paper from her hands. Only Ricky knew that Sears was disturbed, not merely rude.

"Mr. Hawthorne . . . ?" A bit rattled by Sears's coldness, the woman turned to Ricky.

"Yes, thank you, Mrs. Scales," he said. "That's very kind of you." He too accepted several sections of the towelling.

"Their throats were cut," Elmer said to his wife. "What did I tell you? Some crazyman's been out here. *And—*" his voice rose "—a crazyman who can fly, because he didn't leave no prints."

"Tell them," his wife said. Elmer looked at her sharply, and she hurried off to put the coffee together.

Hardesty asked, "Tell us what?" No longer in the Wyatt Earp costume, the sheriff was restored to his proper age of fifty. *He's hitting the bottle worse than ever,* Ricky thought, seeing the broken veins in Hardesty's face, the deepening irresolution. For the truth was that, despite his Texas Ranger appearance, the hawk nose, lined cheeks and gunslinger blue eyes, Walt Hardesty was too lazy to be a good sheriff. It was typical of him that he had had to be told to look at the second pair of sheep. And Elmer Scales was right; he should have taken notes.

Now the farmer was preening himself, about to deliver his bomb-shell. Stringy cords stood out in his neck; his bat ears went a deeper shade of red. "Well hell, I saw him, didn't I?" His mouth dropped comically, and he surveyed each of them in turn.

"Him," his wife said in ironic counterpoint behind him.

"Shit, woman, what else?" Scales thumped the table. "Get that coffee ready and stop interrupting." He turned back to the three men. "As big as me! Bigger! Starin' at me! Damnedest thing you ever saw!" Enjoying his moment, he spread his arms. "Right outside!

Just a little further than that away from me. How's them apples?"

"Did you recognize him?" Hardesty asked.

"Didn't see him that well. Now I'll tell you how it was." He was moving around the kitchen, unable to contain himself, and Ricky was reminded of an old perception, that "Our Vergil" wrote poetry because he was too volatile to believe he was not capable of it. "I was in here last night, late. Couldn't sleep, never could."

"Never could," echoed his wife.

Screeches, thumps came from overhead. "Forget the coffee and get on upstairs, straighten 'em out," Scales said. He paused while she left the room. Soon another voice joined the cacophony above; then the noises ceased.

"Like I said. I was in here, readin' through a couple-two-three equipment and seed catalogues. Then! I hears something from out near the barn. Prowler! Damn! I jumps up and looks out the window. Seen it was snowin'. Uh oh, work to do tomorrow, I says to myself. Then I seen him. By the barn. Well, between the barn and the house."

"What did he look like?" Hardesty said, still not taking notes.

"Couldn't tell! Too dark!" Now his voice had soared from alto to soprano. "Just saw him there, starin'!"

"You saw him in the dark?" Sears asked in a bored voice. "Were your yard lights on?"

"Mr. Lawyer, you gotta be kidding, with electric bills the way they are. No, but I saw him and I knew he was big."

"Now, how did you know that, Elmer?" asked Hardesty. Mrs. Scales was coming down the uncarpeted stairs—*thump thump thump,* hard shoes hitting the wooden risers. Ricky sneezed. A child began to whistle, and abruptly ceased as the footsteps paused.

"Because I saw his eyes! Didn't I? Just starin' out at me! About six feet above the ground."

"You just saw his eyes?" asked Hardesty, incredulous.

"What the hell did this guy's eyes do, Elmer, shine in the dark?"

"You said it," Elmer replied.

Ricky jerked his head to look at Elmer, who regarded them all with evident satisfaction, and then without meaning to, looked across the table at Sears. He had gone tense and immobile at Hardesty's last question, trying to let nothing show on his face, and on Sears's round face he saw the same intention. *Sears too. It means something to him too.*

"Now I expect you to get him, Walt, and you two lawyers of mine to sue his ass from here to summer," Elmer said conclusively. "Excuse my language, honey." His wife was coming into the little kitchen again, and she nodded at his apology, acknowledging its rectitude by tapping it with her chin as it went by, before taking the percolator off the burner.

"Did you see anything last night, Mrs. Scales?" Hardesty asked.

Ricky saw a similar recognition in Sears's eyes and knew that he had given himself away.

"All I saw was a scared husband," she said. "I suppose that's the part he left out."

Elmer cleared his throat; his Adam's apple bobbed. "Well. It looked funny."

"Yes," Sears said. "I think we know all we need to know. Now if you'll excuse us, Mr. Hawthorne and I must be getting back to town."

"You'll drink your coffee first, Mr. James," said Mrs. Scales, putting a steaming plastic cup down before him on the tabletop. "If you're going to sue some monster's ass from here to summer you'll need your strength."

Ricky forced himself to smile, but Walt Hardesty guffawed.

Outside, Hardesty, back in the protective coloration of his Texas Ranger outfit, bent over to speak softly through the three-inch crack Sears had opened in the window. "Are you two going back into town? Could we meet somewhere to have a word or two?"

"Is it important?"

"Might be, might not. I'd like to talk to you, though."

"Right. We'll go straight to your office."

Hardesty's gloved hand went to his chin and caressed it. "I'd rather not talk about this in front of the other boys."

Ricky sat with his hands on the wheel, his alert face turned to Hardesty, but his mind held only one thought: *It's starting. It's starting and we don't even know what it is.*

"What do you suggest, Walt?" asked Sears.

"I suggest a sub rosa stop someplace where we can have a quiet talk. Ah, do you know Humphrey's Place, just inside the town limits on the Seven Mile Road?"

"I believe I've seen it."

"I sorta use their back room as an office when I've got confidential business. What say we meet there?"

"If you insist," Sears said, not bothering to consult Ricky.

They followed Hardesty's car back to town, going a little faster than they had on the way out. The recognition between them—that each knew the frightening thing Elmer Scales had seen—made speech impossible. When Sears finally spoke, it was on an apparently neutral topic. "Hardesty's an incompetent fool. 'Confidential business.' His only confidential business is with a bottle of Jim Beam."

"Well, now we know what he does in the afternoons." Ricky turned off the highway onto the Seven Mile Road. The tavern, the only building in sight, was a gray collection of angles and points two hundred yards down on the right.

"Indeed. He blots up free liquor in Humphrey Stalladge's back room. He'd be better off in a shoe factory in Endicott."

"What do you think this conversation will be about?"

"We'll know all too soon. Here's our rendezvous."

Hardesty was already standing beside his car in the big, now nearly empty parking lot. Humphrey's Place, in fact no more than an ordinary roadside tavern, had a long peaked and gabled façade with two large black windows: in one of these neon spelled out its name; in the other *Utica Club* flashed on and off. Ricky pulled in beside the sheriff's car, and the two lawyers got out into the cold wind.

"Just follow me," Hardesty said on a rising curve of intonation, his voice inflated with false bonhomie. After looking at one another with shared discomfort, they went up the concrete steps after him. Ricky sneezed twice, hard, the moment he was inside the tavern.

Omar Norris, one of the town's small population of full-time drinkers, was seated on a stool at the bar, looking at them in amazement; plump Humphrey Stalladge moved between the booths, dusting ashtrays. "Walt!" he called, and then nodded at Ricky and Sears. Hardesty's bearing had changed: within the bar, he was taller, more signeurial, and his physical attitude to the two older men behind him somehow suggested that they had come to the place for his advice. Then Stalladge glanced more closely at Ricky and said, "Mr. Hawthorne, isn't it?" and smiled and said, "Well," and Ricky knew that Stella had been in here at one time or another.

"Back room okay?" Hardesty asked.

"Always is, for you." Stalladge waved toward a door marked Private, tucked in a corner beside the long bar, and watched the three men across the dusty floor. Omar Norris, still astonished, watched them, Hardesty striding like a G-man, Ricky conspicuous only in his sober neatness, Sears an imposing presence similar to (it only now came to Ricky) Orson Welles. "You're in good company today, Walt," Stalladge called behind their backs, and Sears made one of his disgusted noises deep in his throat—as much at that as at the negligent wave of his gloved hand with which Hardesty acknowledged the remark. Hardesty, princely, opened the door.

But once inside, after indicating that they should go down the dim hallway to the dark room at its end, his shoulders slumped again, his face relaxed, and he said, "Can I get you anything?" Both men shook their heads.

"I'm a little thirsty, myself," Hardesty said, grimaced, and went back through the door.

Wordlessly the two lawyers went down the hall and into the dingy back room. A table, scarred by a thousand generations of cigarettes, stood in the center; six camp chairs circled it. Ricky found the light switch and flicked it down. Between the unseen light bulbs and the table stood cases of beer stacked nearly to the ceiling. The entire room smelled of smoke and stale beer; even with the light on, the front portion of the room was nearly as dark as it had been before.

"What are we doing here?" Ricky asked.

Sears sat heavily in one of the camp chairs, sighed, removed his hat and put it carefully on the table. "If you mean what will come of this fantastic excursion, nothing, Ricky, nothing."

"Sears," Ricky began, "I think we ought to talk about what Elmer saw out there."

"Not in front of Hardesty."

"I agree. Now."

"Not now. Please."

"My feet are still cold," Ricky said, and Sears gave him a rare smile.

They heard the door at the end of the hall sliding open. Hardesty came in, a full glass of beer in one hand and a half-empty bottle of Labatt's and his Stetson in the other. His complexion had become slightly reddened, as if by a rough plains wind. "Beer's the best thing for a dry throat," he said. Beneath the camouflaging mist of beer which floated out with his words was the sharper, darker tang of sour-mash whiskey. "Really wets the pipes." Ricky calculated that Hardesty had managed to swallow one shot of whiskey and half a bottle of beer in the few moments he had been in the bar. "Have you two ever been here before?"

"No," Sears said.

"Well, this is a good place. It's real private, Humphrey makes sure you're not disturbed if you got something private you want to say, and it's kind of out of the way, so nobody is likely to see the sheriff and the two most distinguished lawyers in town sneakin' into a tavern."

"Nobody except Omar Norris."

"Right, and he's not likely to remember." Hardesty swung a leg over a chair as if it were a large dog he intended to ride, lowered himself into it and simultaneously tossed his hat onto the table, where it bumped into Sears's. Then the Labatt's bottle went onto the table; Sears moved his own hat a few inches nearer his belly as the sheriff took a long swallow from his glass.

"If I may repeat a question my partner just asked, what are we doing here?"

"Mr. James, I want to tell you something." The gunfighter eyes had a drunk's shining sincerity. "You'll understand why we had to get away from Elmer. We're never gonna find who or what killed those sheep." He swallowed again; stifled a burp with the back of his hand.

"No?" At least Hardesty's awful performance was taking Sears's mind off his own troubles; he was miming surprise and interest.

"No. No way, no how. This ain't the first time something like this happened."

"It isn't?" Ricky brought out. He too sat down, wondering how much livestock had been slaughtered around Milburn without his hearing of it.

"Not by a long shot. Not here, see, but in other parts of the country."

"Oh," Ricky leaned back against the rickety chair.

"You remember a few years back I went to a national police convention in Kansas City. Flew out, stayed there a week. Real good trip." Ricky could remember this, because after Hardesty's return the sheriff had spoken to the Lion's Club, the Kiwanis, the Rotary, the Jaycees and the Elks, the National Rifle Association, the Masons and the John Birch Society, the VFW and the Companions of the Forest of America—the organizations which had paid for his trip, and to a third of which Ricky by obligation belonged. His topic was the need for "a modern and fully equipped force for law and order in the small American community."

"Well," Hardesty said, gripping the beer bottle in one hand like a hot dog, "one night back at the motel, I got talking to a bunch of local sheriffs. These guys were from Kansas and Missouri and Minnesota. You know. They were talking about just this kind of setup —funny kinds of unsolved crimes. Now my point is this. At least two or three of these guys ran into exactly the same thing we saw today. Bunch of animals lying dead in a field—wham, bam, dead overnight. No cause until you look at 'em and find—you know. Real neat wounds, like a surgeon would do. And no blood. Exsanguinated, they call that. One of these guys said there was a whole wave of this in the Ohio River valley in the late sixties. Horses, dogs, cows—we probably got the first sheep. But, Mr. Hawthorne, you brought it all back to me when you said that about the no blood. That's right, that reminded me. You'd figure those sheep would bleed like crazy. And in Kansas City, the same thing happened just a year back before the conference, around Christmas."

"Nonsense," said Sears. "I'm not going to listen to any more of this rubbish."

"Excuse me, Mr. James. It's not nonsense. It all happened. You could look it up in the *Kansas City Times*. December 1973. Buncha dead cattle, no footprints, no blood—and that was on fresh snow too, just like today." He looked across at Ricky, winked, drained his beer.

"Nobody was ever arrested?" Ricky asked.

"Never. In all of those places, they never found anybody. Just like somethin' bad came to town, put on its show and took off again. My idea is that things like this are somethin's idea of a joke."

"What?" Sears said explosively. "Vampires? Demons? Crazy."

"No, I'm not sayin' that. Hell, I know there's no vampires, just like I know that damned monster in that lake in Scotland isn't there." Hardesty tipped back in his chair and locked his hands behind his head. "But nobody ever found anything, and we ain't gonna either. There isn't even any sense in looking. I figure just to keep Elmer happy by telling him how I'm workin' on it."

"Is that really all you intend to do?" asked incredulous Ricky Hawthorne.

"Oh, I might have a man walk around some of the local farms, ask if they saw anything funny last night, but that's about all."

"And you actually brought us here to tell us that?" Sears asked.

"I actually did."

"Let's go, Ricky." Sears pushed his chair back and reached for his hat.

"And *actually* I thought the two most distinguished lawyers in town might be able to tell me something."

"I could, but I doubt that you'd listen."

"A little less high and mighty, Mr. James. We're both on the same side, aren't we?"

Ricky said, over the inevitable *phht* of expelled air from Sears, "What did you think we could tell you?"

"Why you think you know something about what Elmer saw last night." He fingered a groove in his forehead, smiling. "You two old boys went into deep freeze when Elmer was talking about that. So you know something or heard something or saw something you didn't want to tell Elmer Scales. Well, suppose you support your local sheriff and speak up."

Sears pushed himself up from the chair. "I saw four dead sheep. I know nothing. And that, Walter, is that." He snatched his hat from the table. "Ricky, let's go do something useful."

"He's right, isn't he?" They were turning the corner at Wheat Row. The vast gray body of St. Michael's Cathedral hung in the air to their right; the grotesque and saintly figures above the door and beside the windows wore caps and shirts of fresh snow, as if they had been frozen in place.

"About?" Sears waved toward their office building.

"Miracle of miracles. A parking space right in front of the door."

"About what Elmer saw."

"If it is obvious to Walt Hardesty, then it is obvious indeed. Yes."

"Did you actually see anything?"

"I saw something not there. I hallucinated. I can only assume that I was overtired and somehow emotionally affected by the story I told."

Ricky carefully backed the car into the space before the tall wooden façade of the office building.

Sears coughed, placed his hand on the door latch, did not move; to Ricky, he looked as though he already regretted what he was going to say. "I take it you saw more or less the same thing that Our Vergil did."

"Yes, I did." He paused. "No. I felt it, but I knew what it was."

"Well." He coughed again, and Ricky grew tense with waiting. "What I saw was Fenny Bate."

"The boy in your story?" Ricky was astonished.

"The boy I tried to teach. The boy I suppose I killed —helped to kill."

Sears took his hand from the door and let his weight fall back on the car seat. Now, at last, he wanted to talk.

Ricky tried to take it·in. "I wasn't sure that—" He stopped in midsentence, aware that he was breaking one of the Chowder Society's rules.

"That it was a true story? Oh, it was true enough, Ricky. True enough. There was a real Fenny Bate, and he died."

Ricky remembered the sight of Sears's lighted window. "Were you looking out of the library windows when you saw him?"

Sears shook his head. "I was going upstairs. It was very late, probably about two o'clock. I had fallen asleep in a chair after doing the dishes. I didn't feel very good, I'm afraid—I would have felt worse if I'd known that Elmer Scales was going to wake me up at seven o'clock this morning. Well, I turned off the lights in the library, closed the door, and began to go up the stairs. And then I saw him sitting there, sitting on the stairs. He appeared to be asleep. He was dressed in the rags I remembered him wearing, and his feet were bare."

"What did you do?"

"I was too frightened to do anything at all. I'm no longer a strong young man of twenty. Ricky, I just stood there for—I don't know how long. I thought I might collapse. I steadied myself by putting my hand on the banister, and then he woke up." Sears was clasping his hands together before him, and Ricky could tell that he was gripping hard. "He didn't have eyes. He just had holes. The rest of his face was smiling." Sears's hands went to his face and folded in beneath the wide hat-brim. "Christ, Ricky. He wanted to play."

"He wanted to *play?*"

"That's what went through my mind. I was in such shock I couldn't think straight. When the—hallucination—stood up, I ran back down the stairs and locked myself in the library. I went to bed on the couch. I had the feeling that it was gone, but I couldn't make myself go back out on the staircase. Eventually I fell asleep and had the dream we were discussing. In the morning of course I recognized what had happened. I was 'seeing things,' in the vulgar parlance. And I did not think, nor do I think now, that such things are exactly in the province of Walt Hardesty. Or Our Vergil, for that matter."

"My God, Sears," Ricky said.

"Forget about it, Ricky. Just forget I ever told you. At least until this young Wanderley arrives."

Jesus she moved she can't she's dead spoke in his mind again, and he turned his eyes from the dashboard where they had been resting while Sears told him to do the impossible, and looked straight into the pale face of his law partner.

"No more," Sears said. "Whatever it is, no more. I've had enough."

. . . no put her feet in first . . .

"Sears."

"I can't, Ricky," Sears said, and levered himself out of the car.

Hawthorne got out on his side, and looked across the top of the car at Sears, an imposing man dressed in black, and for a moment he saw on the face of his old friend the waxy features his dream had given him. Behind him, around him, all of the town floated in wintry air, as if it too had secretly died. "But I'll tell you one thing," Sears said. "I wish Edward were still alive. I often wish that."

"So do I," Ricky whispered, but Sears had already turned from him and was beginning to go up the steps to the front door. A rising wind bit at Ricky's face and hands, and he quickly followed, sneezing again.

John Jaffrey

1

The doctor, whose party it had been, woke out of a troubled sleep just at the time when Ricky Hawthorne and Sears James were beginning their walk across a field in the direction of what appeared to be several piles of dirty laundry. Moaning, Jaffrey looked around the bedroom. Everything appeared to be subtly altered, subtly wrong. Even the bare shoulder of Milly Sheehan, who slept on beside him, was somehow wrong—Milly's round shoulder looked insubstantial, like pink smoke floating in the air. This was true of the bedroom as a whole. The fading wallpaper (blue stripes and bluer roses), the table bearing neat piles of coins, a library book *(The Making of a Surgeon)* and a lamp, the doors and handles of the tall white cupboard opposite, his yesterday's gray striped suit and last evening's dinner jacket draped carelessly over a chair: it all seemed drained of several shades of color, wispy as the interior of a cloud. In this room, at once familiar and unreal, he could not stay.

Jesus she moved, his own words, coiled and died in the washed-out air as if he had just spoken them. Pursued by them, he quickly got out of bed.

Jesus she moved, and this time he heard it spoken. The voice was level, without shading or vibrato, not his own. He had to get out of the house. Of his dreams, he could remember only the last startling image: before that there had been the usual business of lying paralyzed in a bare bedroom, no bedroom he'd ever seen in his life, and the coming of a threatening beast which resolved into dead Sears and dead Lewis: he had assumed they'd all been having this dream. But the image which propelled him across the room was this: the face, streaked with blood and distorted with bruises, of a young woman—a woman as dead as Sears and Lewis in the familiar dream—staring at him with glowing eyes and grinning mouth. It was more real than anything about him, more real than himself. *(Jesus she moved she can't she's dead)*

But she moved, all right. She sat up and grinned.

It was coming to an end for him at last, as it had for Edward, and with part of his mind he knew it. And was grateful. A little surprised that his hands did not melt through the brass handles of the dresser drawer, Jaffrey pulled out socks and underwear. Unearthly rose light pervaded the bedroom. He quickly dressed in random articles of clothing, selecting them blindly, and left the bedroom to go down the stairs to the ground floor. There, obeying an impulse stamped into him by ten years' habit, he let himself into a small rear office, opened a cabinet and took out two vials and two disposable hypodermics. He sat on a revolving typing chair, rolled up his left sleeve, took the syringes from their wrappers and put one on the metal-topped table beside him.

The girl sat up on the blood-smeared car seat and grinned at him through the window. She said, *Hurry up, John.* He pushed the first needle through the rubber cap over the insulin compound, pulled back the barrel and socked the needle into his arm. When the hypodermic was empty, he retracted it and tossed it into the waste-basket beneath the table; then he put the other syringe into the second vial, which contained a compound of morphine; this went into the same arm.

Hurry up, John.

None of his friends knew he was a diabetic, and had been since his early sixties; neither did they know of the morphine addiction which had gained on him since the same period, when he had begun administering the drug to himself: they had only seen the effects of the doctor's morning ritual gradually eating into him.

With both syringes at the bottom of the wastebasket, Dr. Jaffrey came out into his entrance hall and waiting room. Empty chairs stood in rows against the walls; on one of these appeared a girl in torn clothing, red smears across her face, redness leaking from her mouth when she said *Hurry up, John.*

He reached into a closet for his overcoat and was surprised that his hand, extended there at the end of his arm, was such a whole, functioning thing. Someone behind him seemed to be helping him get his arms through the sleeves of the coat. Blindly he grabbed a hat from the shelf above the coathooks. He stumbled through his front door.

2

The face was smiling down at him from an upstairs window in Eva Galli's old house. *Get along, now.* Moving a little oddly, as if drunk, he went down the walk, his feet in carpet slippers not registering the cold, and turned in the direction of town. Until he reached the corner, he could feel that house across the street as a presence behind him; when he managed to get as far as the corner, his open coat flapping about the trousers to the gray suit and the dinner jacket, he suddenly saw in his mind that the house was blazing, all of it blanketed in a transparent flame that was even now warming his back. But when he turned around to look it was not burning, there were no transparent flames, nothing had happened.

Thus, when Ricky Hawthorne and Sears James were seated with Walt Hardesty in a farm kitchen drinking coffee, Dr. Jaffrey, a thin figure in a fishing hat, an un-buttoned coat, the trousers to one suit, the jacket to another and carpet slippers, was moving past the front of the Archer Hotel. He was as little aware of it as he was of the wind which whipped his coat back and snapped it behind him. Eleanor Hardie, vacuuming the carpet in the hotel's lobby, saw him go by, holding down his fishing hat, and thought: poor Dr. Jaffrey, he has to go out to see a patient in this weather. The bot-tom of the window excluded the carpet slippers from her view of the doctor. She would have been confused to see him hesitate at the corner and turn down the left side of the square—in effect going back the way he had come.

When he passed the big windows of the Village Pump restaurant, William Webb, the young waiter Stella Haw-thorne had intimidated, was setting out napkins and silverware, working his way toward the back of the res-taurant where he could take a break and have a cup of coffee. Because he was nearer to Dr. Jaffrey than Eleanor Hardie had been, he took in the details of the doctor's pale, confused face beneath the fishing hat, the coat unbuttoned to reveal the doctor's bare neck, the tuxedo jacket over the pajama top. What went through his mind was: *the old fool's got amnesia.* On the half-dozen occasions Bill Webb had seen Dr. Jaf-frey in the restaurant, the doctor had read a book straight through his meal and left a minute tip. Because Jaffrey had begun to hurry, though the expression on his face suggested that he had no proper idea of where he was going, Webb dropped a handful of silverware on the table and rushed out of the restaurant.

Dr. Jaffrey had begun to flap down the sidewalk. Webb ran after him and caught up with him at the traffic lights a block away: the doctor, running, was an angular bird. Webb touched the sleeve of the black coat. "Dr. Jaffrey, can I help you?"

Dr. Jaffrey.

In front of Webb, about to run across the street without bothering to check the traffic—which, in any case, was nonexistent—Jaffrey turned around, having heard a toneless command. Bill Webb then was given one of the most unsettling experiences of his life. A man with whom he was acquainted, a man who had never looked at him with even polite curiosity, now regarded him with utter terror stamped into his features. Webb, who dropped his hand, had no idea that the doctor saw, instead of his ordinary, slightly froggy face, that of a dead girl grinning redly at him.

"I'm going," the doctor said, his face still registering horror. "I'm going now."

"Uh, sure," said Webb.

The doctor turned and fled, and reached the other side of the street without mishap. He continued his bird-like run down the left side of Main Street, elbows hitching, coat twisting out behind him, and Webb was sufficiently unsettled by the look the doctor had given him to stand staring at him open-mouthed until he realized that he was coatless and a block from the restaurant.

3

In Dr. Jaffrey's mind a perfect image had formed, far clearer than the buildings past which he fled. This was of the two-lane steel bridge over the little river into which Sears James had once thrown a blouse wrapped about a large stone. The fishing hat lifted from his head in a buffeting wind, and for a moment that was clear too, sailing handsomely through gray air.

"I'm going now," he said.

Though on any normal day John Jaffrey could have

gone straight to the bridge without even thinking about which streets would take him there, this morning he wandered about Milburn in a growing panic, unable to find it. He could picture the bridge perfectly—he saw even the rivets with their rounded heads, the flat dull face of the metal—but when he tried to picture its location, he saw only fuzz. Buildings? He turned into Market Street, almost expecting to see the bridge lifting up between Burger King and the A&P. Seeing only the bridge, he had forgotten the river.

Trees? A park? The picture the words evoked was so strong that he was surprised, leaving Market Street, to see about him only empty streets, snow heaped at the curbside. *Move on, doctor.* He stumbled forward, righted himself by leaning against a barber pole, went on.

Trees? Some trees, scattered in a landscape? No. Nor these floating buildings.

As the doctor wandered half-blindly through streets he should have known, tacking from the square to Washington Street on the south, then over to Milgrim Lane and down declining Milgrim Lane past three-room wooden houses set between carwashes and drug-stores into the Hollow and real poverty where he would be as close to unknown as he could be and still be in Milburn (here he might have been in trouble if it hadn't been so cold and if *trouble* hadn't become a meaning-less concept to apply to him), several people saw him go. The Hollow people who saw him go thought he was just another crazy, doomed and oddly dressed. When he accidentally turned back in the right direction and crossed back into quiet streets where bare trees stood at the ends of long lawns, those who saw him assumed that the doctor's car was nearby, because he had begun to move in a slow trot and was hatless. A mailman who grabbed his arm and said, "Man, do you need help?" was shocked into helplessness by the same wide-open gaze of terror that had stopped Bill Webb. Eventually Dr. Jaffrey wound back into the business district.

When he had twice circled Benjamin Harrison Oval, both times going right past Bridge Approach Lane, a patient voice in his mind said *Go around once more and take the second right turn, doctor.*

"Thank you," he whispered, having heard amusement as well as patience in the voice he'd once heard as inhumanly toneless.

So once more, exhausted and half-frozen, John Jaffrey forced himself to move painfully past the tire-repair outfits and muffler centers of Benjamin Harrison Oval, and lifting his knees like a worn-out milkhorse, at last made the turn into Bridge Approach Lane.

"Of course," he sobbed, seeing it at last, the gray arch of the bridge over the sluggish river. He could trot no further; by now in fact he could barely walk. One of the slippers had fallen off, and the foot it had covered was entirely without sensation. He had a flaming stitch in his left side, his heart thudded, his lungs were one vast ache. The bridge was an answered prayer. He trudged toward it. *This* was where the bridge belonged, here in this windy area where the old brick buildings gave way to weedy marshland, here where the wind felt like a hand holding him back.

Now, doctor.

He nodded, and as he drew nearer he saw where he could stand. Four big scallops of metal, themselves cross-hatched by girders, formed an undulating line on either side of the bridge. In the middle of the bridge, between the second and third metal curves, a thick steel girder protruded upward.

Jaffrey could not feel the change from the concrete of the road to the steel of the bridge, but he could feel the bridge move beneath him, lifting a little with each particularly strong gust. When he reached the superstructure, he pulled himself along on the rail. After reaching the central girder, he gripped one of the rungs, put his frozen feet on the bottom rung, and tried to climb up to the flat rail.

He could not do it.

For a moment he stood there, hands on one rung and feet on another, like an old man hanging from a rope, breathing so heavily it sounded like sobbing. He managed to lift his slippered foot and put it on the next rung. Then by using what he felt was surely the last of his strength, he pulled his body up onto it. Some flesh from his bare foot adhered to the lower rung. Panting, he stood on the second rung, and saw that he had two more rungs to go before he would be high enough to stand on the flat rail.

One at a time, he transferred his hands to the next highest rung. Then he moved the slippered foot; and with what felt like heroic effort, moved the other.

Pain seared his entire leg, and he clung to the supports, the bare foot lifted into cold wind. For a moment, his foot blazing, he feared that shock would tumble him back down onto the bridge. Once down, he would never be able to climb up again.

Delicately he put the toes of his still-flaming foot on the rung. It was enough to hold him. Again he transferred his numb arms. The slippered foot went up a rung—by itself it seemed. He tried to pull himself up, but his arms merely trembled. It felt as though the muscles in his shoulders were separating. Finally he threw himself up, assisted he thought by a hand pushing upward in the small of his back, his fingers luckily caught the rung, and he was nearly there.

For the first time he noticed his bare foot, bleeding onto the metal. The pain had increased; now his entire left leg seemed to be in flames. He put the foot down onto the flat rail, and held tightly with both exhausted arms while he moved his right foot beside it.

The water glistened feebly beneath him. Wind buffeted his hair, his coat.

Standing before him on a platform of gray wind, dressed in tweed jacket and bow tie, was Ricky Hawthorne. Ricky's hands were clasped, in a characteristic gesture, before his belt buckle. "Good work, John," he said in his dry kind voice. The best of them all, the sweetest, cuckolded little Ricky Hawthorne.

"You take too much guff from Sears," John Jaffrey said, his voice weak and whispery. "You always did."

"I know." Ricky smiled. "I'm a natural subaltern. Sears was always a natural general."

"Wrong," Jaffrey tried to say. "He's not, he's . . ." The thought died.

"It doesn't matter," came the light dry voice. "Just step forward off the bridge, John."

Dr. Jaffrey was looking down at the gray water. "No, I can't. I had something different in mind. I was going . . ." Confusion took it away.

When he looked up again, he gasped. Edward Wanderley, who had been closer to him than any of the others, was standing on the wind instead of Ricky. As on the night of the party, he wore black shoes, a gray flannel suit, a flowered shirt. Black-rimmed spectacles were joined at the bows by a silvery cord. Handsome in his theatrical gray hair and expensive clothes, Edward smiled at him with compassion, concern, warmth. "It's been a little while," he said.

Dr. Jaffrey began to weep.

"It's time to stop messing around," Edward told him. "All it takes is one step. It's simple as hell, John."

Dr. Jaffrey nodded.

"So take the step, John. You're too tired to do anything else."

Dr. Jaffrey stepped off the bridge.

Below him, at the level of the water but protected from the wind by a thick steel plate, Omar Norris saw him hit the water. The doctor's body went under, surfaced a moment later and spun halfway around, face down, before it began to drift downriver with the current. "Shit," he said: he'd come to the one place he could think of where he could finish off a pint of bourbon without being cornered by lawyers, the sheriff, his wife or someone telling him to get on the snowplow and start clearing the streets. He tilted more bourbon into his mouth, closed his eyes. When he opened them it was still there, lower in the water because the heavy coat had begun to weight the body down. "Shit." He capped the bottle, stood up and went back out into the wind to see if he could find someone who would know what to do.

II

Jaffrey's Party

Give place, you ladies, and begone!
Boast not yourselves at all!
For here at hand approacheth one
   whose face will stain you all.

—"A Praise of His Lady"
   Tottel's Miscellany, 1557

1

The following events occurred a year and a day earlier, in the evening of the last day of the golden age. None of them knew it was their golden age, nor that it was coming to an end: in fact they would have seen their lives, in the usual fashion of people with comfortable existences, a sufficiency of friends and the certainty of food on the table, as a process of gradual and even imperceptible improvement. Having survived the crises of youth and the middle years, they thought they had wisdom enough to meet the coming crises of age; having seen wars, adulteries, compromise and change, they thought they had seen most everything they *would* see —they'd make no larger claim.

Yet there were things they had not seen, and which they would see in time.

It is always true in personal, if not historical, terms that a golden age's defining characteristic is its dailiness, its offered succession of the small satisfactions of daily living. If none in the Chowder Society but Ricky Hawthorne truly appreciated this, in time they would all know it.

2

"I suppose we have to go."

"What? You always like parties, Stella."

"I have a funny feeling about this one."

"Don't you want to meet that actress?"

"My interest in meeting little beauties of nineteen was always limited."

"Edward seems to have become rather taken with her."

"Oh, Edward." Stella, seated before her mirror and brushing her hair, smiled at Ricky's reflection. "I suppose it'll be worth going just to see Lewis Benedikt's reaction to Edward's find." Then the smile changed key as the fine muscles beside her mouth moved, became more edged. "At least it's something to be invited to a Chowder Society evening."

"It's not, it's a party," Ricky vainly pointed out.

"I've always thought that women should be allowed during those famous evenings of yours."

"I know that," Ricky said.

"And that's why I want to go."

"It's not the Chowder Society. It's just a party."

"Then who had John invited, besides you and Edward's little actress?"

"Everybody, I think," Ricky answered truthfully. "What's the feeling you said you had?"

Stella cocked her head, touched her lipstick with her little finger, looked into her summery eyes and said, "Goose over my grave."

3

Sitting beside Ricky as he drove her car the short distance to Montgomery Street, Stella, who had been unusually silent since they'd left the house, said, "Well, if everybody really is going to be there, maybe there'll be a few new faces."

As she had meant him to, Ricky felt a mocking blade of jealousy pierce him.

"It's extraordinary, isn't it?" Stella's voice was light, musical, confidential, as if she had intended nothing that was not superficial.

"What is?"

"That one of you is having a party. The only people we know who have parties are us, and we have about two a year. I can't get over it—John Jaffrey! I'm amazed Milly Sheehan let him get away with it."

"The glamour of the theater world, I imagine," Ricky said.

"Milly doesn't think anything is glamorous except John Jaffrey," Stella replied, and laughed at the image of their friend she could find in every glance of his housekeeper. Stella, who in certain practical matters was wiser than any of the men about her, sometimes titillated herself with the notion that Dr. Jaffrey took some sort of dope; and she was convinced that Milly and her employer did not occupy separate beds.

Considering his own remark, Ricky had missed his wife's insight. "The glamour of the theater world," as remote and unlikely as any such thing seemed in Milburn, did seem to have gripped Jaffrey's imagination—he, whose greatest enthusiasm had been for a neatly hooked trout, had become increasingly obsessed with Edward Wanderley's young guest during the previous three weeks. Edward himself had been very secretive about the girl. She was new, she was very young, she was for the moment a "star," whatever that really meant, and such people provided Edward's livelihood: so it was not exceptional that Edward had persuaded her to be the latest subject of his ghosted autobiographies. The typical procedure was that Edward had his subjects talk into a tape recorder for as many weeks as their interest held; then, with a great deal of skill, he worked these memories into a book. The rest of the research was done through the mails and over the telephone with anybody who knew or had once known his subject—genealogical research too was a part of Edward's method. Edward was proud of his genealogies. The recording was done whenever possible at his house; his study walls were lined with tapes—tapes on which, it was understood, many juicy and unpublishable indiscretions were recorded. Ricky himself had only the most notional interest in the personalities and sex lives of actors, and so he thought did the rest of his friends. But when *Everybody Saw the Sun Shine* underwent a month's change of cast which Ann-Veronica Moore spent in Milburn, John Jaffrey had increasingly had one goal—to have this girl come to his house. An even greater mystery was that his hints and schemes had succeeded, and the girl had consented to attend a party in her honor.

"Good Lord," Stella said, seeing the number of cars lined at the curb before Jaffrey's house.

"It's John's coming-out party," Ricky said. "He wants to show off his accomplishment."

They parked down the block and slipped through cold air to the front door. Voices, music pulsed at them.

"I'll be damned," Ricky said. "He's using his offices too."

Which was the truth. A young man pressed up against the door by the crowd let them in. Ricky recognized him as the latest occupant of the Galli house. He accepted Ricky's thanks with a deferential grin, and then smiled at Stella. "Mrs. Hawthorne, isn't it? I've seen

you around town, but we've never been introduced."
Before Ricky could remember the man's name, he had
offered Stella his hand and said, "Freddy Robinson, I
live across the street."

"A pleasure, Mr. Robinson."

"This is some party."

"I'm sure it is," said Stella, the faintest of smiles tip-
ping the edges of her mouth.

"Coats in the consulting room here, drinks upstairs.
I'd be happy to get you while you and your husband
take care of your coats."

Stella looked at his blazer, his plaid trousers, his
floppy velvet bow tie, his absurdly eager face. "That
won't be necessary, I'm sure, Mr. Robinson."

She and Ricky dodged into the consulting room,
where coats were flung everywhere.

"Good God," said Stella. "What does that young
man do for a living?"

"I think he sells insurance."

"I should have known. Take me upstairs, Ricky."

Holding her cool hand, Ricky led her out of the consulting room and through the lower fringe of the party
to the stairs. A record player on a table thumped out
disco music; young people strutted, wriggled before it.
"John's had a brainstorm," Ricky muttered. "If not
sunstroke," Stella said behind him.

"Hiya, Mr. Hawthorne." This was from a tall boy in
his late teens, a client's son.

"Hello, Peter. It's too noisy for us down here. I'm
looking for the Glenn Miller wing."

Peter Barnes's clear blue eyes regarded him expressionlessly. Did he seem that foreign to young people? "Hey, what do you know about Cornell? I think
that's where I want to go to college. I might be able to
get early admission. Hiya, Mrs. Hawthorne."

"It's a good school. I hope you make it," said Ricky.
Stella poked him smartly in the back.

"No sweat. I know I'll get in. I got seven-hundreds
on my trial boards. Dad's upstairs. Do you know
what?"

"No." Stella prodded him again. "What?"

"All of us were invited because we're about the same age as Ann-Veronica Moore, but they just took her upstairs as soon as she and Mr. Wanderley got here. We never even got to talk to her." He gestured around at the couples doing the hustle in the small downstairs room. "Jim Hardie kissed her hand, though. He's always doing things like that. He really grosses everybody out."

Ricky saw Eleanor Hardie's son doing a series of ritualistic dance steps with a girl whose black hair flowed down to the small of her back—it was Penny Draeger, the daughter of a druggist who was a client. She twitched away, spun, lifted a foot, and then placed her behind squarely on Hardie's crotch. "He sounds like a promising boy," Stella purred. "Peter, would you do me a favor?"

"Uh, sure," the boy gulped. "What?"

"Clear a space so that my husband and I can go upstairs."

"Sure, yeah. But you know what? We were just invited to meet Ann-Veronica Moore, and then we were supposed to go home. Mrs. Sheehan said we can't even go upstairs. I guess they thought she'd like to dance with us or something, but they didn't even give her a chance. And at ten o'clock, Mrs. Sheehan said she was going to throw us all out. Except for him, I suppose." He nodded at Freddy Robinson, who had one arm around the shoulders of a giggling high-school girl.

"Terribly unfair," Stella said. "Now be a good boy and carve a way through the undergrowth."

"Oh yeah." He took them across the crowded room to the staircase as if he were reluctantly leading an outing from the local asylum. When they were safely on the stairs and Stella had already begun to go regally up, he bent forward and whispered in Ricky's ear. "Will you do something for me, Mr. Hawthorne?" Ricky nodded. "Say hello to her for me, will you? She's a real piece."

Ricky laughed aloud, causing Stella to turn her head and look at him quizzically. "Nothing, darling," he said, and went up the stairs to the quieter regions of the house.

They saw John Jaffrey standing in the hallway, rubbing his hands together. Soft piano music drifted from the living rooms. "Stella! Ricky! Isn't this wonderful?" He gestured expansively toward the rooms. They were as crowded as those downstairs, but with middle-aged men and women—the parents of the teenagers, Jaffrey's neighbors and acquaintances. Ricky saw two or three of the prosperous farmers from outside town, Rollo Draeger, the druggist, Louis Price, a commodity broker who had given him one or two good ideas, Harlan Bautz, his dentist, who already seem tipsy, some men he didn't know but who he thought were probably from the university—Milly Sheehan had a nephew who taught there, he remembered—Clark Mulligan, who ran the town's movie theater, Walter Barnes and Edward Venuti from the bank, each in a snowy turtleneck, Ned Rowles who edited the local paper. Eleanor Hardie, both hands on a tall glass held at the level of her breasts, was tilting her high-browed face toward Lewis Benedikt. Sears was leaning against a bookcase, looking out of sorts. Then the crowd parted, and Ricky saw why. Irmengard Draeger, the druggist's wife, was blathering in his ear, and Ricky knew what she was saying. *I went to Skidmore, well I had three years before I met Rollo, don't you think I deserve something better than this one-horse town? Honestly, if it wasn't for Penny, I'd pack up and leave this minute.* It was the melody, if not exactly the lyric, and Irmengard had set the past ten years of her life to it.

"I don't know why I never did it before," John said, his face gleaming. "I feel younger tonight than I have in a decade."

"How wonderful, John," Stella said, leaning forward to kiss his cheek. "What does Milly think of it?"

"Not much." He looked bemused. "She couldn't figure out why I wanted to have a party in the first place.

She couldn't understand why I wanted to have Miss Moore here at all."

Milly herself came into view at that moment, holding a tray of canapés before Barnes and Venuti, the two bankers, and from the determined look on Milly's plump face, Ricky saw that she had opposed the idea from the first. "Why did you want to?"

"Excuse me, John, I'm going to mill," said Stella. "Don't worry about getting me a drink, Ricky, I'll take one from someone who isn't using his." She went through the doorway in the direction of Ned Rowles. Lou Price, gangsterish in a double-breasted pinstriped suit, took her hand and pecked her on the cheek.

"She's a wonderful gal," John Jaffrey said, and the two men watched Stella deflect Lou Price with a phrase and continue toward Ned Rowles. "I wish there were a million like her." Rowles was turning around to watch Stella approach him, his face lighting up with pleasure. In his corduroy jacket, with his sandy hair and earnest face, Ned Rowles resembled a journalism student more than an editor. He too kissed Stella, but on the mouth, and held both her hands as he did so. "Why did I want to?" John cocked his head, and four deep wrinkles divided the side of his neck. "I don't know, exactly. Edward's so entranced with this girl that I wanted to meet her."

"Is he? Entranced?"

"Oh, absolutely. You wait. You'll see. And then, you know, I only ever see my patients and Milly and the Chowder Society. I thought it was time to bust out a little. Have a little fun before I dropped dead."

This was very giddy for John Jaffrey, and Ricky glanced at his friend, taking his eyes from his wife, who was still holding hands with Ned Rowles.

"And do you know what I can't get over? One of the most famous actresses in America is upstairs in my house, right this minute."

"Is Edward with her?"

"He said she had to take a few minutes before she joined us. I guess he's helping her with her coat or something." Jaffrey's ravaged face simply gleamed with pride.

"I don't think she's quite yet one of the most famous actresses in America, John." Stella had moved on, and Ned Rowles was saying something vehement to Ed Venuti.

"Well, she will be. Edward thinks so, and he's always right about things like that. Ricky!" Jaffrey gripped his upper arms. "Did you see the kids dancing downstairs? Isn't that fantastic? Kids having a good time in *my* house? I thought they'd enjoy meeting her. It's a fantastic honor, you know. She can only be here a few more days. Edward's got the taping nearly done, and she has to get back to New York to rejoin the play. And here she is, in my house! By God, Ricky."

Ricky felt almost as though he should press a cold cloth to Jaffrey's forehead.

"Did you know that she just came out of nowhere? That she was the most promising student in her drama class, and the next week she got her part in *Everybody Saw the Sun Shine?*"

"No, John."

"Just now I had a wonderful idea. It was about having her here in the house. I was standing here, listening to the kids' disco music from downstairs, and hearing bits and pieces of the George Shearing record from in there, and I thought—downstairs is the raw, animal life, kids jumping around to that beat, on this floor we've got the mental life, doctors and lawyers, all middle-class respectability, and upstairs is grace, talent, beauty—the spirit. You see? It's like evolution. She's the most ethereal thing you've ever seen. And she's only eighteen."

Never in his life had Ricky heard John Jaffrey express such a fanciful concept. He was beginning to worry about the doctor's blood pressure. Then both men heard a door close up on the next landing, followed by Edward's deep voice saying something that had the sly intonation of a joke.

"I thought Stella said she was nineteen," Ricky said.

"Shhh."

A beautiful little girl was coming toward them down the stairs. Her dress was simple and green, her hair was a cloud. After a second Ricky saw that her eyes matched the dress. Moving with a kind of rhythmic idle precision, she gave them the tiniest of smiles— still it was brilliant—and went by, patting Dr. Jaffrey's chest with her fingertips as she passed them. Ricky watched her go, amused and touched. He had seen nothing like it since Louise Brooks in *Pandora's Box*.

Then he looked at Edward Wanderley and saw at once that John Jaffrey was right. Edward's feathers were shining. He had obviously been stirred up by the girl, and it was equally obvious that it was difficult for him to leave her alone long enough to greet his friends. All three men began to move into the crowded living room. "Ricky, you look great," Edward told him, putting an arm easily around Ricky's shoulders. Edward was half a foot taller, and when Edward began to propel him into the room, Ricky could smell an expensive cologne. "Just great. But isn't it time you stopped wearing bow ties? The Arthur Schlesinger era is dead and gone."

"That was the era right after mine," Ricky said.

"No, listen, nobody's older than he feels. I stopped wearing neckties altogether. In ten years, eighty per cent of the men in this country will wear ties only to weddings and funerals. Barnes and Venuti over there will be wearing that getup to the bank." He scanned the room. "Where the hell did she go?" Ricky, in whom new ties evoked a desire to wear them even to bed, looked at Edward's unfettered neck as his friend surveyed the crowded room, saw that it was even more corded than John Jaffrey's, and decided not to change his habits. "I've spent three weeks with that girl, and she's the most fantastic subject I ever had. Even if she makes the stuff up, and maybe she does, it'll be the best book I'll ever do. She's had a horrible life, *horrible*. It makes you weep just to hear it—I sit there and cry. I tell you, she's wasted in that piece of Broadway fluff, wasted. She'll be a great tragic actress. Once she's out of her teens." Red-faced, Edward guffawed at his own preposterousness. Like John, he too was in flight.

"You two seem to have caught that girl like a virus," Ricky said.

John giggled, and Edward said, "The whole world will, Ricky. She's really got that gift."

"Oh," Ricky said, remembering something. "Your nephew Donald seems to be having a great success with his new book. Congratulations."

"It's nice to know I'm not the only talented bastard in the family. And it should help him get over his brother's death. That was an odd story, a very odd story—they both seem to have been engaged to the same woman. But we don't want to think about anything macabre tonight. We're going to have fun."

John Jaffrey nodded in happy agreement.

4

"I saw your son downstairs, Walt," Ricky said to Walter Barnes, the older of the two bankers. "He told me his decision. I hope he makes it."

"Yeah, Pete's decided on Cornell. I always hoped he'd at least apply to Yale—my old school. I still think he'd make it." A heavy-set man with a stubborn face like his son's, Barnes was disinclined to accept Ricky's congratulations. "The kid isn't even interested any-more. He says Cornell's good enough for him. 'Good enough.' His generation's even more conservative than mine. Cornell's the kind of rinky-dink place where they still have food fights. Nine or ten years ago, I used to be worried that Pete would grow up to be a radical with a beard and a bomb—now I'm afraid he'll settle for less than he could get."

Ricky made vague noises of sympathy.

"How are your kids doing? They both still out on the West Coast?"

"Yes. Robert's teaching English in a high school. Jane's husband just got a vice-presidency."

"Vice-president in charge of what?"

"Safety."

"Oh, well." They both sipped at their drinks, refraining from trying to invent comment on what a promotion to vice-president in charge of safety might mean in an insurance company. "They planning to get back here for Christmas?"

"I don't think so. They both have pretty active lives." In fact, neither of their children had written to Ricky and Stella for several months. They had been happy infants, sullen adolescents, and now, both of them nearly forty, were unsatisfied adults—in many ways, still adolescent. Robert's few letters were barely concealed pleas for money; Jane's were superficially bright, but Ricky read desperation in them. ("I'm really getting to like myself now": a statement which to Ricky meant its opposite. Its glibness made him wince.) Ricky's children, the former darlings of his heart, were now like distant planets. Their letters were painful; seeing them was worse. "No," he said, "I don't think they'll be able to make it this time."

"Jane's a pretty girl," Walter Barnes said.

"Her mother's daughter."

Ricky automatically began to look around the room to catch a glimpse of Stella, and saw Milly Sheehan introducing his wife to a tall man with stooping shoulders and thick lips. The academic nephew.

Barnes asked, "Have you seen Edward's actress?"

"She's here somewhere. I saw her come down."

"John Jaffrey seems very excited about her."

"She is really sort of unnervingly pretty," Ricky said, and laughed. "Edward's been unnerved too."

"Pete read in a magazine that she's only seventeen years old."

"In that case, she's a public menace."

When Ricky left Barnes to join his wife and Milly Sheehan, he caught sight of the little actress. She was

dancing with Freddy Robinson to a Count Basie record,
and she moved like a delicate bit of machine tooling,
her eyes shining greenly; his arms about her, Freddy
Robinson looked stupefied with happiness. Yes, the
girl's eyes were shining, Ricky saw, but was it with
pleasure or mockery? The girl turned her head, her
eyes sent a current of emotion across the room to him,
and Ricky saw in her the person his daughter Jane,
now overweight and discontented, had always wanted
to be. As he watched her dance with foolish Freddy
Robinson, he understood that there before him was a
person who would never have cause to utter the damning phrase that she was really getting to like herself:
she was a little flag of self-possession.

"Hello, Milly," he said. "You're working hard."

"Oh poof, when I'm too old to work I'll lay down
and die. Did you have anything to eat?"

"Not yet. This must be your nephew."

"Oh, please *forgive* me. You haven't met." She
touched the arm of the tall man beside her. "This is
the brainy one in my family, Harold Sims. He's a professor at the college and we've just been having a nice
talk with your wife. Harold, this is Frederick Hawthorne, one of the doctor's closest friends." Sims
smiled down at him. "Mr. Hawthorne's a charter member of the Chowder Society," Milly concluded.

"I was just hearing about the Chowder Society,"
Harold Sims said. His voice was very deep. "It sounds
interesting."

"I'm afraid it's anything but."

"I'm speaking from the anthropological point of
view. I've been studying the behavior of male chron-
ologically-related interaction groups. The ritual content is always very strong. Do you, uh, members of the
Chowder Society actually wear dinner jackets when you
meet?"

"Yes, I'm afraid we do." Ricky looked to Stella for
help, but she had mentally abstracted herself, and was
gazing coolly at both men.

"Why is that, exactly?"

Ricky felt that the man was about to pull a notebook from his pocket. "It seemed like a good idea a hundred years ago. Milly, why did John invite half the town if he's going to let Freddy Robinson monopolize Miss Moore?"

Before Milly could answer, Sims asked, "Are you familiar with the work of Lionel Tiger?"

"I'm afraid I'm abysmally ignorant," Ricky said.

"I'd be interested in observing one of your meetings. I suppose that could be arranged?"

Stella laughed at last, and gave him a look which meant, *get out of that.*

"I suppose differently," Ricky said, "but I could probably get you into the next Kiwanis meeting."

Sims reared back, and Ricky saw that he was too unsure of his dignity to take jokes well. "We're just five old coots who enjoy getting together," he quickly said. "Anthropologically, we're a washout. We're of no interest to anyone."

"You're of interest to me," said Stella. "Why don't you invite Mr. Sims and your wife to the next meeting?"

"Yeah!" Sims began to show an alarming quantity of enthusiasm. "I'd like to record for a start, and then the video element—"

"Do you see that man over there?" Ricky nodded in the direction of Sears James, who more than ever resembled a stormcloud in human form. It looked like Freddy Robinson, now separated from Miss Moore, was trying to sell him insurance. "The big one? He'd slit my throat if I did any such thing."

Milly looked shocked; Stella lifted her chin and said, "Very nice meeting you, Mr. Sims," and left them.

Harold Sims said, "Anthropologically, that's a very interesting statement." He regarded Ricky with an interest even more professional. "The Chowder Society must be highly important to you."

"Of course it is," Ricky said simply.

"From what you just said, I'd assume that the man

you just pointed out is the dominant figure in the group—as it were, the honcho."

"Very astute of you," Ricky said. "Now if you'll forgive me, I see someone I must have a word with."

When he had turned his back and gone away only a few steps, he heard Sims ask Milly, "Are those two really married?"

5

Ricky stationed himself in a corner, deciding he'd wait things out. He had a good mostly unobstructed view of the party: he'd be quite happy just watching things until it was time to go home. The record having come to an end, John Jaffrey appeared beside the portable stereo and put another one on the turntable. Lewis Benedikt, drifting up beside him, seemed amused, and when the sound began to issue from the speakers, Ricky heard why. It was a record by Aretha Franklin, a singer Ricky knew only from the radio. Where on earth would John Jaffrey have obtained such a record, and how long ago had he done it? He must have bought it specifically for the party. This was a fascinating concept, but Ricky's deliberations on it were interrupted by a succession of people who joined him, one by one, in his corner.

The first person who found him was Clark Mulligan, the owner of the Rialto, Milburn's only movie theater. His Hush Puppies were unaccustomedly clean, his trousers pressed, his belly successfully contained by his jacket button—Clark had spruced himself up for the evening. Presumably he knew that he had been invited for his relation to show business. Ricky thought it must have been the first time John had had Clark Mulligan in his home. He was glad to see him; he was always glad to see him. Mulligan was the only person in town who shared his love of old movies. Hollywood gossip bored Ricky, but he loved the films of its golden days.

"Who does she remind you of?" he asked Mulligan.

Mulligan squinted across the room. The actress was

standing demurely across the room, listening to something said by Ed Venuti. "Mary Miles Minter?"

"She reminded me of Louise Brooks. Though I don't suppose Louise Brooks's eyes were green."

"Who knows? She's supposed to be a damn fine little actress, though. Cropped up just out of nowhere. Nobody knows anything about her."

"Edward does."

"Oh, he's doing one of his books, isn't he?"

"The interviewing is nearly done. It's always difficult for Edward to say good-bye to his subjects, but this time it will be especially traumatic. I think he fell in love with her." And indeed, Edward had jealously joined Ed Venuti, and managed to interpose himself between the banker and the little actress.

"I'd fall in love with her too," Mulligan said. "Once they get their faces up on the screen, I fall in love with all of them. Have you seen Marthe Keller?" His eyes rolled.

"Not yet, but from the photos I've seen she looks a lot like a modern Constance Talmadge."

"Are you kidding? How about Paulette Goddard?" And from there they went happily on to speak of Chaplin, of *Monsieur Verdoux,* of Norma Shearer and John Ford, Eugene Pallette and Harry Carey, Jr., *Stagecoach* and *The Thin Man,* Veronica Lake and Alan Ladd, John Gilbert and Rex Bell, Jean Harlow, Charlie Farrell, Janet Gaynor, *Nosferatu* and Mae West, actors and films Ricky had seen as a younger man and had never ceased youthfully to cherish, and the fresh memory of them helped to dampen the recollection of what a young man had said about himself and his wife.

"Wasn't that Clark Mulligan?" His second visitor was Sonny Venuti, Edward's wife. "He looks terrible." Sonny herself had changed over the past few years from a slender, pretty woman with a lovely smile to a bony stranger with an uneasy, dazed expression permanently fixed in her eyes. A casualty of marriage. Three months before she had come into Ricky's office and asked what she had to do to get a divorce: "I'm not sure yet, but

I'm definitely thinking about it. I have to find out where
I am." Yes, there was another man, but she would not
name him. "I'll tell you this, though, he's good-looking
and intelligent and he's as close to sophisticated as you
can get in this town." She had left no doubt that the
man was Lewis. Such women always reminded Ricky
Hawthorne of his daughter, and he had led her through
all of her options gently, outlining all the steps, explaining everything carefully and succinctly, though he knew
she would never return.

"She's beautiful, isn't she?"

"Oh, entirely."

"I talked to her for a second."

"Yes?"

"She wasn't interested. She's only interested in men.
She'd love *you*."

At the moment, the actress was talking to Stella, not
ten feet away, which seemed to undercut Sonny Venuti's
statement. Ricky watched the two women conversing
without hearing their words; Sonny went on at some
length to explain why the actress would love him. The
subject of these remarks was listening to Stella, she
responded, both women were lovely, cool, amused.
Then Miss Moore said something that visibly con-
founded Stella: Ricky's wife blinked, opened her mouth,
snapped it shut, patted her hair—if she had been a
man, she'd have scratched her head. Ann-Veronica
Moore, trailed by Edward Wanderley, went off.

"So I'd watch myself," Sonny Venuti was saying. "She
might look like a little angel, but that kind of woman
loves to turn men into hash."

"*Pandora's Box*," said Ricky, reminded of his first
impression of the actress.

"What? Oh, never mind, I know, it's an old movie.
When I came to you that time you mentioned Katharine
Hepburn and Spencer Tracy twice."

"How are things now, Sonny?"

"I'm trying again, Jesus, how I'm trying. Who can
get a divorce in Milburn? But I still want to find out
who I am."

Ricky thought of his daughter, and his heart twisted.

Then Sears James joined Ricky in his corner. "Privacy at last," he said, putting his drink on a table and leaning against the bookshelves.

"I wouldn't count on it."

"An appalling young man tried to sell me insurance. He lives across the street."

"I know him."

Since they were in total agreement on the subject of Freddy Robinson, there was nothing more to say. Eventually Sears broke the silence. "Lewis might need help getting home. He's been a bit bibulous."

"Well, after all, it's not one of our meetings."

"Hmm. I suppose he might pick up a girl who could drive him home."

Ricky glanced at him to see if he meant this personally, but Sears was merely surveying the party blandly, obviously bored. "Did you talk to the guest of honor?"

"I haven't even seen her."

"She's highly visible. I think she's over—" He lifted his drink in the direction he had seen her, but the actress was no longer there. Edward was talking to John, presumably about her, but Ann-Veronica Moore was no longer in the room. "Keep an eye on Edward. He'll find her."

"Isn't that Walter Barnes's son standing by the bar?"

Though it was now long past ten, Peter Barnes and a young girl were indeed by the bar, and the waiter who had relieved Milly of her duties was mixing drinks for them. Doctor Jaffrey's housekeeper had clearly not had the heart to send away the teenagers downstairs, and the bolder ones had invaded the upstairs party. The piano music which had replaced Aretha Franklin abruptly ceased, and Ricky saw Jim Hardie juggling several record albums, trying to decide which was least out of date. "Uh, oh," he said to Sears, "we have a new disc jockey."

"That's it," Sears said. "I'm tired and I'm going home. Noisy music makes me want to bite someone."

He moved massively away. Milly Sheehan stopped his progress and spoke agitatedly to him. Ricky guessed that she was in a tizzy over the sudden appearance of the teenagers. Sears shrugged—it was not his problem.

Ricky wanted to go home then, but Stella had begun to dance with Ned Rowles, and soon several of the wives had enticed their husbands to that part of the room nearest the record player. The teenagers danced energetically, sometimes almost elegantly; the adults looked foolishly imitative beside them. Ricky groaned; it was going to be a long night. All had begun to speak louder, the barman mixed a half dozen drinks at a time, moving an upended bottle over a row of ice-filled glasses. Sears reached the door and disappeared.

Christina Barnes, a tall blonde with an avid face, appeared by Ricky. "Since my son has managed to take over this party, how about dancing with me, Ricky?"

Ricky smiled. "I'm afraid I can't be a gentleman, Christina. I haven't danced in forty years."

"You must do something pretty well to hang on to Stella all these years."

She'd had about three drinks too many. "Yes," he said. "You know what it was? I never lost my sense of humor."

"Ricky, you're wonderful. I'd love to give you a backrub one of these days and see if I could find out what you're made of."

"Old pencil stubs and out-of-date law books."

Clumsily she kissed him, hitting the edge of his jaw. "Did Sonny Venuti see you a couple of months ago? I want to talk to you about it."

"Then come to my office," he said, knowing she would not.

"Excuse me, Ricky, Christina," said Edward Wanderley, who had come up on Ricky's other side.

"I'll leave you men to your private business." Christina went off in search of a dancing partner.

"Have you seen her? Do you know where she is?" Edward's broad face was boyish, anxious.

"Miss Moore? Not for a little while. Have you lost her?"

"Damn. She just vanished."

"She's probably in the bathroom."

"For twenty-five minutes?" Edward rubbed his forehead.

"Don't worry about her, Edward."

"I'm not worried, I just want to find her." He stood on tiptoe and began to look over the heads of the dancers, still grinding his fist into his forehead. "You don't suppose she went off with one of those awful kids?"

"Couldn't say." Edward slapped his shoulder and went rapidly out into the room.

Christina Barnes and Ned Rowles appeared in the vacuum Edward left at the edge of the carpet, and Ricky went around them to look for Stella. After a moment he saw her with Jim Hardie, obviously declining an invitation to learn the Bump. She looked over at him with some relief, and separated from the boy.

The music was so loud they had to speak directly into one another's ears. "That's the most forward boy I've ever met."

"What did he say?"

"He said I looked like Anne Bancroft."

The music abruptly stopped, and Ricky's reply carried over the entire party. "No one under thirty should be allowed to enter a movie theater."

Everyone but Edward-Wanderley, who was quizzing a hostile Peter Barnes, turned to look at Ricky and Stella. Then the ever-hopeful Freddy Robinson took the hand of Jim Hardie's girlfriend, another record fell onto the turntable, and people went back to the business of being at a party. Edward had been speaking softly, insistently, but Peter Barnes's aggrieved voice floated out a moment before the music began: "Jesus, man, maybe she went upstairs."

"Can we go?" he asked Stella. "Sears left a while ago."

"Oh, let's stay a while. We haven't done anything

like this in ages. I'm having fun, Ricky." When she saw his crestfallen face, she said, "Dance with me, Ricky. Just this once."

"I don't dance," he said, making himself heard over the din of the music. "Enjoy yourself. But let's go in about half an hour, all right?"

She winked at him, turned away, and was immediately captured by gangsterish Lou Price, to whom this time she succumbed.

Edward, seeing nothing, rushed by.

Ricky walked around the edges of the party for a time, refusing drinks from the barman. He spoke to Milly Sheehan, who was sitting exhausted on the couch. "I didn't know it would turn out like this," Milly said. "It'll take hours to clean up."

"Make John help you."

"He *always* helps," Milly said, radiance touching her plain round face. "He's wonderful that way."

Ricky wandered on, at last arriving at the top of the stairs. Silence from upstairs and down. Was Edward's actress up there with one of the boys? He smiled, and went downstairs for the quiet.

The doctor's offices were deserted. Lights burned, cigarettes had been stamped out on the floor, half-filled cups stood on every surface. The rooms smelled of sweat, beer, smoke. The little portable record player in the front room spun on, the needle clicking in the empty grooves. Ricky lifted the tone arm, put it on its support and turned the machine off. Milly would have a lot of work down here the next morning. He looked at his watch. Twelve-thirty. Through the ceiling came the thumping of a bass, a tinny echo of music.

Ricky sat in one of the stiff waiting-room chairs, lit a cigarette, sighed and relaxed. He wondered if he might help Milly by beginning to straighten up these downstairs rooms, then realized that he'd need a broom. He was too tired to go scouting for a broom.

A few minutes later footsteps woke him out of a light doze. He straightened up in his chair, listening to someone opening a door at the bottom of the stairs. "Hello?" he called out, not wanting to embarass an illicit couple.

"Who's that? Ricky?" John Jaffrey came into the front waiting room. "What are you doing here? Have you seen Edward?"

"I came down for the quiet. Edward was rushing around trying to find Miss Moore. Maybe he went upstairs."

"I'm worried about him," Jaffrey said. "He looked so—so taut. Ann-Veronica's dancing with Ned Rowles. Couldn't he see her?"

"She vanished a while back. That's why he was anxious."

"Oh, poor Edward. He doesn't have to worry about that girl. She's good as gold. You should see her. She's absolutely lovely. She looks better than she has all night."

"Well." He pushed himself out of the stiff chair. "Do you want help finding Edward?"

"No, no, no. You just carry on. I'll find him. I'll try the bedrooms. Though what he'd be doing there—"

"Still looking, I expect."

John wheeled around, muttering that he couldn't help but worry, and went back through the consulting rooms. Ricky slowly followed.

Harold Sims was dancing with Stella, holding her tightly and keeping up a steady stream of talk into her ear. The music was so loud that Ricky wanted to scream. Nobody but Sears had left, and the young people, many of them now drunk, whirled about, hair and arms flying. The little actress cavorted with the editor, Lewis was talking to Christina Barnes on the couch. Both were oblivious to the presence of sleeping Milly Sheehan, not eight inches away. Ricky wished profoundly that he were in his bed. The noise gave him a headache. His old friends, Sears excepted, seemed to have lost their minds. Lewis had his hand on Christina Barnes's knee, and his eyes were unfocused. Was he really trying to seduce his banker's wife? In the presence of her husband and son?

Upstairs, something heavy fell over, and only Ricky heard it. He went back out onto the landing and saw John Jaffrey standing at the top of the stairs.

"Ricky."

"What's wrong, John?"

"Edward. It's Edward."

"Did he knock something over?"

"Come up here, Ricky."

Ricky went up, growing a little more worried with each step. John Jaffrey seemed very shaken.

"Did he knock something over? Did he hurt himself?"

Jaffrey's mouth opened. Finally sounds emerged. "I knocked a chair over. I don't know what to do."

Ricky reached the landing and looked into Jaffrey's ruined face. "Where is he?"

"The second bedroom."

Since Jaffrey did not move, Ricky went across the hall to the second door. He looked back; Jaffrey nodded, swallowed and finally came toward him. "In there."

Ricky's mouth was dry. Wishing that he were anywhere else, doing anything but what he was doing, he put a hand on the doorknob and turned it. The door swung open.

The bedroom was cold, and almost bare. Two coats, Edward's and the girl's, were lain across an exposed mattress. But Ricky saw only Edward Wanderley. Edward was on the floor, both hands clutched to his chest and his knees drawn up. His face was terrible.

Ricky stepped back and nearly fell over the chair that John Jaffrey had overturned. There was no question that Edward was still alive—he did not know how he knew it, but he knew—yet he asked, "Did you try to feel his pulse?"

"He doesn't have a pulse. He's gone."

John was trembling just inside the door. Music, voices came up the stairwell.

Ricky forced himself to kneel by Edward's side. He touched one of the hands gripping Edward's green shirt. He worked his fingers around to the underside of the wrist. He felt nothing, but he was no doctor. "What do you think happened?" He still could not look again at Edward's distorted face.

John came further into the room. "Heart attack?"

"Do you think that's what it was?"

"I don't know. Yes, probably. Too much excitement. But—"

Ricky stared up at Jaffrey and took his hand from Edward's still warm hand. "But what?"

"I don't know. I can't say. But, Ricky, look at his face."

He looked: rigid muscles, mouth drawn open as if to yell, empty eyes. It was the face of a man being tortured, flayed alive. "Ricky," John said, "it's not a very medical thing to say, but he looks as if he was scared to death."

Ricky nodded and stood. That was just how Edward looked. "We can't let anyone come up here. I'll go down and phone for an ambulance."

6

And that was the ending of Jaffrey's party: Ricky Hawthorne telephoned for an ambulance, switched off the record player and said that Edward Wanderley had "had an accident" and was beyond help, and sent thirty people home. He permitted no one to go upstairs. He looked for Ann-Veronica Moore, but she had already left.

Half an hour later, Edward's body was on its way to hospital or morgue. Ricky drove Stella home. "You didn't see her leave?" he asked.

"One minute she was dancing with Ned Rowles, the next minute she was out the door. I thought she was going to the bathroom. Ricky, how horrible."

"Yes. It was horrible."

"Poor Edward. I don't think I really believe it."

"I don't think I do either." Tears filled his eyes, and for some seconds he drove blindly, seeing only a streaky blur. To try to take the image of Edward's face from his mind, he asked, "What did she say to you that surprised you so much?"

"What? When? I barely spoke to her."

"In the middle of the party. I saw her talking to you, and I thought she said something that startled you."

"Oh." Stella's voice rose. "She asked me if I was married. I said, 'I'm Mrs. Hawthorne.' And then she said, 'Oh, yes, I've just seen your husband. He looks like he'd be a good enemy.'"

"You couldn't have heard her correctly."

"I did."

"It doesn't make sense."

"That's what she said."

And a week later, after Ricky had telephoned the theater where the girl was working, trying to return her coat, he heard that she had returned to New York the day after the party, abruptly quit the play and left town. Nobody knew where she was. She had vanished for good—she was too young, too new, and she left behind not even enough reputation for a legend. That night, at what looked like being the final meeting of the Chowder Society, he had, inspired, turned to a morose John Jaffrey and asked, "What's the worst thing you've ever done?" And John saved them all by answering, "I won't tell you that, but I'll tell you the worst thing that ever happened to me," and told them a ghost story.

Part Two

Dr. Rabbitfoot's Revenge

Follow a shadow, it still flies you;
Seem to fly it, it will pursue.

—Ben Jonson

I

Just Another Field,
but What They Planted There

From the journals of Don Wanderley

1

The old idea of Dr. Rabbitfoot . . . the idea for another book, the story of the destruction of a small town by Dr. Rabbitfoot, an itinerant showman who pitches camp on its outskirts, sells elixirs and potions and nostrums (a black man?), and who has a little sideshow—jazz music, dancing girls, trombones, etc. Fans and bubbles. If I ever saw a perfect setting for this story, Milburn is it.

First about the town, then about the good doctor. My uncle's town, Milburn, is one of those places that seems to create its own limbo and then to nest down in it. Neither proper city nor proper country—too small for one, too cramped for the other, and too self-conscious about its status. (The local paper is called *The Urbanite.* Milburn even seems proud of its minuscule slum, the few streets called the Hollow, seems to point at it and say: See, we've got places where you want to be careful after dark, the age hasn't left us high and dry and innocent. This is almost comedy. If trouble ever comes to Milburn, it won't start in the Hollow.) Three-fourths of the men work somewhere else, in Binghamton mainly—the town depends on the freeway for its life. A feeling of being oddly settled, unmoving, *heavy,* and at the same time nervous. (I bet they gossip about one another endlessly.) Nervous because they'd feel that they were forever missing something—that the age after all has left them high and dry. Probably I feel this because of the contrast between here and California—this is a worry they don't have, there. It does seem a particularly *Northeast* kind of anxiety, peculiar to these little towns. Good places for Dr. Rabbitfoot.

(Speaking of anxiety, those three old men I met today—my uncle's friends—have it bad. Obviously has to do with whatever made them write to me, not knowing that I was getting so sick of California I'd have gone anywhere I thought I might be able to work.)

Physically, of course, it's pretty—all these places are. Even the Hollow has a kind of sepia thirties prettiness. There's the regulation town square, the regulation trees—maples, tamarack pines, oaks, the woods full of mossy deadfalls—a sense that the woods around the town are stronger, *deeper* than the little grid of streets people put in their midst. And when I came in I saw the big houses, some of them big enough to be called mansions.

But still . . . it is wonderful, a heaven-sent setting for the Dr. Rabbitfoot novel.

He's black, definitely. He dresses gaudily, with old-fashioned pzazz: spats, big rings, a cane, a flashy waist-coat. He's chirpy, showbizzy, a marathon talker, slightly ominous—he's the bogeyman. He'll own you if you don't watch out. He'll get you seven ways to Sunday. He's got a killer smile.

You only see him at night, when you pass a piece of land normally deserted and there he is, standing on a platform outside his tent, twirling a cane while the jazz band plays. Lively music surrounds him, it whistles through his tight black hair, a saxophone curls his lips. He's looking straight at you. He invites you in to have a look at his show, to buy a bottle of his elixir for a dollar. He says he is the celebrated Dr. Rabbitfoot, and he's got just what your soul needs.

And what if what your soul needs is a bomb? A knife? A slow death?

Dr. Rabbitfoot gives you a big wink. You're *on*, man. Just pull a dollar out of your jeans.

Now to state what is obvious: Behind this figure I've been carting around in my head for years is Alma Mobley. It also suited her to give you what you wanted.

All the time, the capering smile, the floating hands, the eyes of bleached and dazzling white . . . his sinister gaiety. *An' what about that little Alma Mobley, boy? Suppose you see her when you close your eyes, then what? Is she there, hee hee? Has you ever touched a ghost? Has you ever put your hand on a ghost's white skin? And yo' brutha's peaceful eyes—was they watchin' you?*

2

I went to the office of the lawyer who wrote to me, Sears James, as soon as I got into town—a severe white building on Wheat Row, just alongside the town square. The day, gray in the morning, was cold and bright, and before I saw his receptionist I thought, maybe this is the start of a new cycle for you, but the receptionist told him that both Mr. James and Mr. Hawthorne were at a funeral. That new secretary they hired went too, but it looked a little pushy to her, because she didn't know Dr. Jaffrey at all, did she? Oh, they should be at the cemetery by now. And are you the Mr. Wanderley they've been expecting? I don't suppose you knew Dr.

Jaffrey, either? Oh, he was a dear, dear man, he must have been doctoring here in Milburn for forty years, he was the kindest man you ever saw, not sugary-sweet, you know, but when he put his hands on you, you just felt the kindness flowing out, *she rattled on, looking me over, inspecting me, trying to figure out just what the devil her boss wanted me for,* and then this old woman sitting at her switchboard locked him with an angry smile and slapped the trump card on the table, *she said of course you don't know, but he killed himself five days ago. He jumped off the bridge—can you imagine that? It was just tragic. Mr. James and Ricky Hawthorne were so upset. They still haven't gotten over it. Now that Anna girl is making them do twice as much work, and we've got that crazy Elmer Scales calling up every day, yelling at them about those four sheep of his . . . . what would make a nice man like Dr. Jaffrey do a thing like that, do you imagine?*

(*He listened to Dr. Rabbitfoot, lady.*)

Oh, you'd like to go out to the cemetery?

3

He did. It was on a road called Pleasant Hill, just out of town on one of the state roads (she gave him good directions), long fields dying under snow that came too early, and every now and then the wind picking up a flat sheet of loose snow, making it stand up and wave its arms. *Funny how lost this country seems, though people have been walking back and forth over it for hundreds of years. It looks bruised and regretful, its soul gone or withdrawn, waiting for something to happen that will wake it up again.*

The sign, *Pleasant Hill Cemetery,* was a length of stamped gray metal on one side of a black ironwork gate; if it had not been for the big gates standing at what looked like the entrance to just another hilly field, Don would have missed it. He looked at the gates as they came nearer, wondering what kind of farmer would be grandiose enough to stick up a baronial gate at his tractor path, slowed down, glanced up at the rising narrow road—more than a tractor path—and saw half a dozen cars parked at the top of the hill. Then he saw the little plate. *Just another field, but heavens what they planted there.* He swung his car through the gates.

Don left his car apart from the others, halfway up the hill, and walked to the top: nearest him was the oldest section of the cemetery, tilted slabs with pitted markings, stone angels lifting arms weighted with snow. Granite young women shielded their eyes with forearms hung with drapery. Thin skeletons of weeds mounted up the leaning slabs. The narrow road bisected the old section and led into a larger region of neat small headstones. Purple, gray and white, these were dwarfed by the expanse of land rolling out from them: after a moment, a hundred yards away, Don saw the fences surrounding the cemetery. A hearse was drawn up at the land's lowest point. The black-hatted driver cupped a cigarette so that it would not be seen by the little knot of people clustered around the newest grave. One woman shapeless in a pale blue coat clung to another, taller woman; the other mourners stood as straight and motionless as fenceposts. *When I saw the two old men standing together at the base of the grave, I knew they had to be the two lawyers—if they weren't lawyers they were from Central Casting. I started to come toward them down the slope of the narrow road. Then I thought, if the dead man was a doctor, why aren't there more people—where are his patients?* A silver-haired man beside the two lawyers saw him first and prodded the massive one who wore a black fur-collared coat with his elbow. The big one glanced up at him, and then the little man beside him, the one who looked as if he had a cold, also took his eyes from the minister and looked curiously at Don. Even the minister stopped talking for a moment, stuck one frozen hand in the pocket of his overcoat, and gaped at Don with rubber-faced confusion.

Then, finally, a sign of welcome, a contrast to this

guarded examination: one of the beauties, the younger one (a daughter?), wafted toward him a small genuine smile.

The man with silver-white hair who looked to Don as though he should have been in the movies left the other two and sauntered toward Don. "Are you a friend of John's?" he whispered.

"My name is Don Wanderley," he whispered back. "I got a letter from a man named Sears James, and the receptionist in his office said I could find him out here."

"Hell, you even look a little like Edward." Lewis grabbed his bicep and squeezed. "Look, kid, we're having a rough time here, just hang in there and don't say anything until it's all over. You got a place to stay tonight?"

So I joined them, half-meeting, half-avoiding their glances. The woman in the pale blue coat sagged against the challenging-looking woman holding her up: her face worked and she wailed oh no oh no oh no. Crumpled colored tissues lay at her feet, lifting and scampering in the wind that cut into the hollow. Every now and then one of them shot away like a small pastel pheasant and caught in the mesh of the fence. By the time we left there were dozens of them there, flattened out against the wire.

Frederick Hawthorne

4

Ricky had been pleased with Stella. While the three remaining members of the Society had been trying to adjust to the shock of John's death, only Stella had thought of the plight of Milly Sheehan. Sears and Lewis, he supposed, had thought as he had—that Milly would simply live on in John's house. Or that, if the house was too empty for her, she would put up at the Archer Hotel until she decided where to go and what to do. He and

Sears knew that she had no financial troubles; they had drawn up the will which left Milly John Jaffrey's house and the contents of his bank accounts. If you added it all together, she had been willed assets of somewhere around two hundred thousand dollars: and if she chose to stay in Milburn, there was more than enough in the bank to pay the real estate taxes and give her a comfortable living. We're lawyers, he said to himself, we think like that. We can't help it; we put the pettifogging first and the people second.

Of course they were thinking of John Jaffrey. The news had come near noon of the day following that in which Ricky's premonitions had reached their height: he had known that something dreadful had happened the moment he recognized the shaky voice on the other end of the line as Milly Sheehan's. "It's, it's," she said, her voice trembling and cloudy. "Mr. Hawthorne . . . ?"

"Yes, it's me, Milly," he said. "What's happened?" He pushed the buzzer that communicated to Sears's office and told him to switch on the telephone speaker for his extension. "What is it, Milly?" he asked, knowing that his voice would be much too loud for Sears, but momentarily unable to speak softly—the speakers, while reproducing the client's voice at a normal volume, tripled the noise made by anyone at the other office extension. "You're breaking my eardrums," Sears complained over the line.

"Sorry," Ricky said. "Milly, are you there? It's Milly, Sears."

"So I gathered. Milly, can we help you?"

"Oooo," she wailed and the back of his neck went cold.

The phone went dead. "Milly?"

"Pipe down," Sears commanded.

"Are you there, Milly?"

Ricky heard the telephone clattering against some hard surface.

The next voice was Walt Hardesty's. "Hey, this is the sheriff. Is this Mr. Hawthorne?"

"Yes. Mr. James is on the other line. What's going on, Walt? Is Milly all right?"

"She's standin' lookin' out the window. What is she anyhow, his wife? I thought she was his wife."

Sears burst in impatiently, his voice loud as a cannon in Ricky's office. "She is his housekeeper. Now tell us what is happening out there."

"Well, she's fallin' apart like a wife. You two are Dr. Jaffrey's lawyers?"

"Yes," Ricky said.

"Do you know about him yet?"

Both partners were silent. If Sears felt the way Ricky did, his throat was too tight for speech.

"Well, he was a leaper," Hardesty said. "Hey, hang on, lady. Sit down or something."

"HE WAS A WHAT?" Sears bellowed, his voice booming through Ricky's office.

"Well, he took a dive off the bridge this morning. He was a leaper. Lady, calm down and let me talk."

"The lady's name is Mrs. Sheehan," Sears said in a more normal voice. "She might respond better if you called her that. Now since Mrs. Sheehan evidently wished to communicate with us and is unable to do so, please tell us what happened to John Jaffrey."

"He took a dive off . . ."

"Be careful. He *fell* off the bridge? Which bridge?"

"Hell, the bridge over the river, what do you think?"

"What's his condition?"

"Dead as a doornail. What do you think it would be? Say, who's gonna take care of the arrangements and all that? This lady's in no shape . . ."

"We will," Ricky said.

"And we might take care of more than that," Sears uttered furiously. "Your manner is disgraceful. Your diction is shameful. You are a ninny, Hardesty."

"Just wait a damned—"

"AND! If you are assuming that Dr. Jaffrey committed suicide, then you are on shaky ground indeed, my friend, and you'd be well advised to keep that assumption to yourself."

"Omar Norris saw the whole thing," Hardesty said. "We need ID before we can get set for the autopsy, so why don't you get over here so we can get off the phone?"

Five seconds after Ricky put down his phone Sears appeared in the doorway, already thrusting his arms into his coat. "It's not true," Sears said, pulling on the coat. "It's some mistake, but let's get over there anyway."

The telephone buzzed again. "Don't answer it," Sears said, but Ricky picked it up. "Yes?"

"There's a young woman in reception who wants to see you and Mr. James," said the receptionist.

"Tell her to come back tomorrow, Mrs. Quast. Dr. Jaffrey died this morning, and Mr. James and I are going to his home to meet Walt Hardesty."

"Why . . ." Mrs. Quast, who had been on the verge of indiscretion, changed subjects. "I'm so sorry, Mr. Hawthorne. Do you want me to call Mrs. Hawthorne?"

"Yes, and say I'll be in touch as soon as I can." By now, Sears was in a rage of impatience, and when Ricky moved around his desk, his partner was already in the hallway, twirling his hat. Ricky grabbed his coat and hurried to catch up.

Together they went down the paneled hall. "That ponderous, unthinkable oaf," Sears rumbled. "As if you could believe Omar Norris on any subject except bourbon and snowplows."

Ricky stopped short and put his hand on Sears's arm. "We have to think about this, Sears. John might actually have killed himself." It still hadn't sunk into him, and he could see that Sears was determined not to let it sink into *him*. "He'd never have any reason to go walking on the bridge, and especially not in this weather."

Sears's face suffused with blood. "If you think that, you're a ninny too. I don't care if John was *birdwatching,* he was doing something." His eyes avoided Ricky's. "I don't know and can't imagine what, but something. Did he seem suicidal to you last night?"

"No, but . . ."

"Therefore, let's not wrangle. Let's get over to his house." He sped down the hall ahead of Ricky and banged open the reception room door with his shoulders. Ricky Hawthorne, hurrying after, came out into the reception room and was mildly surprised to see him confronting a tall girl with dark hair, an oval face and small, chiseled features.

"Sears, we don't have time now, and I told this young woman to drop in tomorrow."

"She says—" Sears took off his hat. He looked as if he'd been hit on the head with a plank. "Tell him what you told me," he said to the girl.

She said, "Eva Galli was my aunt, and I'm looking for a job."

(Mrs. Quast turned away from the girl, who had merely smiled at her, and blushed as she dialed the Hawthorne number. The girl moved away to examine the Kitaj graphics with which Stella, two or three years ago, had replaced Ricky's old Audubon prints. Incomprehensible and new, was Mrs. Quast's judgment on both the graphics and the girl. *No,* Stella Hawthorne exhaled when she had heard the news about Dr. Jaffrey. *Oh, poor Milly. Poor everybody, I'm sure, but I'll have to do something about Milly.* When she pulls the jack from the switchboard, Mrs. Quast thinks, my goodness it's very *bright* in here and then thinks, no golly it's *dark,* dark as *sin,* the lights must have blazed up and gone out, but the next instant everything is normal, the lamp on her desk looks just as it always does, and she rubs her eyes and shakes her gray head—*Milly Sheehan had a soft cushy life right along, about time she went out and did a real job of work*—and is astonished to hear Mr. James telling that snip of a girl that if she comes back tomorrow they'll talk about giving her some secretarial work. *I mean, just what the dickens is going on around here?*)

And Ricky, looking at Sears, wondered too—secretarial work? They had a half-time secretary, Mavis

Hodge, who did most of their typing: to find enough work for another girl they'd have to start answering their junk mail. But of course it wasn't the need for more hands on deck that made Sears treat the girl the way he did, it was that name, *Eva Galli,* pronounced in a voice that would taste like port wine if you could drink it . . . Sears suddenly looked very tired, the sleeplessness and the nightmares and the vision of Fenny Bate and Elmer Scales and his damned sheep and how John's death *(he was a leaper)* had all gathered to unstring him if only for a moment. Ricky saw his partner's fear and exhaustion and saw that even Sears could come unglued. "Yes, come back tomorrow," he said to the girl, noticed that the oval face and regular features were more than just attractive, and knew that if there was one thing Sears didn't need reminding of at that moment, it was Eva Galli. Mrs. Quast was staring at him, so he told her to deal with all incoming calls during the afternoon, just to be saying something.

"I gather that a good friend of yours has just died," the girl said to Ricky. "I'm sorry to be coming at such an awkward time," and ruefully smiled with what looked like genuine concern. "Please don't let me delay you."

He glanced once more at her foxlike features before turning to Sears and the door—Sears reflectively buttoning up his coat, white faced—and it seemed to him that maybe Sears's instincts were right, maybe this girl's coming was a part of the puzzle, nothing seemed accidental anymore: as if there were some kind of plan and if they could only get all the pieces together they'd see what it was.

"It's probably not even John," Sears said in the car. "Hardesty is such an incompetent that I wouldn't be surprised if he took Omar Norris's word . . ." His voice died out; both partners knew this was only fancy. "Too cold," Sears said, his lips puckering out childishly. "Too damn cold," Ricky agreed, and finally thought of another thing to say. "At least Milly won't starve." Sears sighed, almost amused. "Good thing too, she'd never get another job with eavesdropping privileges." Then

there was silence again as they recognized that they
were agreeing that John Jaffrey probably had stepped
off the Milburn bridge and drowned in the freezing
river.

After they had picked up Hardesty and driven to the
tiny jail where the body was being kept until the arrival of the morgue truck, they found that Omar Norris
had not been mistaken. The dead man was John—he
looked even more wasted than he had in life. His
sparse hair adhered to his scalp, his lips drew back over
blue gums—his whole being was vacant, as in Ricky
Hawthorne's nightmare. "Jesus," Ricky said. Walt
Hardesty grinned and said, "That ain't the name we got,
Mr. Lawyer." "Give us the forms, Hardesty," Sears
said quietly, and then, being Sears, added, "We'll take
his effects too, unless you managed to lose them along
with his dentures."

They thought they might find a clue to Jaffrey's death
in the few things contained in the manila envelope
Hardesty gave them. But in the collection taken from
John Jaffrey's pockets they could read nothing at all.
A comb, six studs and matching cufflinks, a copy of
The Making of a Surgeon, a ballpoint pen, a bundle of
keys in a worn leather pouch, three quarters and a
dime—Sears spread it over his lap in the front seat of
Ricky's old Buick. "A note was too much to hope for,"
Sears said, and then leaned gigantically back and rubbed
his eyes. "I'm beginning to feel like a member of an
endangered species." He straightened up again and
looked at the mute assortment of objects. "Do you
want to keep any of this yourself, or should we just give
it to Milly?"

"Maybe Lewis would like the studs and cufflinks."

"Let's give them to him. Oh, Lewis. We'll have to
tell him. Do you want to go back to the office?"

They sat numbly on the warm cushions of Ricky's
old car. Sears removed a long cigar from his case,
snipped off the tip, and without bothering to go through
the usual rituals of sniffing and looking, applied his
cigar lighter to it. Ricky wound his window down un-

complaining: He knew that Sears was smoking out of reflex, that he was unconscious of the cigar.

"Do you know, Ricky," he said around it, "John is dead and we've been talking about his cufflinks?"

Ricky started his car. "Let's get back to Melrose Avenue and have a drink."

Sears put the pathetic collection back into the manila envelope, folded it in half and slid it into one of the pockets of his coat. "Watch where you're driving. Has it escaped your attention that it's snowing again?"

"No, it has not," Ricky said. "If it starts this early and if it gets much worse, we could find ourselves snowed in before the end of winter. Maybe we should lay in some canned food, just to be on the safe side." Ricky flicked on his headlights, knowing that Sears would soon begin to issue commands about this. The gray sky which had hung over the town for weeks had darkened nearly to black, broken by clouds like combers.

"Humph," Sears snorted. "The last time that happened—"

"I was back from Europe. Nineteen-forty-seven. Terrible winter."

"And the time before that was in the twenties."

"Nineteen-twenty-six. The snow almost covered the houses."

"People died. A neighbor of mine died in that snow."

"Who was that?" Ricky asked.

"Her name was Viola Frederickson. She was caught in her buggy. She just froze to death. The Fredericksons had John's house, in fact." Sears sighed again, wearily, as Ricky turned into the square and went past the hotel. Snowflakes like balls of cotton streaked past the dark windows of the hotel. "For God's sake, Ricky, your window's open. Do you want to freeze us both?" He raised his hands to lift the fur collar nearer his chin, and saw the cigar protruding from between his fingers. "Oh. Sorry. Habit." He lowered his own window and dropped the cigar through it. "What a waste."

Ricky thought of John Jaffrey's body lying on a

stretcher in a cell; of breaking the news to Lewis; of the bluish skin stretched over John's skull.

Sears coughed. "I can't understand why we haven't heard from Edward's nephew."

"He'll probably just turn up." The snow slackened off. "That's better." Then thought, *well, maybe not:* the air had a peculiar midday darkness which seemed unaffected by his headlights. These were no more than a glow nearly invisible at the front of the car. It was the objects and oddments of the town which instead seemed to glow, not with the yellow glow of headlights but whitely, with the white of the clouds still boiling and foaming overhead—here a picket fence, there a door and molding shone. Here a scattering of stones in a wall, there naked poplars on a lawn. Their bloodless color reminded Ricky eerily of John Jaffrey's face. Above these random shining things the sky beyond the boiling clouds was even blacker.

"Well, what do you think happened?" Sears demanded.

Ricky turned into Melrose Avenue. "Do you want to stop off at your house for anything first?"

"No. Do you have an opinion or don't you?"

"I wish I knew what happened to Elmer Scales's sheep."

Now they were pulling up in front of Ricky's house and Sears was showing obvious signs of impatience. "I don't give a gold-plated damn for Our Vergil's sheep," he said; he wanted to get out of the car, he wanted to end the discussion, he would have growled like a bear if Ricky had mentioned the apparition of barefooted, boneheaded Fenny Bate on his staircase—Ricky saw all this, but after he and Sears had left the car and were walking up the path to the door he said, "About that girl this morning."

"What about her?"

Ricky put his key in the slot. "If you want to pretend that we need a secretary, fine, but . . ."

Stella opened the door from within, already talking. "I'm so glad both of you are here. I was so afraid you'd go back to stuffy Wheat Row and pretend that nothing had happened. Pretend to work and keep me in the dark! Sears, please, come in out of the cold, we don't want to heat all outdoors. Come in!" They shuffled into the hall and moving like two tired cart-horses, took off their coats. "You both look just awful. There's no question of mistaken identity then, it was John?"

"It was John," Ricky said. "We can't really tell you any more, Stella. It looks like he jumped from the bridge."

"Dear me," Stella said, all her momentary brightness gone. "The poor Chowder Society."

"Amen," Sears said.

After late lunch Stella said that she'd make up a tray for Milly. "Maybe she'll want to nibble something."

"Milly?" Ricky asked, startled.

"Milly Sheehan, need I remind you? I couldn't just let her rattle around in that big house of John's. I picked her up and drove her back here. She's absolutely wrecked, the poor darling, so I put her to bed. She woke up this morning and couldn't find John, and she fretted in that house for hours until horrible Walter Hardesty came by."

"Fine," Ricky said.

"Fine, he says. If you and Sears hadn't been so wrapped up in yourselves, you might have spared a thought for her."

Attacked, Sears raised his head and blinked. "Milly has no worries. She's been left John's house and a disproportionate amount of money."

"Disproportionate, Sears? Why don't you take her tray up and tell her how grateful she should be. Do you think that would cheer her up? That John Jaffrey left her a few thousand dollars?"

"Scarcely a few thousand, Stella," said Ricky. "John willed almost everything he owned to Milly."

"Well, that's as it should be," Stella declared, and stamped off to the kitchen, leaving them both mystified.

Sears asked, "You ever have any trouble deciphering what she's talking about?"

"Now and then," Ricky answered. "There used to be a code book, but I think she threw it out shortly after our wedding. Shall we call Lewis and tell him? We've put it off too long already."

"Give me the phone," Sears said.

Lewis Benedikt

5

Not hungry, Lewis made lunch for himself from habit: cottage cheese, Croghan baloney with horseradish and a thick chunk of Otto Gruebe's cheddar, made by old Otto himself in his little cheese factory a couple of miles outside Afton. Feeling a little upset by his experiences of the morning, Lewis enjoyed thinking of old Otto now. Otto Gruebe was an uncomplicated person, built a little like Sears James, but stooped from a lifetime of bending over vats; he had a rubbery clown's face and enormous shoulders and hands. Otto had made this comment on his wife's death: "You hat a liddle trouble over there in Spain, yeah? They told me in town. It's such a *pidy,* Lewis." After everyone else's tact, this had moved Lewis immeasurably. Otto with his curd-white complexion from spending ten hours a day in his factory, Otto with his pack of coon dogs— he'd never been spooked a day in his life. Chewing his way through lunch, Lewis thought he would drive up to see Otto someday soon; he'd take his gun and go out looking for coon with Otto and his dogs, if the snow held off. Otto's Germanic hardheadedness would do him good.

But it was snowing again now; the dogs would be barking in their kennels and old Otto would be skimming off whey, cursing the early winter.

A pity. Yes: a pity was what it was, and more than that: a mystery. Like Edward.

He stood up abruptly and dumped his dishes in the

sink; then he looked at his watch and groaned. Eleven-thirty and lunch already over; the rest of the day loomed over him like an Alp. He did not even have an evening of bubbleheaded conversation with a girl to look forward to; nor, because he was trying to wind things down, could he anticipate an evening of deeper pleasure with Christina Barnes.

Lewis Benedikt had successfully managed what in a town the size of Milburn is generally considered an impossibility: from the first month of his return from Spain, he had constructed a secret life that stayed secret. He pursued college girls, young teachers at the high school, beauticians, the brittle girls who sold cosmetics at Young Brothers department store—any girl pretty enough to be ornamental. He used his good looks, his natural charm and humor and his money to establish himself in the town's mythology as a dependably comic character: the aging playboy, the Suave Old Bird. Boyish, wonderfully unself-conscious, Lewis took his girls to the best restaurants for forty miles around, ordered them the best food and wine, kept them in stitches. He took to bed, or was taken to bed by, perhaps a fifth of these girls—the ones who showed him by their laughter that they could never take him seriously. When a couple—a couple, say, like Walter and Christina Barnes—walked into The Old Mill near Kirkwood or Christo's between Belden and Harpursville, they might half expect to see Lewis's steel-gray head bending toward the amused face of a pretty girl a third his age. "Look at that old rascal," Walter Barnes might say, "at it again." His wife would smile, but it would be difficult to tell what the smile meant.

For Lewis used his comic reputation as a rake to camouflage the seriousness of his heart, and he used his public romances with girls to conceal his deeper, truer relationships with women. He spent evenings or nights with his girls; the women he loved he saw once or twice a week, in the afternoons while their husbands were at work. The first of these had been Stella Haw-thorne, and in some ways the least satisfactory of his

loves, she had set the pattern for the rest. Stella had
been too offhand and witty, too casual with him. She
was enjoying herself, and simple enjoyment was
what the young high-school teachers and beauticians
gave him. He wanted feeling. He wanted emotion—he
needed it. Stella was the only Milburn wife who, tested,
had evaded that need. She had given his playboy
image back to him—consciously. He loved her briefly
and wholly, but their needs were badly mismatched.
Stella did not want *Sturm und Drang;* Lewis, at the
center of his demanding heart, knew that he wanted to
recapture the emotions Linda had given him. Frivolous
Lewis was Lewis only skin deep. Sadly, he had to let
Stella go: she had taken up none of his hints, his offered
emotion had simply rolled off her. He knew that she
thought he'd simply gone on to an empty series of affairs
with girls.

But he had instead gone on, eight years ago, to Leota
Mulligan, the wife of Clark Mulligan. And after Leota,
to Sonny Venuti, then to Laura Bautz, the wife of the
dentist Harlan Bautz, and finally, a year ago, to Christina Barnes. He had cherished each of these women. He
loved in them their solidity, their attachments to their
husbands, their hungers, their humor. He loved talking
to them. They had understood him, and each of them
had known exactly what he was offering: more a hidden
pseudo-marriage than an affair.

When the emotion began to go stale and rehearsed,
then it was over. Lewis still loved each of them; he
still loved Christina Barnes, but—

The but was that the wall was before him. The wall
was what Lewis called the moment when he began to
think that his deep relationships were as trivial as his
romances. Then it was time to draw in. Often, in times
of withdrawal, he found that he was thinking of Stella
Hawthorne.

Well, he certainly could not look forward to an evening with Stella Hawthorne. To fantasize about that
would be to confirm his foolishness to himself.

What was more foolish than that ridiculous scene

this morning? Lewis left the sink to look out the window toward the path into the woods, remembering how he had raced down it, panting, his heart leaping with terror—now there was real asininity. The fluffy snow fell, the familiar wood raised white arms, the return path trailed harmlessly, charmingly off at a screwball angle, going nowhere.

"When you fall off a horse, you get back on," Lewis told himself. "You get right back on that mother." What had happened? He had heard—voices? No; he had heard himself thinking. He had spooked himself by remembering too exactly Linda's last night alive. That and the nightmare—Sears and John advancing toward him—had bamboozled his emotions so that he behaved like someone in a Chowder Society story. No evil stranger had stood behind him on the path back home; you could not walk through the woods without being heard. Everything was explicable.

Lewis went upstairs to his bedroom, kicked off his loafers and pushed his feet into a pair of Dingos, pulled on a sweater and a ski parka and went back down and out the kitchen door.

His morning footprints were already filling with new snow. The air felt delicious, crisp as a winesap apple; light snow continued to come down. If he could not go coon hunting with Otto Gruebe, he might be able to get in some skiing before long. Lewis walked across his brick patio and stepped onto the path. Above him the sky was dark and scattered with shining clouds, but clear gray light filled the day. Snow on the pine branches gleamed, particular and white as moonlight.

He deliberately set off on what was normally his return path. His own fear surprised him, tingling in his mouth and belly like anticipation.

"Well, I'm here, come and get me," he said, and smiled.

He felt the presence of nothing but the day and the woods, his house at his back; he realized after a moment that even his fear had vanished.

And now, walking over new snow toward his woods,

Lewis had a fresh perception. It may have come because he was seeing the woods from an unfamiliar angle,
going at them backward, and it may have been because
he was just walking through them for the first time in
weeks, not jogging. Whatever the reason, the woods
looked like an illustration in a book—not like a real
woods, but a drawing on a page. It was a fairytale
woods, looking too perfect, too composed—drawn in
black ink—to be real. Even the path, winding off in a
pretty indirection, was a fairytale path.

It was the clarity which gave it mystery. Each bare
and spiky branch, each tangle of wiry stalks, stood out
separately, shining with its own life. Some wry magic
hovered just out of sight. As Lewis went deeper into
the woods, where the new snow had not penetrated, he
saw his morning's footprints, and they too seemed
haunting and illustrative and part of the fairytale, these
prints in snow coming toward him.

Lewis was too restless to stay inside after his walk.
The emptiness of the house proclaimed that the house
held no woman; for some time, there would be no woman, unless Christina Barnes came out for one last scene.
A few jobs around the house had been waiting for
weeks—he had to check the sump, the dining room
table was badly in need of polish, as was most of the
silver—but these jobs could wait a while longer. Still
wearing the sweater and parka, Lewis prowled his
house, going from one floor to another, never settling
in one room.

He went into his dining room. The big mahogany
table reproached him; its surface was dull, lightly
scratched here and there from times he'd put Spanish
earthenware down on it without using a mat. The spray
of flowers in a jug on the center of the table had wilted;
a few petals lay like dead bees on the wood. *Did you
really expect to see someone out there?* he asked himself. *Are you disappointed that you didn't?*

Turning out of the dining room with the jug of
wasted flowers in his hands, he saw again the fairytale

tangle of the woods. Branches glistened, thorns shone like thumbtacks, implying some narrative on which he'd already closed the book.

Well. He shook his head and took the dead flowers into the kitchen and dumped them into the waste bin. *Whom did you want to meet? Yourself?*

Unexpectedly, Lewis blushed.

He set down the empty jug on a counter and went back outside, crossing the patio to the old stable some previous owner had converted into a garage and tool shed. The Morgan was parked beside a toolbench covered with screwdrivers, pliers and paintbrushes in cans. Lewis bent his head, unlocked the door and cramped himself in behind the wheel.

He reversed out of the garage, left the car and heaved the door shut, then got in and swung the car around on the bricks and drove down the tree-lined lane to the highway. He immediately felt more like himself: the canvas top of the Morgan bucked in the wind, cold breeze parted his hair in the middle. The tank was almost full.

In fifteen minutes he was surrounded by hills and open country marked off at intervals by stands of trees. He took the little roads, opening the car up to seventy, sometimes eighty when he saw a nice stretch of straight road before him. He skirted the Chenango Valley, followed the line of the Tioughnioga River as far as Whitney Point, and then cut off west toward Richford and Caroline, deep in the Cayuga Valley. Sometimes on curves the little car's back end skittered around, but Lewis corrected the skid expertly, not even thinking about it. Lewis instinctively drove well.

Finally he realized that he was traveling the same route, and in the same way, as when he'd been a student returning to Cornell. The only difference was that exhilarating speed then had been thirty miles an hour.

After nearly two hours of driving, taking little roads past farms and state parks just to see where they'd go, his face was numb with cold. He was in Tompkins County, close to Ithaca, and the country here was more

lyrical than around Binghamton—when he reached the
tops of hills, he could see the black road arrowing
through vales and over tree-lined rises. The sky had
darkened, though it was only midafternoon: Lewis
thought he'd see more snow before nightfall. Then
ahead of him, just far enough away to build up the
right amount of speed, was a wide place in the road
where he knew he could make the Morgan spin completely around. But he reminded himself that he was
sixty-five years old—too old to do stunts in cars. He
used the wide place in the road to turn around toward
home.

Going more slowly, he drove across the valley toward Harford, cutting back east. On the straight ways
he opened the car up a little, but was careful to keep
under seventy. Still, there was pleasure in it, in the
speed and the cold breeze on his face and the dainty
handling of the little car. All this nearly made him feel
that he was a Tau Kappa Epsilon boy again, skimming
over the roads toward home. A few heavy snowflakes
drifted down.

Near the airfield outside Glen Aubrey he passed a
stand of denuded maples and saw in them the gleaming
clarity of his own woods. They seemed suffused with
magic, with some concealed meaning that was part of
a complex story—hero foxes that were princes suffering
a witch's curse. He saw the footprints racing toward
him.

. . . *suppose you went out for a walk and saw yourself running toward you, your hair flying, your face distorted with fear* . . .

His viscera went cold as his face. Ahead of him, standing in the middle of the road, was a woman. He had
time to notice only the alarm in her posture, the hair
which billowed around her shoulders. He twisted the
wheel, wondering where in hell she'd come from—*Jesus
she just jumped out at me*—at the same time as he
realized that he was bound to hit her. The car was
going to slew around.

The rear end of the Morgan drifted slowly toward

the girl. Then the entire car was traveling sideways and he lost sight of her. Panicked, Lewis cramped the wheel the other way. Time whittled down to a solid capsule encasing him as he sat helpless in a flying car. Then the texture of the moment changed, time broke and began to flow, and he knew, as passive as he'd ever been in his life, that the car had left the road: everything was happening with unbelievable slowness, almost lazily, and the Morgan was floating.

It was over in a moment. The car stopped with a boneshaking jolt in a field, its nose pointed toward the road. The woman he might have struck was nowhere in sight. The taste of blood filled Lewis's mouth; locked on the wheel, his hands were trembling. Maybe he *had* hit the woman and thrown her body off into a ditch. He fought the door, opened it and got out. His legs were trembling too. He saw at once that the Morgan was stuck: its rear tires were bolted to the field. He'd need a towtruck. "Hey!" he shouted. "Are you okay?" He forced his legs to move. "Are you all right?"

Lewis went unsteadily toward the road. He saw the crazy streaks his car had made. His hips ached. He felt very old. "Hey! Lady!" He couldn't see the girl anywhere. Heart pounding, he waddled across the road, afraid of what he might see lying in the ditch, limbs splayed out, head thrown back . . . but the ditch cradled only a mound of unblemished snow. He looked up and down the road: no woman anywhere in sight.

Lewis eventually gave up. Somehow the woman had gone away as suddenly as she'd come; or he had just imagined that he'd seen her. He rubbed his eyes. His hips still ached; bones seemed to be rubbing together. He went creakily down the road, hoping to see a farmhouse from which he could call the AAA. When he finally found one, a man with a thick black mattress of a beard and animal eyes let him use his telephone but made him wait outside on an open porch until the truck came.

*   *   *

He did not get home until after seven. Hungry, Lewis was still irritable. The girl had been there only a moment, like a deer jumping out before him, and when he had gone into the skid he had lost sight of her. But on that long straight road, where could she have run to, after he had landed in the field? So maybe she actually was lying dead in a ditch; but even a dog would leave a huge dent in the Morgan's body, and the car was undamaged.

"Hell," he said out loud. The car was still in the drive; he had been in the house only long enough to get warm. The midday restlessness, the feeling that if he did not move some bad thing would happen—that something worse than the accident was aimed at him like a gun—was back. Lewis went up to his bedroom, removed the sweater and parka and put on a clean shirt, a rep tie and double-breasted blazer. He'd go to Humphrey's Place and have a hamburger and a few beers. That was the ticket.

The lot was nearly full, and Lewis had to park in a space close to the road. The light snow had ceased during the early evening, but the air was cold and so sharp it felt as if you could break pieces off it with your bare hands. Beer signs flashed from the windows of the long gray building; country music from the four-piece band came to Lewis across the spaces of the lot. *Wabash Cannonball.*

A keening note on the fiddle stitched into his brain as soon as he was inside, and Lewis frowned at the musician sawing away on the bandstand, hair down to his shoulders, left hip and right foot jigging in time, but the boy's eyes were closed and he never noticed. Then an instant later the music was just music again, but his headache remained. The bar was crowded and so warm that Lewis began to perspire almost immediately. Big shapeless Humphrey Stalladge, an apron over his white shirt, moved back and forth behind the bar. All the tables nearest the band seemed to be filled with kids drinking beer from pitchers. When he looked at the backs of their heads, Lewis honestly couldn't tell the boys from the girls.

What if you saw yourself running toward you, running toward the headlights of your car, your hair flying and your face twisted with fear . . .

"Get you anything, Lewis?" Humphrey asked.

"Two aspirin and a beer. I've got a rotten headache. And a hamburger, Humphrey. Thanks."

Down at the other end of the bar, as far from the bandstand as he could get, looking both damp and filthy, Omar Norris was entertaining a group of men. As he talked his eyes bulged, his hands made swooping motions, and Lewis knew that if you were close enough to him you'd eventually see Omar's spittle shining on your lapels. When he had been younger, Omar's stories of getting out from under his wife's heel and of W. C. Fields-like stratagems for avoiding all work but running the town snowplow and working as the department store Santa had been amusing enough, but Lewis was mildly surprised that he could get anyone to listen to him now. People were even buying him drinks. Stalladge came back with his aspirin tablets and set a glass of beer beside them. "Burger's on the way," he said.

Lewis put the aspirins on his tongue and washed them down. The band had stopped playing *Wabash Cannonball* and was doing something else, a song he didn't recognize. One of the young women at the tables in front of the band had turned around and was staring at him. Lewis nodded to her.

He finished his beer and looked over the rest of the crowd. There were only a few empty booths by the front wall, so he caught Humphrey's eye and pointed to his glass, and when it was filled he started to go across the room to one of them. If he didn't get one early enough, he'd be pinned to the bar all night. Halfway across the room he nodded to Rollo Draeger, the druggist—come out to get away from Irmengard's endless complaints—and belatedly recognized the boy seated beside the girl who had stared at him: Jim Hardie, Eleanor's son, usually seen these days with

Draeger's daughter. He glanced back at the couple, and found them both staring at him now. Jim Hardie was a suspect kid, Lewis thought: he was broad and blond and strong, but he looked like he had a streak of wildness as wide as the county. He was always grinning: Lewis had heard from Walt Hardesty that Jim Hardie was probably the one who had burned down the deserted old Pugh barn and set a field on fire. He could see the boy grinning as he did that. The girl with him tonight was older than Penny Draeger; better-looking, too.

Lewis remembered a time, years ago, when everything had been simple, and it would have been he sitting beside a girl listening to a band, Noble Sissle or Benny Goodman—Lewis with his heart on fire. The memory made him automatically look around the room for Stella Hawthorne's commanding face, but he knew that the moment he'd entered he had half-consciously recorded that she was not in the room.

Humphrey appeared with his hamburger, looked at his glass and said, "If you're gonna drink that fast, maybe you want a pitcher?"

Lewis had not even noticed that his second beer was finished. "Good idea."

"You don't look so hot," Humphrey said.

The band, which had been discussing something, noisily went back to work and spared Lewis the necessity of replying. Humphrey's two relief barmaids, Anni and Annie, came in, releasing a wave of cold into the room. They were just enough reason to stick around. Anni was gypsyish, with curly black hair fluffing out around a sensual face; Annie looked like a Viking and had strong well-shaped legs and beautiful teeth. Both of them were in their mid-thirties and talked like college professors. They lived with men off in the country and were childless. Lewis liked both of them enormously, and sometimes took one or the other out for a meal. Anni saw him and waved, he waved back, and the guitarist, backed by a seesawing fiddle, yelled

*You lost your hot, I lost mine
so* (feedback) *we find
a spare garden to seed our dreams?*

Humphrey moved away to give the women instructions.
Lewis bit into his hamburger.

When he looked up Ned Rowles was standing beside
him. Lewis raised his eyebrows and, still chewing, half-
stood and motioned for Rowles to enter the booth. He
liked Ned Rowles too; Ned had made *The Urbanite* an
interesting newspaper, not just the usual smalltown list
of firemen's picnics and advertisements for sales at the
grocery stores. "Help me drink this," he said, and
poured beer from the pitcher into Ned's nearly empty
glass.

"How about me?" said a deeper, dryer voice over
his shoulder, and, startled, Lewis turned his head to see
Walt Hardesty glinting down at him. That explained
why Lewis had not seen Ned at first; he and Hardesty
had been back in the room where Humphrey stacked
his surplus beer. Lewis knew that Hardesty, who was
year by year surrendering himself to the bottle as surely
as Omar Norris, sometimes spent all afternoon in the
back room—he would not drink in front of his deputies.

"Of course, Walt," he said, "I didn't see you before.
Please join me." Ned Rowles was looking at him oddly.
Lewis was sure that the editor found Hardesty as tiresome as he did himself and had no desire for more of
his company, but did he expect him to send the sheriff
away? Whatever the look meant, Rowles slid over on
his side of the booth to make room for Hardesty. The
sheriff was still wearing his outer jacket; that back
room was probably cold. Like the college student he
resembled, Ned went as long as possible with only a
tweed jacket for protection against winter.

Then Lewis saw that both men were looking at him
oddly, and his heart jumped—had he hit the girl after
all? Had someone written down his license number?
He'd be guilty of hit and run! "Well, Walt," he said,

"is this about anything special, or do you just want a beer?" He filled Hardesty's glass as he spoke.

"Right now, I'll settle for the beer, Mr. Benedikt," Hardesty said, "Quite a day, right?"

"Yes," Lewis said simply.

"A terrible day," said Ned Rowles, and he passed a hand through the hair falling over his forehead. He grimaced at Lewis. "You don't look so good, pal. Maybe you ought to go home and get some rest."

Lewis was even more puzzled than before by this remark. If he had struck the girl and if they knew about it, the sheriff would not just let him go home. "Oh," he said, "I get restless at home. I'd feel a lot better if people stopped telling me I looked terrible."

"Well, it's a miserable business," Rowles said. "I guess we'd all agree to that."

"Hell, yes," Hardesty said, finishing off his beer and pouring another. Ned's face was set in a painful expression of—what? It looked like sympathy. Lewis splashed more beer into his glass. The fiddler had switched to guitar, and now the music had become so loud that the three men had to bend over to be heard. Lewis could hear fragments of lyrics, phrases bawled into the microphones.

wrong way out, baby . . . wrong way out

"I was just thinking of the times when I was a kid and used to go see Benny Goodman," he said. Ned Rowles snapped his head back, looking confused.

"Benny *Goodman?*" Hardesty snorted. "Myself, I like country. Real country, Hank Williams, not the junk these kids play. That's not country. Take your Jim Reeves. That's what I like." Lewis could smell the sheriff's breath—half beer and half some terrible foulness, as if he'd been eating garbage.

"Well, you're younger than I am," he said, pulling back.

"I just wanted to say how sorry I was," Ned interjected, and Lewis looked at him sharply, trying to figure

out just how much trouble he was in. Hardesty was
signaling to Annie, the Viking, for another pitcher. It
came within minutes, slopping over when Annie set it
on the table. When she walked away she winked at
Lewis.

Sometime during the morning, Lewis remembered,
and sometime during his drive . . . bare maples . . . he
had been aware of an odd, dreamy clarity, a sharpness
of vision that was like looking at an etching—a haunted
wood, a castle surrounded by spiky trees—

wrong way out baby, you're on the wrong

—but now he felt muzzy and confused, everything was
strange and Annie's wink was like something in a surreal movie—

you're on the wrong

Hardesty bent forward again and opened his mouth.
Lewis saw a spot of blood in Hardesty's left eye, hovering below the blue iris like a fertilized egg. "I'll tell
you something," Hardesty shouted at him. "We got
these four dead sheep, see? Throats cut. No blood and
no footprints either. What do you make of that?"

"You're the law, what do you make of it?" Lewis
said, raising his voice to be heard over the roar of the
band.

"I say it's a damn funny world—gettin' to be a
damn funny world," Hardesty shouted at him, and
gave Lewis one of his Texas hard-guy looks. *"Real*
damn funny. I'd say that your two old lawyer buddies
know something about it, too."

"That's unlikely," Ned understated. "But I ought
to see if one of them wants to write something about
Dr. John Jaffrey for the paper. Unless you'd like to,
Lewis."

"Write about John for *The Urbanite?"* Lewis asked.

"Well, you know, about a hundred words, maybe

two hundred, anything you can think of to say about him."

"But why?"

"Jesus wept, because you don't want Omar Norris to be the only one—" Hardesty stopped, mouth open. He looked stupefied. Lewis craned his neck to see Omar Norris across the crowded room, still waving his arms and babbling. On the bar before him sat a row of drinks. The feeling of something bad nearby which had dogged him all day intensified. An out-of-tune fiddle chord went through him like an arrow: *this is it, this is it—*

Ned Rowles reached across the table and touched Lewis's hand. "Ah, Lewis," he said. "I was sure you knew."

"I was out all day," he said. "I was—what happened?" *A day after Edward's anniversary,* he thought, and knew that John Jaffrey was dead. Then he realized that Edward's heart attack had come after midnight, and that *this* was the anniversary of his death.

"He was a leaper," Hardesty said, and Lewis saw that he'd read the word somewhere and thought it was the kind of word he should use. The sheriff took a swallow of beer and grimaced at Lewis, full of self-conscious menace. "He went off the bridge before noon today. Probably dead as a mackerel before he hit the water. Omar Norris there saw the whole thing."

"He went off the bridge," Lewis repeated softly. For some reason, he wished that he had hit a girl with his car—it was only a moment's wish, but it would have meant that John was safe. "My God," he said.

"We thought Sears or Ricky would have told you," Ned Rowles informed him. "They agreed to take care of the funeral arrangements."

"Jesus, John is going to be buried," Lewis said, and surprised tears came up in his eyes. He stood up and clumsily began to edge out of the booth.

"Don't suppose you could tell me anything useful," Hardesty said.

"No. No. I have to get over there. I don't know anything. I've got to see the others."

"Tell me if I can help at all," Ned shouted over the noise.

Not really looking where he was going, Lewis brushed into Jim Hardie, who had stationed himself unseen just outside the booth. "Sorry, Jim," Lewis said and would have gone by Jim and the girl, but Hardie closed his fist around Lewis's arm.

"This lady wanted to meet you," Hardie said, grinning unpleasantly. "So I'm making the introductions. She's stopping at our hotel."

"I just don't have the time, I have to leave," Lewis said, Hardie's hand still clamping forcefully on his forearm.

"Hang on. I'm doing what she asked me to do. Mr. Benedikt, this is Anna Mostyn." For the first time since he'd met her glance at the bar, Lewis looked at the girl. She was not a girl, he discovered; she was about thirty, perhaps a year or two on either side. She was anything but a typical Jim Hardie date. "Anna, this is Mr. Lewis Benedikt. I guess he's about the handsomest old coot in five or six counties, maybe the whole damn state, and he knows it too." The girl grew more startling the more you looked at her. She reminded him of someone, and he supposed it must have been Stella Hawthorne. It crossed his mind that he'd forgotten what Stella Hawthorne had looked like when she was thirty.

A ravaged figure from a low-life painting, Omar Norris was pointing at him from the bar. Still grinning ferociously, Jim Hardie let go of his arm. The boy with the fiddle swung his hair back girlishly and counted off another number.

"I know you have to leave," the woman said. Her voice was low, but it slid through the noise. "I heard about your friend from Jim, and I just wanted to tell you how sorry I was."

"I just heard myself," Lewis said, sick with the need to leave the bar. "Nice to meet you, Miss—"

"Mostyn," she said in her effortlessly audible voice.

"I hope we'll be seeing each other again. I'm going to work for your lawyer friends."

"Oh? Well . . ." The meaning of what she had said reached him. "Sears and Ricky gave you a job?"

"Yes. I gather they knew my aunt. Perhaps you did too? Her name was Eva Galli."

"Oh, Jesus," Lewis said, and startled Jim Hardie into dropping his arm. Lewis plunged off into the interior of the bar before changing direction and rushing toward the door.

"Glamour boy musta got the shits or something," Jim said. "Oh. Sorry, lady. I mean, Miss Mostyn."

The Chowder Society Accused

6

The Morgan's canvas top creaking, cold billowing in, Lewis drove to John's house as fast as he could. He did not know what he expected to find there: maybe some ultimate Chowder Society Meeting, Ricky and Sears speaking with eerie rationality over an open coffin. Or maybe Ricky and Sears themselves magically dead and wrapped in the black robes of his dream, three bodies lying in an upper bedroom . . .

Not yet, his mind said.

He pulled up beside the house on Montgomery Street and got out of the car. The wind pulled the blazer away from his body, yanked at his necktie: he realized that like Ned Rowles he was coatless. Lewis looked despairingly at the unlighted windows, and thought that at least Milly Sheehan would be in. He trotted up the path and pushed the bell. Far away and dim, it rang. Immediately below it was the office bell for John's patients, and he pushed that one too and heard an impatient clamor go off just on the other side of the door. Lewis, standing as if naked in the cold, began to shake.

Cold water lay on his face. At first he thought it was snow, then realized that he was crying again.

Lewis pounded on the door futilely, turned away, the tears like ice on his face, and looked across the street and saw Eva Galli's old house.

His breath froze. He almost thought he saw her again, the enchantress of their youth, moving across a downstairs window.

For a moment everything had the hard clarity of the morning and his stomach froze too, and then the door opened and he saw that the figure coming out was a man. Lewis wiped his brow with his hands. The man obviously wanted to speak with him. As he approached, Lewis recognized him as Freddy Robinson, the insurance salesman. He too was a regular at Humphrey's Place.

"Lewis?" he called. "Lewis Benedikt? Hey, good to see you, man!"

Lewis began to feel as he had in the bar—he wanted to get away. "Yes, it's me," he said.

"Gee, what a pity about old Dr. Jaffrey, hey? I heard about it this afternoon. He was a real buddy of yours, wasn't he?" Robinson was by now close enough to shake hands, and Lewis was unable to avoid grasping the salesman's cold fingers. "Hell of a note, hey? Goddamned tragedy, I call it. Boy." He was shaking his head sagely. "I'll tell you something. Old Dr. Jaffrey pretty much kept to himself, but I loved that old guy. Honest. When he invited me over to that party he had for the actress, you could have knocked me down with a feather. And man, what a party! Really, I had the time of my life. Great party." He must have seen Lewis stiffen, for he added, "Until the end, of course."

Lewis was looking at the ground, not bothering to reply to these horrible remarks, and Freddy Robinson rushed into the silence to add, "Hey, you look kind of crapped out. You don't want to stand here in the cold. Why don't you come over to my place, have a good stiff drink? I'd like to hear about your experiences, chew the fat a little bit, check out your insurance situation, just for the record—there's nobody at home here anyhow—" Like Jim Hardie, he grabbed Lewis's arm, and Lewis, harassed and miserable as he was, sensed desperation and hunger in the man. If Robinson could have handcuffed Lewis and dragged him across the street, he would have. Lewis knew that Robinson, for whatever private reasons, would fasten on him like a barnacle if he allowed him to.

"I'm afraid I can't," he said, more polite than if he had not felt the enormity of Robinson's need. "I have to see some people."

"You mean Sears James and Ricky Hawthorne, I guess," Robinson said, defeated already. He released Lewis's arm. "Gosh, what you guys do is so great, I mean I really admire you, with that club you have and everything."

"Christ, don't admire *us*," Lewis said, already moving toward his car. "Someone's picking us off like flies."

It was uttered almost casually, a merely dismissive remark, and within five minutes Lewis had forgotten he'd said it.

He drove the eight blocks to Ricky's house because it was unthinkable that Sears would have taken Milly Sheehan to his place, and when he got there he saw that he'd been correct. Ricky's old Buick was still in the drive.

"Oh, so you've heard," Ricky said when he opened the door. "I'm glad you came." His nose was red, with crying Lewis thought, and then saw that he had a bad cold.

"Yes, I saw Hardesty and Ned Rowles and they told me. How did you hear?"

"Hardesty called us at the office." The two men entered the living room, and Lewis saw Sears James, seated in an easy chair, scowl when the sheriff was named.

Stella came in from the dining room, gasped, and ran across the room to embrace him. "I'm so sorry, Lewis," she said. "It's such a damn shame."

"It's impossible," said Lewis.

"That may be so, but it certainly was John who was taken to the county morgue this noon," Sears said in a thick voice. "Who's to say what is impossible? We've all been under a strain. I may go off the bridge tomorrow." Stella gave Lewis an extra squeeze and went to sit beside Ricky on the Hawthorne's couch. The Italian coffee table in front of them looked the size of an ice rink.

"You need coffee," Stella said, scrutinizing Lewis more carefully, and got up again to go into the kitchen.

"You'd think it impossible," Sears went on, unruffled by the interruption, "that three adult men like ourselves would have to huddle together for warmth, but here we are."

Stella returned with coffee for all of them, and the desultory conversation ceased for a moment.

"We tried to reach you," Ricky said.

"I was out for a drive."

"It was John who wanted us to write to young Wanderley," Ricky said after a moment.

"Write to whom?" Stella asked, not understanding. Sears and Ricky explained. "Well, that's the craziest thing I ever heard," she finally said. "It's just like the three of you, to get all worked up and then ask someone else to solve your problems. I wouldn't have expected it from John."

"He's supposed to be an expert, Stella," Sears said in exasperation. "As far as I'm concerned, John's suicide proves that we need him more than ever."

"Well, when's he coming?"

"Don't know," Sears admitted. He looked rumpled, a fat old turkey at the end of winter.

"If you ask me, what you ought to do is stop those Chowder Society meetings," Stella told him. "They're destructive. Ricky woke up screaming this morning— all three of you look like you've seen ghosts."

Sears remained cool. "Two of us saw John's body. That should be reason enough for looking a little out of sorts."

"How did—" Lewis began, and then stopped. *How did he look?* was a singularly stupid question.

"How did what?" demanded Sears.

"How did you happen to hire Eva Galli's niece as a secretary?"

"She asked for a job," Sears said. "We had some extra work."

"Eva Galli?" asked Stella. "Wasn't she that rich woman who came here, oh, a long time ago? I didn't know her very well; she was much older than I. Wasn't she going to marry someone? Then she just upped and left town."

"She was going to marry Stringer Dedham," Sears said impatiently.

"Oh yes, Stringer Dedham," Stella remembered. "My goodness, he was a handsome man. There was that awful accident—something at a farm."

"He lost both arms in a threshing machine," Ricky said.

"Ugh. What a conversation. This must be like one of your meetings."

All three men had been thinking the same thing.

"Who told you about Miss Mostyn?" asked Sears. "Mrs. Quast must gossip overtime."

"No, I met her. She was at Humphrey's Place with Jim Hardie. She introduced herself to me."

The feeble conversation died again.

Sears asked Stella if there was any brandy in the house, and Stella said she'd get some for everybody and disappeared again into the kitchen.

Sears yanked savagely at his jacket, trying to make himself comfortable in the leather and metal chair. "You took John home last night. Did he seem unusual in any way?"

Lewis shook his head. "We didn't talk much. He said your story was good."

"He didn't say any more than that?"

"He said he was cold."

"Humph."

Stella returned with a bottle of Rémy Martin and

three glasses on a tray. "You should see yourselves. You look like three owls."

They did not so much as nod.

"Gentlemen, I'll leave you with the brandy. I'm sure you have things you want to talk about." Stella looked them over, autocratic and benign as a primary teacher, and then moved quickly out of the room without saying good-bye. Her disapproval stayed with them.

"She's upset," Ricky said apologetically. "Well, we all are. But Stella's more affected by this than she wants to show." As if to make amends for his wife, Ricky leaned forward over the glass ice-rink table and poured a generous amount of cognac into each glass. "I need this too. Lewis, I just don't understand what would make him do it. Why would John Jaffrey want to kill himself?"

"I don't know why," said Lewis, taking one of the glasses. "Maybe I'm glad I don't."

"Talk sense for a change," Sears growled. "We're men, Lewis, not animals. We're not supposed to stay cowering in the darkness." He too accepted a glass and sipped. "As a species, we hunger for knowledge. For enlightenment." His pale eyes angrily fixed on Lewis. "Or perhaps I misunderstood you, and you did not actually intend to defend ignorance."

"Overkill, Sears," Ricky said.

"Less jargon, Ricky," Sears retorted. " 'Overkill,' indeed. That might impress Elmer Scales and his sheep, but it does not impress me."

There was something about sheep—but Lewis had forgotten it. He said, "I don't mean to defend ignorance, Sears. I just meant that—hell, I don't know anymore. I guess I meant that it might be too much to take." What he did not articulate but was half aware of was the notion that he feared to peer too closely into the last moments of any suicide's life, be it friend or wife.

"*Yes*," breathed Ricky.

"Twaddle," said Sears. "I'd be relieved to learn that John was merely despairing. It's the other explanations that frighten me."

Lewis said, "I have the feeling that I'm sort of missing something," and proved to Ricky for the thousandth time that he was not the dullard of Sears's imagination.

"Last night," Ricky said, holding his glass with both hands and smiling fatalistically, "after the other three of us had gone, Sears saw Fenny Bate on his staircase."

"Christ."

"That's enough," Sears warned. "Ricky, I forbid you to go into this. What our friend means, Lewis, is that I thought I saw him. I was badly frightened. It was an hallucination—a ha'nt, as they used to say in these parts."

"Now you're arguing both ways," Ricky pointed out. "For my part, I'd be happy to think you're right. I don't want to see young Wanderley here. I think we might all be sorry, just about the time it's too late."

"You misread me. I want him to come and say: give it up. My Uncle Edward died of smoking and excitement, John Jaffrey was unstable. That's the reason I agreed to John's suggestion. I say, let him come, and the sooner the better."

Lewis said, "If you feel that, I agree with you."

"Is that fair to John?" Ricky asked.

"John's past being fair to," Sears said. He finished the cognac in his glass and leaned forward to pour more from the bottle.

Sudden footsteps on the stairs made all three swivel their heads toward the entrance from the hall.

Turned that way in his chair, Lewis could see Ricky's front window, and he noticed with surprise that it had begun to snow again. Hundreds of big flakes hammered the black window.

Milly Sheehan came in, her hair all flattened on one side and all frowsy on the other. She was sausaged into one of Stella's old dressing gowns. "I heard that, Sears James," she said in a voice like the wail of an ambulance. "You'll bully John even when he's dead."

"Milly, I meant no disrespect," Sears said. "Shouldn't you—"

"*No.* You won't get rid of me now. I won't give you coffee now and bow and scrape. I have something to say to you. John didn't commit suicide. Lewis Benedikt, you listen too. He didn't. He wouldn't have. John was murdered."

"Milly," Ricky began.

"Do you think I'm deaf? Do you think I don't know what's going on? John was killed, and do you know who killed him? Well, I do." Footsteps, this time Stella's, came hurrying down the stairs. "I know who killed him. It was you. You—you Chowder Society. You killed him with your terrible stories. You made him sick—you and your Fenny Bates!" Her face twisted; Stella rushed in too late to stop Milly's final words. "They ought to call you the Murder Society! They ought to call you Murder Incorporated!"

7

So there they stood, Murder Incorporated, beneath a bright sky in late October. They felt grief, anger, despair, guilt—they had been talking of graves and corpses compulsively for a year, and now they were burying one of their own. The unexpected findings of the autopsy had puzzled and distressed them all; Sears had blown up, choosing to disbelieve. Ricky too had not at first believed that John could have been a dope addict. "Evidence of massive, habitual and longstanding introduction of narcotic substance . . ." then a lot of fancy medical language, but the point was that the coroner had publicly defamed John Jaffrey. Sears's ranting had been of no use—the man would not change his story. Sears would not alter his opinion that in the course of one autopsy the man had changed from a skillful professional to an incompetent and dangerous fool. The coroner's findings had circulated through Milburn, and some citizens said they sided with Sears and some accepted the autopsy's conclusions, but none came to the funeral. Even the Reverend Neil Wilkinson seemed embarrassed. The funeral of a suicide and drug addict—well!

The new girl, Anna, had been wonderful: she'd helped deal with Sears's rage, cushioning Mrs. Quast from the worst effects of it, she'd been as marvelous with Milly Sheehan as Stella had, and she'd transformed the office. She had forced Ricky to realize that Hawthorne, James had plenty of work if Hawthorne and James wanted to do it. Even during the terrible period of arranging John's funeral, even on the day he took a suit from John's closet and bought a coffin, he and Sears found themselves responding to more letters and answering more phone calls than they had for weeks. They had been drifting toward retirement, sending clients elsewhere as if automatically, and Anna Mostyn seemed to have brought them back to life. She had mentioned her aunt only once, and in the most harmless way: she had asked them what she was like. Sears had come close to blushing and muttered, "Almost as pretty as you, but not as fierce." And she had been staunchly on Sears's side in the matter of the autopsy. Even coroners make mistakes, she had pointed out with placid, undeniable common sense.

Ricky was not so sure; he was not even sure it mattered. John had functioned perfectly well as a doctor; his own body had weakened but he had remained competent at curing other bodies. Surely a "massive, habitual, etc." drug habit would account for the physical decline John had exhibited. A daily insulin injection would have got John used to needles. He found that if John Jaffrey had been an addict, it did not much affect what he thought of him.

And this: it made his suicide explicable. No emptyeyed barefooted Fenny Bate, no Murder Incorporated, no mere stories had killed him—the drug had eaten into his brain as it had eaten into his body. Or he could not take it anymore, the "shame" of addiction. Or something.

Sometimes it was convincing.

In the meantime his nose ran and his chest tickled. He wanted to sit down; he wanted to be warm. Milly Sheehan was gripping Stella as if the two of them were battered by a hurricane, now and then using one hand to pluck another tissue from the box, wipe her eyes, and drop the tissue on the ground.

Ricky took a damp tissue from his own coat pocket, discreetly wiped his nose, and returned it to his pocket.

All of them heard the car coming up the hill to the cemetery.

From the journals of Don Wanderley

8

It seems I am an honorary member of the Chowder Society. It's all very odd—in fact, just the peculiarity of it all is a shade unsettling. Maybe the oddest part of my being here is that my uncle's friends almost seem to fear that they are caught in some kind of real-life horror story, a story like *The Nightwatcher*. It was because of *The Nightwatcher* that they wrote me. They saw me as some sort of steel-plated professional, an expert in the supernatural—they saw me as a Van Helsing! My original impressions were correct; they all do feel a distinct foreboding—I suppose you could say they're on the verge of being scared of their own shadows. My role is to *investigate,* of all things. And what they haven't told me directly, but have implied, is that I am supposed to say, nothing to worry about, boys. There's a rational, reasonable explanation for everything—but of that I have little doubt.

They want me to be able to write, too—they're very firm about that. Sears James said, "We didn't ask you here so that we could interrupt your career!" So they want me to give about half of my day to Dr. Rabbitfoot, and the other half to them. There's the feeling, definite-

ly, that part of what they want is just someone to talk
to. They've been talking to themselves for too long.

Not long after the secretary, Anna Mostyn, left, the
dead man's housekeeper said that she wanted to lie
down, and Stella Hawthorne took her upstairs. When
she came back down, Mrs. Hawthorne gave us all large
glasses of whiskey. In Milburn high society, which I
guess this is, you drink whiskey English style, neat.

We had a painful, halting conversation. Stella Hawthorne said, "I hope you knock some sense into these
characters' heads," which mystified me. They hadn't
yet explained the real reason why they asked me to
come. I nodded, and Lewis said, "We have to talk
about it." That silenced them again. "We want to talk
about your book, too," Lewis said. "Fine," I said.
More silence.

"I might as well feed you three owls," Stella Hawthorne said. "Mr. Wanderley, will you please give me
a hand?"

I followed her into the kitchen, expecting to be
handed plates or cutlery. What I did not expect was
for the elegant Mrs. Hawthorne to whirl around, slam
the door behind her and say, "Didn't those three old
idiots in there say why they wanted you to come here?"

"I guess they fudged a little," I said.

"Well, you better be good, Mr. Wanderley," she said,
"because you're going to have to be Freud to deal with
those three. I want you to know that I don't approve of
your being here at all. I think people should solve their
problems by themselves."

"They implied they just wanted to talk to me about
my uncle," I said. Even with her gray hair, I thought
she could be no older than about forty-six or seven,
and she looked as beautiful and stern as a ship's figure-
head.

"Your uncle! Well, maybe they do. They'd never
deign to tell me," and I understood part of the reason
for her fury. "How well did you know your uncle, Mr.
Wanderley?"

I asked her to use my first name. "Not very well. After I went to college and moved to California, I didn't see him more than once every couple of years. I hadn't seen him at all for several years before his death."

"But he left you his house. Doesn't it strike you a little bit funny that those three characters out there didn't suggest you stay there?"

Before I could reply she went on. "Well, even if it doesn't, it does me. And not only funny, but pathetic. They're afraid to go into Edward's house. They just all came to a kind of—a kind of silent agreement. They've never entered that house. They're superstitious, that's why."

"I thought I felt—well, when I came to the funeral I thought I saw—" I stammered, not sure of how far I could go with her.

"Bully for you," she said. "Maybe you're not as big a blockhead as they are. But I tell you this, Don Wanderley, if you make them any worse than they are already, you'll have me to answer to." She put her hands on her hips, her eyes sizzling, and then she exhaled. Her eyes changed; she gave me a tight, pained smile and said, "We'd better get busy or I suppose they'll start to gossip about you."

She opened the refrigerator and pulled out a platter holding a roast the size of a young pig. "Cold roast beef all right for you? The carving things are in the drawer to your right. Start cutting."

Only after Stella rather abruptly left the house for what she called an "appointment"—after the strange scene in the kitchen, I had a passing notion of its character, and the momentary expression of utter misery which crossed Ricky Hawthorne's face confirmed it—did the three men open up to me. Bad choice of words: they did not "open up" at all, at least not until much later, but after Stella Hawthorne had driven off, the three old men began to show me why they had asked me to come to Milburn.

It began like a job interview.

"Well, here you are at last, Mr. Wanderley," said Sears James, pouring more cognac into his glass and removing a fat cigar case from the inside pocket of his jacket. "Cigar? I can vouch for their merit."

"No thanks," I said. "And please call me Don."

"Very well. I have not welcomed you properly, Don, but I will do so now. We were all great friends of your uncle Edward's. I am, and I speak for my two friends as well, very grateful that you have come across the country to join us. We think that you can help us."

"Does this have to do with my uncle's death?"

"In part. We want you to work for us." Then he asked me if we could talk about *The Nightwatcher*.

"Of course."

"It was a novel, therefore in large part an invention, but was this invention based on an actual case? We assume you did research for the book. But what we want to know is whether in the course of your research you discovered any corroborating evidence for the ideas in your book. Or perhaps your research was inspired by some inexplicable occurrence in your own life."

I could almost feel their tension on my fingertips, and perhaps they could feel mine on theirs. They knew nothing about David's death, but they had asked me to expose the central mystery of both *The Nightwatcher* and my life.

"The invention, as you put it, was based on an actual case," I said, and the tension broke.

"Could you describe that to us?"

"No," I said. "It's not clear enough to me. Also, it's too personal. I'm sorry, but I can't go into it."

"We can respect that," Sears James said. "You seem nervous."

"I am," I admitted, and laughed.

"The situation in *The Nightwatcher* was based on a real situation that you knew about?" asked Ricky Hawthorne, as if he hadn't been paying attention, or could not believe what he had just heard.

"That's right."

"And you know of other similar cases?"

"No."

"But you do not reject the supernatural out of hand," Sears said.

"I don't know if I do or not," I said. "Like most people."

Lewis Benedikt sat up straight and stared at me. "But you just said . . ."

"No, he didn't," Ricky Hawthorne put in. "He just said his book was *based on* a real event, not that it recounted the event exactly. Is that right, Don?"

"More or less."

"But what about your research?" asked Lewis.

"I didn't actually do much," I said.

Hawthorne sighed, glanced at Sears with what looked like irony: *I told you so.*

"I think you can help us anyway," Sears said, as if he were contradicting a voiced opinion. "Your skepticism will do us good."

"Maybe," Hawthorne muttered.

I was still feeling that they had blundered into my most private space. "What does all this have to do with my uncle's heart attack?" I asked. There was a lot of self-defense in the question, but it was the right question to ask.

It all came out—James had decided to tell me everything.

"And we've been having unthinkable nights. I know that John did too. It is not exaggerating to say that we fear for our reason. Would either of you dispute that?"

Hawthorne and Lewis Benedikt looked as though they were remembering things they'd rather not, and shook their heads.

"So we want your expert help, and as much time as you can reasonably give us," Sears concluded. "John's apparent suicide has shaken us all very deeply. Even if he was a drug addict, which I dispute, I do not think he was a potential suicide."

"What was he wearing?" I asked. It was just a stray thought.

"Wearing? I don't recall . . . Ricky, did you look at his clothing?"

Hawthorne nodded. "I had to throw it out. It was the most astounding assortment of things—his evening jacket, a pajama shirt, the trousers to another suit. No socks."

"That's what John put on when he got up the morning he died?" Lewis asked, astonished. "Why didn't you tell us before?"

"At first I was shocked by it, and then I forgot. Too much was happening."

"But he was usually such a fastidious man," Lewis said. "Damn it, if John jumbled his clothes up like that, his mind must have been jumbled too."

"Precisely," Sears said, and smiled at me. "Don, that was a perceptive question. None of us thought of it."

I could see him beginning to snatch up all the available rationalizations. "It doesn't simplify things to point out that his mind was jumbled," I pointed out. "In the case I had in mind when I did my book, a man killed himself, and I'm damn sure his mind was shaken, but I never found out what really happened to him."

"You're talking about your brother, aren't you?" asked Ricky Hawthorne cleverly. Naturally. So they all knew, after all; my uncle had told them about David. "And that was the 'case' you alluded to?"

I nodded.

"Uh oh," Lewis said.

I said, "I just turned it into a ghost story. I don't know what really happened."

For a moment all three of them looked embarrassed.

"Well," Sears James said, "even if you are not accustomed to doing research, I'm sure that you're capable of it."

Ricky Hawthorne leaned back into his eccentric couch; his bow tie was still immaculate, but his nose was red and his eyes bleary. He looked small and lost, in the midst of his giant furniture. "It will obviously make my two friends happier if you stay with us for a while, Mr. Wanderley."

"Don."

"Don, then. Since you seem prepared to do that, and since I am exhausted, I suggest we all say good night. You'll spend the night at Lewis's?"

Lewis Benedikt said, "That's fine," and stood up.

"I have one question," I said. "Are you asking me to think about the supernatural—or whatever you want to call it—because that absolves you from thinking about it?"

"Perceptive, but inaccurate," Sears James said, looking at me with his rifle shot's blue eyes. "We think about it all the time."

"That reminds me," Lewis said. "Are you going to stop the Chowder Society meetings? Does anyone think we should?"

"No," Ricky said with an odd defiance. "For heaven's sake let's not. For our sakes, let's continue to meet. Don will be included."

So here I am. Each of the three men, my uncle's friends, seems admirable in his own way: but are they losing their minds? I can't even be sure they have told me everything. They *are* frightened, and two of them *have* died; and I wrote earlier in this journal that Milburn feels like the sort of town where Dr. Rabbitfoot would go to work. I can feel reality slithering away from me, if I start to imagine that one of my own books is happening around me.

The trouble is, I could almost start to imagine that. Those two suicides—David's and Dr. Jaffrey's—that's the problem, that simple coincidence. (And the Chowder Society shows no signs of recognizing that this coincidence is the main reason I am interested in their problem.) What *am* I involved in here? A ghost story? Or something worse, something not just a story? The three old men have only the sketchiest knowledge of the events of two years ago—and they can't possibly know that they've asked me to enter the strangest part of my life again, to roll myself back through the calendar to the worst, most destructive days: or to roll myself up again in the pages of a book which was my attempt to reconcile myself with them. But can there really be any connection, even if it is just the connection of one ghost story leading to another, as it did with the Chowder Society? And can there truly be any *factual* connection between *The Nightwatcher* and what happened to my brother?

II

Alma

Everything that has beauty has a body, and is a body;
everything that has being has being in the flesh:
and dreams are only drawn from the bodies that are.

—"Bodiless God," D. H. Lawrence

From the journals of Don Wanderley

1

There is only one way to answer that question. I have
to spend a little time, over the next week or two, in
writing out in some detail the facts as I remember them
about myself and David and Alma Mobley. When I
fictionalized them in the book I inevitably sensational-
ized them, and doing so falsified my own memories. If
I were satisfied with that, I would never have considered writing the Dr. Rabbitfoot novel—he's no more
than Alma in blackface, Alma with horns, tail and a

soundtrack. Just as "Rachel Varney" in *The Night-watcher* was no more than Alma in fancy dress. Alma was far stranger than "Rachel." What I want to do now is not invent fictional situations and fictional peculiarities, but look at the peculiarities that existed. In *The Nightwatcher* everything was solved, everything came out even; in life nothing came out even and nothing was solved.

I met Alma not as "Saul Malkin" met "Rachel Varney," in a Paris dining room, but in surroundings utterly banal. It was at Berkeley, where good notices for my first book had obtained me a year's teaching job. The post was a coup for a first-book writer, and I took it seriously. I taught one section of Creative Writing and two sections of an undergraduate course in American literature. It was the second of these that caused most of my work. I had to do so much reading of work which I didn't know well and so much theme-grading that I had little time to write. And if I had barely read Howells or Cooper, I had never looked at the criticism about them which the structure of the course demanded I know. I found myself falling into a routine of teaching my courses, taking the creative writing work home to read before I ate dinner at a bar or café, and then spending my evenings at the library going through bibliographies and hunting up copies of *PMLA*. Sometimes I was able to work on a story of my own when I got back to my apartment; more often, my eyes burned and my stomach was in an uproar from English Department coffee and my instincts for prose were deadened by scholarly waffle. From time to time I took out a girl in the department, an instructor with a mint-condition PhD from the University of Wisconsin. Her name was Helen Kayon, and our desks, along with twelve others, were next to one another in a communal office. She had read my first book, but it had not impressed her.

She was stern about literature, frightened of teaching, careless about her appearance, hopeless about men.

Her interests were in Scots contemporaries of Chaucer and linguistic analysis; at twenty-three, she already had something of the feather impracticality of the old scholar-spinster. "My father changed his name from Kavinski, and I'm just a hard-headed Pole," she said, but it was a classic self-deception: she was hard-headed about Scots Chaucerians and nothing else. Helen was a large girl with big glasses and loose hair which always seemed on its way from one style to another; it was hair with unfulfilled intentions. She had decided some time before that what she had to offer the university, the planet, men was her intelligence. It was the only thing about herself that she trusted. I asked her out for lunch the third time I saw her in the office. She was revising an article, and she nearly jumped out of her chair. I think I was the first man at Berkeley to ask her to lunch.

A few days later I met her in the office after my last class. She was sitting at her desk staring at her typewriter. Our lunch had been awkward: she had said, comparing the articles she was trying to write with my work, "But I'm trying to describe reality!"

"I'm leaving," I said. "Why don't you come with me? We'll have a drink somewhere."

"I can't, I hate bars and I have to work on this," she said. "Oh, look. You could walk me back to my place. Okay? It's up the hill. Is that okay for you?"

"That's where I live too."

"I'm fed up with this anyhow. What are you reading?" I held up a book. "Oh. Nathaniel Hawthorne. Your survey course."

"Harvey Lieberman just told me that in three weeks I'm giving the main lecture on Hawthorne. I haven't read *The House of the Seven Gables* since high school."

"Lieberman is a lazy so and so."

I was inclined to agree: so far, three of his other assistants had also given lectures for him. "I'll be all right," I said, "as long as I can figure out some angle to tie it all up, and get all the reading done."

"At least you don't have tenure to worry about," she said, gesturing toward her typewriter.

"No. Just eating." This had the tone of our lunch.

"Sorry." She bowed her head, suffering already, and I touched her shoulder and told her not to take herself so seriously.

As we were going down the stairs together, Helen carrying a huge worn briefcase straining with books and essays, me carrying only *The House of the Seven Gables,* a tall freckled blond girl slipped between us. The first impression I had of Alma Mobley was of a general paleness, a spiritual blurriness suggested by her long expressionless face and hanging straw-colored hair. Her round eyes were a very pale blue. I felt an odd mixture of attraction and revulsion; in the dim light of the staircase, she looked like an attractive girl who'd spent all her life in a cave—she appeared to be the same ghostly shade of white all over. "Mr. Wanderley?" she asked.

When I nodded, she muttered her name, but I did not catch it.

"I'm a graduate student in English," she said. "I wondered if you'd mind if I came to your lecture on Hawthorne. I saw your name posted on Professor Lieberman's schedule in the departmental office."

"No, please come," I said. "But it's just a survey class, you know. It'll probably be a waste of time for you."

"Thank you," she said and abruptly continued on up the stairs.

"How did she know who I was?" I whispered to Helen, concealing my pleasure in what I thought was my heretofore invisible celebrity. Helen tapped the book in my hand.

She lived only three blocks from my own apartment; hers was a random collection of rooms at the top of an old house, and she shared it with two other girls. The rooms seemed arbitrarily placed, and so did the things in them—the apartment looked as if no one had ever considered where bookcases and chairs and tables ought to go; where delivery men put them, they stayed. Here a lamp had been put next to a chair, there a table heaped with books shoved beneath a window, but everything else was so haphazard that you had to weave around the furniture to reach the hall.

The roommates too seemed arbitrary. Helen had described them to me on the walk up the hill. One of them, Meredith Polk, was also from Wisconsin, a new instructor in the Botany Department. She and Helen had met while hunting for a place to live, found they had done graduate work at the same university and decided to live together. The third girl was a theater graduate student named Hilary Lehardie. Helen said, "Hilary never leaves her room and stays high all day, I think, and she plays rock music most of the night. I put in ear plugs. But Meredith is better. She's very intense and a little bit odd, but I think we're friends. She tries to protect me."

"Protect you from what?"

"Vileness."

Both of the roommates were at home when I reached Helen's apartment. As soon as I came in behind Helen, an overweight black-haired girl in blue jeans and a sweatshirt shot out of the door from the kitchen and glared at me through thick glasses. Meredith Polk. Helen introduced me as a writer in the English Department, and Meredith said "Dja do?" and zipped back into the kitchen. Loud music came from a side bedroom.

The spectacled black-haired girl cannoned out of the kitchen again as soon as Helen had gone in to get me a drink. She wove through the furniture to a camp chair near a wall against which stood what looked like hundreds of cacti and plants in pots. She slotted a cigarette in her mouth and stared at me with an intent suspicion.

"You're not an academic? Not on the regular staff?" This from a first-year instructor, years from tenure.

I said, "I just have a year's appointment. I'm a writer."

"Oh," she said. More staring for a moment. Then: "So you're the one who took her to lunch."

"Yes."

"Ah."

The music boomed through the wall. "Hilary," she said, nodding in the direction of the music. "Our roommate."

"Doesn't it bother you?"

"I don't hear it most of the time. Concentration. And it's good for the plants."

Helen came out with a tumbler too full of whiskey, one ice cube floating at the top like a dead goldfish. She carried a cup of tea for herself.

" 'Scuse me," Meredith said, and darted off in the direction of her room.

"Oh, it's nice to see a man in this awful place," Helen said. For a moment all the worry and self-consciousness left her face, and I saw the real intelligence that lay beneath her academic cleverness. She looked vulnerable, but less so than I had thought.

We went to bed a week later, at my apartment. She was not a virgin, and she was firm about not being in love. In fact she went about the entire matter of deciding to do it and then doing it with the brisk precision she brought to the Scots Chaucerians. "You'll never fall in love with me," she said, "and I don't expect you to. That's fine."

She spent two nights at my apartment, that time. We went to the library together in the evenings, vanishing into our separate carrels as if there were no emotion at all between us. The only actual sign I had that this was not so came one evening a week later when I found Meredith Polk outside my door when I came home. She was still wearing the jeans and sweatshirt. "You shit," she hissed at me, and I quickly opened the door and got her inside.

"You cold-hearted bastard," she said. "You're going to wreck her chances for tenure. And you're breaking her heart. You treat her like a whore. She's much too good for you. You don't even have the same values.

Helen's committed to scholarship—it's the most important thing in her life. I understand that, but I don't think you do. I don't think you're committed to anything but your sex life."

"One thing at a time," I said. "How can I possibly be wrecking her chances for tenure? Let's just take that one first."

"This is her first semester here. They watch us, you know. How do you think it looks if a new instructor jumps in the sack with the first guy who comes along?"

"This is Berkeley. I don't think anyone notices or cares."

"You pig. You don't notice or care, you don't notice anything or care about anything, that's the truth—do you love her?"

"Get out," I said. I was losing my temper. She looked like an angry frog, croaking at me, defining her territory.

Helen herself arrived three hours later, looking pale and bruised. She would not discuss Meredith Polk's astounding accusations, but she said she had talked to her the night before. "Meredith is very protective," she said. "She must have been to you. I'm sorry, Don." Then she began to cry. "No, don't rub my back like that. Don't. It's just foolish. It's only that I haven't been able to work, the past few nights. I guess I've been unhappy whenever I haven't been with you." She looked up at me, stricken. "I shouldn't have said that. But you don't love me, do you? You couldn't, could you?"

"There's no answer to that. Let me get you a cup of tea."

She was lying on the bed in my little apartment, curled up like a fetus. "I feel so guilty."

I came back with her tea. "I wish we could take a trip together," she said. "I wish we could go to Scotland together. I've spent all these years reading about Scotland, and I've never been there." Her eyes were brimming behind the big glasses. "Oh, I'm a horrible mess. I knew I should never have come out here. I was happy in Madison. I should never have come to California."

"You belong here more than I do."

"No," she said, and rolled over to hide her face. "You can go anywhere and fit in. I've never been anything but a working-class drudge."

"What's the last really good book you read?" I asked.

She rolled back over to face me, curiosity defeating the misery and embarrassment on her face. Squinting, she considered it for a moment. *"The Rhetoric of Irony* by Wayne Booth. I just reread it."

"You belong at Berkeley," I said.

"I belong in a zoo."

It was an apology for everything, for Meredith Polk as much as for her own feelings, but I knew that if we went on I could only hurt her more. She was right: it was not possible that I could ever love her.

Afterward I thought that my Berkeley life had settled into a pattern to which the rest of my life would adhere. It was, except for my work, essentially empty. But wasn't it better to continue seeing Helen than to wound her by insisting on a break? In the workbound world I saw as mine, expedience was a synonym for kindness. When we parted between us was the understanding that we would not meet for a day or two, but that all would continue as before.

But a week later the conventional period of my life came to an end; after it I saw Helen Kayon only twice.

2

I had found the hook for the Hawthorne lecture; it was in an essay by R. P. Blackmur: "When every possibility is taken away, *then* we have sinned." The idea seemed to radiate throughout Hawthorne's work, and I could connect the novels and stories by this black Christianity, by the impulse in them for nightmare—by what was almost their desire for nightmare. For to imagine a nightmare is to put it at one remove. And I found a statement by Hawthorne which helped to explain his method: "I have sometimes produced a singular and not unpleasing effect, so far as my own mind was concerned, by imagining a train of incidents in which the spiritual mechanism of the faery legend should be combined with the characters and manners of everyday life." When I had the ideas which would structure the lecture, the details fell onto the pages of my notebook.

This work and my writing students kept me fully occupied for the five days before the lecture. Helen and I met fleetingly, and I promised her that we would get away for a weekend when my immediate work was done. My brother David owned a "cottage" in Still Valley, outside Mendocino, and he'd told me to use it whenever I wanted to get away from Berkeley. This was typical of David's thoughtfulness; but a kind of perversity had kept me from using the house. I did not want to have to be grateful to David. After the lecture I would take Helen to Still Valley and kill two scruples at once.

On the morning of the lecture I reread D. H. Lawrence's chapter about Hawthorne and saw these lines:

And the first thing she does is seduce him.
And the first thing he does is to be seduced.
And the second thing they do is to hug their sin
   in secret, and gloat over it, and try to under-
   stand.
Which is the myth of New England.

That was what I had been looking for all along. I put down my cup of coffee and started to restructure my remarks. Lawrence's insight extended my own, I could see all the books in a new way. I discarded paragraphs and wrote in new ones between the crossed-out lines ... I forgot to call Helen, as I had promised to do.

In the end I used my notes very sparingly. Once, straining for a metaphor, I leaned on the lectern and saw Helen and Meredith Polk seated together in one of the last rows, up at the top of the theater. Meredith Polk was frowning, suspicious as a Berkeley cop. When scientists hear the kinds of things that go on in literature classrooms, they often begin to look that way. Helen merely looked interested, and I was grateful that she had come.

When it was over Professor Lieberman came up from his aisle seat to tell me that he had enjoyed my remarks very much, and would I consider taking his Stephen Crane lecture in two months' time? He was due at a conference in Iowa that week, and since I had done such an "exemplary" job, especially considering that I was not an academic . . . in short, he might find it possible to extend my appointment to a second year.

I was stunned as much by the bribe as by his arrogance. Lieberman, still young, was a famous man, not so much a scholar in Helen's sense as a "critic," a generalizer, a sub-Edmund Wilson; I did not respect his books, but I expected more of him. The students were filing up toward the exits, a solid mass of T-shirts and denim. Then I saw a face lifted expectantly toward me, a slim body clothed not in denim but in a white dress. Lieberman was suddenly an interference, an obstacle, and I agreed to give the Crane lecture to get rid of him. "*Very* good, Donald," he said, and disappeared. As quickly as that: one moment the seersuckered young professor was before me, and the next I was looking into the face of the girl in the white dress. It was the graduate student who had stopped Helen and me on the stairs.

She looked completely different: healthier, with a light golden layer of tan on her face and arms. The straight blond hair glowed. So did her pale eyes: in them I saw a kaleidoscope of shattered lights and colors. Her mouth was bracketed by two faint lines of irony. She was ravishing, one of the most beautiful girls I'd ever seen—no small statement, for Berkeley was so populated by beauties that you saw two new ones every time you looked up from your desk. But the girl before me had none of the gaucheness or assertive, testing vulgarity of the usual undergraduate knockout: she simply looked *right*, perfectly at home in herself. Helen Kayon didn't have a chance.

"That was good," she said, and the faint lines beside her mouth twitched as if at a private joke. "I'm happy I came after all." For the first time, I heard the Southern accent: that sunny drawl, that lilt.

"So am I," I said. "Thank you for the compliment."

"Do you want to relish it in private?"

"Is that an invitation?" And then I saw that I was being too quick, too self-consciously flattered and one-dimensional.

"A what? No, I'm not aware that it was." Her mouth moved: *what an idea.*

I looked up to the top of the lecture theater. Helen and Meredith Polk were already in the aisle, going toward the door. Helen must have begun to move as soon as she'd seen me look at the blond. If she knew me as well as she had said she did, she had known just what I was thinking. Helen went through the exit door without turning around, but Meredith Polk tried to assassinate me with a glance.

"Are you waiting for someone?" the girl said.

"No, it's nothing important," I said. "Would you join me for lunch? I never did have lunch, and I'm starving."

I was behaving, I knew, with appalling selfishness; but I also knew that the girl before me was already more important to me than Helen Kayon, and by letting Helen go at once—by being the bastard Meredith Polk said I was—I was eliminating weeks, perhaps months of painful scenes. I had not lied to Helen; she had always known that our relationship was fragile.

The girl walking beside me across the campus lived in perfect consonance with her femininity; even then, moments after I had first seen her in good light, she seemed ageless, even timeless, beautiful in a nearly hieratic and mythic way. Helen's separation from herself had kept her from gracefulness, and she was blatantly a person of my own blink of history; my first impression of Alma Mobley was that she could have moved with that easy grace over an Italian piazza in the sixteenth century; or in the twenties (more to the point) could have earned an appreciative glance from Scott Fitzgerald, flying past the Plaza Hotel on her devastating legs. Set down like that, it sounds absurd. Obviously I had noticed her legs, I had a sense of her body; but images of Italian piazzas and Fitzgerald at the Plaza are more than unlikely metaphors for carnality. It was as though every cell of her possessed ease; nothing less typical of the usual Berkeley graduate student in English can be imagined. The gracefulness went so deep in her that it seemed, even then, to mark an intense passivity.

Of course I am condensing six months' impressions into a single moment, but my justification is that the seeds of the impression were present as we left the campus to go to a restaurant. Her going with me so willingly, with such unconcern that it resounded with unspoken judgments, did contain a whiff of the passive —the ironic tactful passivity of the beautiful, of those whose beauty has sealed them off inside it like a princess in a tower.

I steered her toward a restaurant I had heard Lieberman mention—it was too expensive for most students, too expensive for me. But the ceremony of luxurious dining suited both her and my sense of celebration.

I knew immediately that it was she I wanted to take to David's house in Still Valley.

Her name, I learned, was Alma Mobley, and she had been born in New Orleans. I gathered more from her manner than from anything explicitly stated that her parents had been well off; her father had been a painter, and long stretches of her childhood had been spent in Europe. Speaking of her parents, she used the past tense, and I gathered that they had died some time ago. That too fit her manner, her air of disconnection from all but herself.

Like Helen, she had been a student in the Midwest. She had gone to the University of Chicago—this seemed next to impossible, Alma in Chicago, that rough knockabout city—and had been accepted as a PhD student at Berkeley. From what she said, I understood that she was just drifting through the academic life, that she had none of Helen's profound commitment to it. She was a graduate student because she had a talent for the mechanics of literary work and was bright; it was better than anything else she could think of doing. And she was in California because she had not liked the Chicago climate.

Again, and overwhelmingly, I had the sense of the irrelevance to her of most of the furniture of her life; of her passive self-sufficiency. I had no doubt that she was bright enough to finish her thesis (Virginia Woolf), and then with luck to get a teaching job at one of the little colleges up and down the coast. Then, suddenly and shockingly, she lifting a spoonful of mint-green avocado to her mouth, I had another vision of her. I saw her as a whore, a 1910 Storyville prostitute, her hair exotically twisted, her dancer's legs drawn up—her naked body was very clear for a moment. Another image of professional detachment, I supposed, but that did not explain the force of the vision. I had been sexually moved by it. She was talking about books—talking not as Helen did, but in a general-reader way—and I looked across the table and I knew that I wanted to be the man who mattered to her, I wanted to grab that passivity and shake it and make her truly see me.

"Don't you have a boyfriend?" I asked her.

She shook her head.

"So you're not in love?"

"No," and she gave a minute smile at the obviousness of the question. "There was a man in Chicago, but that's finished."

I pounced on the noun. "One of your professors."

"One of my associate professors." Another smile.

"You were in love with him? Was he married?"

She looked at me gravely for a moment. "No. It wasn't like what you're thinking. He wasn't married, and I wasn't in love with him."

Even then I recognized that she would find it very

easy to lie. This did not repulse me; instead it was proof of how lightly her life had touched her, and was a part of all that I already wanted to change in her. "He was in love with you," I said. "Was that why you wanted to leave Chicago?"

"No it was already over by then. Alan didn't have anything to do with it. He made a fool of himself. That's all."

"Alan?"

"Alan McKechnie. He was very sweet."

"A very sweet fool."

"Are you determined to know about this?" she asked, with her characteristic trick of adding a soft, almost invisible irony which denied the question any importance.

"No. Just a little curious."

"Well." Her eyes, full of that shattered light, met mine. "It's not much of a story. He became . . . infatuated. I was in a tutorial with him. There were only four of us. Three boys and myself. The tutorial met twice a week. I could tell he was getting interesed in me, but he was a very shy man. He was very inexperienced with women." Again that soft, lobbing deflection in her voice and eyes. "He took me out a few times. He didn't want us to be seen, so we had to go places not in Hyde Park."

"Where did you go?"

"Hotel bars. Places like that. Around the Loop. I think it was the first time he'd ever done anything like that with a student, and it made him nervous. I don't think he'd had much fun in his life. Eventually I became too much for him. I realized that I didn't want him in the way he wanted me. I know what you're going to ask next, so I'll answer it. Yes, we slept together. For a while. It wasn't much good. Alan was not very —physical. I began to think that what he really wanted to do was go to bed with a boy, but of course he was too whatever to do that. He couldn't."

"How long did it last?"

"A year." She finished her meal and dropped her

napkin beside the plate. "I don't know why we're talking about this."

"What do you really like?"

She pretended to consider it seriously. "Let's see. Really like. Summer. Movies. English novels. Waking up at six and seeing very early morning out of the window—everything is so empty and pure. Lemon tea. What else? Paris. And Nice. I really do like Nice. When I was a little girl, we went there four or five summers in a row. And I like very good meals, like this one."

"It doesn't sound like the academic life is the one for you," I said. It was as though she had told me everything and nothing.

"It doesn't, does it?" She laughed, as at something of no importance. "I suppose what I need is a Great Love."

And there she was again, the princess locked in the tower of her own self-regard. "Let's go to a movie tomorrow night," I said, and she agreed.

The next day I persuaded Rex Leslie, whose office was down the hall from mine, to exchange desks with me.

The art cinema was showing Renoir's *La Grande Illusion,* which Alma had never seen. Afterward we went to a coffee shop, a place packed with students, and bits of conversation from adjoining tables filtered through into our own. For a moment after we sat down, I experienced a flash of guilty fear, and recognized a second later that I was afraid of seeing Helen Kayon. But it was not her sort of place; and anyhow at this hour Helen usually was still at the library. I felt a moment of intense gratitude that I was not there too, grinding away at a discipline that was not only my own but merely a condition of employment.

"What a beautiful movie," she said. "I still feel like I'm in it."

"You feel movies very deeply, then."

"Of course." She looked at me, puzzled.

"And literature?"

"Of course." She looked at me again. "Well. I don't know. I enjoy it."

A bearded boy in a lumberjack shirt near us said in a carrying voice, "Wenner is naive and so is his magazine. I'll start buying it again when I see a picture of Jerry Brown on the cover."

His friend said, "Wenner *is* Jerry Brown."

"Berkeley," I said.

"Who is Wenner?"

"I'm surprised you don't know. Jann Wenner?"

"Who is he?"

"He was the Berkeley student who founded *Rolling Stone*."

"Is that a magazine?"

"You're full of surprises," I said. "You mean you've never heard of it?"

"I'm not interested in most magazines. I never look at them. What kind of magazine is it? Is it named after that band?"

I nodded. At least she had heard of them. "What kind of music do you like?"

"I'm not very interested in music."

"Let's try some other names. Do you know who Tom Seaver is?"

"No."

"Have you ever heard of Willie Mays?"

"Didn't he used to be an athlete? I'm also not very interested in sports."

"It shows." She giggled. "You're getting even more intriguing. How about Barbra Streisand?"

She pouted charmingly, self-parodyingly. "Of course."

"John Ford?" No. "Arthur Fonzarelli?" No. "Grace Bumbry?" No. "Desi Arnaz?" No. "Johnny Carson?" No. "Andre Previn?" No. "John Dean?" No.

"Don't ask me any more or I'll start saying yes to everything," she said.

"What do you *do?*" I asked. "Are you sure you live in this country?"

"Let me try you. Have you heard of Anthony Powell

or Jean Rhys or Ivy Compton-Burnett or Elizabeth Jane Howard or Paul Scott or Margaret Drabble or—"

"They're English novelists and I've heard of all of them," I said. "But I take your point. You're really not interested in the things you're not really interested in."

"Exactly."

"You never even read newspapers," I said.

"No. And I never watch television." She smiled. "Do you think I should be stood against a wall and shot?"

"I'm just interested in who your friends are."

"Do you? Well, you are a friend of mine, aren't you?" Over it, as over our entire conversation, was that veneer of disinterested irony. I wondered for a moment if she were actually entirely human: her nearly complete ignorance of popular culture demonstrated more than any assertion how little she cared what people thought of her. What I had thought of as her integrity was more complete than I could have imagined. Maybe a sixth of the graduate students in California had never heard of an athlete like Seaver; but who in America could have avoided hearing of the Fonz?

"But you do have other friends. You just met me."

"I do, yes."

"In the English Department?" It was not impossible: for all I knew of my temporary colleagues, there might have been an extensive cell of Virginia Woolf fanciers who never looked at the newspapers. In them however this remoteness from their surroundings would have been an affectation; of Alma the reverse would have been true.

"No. I don't know many people there. I know some people who are interested in the occult."

"The *occult?*" I could not imagine what she meant. "Séances? Ouija boards? Madame Blavatsky? Planchettes?"

"No. They're more serious than that. They belong to an order."

I was stunned; I had fallen into an abyss. I envisioned Satanism, covens; California lunacy at its worst.

She read my face and said, "I'm not in it myself. I just know them."

"What is the name of the order?"

"X.X.X."

"But—" I leaned forward, scarcely believing that I had heard correctly. "It can't be X.X.X.? Xala . . ."

"Xala Xalior Xlati."

I felt disbelief, shock; I felt a surprised fear, looking at her beautiful face. X.X.X. was more than a group of California screwballs dressing themselves in robes; they were frightening. They were known to be cruel, even savage: they'd had some minor connection with the Manson family, and that was the only reason I had read about them. After the Manson affair they were supposed to have gone elsewhere—to Mexico, I thought. Were they still in California? From what I had read, Alma would have been better off knowing button men in the Mafia: from the Mafia you would expect the motives, rational or not, of our phase of capitalism. The X.X.X. was raw material for nightmares.

"And those people are your friends?" I asked.

"You asked."

I shook my head, still astonished.

"Don't worry about it. Or about them. You'll never see them."

It gave me an entirely different picture of her life; sitting across from me, faintly smiling, she was for a moment sinister. It was as though I had stepped off a sunlit path into jungle: and I thought of Helen Kayon working on Scots Chaucerians in the library.

"Even I don't see them all that much," she said.

"But you've been to their meetings? You go to their houses?"

She nodded. "I said. They're my friends. But don't worry about it."

It could have been a lie—another lie, for I thought she had not always been truthful with me. But her entire manner, even her concern for my feelings, demonstrated that she was being truthful. She raised her cup of coffee to her lips, smiling at me with a trace of concern, and I saw her standing before a fire, holding a bleeding something in her hands . . .

"You *are* worrying about it. I'm not a member. I know people in it. You asked me. And I thought you should know."

"Have you been to meetings? What goes on?"

"I can't tell you. That is just another part of my life. A small part. It won't touch you."

"Let's get out of here," I said.

Was I thinking even then that she would give me material for a novel? I do not think so. I thought that her contact with the group was probably much slighter than she had suggested; I had only one hint, much later, that it may not have been. She was romancing, exaggerating, I told myself. The X.X.X. and Virginia Woolf? And *La Grande Illusion?* It was very far-fetched.

Sweetly, almost teasingly, she invited me back to her apartment. It was a short walk from the coffeehouse. As we left the busy street and turned into a darker area of tall houses, she began to talk inconsequentially of Chicago and her life there. For once I did not have to question her to get information about her past. I thought I could detect a glancing relief in her voice: because she had "confessed" her acquaintance with the X.X.X? Or was it because I had not quizzed her about it? The latter, I thought. It was a typical late summer Berkeley evening, somehow warm and chilly at once— cold enough for a jacket, but with a sense of hidden warmth in the texture of the air. Despite the unpleasant surprise she had given me, the young woman beside me —her unconscious grace, her equally natural wit which lay embedded in her talk, her rather unearthly beauty— enlivened me, made me happier for life than I had been in months. Being with her was like coming out of hibernation.

We reached her building. "Ground floor," she said, and went up the steps to the door. For the pleasure of looking at her, I hung back. A sparrow lighted on the railing and cocked its head; I could smell leaves burning; she turned around and her face was washed into a pale blur by the shadows of the porch. Somewhere in the neighborhood a dog barked. Miraculously, I could still see her eyes, as if they shone like a cat's. "Are you as circumspect as your novel, or are you going to come in with me?"

I simultaneously recorded the fact that she had read my book and the featherlight criticism of it, and went up the steps to the door.

I had not imagined what her apartment would be like, but I should have known that it would be nothing like Helen Kayon's untidy menage. Alma lived alone— but that I had suspected. Everything in the large room into which she brought me was unified by a single taste, a single point of view: it was, though not obviously, one of the most luxurious private rooms I have ever seen. A long thick Bokhara rug lay over the floor; a painted firescreen was flanked by tables which looked to my untrained eye to be Chippendale. A vast desk was placed before the bay window. Striped Regency chairs; big cushions; a Tiffany lamp on the desk. I saw that I had been right to think that her parents were moneyed. I said, "You're not the typical grad student, are you?"

"I decided it was more sensible to live with these things than to put them in storage. More coffee?"

I nodded. So much about her now made sense, fit a pattern I hadn't seen before. If Alma was remote, it was because she was genuinely different; she had been raised in a manner that ninety per cent of America never sees and in which it only provisionally believes, the manner of the bohemian ultra-rich. And if she was essentially passive, it was because she had never had to make a decision for herself. On the spot I invented a childhood of nursemaids and nannies, schooling in Switzerland; holidays on yachts. That, I thought, explained her air of timelessness; it was why I had imagined her flying past the Plaza Hotel in the Fitzgerald twenties: that kind of wealth seemed to belong to another age.

When she came back in with the coffee I said, "How would you like to take a trip with me in a week or two? We could stay in a house in Still Valley."

Alma raised her eyebrows and cocked her head. It struck me that there was an androgynous quality to her passivity; just as there is, perhaps, an androgynous quality to a prostitute.

"You're an interesting girl," I said.

"A *Reader's Digest* character."

"Hardly."

She sat, her knees drawn up, on a fat cushion before me; she was strongly sexual and ethereal at once, and I dismissed the notion of her being somehow androgynous. It seemed impossible that I had just thought it. I knew that I had to sleep with her; I knew I would, and the knowledge made the act even more imperative.

Jus' put yo money on the table, boy . . .

By morning my infatuation was total. Going to bed had taken place in the most understated manner possible; after we had spent an hour or two talking, she had said, "You don't want to go home, do you?" "No." "Well then, you'd better stay here tonight." What followed was not just the ordinary limping round of the body, lust's three-legged race; in fact she was as passive in bed as in all else. Yet she had effortless orgasms, first during the minuet stage and then later during the hell-for-leather period; she clung to my neck like a child while her hips bucked and her legs strained against my back; but even during this surrendering she was separate. "Oh, I love you," she said after the second time, gripping my hair in her fists, but the pressure of her hands was as light as her voice. Reaching one mystery in her, I found another mystery behind it. Alma's passion seemed to come from the same section of her being as her table manners. I had made love with a dozen girls who were "better in bed" than Alma Mobley, but with none of them had I experienced that delicacy of feeling, Alma's ease with shades and colors of feeling. It was like being perpetually on the edge of some other sort of experience; like being before an unopened door.

I understood for the first time why girls fell in love with Don Juans, why they humiliated themselves pursuing them.

And I knew that she had given me a highly selective version of her past. I was certain that she had been nearly as promiscuous as a woman could be. That fit in with the X.X.X., with a sudden departure from Chicago; promiscuity seemed the unspoken element of Alma's mode of being.

What I wanted, of course, was to supplant all the others; to open the door and witness all of her mysteries; to have the grace and subtlety directed entirely toward me. In a Sufi fable, the elephant fell in love with a firefly, and imagined that it shone for no other creature but he; and when it flew long distances away, he was confident that at the center of its light was the image of an elephant.

3

Which is to say no more than that love cut me off at the knees. My notions of getting back to novel-writing vanished. I could not invent feelings when I was so taken over by them myself; with Alma's enigma before me, the different enigma of fictional characters seemed artificial. I would do that, but I had to do *this* first.

Thinking of Alma Mobley incessantly, I had to see her whenever I could: for ten days, I was with her almost every minute I was not teaching. Unread student stories piled up on my couch, matching the piles of essays about *The Scarlet Letter* on my desk. During this time our sexual bravado was outrageous. I made love to Alma in temporarily deserted classrooms, in the unlocked office I shared with a dozen others; once I followed her into a woman's lavatory in Sproul Hall and went into her as she balanced on a sink. A student in the creative writing class, after I had been very rhetorical, asked, "How do you define man, anyhow?" "Sexual and imperfect," I answered.

I said that I spent "almost" every moment with her that I did not spend in class. The exceptions were two evenings when she said that she had to visit an aunt in San Francisco. She gave me the aunt's name, Florence de Peyser, but while she was gone I still sweated with doubt. The next day, however, she was back unaltered —I could see no traces of another lover. Nor of the X.X.X., which was the greater worry. And she surrounded Mrs. de Peyser with so much circumstantial detail (a Yorkshire terrier named Chookie, a closetful of Halston dresses, a maid named Rosita) that my suspicions died. You could not return from an evening with the sinister zombies of the X.X.X. full of stories about a dog named Chookie. If there were other lovers, if the promiscuity I had sensed that first night still clung to her, I saw no sign of it.

In fact, if one thing bothered me it was not the hypothetical rivalry of another man but a remark she had made during our first morning together. It might have been no more than an oddly phrased statement of affection: "You have been approved," she said. For a lunatic moment, I thought she meant by our surroundings—the Chinese vase on the bedside table and the framed drawing by Pissarro and the shag carpet. (All of this made me more insecure than I recognized.)

"So you approve," I said.

"Not by me. Well of course by me, but not only by me." Then she put a finger to my lips.

Within a day or two I had forgotten this irritatingly unnecessary mystery.

Of course I had forgotten my work too, most of it. Even after the first frantically sensual weeks, I spent much less time on teaching than I had before. I was in love as I had never been: it was as though all my life I had skirted joy, looked at it askance, misunderstood it; only Alma brought me face to face with it.

Whatever I had suspected or doubted in her was burned away by feeling. If there were things I didn't know about her, I didn't give a damn; what I did know was enough.

I am sure it was she who first brought up the question of marriage. It was in a sentence like "When we're married, we ought to do a lot of traveling" or "What kind of house do you want after we're married?" Our conversation slipped into these discussions with no strain—I felt no coercion, only an increase in happiness.

"Oh, you really have been approved," she said.

"May I meet your aunt someday?"

"Let me spare you," she said, which did not answer the implied question. "If we get married next year, let's spend the summer on the Greek islands. I have some friends we can stay with—friends of my father's who live on Poros."

"Would they approve of me too?"

"I don't care if they do or not," she said, taking my hand and making my heart speed.

Several days later she mentioned that after we had visited Poros, she would like to spend a month in Spain.

"What about Virginia Woolf? Your degree?"

"I'm not really much of a student."

Of course I did not really imagine that we would spend months and months traveling, but it was a fantasy which seemed at least an image of our shared future; like the fantasy of my continued unspecified approval.

As the day of my Stephen Crane lecture for Lieberman drew nearer, I realized that I had done virtually no preparation, and I told Alma that I'd have to spend at least a couple of evenings at the library: "It'll be an awful lecture anyhow, I don't care if Lieberman tries to get me another year here because I think that we both want to get out of Berkeley, but I have to get some ideas together." She said that was fine, that she was planning to visit Mrs. de Peyser anyhow for the next two or three nights.

When we parted the next day, we gave each other a

long embrace. Then she drove off. I walked back to my apartment, in which I had spent very little time during the previous month and a half, straightened things up and went off to the library.

On the library's ground floor I saw Helen Kayon for the first time since she had left the lecture theater with Meredith Polk. She did not see me; she was waiting for an elevator with Rex Leslie, the instructor with whom I had swapped desks. They were deep in conversation, and while I glanced at them Helen placed the flat of her hand on Rex Leslie's back. I smiled, silently wished her well and went up the stairs.

That night and the next I worked on the lecture. I had nothing to say about Stephen Crane; I was not interested in Stephen Crane; whenever I looked up from the pages, I saw Alma Mobley, her eyes glimmering and her mouth widening.

On the second night of Alma's absence I left my apartment to go out for a pizza and a beer and saw her standing in the shadows beside a bar called The Last Reef; it was a place I would have hesitated to enter, since by repute it was a haunt for bikers and homosexuals looking for rough trade. I froze: for a second what I felt was not betrayal but fear. She was not alone, and the man with her had obviously been in the bar— he carried a glass of beer—but was not apparently a biker or a gay in search of company. He was tall and his head was shaven and he wore dark glasses. He was very pale. And though he was dressed nondescriptly, in tan trousers and a golf jacket (over a bare chest? I thought I saw chains of some sort flattened against skin), the man looked animal, a hungry wolf in human skin. A small boy, exhausted and barefooted, sat on the pavement by his feet. The three of them were strikingly odd, grouped together in the shadows by the side of the bar. Alma seemed comfortable with the man; she spoke desultorily, he answered, they seemed closer than Helen Kayon and Rex Leslie though there were no gestures of familiar warmth between them. The child slumped at the man's feet, shaking himself at times as though he feared to be kicked. The three of them looked like a perverse, nighttime family—a family by Charles Addams: Alma's characteristic grace, her way of holding herself, seemed, beside the werewolflike man and the pathetic child, unreal, somehow wicked. I backed away, thinking that if the man saw me he would turn savage in an instant.

For that *is* what a werewolf looks like, I thought, and then thought: the X.X.X.

The man jerked the twitching boy off the pavement, nodded to Alma, and got into a car by the curbside, still holding his glass of beer. The boy crept into the back seat. In a moment the car had roared off.

Later that night, not knowing if I were making a mistake but unable to wait until the next day, I telephoned her. "I saw you a couple of hours ago," I said. "I didn't want to disturb you. Anyhow, I thought you were in San Francisco."

"It was too boring and I came back early. I didn't call because I wanted you to get your work done. Oh, Don, you poor soul. You must have imagined something awful."

"Who was the man you were talking to? Shaven head, dark glasses, a little boy with him—alongside a biker's bar."

"Oh, him. Is *that* who you saw me with? His name is Greg. We knew each other in New Orleans. He came here to go to school and then dropped out. The boy is his little brother—their parents are dead, and Greg takes care of him. Though I must say not very well. The boy is retarded."

"He's from New Orleans?"

"Of course."

"What's his last name?"

"Why, are you suspicious? His last name is Benton. The Bentons lived on the same street as we did."

It sounded plausible, if I didn't think about the appearance of the man she was calling Greg Benton. "Is he in the X.X.X.?" I asked.

She laughed. "My poor darling is all worked up, isn't

he? No, of course he isn't. Don't think about that, Don.
I don't know why I told you."

"Do you really know people in the X.X.X.?" I demanded.

She hesitated. "Well, just a few." I was relieved: I
thought she was glamorizing herself. Maybe my "werewolf" really was just an old neighbor from New Orleans;
in fact, the sight of him in the bar's shadows had reminded me of my first sight of Alma herself, standing
colorless as a ghost on a shadowy campus staircase.

"What does this . . . Benton do?"

"Well, I think he has an informal trade in pharma-
ceuticals," she said.

Now that made sense. It suited his appearance, his
hanging around a bar like The Last Reef. Alma sounded
as close to embarrassment as I had ever heard her.

"If you're through with your work, please come over
and give your fiancée a kiss," she said. I was out the
door in less than a minute.

Two peculiar things happened that night. We were
in Alma's bed, watched over by the objects I have
already enumerated. I had been dozing more than
sleeping for most of the night, and I reached over lightly
to touch Alma's bare rounded arm; I did not want to
wake her. But it was as if her arm gave my fingers a
shock: not an electrical shock, but a shock of concentrated feeling, a shock of revulsion—as though I had
touched a slug. I snatched back my hand, she turned
over and mumbled, "All right, darling?" and I mumbled
something back. Alma patted my hand and went back
to sleep. Sometime later I dreamed of her. I saw merely
her face; but it was not the face I knew, and the
strangeness of it made me groan with anxiety; and for
the second time I came wholly awake, not sure where
I was or by whose side I lay.

4

So that may be when the change began, but our relationship remained superficially as it had been, at least
until the long weekend in Still Valley. We still made
love often and happily, Alma continued to speak en-
chantingly of the way we would live after we married.
And I continued to love her even while I doubted the
absolute veracity of some of her statements. After all,
as a novelist wasn't I too a kind of liar? My profession
consisted of inventing things, and of surrounding them
with enough detail to make them believable; a few
inventions on someone else's part did not upset me un-
duly. We had decided to get married in Berkeley at the
end of the spring semester, and marriage seemed a
ceremonious seal to our happiness. But I think the
change had already begun, and that my recoiling from
the touch of her skin in the middle of the night was the
sign that it had started weeks before without my seeing
it.

Yet a factor in the change was certainly the "approval" I had so mysteriously earned. I finally asked
her about it outright on the morning of the Crane lecture; it was a tense morning for me since I knew I was
to do a bad job, and I said, "Look. If this approval
you keep mentioning isn't yours and if it isn't Mrs. de
Peyser's, then whose is it? I can't help but wonder. It's
not your friend in the drug trade, I suppose. Or is it his
idiot brother?"

She looked up, a bit startled. Then she smiled. "I
ought to tell you. We're close enough."

"We ought to be."

She was still smiling. "It's going to sound a little
funny."

"I don't care. I'm just tired of not knowing."

"The person who has been approving of you is an old
lover of mine. Wait, Don, don't look like that. I don't
see him any more. I *can't* see him anymore. He's dead."

"Dead?" I sat down. I sounded surprised, and I am

sure I looked surprised, but I think that I had expected
something of this order of weirdness.

She nodded; her face serious and playful at once—
the "doubling" effect. "That's right. His name is Tasker
Martin. I'm in touch with him."

"You're in touch with him."

"Constantly."

"Constantly."

"Yes. I talk with him. Tasker likes you, Don. He
likes you very much."

"He's okayed me, as it were."

"That's right. I talk to him about everything. And
he's told me over and over that we're right for each
other. Besides that, he just *likes* you, Don. He'd be a
good friend of yours if he were alive."

I just stared at her.

"I told you it would sound a little funny."

"It does."

She lifted her hands. *"So?"*

"Um. How long ago did—Tasker die?"

"Years ago. Five or six years ago."

"Another old New Orleans friend?"

"That's right."

"And you were close to him?"

"We were lovers. He was older—a lot older. He died
of a heart attack. Two nights after that, he started to
talk to me."

"It took him two days to get change for the phones."
She did not reply to this. "Is he talking to you now?"

"He's listening. He's glad you know about him now."

"I'm not so sure I'm glad I do."

"Just get used to the idea. He really likes you, Don.
It'll be all right—it'll be just the same as it was before."

"Does Tasker pick up his phone when we're in bed?"

"I don't know. I suppose he does. He always liked
that side of things."

"And does Tasker give you some of your ideas about
what we'll do after we get married?"

"Sometimes. It was Tasker that reminded me about

my father's friends on Poros. He thinks you'll love the island."

"And what does Tasker think I'm going to do now that you've told me about him?"

"He says you'll be upset for a little while and that you'll think I'm crazy for a while, but that you'll just get used to the idea. After all, he's here and he isn't going anywhere, and you're here and we're going to be married. Don, just think about Tasker as though he were a part of me."

"I suppose he must be," I said. "I certainly can't believe that you're actually in communication with a man who died five years ago."

In part, I was fascinated by all this. A nineteenth-century habit like talking with departed spirits suited Alma down to the ground—it harmonized even with her passivity. But also it was creepy. The talkative ghost of Tasker Martin was obviously a delusion: in the case of anybody but Alma, it would have been the sympton of mental illness. Creepy too was the concept of being okayed by former lovers. I looked across the table at Alma, who was regarding me with a kindly expression of expectancy, and thought: she does look androgynous. She could have been a pretty nineteen-year-old freckled boy. She smiled at me, still with expectation kindling in her face. I wanted to make love to her, and I also felt a separation from her. Her long beautifully shaped fingers lay on the polished wood of her table, attached to hands and wrists equally beautiful. These too both attracted and repelled.

"We'll have a beautiful marriage," Alma said.

"You and me and Tasker."

"See? He said you'd be like that at first."

On the way to the lecture I remembered the man I had seen her with, the Louisianian Greg Benton with his dead ferocious face, and I shuddered.

For one sign of Alma's abnormality, one indication that she was no one else I had ever known, was that she suggested a world in which advisory ghosts and men who were disguised wolves could exist. I know of no other way to put this. I do not mean that she made me believe in the paraphernalia of the supernatural; but she suggested that such things might be fluttering invisibly about us. You step on a solid-looking piece of ground and it falls away under your shoe; you look down and instead of seeing grass, earth, the solidity you had expected, you are looking at a deep cavern where crawling things scurry to get out of the light. Well, so here is a cavern, a chasm of sorts, you say; how far does it go? Does it underlie everything, and is the solid earth merely a bridge over it? No; of course it is not; it very likely is not. I do love Alma, I told myself. We will be married next summer. I thought of her extraordinary legs, of her fine lovely face; of the sense I had with her that I was deep in a half-understood game.

My second lecture was a disaster. I brought out secondhand ideas, unsuccessfully tried to relate them and got lost in my notes; I contradicted myself. My mind on other things, I said that *The Red Badge of Courage* was "a great ghost story in which the ghost never appears." It was impossible to disguise my lack of preparation and interest in what I was saying. There were a few ironic hand-claps when I left the podium. I was grateful that Lieberman was far away in Iowa.

After the lecture I went to a bar and ordered a double Johnny Walker Black. Before I left I went to the telephones at the back and took out the San Francisco directory. I looked under P first and found nothing and started to sweat, but when I looked under D I found de Peyser, F. The address was in the right section of town. Maybe the earth was solid ground after all; of course it was.

The next day I rang David at his office and told him that I'd like to go to his place in Still Valley. "Fantastic," he said, "and about time, too. I've got some people looking in to see that nobody steals anything, but I wanted you to use the place all along, Don."

"I've been pretty busy," I said.

"How are the women out there?"

"Strange and new," I said. "In fact I think I'm engaged."

"You don't sound so sure about it."

"I'm engaged. I'm getting married next summer."

"What the hell's her name? Have you told anybody? Wow. I've heard about being understated, but . . ."

I told him her name. "David, I haven't told anybody else in the family. If you're in touch with them, say I'll be writing soon. Being engaged takes up most of my time."

He told me how to get to his place, gave me the name of the neighbors who had the key and said, "Hey, little brother, I'm happy for you." We made the usual promises to write.

David had bought the Still Valley property when he had a job in a California law firm; with his usual sagacity, he had chosen the place carefully, making sure that the house he would have as a vacation home had plenty of land around it—eight acres—and was close to the ocean, and then had spent all of his spare cash having the building completely renewed and redecorated. When he left for New York he kept the place, knowing that property values in Still Valley were going to take off. The house had probably quadrupled in value since then, proving once again that David was no fool. After Alma and I had picked up the keys from the painter and his pottery-making wife several miles down the valley road, we turned off onto a dirt road in the direction of the ocean. We could hear and smell the Pacific before we saw the house. And when Alma saw it she said, "Don, this is where we should come for our honeymoon."

I had been misled by David's constant description of the place as a "cottage." What I expected was a two- or three-room frame building, probably with outdoor plumbing—a beer and poker shack. Instead it looked just like what it was, the expensive toy of a rich young lawyer.

"Your brother just lets this place stay empty?" Alma asked.

"I think he comes here two or three weeks every year."

"Well."

I had never before seen her impressed. "What does Tasker think?"

"He thinks it's incredible. He says it looks like New Orleans."

I should have known better.

Yet the description was not inaccurate: David's "cottage" was a tall two-story wooden structure, dazzling white and Spanish in conception, with black wrought-iron balconies outside the upper windows. Thick columns flanked the massive front door. Behind the house we could see the endless blue ocean, a long way down. I took our suitcases from the trunk of the car and went up the steps and opened the door. Alma followed.

After going through a small tiled vestibule, we were in a vast room where various areas were raised and others sunken. A thick white carpet rolled over it all. Massive couches and glass-topped tables stood in the different areas of the room. Exposed beams had been polished and varnished across the width of the ceiling.

I knew what I would find even before we inspected the house, I knew there would be a sauna and a Jacuzzi and a hot tub, an expensive stereo system, a Cuisinart in the kitchen, a bookshelf filled with educational porn in the bedroom—and all this we found as we went through the house. Also a Betamax, a French bread rack serving as shelf space for Art Deco gewgaws, a bed the size of a swimming pool, a bidet in every bathroom . . . almost immediately I felt trapped inside someone else's fantasy. I'd had no idea David had made so much money during his years in California; neither had I known that his taste stayed on the level of a hustling young Jaycee.

"You don't like it, do you?" asked Alma.

"I'm surprised by it."

"What's your brother's name?"

I told her.

"And where does he work?"

She nodded when I named the firm, not as "Rachel Varney" would have done, with a detached irony, but as though she were checking the name against a list.

Yet of course she was correct: I did not like David's Xanadu.

Still, there we were: we had to spend three nights in the house. And Alma accepted it as if it were hers. But as she cooked in the gadget-laden kitchen, as she reveled in David's collection of expensive toys, I grew increasingly sour. I thought she had adapted to the house in some uncanny fashion, had subtly altered from the student of Virginia Woolf to a suburban wife: suddenly I could see her stocking up on chip dip at the supermarket.

Once again I am compressing ideas about Alma into a single paragraph, but in this case I am condensing the impressions of two days, not of three times that many months; and the change in her was merely a matter of degree. Yet I had the uneasy feeling that, just as in her apartment she was perfectly the embodiment of the Bohemian rich girl, in David's house she threw off hints of a personality suited to Jacuzzi baths and home saunas. She became more garrulous. The sentences about how we would live after our marriage became essays: I found out where we would make our base while we traveled (Vermont), how many children we would have (three)—on and on.

And worse, she began to talk endlessly about Tasker Martin.

"Tasker was a big man, Don, and he had beautiful white hair and a strong face with the most piercing blue eyes. What Tasker used to like was . . . Did I ever tell you about Tasker's . . . One day Tasker and I . . ."

This more than anything marked the end of my infatuation.

But even then I found it difficult to accept that my feelings had changed. While she described the characters of our children, I would find myself mentally crossing my fingers—almost shuddering. Realizing what I was doing, I would say to myself: "But you're in love, aren't you? You can even put up with the fantasy of Tasker Martin, can't you? For her sake?"

The weather made everything worse. Though we had had warm sunshine on the day we arrived, our first night in Still Valley was submerged in dark dense fog that endured for the next three days. When I looked out the rear windows toward the ocean, it was as though the ocean were all around us, gray and deadening. (Of course, this is what "Saul Malkin" imagines in his Paris hotel room with "Rachel Varney.") At times you could see halfway down to the valley road, but at other times you saw about as far ahead as you could extend your arms. A flashlight in that damp grayness simply lost heart.

Thus, there we are, mornings and afternoons in David's house while gray fog slides past the windows and the noise of waves slapping the beach far down suggests that any minute water will begin to come in through the bottom of the door. Alma is elegantly curled on one of the sofas, holding a cup of tea or a plate with an orange divided into equal sections. "Tasker used to say that I'd be the most beautiful woman in America when I was thirty. Well, I'm twenty-five now, and I think I'll disappoint him. Tasker used to . . ."

What I felt was *dread*.

On the second night she rolled out of bed naked, waking me. I sat up in bed, rubbing my eyes in the gloom. Alma walked across the cold gray bedroom to the window. We had not closed the drapes, and Alma stood with her back to me, staring at—at nothing at all. The bedroom windows faced the ocean, but though we could hear the cold noises of water all through the night, the window revealed nothing but surging gray.

I expected her to speak. Her back looked very long and pale in the murky room.

"What is it, Alma?" I asked.

She did not move or speak.

"Is anything wrong?" Her skin seemed lifeless, white cold marble. "What happened?"

She turned very slightly toward me and said, "I saw a ghost." (That, at any rate, is what "Rachael Varney" tells "Saul Malkin"; but did Alma actually say, "I *am* a ghost?" I could not be sure; she spoke very softly. I'd had more than enough of Tasker Martin, and my first response was a groan. But if she had said *I am a ghost,* would I have responded differently?)

"Oh, Alma," I said, not as fed up as I would have been in the daytime. The chill in the room, the dark window and the girl's long white body, these made Tasker a more real presence than he had been. I was a little frightened. "Tell him to go away," I said. "Come back to bed."

But it was no good. She picked her robe off the bed, put it around her and sat down, turning her chair toward the window. "Alma?" She would not answer or turn around. I lay down again and finally went back to sleep.

After the long weekend in Still Valley things moved to their inevitable conclusion. I often thought that Alma was half-mad. She never explained her behavior of that night, and after what happened to David, I wondered if all her actions comprised what I had once called a game: if she had been playfully, consciously manipulating my mind and feelings. Passive rich girl, terrorist of the occult, student of Virginia Woolf, semilunatic—she did not cohere.

She continued to project us into our future, but after Still Valley I began to invent excuses for avoiding her. I thought that I loved her, but the love was overshadowed by dread. Tasker, Greg Benton, the zombies of the X.X.X.—how could I marry all *that?*

And then I felt a physical as well as a moral revulsion. Over the two months following Still Valley, we had generally ceased making love, though I sometimes spent the night in her bed. When I kissed her, when I held or touched her, I overheard my own thinking: *not much longer*.

My teaching, except for rare flashes in the writing classes, had become remote and dull; I had stopped my own writing altogether. One day Lieberman asked me to see him in his office and when I arrived he said, "One of your colleagues described your Stephen Crane lecture to me. Did you actually say that *The Red Badge* was a ghost story without a ghost?" When I nodded, he asked, "Would you mind telling me what that means?"

"I don't know what it means. My mind was wandering. My rhetoric got out of hand."

He looked at me in disgust. "I thought you made a good start," he said, and I knew there was no longer any question of my staying on another year.

5

Then Alma disappeared. She had forced me, as dependent people can force others to do as they wish, to meet her for lunch at a restaurant near the campus. I went, got a table, waited half an hour and at last realized that she was not coming. I had been braced for more stories of what we were going to do in Vermont, and I was not hungry, but ate a salad out of general relief and went home.

She did not call that night. I dreamed of her sitting in the prow of a small boat, drifting away down a canal and smiling enigmatically, as if giving me a day and a night of freedom was the last act of the charade.

By morning I had begun to worry. I telephoned her several times during the day, but either she was out or not answering the phone. (This evoked a clear picture. A dozen times while I had been in her apartment, she had let the phone ring until it stopped.) By evening, I had begun to imagine that I was really free of her, and I knew that I would do anything to avoid seeing her again. I telephoned twice more during the night, and was happy to get no answer. Finally I stayed up until two writing a letter breaking it off.

Before my first class I went over to her building. My heart was beating fast: I was afraid I'd see her by accident and have to mouth the phrases which were so much more convincing on paper. I went up the steps of her building and saw that the drapes were drawn over her windows. I pushed at the locked door. I almost pushed the bell. Instead I slid the letter between the window and the frame, where she would see it and the inscription *Alma* as soon as she came up the stairs. Then I—no other word for it—fled.

Of course she knew my teaching schedule, and I half-expected to see her loitering outside a classroom or lecture theater, my smug letter in her hand and a provoking expression on her face. But I went through my teaching day without seeing her.

The following day was a repetition of the last. I worried that she might have killed herself; I dismissed the worry; I went off to my classes; in the afternoon I rang and got no reply. Dinner at a bar; then I walked to her street and saw the white oblong of my treachery still in her window. At home I debated taking my phone off the hook but left it on, by now almost ready to admit that I was hoping she would call.

The next day I had a section of the American literature class at two o'clock. To get to the building where it met I had to cross a wide brick plaza. This plaza was always crowded. Students set up desks where you could sign petitions for legalizing marijuana or declare yourself in favor of homosexuality and the protection of whales; students thronged by. In their midst I saw Helen Kayon, for the first time since the evening in the library. Rex Leslie was walking beside her, holding her hand. They looked very happy—animal contentment encased them as in a bubble. I turned away from that sight, feeling like a Skid Row derelict. I realized that

I had not shaved in two days, had not looked at myself in the mirror nor changed my clothes.

And when I turned away from Helen and Rex, I saw a tall pale man with a shaven head and dark glasses staring at me from beside a fountain. The vacant-faced boy, barefoot and in ragged dungarees, sat at his feet. Greg Benton seemed even more frightening than he had outside The Last Reef; standing in the sun beside a fountain, he and his brother were extraordinary apparitions—a pair of tarantulas. Even the Berkeley students, who had seen a great deal in the way of human oddity, visibly skirted them. Now that he knew I had noticed him, Benton did not speak or gesture to me, but his whole attitude, the tilt of the shaven head, the way he held his body, was a gesture. It all expressed anger—as though I'd enraged him by getting away with something. He was like an angry blot of darkness on the sunny plaza: like cancer.

Then I realized that for some reason he was helpless. He was glaring at me because that was all he *could* do. I immediately blessed the protection of the thousands of students: and then I thought that Alma was in trouble. In danger. Or dead.

I turned away from Benton and his brother and sprinted toward the gate at the bottom of the plaza. When I had crossed the street, I turned around to look back at Benton: I'd felt him watching me run—felt his cold satisfaction. But he and his brother had vanished. The fountain splashed, students milled. I even had a glimpse of Helen and Rex Leslie going into Sproul Hall, but the cancer had melted away.

By the time I reached Alma's street my fear seemed absurd. I knew that I was reacting to my own guilt. But had she not marked our final separation by standing me up at the restaurant? That I should have been in a sweat for her safety seemed a final manipulation. I caught my breath. Then I noticed that the drapes in Alma's windows were parted and the envelope was gone.

I ran down the block and up the stairs. Leaning sideways, I could see in her windows. Everything was gone. The room had been stripped bare. On the floor-boards which had been covered by Alma's rugs I saw my envelope. It was unopened.

6

I went home dazed and stayed that way for weeks. I could not understand what had happened. I felt enormous relief and enormous loss. She must have left her rooms on the day we were to meet at the restaurant: but what had been in her mind? A last joke? Or had she known that everything was over, had been ever since Still Valley? Was she in despair? That was difficult to believe.

And if I had been so eager to be rid of her, why did I now feel that I was shuffling through a less significant world? Alma gone, I was left with the bare world of cause and effect, the arithmetic world—if without the odd dread she had aroused in me, without the mystery too. The only mystery I had left was that of where she had gone; and the larger mystery of who she had been.

I drank a good deal and cut my classes: I slept most of the day. It was as though I had some generalized disease that took my energy and left me with no occupation but sleeping and thinking about Alma. When after a week I began to feel healthier, I remembered seeing Benton in the plaza and imagined that he'd been angry because he had known that what I had gotten away with was my life.

After I started to meet my classes again I saw Lieberman in the halls after a lecture and at first he ducked his head and intended to snub me, but he thought better of it and flicked his eyes at mine and said, "Step into my office for a second, will you, Wanderley?" He too was angry, but it was anger I could deal with; I want to say it was only human anger: but what anger is not? A werewolf's?

"I know I've disappointed you," I said. "But my life got out of hand. I got sick. I'll finish out the term as honorably as I can."

"Disappointed? That's a mild word for it." He leaned back in his leather chair, his eyes blazing. "I don't think we've ever been let down so much by one of our temporary appointments. After I entrusted you with an important lecture, you apparently threw together the worst mishmash—the worst *garbage*—" He collected himself. "And you've missed more classes than anyone in our history since we had an alcoholic poet who tried to burn down the recruitments office. In short, you've been lax, slipshod, lazy—you've been disgraceful. I just wanted you to know what I thought of you. Single-handedly, you've endangered our entire program of bringing in writers. This program is supervised, you know. We have a board to answer to. I'll have to defend you to them, as much as I detest the thought."

"I can't blame you for feeling as you do," I said. "I just got into an odd situation—I think I've sort of been cracking up."

"I wonder when you so-called creative people are going to realize that you can't get away with murder." The outburst made him feel better. He steepled his fingers and looked at me over them. "I hope you don't expect me to give you a glowing recommendation."

"Of course not," I said. Then I thought of something. "I wonder if I can ask you a question."

He nodded.

"Have you ever heard of an English professor at the University of Chicago named Alan McKechnie?" His eyes widened; he folded his hands. "I don't really know what I'm asking. I wondered if you knew anything about him?"

"What the hell are you saying?"

"I'm curious about him. That's all."

"Well, for what it's worth," he said, and stood up. He marched over to his window, which gave a splendid view of the plaza. "I dislike gossip, you know."

What I knew was that he loved gossip, like most

academics. "I knew Alan slightly. We were on a Robert
Frost symposium five years ago—sound man. A bit too
much the Thomist, but that's Chicago, isn't it? Still, a
good mind. Had a lovely family too, I gather."

"He had children? A wife?"

Lieberman looked at me suspiciously. "Of course.
That's what made it so tragic. Apart from the loss of
his contributions to the field, of course."

"Of course. I forgot."

"Look? What do you know? I'm not going to
slander a colleague for the sake of—the sake of—"

"There was a girl," I said.

He nodded, satisfied. "Yes. Apparently. I heard
about it at the last MLA convention. One of the fellows
from his department told me about it. He was *vamped*.
This girl simply pursued him. Dogged him. La Belle
Dame Sans Merci, in a word—I gather he finally did
become enchanted by her. She was a graduate student
of his. These things happen of course, they happen all
the time. A girl falls for her professor, manages to
seduce him, sometimes she makes him leave his wife,
most times not. Most of us have more sense." He
coughed. I thought: you really are a turd. "Well. He
did not. Instead he went to pieces. The girl ruined him.
In the end he killed himself. The girl, I gather, did a
midnight flit—as our English friends have it. Though
what this has to do with you, I can't imagine."

She had falsified nearly everything in the McKechnie
story. I wondered what else might have been a lie.
When I got home, I rang de Peyser, F. A woman answered the phone.

"Mrs. de Peyser?"

It was.

"Please excuse me for calling you on what may be a
case of mistaken identity, Mrs. de Peyser, but this is
Richard Williams at the First National of California.
We have a loan application from a Miss Mobley who
lists you as a reference. I'm just running the usual
routine information check. You're named as her aunt.

"As her what? What's her name?"

"Alma Mobley. The problem is that she forgot to give your address and phone number, and there are several other Mrs. de Peysers in the Bay area, and I need the correct information for our files."

"Well it's not me! I've never heard of anybody named Alma Mobley, I can assure you of that."

"You do not have a niece named Alma Mobley who is a graduate student at Berkeley?"

"Certainly not. I suggest you get back to this Miss Mobley and ask her for her aunt's address so you don't go wasting your time."

"I'll do that right now, Mrs. de Peyser."

The second semester was a rainy blur. I pushed at a new book, but it would not budge. I never knew what to make of the Alma character: was she a La Belle Dame Sans Merci, as Lieberman had said; or was she a girl on the far borders of sanity? I didn't know how to treat her, and the first draft took so many misdirections it could have been an exercise in the use of the unreliable narrator. And I felt that the book needed another element, one I couldn't yet see, before it would work.

David telephoned me in April. He sounded excited, happy, more youthful than he'd been in years. "I have amazing news," he said. "Astounding news. I don't know how to tell you."

"Robert Redford bought your life story for the movies."

"What? Oh, come off it. No, really, this is hard for me to tell you."

"Why don't you just start at the beginning?"

"Okay. Okay, that's what I'll do, wiseass. Two months ago, on February third" —this was really the lawyer at work—"I was up on Columbus Circle, seeing a client. The weather was terrible, and I had to share a cab back to Wall Street. Bad news, right? But I found myself sitting next to the most beautiful woman I'd ever seen in my life. I mean, she was so good-looking my mouth went dry. I don't know where I got the guts, but by the time we got to the Park, I asked her out to dinner. I don't usually do things like that!"

"No, you don't." David was too lawyerly to ask strange girls for dates. He'd never been in a singles bar in his life.

"Well, this girl and I really hit it off. I saw her every night that week. And I've gone on seeing her ever since. In fact, we're going to get married. That's half of the news."

"Congratulations," I said. "I wish you better luck than I had."

"Now we come to the difficult part. The name of this astounding girl is Alma Mobley."

"It can't be," I said.

"Wait. Just wait. Don, I know this is a shock. But she told me all about what happened between you, and I think it's essential that you know how sorry she is for everything that happened. We've talked about this a long time. She knows she hurt your feelings, but she knew that she just wasn't the right girl for you. And *you* weren't right for *her*. Also, she was in a bad patch in California. She wasn't herself, she says. She's afraid you have absolutely the wrong idea of her."

"That's just what I do have," I said. "Everything about her is wrong. She's some kind of witch. She's destructive."

"Hold on. I *am* going to marry this girl, Don. She's not the person you think she is. God, how we've talked about this. Obviously you and I have to talk about it a hell of a lot ourselves. In fact I was hoping you could hop a plane to New York this weekend so we could have a good long talk and really work through it. I'd be glad to pay your fare."

"That's ridiculous. Ask her about Alan McKechnie. See what she tells you. Then I'll tell you the truth."

"No, wait, buddy, we've already been through all that. I know she gave you a garbled version of the McKechnie affair. Can't you imagine how shattered she was? Please come out here, Don. All three of us have to have a long session."

"Not on your life," I said. "Alma's a kind of Circe."

"Look, I'm at the office, but I'll call you later in the week, okay? We have to get things straight. I don't want my brother having bad feelings about my wife."

Bad feelings? I felt horror.

That night David rang again. I asked him if he'd met Tasker yet. Or if he knew about Alma and the Xala Xalior Xlati.

"See, that's where you got the wrong idea. She just made all that stuff up, Don. She was a little unsteady out there on the Coast. Besides who can take all that stuff seriously anyhow? Nobody here in New York ever heard of the X.X.X. In California, people get all cranked up about trivia."

And Mrs. de Peyser? She had told him that I was terribly possessive; Mrs. de Peyser was a tool to get time by herself.

"Let me ask you this, David," I said. "Sometimes, maybe only once, haven't you looked at her or touched her and just felt—something funny? Like that, no matter how strongly attracted you are to her, you're squeamish about touching her?"

"You've got to be kidding."

David would not permit me to creep away from the whole issue of Alma Mobley, as I wanted to do. He would not let it go. He telephoned me from New York two or three times a week, increasingly disturbed by my refusal to see reason.

"Don, we have to talk this thing out. I feel terrible about you."

"Don't."

"I mean, I just don't understand your attitude about this thing. I know you must feel terrible resentment. Jesus, if things had worked out the other way around and Alma had walked out of my life and decided to marry you, I'd be tied in knots. But unless you admit your resentment, we can never get to the point of doing something about it."

"I don't resent anything, David."

"Come off it, kid brother. We have to talk about it sometime. Alma and I both feel that way."

One of my problems was that I didn't know to what extent David's assumptions were correct. It was true that I resented both David and Alma: but was it merely resentment that made me recoil from the thought of them marrying?

A month or so after that, many seesawing conversations later, David called to say that I was "going to have a break from being hounded by your brother. I've got a little business in Amsterdam, so I'm flying there tomorrow for five days. Alma hasn't seen Amsterdam since she was a child, and she'll be coming with me. I'll send you a postcard. But do me a favor and really think about our situation, will you?"

"I'll do my best," I said. "But you care too much about what I think."

"What you think is important to me."

"All right," I said. "Be careful."

Now what did I mean by *that?*

At times I thought that both David and myself had underestimated her calculation. Suppose, I thought, that Alma had engineered her meeting with David. Suppose that she had deliberately sought him out. When I thought about this, Gregory Benton and the stories of Tasker Martin seemed more sinister—as if they, like Alma, were stalking David.

Four days later I got a call from New York telling me that David was dead. It was one of David's partners, Bruce Putnam; the Dutch police had wired the office. "Do you want to go out there, Mr. Wanderley?" Putnam asked. "We'd like to leave it to you to take it from here. Just keep us informed, will you? Your brother was greatly liked and respected here. None of us can figure out what happened. It sounds like he fell out of a window."

"Have you heard from his fiancée?"

"Oh, did he have a fiancée? Imagine that—he never let on. Was she with him?"

"Of course she was," I said. "She must have seen everything. She must know what happened. I'll get on the first plane going."

There was a plane the next day to Schiphol Airport, and I took a cab to the police station which had cabled David's office. What I learned can be set down very barely: David had gone through a window and over a chest-high balcony. The hotel owner had heard a scream, but nothing more—no voices, no arguments. Alma was thought to have left him; when the police entered their room, none of her clothing was still in the closets.

I went to the hotel, looked at the high iron balcony, and turned away to the open wardrobe closet. Three of David's Brooks Brothers suits hung on the rail, two pairs of shoes beneath them. Counting what he must have been wearing at the time of his death, he had brought four suits and three pairs of shoes for a five-day visit. Poor David.

7

I arranged for the cremation and, two days later, stood in a cold crematorium while David's coffin slid along rails toward a fringed green curtain.

Two days after that I was back in Berkeley. My little apartment seemed cell-like and foreign. It was as though I had grown irretrievably apart from the person I had been in the days when I hunted down references to James Fenimore Cooper in *PMLA*. I began to sketch out *The Nightwatcher*, having only the most nebulous ideas for it, and to prepare for my classes again. One night I telephoned Helen Kayon's apartment, thinking that I would ask her out for a drink so that I could talk about Alma and my brother, and Meredith Polk told me that Helen had married Rex Leslie the week before. I found myself falling asleep at intervals all during the day and going to bed before ten at night; I drank too much but could not get drunk. If I survived the year,

I thought, I would go to Mexico and lie in the sun and work on my book.

And escape my hallucinations. Once I had come awake near midnight and heard someone moving around in my kitchen; when I got out of bed and went in to check, I had seen my brother David standing near the stove, holding the coffeepot in one hand. "You sleep too much, kid," he said. "Why not let me give you a cup?" And another time, teaching a Henry James novel to my section of the survey class, I had seen on one of the chairs not the red-haired girl I knew was there, but—again—David, his face covered in blood and his suit torn, nodding happily at how bright I could be about *Portrait of a Lady*.

But I had one more discovery to make before I could go to Mexico. One day I went to the library and instead of going to the stack of critical magazines, went to the reference library and found a copy of *Who's Who* for the year 1960. It was nearly an arbitrary year; but if Alma was twenty-five when I met her, then in 1960 she should have been nine or ten.

Robert Mobley was in the book. As nearly as I can remember it, this was his entry—I read it over and over and finally had it photocopied.

MOBLEY, ROBERT OSGOOD, painter and watercolorist. b. New Orleans, La, Feb 23. 1909; s. Felix Morton and Jessica (Osgood); A.B. Yale U. 1927; m. Alice Whitney Aug 27, 1936; children—Shelby Adam, Whitney Osgood. Shown at: Flagler Gallery, New York; Winson Galleries, New York; Galerie Flam, Paris; Schlegel, Zurich; Galeria Esperance, Rome. Recipient Golden Palette 1946; Southern Regional Painters Award 1952, 1955, 1958. Collected in: Adda May Lebow Museum, New Orleans; Louisiana Fine Arts Museum; Chicago Institute of the Arts; Santa Fe Fine Arts; Rochester Arts Center; many others. Served as Lt Cmdr. USNR, 1941–1945. Member Golden Palette Society; Southern Regional Arts

League; American Water Color Society; American League of Artists; American Academy of Oil Painting. Clubs: Links Golf; Deepdale Golf; Meadowbrook; Century (New York); Lyford Cay (Nassau); Garrick (London). Author: I Came This Way. Homes: 38957 Canal Blvd New Orleans, La; 18 Church Row, London NW3 UK; "Dans Le Vigne," Route de la Belle Isnard, St Tropez 83 France.

This wealthy clubman and artist had two sons, but no daughter. Everything Alma had told me—and David, presumably—had been invention. She had a false name and no history: she might as well have been a ghost. Then I thought of "Rachel Varney," a brunette with dark eyes, the trappings of wealth and an obscure past, and I saw that David had been the missing element in the book I'd tried to write.

8

I've spent nearly three weeks writing all this out, and all I've done is remember—I'm no closer to understanding it than I was before.

But I've come to one perhaps foolish conclusion. I'm no longer so ready to reject the notion that there might be some factual connection between *The Nightwatcher* and what happened to David and myself. I find myself in the same position as the Chowder Society, no longer sure of what to believe. If I am ever invited to tell a story to the Chowder Society, I'll tell them what I've written out here. This account of my history with Alma—not *The Nightwatcher*—is my Chowder Society story. So perhaps I have not wasted my time after all; I've given myself a base for the Dr. Rabbitfoot novel, and I'm prepared to change my mind on an important question—right now, maybe *the* important question. When I started this, the night after Dr. Jaffrey's funeral, I thought it would be destructive to imagine myself in the landscape and atmosphere of one of my own books. Yet—was I not in that landscape, back at Berkeley? My imagination may have been more literal than I thought.

Various odd things have been happening in Milburn. Apparently a group of farm animals, cows and horses, were killed by some kind of beast—I heard a man in the drugstore say that creatures from a flying saucer killed them! And far more seriously, a man either died or was killed. His body was found down near a disused railway siding. He was an insurance salesman named Freddy Robinson. Lewis Benedikt in particular seemed to take this death hard, though it appears to have been accidental. In fact, something very peculiar seems to be happening to Lewis: he's become absentminded and fretful, almost as if he were blaming himself for Robinson's death.

I too have an unusual feeling which I'll record here at the risk of feeling idiotic whenever I see it in later years. This feeling is absolutely unfounded: more a hunch than a *feeling*. It's that if I start to look more closely into Milburn and do what the Chowder Society asks, I'll find what sent David over that railing in Amsterdam.

But the oddest feeling, the feeling that makes the adrenalin go, is that I am about to go inside my own mind: to travel the territory of my own writing, but this time without the comfortable make-believe of fiction. No "Saul Malkin" this time; just me.

He ran back to his house and did not dare to come out again until he could see dawn, when at any rate it was again time for chores and he had to go out. His description of the figure he had seen inspired, among a very few of the most excitable souls of Milburn, the story of a creature from a flying saucer which Don had heard in the drugstore. Both Walt Hardesty and the County Farm Agent, who inspected the dead cows, had heard the story, but neither was gullible enough to accept it. Walt Hardesty, as we know, had his own ideas; he had what he considered good reason for assuming that a few more animals would be bled white and then that would be that. His experience with Sears James and Ricky Hawthorne made him keep his theory to himself and not share it with the County Farm Agent, who chose to overlook certain obvious facts and form the conclusion that somewhere in the area an oversize dog had turned killer. He filed a report to this effect and went back to the county seat, having completed his business. Elmer Scales, who had heard about Norbert Clyde's cows and was constitutionally half inclined to believe in flying saucers anyhow, sat up three nights in a row by his living-room window, holding a loaded twelve-gauge shotgun across his knees (. . . *come from Mars boy maybe you do but we'll see how you glow when you got a load of shot in you*). He could not possibly have foreseen or understood what he would be doing with that shotgun in two months' time. Walt Hardesty, who would have to clean up Elmer's mess, was content to take things easy until the next weirdo happening and think about how he could get the two old lawyers to open up to him—them and their friend Mr. Lewis Snob Benedikt. They knew something they weren't telling, and they knew something too about their other old buddy, Dr. John Dope Fiend Jaffrey. They just didn't take that *normal,* Hardesty told himself as he bedded down in the spare room behind his office. He put a bottle of County Fair on the floor beside his cot. No sir. Mr. Ricky Snob Hawthorne-With-Horns and Mr. Sears and Roebuck Snob James just didn't act normal at all.

But Don does not know, so he cannot put in his journal, that after Milly Sheehan leaves the Hawthorne house to return to the house on Montgomery Street where she lived with John Jaffrey, she remembers one morning that the doctor never did get around to putting up the storm windows and yanks on a coat and goes outside to see if she can do it herself and while she looks up despairingly at the windows (knowing that she'll never be able to lift the big storms that high), Dr. Jaffrey walks around the side of the house and smiles at her. He is wearing the suit Ricky Hawthorne picked out for his funeral but no shoes or socks, and at first the shock of seeing him outside barefoot is worse than the other shock. "Milly," he says, "tell them all to leave—tell them all to get out. I've seen the other side Milly, and it's *horrible*." His mouth moves, but the words sound like a badly dubbed film. *"Horrible.* Be sure to tell them now," he says, and Milly faints. She is out only a few seconds, and comes to whimpering, her hip aching from the fall, but even through her fear she can see no footprints in the snow beside her and knows that she was just seeing things—she'll never tell anyone. They put you away for things like that. "Too many of those darned stories, and a little too much of *Mr.* Sears James," she mutters to herself before picking herself up and limping back inside.

Don, sitting alone in room 17, of course does not know most of the things that happen in Milburn while he takes a three-week tour of his past. He barely sees the snow, which continues to fall heavily; Eleanor Hardie does not skimp on heating any more than she allows the lobby carpet to go unvacuumed, so he is warm, up in his room. But one night Milly Sheehan hears the wind shift to the north and west and getting out of bed to put on another blanket, sees stars between the rags of clouds. Back in bed, she lies listening to the wind blow more strongly—and then even more strongly than that, shaking the sash of the window, forcing itself in. The curtain billows, the shade rattles. When she wakes in the morning, she finds a drift of snow covering the sill.

And here are some other events from two weeks in Milburn, all of which happened while Don Wanderley consciously, willfully and at length evoked the spirit of Alma Mobley:

Walter Barnes sat in hs car at Len Shaw's Exxon station and thought about his wife while Len filled the tank. Christina had been moping around the house for months now, staring at the telephone and burning dinners and at last he had begun to think that she was having an affair. Disturbingly, he still carried in his mind a clear picture of a drunken Lewis Benedikt fondling Christina's knees at Jaffrey's tragic party: and of a drunken Christina letting him do it. It was true that she was still an attractive woman, and he had become an overweight small-town banker, not the financial power he had once envisaged: most of the men of their class in Milburn would have been happy to go to bed with Christina, but it had been fifteen years since a woman had looked at him in a challenging way. Misery settled over him. His son would be leaving home in a year, and then it would be just he and Christina, pretending that they were happy. Len coughed and said, "How's your friend Mrs. Hawthorne? Thought she looked a little peaked last time she was in here—thought maybe she had a touch of the flu." "No, she's fine," Walter Barnes replied, thinking that Len, like ninety per cent of the men in town, coveted Stella: as he did himself. What he ought to do, he thought, was run away with Stella Hawthorne; go someplace like Pago Pago and forget about being lonely and married in Milburn; not knowing that the loneliness which would in fact visit him would be worse than anything he could imagine;

and Peter Barnes, the banker's son, sat in another car with Jim Hardie while they drove at twenty miles over the limit to a rundown tavern, listening to Jim, who was six-two and muscular and the kind of boy described forty years earlier as "born to hang," and who had set fire to the old Pugh barn because he'd heard the Dedham girls kept their horses in it, tell stories of his sexual relations with the new woman at the hotel, this Anna woman, stories which would never be true, not in the way Jim meant them;

and Clark Mulligan sat in the projection booth of his theater, watching *Carrie* for the sixtieth time and worried about what all this snow would do to his business and if Leota would have something besides hamburger casserole for dinner and if anything exciting would ever happen to him again;

and Lewis Benedikt paced the rooms in his enormous house tormented by an impossible thought: that the woman who had appeared before him on the highway and whom he had nearly killed was his dead wife. The set of the shoulders, the swing of the hair . . . the more he thought back to those seconds, the more agonizingly quick and vague they were;

and Stella Hawthorne lay on a motel bed with Milly Sheehan's nephew, Harold Sims, wondering if Harold would ever stop talking: "And then, Stel, some of the guys in my department are looking into myth survival among the Amerinds because they say the whole group dynamic thing is a dead letter, can you believe it? Hell, I only finished my thesis four years ago, and now the whole thing's out of style, Johnson and Leadbeater don't even *mention* Lionel Tiger anymore, they're getting into field work, and the other day, for Chrissake, a guy stopped me in the corridor and asked me if I've ever read any of the stuff on the Manitou—the *Manitou*, for Chrissake. Myth survival, for Chrissake."

"What's a Manitou?" she asked him, but didn't pay any attention to his answer—some story about an Indian who chased a deer for days up a mountain, but when he got to the top the deer turned on him and wasn't a deer anymore. . . .

and bundled-up Ricky Hawthorne, driving to Wheat Row one morning (he now had his snow tires) saw a man wearing a pea jacket and a blue watch cap beating a child on the north side of the square. He slowed, and just had time to see the boy's bare feet kicking in the snow. For a moment he was so shocked that he could not think what to do; but he stopped, pulling the car over to the curb, and got out. "That's enough," he shouted, "that's *quite* enough," but the man and the child both turned to stare at him with such peculiar force that he put down his arm and got back in the car;

and the next night, sipping camomile tea, looked out of an upstairs window and nearly dropped the cup, seeing a forlorn face staring in at him—gone in an instant when he jerked to one side. In the next instant, he realized that it was his own face;

and Peter Barnes and Jim Hardie come out of a country bar, and Jim, who is only half as drunk as Peter, says *hey, shithead, I got a great idea,* and laughs most of the way back to Milburn;

and a dark-haired woman sits facing the window in a dark room in the Archer Hotel and watches the snow fall and smiles to herself;

and at six-thirty in the evening an insurance salesman named Freddy Robinson locks himself in his den and telephones a receptionist named Florence Quast and says, "No, I don't think I need to bother either of them, I think that new girl of theirs could answer my questions. Could you give me her name? And just where is she staying again?"

and the woman in the hotel sits and smiles, and several more animals, part of the fun, are butchered: two heifers in Elmer Scales's barn (Elmer having fallen asleep with the shotgun across his lap) and one of the Dedham girls' horses.

2

That was how Freddy Robinson came in. He had written the policy for the two Dedham girls, the daughters of the late Colonel and the sisters of long-deceased Stringer Dedham. Nobody bothered about the Dedham girls much anymore: they lived out in their old house on Willow Mile Road, they had their horses but rarely sold one, they kept to themselves. The same age as most of the men in the Chowder Society, they had not aged as well. For years they had talked obsessionally about Stringer, who had not died immediately when the threshing machine pulled off his arms but had lain on the kitchen table, wrapped in three blankets during a sweltering August, babbling and passing out and then babbling again until the life ran out of him. People in Milburn got tired of hearing about what Stringer was trying to say while he died, especially since it didn't make much sense; even the Dedham girls couldn't properly explain it—what they wanted you to know was that Stringer had *seen* something, he was upset, he wasn't fool enough to get caught in the thresher if he was really himself, was he? And the girls seemed to blame Stringer's fiancée, Miss Galli, and for a little while eyebrows were raised at her; but then Miss Galli just upped and left town, and after that people lost interest in whatever the Dedham girls thought of her. Thirty years later not many people in town even remembered Stringer Dedham, who had been handsome and a gentleman and would have turned the horses into a business and not just a half-hearted hobby for a couple of aging women, and the Dedham girls got tired of their own obsession—after so many years, they weren't so sure what Stringer had been trying to say about Miss Galli—and decided that their horses were better friends than Milburn people. Twenty years after that they were still alive, but Nettie was paralyzed with a stroke and most young people in Milburn had never seen either of them.

Freddy Robinson had driven past their farm one day not long after he had moved to Milburn and what made him reverse and go up the drive was the name on the mailbox, Col. T. Dedham—he didn't know that Rea Dedham repainted her father's name on the box every two years. Even though Colonel Thomas Dedham had died of malaria in 1910, she was too superstitious to

take it off. Rea explained it to him; and she was so
pleased to have a spruce young man across the table
from her that she bought three thousand dollars' worth
of insurance. What she insured were her horses. She
was thinking of Jim Hardie, but she didn't tell that to
Freddy Robinson. Jim Hardie was a bad 'un, and he'd
had a grudge against the girls ever since Rea shooed
him away from the horse barn when he was a little
boy: the way young Robinson explained it to her, a little
insurance was just what she needed, in case Jim Hardie
ever came back with a can of gasoline and a match.

At that time, Freddy was a new agent and his ambi-
tion was to become a member of the Million Dollar
Roundtable; eight years later he was close to making
it, but it no longer mattered to him—he knew that if
he'd been in a bigger town he'd have had it long before.
He had been to enough conferences and conventions
and sales meetings to think that he knew most that
there was to know about the insurance business; he
knew how the business worked, and he knew just how
to sell life and property insurance to a scared young
farmer whose soul belonged to the bank and whose
nest egg had just vanished into a new milking system—
now a fellow like that really needed insurance. But
eight years of living in Milburn had changed Freddy
Robinson. He no longer took pride in his ability to sell,
since he had learned that it was based on an ability to
exploit fear and greed; and he had learned half-consciously to despise most of his fellow salesmen—in the
company's phrase, the "Humdingers."

It was not his marriage or children which had
changed Freddy, but living across the street from John
Jaffrey's house. At first, he had thought that the old
boys he saw trooping in once a month or so were comic,
unbelievably stuffy-looking. Dinner jackets! They had
looked unprecedentedly grave—five Methuselahs padding out their time.

Then he began to notice that after sales meetings in
New York he returned home with relief; his marriage

was going badly (he was finding himself attracted to the high school girls his wife, two children ago, had rather resembled), but home was more than Montgomery Street—it was all of Milburn, and most of Milburn was quieter and prettier than anywhere he'd ever lived. Gradually he felt that he had a secret relationship to Milburn; his wife and children were eternal, but Milburn was a temporary restful oasis, not the provincial backwater he had first thought it. And once at a conference, a new agent sitting next to him unpinned his Humdinger badge and dropped it under the table, saying, "I can stand most of it, but this Mickey Mouse crap drives me up the wall."

Two further events, as unremarkable as these, assisted Freddy's conversion. One night, aimlessly walking about an ordinary section of Milburn, he went past Edward Wanderley's house on Haven Lane and saw the Chowder Society through a window. There they sat, his Methuselahs, talking among themselves; one raised a hand, one smiled. Freddy was lonely, and they seemed very close. He stopped to stare in at them. Since moving to Milburn, he had gone from twenty-six to thirty-one, and the men no longer seemed so old; while they had stayed the same, he had aged toward them. They were not grotesque, but dignified. Also, something he had never considered, they were enjoying themselves. He wondered what they were talking about, and was assailed by the sense that it was something *secret*—something not business, not sport, not sex, not politics. It simply washed through him that their conversation would be of a sort he had never heard. Two weeks later he took one of the high school girls to a restaurant in Binghamton, and saw Lewis Benedikt across the room with one of the waitresses from Humphrey Stalladge's bar. (Both had sweetly rejected Freddy's advances.) He had begun to envy the Chowder Society; before long he would begin to love what he considered they represented, a way of combining civilization with a quiet good time.

Lewis was the focus of Freddy's feelings. Closer to

Freddy's age than the others, he showed what Freddy might become.

He watched his idol at Humphrey's Place, noticing how he raised his eyebrows before answering a question and how he tilted his head to one side, often, when smiling; how he used his eyes. Freddy began to copy these mannerisms. He copied too what he thought was Lewis's sexual pattern, but scaling down the ages of the girls from Lewis's twenty-five or twenty-six to seventeen or eighteen, which was the age of the girls who interested him anyhow. He bought jackets like those he saw Lewis wearing.

When Dr. Jaffrey invited him to his party for Ann-Veronica Moore, Freddy thought the doors of heaven had opened. He pictured a quiet evening, the Chowder Society and himself and the actress, and told his wife to stay home; when he saw the crowd, he began behaving like a fool. He stayed downstairs, too shy and disappointed to approach the older men he wanted to befriend; he made eyes at Stella Hawthorne; when he finally gathered the nerve to approach Sears James—who had always terrified him—he found himself talking about insurance as if under a curse. After Edward Wanderley's body was discovered, Freddy crawled away with the other guests.

After Dr. Jaffrey's suicide, Freddy was desperate. The Chowder Society was disintegrating before he had even had a chance to prove his worthiness for it. On that night, he saw Lewis's Morgan pull up to the doctor's house, and ran out to comfort Lewis—to make his impression. But again it had not worked. He was too nervous, he had been fighting with his wife, and he had been unable to keep from mentioning insurance; he had lost Lewis again.

Therefore, knowing nothing of what Stringer Dedham may have tried to describe to his sisters as he lay bleeding to death into a blanket on his kitchen table, Freddy Robinson, whose children were already noisy strangers and whose wife wanted a divorce, had no idea of what lay before him when Rea Dedham called him one morning and said that he had to come out to the farm. But he thought that what he saw there, a bit of silk scarf fluttering on a wire fence, gave him a way into the gracious company of friends he needed.

At first it seemed like another morning's work—another tiresome claim to be settled. Rea Dedham made him wait ten minutes on her frozen porch. From time to time he heard a horse neighing in the stables. Finally she appeared, wrinkled and hunched in a plaid shawl over her dress, saying that she knew who did it, yessir, she knew, but she'd looked at her policy and it didn't say anywhere that you didn't get your money if you knew, did it? And would he like any coffee?

"Yes, thank you," Freddy said, and pulled some papers from his briefcase. "Now if we could get into some of these claim forms, the company can start processing them as soon as possible. I'll have to look at the damage, of course, Miss Dedham. I guess you had some kind of accident?"

"I told you," she said. "I know who did it. It wasn't any accident. Mr. Hardesty is coming out too, so you'll just have to wait for him."

"So this is a case of criminal loss," Freddy said, checking off a box on one of his papers. "Could you just tell me about it in your own words?"

"They're the only words I have, Mr. Robinson, but you'll wait until Mr. Hardesty is here. I'm too old to say it all twice. And I'm not going out in that cold twice, not even for money. Brr!" She hugged herself with her bony arms and shivered theatrically. "Now you sit still and get some coffee into yourself."

Freddy, who had been awkwardly holding all his papers, his pen and his briefcase, looking around for a vacant chair. The Dedham girls' kitchen was a dirty cave filled with junk. One chair supported a couple of table lamps, another a stack of *Urbanites* so old they were yellow. A tall mirror in an oak-leaf frame on one wall dully gave him back his reflection, a figure of bureaucratic incompetence engulfed by disorderly papers. He backed up to one dark wall, bent down and knocked a cardboard box off a chair with his bottom. It fell to the floor with a loud crash. The only sunlight in the room streamed over him. "Heavens," Rea Dedham said, shrugging. "Noise!" Freddy cautiously extended his legs and arranged his papers on his lap. "Dead horse, is that it?"

"That's it. You people owe me some money—a *lot* of money, the way I see it."

Freddy heard something heavy rolling toward the kitchen through the house, and soundlessly groaned. "I'll just get started on the preliminary details," he said, and bent over so that he would not have to look at Nettie Dedham.

"Nettie wants to say hello," Rea said. So he had to look up anyhow.

A moment later the door creaked inward, admitting a heap of blankets in a wheelchair. "Hello, Miss Dedham," Freddy said, half-standing and clutching the briefcase with one hand, the papers with the other. He gave her a quick glance, then fled back into his papers. Nettie uttered a noise. Her head seemed to Freddy to be chiefly gaping mouth. Nettie was covered up to the chin in blankets, and her head was pulled back by some terrible constriction of the muscles so that her mouth was permanently open.

"You remember nice Mr. Robinson," Rea said to her sister, putting down cups of coffee on the table. Rea apparently ate all her meals standing up, for she made no move to sit now. "He's going to get our money for poor dear Chocolate. He's filling out the forms now, isn't he? He's filling out the forms."

"Ruar," Nettie uttered, waggling her head as she spoke. *"Glr ror."*

"Get us our money, that's right," Rea said. "There's nothing wrong with Nettie, Mr. Robinson."

"I should say not," he said, and looked away again. His eye fell on a stuffed robin under a glass bell, surrounded by dark brown leaves. "Let's get down to business, shall we? I gather the animal was named—"

"Here's Mr. Hardesty," Rea said. Freddy could hear another car coming up the drive, and lay the pen across the papers in his lap. He glanced uneasily at Nettie who was working her mouth and staring dreamily at the mottled ceiling. Rea set down her cup and began to struggle toward the door. *Lewis would open it for her,* he thought, still clutching his awkward pile of papers.

"Sit down, for heaven's sake," the old woman snapped.

Hardesty's boots crunched across the snow, mounted the porch. He had knocked twice before Rea got to the door.

Freddy had seen Walt Hardesty in Humphrey's place too often, sneaking into the back room at eight and lurching out at twelve, to think much of him as a sheriff. He looked like a bad-tempered failure, the sort of cop who'd enjoy using his gunbutt on someone's head. When Rea got the door open, Hardesty stood on the porch with his hands in his pockets, his sunglasses like armor over his eyes, and made no move to come in. " 'Lo, Miss Dedham," he said. "Well, where's your problem?"

Rea pulled the shawl more tightly around herself and went through the door. Freddy hesitated a moment and then realized that she was not coming back in; he dumped his papers on the chair and followed. Nettie waggled her head at him as he passed.

"I know who did it," he heard her saying to Hardesty as he went toward them. The old lady's voice was high and indignant. "It was that Jim Hardie, that's who."

"Oh, yeah?" Hardesty said. Freddy joined them, and the sheriff nodded at him over Rea's head. "Didn't take you long to get here, Mr. Robinson."

"Company paperwork," Freddy mumbled. "Official paperwork."

"Guys like you always got papers up the old kazoo," Hardesty said, and gave him a taut smile.

"It was Jim Hardie for sure," Rea insisted. "That boy's crazy."

"Well, we'll see about that," Hardesty said. They were nearly at the stables. "You find the dead animal?"

"We have a boy these days," Rea said. "He comes out to feed and water and change the straw. He's a nancy-boy," she added, and Freddy jerked his head up in surprise. Now he could smell the stables. "He found Chocolate in his stall. That's six hundred dollars' worth of horsemeat, Mr. Robinson, no matter who did it."

"Uh, how did you reach that figure?" Freddy asked. Hardesty was opening the stable doors. One horse whinnied, another kicked at its stall door. All the horses, to Freddy's untrained eye, looked dangerous. Their enormous lips and eyes flared at him.

"Because his sire was General Hershey and his dam was Sweet Tooth and they were two fine horses, that's because why. We could have sold General Hershey for stud anywhere—he looked just like Seabiscuit, Nettie used to say."

"Seabiscuit," Hardesty said under his breath.

"You're too young to remember any of the good horses," Rea said. "You write that down in your papers. Six hundred dollars." She was leading them into the stables, and the horses in the stalls shied back or swung their heads, according to their nature.

"These animals ain't too damn clean," Hardesty said. Freddy looked more closely and saw a huge patch of dried mud on the side of a gray.

"Skittish," Freddy said.

"He says they're skittish, the other one says they're dirty. I'm too *old,* that's the problem. Well, here's poor old Chocolate." The statement was unnecessary; the two men were staring over the stall door at the body of a big reddish animal on the straw-littered floor. To Freddy it looked like the body of a huge rat.

"Hell," Hardesty said, and opened the stall door. He stepped over the stiff legs and began to straddle the neck. The horse in the next stall whinnied, and Hardesty nearly fell down. "Hell." He steadied himself by propping an arm against the wooden side of the stall. "Hell, I can see it from here." He reached down to the horse's nose and tugged the entire head back toward him.

Rea Dedham screamed.

The two men half-carried, half-lifted her out of the stables past two rows of terrified horses. "Settle down now, settle down," Hardesty kept repeating, as if the old lady were herself a horse.

"Who the hell would do a thing like that?" Freddy asked, still shocked by the sight of the long wound in the horse's neck.

"Norbert Clyde claims it's Martians. Says he saw one. Didn't you hear about that?"

"I heard something," Freddy admitted. "Are you going to check into where Jim Hardie was last night?"

"Mister, I'd be a damn sight happier if people didn't tell me how to do my job." He bent over the old woman. "Miss Dedham, you settled down now? You like to sit?" She nodded, and Hardesty said to Freddy, "I'll hold her up, you open the door of my car."

They propped her up on the car seat, her legs dangling out. "Poor Chocolate, poor Chocolate," she moaned. "Horrible . . . poor Chocolate."

"All right, Miss Dedham. Now, I want to tell you something." Hardesty leaned forward and propped a foot up on the car. "Jim Hardie didn't do this, you hear me? Jim Hardie was out drinking beer with Pete Barnes last night. They drove up to a beer joint outside Glen Aubrey, and we got them checked in there till damn near two o'clock. I know about your little feud with Jim, so I asked around."

"He could have done it after two," Freddy said.

"He was playing cards with Peter Barnes in the Barnes's basement until daylight. That's what Pete says anyhow. Jim's been spending a lot of time with Pete Barnes, but I don't think the Barnes kid would do a thing like this or cover up for someone who did, do you?"

Freddy shook his head.

"And when Jim hasn't been with the Barnes kid,

he's been with that new dame, you know who I mean. The good-looker—looks like a model."

"I know who you mean. That is, I've seen her."

"Yeah. So he didn't kill this horse, and he didn't kill Elmer Scales's heifers either. The State Farm Agent says it was a dog turned killer. So if you see a big flying dog with teeth like razors, I guess you got it." He looked at Freddy hard, and turned back to Rea Dedham. "You about ready to go inside now? Too cold out here for a old lady like you. I'll get you inside, and go back and get someone to get rid of that horse for you."

Freddy stepped back, rebuffed by Hardesty. "You know it wasn't a dog."

"Yep."

"So what do you think it was? What's going on?" He looked around, knowing that he was missing something. Then he had it, and opened his mouth just as he saw a bright bit of cloth fluttering on the barbed-wire fence near the stables.

"You want to say?"

"There wasn't any blood," Freddy said, looking at the cloth.

"Good for you. Farm Agent decided not to notice that. You gonna help me with this old lady?"

"I dropped something back there," Freddy told him, and walked back toward the stables. He heard Hardesty grunt, picking up Miss Dedham, and when he got to the stables, turned around to see him carrying her in the door. Freddy went over to the barbed wire and pulled the long bit of cloth from it—silk. It was torn from a scarf, and he knew where he had seen it.

Freddy began—it was not the word he would have chosen—to scheme.

Back home, after he had typed up his report and mailed it and the signed forms off to the head office, he dialed Lewis Benedikt's telephone number. He did not really know what he would say to Lewis; but he thought he had the key he'd been looking for.

"Hey, Lewis," he said. "Hey, how are you? This is Freddy."

"Freddy?"

"Freddy Robinson. You know."

"Oh yes."

"Ah, are you busy right now? I've got something I want to talk to you about."

"Go ahead," Lewis said, not very promisingly.

"Yeah. If I'm not taking up your time? . . . Okay. You know about those animals that were killed? Did you know there was another one? One of those old horses the Dedham sisters own, I wrote the policy on it, well I don't think any Martian killed it. I mean, do you?" He paused, but Lewis said nothing. "I mean, that's screwball. Uh, look, isn't that woman who just moved into town, the one who sometimes hangs around with Jim Hardie, isn't she working for Sears and Ricky?"

"I've heard something to that effect." Lewis said, and Freddy heard in his voice that he should have said Hawthorne, James instead of Sears and Ricky.

"Do you know her at all?"

"Not at all. Do you mind if I ask what the point is?"

"Well, I think there's more going on than Sheriff Hardesty knows about."

"Could you explain yourself, Freddy?"

"Not on the phone. Could we meet somewhere to talk about it? See, I found something out at the Dedham place, and I didn't want to show it to Hardesty until I had talked with you and maybe with, ah, Mr. Hawthorne and Mr. James."

"Freddy, I don't have a clue what you're talking about."

"Well, to tell you the truth I'm not so sure myself, but I wanted to get together with you, have a few beers maybe and bat a few ideas around. Sort of see what we can come up with on this."

"On what, for God's sake?"

"On a few ideas I have. I think all you guys are just terrific, you know, and I want you to know if there's any kind of trouble coming your way . . ."

"Freddy, I've got all the insurance I need," Lewis said. "I'm not in the mood to go out. Sorry."

"Well, maybe I'll see you in Humphrey's Place anyhow? We could talk there."

"It's a possibility," Lewis said, and hung up.

Freddy put his receiver down, satisfied that he had planted enough hooks in Lewis for now. Lewis was bound to call him back once he'd thought about everything Freddy had told him. Of course if everything he was thinking was true, then it was his duty to go to Hardesty, but there was plenty of time for that—he wanted to think out the implications before he spoke to Hardesty. He wanted to make sure that the Chowder Society was protected. His thoughts went more or less in this order: he had seen the scarf from which the piece had been torn around the neck of the girl Hardesty called "the new dame." She had worn the scarf at Humphrey's Place on a date with Jim Hardie. Rea Dedham suspected Jim Hardie of killing the horse; Hardesty had said something about a "feud" between the Hardie boy and the Dedham sisters. The scarf proved that the girl had been there, so why not Hardie too? And if these two had for whatever reason killed the horse, why not the other animals? Norbert Clyde had seen a big form, something peculiar about the eyes: it could have been Jim Hardie caught in a ray of moonlight. Freddy had read about modern witches, crazy women who organized men into covens. Maybe this new girl was one of them. Jim Hardie was fodder for any lunatic who came down the pike, even if his mother would never see it. But the reputation of the Chowder Society would be damaged if all this were true, and if it got out. Hardie could be shut up, but the girl would have to be paid off and forced to leave.

He waited two days, anxiously waiting for Lewis to return his call.

When Lewis did not, he decided that the time for aggression had come and once again dialed Lewis's number.

"It's me again, Freddy Robinson."

"Oh, yes." Lewis said, already distant.

"I really think we ought to get together. Hey? Honestly, Lewis, I think we should. I've got your best interests at heart." Then, searching for an unanswerable appeal, "What if the next body is human, Lewis? Think about that."

"Are you threatening me? What the hell are you saying?"

" 'Course not." He was flattened. Lewis had taken it the wrong way. "Listen, how about tomorrow evening some time?"

"I'm going coon hunting," Lewis immediately said.

"Gosh," Freddy said, startled by this new facet of his idol. "I didn't know you did that. You hunt raccoon? That's really great, Lewis."

"It's relaxing. I go out with an old boy who has a few dogs. We just go off and waste time in the woods. Great if you like that sort of thing." Freddy heard the unhappiness in Lewis's voice, and for a moment was too disturbed by it to reply. "Well, good-bye," Lewis said, and hung up.

Freddy stared at the phone, opened the drawer where he had put the section of scarf, looked at it. If Lewis could go hunting, so could he. Not really knowing why he felt it was necessary, he went to the door of his study and locked it. He searched his memory for the name of the old woman who worked as receptionist for the law firm: Florence Quast. Then he got her number from the book and mystified the old lady with a long story about a nonexistent policy. When she suggested that he call either Mr. James or Mr. Hawthorne, he said, "No, I don't think I need bother either of them, I think that new girl of theirs could answer my questions. Could you give me her name? And just where is she staying again?"

(Are you thinking, Freddy, that somehow she will be living in your house very soon? And is that why you locked the door of your study? Did you want to keep her out?)

Hours later, he rubbed his forehead, buttoned his jacket, wiped his palms on his trousers and dialed the Archer Hotel.

"Yes, I'd be happy to see you, Mr. Robinson," the girl said, sounding very calm.

(Freddy, you're not really afraid of meeting a pretty girl for a late-night conversation, are you? What's the matter with you, anyhow? And why did you think she knew exactly what you were going to say?)

3

Do you get the point? Harold Sims asked Stella Haw-thorne, absently stroking her right breast. Do you see? It's just a story. That's the kind of thing my colleagues are into now. Stories! The point about this thing the Indian was chasing is that it has to show itself—it can't resist identifying itself—it's not just evil, it's vain. And I'm supposed to tell dumb horror stories like that, dumb stories like some stupid hack . . .

"All right, Jim, what's the story?" Peter Barnes asked. "What's this big idea of yours?" The cold air rushing into Jim Hardie's car had sobered Peter considerably: now when he concentrated he could make the four yellow beams of their headlights slide together into two. Jim Hardie was still laughing—a mean, determined laughter, and Peter knew that Jim was going to do something to somebody whether he was with him or not.

"Aw, this is great," Hardie said, and banged the horn. Even in the dark his face was a red mask in which the eyes were slits: that was the way Jim Hardie always looked while he was doing his most outrageous stunts, and whenever Peter Barnes ever took the time really to think about it, he was grateful that in a year he was going off to college and getting away from a friend who could look as crazy as that. Jim Hardie, drunk or otherwise stimulated, was capable of frightening wildness. What was either almost admirable or even more frightening was that he never lost his physical or verbal efficiency, no matter how drunk he was. Half-drunk, like now, he never slurred his words or staggered; wholly drunk, he was a figure of pure anarchy. "We're gonna tear things up," he said.

"Great," Peter said. He knew better than to protest; besides, Jim always got away with everything he did. Ever since they had met in grade school, Jim Hardie had talked his way out of trouble—he was wild, but not stupid. Even Walt Hardesty had never gotten anything on him—not even burning down the old Pugh barn because dumb Penny Draeger had told him that the Dedham girls, whom he hated, were using it as a stable.

"Might as well catch a few grins before you go to Cornell, hey?" Jim said. "Might as well catch all the grins you can get, because I hear that place is the pits." Jim had always said that he saw no point in going to college, but he occasionally showed that he resented Peter's acceptance, by early admission, to Cornell. Peter knew that all Jim Hardie wanted was for them to go on raising hell, a perpetual eighteen, forever.

"So is Milburn," Peter said.

"Good point, my son. It sure as shit is. But let's at least liven the place up, huh? So that's what we're going to do tonight, Priscilla. And just in case you thought you were going to dry up in the course of our adventures, your old friend James took care of that." Hardie unzipped his coat and pulled out a bottle of bourbon. "Golden hands, you turd, golden hands." He unscrewed the cap with one hand and drank while he drove, and his face grew red and taut. "You want a shluck?"

Peter shook his head; the smell nauseated him.

"Stupid bartender turned his back, right? *Zoom.* Asshole knew it was gone, too, but he was too much of a dipshit to say anything to me. You know something, Peter? It's depressing, having competition no better than that." He laughed, and Peter Barnes laughed too.

"Well, what are we going to do?"

Hardie passed him the bottle again, and this time he drank. The headlights swam apart and became four, and he shook his head, forcing them back to two.

"Hah! We are gonna peep, my boy, we are gonna

take a look at a lady." Hardie pulled at the bottle, chuckled, dribbled bourbon down his chin.

"Peep? Like a peeping Tom?" He let his head roll toward Hardie, who could obviously steam on to morning and through the next day, getting less predictable all the time.

"Peep. Look. Shoot a beaver. If you don't like it, jump out of the car."

"On a lady?"

"Well, not on a man, shitface."

"What, hide in a bush and look through . . ."

"Not exactly. Not exactly. Someplace much better."

"Who is it?"

"That bitch at the hotel."

Peter was now more confused than ever. "The one you were talking about? The one from New York?"

"Yeah." Jim swung the car around the square, passing the hotel without even bothering to look at it.

"I thought you were balling her."

"Well, I lied, man. So what? So I exaggerate a little. Truth is, she never let me put a hand on her. Look, I'm sorry I made up a little adventure about her, okay? She made me feel like a jerk. Taking her out to Humphrey's, giving her all my best lines—well, I want to take a look at her when she doesn't know I'm there."

Jim bent forward and, disregarding the road altogether for a reckless amount of time, groped under his seat. When he straightened up again, he was grinning widely and holding a long brass-trimmed telescope. "With this. Hell of a good scope, Junior—cost me sixty bucks in the Apple."

"Mmn." Peter lolled back against the seat. "This is the grungiest thing I ever heard of."

A moment later, he became aware that Jim was stopping the car. He pushed himself forward and peered through the window. "Oh no. Not here."

"This is it, babe. Move your ass."

Hardie shoved his shoulder, and Peter opened the door and half-rolled out of the car. St. Michael's cathedral loomed before them, huge and forbidding in the darkness.

Both boys stood shivering in their windbreakers by a side door of the cathedral. "Now what are you going to do, kick the door in? There's a padlock on it, if you haven't noticed."

"Shut your trap. I work in a hotel, remember?" Hardie produced a bundle of keys on a ring from beneath his jacket. The other hand held the telescope and the bottle. "Go over there and take a piss or something while I try the keys." He set the bottle down on the step and bent toward the lock.

Peter walked away down the long gray side of the church. From this side, it looked like a prison. He unzipped, steamingly pissed, staggered and splashed on his boots. Then he leaned against the church with one arm, stood as if deep in reflection, and quietly vomited between his feet. That too steamed. He was thinking about walking home when Jim Hardie called, "Come on, Clarabelle." He turned around and there was Hardie grinning at him, waving the keys and the bottle at him beside an open door. He resembled one of the gargoyles on the cathedral's façade.

"No," he said.

"Come *on*. Or don't you have hair on your balls?"

Peter trudged forward, and Hardie reached out and yanked him through the door.

Inside, the cathedral was cold, and dark with an undersea darkness. Peter stopped still, his feet on brick, feeling an immense space around him. He reached out his hands and touched chill air. Behind him, he heard Jim Hardie getting all of his things together. "Hey, where's your goddamned hand? Here, take this." The telescope slapped against his palm. Hardie's footsteps went away off to the side, clicking on the brick floor.

He turned and saw Hardie's hair flickering in the dark. "Move it. There are some stairs around here someplace . . ."

Peter took a step forward and crashed into some sort of bench.

"Quiet."

"I can't see you!"

"Shit. Over here." There was a movement in the darkness: he understood that Jim was waving, and cautiously moved toward him.

"You see the stairs? We go up there. To a sort of balcony."

"You did this before," Peter said, amazed.

"Sure I did it before. Don't be a dope. Sometimes I used to take Penny here and screw around in the pews. What the hell? She's not Catholic either."

Peter's eyes were adjusting, and diffused light from a high circular window helped him to see the interior of the church. He had never been inside St. Michael's before. It was much larger than the white suburban box in which his parents spent an hour on Easter and Christmas day. Enormous pillars divided the vast space; an altar cloth shone like a ghost. He burped and tasted vomit. The staircase Jim was pointing to was wide, of brick, and curved against the inner skin of the cathedral.

"We go up there, and we wind up right in the front, facing the square. Her room is on the square, see? With a good telescope we can look right in."

"It's dumb."

"I'll explain later, shithead. Let's go up." He began to go quickly up the stairs. Peter stayed behind. "Wait," Hardie said, turning around and descending a couple of the steps. "You need a cigarette." He grinned at Peter, pulled out his cigarettes and gave one to Peter.

"Here?"

"Shit, yes. Nobody's going to see you." He lit his cigarette and Peter's. The flame of the lighter reddened the walls, made everything else disappear. The smoke helped the taste in Peter's mouth, somehow making the vomit taste more like beer again. "Take a drag or two. See? It's okay." He blew out smoke, but with the flame extinguished, Peter could only hear him exhale. He

"Well, the first day she comes to the hotel I tried to come on with her, right? She puts me down. Then a little bit later *she* asks *me* if I'll take her out. She says she wants to see Humphrey's Place. So I take her there, but she's barely paying attention to me. Really pissed me off, man. I mean, why waste my time if she's not interested, right? Well, you know why? She wanted to meet Lewis Benedikt. You know him, right? The guy who was supposed to of offed his wife over in France."

"Spain," said Peter, who had very complicated ideas about Lewis Benedikt.

"Who cares? Anyhow, I'm sure that's why she asked me to take her there. So she's hot for wife-killers."

"I don't think he did it." Peter said. "He's a good guy. I mean, I think he's a good guy. I think that women sometimes sort of—you know—"

"Shit, I don't care if he did it or not. Hey, she's moving. He was silent; Peter was startled a moment later to have the telescope thrust into his hands. "Take a look. Fast."

Peter lifted the telescope, searched for the window, scanned past the top of the A in the hotel's sign. Back to the A; then straight up. He involuntarily moved several inches back on the sill. The woman stood at the window, smiling, holding a cigarette, looking right into his eyes. He thought he might have to vomit again. "She's looking at us!"

"Get serious. We're way across the square. It's dark out. But you see what I mean."

Peter gave the telescope back to Jim, who resumed looking at the woman's window. "See what you mean about what?"

"Well, she's weird. Two o'clock, and she's in her room in the dark with all her clothes on, smoking?"

"So what?"

"Look, I lived in that hotel all my life, right? So I know how people act in hotels. Even the old farts who stay with us. They watch television, they want room service, they leave their clothes all over the room, you get bottles on cabinets and rings on the tables, they

drew on his own cigarette again. Hardie wa
calmed him. "Just come on up now." He star   c
and Peter followed.   )

At the top, far up inside the church, they fo   s
narrow gallery around to the front of the churc
a window with a broad stone sill looked ac
square. Jim was sitting with his legs up on the s
Peter reached him. "Would you believe it," he
once had a beautiful moment with Penny right
spot." He dropped his cigarette on the floor and
it out. Peter saw him wink in the gray illum
from the window. "Drives 'em crazy. They can'
out who was smoking. Here. Have a drink." H
the bottle out.

Peter shook his head and gave him the tele
"Okay, we're here. Now explain." He sat on the
sill and jammed his hands into the windbre
pockets.

Hardie looked at his watch. "First, some magic.
Look out the window." Peter looked: the square, the
dark buildings, bare trees. The Archer Hotel across
the square had no lighted windows. "One, two, three."
On *three* the lights in the square switched off. "It's two
o'clock."

"Some magic."

"Well, if you're so hot, turn them back on." Hardie
swung around, kneeling on the stone, and put the telescope to his eyes. "Too bad her light's not on. But if
she gets near the window I'll be able to see her. You
want a look?"

Peter took the telescope and trained it on the hotel.

"She's in the room above the front door. Straight
across and a little bit down."

"I got the window. There's nothing there." Then he
saw a red flash in the blackness of the room. "Wait.
She's smoking."

Hardie grabbed the telescope from him. "Right.
Sitting there smoking."

"So explain why we broke into a church to watch
her smoke."

have little parties in their rooms and you have to scrub the carpet afterward. At night you can hear them talking to themselves, snoring, spitting—well, you can hear everything they do. You can hear them pissing in the sink. The walls are thick but the *doors* aren't, see? If you're out in the hall you can practically hear them brush their teeth."

"So what?" Peter asked again.

"So she doesn't do any of that. She never makes any noise at all. She doesn't watch TV. Her room hardly ever needs to be cleaned. Even the bed is always made up. Strange, huh? So what does she do, sleep on top of the covers? Stay up all night?"

"Is she still there?"

"Yeah."

"Let me see." Peter took the telescope. The woman was still standing at her window, smiling faintly as if she knew they were talking about her. Peter shivered. He gave back the telescope.

"I'll tell you some more. I carried her suitcase up when she checked in. Now I've toted about a million suitcases, believe me, and that one was empty. She might have had a few newspapers in it, nothing more. Once when she was at work I looked in her closets— nothing. No clothes. But *she didn't always wear the same thing,* man. So what the hell did she do, wear them in layers? Two days later I checked again, and this time the closet was full of clothes—just like she knew someone came in to look. That was the night she asked me to take her to Humphrey's, and I figured she was going to chew me out. But no, she hardly talked to me at all. About the only thing she said was, 'I want you to introduce me to that man.' 'Lewis Benedikt?' I said, and she nodded, like she already knew his name. I took her up to him, and he ran away like a rabbit."

"Benedikt did? What for?"

"I thought he was afraid of her." Jim put the telescope down and lit another cigarette, looking at Peter all the time. "And you know something? I was too.

There's just something in the way she looks at you sometimes."

"Like if she thinks you were poking around in her room."

"Maybe. But it's a heavy look, man. It really gets you. There's one other thing too. If you walk along the halls at night, you can tell if people have their lights on, right? The light comes through the bottom of the door. Well, she never has her lights on. *Never*. But one night —well, this is crazy."

"Tell me."

"One night I saw some flickering underneath her door. Flickering light—like radium or something, you know? A kind of greenish light. Cold light. It wasn't a fire or anything, and it wasn't from our lamps."

"That's stupid."

"I saw it."

"But it doesn't mean anything. Green light."

"Not just green—sort of glowing. Sort of silvery. Anyhow, that's why I wanted us to take a look at her."

"Well, you did, so let's go home. My father'll be angry if I'm late!"

"Hold on." He looked through the telescope again. "I think something's happening. She's not at the window any more. Holy shit." He lowered the telescope. "She opened the door and went out. I saw her go into the hall."

"She's coming over here!" Peter scuttled off the sill and moved down the gallery toward the stairs.

"Don't wet your pants, Priscilla. She isn't coming here. She couldn't see us, remember? But if she's going somewhere, I want to see where. You coming or not?" He was already gathering up his cigarettes, the bottle, his bundle of keys. "Come on. We gotta hurry. She'll be out of the door in two minutes."

"I'm hurrying, I'm hurrying!"

They pounded along the gallery and down the stairs. Hardie ran through the side aisles of the cathedral and pushed the door open, which gave stumbling Peter enough light to avoid the pillars and the edges of the pews. Out in the night, Jim clipped the padlock back on the door and ran to the car. Peter's heart beat rapidly, in part from relief at being out of the church. Yet he was still tense. He pictured the woman he had seen in the window coming across the snowy square toward them, the wicked queen from *Snow White*, a woman who never turned on a light or slept in a bed and who could see him on a black night through a church window.

He realized that his head was clear. As he got into the car beside Jim, he said, "Fear sobers you up."

"She wasn't coming here, idiot," Hardie said, but pulled away from the side of the cathedral out to the south side of the square so rapidly that his tires squealed. Peter looked anxiously into the long expanse of the square—white ground broken by bare trees and the dim statue—but saw no evil queen drifting toward them. The picture had been so clear in his mind that, disbelieving, he continued to scan the town square after Jim had turned into Wheat Row.

"She's on the steps," Jim whispered when they were nearly to the corner. Looking toward the hotel through the bare trees, Peter saw the woman calmly descending to the sidewalk. She wore the long coat, a fluttering scarf, a hat. She looked so absurdly normal in this clothing, turning out into the deserted street past two in the morning, that Peter laughed and shuddered at once.

Jim switched off the headlights and rolled quietly up to the stoplight. Off to their left and across the street, the woman moved quickly into darkness.

"Hey, let's just go home," Peter said.

"Screw that. I want to see where she's going."

"What if she sees us?"

"She won't." He turned left and went slowly down the top of the square past the hotel, his lights still off. Though the lights in the square were not on, the street lamps would remain lighted until dawn, and both boys saw her entering a pool of light at the end of the first block across Main Street. Jim drove slowly across, and then waited until she had walked another block before going further.

"She's just taking a walk." Peter said. "She has insomnia, and she takes walks at night."

"Like hell."

"I don't like doing this."

"Okay. Okay. Get out of the car and walk home," Jim whispered fiercely at him. He reached across Peter and opened the passenger door. "Get out and run home."

Peter sat in the blast of cold from the door, almost ready to get out. "You should too."

"Jesus. God damn you! Get out or close the door," Jim hissed. "Hey! Wait a second!" Both boys watched as another car swung onto the street ahead of them and paused under a street lamp two blocks ahead. The woman went unconcernedly up to the car, the door swung open, and she got in.

"I know that car," Peter said. "I've seen it around."

"Of course you have, you dodo. Seventy-five blue Camaro—it belongs to that turkey, Freddy Robinson." He picked up speed as Robinson's car drove away.

"Well, now you know where she goes at nights."

"Maybe."

"Maybe? What else? Robinson's married. In fact, my mother heard from Mrs. Venuti that his wife wants to divorce him."

"That's because he sucks around high school girls, right? You know that Freddy Robinson likes 'em young. Haven't you ever seen him out with a girl?"

"Yeah."

"Who was it?"

"A girl from school," Peter said, not wanting to say that it was Penny Draeger.

"Okay. So whatever that jerk is doing, he's not just out on a date. Now, where the hell's he going?"

Robinson was leading them through northwest Milburn, making turns that seemed random, going further from the center of town. These houses under a black sky, snow drifted on their front lawns, looked sinister to Peter Barnes: the scale of the night diminished them to something larger than dollhouses, smaller than themselves. Freddy Robinson's taillights moved ahead of them like the eyes of a cat.

"All right. Let's see, he's going to turn right up ahead, and go west on Bridge Road."

"How do you—?" Peter stopped talking and watched Robinson's car do as Jim had predicted. "Where is he going?"

"To the only thing out this way that doesn't have a set of swings in the back yard."

"The old railroad station."

"You win a cigar. Or better yet, a cigarette." Both boys lit Marlboros; in the next minute, Robinson's car swung into the parking lot of Milburn's disused station. The railway had tried for years to sell the building; it was an empty shell with a board floor and a ticket window. Two old boxcars had stood on the overgrown tracks for as long as the boys could remember.

As they watched from an unlighted car down Bridge Road, first the woman, then Robinson, left the Camaro. Peter looked at Jim, afraid that he knew what Hardie was going to do. Hardie waited until Robinson and the woman had gone around the side of the station and then opened his door.

"No," Peter said.

"Fine. Stay here."

"What's the point? Catch them with their pants down?"

"That's not what they're going to do, idiot. Out here? Or in that freezing old station, with the rats? He's got enough money to hit a motel."

"Then *what?*" Peter pleaded.

"I want to know what she says. She brought him here, didn't she?"

And he closed the door and began to move quietly up Bridge Road.

Peter touched the door handle, pushed it down and heard the lock disengage. Jim Hardie was crazy: why should he follow him any futher into pointless trouble?

Already they had invaded a church and smoked cigarettes and drunk whiskey there, and here was Jim
Hardie, not satisfied, creeping along after cradle-rob-
bing Freddy Robinson and that spooky woman.

What? The ground vibrated and from nowhere a
freezing wind slammed into him. More than two voices
seemed to lift beyond the station, screeching into the
sudden wind. It felt as though a hand were banging
inside Peter's skull.

The night deepened about him, and he thought he
was fainting; he dimly heard Jim Hardie falling into the
snow up ahead, and then they and the old station
seemed surrounded by a moment of pure brightness.

He was out of the car, standing up on earth that
seemed to bounce, looking toward Jim: his friend sat
up in the snow, his body covered with white; Jim's eyebrows gleamed, greenish, like the dial of a watch—
snow did that sometimes, caught by angled moonlight—

Jim ran toward the station and Peter was able to
think: *That's how he gets in trouble, he's not just crazy,
he never gives up—*

and they both heard Freddy Robinson scream.

Peter squatted down beside the car as if he expected gunshots. He could hear Jim's footsteps receding
in the direction of the station. The footsteps paused;
terrified, Peter looked cautiously around the fender of
the car. Back and legs dusted with gleaming snow, Jim
was unknowingly miming his own posture, and peering
around the side of the station.

He wished he were two hundred yards off, watching
through a telescope.

Jim crawled a few yards farther: Peter knew that
now he would be able to see the entire rear of the station. Beyond the platform, stone steps led down into
the railbed. The two abandoned boxcars sat, mired in
weeds, at either end of the station.

He shook his head, and saw Jim running, bent over,
back to the car. Jim did not speak to him or even look at
him, but opened the door and scrambled in. Peter got

in—his knees stiff from kneeling—just as Jim started the car.

"Well, what happened?"

"Shut up."

"What did you see?"

Hardie hit the accelerator and popped the clutch; the car shot widely forward. A film of snow covered Hardie's jacket and jeans.

"Did you see anything?"

"No."

"Did you feel the ground shake? Why did Robinson yell?"

"I don't know. He was lying down on the tracks."

"You didn't see that woman?"

"No. She must have been around the side."

"Well, you saw something. You ran like hell."

"At least I went!"

The rebuke quieted Peter, but more was to come. "You damn chicken-shit, you just hid behind the car like a little girl—you got the balls of a pigeon—now listen, if anybody asks where you were tonight, you were playing poker with me, we were playing poker in your basement just like last night, right? Nothing happened, you get it? We had a few beers and then we picked up the game from last night. Okay?"

"Okay, but . . ."

"*Okay.*" Hardie turned to glare at Peter. "Okay. You want to know what I saw? Well, something saw *me*. You know what? There was a little kid sitting on the top of the station, and he must have been watching me all the time."

This was totally unexpected. "A little kid? That's crazy. It's almost three in the morning. And it's cold, and there's no way to get up to the roof of the station anyhow. We used to try it often enough, back in grade school."

"Well, he was there and he was watching me. And here's another little tidbit." Hardie savagely cramped the car around a corner, and nearly went sideways into a row of mailboxes. "He was barefoot. And I don't think he had a shirt on either."

Peter was silenced.

"Man, he gave me the flying shits. So I got out. And I think Freddy Robinson is dead, man. So if anybody asks, we played poker all night."

"Whatever you say."

"Whatever I say."

Omar Norris had an unpleasant awakening. After his wife had thrown him out of his house, he had spent the night in what he considered his last refuge, one of the boxcars near the abandoned station, and if he had heard any noises during his sodden sleep, he no longer remembered them. Therefore, he was particularly disgruntled to see what he had taken for a bundle of old rags on the tracks outside was a human body. He did not say "Not again" (what he said was "Shit on this"), but "Not again" was what he meant.

4

Over the next few nights and days several events of varying immediate importance took place in Milburn. Some of these events seemed trivial to the people involved, some were confusing or annoying, yet others were commanding and significant: but all were part of the pattern which would eventually bring so many changes to Milburn, and as a part of the pattern, all were important.

Freddy Robinson's wife learned that her husband had carried only the skimpiest life insurance coverage on himself, and that Humdinger Fred, the prospective member of the Million Dollar Roundtable, was worth only fifteen thousand dollars dead. She made a tearful long-distance call to her unmarried sister in Aspen, Colorado, who said, "I always told you he was a cheap so and so. Why not sell your house and come out here where it's healthy? And what kind of accident was that anyhow, honey?"

Which was the question that Broome County deputy coroner was asking himself, faced with the corpse of a thirty-four-year-old man from which most of the internal organs and all the blood had been removed. For a moment he considered writing under CAUSE OF DEATH the word "Exsanguination," but instead wrote "Massive internal insult," with a long appended note ending with the speculation that the "insult" had been caused by a marauding animal.

And Elmer Scales sat up every night with the shotgun across his lap, not knowing that the last cow had been killed and that the figure he had tauntingly half-seen was looking for bigger game;

and Walt Hardesty bought Omar Norris a drink in the back room at Humphrey's Place and heard Omar say that now that he had time to think about it, maybe he did hear a car or two that night, and it seemed to him that wasn't all, it seemed to him there was some kind of *noise* and some kind of *light*. "Noise? Light? Get the hell out of here, Omar," Hardesty said, but stayed nursing his beer after Omar left, wondering just what the hell was going on;

and the excellent young woman Hawthorne, James had hired told her employers that she wanted to leave the Archer Hotel and had heard in town that Mrs. Robinson was putting her house up for sale, and could they talk to their friend at the bank and set up the financing? She had, it turned out, a healthy account at a savings and loan in San Francisco;

and Sears and Ricky looked at one another with something surprisingly close to relief, as if they hadn't liked the thought of that house sitting empty, and said they could probably arrange something with Mr. Barnes;

and Lewis Benedikt promised himself he'd call his friend Otto Gruebe to make a date to go out with the dogs for a day's coon hunting;

and Larry Mulligan, laying out Freddy Robinson's

body for burial, looked at the corpse's face and thought.
he must have seen the devil coming to carry him off;

and Nettie Dedham, penned in her wheelchair as she
was penned within her paralyzed body, sat looking out
of the dining-room window as she liked to do while Rea
busied herself with the horses' evening feed and tilted
her head so that she could see the evening light on the
field. Then she saw a figure moving around out there
and Nettie, who understood more than even her sister
credited, fearfully watched it approach the house and
barn. She uttered a few choked sounds, but knew that
Rea would never hear them. The figure came nearer,
hauntingly familiar. Nettie was afraid it was the boy
from town Rea talked about—that wild boy in a rage
that Rea had named him to the police. She trembled,
watching the figure come nearer across the field, imagining what life would be like if the boy did anything to
Rea; and then squawked in terror and nearly tipped
over the wheelchair. The man walking toward the barn
was her brother Stringer, wearing the brown shirt he'd
had on the day he died: it was covered with blood, just
as it had been when they'd put him on the table and
wrapped him in blankets, but his arms were whole.
Stringer looked across the small yard to her window,
then held the strands of barbed wire with his hands,
stepped through the fence and came toward the window. He smiled in at her, Nettie with her head rolling
back on her shoulders, and then turned again toward
the stable.

And Peter Barnes came down to the kitchen for his
usual rushed breakfast, even more rushed these days
when his mother had turned so introspective, and found
his father, who should have left the house fifteen minutes earlier, sitting at the table before a cold cup of
coffee. "Hey, dad," he said, "you're late for the bank."

"I know," his father said. "I wanted to talk to you
about something. We haven't talked much lately, Pete."

"Yeah, I guess. But can't it wait? I have to get to
school."

"You'll get there, but no, I don't think it can wait. I've been thinking about this for a couple of days."

"Oh?" Peter poured milk into a glass, knowing that it was likely to be serious. His father never came out with the serious things right away: he brooded about them as if they were bank loans, and then hit you with them when he had a plan all worked out.

"I think you've been seeing too much of Jim Hardie," his father said. "He's no good, and he's teaching you bad habits."

"I don't think that's true," Peter said, stung. "I'm old enough to have my own habits. Besides, Jim's not half as bad as people say—he just gets wild sometimes."

"Did he get wild Saturday night?"

Peter set down the glass and looked with feigned calm at his father. "No, weren't we quiet enough?"

Walter Barnes took off his glasses and polished them on his vest. "You're still trying to tell me you were here that night?"

Peter knew better than to stick to the lie. He shook his head.

"I don't know where you were, and I'm not going to ask. You're eighteen, and you have a right to your privacy. But I want you to know that at three o'clock your mother thought she heard a noise and I got up and walked all through the house. You weren't downstairs in the family room with Jim Hardie. In fact you weren't anywhere in the house." Walter put his glasses back on and looked seriously at his son, and Peter knew that now he was going to produce whatever plan he'd thought up.

"I haven't told your mother because I didn't want her to worry about you. She's been tense lately."

"Yeah, what's she so angry about, anyhow?"

"I don't know," said his father, who had an approximate idea. "I think she's lonely."

"But she's got a lot of friends, there's Mrs. Venuti, she sees her every day almost—"

"Don't try to get me off the track. I'm going to ask

you a few questions, Pete. You didn't have anything to do with the Dedham girls' horse being killed, did you?"

"No," Peter uttered, shocked.

"And I don't really suppose you know anything about Rea Dedham being murdered."

To Peter, the Dedham girls were illustrations from a history book. "Murdered? God, I—" He looked wildly around the kitchen. "I didn't even know."

"I thought so. I just heard about it myself yesterday. The boy who cleans their stables found her yesterday afternoon. It'll be on the news today. And in tonight's paper."

"But why ask me?"

"Because people are going to think that Jim Hardie might possibly be involved."

"That's crazy!"

"I hope for Eleanor Hardie's sake that it is. And to tell you the truth, I can't see her son doing anything like that."

"No, he couldn't, he's just sort of wild, he doesn't stop when the ordinary guy would . . ." Peter shut up, hearing his own words.

His father sighed. "I was worried . . . people knew that Jim has something against those poor old women. Well. I'm sure that he had nothing to do with it, but Hardesty will undoubtedly be asking him questions." He put a cigarette in his mouth, but did not light it. "Okay. Scout, I think we have to be closer. You're going to college next year, and this is probably our last year together as a family. We're going to give a party weekend after next, and I'd like you to loosen up and come and be a part of it. Will you do that?"

So that was the plan. "Sure," he said, relieved.

"And you'll stay for the entire party? I'd like it if you could really get in the swing of things."

"Sure." Looking at his father, Peter saw him for a moment as already surprisingly old. His face was lined and pouchy, marked by a lifetime of worry.

"And we'll have more talks in the mornings?"

"Yes. Whatever you say. Sure."

"And there'll be less hanging around in beer joints with Jim Hardie." This was a command, not a question, and Peter nodded. "He could get you in real trouble."

"He's not as bad as everyone thinks," Peter said. "He just won't *stop*, you know, he keeps on going and—"

"That's enough. Better get to school. Can I give you a lift?"

"I'd like to walk. I get there too early otherwise."

"Okay, scout."

Five minutes later, books under his arm, Peter left the house; his viscera still retained the imprint of the fear he had felt when he thought his father would ask about Saturday night—that was an episode he planned to put out of his mind as completely as possible—but the fear was only a trembling area surrounded by a sea of relief. His father was far more concerned about being closer to him than about whatever he got up to with Jim Hardie: Saturday night would slip backward into time and become as remote as the Dedham girls.

He rounded the corner. His father's tact lay between him and whatever mysterious thing had happened out there two nights ago. In some way, his father was a protection against it; the terrible things would not happen; he was protected even by his immaturity. If he did not do anything bad, the terrors wouldn't get him.

By the time he reached the top of the square, the fear had almost entirely vanished. His normal route to school would have taken him past the hotel, but he did not want to take the slightest chance of seeing that woman again, and he turned off into Wheat Row. The cool air clipped against his face; sparrows thronged and cheeped across the snowy square, moving in quick zigs and zags. A long black Buick passed him, and he looked in the windows to see the two older lawyers, his father's friends, in the car's front seat. They both looked gray and tired. He waved, and Ricky Hawthorne lifted a hand in a returned greeting.

He was nearly at the bottom of Wheat Row and walking past the parked Buick when a commotion in the square took his attention. A muscular man in sunglasses, a stranger, wandered over the snow. He wore a pea jacket and a knit watch cap, but Peter saw from the white skin around his ears that his head was shaven. The stranger was clapping his hands together, making the sparrows scatter like spray from a shotgun: he looked irrational as a beast. Nobody else, neither the businessmen going up the pretty eighteenth-century steps of Wheat Row nor the secretaries following in short coats and long legs, saw him. The man clapped his hands again, and Peter realized that the man was looking directly at him. He was grinning like a hungry leopard. He started to lope toward Peter: Peter, frozen, sensed that the man was moving more rapidly than his steps could explain. He turned to run and saw, seated on one of the tilting tombstones before St. Michael's, a little boy with ragged hair and a slack grinning face. The boy, less fierce, was of the same substance as the man. He too was staring at Peter, who remembered what Jim Hardie had seen at the abandoned station. The stupid face twisted into a giggle. Peter nearly dropped his books, ran, kept running without looking back.

Our Miss Dedham Will Now Say a Few Words

5

The three men sat in the corridor on the third floor of University Hospital, Binghamton. None of them liked being there: Hardesty because he suspected he looked like a fool in the larger city, where no one immediately knew of his authority, and suspected also that he was on a useless mission; Ned Rowles because he disliked being away from *The Urbanite*'s offices at most times of the day, and especially disliked leaving layout entirely to the staff; and Don Wanderley because he had been out of the East too long to drive instinctively well on icy roads. Yet he thought that seeing the old woman whose sister had died so bizarrely might help the Chowder Society.

The suggestion had been Ricky Hawthorne's. "I haven't seen her in an age, and I understand she had a stroke some time back, but we might learn something from her. If you're willing to make the journey on a day like this." It was a day when noon was as dark as evening; storms hung over the town, waiting to happen.

"You think there might be some connection between her sister's death and your own problem?"

"There might be," Ricky admitted. "I don't really think so, of course, but it wouldn't do to overlook even these peripheral things. Trust me that there is some relevance, anyhow. We'll have it all out later. Now that you're here, we shouldn't keep you in the dark about anything. Sears might not agree with me, but Lewis probably would." Then Ricky had added wryly, "Besides, it might do you good to get out of Milburn, however briefly."

And that had been true at first. Binghamton, four or five times the size of Milburn, even on a dark, lowering day was another, brighter world: full of traffic, new buildings, young people, the sound of urban life, it was of its decade; it pushed little Milburn back into some novelettish period of Gothic romance. The larger city had made him recognize how enclosed Milburn was, how much an appropriate field for speculation like the Chowder Society's—it was the aspect of the town which had initially reminded him of Dr. Rabbitfoot. It seemed he had become accustomed to this. In Binghamton there was no drone of the macabre, no lurking abnormality to be sniffed out in stories over whiskey and in nightmares by old men.

But on the third floor of the hospital, Milburn held sway. Milburn was in Walt Hardesty's suspicion and nervousness, his rude "What the hell are *you* doing here? You're from town. I've seen you around—I saw you in Humphrey's." Milburn was even in Ned Rowles's lank hair and rumpled suit: at home, Rowles looked conventional and even well dressed; outside, he looked almost rubelike. You noticed that his jacket was too short, his trousers webbed with wrinkles. And Rowles's manner, in Milburn low-key and friendly, here seemed tinged with shyness.

"Just struck me as funny, old Rea going so soon after that Freddy Robinson being found dead. He was out at their place, you know, not more than a week before Rea died."

"How did she die?" Don asked. "And when can we see her sister? Aren't there evening visiting hours?"

"Waiting for a doctor to come out," Rowles said. "As to how she died, I decided not to put that in the paper. You don't need sensationalism to sell papers. But I thought anyone might have heard, around town."

"I've been working most of the time," Don said.

"Ah, a new book. Splendid."

"Is *that* what this guy is?" Hardesty asked. "That's just what we need, a writer. Sweet jumping Jesus. Great. I'm gonna be talking to a witness in front of the fearless editor and some writer. And this old dame, how the hell is she going to know who I am, anyhow? How is *she* gonna know I'm sheriff?"

That's what is worrying him, Don thought: he looks like Wyatt Earp because he's so insecure that he wants everybody to know that he wears a badge and carries a gun.

Some of this must have shown on his face, because Hardesty became more aggressive. "Okay, let's have your story. Who sent you here? Why are you in town?"

"He's Edward Wanderley's nephew," Rowles said in a tired voice. "He's doing some work for Sears James and Ricky Hawthorne."

"Jesus, those two," Hardesty moaned. "Did they ask you to come here to see the old lady?"

"Mr. Hawthorne did," Don answered.

"Well, I suppose I ought to fall down and pretend I'm a red carpet." Hardesty lit a cigarette, ignoring the no smoking sign at the end of the corridor. "Those two old birds have something up their sleeves. Up their sleeves. Hah! That's rich."

Rowles looked away, obviously embarrassed; Don glanced at him for an explanation.

"Go on, tell him, Fearless. He asked you how she died."

"It's not very appetizing." Rowles, wincing, caught Don's eye.

"He's a big boy. He's built like a running back, ain't he?"

That was another thing about the sheriff: he would always be measuring the size of another man against his own.

"Go on. It's not a goddamned state secret."

"Well." Rowles leaned wearily back against the wall. "She bled to death. Her arms were severed."

"My God," Don said, sickened and sorry that he had come. "Who would . . ."

"You got me, you know?" Hardesty said. "Maybe your rich friends could give us a hint. But tell me this— who would go around doing operations on livestock, like happened out at Miss Dedham's? And before that, at Norbert Clyde's. And before that, at Elmer Scales's?"

"You think there's one explanation for all of that?" This was, he assumed, what his uncle's friends had asked him to discover.

A nurse went by and scowled at Hardesty, who was shamed into stamping out his cigarette.

"You can go in now," the doctor said, leaving the room.

Don's first shocked thought, seeing the old woman, was *she's dead too:* but he noticed her bright panicked eye, which was darting from one of them to another. Then he saw her mouth working and knew that Nettie Dedham was beyond communication.

Hardesty, thrusting forward, was bustlingly untroubled by the patient's gaping mouth and signs of agitation. "I'm the sheriff, Miss Dedham," he said, "Walt Hardesty, the sheriff from over in Milburn?"

Don looked into the flat panic in Nettie Dedham's eye and wished him luck. He turned to the editor.

"I knew she had a stroke," the editor said, "but I didn't know she was as bad as this."

"We didn't meet the other day," Hardesty was saying, "but I talked to your sister. Do you remember? When the horse was killed?"

Nettie Dedham made a rattling sound.

"Is that yes?"

She repeated the sound.

"Good. So you remember, and you know who I am." He sat down and began speaking in a low voice.

"I suppose Rea Dedham could understand her," Rowles said. "Those two were supposed to be beauties, once. I remember my father talking about the Dedham girls. Sears and Ricky would remember."

"I guess they would."

"Now I want to ask you about your sister's death," Hardesty was saying. "It's important that you tell me anything you saw. You say it, and I'll try to understand it. Okay?"

"Gl."

"Do you remember that day?"

"Gl."

"This is impossible," Don whispered to Rowles, who twitched his face and went around to the other side of the bed to look out of the window. The sky was black and neon purple.

"Were you sitting in a position where you could see the stables where your sister's body was found?"

"*Gl.*"

"That's affirmative?"

"*Gl!*"

"Did you see anybody approach the barn or stables prior to your sister's death?"

"*GL!*"

"Could you identify that person?" Hardesty was sitting forward at an exaggerated angle. "Say if we brought him here, could you make a noise to say he was the one?"

The old woman made a sound Don eventually recognized as crying. He felt debased by his presence in the room.

"Was that person a young man?"

Another series of strangled noises. Hardesty's excitement was turning into an iron impatience.

"Let's say it was a young man, then. Was it the Hardie boy?"

"Rules of evidence," Rowles muttered to the window.

"Screw the rules of evidence. Was that who it was, Miss Dedham?"

"Glooorgh," moaned the old woman.

"Shit. Do you mean to say no? It wasn't?"

"Glooorgh."

"Could you try to name the person you saw?"

Nettie Dedham was trembling. "Glngr. Glnger." She made an effort which Don could feel in his own muscles. "Glngr."

"Ah, let's let that go for now. I got a couple more things." He rotated his head to look angrily at Don, who thought he saw embarrassment too on the sheriff's face. Hardesty turned back to the old woman and pitched his voice lower, but Don could still hear.

"I don't suppose you heard any funny noises? Or saw any funny lights or anything?"

The old woman's head wobbled; her eyes darted.

"Any funny noises or lights, Miss Dedham?" Hardesty hated having to ask her this. Ned Rowles and Don shared a glance of puzzled interest.

Hardesty wiped his forehead, giving up. "That's it. It's no good. She thinks she saw something, but who the hell can figure out what it was? I'm getting out of here. You stay or not, do what the hell you like."

Don followed the sheriff out of the room, and paused in the corridor as Hardesty spoke to a doctor. When Rowles emerged, his aging boy's face was pensive and considering.

Hardesty turned from the doctor and glanced at Rowles. "You make any sense out of that?"

"No, Walt. No sense that makes sense."

"You?"

"Nothing," Don said.

"Well, I'll be damned if I'm not going to start believing in spacemen or *vampires* or *something* pretty soon myself," Hardesty said, and went off down the corridor.

Ned Rowles and Don Wanderley followed. When they reached the elevators, Hardesty was standing inside one, stabbing a button. Before Don could reach the elevator, the door had whooshed shut unimpeded by the sheriff, who obviously wanted to escape the other two.

A moment later another elevator appeared, and the two men stepped inside it. "I've been thinking about what Nettie might have been trying to say," Rowles told him. The doors closed and the elevator smoothly descended. "I promise you, this is crazy."

"I haven't heard anything lately that isn't."

"And you're the man who wrote *The Nightwatcher*."

Here we go, Don thought.

Don buttoned up his coat and followed Rowles outside into the parking lot. Though he wore only his suit, Rowles did not appear to notice the cold. "Here, get in my car for a second," the editor said.

Don got into the passenger seat and looked over at Rowles, who was rubbing his forehead with one hand. The editor looked much older in the interior of the car: shadows poured into his wrinkles. " 'Glngr?' Isn't that what she said, that last time? You agree? It was a lot like that anyhow, wasn't it? Now. I never knew him myself, but a long time ago the Dedham girls had a brother, and I guess they talked about him for quite a while after he died . . ."

Don drove back toward Milburn on the field-bordered highway under the lurid sky purpled with glowing strips. Back, back to Milburn, with part of the story of Stringer Dedham riding with him; back to Milburn, where people were beginning to close themselves up as the snows grew worse and the houses seemed to melt closer together; where his uncle had died and his uncle's friends dreamed of horrors; away from the century and back to the confinement of Milburn, more and more like that of his own mind.

Housebreaking, Part One

6

"My father says I'm not supposed to see you so much anymore."

"So what? Do you care? How old are you anyhow, five?"

"Well, he's worried about something. He doesn't look very happy."

"He doesn't look happy," Jim mimicked. "He's old. I mean, what is he, fifty-five? He's got a boring job and an old car and he's too fat and his favorite little boy is going to fly out of the nest in nine or ten months. Just take a look around this town, friend. How many folks do you see with big smiles on their wrinkly old faces? This town is loaded with miserable old suckers. Are you gonna let them run your life?" Jim leaned back on his barstool and smiled at Peter, clearly assuming that the old argument was still persuasive.

Peter felt himself sinking back into uncertainty and ambiguity—these arguments were persuasive. His father's worries were not his: and the issue had never been that he did not love his father, for he did, but merely whether he should always obey his father's infrequent orders—or as Jim put it, "let him run your life."

For had he, after all, done anything truly bad with Jim? Because of Jim's keys, they had not even broken into the church; then they had followed a woman. That was all. Freddy Robinson had died, and that was a shame even if they had not liked him, but nobody was saying that his death had not been natural; he'd had a heart attack, or had fallen down and hurt his head . . .

And there had been no little boy on top of the station.

And there had been no little boy sitting on the gravestone.

"I suppose I should be grateful your old man let you come out tonight."

"No, it's not that bad. He just thinks we ought to spend less time together, not that we shouldn't spend any time at all together. I guess he doesn't like me sitting in places like this."

"This? What's wrong with this?" Hardie gestured comically around at the seedy tavern. "Hey, you— Sunshine!" Jim shouted. "This is a hell of a great place, isn't it?" The bartender looked back over his shoulder and grimaced stupidly. "Civilized as shit, Lady Jane. The Duke down there agrees with me. I know what your old man is afraid of. He doesn't want you to get in with the wrong crowd. Well, I am the wrong crowd, that's true. But if I am, then so are you. So the worst has already happened, and as long as you're here, you might as well relax and enjoy it."

If you wrote down the things Hardie said and looked at them afterward, you'd find the errors, but just listening to him talk, you'd be convinced of anything.

"See, what the old boys all think is craziness is just another way of stayin' sane—you live in this town long enough you're in danger of woodworm in the headboard, and you have to keep reminding yourself that the whole world isn't just one big Milburn." He looked over at Peter, sipped his beer and grinned, and Peter saw the fractured light in his eyes and knew, as he had all along, that underneath the "stayin' sane" kind of craziness there was another, real craziness. "Now admit it, Pete." He said, "Aren't there times when you'd like to see the whole damn town go up in flames? The whole thing knocked down and plowed over? It's a ghost town, man. The whole place is full of Rip Van Winkles, it's just one Rip Van Winkle after another, a bunch of weird Rip Van Winkles with vacuums for brains, with a knothead drunk for a sheriff and crummy bars for a social life—".

"What happened to Penny Draeger?" Peter interrupted. "You haven't gone out with her for three weeks."

Jim hunched over the bar and wrapped his hand around his beer-glass. *"One.* She heard I took that Mostyn dame out, so she got pissed off at me. *Two.* Her parents, old Rollie and Irmengard, heard that she went out a couple of times with the late F. Robinson. So they grounded her. She never told me about that, you know? Good thing she didn't. I would have grounded her, all right."

"Do you think she went out with him because you took that woman to Humphrey's?"

"How the hell do I know why she does things, man? Do you see a sequence there, my boy?"

"Don't you?" It was sometimes safer to give Jim's questions back to him.

"Hell." He bent all the way forward and lay his shaggy head on the wet wood of the bar. "All these women are mysteries to me." He was speaking softly, as if regretfully, but Peter saw his eyes gleaming between his lashes and knew it was an act. "Yeah. Well you might have a point. There might be a sequence there after all, Clarabelle. There just might be. And if there is, then that Anna dame besides not giving me any herself after teasing me along, also screwed up the sex life I had. In fact, if you look at it that way, you could definitely say that she owes me a few." He rolled his head a quarter turn up on the bar, and his eyes gleamed at Peter. "Which had occurred to me, to tell you the truth." He sat there, bent over, his head like a separate object on the bar, grinning maniacally up at Peter. "Yes, it had, old pal."

Peter swallowed.

Jim straightened up and knocked on the bar. "Two more flagons here, Sunshine."

"What do you want to do?" Peter asked, knowing that he would inevitably be carried along with it, and looked through the tavern's greasy windows at a pane of darkness flecked with white.

"Let's see. What do I want to do?" Jim mused, and Peter realized sickeningly that Jim had known all along what he wanted to do, and that inviting him out for a beer was only the first moment of the plan; he'd been steered into this conversation as surely as he'd been driven out into the country, and all of it, "another way of stayin' sane" and the ghost town business, was enumerated on a list somewhere in Hardie's mind. "What do I want to do?" He cocked his head. "Even this palace gets a little boring after a flagon or six, so I guess going back to dear little Milburn would be pleasant. Yes, I think we'll definitely be going back to dear little Milburn."

"Let's stay away from her," Peter said.

Jim ignored this. "You know, our dear lovely sexy friend moved out of the hotel two weeks ago. Oh, she is missed. She is *missed*, Pete. I miss seeing that great ass going up the stairs. I miss those eyes flashing in the corridors. I miss her empty suitcase. I miss her amazing body. And I'm sure you know where she went."

"My father arranged the mortgage. *His* house." Peter nodded more vigorously than he needed to, and realized he was getting drunk again.

"Your old man's a useful old gnome, isn't he?" Jim asked, smiling pleasantly. "Innkeeper!" He banged on the bar. "Give my friend and myself a couple of shots of your best bourbon." The bartender resentfully poured out shots of the same brand that Jim had stolen. "Now, back to the point. Our friend who is so sincerely missed moves out of our excellent hotel and into Robinson's house. Now isn't that a curious sort of coincidence? I suppose that you and I, Clarabelle, are the only two people in the world who know that it is a coincidence. Because we're the only people who knew she was out at the station when old Freddy passed."

"His heart," Peter muttered.

"Oh, she does get you in the heart. She gets you by the heart and the balls. But funny though, isn't it? Freddy falls down onto the tracks—did I say falls? No: *floats*. I saw it, remember. He floats down onto the tracks like he's made out of tissue paper. Then she gets all hot to own his house. Is that also one, old buddy? Do you see a sequence there too, Clarabelle?"

"No," he whispered.

"Now, Pete, that's not how you got early admission to Cornhole U. Use those powerful brain cells, baby." He put his hand on Peter's back and leaned toward him, breathing the clear odor of alcohol into Peter's face. "Our sexy friend wants something in that house. Just think of her in there. Man, I'm curious, aren't you? That sexy lady moving around in Freddy's old house— what's she looking for? Money? Jewelry? Dope? Well, who knows? But she's looking for something. Moving that sexy frame of hers around those rooms, checking everything out . . . that'd be a sight to see, wouldn't it?"

"I can't," Peter said. The bourbon moved in his guts like oil.

"I think," said Jim, "that we will begin to move toward our transportation."

Peter found himself standing outside in the cold by Jim's car: he could not remember why he was alone. He stamped his feet, rotated his head on his shoulders; said, "Hey, Jim."

Hardie emerged a moment later, grinning like a shark. "Sorry to keep you waiting. Just had to tell our friend in there how much I enjoyed his company. He didn't seem to believe me, so I had to repeat my message several times. He demonstrated what you could call a lack of interest. Fortunately, I managed also to take care of our liquid requirements for the remainder of this pleasant evening." He partially unzipped his jacket and let the neck of a bottle protrude.

"You're a madman."

"I'm crazy like a fox, you mean." Jim opened the car and leaned across the seat to unlock Peter's door. "Now to return to the subject of our previous discussion."

"You really ought to go to college," Peter said as

Jim started the car. "With your talent for bull, you'd be Phi Beta Kappa."

"Well, I used to think I'd be a pretty good lawyer," Jim said surprisingly. "Here, have a jolt." He passed Peter the bottle. "What's a good lawyer besides a superior bullshitter? Look at that old Sears James, man. If I ever saw a guy who looks like he could shit you from here to Key West . . ."

Peter remembered his last sight of Sears James, seated massively in a car, his face pale behind the bleary window. Then he remembered the face of the boy sitting on the headstone in front of St. Michael's. "Let's stay away from that woman," he said.

"Now that's just the point I want to discuss." He gave Peter a bright look. "Didn't we reach the point where this mysterious lady is wandering around the house looking for something? As I recall, Clarabelle, I invited you to picture that."

Peter nodded miserably.

"And give me back that bottle if you're not going to do anything with it. Now. There's something in that house, isn't there? Aren't you a little curious about what it is? There's something going on, anyhow, and you and me, old buddy, are the only people who know about it. Am I right so far?"

"You might be."

"CHRIST!" Hardie yelled, making Peter jump. "You dumb SHIT! What else can I be? There's some reason she wanted that house—that's the only thing that makes sense. There's something in there she wants."

"You think she got rid of Robinson?"

"I don't know about that. I didn't see anything but him sort of floating down onto the tracks. What the hell? But I can tell you one thing, I want to get a look at that house."

"Oh no," Peter moaned.

"There's nothing to be afraid of," Jim protested. "She's just a broad, after all. She's got strange habits, but she's just a woman, Clarabelle. And for shit's sake, I'm not really stupid enough to go in there when she's there.

And if you're too chicken-shit to go in with me, you can walk from here."

Down, down the dark country road; down the dark road to Milburn.

"How will you know if she's out? She sits in the dark every night, you said."

"You ring the bell, dummy."

On the crest of the last low hill before the turnoff, Peter, already sick with worry, looked down the highway and saw the lights of Milburn—gathered in a little depression in the land, they looked as though one hand could gather them up. It looked arbitrary, Milburn, like a nomad city of tents, and though Peter Barnes had known it all his life—though it was, in effect, all he *had* known—it looked unfamiliar.

Then he saw why. "Jim. Look. All the lights on the west side of town are out."

"Snow pulled down the wires."

"But it's not snowing."

"It snowed when we were in the bar."

"Did you really see a little kid sitting on top of the station that night?"

"Nah. Just thought I did. It must have been snow, or some newspaper or something—shit, Clarabelle, can a kid get up there? You know he can't. Let's be straight, Clarabelle, it was a little spooky out there that night."

They continued on to Milburn through the growing dark.

7

There, in town, Don Wanderley sat at his desk on the west side of the Archer Hotel, and saw darkness suddenly spread over the street below his window while his desk lamp still burned;

and Ricky Hawthorne gasped as dark surged through his living room, and Stella said to get the candles, it

was only that spot on the highway where the lines always blew down at least twice every winter;

and Milly Sheehan, going for her own candles, heard
a slow knocking at the front door which she would
never, ever, not in a thousand years, answer;

· and Sears James, locked in his suddenly dark library,
heard a rattle of happy footsteps on his stairs and told
himself he was dozing;

and Clark Mulligan, who had been showing two
weeks of science fiction and horror pictures and had a
head full of lurid images—*you can show it, man, but
nobody makes you watch it*—walked out of the Rialto
for the fresh air in the middle of a reel and thought he
saw in the sudden blackout a man who was a wolf lope
across the street, on a fierce errand, in an evil hurry
to get somewhere *(nobody makes you watch the stuff,
man)*.

Housebreaking, Part Two

8

Jim stopped the car half a block away from the house.
"If only the goddamned lights didn't go off." They
were both looking at the building's blank façade, the
curtainless windows behind which no figure moved, no
candle shone.

Peter Barnes thought of what Jim Hardie had seen,
Freddy Robinson's body floating down onto the overgrown railway tracks, and of the-little-boy-who-wasn't-
there but perched on the tops of stations and headstones.
And then he thought: *I was right the last time. Fear
sobers you up.* When he looked at Jim, he saw him tense
with excitement.

"I thought she never turned them on anyhow."

"Man, I still wish they didn't go off," Jim said, and
shivered, his face a grinning mask. "In a place like
this"—gesturing out at the respectable neighborhood of

three-story houses—"you know, in a Rotarian pig heaven like this, our lady friend might sort of want to blend in. She might keep her lights on just so nobody thinks there's nothing funny about her." He tilted his head. "Like, you know, that old house on Haven Lane where that writer guy lived—Wanderley? You ever go past there at night? All these houses around are all lit up and there's old Wanderley's place as dark as a tomb, man. Gives you the frights."

"*This* gives me the frights," Peter admitted. "Besides that, it's illegal."

"You really *are* the pits, you know that?" Hardie turned on his seat and stared at Peter, who saw his barely controlled urge to get *moving*, to *do*, to flail out again at whatever obstacle the world had put in his way. "Do you get the feeling that our lady friend worries about what's legal and what isn't? Do you think she got that house because she was worried about the damned law—about Walt Hardesty, for Chrissake?" Hardie shook his head, either disgusted or pretending to be disgusted. Peter suspected that he was working himself up for an action even he thought might be reckless.

Jim turned away from him and started the car moving; Peter hoped for a moment that Hardie was going to circle around the block and go back to the hotel, but his friend kept the car in first gear and merely crept up the block until they were directly in front of the house.

"You're either with me or you're a jerk, you jerk," he said.

"What are you going to do?"

"First off, take a look in a downstairs window. Do you have balls enough for that, Clarabelle?"

"You won't be able to see anything."

"Jesus," Hardie said, and got out of the car.

Peter hesitated only a second. Then he too got out and followed Hardie up across the snowy lawn and around the side of the building. Both boys moved quickly, hunching over to avoid being seen by the neighbors.

In a moment they were sitting on their haunches in drifted snow beneath one of the side windows. "Well, at least you have guts enough to look in a window, Clarabelle."

"Don't call me that," Peter whispered. "I'm sick of that."

"Great time you picked to tell me." Hardie grinned at him, then lifted his head to peer over the sill. "Hey, look at this."

Peter slowly raised his head above the sill. He was looking into a small side room just visible in the moonlight falling in over their shoulders. The room had neither furniture nor carpet.

"Weird lady," Hardy said, and Peter heard laughter hidden in his voice. "Let's go around the back." He scuttled away, still hunching over. Peter followed.

"I'll tell you what, I don't think she's here," Hardie said when Peter reached the back of the building. He was standing up and leaning against the wall between a small window and the back door. "I just get the feeling this house is empty." Here in the back where no one could see them, both boys felt more comfortable.

The long back yard ended in a white hillock of snow which was a buried hedge; a plaster birdbath, the basin covered with snow like frosting on a cake, sat between them and the hedge. Even by moonlight this was a reassuringly commonplace object. You couldn't be frightened with a birdbath looking at you, Peter thought, and managed a smile.

"Don't you believe me?" Hardie challenged.

"It's not that." Both were speaking in their normal voices.

"Okay, you look in there first."

"Okay." Peter turned and stepped boldly in front of the small window. He saw a sink gleaming palely, a hardwood floor, a stove Mrs. Robinson must have left behind. A single water glass, left on the breakfast bar, caught an edge of moonlight. If the birdbath had looked homely, this looked forlorn—one glass gathering dust on the counter—and Peter at once began to agree with Jim that the house was empty. "Nothing," he said.

Hardie nodded beside him. Then he jumped up to the small concrete step before the back door. "Man, if you hear anything, run like hell." He pushed the bell.

The sound of the doorbell trilled through the house.

Both boys braced themselves; held their breath. But no steps came, no voices called.

"Hey?" Jim said, smiling seraphically at Peter. "How about that?"

"We're doing this all wrong," Peter said. "What we ought to do is walk around in front and act like we just came. If anybody sees us, we'll just be two guys looking for her. If she doesn't answer the front doorbell, we'll do what people always do and look in the front windows. If someone sees us crawling around like we did before, they'll call the cops."

"Not bad," Jim said after a moment. "Okay, we'll try it. But if nobody answers, I'm coming around back here and going in. That was the point, remember?"

Peter nodded; he remembered.

As if he too were relieved at having found a way to stop skulking, Jim walked freely and naturally to the front of the house. Peter coming more slowly behind him, Jim went across the lawn to the front door. "Okay, sport," he said.

Peter stood beside him and thought: *I can't go in there*. Empty, but filled with bare rooms and the atmosphere of whatever kind of person chose to live in them, the house seemed to be feigning stillness.

Jim rang the front bell. "We're wasting time," he said, and betrayed his own unease.

"Just wait. Just act normal."

Jim stuck his hands in the pockets of his jacket and fidgeted on the doorstep. "Long enough?"

"A few more seconds."

Jim exhaled a billowing cloud of steam. "Okay. A few more seconds. One—two—three. Now what?"

"Ring it again. Just like you would if you thought she was at home."

Jim stabbed the bell a second time: the trilling flared and died inside the house.

Peter looked up and down the block of houses across the street. No cars. No lights. The dim glow of a candle shone in a window four houses away, but no curious faces looked out at the two boys standing on the steps of the new neighbor's house. Old Dr. Jaffrey's house directly across the street looked mournful.

From nowhere at all, utterly inexplicably, distant music floated in the air. A buzzing trombone, an insinuating saxophone: jazz, played a long way off.

"Huh?" Jim Hardie lifted his head and turned from the door. "Sounds like—what?"

Peter had an image of flatbed trucks, black musicians playing freely into the night. "Sounds like a carnival."

"Sure. We get a lot of those in Milburn. In November."

"Must be a record."

"Somebody's got his window open."

"Has to be."

And yet—as if the idea of carnival musicians suddenly appearing to play in Milburn was frightening—neither boy wanted to admit that these lilting sounds were too true to come from a record.

"Now we look in the window," Jim said. "Finally."

He jumped off the steps and went to the large front window. Peter stayed on the porch, softly clapping his hands together, listening to the fading music: the flatbed was going into the center of town, toward the square, he thought. But what sense did that make? The sound died away.

"You'll never guess what I'm looking at," Jim said.

Startled, Peter looked at his friend. Jim's face was determinedly bland. "An empty room."

"Not quite."

He knew that Jim would not tell him: he would have to look for himself. Peter jumped off the step and walked up to the window.

At first he saw what he had expected: a bare room where the carpet had been taken up and invisible dust lay everywhere. On the other side, the black arch of a doorway; on his side, the reflection of his own face, looking out from the glass.

He felt for a second the terror of being trapped in there like his reflection, of being forced to go through that doorway, to walk the bare floorboards: the terror made no more sense than the band music, but like it, it was there.

Then he saw what Jim had meant. On one side, up against the baseboards, a brown suitcase lay on the floor.

"That's hers!" Jim said in his ear. "You know what that means?"

"She still there. She's in there."

"No. Whatever she wanted is still in there."

Peter backed away from the window and looked at Jim's set, red face. "That's enough screwing around," Jim said. "I'm going inside. You coming—Clarabelle?"

Peter could not answer; Jim simply stepped around him and set off around the side of the house.

Seconds later he heard the pop and tinkle of breaking glass. He groaned; turned around and saw his features reproduced in the window; they were pulled by fear and indecision.

Get out. No. You have to help him. Get out. No, you have to—

He went around the side of the house as quickly as he could without running.

Jim was up on the back steps, reaching in through the little pane of glass he had broken. In the dim light, bent over, he was the image of a burglar: Jim's words came back to him. *So the worst has already happened, and you might as well relax and enjoy it.*

"Oh, it's you," Jim said. "Thought you'd be home under the bed by now."

"What happens if she comes home?"

"We run out the back, idiot. Two doors in this house, remember? Or don't you think you can run as fast as a woman?" His face stilled with concentration for a moment; then the lock clicked open. "Coming?"

"Maybe. But I'm not going to steal anything. And you aren't either."

Jim snorted derisively and went through the door.

Peter went up the steps and peered in. Hardie was moving across the kitchen floor, going deeper into the house, not bothering to look back.

Might as well relax and enjoy it. He stepped over the doorframe. Ahead of him, Hardie was thumping around in the hallway, opening doors and cabinets.

"Quiet," Peter hissed.

"Quiet yourself," Jim called back, but the noises immediately ceased, and Peter understood that whether or not he admitted it, Jim also was afraid.

"Where do you want to look?" Peter asked. "What are we looking for, anyway?"

"How should I know? We'll know when we see it."

"It's too dark in here to see anything. You could see better from the outside."

Jim pulled his matches out of his jacket and lit one. "How is that?" In truth, it was worse: where they previously had a dim vision of the entire hallway, now they could see only within a small circle of light.

"Okay, but we stick together," Peter said.

"We could cover the house faster if we split up."

"No way."

Jim shrugged. "Whatever you want." He led Peter down the hall into the living room. This was even bleaker than they had been able to see from the outside. The walls, dotted here and there by children's crayons, also showed the pale rectangles where pictures had hung. Paint flaked off in chips and patches. Jim was going around the room, knocking on the walls, lighting one match after another.

"Look at the suitcase."

"Oh yeah, the suitcase."

Jim knelt down and opened the case. "Nothing." Peter watched over his shoulder as Jim turned the suitcase over, shook it, and replaced it on the bare floor.

He whispered, "We're not going to find anything."

"Christ, we look in two rooms and you're ready to give up." Jim stood up abruptly, and his match went out.

For a moment pure blackness enveloped them. "Light another one," Peter whispered.

"Better this way. No one outside can see a light. Your eyes'll adjust."

They stood in silence and darkness for five or six seconds, letting the image of flame fade from their eyes, become a pinpoint in sheer black; then waited longer seconds while the features of the house took shape around them.

Peter heard a noise from somewhere in the house and jumped.

"For God's sake, calm down."

"What was that?" Peter whispered, and heard the hysteria rising in his voice.

"A stair creaked. The back door clicked shut. Nothing."

Peter touched his forehead with his fingers and felt them trembling against his skin.

"Listen. We've been talking, pounding walls, we broke a window—don't you think she'd come out if she was here?"

"I guess so."

"Okay, let's try the next floor."

Jim grabbed the sleeve of his jacket and pulled him out of the living room back into the hall. Then he let go and led Peter down the hall to the foot of the stairs.

Up there it was dark—up there it was new territory. Peter felt more profoundly uneasy, looking at the stairs, then he had since entering the house.

"You go up and I'll stay here."

"You want to hang around in the dark by yourself?"

Peter tried to swallow, but could not. He shook his head.

"All right. It's got to be up there, whatever it is."

Jim put his foot on the second of the unpainted steps. Here too the carpet had been removed. He lifted himself up; looked back. "Coming?" Then he began to mount the stairs, taking them by twos. Peter watched: when Jim was halfway up, he willed himself to follow.

The lights snapped on again when Jim was at the top and Peter was two-thirds of the way up.

"Hello, boys," said a deep unruffled voice from the bottom of the stairs.

Jim Hardie shrieked.

Peter fell backward on the stairs and, half-paralyzed with fright, thought he'd slide right down into the grasp of the man looking up at them.

"Let me take you to your hostess," he said, giving them a dead smile. He was the strangest-looking man Peter had ever seen—a blue knit cap was shoved down over blond curly hair like Harpo Marx's, sunglasses rode on his nose; he wore overalls but no shirt, and his face was white as ivory. It was the man from the square. "She will be delighted to see you again," the man said. "As her first visitors, you can count on an especially warm welcome." The man's smile broadened as he began to come up the stairs after them.

When he had come up only a few of the steps he lifted a hand and pulled the blue cap off his head. The Harpo curls, a wig, came off with it.

When he took off the dark glasses his eyes shone a uniform golden yellow.

9

Standing at his window in the hotel and looking out over the darkened section of Milburn, Don heard the far off convolutions of saxophones and trombones blaring on the cold air and thought: *Dr. Rabbitfoot's come to town.*

His telephone rang behind him.

Sears was facing his library door, listening for footsteps padding on his stairs, when his telephone rang.

Ignoring it, he unlocked his door; opened it. The stair-case was empty.

He went to answer his phone.

Lewis Benedikt, whose mansion was on the furthest periphery of the area affected by the power failure, heard neither music nor childish footsteps. What he heard, blown on the wind or from inside his own mind or drifting on a draft through his dining room and wind-ing around a newel post on its way toward him, was the most despairing sound he knew: the languishing, nearly inaudible voice of his dead wife, calling over and over again, "Lewis. Lewis." He had been hearing it, on and off, for days. When his telephone rang he turned to it with relief.

And with relief too heard Ricky Hawthorne's voice: "I'm going batty sitting here in the dark. I've spoken to Sears and Edward's nephew and Sears graciously said that we can get together at this short notice at his house. I'd say we need to. Do you agree? We'll break a rule and just come as we are, shall we?"

Ricky thought that the young man was getting to look like a true member of the Chowder Society. Beneath the mask of sociability anyone would expect from a nephew of Edward's, he had the jim-jams. He leaned back in one of Sears's wonderful leather chairs, he sipped his whiskey and looked (with his uncle's reflex amuse-ment) around the cherished interior of the library (did it look as old-fashioned to him as Edward had said it was?), he spoke at intervals, but there was an under-current of tension in all of it.

Maybe that makes him one of us, Ricky thought: and he saw that Don was the sort of person they would have befriended, years and years back; if he had been born forty years earlier, he would have been one of them as if by birthright.

Still, there was a streak of secrecy in him. Ricky could not imagine what he had meant by asking if any of them had heard music during the early evening.

Pressed about this, he had evaded explanations; pressed further, he had said, "I was just getting the feeling that everything happening has a direct relationship to my writing."

This remark, which would have seemed egotistical at any other time, was given density by the candlelight; each of the men stirred in his chair.

"Isn't that why we asked you here?" Sears said.

And then he had explained: Ricky listened puzzled to Don's account of his idea for a new book and the description of the Dr. Rabbitfoot character, and how he had heard the showman's music just before Ricky's call.

"Are you saying that events in this town are occurrences from an unwritten book?" Sears asked incredulously. "That's sheer poppycock."

"Unless," Ricky said, thinking, "unless . . . well, I'm not really sure how to put this. Unless things here in Milburn have focused lately—have come to a focus they did not have before."

"You mean that I'm the focus," Don said.

"I don't know."

"This is nonsense," Sears interjected. "Focused, unfocused—all that's happened is that we are managing to frighten ourselves even more. That's your focus. The daydreams of a novelist can't have anything to do with it."

Lewis sat apart from all this, wrapped in some private misery. Ricky asked him what he thought, and Lewis replied, "Sorry. I was thinking about something else. Can I get myself another drink, Sears?"

Sears nodded grimly; Lewis was drinking at twice his normal rate, as if his appearance at a meeting in an old shirt and a tweed jacket gave him license to break another of their old rules.

"What's supposed to indicate this mysterious focus?" Sears asked belligerently.

"You know as well as I do. John's death, first of all."

"Coincidence," Sears said.

"Elmer's sheep—all the animals that have died."

"Now you believe in Hardesty's Martians."

"Don't you remember what Hardesty told us? That it was sort of a *game*—an amusement some sort of creature gave itself. What I'm suggesting is that the stakes have been raised. Freddy Robinson. Poor old Rea Dedham. I felt, months ago, that our stories were bringing something about—and I fear, I very much fear, that more people are going to die. I'm saying that our lives and the lives of many people in this town may be endangered."

"Well, what I said stands. You have certainly managed to frighten yourself," Sears said.

"We're all frightened," Ricky pointed out. His cold made his voice raw and his throat throbbed, but he forced himself to go on. "We are. But what I think is that Don's arrival here was like the fitting of the last piece into a puzzle—that when all of us were joined by Don, the forces, whatever you want to call them, were increased. That we invoked them. We by our stories, Don in his book and in his imagination. We see things, but we don't believe them; we feel things—people watching us, sinister things following us—but we dismiss them as fantasies. We dream horrors, but try to forget them. And in the meantime, three people have died."

Lewis stared at the rug, then nervously spun an ashtray on the table before his chair. "I just remembered something I said to Freddy Robinson on the night he cornered me outside John's house. I said that someone was picking us off like flies."

"But why should this young man, whom none of us had seen until a short time ago, be the last element?" Sears asked.

"Because he was Edward's nephew?" Ricky asked. It came to him straight from the blue sky of inspiration; a moment later he felt a painful spasm of relief that his children were not coming to Milburn for Christmas. "Yes. Because he is Edward's nephew."

All three of the older men almost palpably felt the

gravity of what Ricky had called "the forces" about them. Three frightened men, they sat in the molten light of the candles and looked back into their past.

"Maybe," Lewis at last said. He drained his whiskey. "But I don't understand about Freddy Robinson. He wanted to meet with me—he called me twice. I just put him off. Made a vague promise to see him in a bar sometime."

Sears asked, "He had something to tell you before he died?"

"I didn't give him the chance to tell it. I thought he wanted to sell me insurance."

"Why did you think that?"

"Because he said something about trouble coming your way."

They were silent again. "Maybe," Lewis said, "if I met him, he'd still be alive."

Ricky said, "Lewis, that sounded just like John Jaffrey. He blamed himself for Edward's death."

For a moment all three men glanced at Don Wanderley.

"Maybe I'm not here just because of my uncle," Don said. "I want to buy my way into the Chowder Society."

"What?" Sears exploded. *"Buy?"*

"With a story. Isn't that the admission fee?" He smiled tentatively around the circle. "It's very clear in my mind because I just spent some time writing it all in a journal. And," he said, breaking another of their rules, "this isn't fiction. This happened just in the way I'll tell it—you couldn't use it as fiction because it didn't have a real ending. It just slipped backward when other things happened. But if Mr. Hawthorne" ("Ricky," the lawyer breathed) "is right, then five people, not four, have died. And my brother was the first of them."

"You were both engaged to the same girl," Ricky said, remembering one of the last things Edward had said to him.

"We were both engaged to Alma Mobley, a girl I met at Berkeley," Don began, and the four of them

settled into their chairs. "I think this is a ghost story,"
he said, pulling, in Dr. Rabbitfoot's image, the dollar
from his jeans.

He held them with the story, speaking into the flame
of the candles as if into an unquiet place in his mind;
he did not tell it as he had in his journal, deliberately
invoking all the detail he could remember, but he told
most of it. The story took him half an hour.

"So the *Who's Who* entry proved that everything she
had said was false," Don concluded. "David was dead,
and I never saw her again. She had simply disappeared."
He wiped his face; exhaled loudly. "That's it. Is it a
ghost story or not? You tell me."

None of the men spoke for a moment. *Tell him,
Sears,* Ricky silently prayed. He looked over at his old
friend, who had steepled his fingers before his face.
Say it, Sears. Tell him.

Sears eyes met his. *He knows what I'm thinking.*

"Well," Sears said, and Ricky closed his eyes. "As
much as any of our stories is, I guess. Is that the series
of events on which you based your book?"

"Yes."

"They make a better story than the book," Sears said.

"But they don't have an ending."

"Not yet, perhaps," Sears said. He scowled at the
candles, which had burned down into the silver holders.
Now, Ricky prayed, his eyes still closed. "This young
man you imagined to look like a werewolf was named—
ah, Greg? Greg Benton?" Ricky opened his eyes again,
and if anyone had been looking at him they would
have seen gratitude written on his every feature.

Don nodded, clearly not understanding why this was
important.

"I knew him under a different name," Sears said.
"A long time ago, he was called Gregory Bate. And
his half-witted brother was called Fenny. I was present
when Fenny died." He smiled with the bitterness of a
man compelled to eat a meal he hates. "That would

have been quite some time before your—Benton—
decided to affect a shaven head."

"If he can make two appearances, then he can make
three," Ricky said. "I saw him on the square not two
weeks ago."

The lights, violently bright after so long a time of
candlelight, came suddenly on. The four men in Sears's
library, their distinction and whatever of ease the
candlelight had given them erased by the harsher light,
looked fearful: *we look half-dead already,* Ricky
thought. It was as though the candles had drawn them
into a warm circle, the warmth of a candle and a group
and a story; now they were blown apart, scattered on a
wintry plain.

"Looks like he heard you," Lewis, drunk, said. "Maybe that's what Freddy Robinson saw. Maybe he saw
Gregory turning into a wolf. Hah!"

Housebreaking, Part Three

10

Peter picked himself up on the stairs and, with no
awareness of willing himself to move, went backward up
the stairs to stand beside Jim on the landing.

The werewolf came slowly, unstoppably toward them,
in no hurry at all. "You want to meet her, don't you?"
His grin was ferocious. "She will be so pleased. You
will have quite a welcome, I promise you."

Peter looked wildly around; saw phosphorescent light
leaking from beneath a door.

"She is not perhaps quite in shape to see you yet, but
that makes it all the more interesting, don't you think?
We all like to see our friends with their masks off."

He's talking to keep us still, Peter thought. *It's like
hypnotism.*

"Aren't you the two boys interested in scientific exploration? In telescopes? How nice it is to meet two fine young fellows with inquiring minds, two fellows who want to extend their knowledge. So many young people merely coast along, don't they, so many are afraid to take risks. Well, we certainly can't say that about you now, can we?"

Peter glanced at Jim Hardie's face: Jim's mouth hung open.

"No, you have been extremely brave. Now I will be with you in a moment, and I want you to relax and wait for me . . . just relax and wait."

Peter slammed the back of his hand into Jim's ribs, but Jim did not move. He glanced back at the terrible figure coming toward him, and made the mistake of looking directly into the blank golden eyes. Immediately he heard a voice like music coming not from the man but speaking directly inside his head: *Relax, Peter, relax, you will meet her . . .*

"Jim!" he screamed.

Hardie gave a convulsive shudder, and Peter knew that he was lost already.

Settle down, boy, no need for all that noise . . .

The golden-eyed man was nearly to them, reaching out his left hand. Peter stepped backward, too frightened for coherent thought.

The man's white hand glided nearer and nearer Jim's own left hand.

Peter turned his back and pounded halfway up the next flight of stairs. When he looked around the light beneath the door on the landing was spilling out with such intensity that the walls were tinted faintly green: green too was Jim, in that light.

"Just take my hand," the man said. He was two steps below Jim, and their hands nearly touched.

Jim brushed his fingers against the palm of the man's hand.

Peter looked up the stairs, but could not leave Jim.

The man beneath was chuckling. Peter's heart froze,

and he looked down again. The man was grasping Jim's
wrist with his left hand. The wolfish eyes glowed wide.

Jim screeched.

The man holding him moved his hands to Jim's
throat and twisted his body with immense force, slamming the boy's head against the wall. He planted his
feet on the boards of the landing and again smashed
Jim's head into the wall.

Your turn.

Jim fell onto the boards and the man kicked him
aside as if he were as weightless as a paper bag. A bright
smear of blood like a child's finger-painting lay on the
wall.

Peter ran down a long corridor lined with doors;
opened one at random and slipped in.

Just inside the door, he froze. The outline of a man's
head showed against a window. "Welcome home," the
man's toneless voice said. "Have you met her yet?" He
stood up from the bed. "You haven't? Once you do,
you'll never forget it. An incredible woman."

The man, still only a black outline against a window,
began to shuffle toward Peter, who remained stock-still
just inside the door. As the man drew nearer, he saw
that it was Freddy Robinson.

"Welcome home," Robinson said.

Found you.

Footsteps in the corridor paused outside the bedroom
door. *Time. Time. Time. Time.*

"You know, I don't exactly remember—"

Panicked, Peter rushed at Robinson with his arms
extended, intending to shove him out of the way: the
moment his fingers touched his shirt, Robinson broke
up into a shapeless pattern of glowing points of light;
his fingers tingled. It was gone utterly in an instant, and
Peter rushed through the air where it had been.

"Come out, Peter," said the voice outside the door.
"We all want you to come out"; and the other voice in
his mind repeated *Time.*

Standing in front of the bed, Peter heard the doorknob moving. He scrambled onto the bed and banged

the heels of his hands against the top of the window frames.

The window slid up as if on grease. Cold air streamed over him. He felt the other mind reaching for him, telling him to come to the door, not to be silly, didn't he want to see that Jim was all right?

Jim!

He crawled out of the window as the door opened. Something rushed toward him, but he was already across the upper roof and jumping down onto the next level. From there he let himself drop onto the roof of the garage; and from the garage he jumped onto a snowdrift.

As he ran past Jim's car he looked sideways at the house; but it was as solidly ordinary as it had looked at first: only the lights in the stairwell and front hall burned, casting an inviting rectangle of yellow onto the walk. That too seemed to speak to Peter Barnes, to say *imagine the peace of lying down with your hands crossed on your chest, imagine sleeping under ice . . .*

He ran all the way home.

11

"Lewis, you're already drunk," Sears said gruffly. "Don't make more of an ass of yourself."

"Sears," Lewis said, "it's a funny thing, but it's hard not to make an ass of yourself when you talk about stuff like this."

"That's a point. But for God's sake, stop drinking."

"You know, Sears," Lewis said. "I get the feeling our little decorums aren't going to be much good anymore."

Ricky asked him, "Do you want to stop meeting?"

"Well, what the hell are we? The Three Musketeers?"

"In a way. We're what's left. Plus Don, of course."

"Oh, Ricky." Lewis smiled. "The sweetest thing about you is that you're so damned loyal."

"Only to the things worth being loyal to," Ricky said,

and sneezed loudly twice. "Excuse me. I ought to be home. Do you really want to give up the meetings?"

Lewis shoved his glass toward the middle of the table and slumped down in his chair. "I don't know. I suppose not. I'd never get any of Sears's good cigars if we didn't meet twice a month. And now that we have a new member, well . . ." Just as Sears was about to burst out, Lewis looked up at them and was as handsome as he'd ever been in his life. "And maybe I'd be scared not to meet. Maybe I believe everything you said, Ricky. I've had a couple of funny experiences since October—since the night Sears talked about Gregory Bate."

"So have I," Sears said.

"So have I," echoed Ricky. "Isn't that what we've been saying?"

"So I guess we should tough it out," Lewis said. "You guys are in another league intellectually from me, maybe this kid here is too, but I guess it's a hang together or hang separately kind of situation. Sometimes, out at my place, I get really spooked—like something is out there just counting the seconds until it can nail me. Like it nailed John."

"Do we believe in werewolves?" Ricky asked.

"No," Sears said, and Lewis shook his head.

"I don't either," said Don. "But there's something . . ." He paused, thinking, and looked up to see all three of the older men looking expectantly at him. "I don't have it worked out yet. It's just an idea. I'll think about it some more before I try to explain it."

"Well, the lights have been on for some time now," Sears said pointedly. "And we had a good story. Perhaps we've made some progress, but I don't see how. If the Bate brothers are in Milburn, I'd like to assume that they'll do as the ineffable Hardesty suggests, and move on when they're tired of us."

Don read the expression in Ricky's eyes and nodded.

"Wait," Ricky said. "Excuse me, Sears, but I sent Don out to see Nettie Dedham at the hospital."

"Oh, yes?" Sears was already magisterially bored.

"I went, yes," Don said. "I met the sheriff and Mr. Rowles there. We all had the same idea."

"To see if she'd say anything," Ricky said.

"She couldn't. She isn't able to." Don looked at Ricky. "You must have called the hospital."

"I did," Ricky said.

"But when the sheriff asked her if she had seen anyone on the day her sister died, she tried to say a name. It was obvious that that's what she was doing."

"And the name?" Sears demanded.

"What she said was just a garble of consonants—like Glngr. Glngr. She said it two or three times. Hardesty gave up—couldn't make any sense out of it."

"I don't suppose anyone could," Lewis said, glancing at Sears.

"Mr. Rowles took me aside out in the parking lot and said that he thought she was trying to say her brother's name. Stringer? Isn't that right?"

"Stringer?" Ricky said. He covered his eyes with the palm of a hand.

"I'm missing something," Don said. "Would somebody explain to me why that's so important?"

"I knew this was going to happen," Lewis said. "I knew it."

"Get a hold of yourself, Lewis," Sears ordered. "Don, we will have to discuss this among ourselves first. But I think that we owe you a story to match the one you told us. You will not hear it tonight, but after we've discussed it, I imagine that you will get the ultimate Chowder Society story."

"Then I want to ask another favor," Don said. "If you decide to tell it to me, could we have it at my uncle's house?"

He saw the reluctance pass through the three men; they looked suddenly older—even Lewis seemed frail.

"That may not be a bad idea," Ricky Hawthorne said. He looked like one vast cold wrapped in mustache and spotted bow tie. "A house of your uncle's was where it started for us." He managed to smile at Don.

"Yes. I think you'll hear the ultimate Chowder Society story."

"And may the Lord protect us until then," Lewis said.

"May He protect us afterward," Sears added.

12

Peter Barnes entered his parents' bedroom and sat on the bed, watching his mother brush her hair. She was in her distant, abstracted mood: for months now, she had alternated between this glacial coldness—cooking TV dinners and taking long walks by herself—and an intrusive maternalism. In that mood she gave him new sweaters, cooed over him at dinner and pestered him about his homework. In her maternal periods he often sensed that she was almost on the verge of crying: the weight of unshed tears hung in her voice and charged her gestures.

"What's for dinner tonight, mom?"

She tilted her head and looked at his reflection in the mirror for approximately a second. "Hot dogs and sauerkraut."

"Oh." Hot dogs were fine with Peter, but his father detested them.

"Is that what you wanted to ask, Peter?" She did not look at him this time, but kept her eyes on the reflection of her hand pulling the brush through her hair.

Peter had always been conscious that his mother was an exceptionally attractive woman—maybe not a fabulous beauty like Stella Hawthorne, but more than merely pretty all the same. She had a high, youthful blond attractiveness; she had always had an unencumbered look, like a sailboat one sees far out in a bay, nipping into the breeze. Men desired her, he knew, though he did not wish to think about that; on the night of the party for the actress, he had seen Lewis Benedikt caress his mother's knees. Until then he had blindly (he now thought) imagined that adulthood and marriage meant release from the passionate confusions of youth. But his mother and Lewis Benedikt could have been Jim Hardie and Penny Draeger; they looked a more natural couple than she and his father. And not long after the party he had felt his parents' marriage begin to unravel.

"No, not really," he said. "I like to watch you brushing your hair."

Christina Barnes froze, her hand lifted to the crown of her head; then brought it down in a smooth heavy stroke. She found his eyes again, then looked quickly, almost guiltily away.

"Who's going to come to your party tomorrow night?" he asked.

"Oh, just the usual people. Your father's friends. Ed and Sonny Venuti. A few other people. Ricky Hawthorne and his wife. Sears James."

"Will Mr. Benedikt be here?"

This time she deliberately met his eyes. "I don't know. Maybe. Why? Don't you like Lewis?"

"Sometimes I guess I do. I don't see him all that much."

"Nobody sees him all that much, darling," she said, lifting his mood a little. "Lewis is a recluse, unless you're a twenty-five-year-old girl."

"Wasn't he married once?"

She looked at him again, this time more sharply. "What's the point of all this, Peter? I'm trying to brush my hair."

"I know. I'm sorry." Peter nervously smoothed the counterpane with his hand.

"Well?"

"I guess I was just wondering if you were happy."

She laid down the brush on her dressing table, making its ivory back click against the wood. "Happy? Of course I am, sweetie. Now go downstairs and tell your father to get ready for dinner."

Peter left the bedroom and went downstairs to the small side room where his father was undoubtedly watching television. That was another sign that things

were going wrong: Peter could not remember his
father ever choosing to watch television at night before,
but for months he had taken his briefcase into the television room, saying that he wanted to work on a few
papers; minutes later the theme music of "Starsky and
Hutch" or "Charlie's Angels" would come faintly
through the closed door.

He peeked into the room, saw the Eames chair pulled
up in front of the flickering screen—"The Brady
Bunch"—the salted nuts on the bowl on the table, a
pack of cigarettes and lighter beside them, but his
father was not there. His briefcase, unopened, lay on
the floor beside the Eames chair.

Out of the television room, then, with its images of
lonely comfort, and down the hall to the kitchen. When
Peter walked in, Walter Barnes, dressed in a brown suit
and worn brown wingtip shoes, was just dropping two
olives into a martini. "Peter, old scout," he said.

"Hi, dad. Mom says dinner's going to be ready soon."

"I wonder what that means. An hour—an hour and
a half? What did she make anyhow, do you know?"

"It's going to be hot dogs."

"Whoof. Ugh. Christ. I guess I'll need a few of these,
hey, Pete?" He raised his glass, smiled at Peter, and
sipped.

"Oh, dad . . ."

"Yes?"

Peter stepped sideways, shoved his hands in his
pockets, suddenly inarticulate. "Are you looking forward to your party?"

"Sure," his father said. "It'll be a good time, Pete,
you'll see. Everything's going to work out fine."

Walter Barnes began to walk out of the kitchen
toward the television room, but some instinct made him
look back at his son, who was spinning from side to
side, hands still in his pockets, his face snagged with
emotion. "Hey there, scout. Having trouble at school?"

"No," Peter said, shifting miserably: side to side, side
to side.

"Come on with me."

They went down the hall, Peter hanging back. At the door to the television room, his father said, "Your friend Jim Hardie still hasn't come back, I hear."

"No." Peter started to sweat.

His father placed the martini on a mat and put himself heavily into the Eames chair. They both glanced at the screen. Most of the Brady children and their father were crawling around the furniture of their living room—a living room much like the Barnes's own—looking for a lost pet, a turtle or a kitten (or perhaps, since those Brady kids were cute little rascals, a rodent).

"His mother's worried sick," his father said, and popped a handful of macadamia nuts into his mouth. When those had gone down his throat, he said, "Eleanor's a nice woman. But she never understood that boy. You have any idea where he might have gone?"

"No," Peter said, looking to the rodent hunt as if for clues to the conduct of family life.

"Just took off in his car."

Peter nodded. He had walked over toward Montgomery Street on his way to school the day after his escape from the house and from halfway down the block had seen that the car was gone.

"Rollie Draeger's a bit relieved, is my guess," said his father. "Probably just good luck his daughter's not pregnant."

"Um hum."

"You wouldn't have any idea where Jim went?" His father glanced at him.

"No," Peter said, and risked a look in return.

"He didn't confide in you during one of your beer-drinking sessions?"

"No," Peter said unhappily.

"You must miss him," his father said. "Maybe you're even worried about him. Are you?"

"Yeah," Peter said, by now as close to tears as he sometimes thought his mother was.

"Well, don't be. A kid like that will always cause

more trouble than he'll ever be in himself. And I'll tell you something—I know where he is."

Peter looked up at his father.

"He's in New York. Sure he is. He's on the run for some reason or other. And I wonder if he might not have had something to do with what happened to old Rea Dedham after all. Looks funny that he ran out, don't you think?"

"He didn't," Peter said. "He just didn't. He couldn't."

"Still, you're better off with a couple of old farts like us than with him, don't you think?" When Peter did not give him the agreement he expected, Walter Barnes reached out toward his son and touched his arm. "One thing you have to learn in this world, Pete. The trouble-makers might look glamorous as hell, but you're better off steering clear of them. You stay with people like our friends, like the ones you'll be talking to at our party, and you'll be on your way. This is a hard enough world to get through without asking for trouble." He released Peter's arm. "Say, why don't you pull up a chair and watch TV a little while with me? Let's spend a little time together."

Peter sat down and pretended to watch the television. From time to time he heard the grinding of the snow-plow, gradually working past their house and then continuing on in the direction of the square.

13

By the next day both atmospheres—internal and external—had changed. His mother was in neither of her moods, but moved happily through the house, vacuuming and dusting, talking on the telephone, listening to the radio. Peter, up in his room, listened to music interspersed with snow reports. The roads were so bad that school had been called off. His father had walked to the bank: from his bedroom window, Peter had seen his father setting off in hat, topcoat and rubber boots, looking small and Russian. Several other Russians, their neighbors, had joined him by the time he reached the end of the block. The snow reports repeated a monotonous theme: *break out the snowmobiles, kids, eight inches last night and more predicted for the weekend, accident on Route 17 has stalled traffic between Damascus and Windsor . . . accident on Route 79 has stopped traffic between Oughuoga and Center Village . . . overturned camper van on Route 11 four miles north of Castle Creek . . .* Omar Norris came by on the snowplow just before noon, burying two cars under an immense drift. After lunch his mother made him beat egg whites to a stiff froth. The day was a long bolt of gray cloth; endless.

Alone again in his room he looked up *Robinson, F,* in the directory and dialed the number, his heart trying to bump the roof of his mouth. After two rings, someone picked up the receiver and immediately replaced it.

The radio brought disasters. A fifty-two-year-old man in Lester died of a heart attack while shoveling out his driveway; two children were killed when their mother's car struck a bridge abutment near Hillcrest. An old man in Stamford died of hypothermia—no money for the heating.

At six the snowplow again rattled past the house. By then Peter was in the television room, waiting for the news. His mother looked in, a blond head in a swirl of cooking orders: "Remember to change for dinner, Pete. Why don't you go all out and wear a tie?"

"Is anybody coming in this weather?" He pointed to the screen—a blur of falling snow, blocked traffic. Men with a stretcher carried the body of the hypothermia victim, seventy-six-year-old Elmore Vesey, out of a rotting snowbound shack.

"Sure. They don't live far away." Inexplicably happy, she sailed off.

His father came home gray-faced half an hour later, looked in and said, "Hiya, Pete. Okay?" and went upstairs to roll into a hot tub.

At seven his father joined him in the television room, martini in hand, cashews in the bowl. "Your mother says she'd like to see you in a tie. Since she's in a good mood, why not oblige her this once?"

"Okay," he said.

"Still no word from Jim Hardie?"

"No."

"Eleanor must be losing her mind with worry."

"I guess."

He went back up to his room and lay on his bed. Being in attendance at a party, answering all the familiar questions ("Looking forward to Cornell?"), walking around with a tray and pitchers of drinks, were what he felt least in the world like doing. He felt most like curling up in a blanket and staying in bed for as long as they'd let him. Then nothing could happen to him. The snow would build up around the house, the thermostats would click on and off, he would fall into great arcs of sleep . . .

At seven-thirty the bell rang, and he got up from bed. He heard his father opening the door, voices, drinks being offered: the arrivals were the Hawthornes and another man whose voice he did not recognize. Peter slid his shirt up over his head and replaced it with a clean one. Then he pulled a tie under the collar, knotted it, combed his hair with his fingers and left the bedroom.

When he reached the landing and was able to see the door, his father was hanging up coats in the guest closet. The stranger was a tall man in his thirties— thick blond hair, squarish friendly face, tweed jacket and blue shirt without a tie. *No lawyer,* Peter thought.

"A *writer,*" his mother said at that instant, her voice way up out of its normal register. "How interesting," and Peter winced.

"Here's our boy Pete," his father said, and all three guests looked up at him, the Hawthornes with smiles, the stranger merely with an appraising glance of interest. He shook their hands and wondered, taking Stella Hawthorne's hand, as he always did seeing her, how a woman that old managed to be as good-looking as anyone you saw in the movies. "Nice to see you, Peter,"

Ricky Hawthorne said, and gave him a brisk dry hand-shake. "You look a little beat."

"I'm okay," he said.

"And this is Don Wanderley, he's a writer, and he was the nephew of Mr. Wanderley," his mother said. The writer's handshake was firm and warm. "Oh, we must talk about your books. Peter, would you please go in the kitchen and get the ice ready?"

"You look sort of like your uncle," Peter said.

"Thank you."

"Pete, the *ice*."

Stella Hawthorne said, "On a night like this I think I want my drinks steamed, like clams."

His mother cut off his laugh—"Pete, the ice, please" —and then turned to Stella Hawthorne with a fast nervous grin. "No, the streets seem all right for the moment," he heard Ricky Hawthorne say to his father; he went down the hall into the kitchen and began cracking ice into a bowl. His mother's voice, too loud, carried all the way.

A moment later she was beside him, taking things from under the grill and peering into the oven. "Are the olives and rice crackers out?" He nodded. "Then get these on a tray and hand them around, please, Peter." They were egg rolls and chicken livers wrapped in bacon. He burned his fingers transferring them to a tray, and his mother crept up behind him and kissed the nape of his neck. "Peter, you're so sweet." Without having had a drink, she acted drunk. "Now, what do we have to do? Are the martinis ready? Then when you come back with the tray, come back in for the pitcher and put it on another tray with the glasses, will you? Your father'll help. Now. What do I have to do? Oh—mash up capers and anchovies to put in the pot. You look just lovely, Peter, I'm so glad you put on a tie."

The bell rang again: more familiar voices. Harlan Bautz, the dentist, and Lou Price, who looked like the villain of a gangster movie. Their wives, brassy and meek respectively.

He was passing the first tray around when the Venutis arrived. Sonny Venuti popped an egg roll in her mouth, said, "Warmth!" and kissed him on the cheek. She looked pop-eyed and haggard. Ed Venuti, his father's partner, said, "Looking forward to Cornell, son?" and breathed gin in his face.

"Yes, sir."

But he was not listening. "God bless the Martoonerville Trolley," he said as his father put a filled glass in his hand.

When he offered the tray to Harlan Bautz, the dentist slapped his back and said, "Bet you can't wait to get to Cornell, hey, boy?"

"Yes, sir." He fled back into the kitchen.

His mother was spooning a greenish mixture into a steaming casserole. "Who just came?"

He told her.

"Just finish adding this goop and then put it back in the oven," she said, handing him the bowl. "I have to get out and say hello. Oh, I feel so *festive* tonight."

She left, and he was alone in the kitchen. He dropped the rest of the thick green substance into the casserole and twirled a spoon around in it. When he was putting it back into the oven, his father appeared and said, "Where's the drinks tray? I shouldn't have made so many martinis, we got a crowd of whiskey drinkers. Oh, I'll just take out the pitcher and use the other glasses in the dining room. Hey, the joint's jumping already, Pete. You ought to talk to that writer, he's an interesting fella, guess he writes chillers—I remember Edward telling me something about it. Interesting, no? I knew you'd have a good time if you spent some time with our friends. You are, aren't you?"

"What?" Peter closed the oven door.

"Having a good time."

"Sure."

"Okay. Get out there and talk to people." He shook his head as if in wonderment. "Boy. Your mother's all wound up. She's having a great time. Nice to see her like this again."

"Yes," Peter said, and drifted out to the living room, carrying a tray of canapés his mother had left behind.

There she was, "all wound up," as his father had said: almost as if literally wound up, talking rapidly through a cloud of exhaled smoke, darting from Sonny Venuti to pick up a bowl of black olives and offer them to Harlan Bautz.

"They say if this keeps up Milburn could be cut off entirely," Stella Hawthorne said, her voice lower and more listenable to than his mother's and Mrs. Venuti's. Perhaps for that reason, it stopped all conversation. "We only have that one snowplow, and the county's plow will be kept busy on the highway."

Lou Price, on the couch beside Sonny Venuti, said, "And look who's driving our plow. The council should never have let Omar Norris's wife talk them into it. Most of the time Omar's too boiled to see where he's going."

"Now, oh, Lou, now, that's the only work Omar Norris does all year round—and he came by here twice today!" His mother defended Omar Norris overbrightly: Peter saw her looking at the door, and knew that her febrile high spirits were caused by someone who had not arrived yet.

"He must be sleeping out in the boxcars these days," Lou Price said. "In boxcars or in his garage, if his wife lets him get that close. You want a guy like that running a two-ton snowplow past your car? He could run the damn thing on his breath."

The doorbell rang, and his mother nearly dropped her drink.

"I'll get it," Peter said, and went to the door.

It was Sears James. Beneath the wide brim of his hat, his face was worn and so white his cheeks looked almost blue. Then he said, "Hello, Peter," and looked normal again, taking off his hat and apologizing for being late.

For twenty minutes Peter took canapés around on trays, refilled drinks and evaded conversation. (Sonny Venuti, grabbing his cheek with two fingers: "I bet you

can't wait to get away from this awful town and start
chasing college girls, right, Pete?") Whenever he looked
at his mother, she was in the middle of a sentence, her
eyes darting to the front door. Lou Price was loudly
explaining something about soybean futures to Harlan
Bautz; Mrs. Bautz was boring Stella Hawthorne with
advice about redecoration. ("I'd say, go rosewood.")
Ed Venuti, Ricky Hawthorne and his father were talking off in a corner about the disappearance of Jim
Hardie. Peter returned to the sterile peacefulness of
the kitchen, loosened his tie and cradled his head on
a counter spattered with green. Five minutes later the
telephone rang. "No, don't bother, Walt, I'll get it," he
heard his mother cry in the living room.

The kitchen extension stopped ringing a few seconds
later. She was on the phone in the television room.
Peter looked at the white telephone on the kitchen
wall. Maybe it was not what he thought; maybe it was
Jim Hardie to say *hey don't worry, man, I'm in the
Apple* . . . he had to know. Even if it was what he
thought. He picked up the receiver: he would listen
only for a second.

The voice was Lewis Benedikt's, and his heart folded.
". . . can't come, no, Christina," Lewis was saying.
"I just can't. My drive is six feet deep in snow."

"Someone's on the line," his mother said.

"Don't be paranoid," Lewis said. "Besides, Christina,
it would be a waste of time for me to come out. You
know."

"Pete? Is that you? Are you listening?"

Peter held his breath; did not hang up.

"Oh, Peter's not listening. Why would he?"

"Damn you, are you there?" His mother's voice:
sharp as the buzz of a hornet.

"Christina, I'm sorry. We're still friends. Go back to
your party and have a great time."

"You can be such a shallow creep," his mother said,
and slammed down the phone. A second later, in shock,
Peter also put down his receiver.

He stood on wobbly legs, almost certain of the meaning of what he had overheard. He blindly turned to the kitchen window. Footsteps. The door behind him opened and closed. Behind his own blank reflection— as drained as when he had looked into an empty room on Montgomery Street—was his mother's, her face an angry blur. "Did you get an earful, spy?" Then there was another reflection between them—it was like that for a moment, another pale blur sliding between his face and his mother's. It shifted closer, and Peter was looking at a small face not in reflection, but directly outside the window: an imploring, twisted childish face. The boy was begging him to come out. "Tell me, you little spy," his mother ordered.

Peter screamed; and jammed his fist in his mouth to stop the noise. He closed his eyes.

Then his mother's arms were around him and her voice was going, muttering apologies, the tears now not latent but warm on his neck. He could hear, above the noise his mother was making, the voice of Sears James declaiming: "Yes, Don came here to take possession of his house, but also to help us out with a little problem—a research problem." Then a muffled voice that might have been Sonny Venuti's. Sears replied, "We want him to look into the background of that Moore girl, the actress who disappeared." More muffled voices: mild surprise, mild doubt, mild curiosity. He took his fist out of his mouth.

"It's okay, mom," he said.

"Peter, I'm so sorry."

"I won't tell."

"It's not—Peter, it wasn't what you think. You can't let it upset you."

"I thought maybe it was Jim Hardie calling," he said.

The doorbell rang.

She loosened her grip on his neck. "Poor darling, with a crummy runaway friend and a psycho mother like me." She kissed the back of his head. "And I cried all over your clean shirt."

The bell rang again.

"Oh, there's one more," Christina Barnes said. "Your father will make the drinks. Let's get back to normal before we're seen in public again, okay?"

"It's someone you invited?"

"Why sure it is, Pete, who else could it be?"

"I don't know," he said, and looked at the window again. No one was there: only his mother's averted face and his own, glowing like pale candles in the glass. "Nobody."

She straightened up and wiped her eyes. "I'll get the food out of the oven. You better get in and say hello."

"Who is it?"

"Some friend of Sears and Ricky's."

He walked to the door and looked back, but she was already opening the oven door and reaching in, an ordinary woman getting the dinner ready for a party.

I don't know what's real and what isn't, he thought, and turning his back on her went out into the hall. The stranger, Mr. Wanderley's nephew, was talking near the living-room arch. "Well, what I'm interested in now, to tell the truth, is the difference between invention and reality. For example, did you happen to hear music a few days ago? A band, playing outside somewhere in town?"

"Why no," breathed Sonny Venuti. "Did you?"

Peter stopped dead just inside the arch and gaped at the writer.

"Hey, Pete," his father said. "I want you to meet your dinner partner."

"Oh, *I* wanted to sit next to this handsome young man," Sonny Venuti crooned, smiling at him popeyed.

"You're stuck with me," said Lou Price.

"Come on over here, scout," his father called.

He pulled himself away from Don Wanderley, who was looking at him curiously, and turned to his father. His mouth dried. His father was standing with his arm around a tall woman with a lovely fox-sharp face.

It was the face which had looked the wrong way

through a telescope across a dark square and found him.

"Anna, this is my son Pete. Pete, Miss Mostyn."

Her eyes licked at him. He was conscious for a moment of standing halfway between the woman and Don Wanderley, Sears James and Ricky Hawthorne looking on like spectators at a tennis match; but himself and the woman and Don Wanderley forming the points of a long narrow triangle like a burning-glass, and then her eyes moved over him again, and he was conscious only of the danger he was in.

"Oh, I think Peter and I will have lots to talk about," said Anna Mostyn.

From the journals of Don Wanderley

14

What was to have been my introduction to a wider Milburn community ended in a disastrous shambles.

Peter Barnes, a tall black-haired boy who looks both capable and sensitive, was the dropped bomb. He seemed merely uncommunicative at first—understandable in a seventeen-year-old playing servant at his parents' party. Flashes of warmth for the Hawthornes. He too responds to Stella. But underneath the distance was something else—something I gradually imagined was—panic? Despair? Apparently a friend of his disappeared under a cloud, and his parents evidently assumed that to be the cause of his moroseness. Yet it was more than that, and what I thought I saw in him was fear—the Chowder Society had either tuned me to this, or caused me mistakenly to project it. When I was making my pompous remarks to Sonny Venuti, Peter stopped in his tracks and stared at me; he really searched me with his eyes, and I had the idea that he wanted badly to talk to me—not about books. The startling thing was that I thought that he too had heard the Dr. Rabbitfoot music.

And if that's true—

if that's true—

then we are in the middle of Dr. Rabbitfoot's revenge. And all Milburn is about to blow up.

Oddly, it was something Anna Mostyn said that caused Peter to faint. He trembled when he first saw her: I am sure of that. He was afraid of her. Now Anna Mostyn is a woman not far short of beauty, even the awesome Stella Hawthorne sort; her eyes seem to go all the way back to Norfolk and Florence, where she says her ancestors came from. She has apparently made herself indispensable to Sears and Ricky, but her greatest gift is for merely being politely there, helpful when that is needed, as on the day of the funeral. She suggests kindness and sympathy and intelligence but does not overwhelm you with her excellence. She is discreet, quiet, on the surface of things a supremely self-contained, self-possessed young woman. She really is remarkably unobtrusive. Yet she is sensual in an inexplicably unsettling way. She seems *cold,* sensually cold: it is a self-referring, self-pleasing sensuality.

I saw her fix Peter Barnes with this challenge for a moment during dinner. He had been staring at his plate, forcing his father into yet more bluster and bonhomie, and annoying his mother; he never looked at Anna Mostyn, though he was sitting next to her. The other guests ignored him and chattered away about the weather. Peter was burning to get away from the table. Anna took his chin in her hand, and I knew the sort of look he was getting. Then she said to him very quietly that she wanted some of the rooms of her new house repainted, and she thought that he and one or two of his school friends might like to come to her house to do it. He swooned. That old-fashioned word fits perfectly. He fainted, passed out, pitched forward— swooned. I thought at first that he'd had a fit; so did most other people present. Stella Hawthorne calmed us down, helped Peter off his chair, and his father took him upstairs. Dinner ended shortly afterward.

And now I notice this for the first time: Alma Mobley. Anna Mostyn. The initials, the great similarity of the names. Am I at a point where I can afford to call anything coincidental "a mere coincidence"? She is not like Alma Mobley in any way; yet she *is* like her.

And I know how. It is their air of timelessness: but where Alma would have flown past the Plaza Hotel in the twenties, Anna Mostyn would have been inside, smiling at the antics of men with flasks in their pockets, men cavorting, talking about new cars and the stock market, doing their best to knock her dead.

Tonight I am going to take the pages of the Dr. Rabbitfoot novel down to the hotel's incinerator and burn them.

Part Three

The Coon Hunt

But the civilized human spirit, whether one calls
it bourgeois or merely leaves it at civilized,
cannot get rid of a feeling of the uncanny.

—*Dr Faustus*, Thomas Mann

avoided; and as the snows melted, the river—grayer and faster than on the day John Jaffrey stepped off the bridge—came nearly up to its banks. For the first time in five years Walt Hardesty and his deputies, aided by the fire volunteers, piled sandbags along the banks to prevent a flood. Hardesty kept on his Wild West costume all during the heavy hard work of carrying the sandbags from the truck, but a deputy named Leon Churchill stripped to his waist and thought maybe the worst of it was over until the bitter days of February and March.

Metaphorically, Milburn people in general took off their shirts. Omar Norris happily went back on the bottle full time, and when his wife kicked him out of the house, returned to his boxcar without a qualm and prayed into the neck of a half-empty fifth that the heavy snow was gone for good. The town relaxed during these days of temporary, warming relief. Walter Barnes wore a gaudy pink-and-blue-striped shirt to the bank, and for eight hours felt deliciously unbankerlike; Sears and Ricky made timeworn jokes about Elmer Scales suing the weatherman for inconstancy. For two days lunchtimes at the Village Pump were crowded with strangers out for drives. Clark Mulligan's business doubled during the final two days of his Vincent Price double feature, and he held the pictures over for another week. The gutters ran with black water; if you weren't careful, cars dodging too close to the curbs could drench you from the neck down. Penny Draeger, Jim Hardie's former girlfriend, found a new man, a stranger with a shaven head and dark glasses who said to call him G and was exciting and mysterious and came from nowhere and said he was a sailor—heady stuff for Penny. In the sunlight, with the sound of water everywhere, Milburn was a spacious town. People pulled on rubber boots to keep their shoes dry and went for walks. Milly Sheehan hired a boy from down the block to hang her storm windows and the boy said, "Gee, Mrs. Sheehan, maybe you won't even need these until Christmas!" Stella Hawthorne, lying in a scented tub, decided that it was time to send Harold Sims back to the spinster librarians who would be impressed by him: she'd rather have her hair done. Thus for two days resolutions were made, long hikes were taken; men did not resent getting out onto the highway in the morning and driving to their offices; in this false spring, spirits lifted.

But Eleanor Hardie grew exhausted with worry and polished the hotel's banisters and counters twice in one day, and John Jaffrey and Edward Wanderley and the others lay underground, and Nettie Dedham was taken off to an institution still mouthing the only two syllables she would ever wish to say; and Elmer Scales's gaunt body thinned down even further as he sat up with the shotgun across his lap. The sun went down earlier each evening, and at night Milburn contracted and froze. The houses seemed to draw together; the streets which were spangled by day darkened, seemed to narrow to ox-cart width; the black sky clamped down. The three old men of the Chowder Society forgot their feeble jokes and trekked through bad dreams. Two spacious houses stood ominously dark; the house on Montgomery Street contained horrors, which flickered and shifted from room to room, from floor to floor; in Edward Wanderley's old house on Haven Lane, all that walked was mystery: and for Don Wanderley, when he would see it, the mystery would lead to Panama City, Florida, and a little girl who said "I am you."

Lewis spent the first of these days shoveling out his drive, deliberately overexerting himself and working so hard that he sweated through the running suit and khaki jacket he wore; by noon his arms and back were aching as if he'd never worked in his life. After lunch he napped for half an hour, showered, and forced himself to finish the job. He shoveled the last of it out of his drive—by then the snow was damp and much heavier than when he'd started—at six-thirty. Lewis went in, having created what looked like a mountain range down the side of his drive, showered again, took his telephone off the hook and consumed four bottles of beer and two hamburgers. He did not think he would be able to get up the stairs to bed. When he made it into his bedroom, he painfully removed his clothes, dropped them on the floor, and fell onto his blankets, instantly asleep.

He was never sure whether this was a dream: in the night he heard a dreadful noise, the sound of the wind blowing all that snow back over his drive. It seemed like wakefulness; and it seemed too that he heard another sound—a sound like music blown on the wind. He thought: *I'm dreaming this*. But his muscles ached and wobbled as he got out of bed, and his head spun. He went to his window, which looked down the side of the house onto the roof of the old stables and the first third of his drive. He saw a three-quarter moon hanging above desolate trees. The next thing he saw was so much like a scene from one of Ricky's odder movies that afterward he knew that he could not actually have witnessed it. The wind blew, as he had feared, and gauzy sheets of snow drifted onto his drive; everything was starkly black and white. A man dressed in minstrel's clothing stood on top of the snow-mountain going down to the road. A saxophone white as his eyes hung from his mouth. As Lewis looked, not even trying to force his foggy mind to make sense of this vision, the musician blew a few half-audible bars, lowered the saxophone and winked. His skin seemingly as black as the sky, he stood weightlessly on snow into which he should have sunk up to his waist. Not one of your old spirits, Lewis, jealous of your tenancy, come for your blackbirds and snowdrops; go back to bed and dream in peace. But still stupid with exhaustion, he watched on and the figure changed—it was John Jaffrey grinning at him from the impossible perch, shoe-blacking spread on his face and hands: white eyes, white teeth. Lewis stumbled back into bed.

After he had steamed most of the soreness out of his muscles in a long hot shower Lewis went downstairs and looked out of his dining-room windows with astonishment. Most of the snow had already disappeared

from the trees in front of his house, leaving them wet
and shiny. Black pools of water lay over the brick court
which extended from his house to the old stables. The
range of snow down the drive was only half its height
of yesterday. The shift in weather had held. The sky
was cloudless and blue. Lewis looked a second time at
the diminished range of snow beside his drive and
shook his head: another dream. Edward's nephew had
planted that picture in his mind, with his account of the
leading character in his unwritten book, the black carni-
val-bandleader with the funny name. *He has us dreaming his books for him,* he thought, and smiled.

He went to the entry hall, kicked off his loafers and
put on his boots.

Pulling his khaki jacket over his shoulders, he went
back through the house to the kitchen. Lewis put a
kettle full of cold water on a burner and looked through
the kitchen window. Like the trees in front of the house,
his woods shone and glistened; snow lay damp and
squashy on the lawn, whiter and deeper beneath the
wet trees further away. He would take his walk while
the kettle boiled, and then come back and have breakfast.

Outside, warmth surprised him; and more than that,
the warm, almost laundered-feeling air seemed a protection, a cocoon of safety. The menacing suggestive-
ness of his woods had been rinsed away—shining with
their beautiful muted colors of tree bark and lichen,
with the mushy snow beneath like a swipe of watercolor, Lewis's woods had none of the hard-edged illus-
trationlike quality he had seen in them before.

He took his path backward again, loafing along and
breathing deeply; he smelled the mulch of wet leaves
beneath the snow. Feeling youthful and healthy, his
chest full of delicate air, he regretted drinking too much
at Sears's house. It was foolish to blame himself for
Freddy Robinson's death; as for whispers of his name,
hadn't he heard those all his life? It was snow falling
from a branch—meaningless noise to which his guilty
soul gave meaning.

He needed a woman's company, a woman's conversation. Now that it was finally over with Christina Barnes, he could invite Annie, the blond waitress from Humphrey's, out to his house for a good dinner and let her talk to him about painters and books. Her intelligent conversation would be an exorcism of the past month's worries; maybe he would invite Anni too, and they both would talk about painters and books. He'd stumble a bit, trying to keep up, but he would learn something.

And then he thought that maybe he'd get Stella Hawthorne away from Ricky for an hour or two and just luxuriate in the fact of that astonishing face and bristling personality sitting across the table from him.

Blissful, Lewis turned around and realized why he had always run his path in the opposite direction: on this long return stretch with its two angled sections, you were nearly at the house before you could see it. Going the other way preserved for as long as possible his illusion that he was the only white man on a densely wooded continent. He was surrounded by quiet trees and dripping water, by white sunshine.

There were two points that destroyed Lewis's illusion of being Daniel Boone striking out through alien wilderness, and he reached the first of these after ten minutes of walking. Midpoint on his walk: he saw the tubular top half of a yellow oil truck, its lower section cut off by the curve of the long field, steaming toward Binghamton. So much for Daniel Boone. He turned down the straight path to the kitchen door.

By now he was hungry, and glad that he had remembered to buy bacon and eggs the last time he was in Milburn. He had coffee beans to grind, stoneground bread to toast, tomatoes to grill. After breakfast he'd call the girls and invite them out for dinner and let them tell him what books to read: Stella would wait.

He was halfway home when he began to smell food. Puzzled, he cocked his head. Unmistakably, it was the smell of breakfast—the breakfast he had just imagined. Coffee, bacon, eggs. *Uh oh,* he thought, *Christina.* After

Walter had left for work and Peter for school, she had climbed into the station wagon and come out for a scene. She still had a key to the back door.

Soon he was close enough to see the house through the last of the trees, and the breakfast smells were stronger. His boots heavy, he trudged forward, thinking of what he could say to Christina. It would be difficult, especially if she were affecting a meek repentant mood, as the breakfast odors seemed to prove she was . . . then, still in the last section of the woods, he realized that her car was not drawn up before the garage.

And that was where she always put her car: the parking area was out of sight of the road, near the back door: in fact it was where everyone parked. But not only was Christina's station wagon not drawn up on the puddly brick court, no car at all was there.

He stopped walking and looked carefully at the gray stone height of the house. Only a few trees stood in his way, and the size of the house made them insignificant —thin stalks. For a moment the house looked even larger than he knew it was.

As a drift of breeze brought the odors of coffee and bacon to him, Lewis looked at his house as if for the first time: an architect's copy of an illustrator's idea of a Scottish castle, a folly of a kind, the building too appeared to glisten, as the wet trees had. It was the end of a quest in a story. Lewis with his soaking boots and hungry belly looked at the house with a frozen heart. The windows glittered in their casements.

It was the castle of a dead, not a captive, princess.

Slowly Lewis approached the house and left the temporary safety of the woods. He crossed the brick court where the car should have been. The odors of breakfast were maddeningly strong. Lewis cautiously opened the kitchen door; he entered.

The kitchen was empty, but not undisturbed. Signs of occupation and activity lay everywhere. Two plates were laid out on the kitchen table—his best china. Polished silver had been set beside the plates. Two candles, not lighted, stood in silver holders near the plates. A can of frozen orange juice had been set out before his blender. Lewis turned to the stove: empty pans sat atop unlighted burners. The smell of cooking was overwhelming. His kettle whistled, and he turned it off.

Two slices of bread had been placed beside the toaster.

"Christina?" he called, thinking—not very rationally —that it still might be a practical joke. There was no answer.

He turned back to the stove and sniffed the air over the pans. Bacon. Eggs in butter. Superstitiously he touched the cold iron.

The dining room was just as he had left it; and when he went into the living room, that too was undisturbed. He picked up a book on the arm of a chair and looked at it quizzically, though he had put it there the night before. He stood in the living room for a moment, here where no one had come, smelling a breakfast no one had cooked, as if the room were a refuge. "Christina?" he called. "Anybody?"

Upstairs a familiar door clicked shut.

"Hello?"

Lewis moved to the base of the stairs and looked up. "Who's there?" Sunlight drifted in from a window on the landing; he saw dust motes spinning lazily above the stairs. The house was noiseless; for the first time its vast size seemed a threat. Lewis cleared his throat.

"Who's there?"

After a long moment he began to climb the stairs. When he reached the landing he looked out of the little window set in its casement—sunlight, dripping trees— and continued on to the top.

Here the hallway was light, silent, empty. Lewis's bedroom was on the right, two old rooms with the adjoining wall removed. One of the old doors had been sealed off, the other replaced with an elaborately grained slab of monkeywood hand-fashioned into a door. With its heavy brass knob, Lewis's bedroom door closed with a distinctively chunky sound, and that was the sound he had heard.

Lewis stood before the door, unable to make himself open it. He cleared his throat again. He could see the double expanse of his bedroom, the carpet, his slippers beside the bed, his pajamas over a chair, the windows from which he had looked that morning. And he could see the bed. What made him afraid to open the door was that on the bed he envisioned the fourteen years' dead body of his wife. He raised his hand to knock; he held his fist an inch from the door; lowered it again. Lewis touched the doorknob.

He forced himself to turn the heavy knob. The lock disengaged. Lewis closed his eyes and pushed.

He opened them to hazy sunlight from the long windows opposite the door; an edge of a chair, hung with blue-striped pajamas; the reek of rotting flesh.

Welcome, Lewis.

Lewis bravely stepped around the door and into the pool of early light that was his bedroom. He looked at the empty bed. The foul odor dissipated as quickly as it had come. Now he could smell only the cut flowers on the table before the window. He went to the bed and hesitantly touched the bottom sheet, which was warm.

A minute later he was downstairs holding the telephone. "Otto. Are you afraid of the game wardens?"

"Ach, Lewis. They run when they see me. On a day like this you want to go out with the dogs? Come for schnapps instead."

"Then we go out," Lewis said. "Please."

2

Peter walked out of his homeroom when the bell rang and went down the corridor to his locker. While the rest of the school pushed past to various parts of the building and most of his class filed into Miller's room for history, he pretended to search for a book. Tony Drexler, a friend of his, loitered beside him for unbearable seconds and finally asked, "Heard from Jim Hardie yet?"

"No," Peter said, burying himself deeper in his locker.

"I bet he's in Greenwich Village already."

"Yeah."

"Time to get to History. You read the chapter?"

"No."

"Bullshit," Drexler laughed. "See you there."

Peter nodded. Not long after he was alone. Leaving his books in his locker but taking his coat, he slammed the metal panel shut and ran down the hall to the bathroom. He shut himself in a toilet and waited for the first period bell to ring.

Ten minutes later he peeked out of the bathroom door. The hallway was empty, and he raced down the corridor. Then he continued unseen down the stairs and out the door.

A hundred yards off to the side, a first-period gym class sweated over calisthenics on the muddy field; two girls were already doing punishment laps around the track. Nobody saw him: school was already deep in its round of self-enclosed activity, marching to the sound of bells.

A block away on School Road, Peter turned off into a sidestreet and from there zigzagged through town, avoiding the square and the shopping district, until he reached Underhill Road, which led to Route 17. He jogged down Underhill Road for half a mile, by now well out of town and in sight only of bare fields ending in stands of trees.

When the highway came in sight, he walked across a squelchy knoll and climbed over a double strip of thick aluminum nailed to a series of white posts. Peter ran across the lanes to the median, climbed another aluminum fence, waited for a break in the traffic and then ran across to the other side of the highway. Then he held out his arm, thumb extended, and began to walk backward down the highway.

He had to see Lewis: he had to talk to Lewis about his mother.

From the bottom of his mind floated the image of himself leaping on Lewis, swinging at him with his fists, battering at the handsome face . . .

But then came the opposite image of Lewis laughing, Lewis telling him not to worry about anything, that he had not come back from Spain to have affairs with people's mothers.

If Lewis said that, he could tell him about Jim Hardie.

Peter had been hitchhiking for fifteen minutes when a blue car finally pulled over to the side of the road. The middle-aged man behind the wheel leaned sideways and opened the passenger door. "Where you going, son?" He was a tubby man in a wrinkled gray suit with a green necktie knotted too tightly. Advertising leaflets of some kind littered the back seat. "Just down the road six or seven miles," Peter said. "I'll tell you when we get close." He got in.

"This is against my principles," the man said, rolling away.

"Pardon?"

"Against my principles. Hitchhiking is pretty dangerous, especially for good-looking kids like you. I don't think you should do it."

Peter laughed out loud, startling both the driver and himself.

The man stopped at the end of Lewis's drive, but would not leave without giving him more advice. "Listen, son. You never know who you're going to meet out on these roads. Could be any kind of pervert." He grabbed Peter's arm just as the boy was opening the door.

"Promise me you won't do it again. Promise me, son."

"Okay, I promise," Peter said.

"The Lord knows you made that promise." The man released Peter's arm, and the boy scrambled out of the car. "Hold on, son, wait up. Just a sec." Peter fidgeted by the side of the car, shifting on his feet, while the man leaned over and picked up one of the leaflets on the back seat. "This will help you, son. Read it and keep it. It's got an answer in it."

"An answer?"

"That's right. Show it to your friends." He handed Peter a cheaply printed pamphlet: *The Watchtower*.

The driver picked up speed on the highway; Peter shoved the little magazine in his pocket and turned around to go up Lewis's drive.

The drive had been pointed out to him, but he had never seen Lewis's house—never seen more of it than the gray peaks which could be glimpsed from the highway. As he began to walk up the drive, these peaks disappeared. The drifted snow had melted, and the drive shone, catching the sun at a hundred mirrorlike points. Seeing the top of the house from the road, Peter had never recognized how far the house sat from the highway, how enclosed it was by trees. When he reached the first curve of the drive, he was able partially to see the house between their trunks, and for the first time he began to question what he was doing.

He came closer. A smaller extension of the drive curved off to the front of the house, which looked as long as a city block. Faceted windows threw back the light. The major section of the drive trailed around the side of the house and ended at a brick courtyard flanked by what looked to Peter like stables—he saw only a corner of these. He could not imagine himself entering such an imposing place: it looked like you could wander a week in it without finding your way out. This evidence of Lewis's separateness, his otherness, put all of Peter's plans in doubt.

Going in there seemed ominously like going into the silent house on Montgomery Street.

Peter walked around to the rear of the building, trying to relate this massive grandeur to what he thought of Lewis. For Peter, who knew nothing of the house's history, it seemed regal: it demanded a different conception of its owner. Still, the rear of the house was better: a door on a brick court, the homely wooden fronts of the stables, this was at a level with which he was more comfortable. He had just noticed the paths leading into the woods when he heard a voice speaking in his mind.

Imagine Lewis in bed with your mother, Peter. Imagine him lying on top of her.

"No," he whispered.

Imagine how she looks moving under him naked, Peter. Imagine—

Peter froze and the voice ceased simultaneously. A car had turned into the drive from the highway. Lewis had come home. Peter thought for a second if he should wait exposed in the courtyard for Lewis to see him as he drove in, and then the car shifted up and was too near the house and he could not bear to see Lewis while the echo of the voice still hung in his mind, and he ran to the side of the stables and crouched down. His mother's station wagon rolled into the courtyard behind the house.

Peter groaned softly, and heard laughter whispering along the painted boards of the old stables.

He flattened himself out on the snow and looked through the gnarled stalks of a rosebush as his mother got out of the station wagon. Her face was drawn, pale with concentrated feeling—a taut angry expression he had never seen. As he watched from beside the stables, she leaned back into the car and tapped the horn twice. Then she straightened up, walked around the front of the car, skirted the puddles on the flat red bricks and went up to the little door in the rear of the house. He thought she would knock, but she dug in her bag for a moment, took out a key and let herself in. He heard her call Lewis's name.

3

Lewis steered the Morgan around a black pool on the rutted drive which led to the back of the cheese factory. This was a bungalow-sized square wooden building Otto had built himself in a valley outside Afton, below a range of wooded hills. Dogs yapped in the kennels to the side of the factory. Lewis parked his car just outside the platform that served as Otto's loading bay, jumped up onto the platform, swung open the metal doors and went into the factory. He inhaled the pervasive odor of curdled milk.

"Lew-iss!" Otto stood in diffuse light on the other side of the little factory surrounded by white machinery, supervising while cheese was poured into round flat wooden molds. As each mold was filled, Otto's son, Karl, took it to the weighing machine, recorded its weight and the mold number, and then stacked it in a corner. Otto said something to Karl and then came across the wooden floor to grasp Lewis's hand. "How good to see you, my friend. But Lew-iss, you look so got-awful tired! You need some of my homemade schnapps."

"And you look busy," Lewis said. "But I'd be grateful for the schnapps."

"Busy, don't worry about busy. Karl is handling everything now, I should worry about Karl? He is a good cheesemaker. Almost as good as me."

Lewis smiled and Otto slapped him on the back and lumbered off to his office, a small enclosure near the loading bay. Otto sank down in his ancient chair behind the desk, making the springs creak; Lewis across the desk from him. "Now, my friend." Otto bent over and removed a decanter and two thimble glasses from a drawer. "Now we have a good drink. To make your cheeks red again." He tipped liquid from the decanter into the glasses.

The liquor burned Lewis's throat, but tasted like a distillation of massed flowers. "Delicious."

"Of course it is delicious. I make it myself. I suppose you brought your gun, Lew-iss?"

Lewis nodded.

"So. I thought you were the kind of friend who comes into my office and drinks my schnapps and eats my beautiful new cheese"—Otto pushed himself out of his chair and went the short distance to a low refrigerator —"but all the time thinks only about going out and shooting something." He placed a block of cheese veined with wine down before Lewis and cut off sections with his knife. This was one of the speciality cheeses Otto made to sell under his own name; the wheels of cheddar went to a combine. "Now tell me. Am I right?"

"You're right."

"I thought so. But it is fine, Lew-iss. I bought a new dog. *Very* good dog. This dog can see two-three miles— can smell for ten! Pretty soon I think I give this dog Karl's job."

The winy cheese was as good as Otto's schnapps. "Do you think it might be too wet to take a dog out?"

"No, no. Under those big trees it won't be so wet. You and me, we'll find some animal. Maybe even a fox, huh?"

"And you're not afraid of the game warden?"

"No! They run when they see me. They say, uh uh, here is that crazy old German—with a gun yet!"

Listening to Otto Gruebe's buffoonery, sitting in his office with a fresh glass of the powerful brandy and his mouth full of intricate tastes, Lewis thought that Otto represented a kind of alternative Chowder Society— a less complicated, but equally valuable friendship.

"Let's go out and see that dog," he said.

"Let's see the dog, hey? Lew-iss, when you see my new dog, you will go down on your knees and propose marriage to her."

Both men put on their coats and left the office. Outside, Lewis noticed a tall skinny boy of roughly Peter Barnes's age up on the loading bay. He wore a purple shirt and tight jeans, and he was piling up the heavy molds for pickup. He stared at Lewis for a moment, than ducked his head and smiled.

As they walked toward the kennels Lewis said, "You hired a new boy?"

"Yes. You saw him? He was the poor boy who found the body of the old lady who kept the horses. She lived near you."

"Rea Dedham," Lewis said. When he glanced over his shoulder, the boy was still looking at him, half-smiling; Lewis swallowed and turned away.

"Ya. He was very disturbed, and he could not stand to live near there anymore, he is a very sensitive boy, Lew-iss, and so he asked me for a job and got a room in Afton. So I gave him a broom and let him clean the machinery and stack the cheese. It is good until after Christmas, then we cannot afford him so much anymore."

Rea Dedham; Edward and John; it pursued him even here.

Otto let the new dog out of its kennel, and was hunkering down beside it, rubbing his hands up and down its coat. It was a hound, lean and gray with muscular shoulders and haunches; the bitch did not yip like the other dogs or leap around with joy to be out of the kennel, but stood attentively beside Otto, looking about with alert blue eyes. Lewis too bent to pet it, and the hound accepted his hand and sniffed his boots. "This is Flossie," Otto said. "What a dog, hey? What a beauty you are, my Flossie. Shall we take you out now for a liddle while, my Flossie?"

For the first time the bitch showed animation, tilting its head and swishing its tail. The well-schooled animal, Otto jug-eared and happy beside it, the nearness of the trees and the pervasive odors of cheese-making, all of this seemed to swing Lewis in an arc away from the blue-jeaned boy behind him and the Chowder Society which lurked behind the boy, and he said, "Otto, I want to tell you a story."

"Ya? Good. Tell me, Lew-iss."

"I want to tell you about how my wife died."

Otto cocked his head and for a moment absurdly resembled the hound kneeling before him. "Ya. Good." He nodded, and reflectively ran a finger around the base of the hound's ears. "You can tell me when we go up in the woods for an hour or two, hey? I'm glad, Lew-iss. I'm glad."

Lewis and Otto called what they did when they went out with rifles and a dog coon-hunting, and Otto chortled about the possibility of seeing a fox, but it had been at least a year since they had shot anything. The rifles and the dog were chiefly an excuse to go rambling through the long wood which lay above the cheese factory—for Lewis, it was a sportier version of his morning runs. Sometimes they shot off their guns, sometimes one of the dogs treed something: Lewis might have tried to shoot it, but at least half the time Otto looked at the banded, angry animal up on the branch of a tree and laughed. "Come on, Lew-iss, this one is too pretty. Let's find an ugly one."

Lewis suspected that if they tried anything like that this time, they'd have to clear it with Flossie first. The sleek little animal was wholly businesslike. She did not go after birds or squirrels like half the other dogs, but padded along in front of them, tilting her head from side to side, her tail switching. "Flossie is going to make us work," he said.

"Ya. I paid two hundred dollars to look like a fool in front of a dog, hey?"

Once they were up the valley and into the trees Lewis felt his tension begin to leave him. Otto was showing off the dog, whistling to make it go out on a wide tangent, whistling again to call it back.

Now they were moving through thick woods. As Otto had predicted, it was colder and dryer up here than in the valley. In exposed territory melting snow made rivulets, and marshy ground beneath the remaining snow sucked at their boots, but under a curtain of conifers it was as if the thaw had never come. Lewis lost sight of Otto for ten minutes at a time, then caught flashes of his red jacket between green fir needles and heard him communicating with the dog. Lewis lifted his Remington to his shoulder and sighted down on a pine cone; the dog switched and skirmished up ahead, looking for a scent.

Half an hour later, when she found one, Otto was too tired to follow it. The dog began baying, and streaked off to their right. Otto lowered his blunderbuss and said, "Ach, let it go, Flossie." The dog whimpered, turned around to stare disbelievingly at the two men: *What are you clowns doing, anyhow?* Then it lowered its tail and walked back. Ten yards off, it sat down and began licking its hindquarters.

"Flossie has given up on us," Otto said. "We are not in her class. Have a liddle drink." He offered Lewis a flask. "I think we need to be warm, hey, Lewis?"

"Can you build a fire around here?"

"Sure I can. I saw a liddle deadfall back a teeny bit —lots of dry wood in there. You just scoop a hole in the snow, get your tinder and presto. Fire."

Seeing that the hill came to its rise only twenty yards above them, Lewis climbed up while Otto went back to the deadfall to collect dry wood and tinder. Flossie, no longer interested, watched him stumble upward toward the ridge.

He did not expect what he found: they had come farther than he had thought and below him, down a long forested slope, was a streak of highway. On the other side of the highway the woods resumed again, but the few cars traveling the highway were a despoilation. They ruined his fragile mood of well-being.

And then it was as if Milburn had reached out even here, to point at him on the crest of a wooded hill: one of the cars moving rapidly down the highway was Stella Hawthorne's. "Oh, God," Lewis muttered, watching Stella's Volvo cross through the space directly before him. It, and the woman driving it, brought the night and the morning back to him. He might as well have pitched a tent on the square; even out in the woods, Milburn whispered behind him. Stella's car traveled up the road; her turn indicator flashed, and she pulled onto the shoulder. A moment later another car pulled in beside her. A man got out and went around to Stella's window and rapped until she opened her door.

Lewis turned away and went back down the slippery hill to Otto.

He had already started a little fire. At the bottom of a hole scooped in the snow, on a bed of stones, a flame licked at tinder. Otto fed it a larger twig, then another, then a handful, and the single flame grew into a dozen. Above this Otto built a foot-high tepee of sticks. "Now, Lew-iss," he said, "warm your hands."

"Any schnapps left?" Lewis took the flask and joined Otto on a fallen log dusted of its snow. Otto dug in his pockets and withdrew a homemade sausage sliced neatly in half. He gave half to Lewis, and bit into his own half. The fire leaped up into the tepee and warmed Lewis's ankles through his boots. He extended his hands and feet and around a bit of sausage said, "One night Linda and I went to a dinner in one of the suites of the hotel I owned. Linda didn't live through the night. Otto, I think the same thing that got my wife is after me."

4

Peter stood up beside the stables, crossed the court and peeked in the kitchen window. Pans on the stove, a round table laid for two: his mother had come for breakfast. He heard her footsteps as she went further into the house, obviously looking for Lewis Benedikt. What would she do when she found out he wasn't there?

Of course she isn't in danger, he told himself: this isn't *her* house. She can't be in danger. She'll find out Lewis isn't here and then she'll go back home. But it was too much like the other time, he looking in a window and waiting at a door while another person prowled within an empty house. *She'll just go home.*

He touched the door, expecting it to be locked; but it swung open an inch.

This time he would not go in. He was afraid of too much—only part of it was the possibility of meeting his mother in the house and having to invent an explanation for his being there.

But he could do that. He could say that he wanted to talk to Lewis about—about anything. Cornell University. Fraternities.

He saw Jim Hardie's crushed head sliding down a mottled wall.

Peter took his hand off the door and stepped down into the brick court. He took several steps backward, looking up at the rear of the house. It was a fantasy anyhow: his mother's angry face had made it clear that she would not accept any fairytales about advice on fraternities.

He backed up further, the fortresslike back of Lewis's house seeming for a moment almost to lean over and follow him. A curtain twitched, and Peter was unable to move further. Someone was behind the curtain, someone not his mother. He could see only white fingers holding back the fabric. Peter wanted to run, but his legs would not move.

The figure with white hands was lowering its face to the glass and grinning down at him. It was Jim Hardie.

Inside the house, his mother screamed.

Peter's legs unlocked, and he ran across the court and through the back door.

He went rapidly through the kitchen and found himself in a dining room. Through a wide doorway he could see living-room furniture, light coming in through the front windows. "Mom!" He ran into the living room. Two leather couches flanked a fireplace, antique weapons hung on one wall. "Mom!"

Jim Hardie walked into the room, smiling. He showed the palms of his hands, demonstrating to Peter that his intentions were not violent. "Hi," he said, but the voice was not Jim's. It was not the voice of any human being.

"You're dead," Peter said.

"It's funny about that," the Hardie-thing replied. "You don't really feel that way after it happens. You don't even feel pain, Pete. It feels almost good. No, it definitely feels pretty good. And of course there's nothing left to worry about. That's a big plus."

"What did you do to my mother?"

"Oh, she's fine.. He's upstairs with her now. You can't go up there. I'm supposed to talk to you. Hi!"

Peter looked wildly at the wall of spears and pikes, but it was too far away. "You don't even *exist*," he shouted, almost crying. "They killed you." He pulled a lamp from a table beside one of the couches.

"It's hard to say," Jim said. "You can't say I don't exist, because here I am. Did I say Hi yet? I'm supposed to say that. Let's—"

Peter threw the lamp at the Hardie-thing's chest as hard as he could.

It went on talking for the seconds the lamp was in the air. "—sit down and—"

The lamp exploded it into a shower of lights like sparks and crashed into the wall.

Peter ran down the length of the living room, almost sobbing with impatience. At the room's other end he passed through an arch, and his feet skidded on black and white tiles. To his right was the massive front door, to his left a carpeted staircase. Peter ran up the stairs.

When he reached the first landing he stopped, seeing that the staircase continued. Down at the other end of the gallerylike hall, he could see the foot of another staircase, which evidently led to another area of the house. "Mom!"

Then he heard a whimpering noise, very near. He moved to Lewis's monkeywood door and opened it— his mother made another strangled whimpering noise. Peter ran into the room.

And stopped. The man from Anna Mostyn's house stood near a large bed that Peter knew must have been Lewis's. Striped pajamas hung from a chair. The man wore the dark glasses and knit cap. His hands were around Christina Barnes's neck. "Master Barnes," he said. "How you young people get around. And how you poke your charming noses into other people's business. You'll be needing the ferule, I'm thinking."

"Mom, they're not real," he said. "You can make them disappear." His mother's eyes protruded and her body moved convulsively. "You just can't listen to what they say, they get inside your head and make you hypnotized."

"Oh, we had no need to do that," the man said.

Peter moved to the broad shelf beneath the windows and picked up a vase of flowers.

"Boy," the man said.

Peter cocked his arm. His mother's face was turning blue, and her tongue protruded. He made a frantic mewing sound in his throat and took aim at the man. Two cold small hands closed around his wrist. A wave of rotten air, the odor of an animal left dead for days in the sun, went over him.

"That's a good boy," the man said.

Hatpin

5

Harold Sims got angrily into the car, forcing Stella to move sideways on the seat. "What's the big idea? What the hell do you mean, acting like this?"

Stella took a pack of cigarettes from her bag, lit one and then silently offered the pack to Harold.

"I said, what's the big idea? I had to drive twenty-five miles to get here." He pushed the cigarettes away.

"It was your idea to meet, I believe. At least that is what you said on the telephone."

"I meant at your house, goddamnit. You knew that."

"And then I specified here. You did not have to come."

"But I wanted to see you!"

"Then what is the difference to you whether we meet here or in Milburn? You can say what you want to say here."

Sims punched the dashboard. "Damn you. I'm under stress. A great deal of stress. I don't need problems from you. What's the point of meeting out here on this godforsaken part of the highway?"

Stella looked around them, "Oh, I think it's really a rather pretty spot. Don't you? It's quite a beautiful spot. But to answer your question, the point of course is that I did not want you to come to my house."

He said, "You don't want me to come to your house," and for a moment looked so stupid that Stella knew she was an enigma to him. Men to whom you were an enigma were thoroughly useless.

"No," she said gently. "I did not."

"Well, Jesus, we could have met in a bar somewhere, or in a restaurant, or you could have come to Binghamton—"

"I wanted to see you alone."

"Okay, I give up." And he lifted his hands as if literally giving something away. "I suppose you're not even interested in what my problem is."

"Harold," she said, "you've been telling me all about your problems for months now, and I have listened with every appearance of interest."

Abruptly, he exhaled loudly, put a hand over hers and said, "Will you leave with me? I want you to go away with me."

"That's not possible." She patted his hand, then lifted the hand off hers. "Nothing like that is going to happen, Harold."

"Come away with me next year. That gives us plenty of time to break the news to Ricky." He squeezed her hand again.

"Besides being impertinent, you are being foolish. You are forty-six. I am sixty. And you have a job." Stella felt almost as though she were speaking to one of her children. This time she very firmly removed his hand and placed it on the steering wheel.

"Oh hell," he moaned. "Oh hell. Oh goddam it. I only have a job until the end of the year. The department isn't recommending me for promotion, and that means I have to go. Holz broke the news to me today. He said he was sorry to do it, but that he was trying to move the department in a new direction, and I wasn't cooperating. Also, I haven't published enough. Well, I haven't published anything in two years, but that isn't my fault, you know I did three articles and every other anthropologist in the country got published—"

"I *have* heard all this before," Stella interrupted. She stubbed out her cigarette.

"Yeah. But now it's really important. The new guys in the department have just aced me out. Leadbeater got a grant to live on an Indian reservation next term and a contract with Princeton University Press and Johnson's got a book coming out next fall . . . and I get the axe."

What he was saying finally reached Stella through her impatience with the sound of his voice. "Do you mean to say, Harold, that you invited me to run away with you when you don't even have a job?"

"I want you with me."

"Where did you plan to go?"

"I dunno. Maybe California."

"Oh, Harold, you are being insufferably banal," she exploded. "Do you want to live in a trailer park? Eat tacoburgers? Instead of moaning to me you ought to be writing letters and trying to find a new job. And why should you think that I would enjoy sharing your poverty? I was your mistress, not your wife." At the last second she restrained herself from adding, "Thank God."

In a muffled voice, Harold said, "I need you."

"This is ridiculous."

"I do. I do need you."

She saw that he was working himself up to the point

of tears. "Now you are being not only banal, but self-pitying. You really are a very self-pitying man, Harold. It took me a long time to see it, but lately when I have thought of you, I have seen you with a big placard around your neck which reads 'Deserving Case.' Admit it, Harold, things have not been very satisfactory between us lately."

"Well, if I disgust you so much why do you go on seeing me?"

"You did not have much competition. And in fact, I do not intend to go on seeing you. In any case you will be far too busy applying for jobs to cater to my whims. And I will be too busy looking after my husband to listen to your complaints."

"Your husband?" Sims said, now really stunned.

"Yes. He is far more important to me than you, and at this moment he needs me much more. So I am afraid this is it. I will not see you anymore."

"That dried up little . . . that old clothes horse . . . ? He can't be."

"Watch out," Stella warned.

"He's so insignificant," Sims wailed. "You've been making a fool of him for years!"

"All right. He is anything but dried up, and I will not listen to you insult him. If I have had an experimental approach to men during my life, Ricky has accommodated himself to it, which I dare say is more than you would be capable of doing, and if I have made a fool of anyone it is myself. I think it is time I retired into respectability. And—if you cannot see that Ricky has four or five times your own significance, then you are deluding yourself."

"Jesus, you can really be a bitch," Harold said, his little eyes as wide as they could get.

She smiled. " 'You're the most terrifying, ruthless creature I've ever known,' as Melvyn Douglas said to Joan Crawford. I cannot remember the name of the movie, but Ricky is very fond of the line. Why don't you call him up and ask him the name of the picture?"

"God, when I think of the men you must have turned into dogshit."

"Few of them made the transformation so successfully."

"You bitch." Harold's mouth was thinning dangerously.

"You know, like all intensely self-pitying men, you really are very crude, Harold. Would you please get out of my car?"

"You're angry," he said in disbelief. "I lose my job and you just dumped on me, and *you're* angry."

"Yes, I am. Please get out, Harold. Go back to your little heaven of self-regard."

"I could. I could get out right now." He leaned forward. "Or I could force you to see reason by making you do what you enjoy so much."

"I see. You're threatening to rape me, are you, Harold?"

"It's more than a threat."

"It's a promise, is it?" she asked, seeing real brutishness in him for the first time. "Well, before you start slobbering over me, I'll make you a promise too." Stella lifted a hand to the underside of her lapel and pulled out a long hatpin: she had carried it with her for years now, ever since a man in Schenectady had followed her all day through shops. She held the hatpin out before her. "If you make one move toward me, I promise you I'll plant this thing in your neck." Then she smiled: and it was the smile that did it.

He scrambled out of the seat as if given an electric shock and slammed the door behind him. Stella reversed the car to the restraining fence, changed gears and shot out across the oncoming traffic.

"GOD DAMN IT!" He pounded a fist into the palm of the other hand. "I HOPE YOU HAVE AN ACCIDENT!"

Sims picked up a stone from the gravelly shoulder and threw it across the highway. Then he stood for a moment, breathing heavily. "Jesus, what a bitch." He ran his fingers through his cropped hair; he was far too

angry to drive all the way back to the university. Sims
looked at the forest which began down the slope, saw
the puddles of icy water between the trees, and then
looked across the four lanes of road to the dry higher
ground.

Story

6

"We'd just had a fight," Lewis said. "We didn't have
many, and when we had one I was usually wrong. This
time it was because I fired one of the maids. She was
just a girl from the country around Málaga. I can't even
remember her name anymore, but she was a crank, or
so I thought." He cleared his throat and leaned toward
the fire. "The reason was that she was all caught up in
the occult. She believed in magic, evil spirits—Spanish
peasant spiritualism. That didn't bother me enough to
fire her, even though she spooked some of the help by
seeing omens in everything. Birds on the lawn, unexpected rain, a broken glass—all omens. The reason I
fired her was that she refused to clean one of the
rooms."

"It is a pretty damn good reason," Otto said.

"I thought so too. But Linda thought I was being
hard on the girl. She'd never refused to clean the room
before. The girl was upset by the guests, said they were
bad or something. It was crazy."

Lewis took another slug of the brandy, and Otto
added a branch to the fire. Flossie came nearer and lay
with her hindquarters close to the flames.

"Were these guests Spanish, Lew-iss?"

"Americans. A woman from San Francisco named
Florence de Peyser and a little girl, her niece. Alice
Montgomery. A cute little girl about ten. And Mrs. de
Peyser had a maid who traveled with her, a Mexican-

American woman named Rosita. They stayed in a big suite at the top of the hotel. Really, Otto, you couldn't imagine people less spooky than those three. Of course, Rosita could have kept the suite clean and probably did, but it was our girl's job to go in there once a day and she refused, so I fired her. Linda wanted me to change the schedule around and let one of the other girls do it."

Lewis stared into the fire. "People heard us fighting about it, and that was rare too. We were out in the rose garden, and I guess I yelled. I thought it was a matter of principle. So did Linda. Of course. I was stupid. I should have switched the schedule like Linda wanted. But I was too stubborn—in a day or two, she would have swung me around to her point of view, but she didn't live long enough." Lewis bit off a piece of the sausage and for a time chewed silently without tasting. "Mrs. de Peyser invited us to dinner in the suite that same night. Most nights we ate by ourselves and stayed out of people's way, but now and then a guest would invite us to join them for lunch or dinner. I thought Mrs. de Peyser was extending herself to be gracious, and I accepted for us.

"I should not have gone. I was very tired—exhausted. I'd been working hard all day. Besides arguing with Linda, I had helped load two hundred cases of wine into the storeroom in the morning, and then I played obligation games in a tennis tournament all afternoon. Two doubles matches. What I really needed was a quick snack and then bed, but we went up to the suite around nine. Mrs. de Peyser gave us drinks, and then we had arranged with the waiter that the meal was to be brought up around a quarter to ten. Rosita would serve it, and the waiter could go back to the dining room.

"Well, I had one drink and felt woozy. Florence de Peyser gave me another, and all I was fit for was trying to make conversation with Alice. She was a lovely little girl, but she never spoke unless you asked her a question. She was suffocated by good manners, and so passive that you thought she was simple-minded. I gathered that her parents had shunted her off onto her aunt for the summer.

"Later I wondered if my drink had been drugged. I began to feel odd, not sick or drunk exactly, but dissociated. Like I was floating above myself. But Florence de Peyser, who had given us a jaunt on her yacht—well, it was just impossible. Linda noticed that I wasn't feeling well, but Mrs. de Peyser pooh-poohed her. And of course I said I felt fine.

"We sat down to eat. I managed to get down a few bites, but I did feel very light-headed. Alice said nothing during the meal, but looked at me shyly from time to time, smiling as if I were an unusual treat. That was not how I felt. In fact, it may have been only alcohol on top of weariness. My senses were screwy—my fingers felt numb, and my jaw, and the colors in the room seemed paler than I knew they were—I couldn't taste the food at all.

"After dinner, her aunt sent Alice to bed. Rosita served cognac, which I didn't touch. I was able to talk, I know, and I may have seemed normal to anyone but Linda, but all I wanted to do was get to bed. The suite, large as it was, seemed to tighten down over me—over the three of us at the table. Mrs. de Peyser kept us there, talking. Rosita melted away.

"Then the child called me from her room. I could hear her voice saying 'Mr. Benedikt, Mr. Benedikt,' over and over again, very softly. Mrs. de Peyser said 'Would you mind? She likes you very much.' Sure, I said, I'd be happy to say good night to the girl, but Linda stood up before I could and said, 'Darling, you're too tired to move. Let me go.' 'No,' said Mrs. de Peyser. 'The child wants him.' But it was too late. Linda was already going toward the girl's bedroom.

"And then it was too late for everything. Linda went into the bedroom and a second later I knew something was horribly wrong. *Because there wasn't any noise.* I had heard the child half-whispering when she called to me, and I should have heard Linda speaking to her.

It was the loudest silence of my life. I was aware, fuzzy as I was, of Mrs. de Peyser staring at me. That silence ticked on. I stood up and began to go toward the bedroom.

"Linda began to shriek before I got halfway. They were terrible shrieks . . . so piercing . . ." Lewis shook his head. "I banged open the door and burst in just as I heard the noise of breaking glass. Linda was frozen in the window, glass showering all over. Then she was gone. I was too shocked and terrified even to call out. For a second I couldn't move. I looked at the girl, Alice. She was standing on her bed with her back flattened against the wall. For a second—for less than a second—I thought she was smirking at me.

"I ran to the window. Alice started sobbing behind me. It was much too late to help Linda, of course. She was lying dead, way down on the patio. A little crowd of people who had come out of the dining room for the evening air stood around her body. Some of them looked up and saw me leaning out of the broken window. A woman from Yorkshire screamed when she saw me."

"She thought you had pushed her," Otto said.

"Yes. She made a lot of trouble for me with the police. I could have spent the rest of my life in a Spanish jail."

"Lew-iss, couldn't this Mrs. de Peyser and the liddle girl explain what really happened?"

"They checked out. They were booked for another week, but while I was making statements to the police, they packed up and left."

"But didn't the police try to find them?"

"I don't know. I never found them again. And I'll tell you a funny thing, Otto. The story has a joke ending. When she checked out, Mrs. de Peyser paid with an American Express card. She made a little speech to the desk clerk too—said she was sorry to go, that she wished she could do something to help me, but that it was impossible, after the shock she and Alice had had, for them to stay on. A month later we heard from

American Express that the card was invalid. The real Mrs. de Peyser was dead, and the company could not honor any debts on her account." Lewis actually laughed. One of the sticks in the fire tumbled down onto the coals, showering sparks out over the snow. "She stiffed me," he said, and laughed again. "Well, what do you think of that story?"

"I think it is a very American sort of story," Otto said, "You must have asked the child what happened— at least what made her stand up on the bed."

"Did I! I grabbed her and shook her. But she just cried. Then I carried her over to her aunt and got downstairs as fast as I could. I never had another chance to talk to her. Otto, why did you say it was an American sort of story?"

"Because, my good friend, everyone in your story is haunted. Even the credit card was haunted. Most of all the teller. And that, my friend, is *echt Amerikanisch.*"

"Well, I don't know," said Lewis. "Look, Otto, I sort of feel like going off by myself for a little while. I'll just wander around for a few minutes. Do you mind?"

"Are you going to take your fancy rifle?"

"No. I'm not going to kill anything."

"Take poor Flossie along."

"Fine. Come on, Flossie."

The dog jumped up, all alertness again, and Lewis, who was now really unable to sit still or to pretend in any way that he was unaffected by the feelings which had sprung out at him from his memories, walked off into the woods.

Witness

7

Peter Barnes dropped the vase, half-nauseated by the foul smell which had swept over him. He heard a high-pitched giggling; his wrist was already cold where the unseen boy gripped him. Already knowing what he would see, he turned around to see it. The boy who had been sitting on the gravestone was holding onto his wrist with both hands, looking up at Peter's face with the same idiot mirth. His eyes were blank gold.

Peter chopped at him with his free hand, expecting that the scrawny reeking child would blow apart like the Jim Hardie-thing downstairs. Instead the boy ducked the blow and kicked at his ankles with a bony foot which hit him like a sledgehammer. The kick dumped Peter on the ground.

"Make him look, brat," the man said.

The boy nipped behind Peter, clamped his head between two ice-hard hands and turned him around by force. The terrible foulness intensified. Peter realized that the boy's head was just behind his own and screamed "Get away from me!" but the hands on his head increased their pressure. It felt as though the sides of his skull were being pushed together. "Let me go!" he yelled, and this time he did fear that the boy would crush his skull.

His mother's eyes were closed. Her tongue stuck out further.

"You killed her," he said.

"Oh, she is not dead yet," the man said. "She is merely unconscious. We need her to be alive, don't we, Fenny?"

Peter heard horrible squeals from behind him. "You strangled her," he said. The pressure of the boy's hands lessened to its original level: enough to hold him as if in a clamp.

"But not to *death*," the man said, giving a mock-pedantic inflection to the words. "I may have crushed her poor little windpipe a little, and the poor darling probably has a very sore throat. But she does have a pretty neck, doesn't she, Peter?"

He dropped one hand, and held Christina Barnes up with the other as if she weighed no more than a cat. The exposed portion of her neck wore large purple bruises.

"You hurt her," Peter said.

"I am afraid that I did. I only wish that I could perform the same service to you. But our benefactor, the charming woman whose house you broke into with your friend, has decided that she wants you for herself. At the moment, she is occupied with more urgent business. But great treats are in store for you, Master Barnes, and for your older friends. By that time, neither you nor they will know up from down. You will not know if you're reaping or sowing, isn't that right, idiot brother?"

The boy gripped Peter's head painfully tightly and made a whinnying noise.

"What are you?" Peter said.

"I am you, Peter," the man said. He was still holding his mother up with one hand. "Isn't that a nice simple answer? Of course it is not the only answer. A man named Harold Sims who knows your older friends would undoubtedly say that I am a Manitou. Mr. Donald Wanderley has been told that my name is Gregory Benton, and that I am a resident of the city of New Orleans. Of course I once spent several entertaining months in New Orleans, but I can't be said to be from there. I was born with the name Gregory Bate, and that was how I was known until my death in the year 1929. Fortunately, I had entered into an agreement with a charming woman known as Florence de Peyser which spared me the usual indignities attendant upon death, which I am afraid I rather feared. And what do you fear, Peter? Do you believe in vampires? In were-wolves?"

The resonant voice had been unreeling in Peter's
mind, lulling and soothing him, and it was a moment
before he realized that he had been asked a direct question. *"No,"* he whispered, and then:

(*Liar* went through his mind)

and the man holding his mother by the throat altered
and Peter knew in every cell that what he was looking
at was not merely a wolf, but a supernatural being in
wolf form whose only purpose was to kill, to create
terror and chaos and to take life as savagely as possible: saw that pain and death were the only poles of its
being. He saw that this being had nothing in it that was
human, and that it only dressed in the body it had once
owned. He saw too, now that it was letting him see
deeply into it, that this pure destructiveness was not its
own master any more than a dog is: another mind
owned and directed it as surely as the creature owned
the dreadful purity of its evil. All of this Peter saw in a
second. And the next second brought an even worse
recognition: that in all of this blackness lived a morally fatal glamour.

"I don't . . ." he uttered, trembling.

"Oh, but you do," the werewolf said, and put his dark
glasses back on. "I saw perfectly well that you do. I
could have been a vampire just as easily. That is even
more beautiful. And perhaps even closer to the truth."

"What are you?" Peter asked again.

"Well, you could call me Dr. Rabbitfoot," the creature said. "Or you could call me a nightwatcher."

Peter blinked.

"Now I am afraid we must leave you. Our benefactor
will arrange another meeting with you and your friends
in due time. But before we take our leave, we must
satisfy our hunger." It smiled. Its teeth were gleam-
ingly white. "Hold him very still," it commanded, and
the hands pushed with terrible force on the sides of
Peter's head. He began to cry.

Still smiling, the creature pulled Christina Barnes
closer to him and, dipping its head to her neck, slid its

mouth over her skin. Peter tried to leap forward, but the frozen hands held him back. The creature began to eat.

Peter tried to scream, and the dead child holding him moved its hands to cover his mouth. It pressed Peter's head against its chest. The smell of putrefaction, his terror and despair, the horror of being clasped against the revolting body and the greater horror of what was happening to his mother—he blacked out.

When he awakened he was alone. The stench of corruption still hung in the room. Peter moaned and pushed himself up into a kneeling position. The vase he had dropped lay on its side near him. Flowers, still brilliant, were strewn out across a puddle on the carpet. He raised his hands to his face and caught on them the reek of the dead boy who had held him. He gagged. The awful smell must have covered his mouth too, rubbed off the boy's hand: it was as though his mouth and cheek were covered with decay.

Peter ran out of the bedroom and down the hall until he found a bathroom. Then he turned on the hot water and scrubbed his face and hands over and over, working up the lather and rinsing it off, then taking the soap again and working it between his palms. He was sobbing. His mother was dead: she had come to see Lewis, and they had killed her. They had done to her what they did to animals: they were dead creatures that lived like vampires on blood. But they were not vampires. Nor were they werewolves; they could just make you think they were. They had sold themselves long ago to whatever owned them. Peter remembered green light leaking from beneath a door, and nearly vomited into the sink. *She* owned them. They were nightwatchers— night-things. He smeared Lewis's soap over his mouth, rubbing and rubbing to rid himself of the smell of Fenny's hands.

Peter remembered Jim Hardie seated at the bar in a seedy country tavern, asking him if he would like to see all of Milburn go up in flames, and knew that unless he could be stronger, braver and smarter than Jim, that what would happen to Milburn would be worse than that. The nightwatchers would systematically ruin the town—make it a ghost town—and leave behind only the stench of death.

Because that's all they want, he said to himself, remembering Gregory Bate's naked face, *all they want is to destroy.* He saw Jim Hardie's taut face, the face of Jim drunk and hurling himself into a wild scheme; the face of Sonny Venuti leaning toward him with her pop eyes; of his mother as she left the station wagon on the brick court; and chillingly, of the actress at the party last year, looking at him with a smiling mouth and expressionless eyes.

He dropped Lewis's towel on the bathroom floor.

They've been here before.

There was only one person who could help him— who might not think he was lying or crazy. He had to get back to town and see the writer who was staying in the hotel.

The loss of his mother went through him once again, shaking tears from him; but he did not have time to cry now. He went out into the hall and past the heavy door. "Oh, mom," he said. "I'll stop them. I'll *get* them. I'll—" But the words were hollow, just a boy's defiance. *They want you to think that.*

Peter did not look back at the house as he ran down the drive, but he felt it back there, watching him and mocking his puny intentions—as if it knew that his freedom was only that of a dog on a leash. At any second he could be pulled back, his neck bruised, his wind cut off . . .

He saw why when he reached the end of Lewis's drive. A car was parked on the verge of the highway, and the Jehovah's Witness who had given him a lift was inside it, looking at him. He blinked his lights at Peter: glowing eyes. "Come along," the man called. "Just come along, son."

Peter ran out into the traffic. An oncoming car

squealed around him, another car skidded to a stop.
Half a dozen horns cried out. He reached the median
and ran across the empty other half of the highway. He
could still hear the Witness calling to him. "Come back.
It's no good."

Peter disappeared into the underbrush on the far side
of the highway. Among the noises and confusions of
traffic, he clearly heard the Witness starting up his car
to track him back to town.

8

Five minutes after Lewis left Otto's fire, he began to
feel tired. His back ached from all the shoveling he had
done the day before; his legs threatened to give out.
The hound trotted before him, forcing him to go on
when he'd rather just go down the hill back to his car.
Even that was at least a half hour walk away. Better to
go on after the dog and settle down and then return
to the fire.

Flossie sniffed at the base of a tree, checked that he
was still there, and trotted on.

The worst part of the story was that he had allowed
Linda to go into the child's room alone. Sitting at the
de Peyser table, woozy, even more exhausted than he
was now, he had sensed that the entire situation was
somehow false, that he was unknowingly playing a part
in a game. That was what he had not told Otto: that
sense of wrongness which had come over him during
dinner. Beneath the food's absence of taste had lain the
faint taste of garbage, and in the same way beneath the
superficial chatter of Florence de Peyser had lain something which had made him see himself as a marionette
forced into dance. Feeling that, why had he continued
to sit, to struggle to appear normal—why hadn't he
taken Linda by the arm and hurried out?

Don too had said something about feeling like a
player in a game.

Because they know you well enough to know what

*you will do. That is why you stayed. Because they knew
you would.*

The slight wind shifted; turned colder. The hound
lifted its nose, sniffed and turned into the direction of
the wind. She began to move more quickly.

"Flossie!" he yelled. The hound, already thirty yards
ahead of him and visible only when he saw it coursing
between the trees, emerged into an opening and glanced
back at Lewis over its shoulder. Then she amazed Lewis
by lowering her head and growling. The next second
she flashed away.

Looking ahead, he saw only the bushy shapes of fir
trees, interspersed with the bare skeletons of other trees,
standing on ground mottled white. Melting snow moved
sluggishly downhill. His feet were cold. Finally he heard
the dog barking, and went toward the sound.

When he finally saw the dog, she began to whine. She
was standing in a small glacial hollow, and Lewis was
at the hollow's upper edge. Boulders like Easter Island
statues, crusted with quartz, littered the bottom of the
hollow. The dog glanced up at him, whined again, wriggled her body, and then flattened out alongside one of
the boulders. "Come back, Flossie," he said. The dog
pressed herself onto the ground, switching her tail.

"What is it?" he asked her.

He stepped into the hollow and slipped two yards
down on cold mud. The dog barked once sharply, then
turned in a tight circle and flattened herself out again
on the ground. She was looking at a stand of fir trees
growing up on the far side of the hollow. As Lewis
slogged through the mud, Flossie crept forward toward
the trees.

"Don't go in there," he said. The dog crept up to the
first of the trees, whining; then it disappeared under
the branches.

He tried to call it out. The hound would not return.
No sound came from within the thick cluster of firs.
Frustrated, Lewis looked up at the sky and saw heavy
clouds scudding on the north wind. The two days'
respite from snow was over.

"Flossie."

The dog did not reappear, but as he looked at the dense curtain of fir needles he saw an astonishing thing. Stitched into the pattern of needles and branches was the outline of a door. A clump of dark needles formed the handle. It was the most perfect optical illusion he had ever seen: even the hinges were represented.

Lewis took a step forward. He was at the spot where Flossie had flattened herself out on the ground. The illusion grew more perfect the closer to the trees he went. Now the needles seemed almost to be suggesting the grain of polished wood. It was the way they alternated colors and shades, darker green above lighter above darker, a random pattern solidifying into the whorls on a slab of monkeywood.

It was the door to his bedroom.

Lewis slowly went up the other side of the hollow toward the door. He went close enough to touch the smooth wood.

It wanted him to open it. Lewis stood in his wet boots in a cold, lifting breeze and knew that all the inexplicable occurrences of his life since that day in 1929 had led him to this: they put him in front of an impossible door to an unforseeable experience. If he had just been thinking that the story of Linda's death was—as Don said of the story of Alma Mobley—without point or ending, then there behind the door was its meaning. Even then Lewis knew that the door led not to one room but many.

Lewis could not refuse it. Otto, rubbing his hands before a twigfire, was only a part of an existence too trivial to insist on its worth—too trivial to hold to. For Lewis, who had already made his decision, his past, especially the latest years in Milburn, was dull lead, a long ache of boredom and uselessness from which he had been shown the way out.

Thus Lewis turned the brass knob and fell into his place in the puzzle.

He stepped, as he knew he would, into a bedroom. He recognized it immediately: the sunny bedroom, filled with Spanish flowers, of the ground-floor apartment he and Linda had kept in the hotel. A silky Chinese rug stretched beneath his feet to each of the room's corners; flowers in vases, still hungry for the sun, picked up the golds, reds and blues of the rug and shone them back. He turned around, saw the closing door, and smiled. Sun streamed through the twin windows. Looking out, he saw a green lawn, a railed precipice and the top of the steps down to the sea which glimmered below. Lewis went to the canopied bed. A dark blue velvet dressing gown lay folded across its foot. At peace, Lewis surveyed the entire lovely room.

Then the door to the lounge opened, and Lewis turned smiling to his wife. In the haze of his utter happiness, he moved forward, extending his arms. He stopped when he saw that she was crying.

"Darling, what's wrong? What happened?"

She raised her hands: across them lay the body of a short-haired dog. "One of the guests found her lying on the patio. Everybody was just coming out from lunch, and when I got there they were all standing around staring at the poor little thing. It was horrible, Lewis."

Lewis leaned over the body of the dog and kissed Linda's cheek. "I'll take care of it, Linda. But how the devil did it get there?"

"They said someone threw it out of a window . . . oh, Lewis, who in the world would do a thing like that?"

"I'll take care of it. Poor sweetie. Just sit down for a minute." He took the corpse of the dog from his wife's hands. "I'll straighten it out. Don't worry about it anymore."

"But what are you going to do with it?" she wailed.

"Bury it in the rose garden next to John, I guess."

"That's good. That's lovely."

Carrying the dog, he went toward the lounge door, then paused. "Lunch went all right otherwise?"

"Yes, fine. Florence de Peyser invited us to join her

in the suite for dinner tonight. Will you feel like it after all that tennis? You're sixty-five, remember."

"No, I'm not." Lewis faced her with a puzzled expression. "I'm married to you, so I'm fifty. You're making me old before my time!"

"Absentminded me," Linda said. "Really, I could just kick myself."

"I'll be right back with a much better idea," Lewis said, and went through the door to the lounge.

The dog's weight slipped off his hands, and everything changed. His father was walking toward him across the floor of the parsonage living room. "Two more points, Lewis. Your mother deserves a little consideration, you know. You treat this house as though it were a hotel. You come in at all hours of the night." His father reached the armchair behind which Lewis stood, swerved off in the direction of the fireplace, and then marched back to the other side of the room, still talking. "Sometimes, I am told, you drink spirits. Now I am not a prudish man, but I will not tolerate that. I know you are sixty-five—"

"Seventeen," Lewis said.

"Seventeen, then. Don't interrupt. No doubt you think that is very grown up. But you will not drink spirits while you live under this roof, is that understood? And I want you to begin showing your age by helping your mother with the cleaning. This room is henceforth your responsibility. You must dust and clean it once a week. And see to the grate in the mornings. Is that clear?"

"Yes, sir," he said.

"Good. That is point one. Point two concerns your friends. Mr. James and Mr. Hawthorne are both fine men, and I would say I have an excellent relationship with both of them. But age and circumstance divide us. I would not call them friends, nor would they call me their friend. For one thing, they are Episcopalians, just one step from popery. For another, they possess a good deal of money. Mr. James must be one of the richest

men in all of New York. Do you know what that
means, in 1928?"

"Yes, sir."

"It means that you cannot afford to keep up with his
son. Nor can you keep up with Mr. Hawthorne's son.
We lead respectable and godly lives, but we are not
wealthy. If you continue to associate with Sears James
and Ricky Hawthorne, I foresee the direst consequences. They have the habits of the sons of wealthy
men. As you know, it is my plan to send you to the university in the autumn, but you will be one of the poorest
students at Cornell, and you must not learn such habits,
Lewis, they will lead only to ruin. I will forever regret
your mother's generosity in using her own funds to
provide the wherewithal to purchase you a motorcar."
He was on another circuit of the room. "And people
are already gossiping about the three of you and that
Italian woman on Montgomery Street. I know clergy-
men's sons are supposed to be wild, but . . . well, words
fail me." He paused midpoint on the track from the
corner of the room and looked seriously into Lewis's
eyes. "I assume that I am understood."

"Yes, sir. I understand. Is that all?"

"No. I am at a loss to account for this." His father
was holding out to him the corpse of a short-haired
hound. "It was lying dead on the walk to the church
door. What if one of the congregation had seen it there?
I want you to dispose of it immediately."

"Leave it to me," Lewis said. "I'll bury it in the rose
garden."

"Please do so immediately."

Lewis took the dog out of the living room, and at the
last minute turned to ask, "Do you have Sunday's ser-
mon prepared, father?"

No one answered. He was in an unused bedroom at
the top of the house on Montgomery Street. The room's
only furniture was a bed. The floorboards were bare,
and greasepaper had been nailed over the only window.
Because Lewis's car had a flat tire, Sears and Ricky
were off borrowing Warren Scales's old flivver while

Warren and his pregnant wife shopped. A woman lay on the bed, but she would not answer him because she was dead. A sheet covered her body.

Lewis moved back and forth on the floorboards, willing his friends to return with the farmer's car. He did not want to look at the covered shape on the bed; he went to the window. Through the greasepaper he could see only vague orange light. He glanced back at the sheet. "Linda," he said miserably.

He stood in a metal room, with gray metal walls. One light bulb hung from the ceiling. His wife lay under a sheet on a metal table. Lewis leaned over her body and sobbed. "I won't bury you in the pond," he said. "I'll take you into the rose garden." He touched his wife's lifeless fingers under the sheet and felt them twitch. He recoiled.

As he watched horrified, Linda's hands crept up beneath the sheet. Her white hands folded the sheet down over her face. She sat up, and her eyes opened.

Lewis cowered at the far end of the little room. When his wife swung her legs off the morgue table, he screamed. She was naked, and the left side of her face was broken and scraped. He held his hands out in front of him in a childish gesture of protection. Linda smiled at him, and said, "What about that poor dog?" She was pointing to the uncovered slab of table, where a short-haired hound lay on its side in a puddle of blood.

He looked back in horror at his wife, but Stringer Dedham, his hair parted in the middle, a brown shirt concealing his stumps, stood beside him. "What did you see, Stringer?" he asked.

Stringer smiled at him bloodily. "I saw you. That's why I jumped out of the window. Don't be a puddin' head."

"You saw me?"

"Did I say I saw you? Guess I'm the puddin' head. *I* didn't see you. Your wife's the one saw *you*. What *I* saw was my girl. Saw her right through her window, morning of the day I helped out on the thresher. Gosh, I must be a real moron."

"But what did you see her doing? What did you try to tell your sisters?"

Stringer bent back his head and laughed, and blood gushed out of his mouth. He coughed. "Golly gee, I couldn't hardly believe it, it was just amazin', friend. You ever see a snake with its head cut off? You ever see that tongue dartin' out—and that head just a stump of a thing no bigger than your thumb? You ever see that body workin' away, beatin' itself in the dust?" Stringer laughed loudly through the red foam in his mouth. "Holy Moses, Lewis, what a godforsaken thing. Honestly, ever since it's been like I can't hardly think straight, like my brain's all mixed up and leakin' outa my ears. It's like that time I had the stroke, in 1940, remember? When one side of me froze up? And you gave me baby food on a spoon? *Grrr*, what a godawful taste!"

"That wasn't you," Lewis said, "That was my father."

"Well, what did I tell you? It's all mixed up—like someone cut my head off, and my tongue keeps moving." Stringer gave an abashed red smile. "Say, wasn't you goin' to take that poor old dog and drop it in the pond?"

"Oh, yes, when they get back," Lewis said. "We need Warren Scales's car. His wife is pregnant."

"The wife of a Roman Catholic farmer is of no concern to me at the moment," his father said. "One year at college has coarsened you, Lewis." From his temporary mooring beside the mantel, he looked long and sadly at his son. "And I know too that this is a coarsening era. Pitch defileth, Lewis. Our age is pitch. We are born into damnation, and for our children all is darkness. I wish that I could have reared you in more stable times—Lewis, once this country was a paradise! A paradise! Fields as far as you could see! Filled with the bounty of the Lord! Son, when I was a boy I saw Scripture in the spider webs. The Lord was watching us then, Lewis, you could feel His presence in the sunlight and the rain. But now we are like spiders dancing in a fire." He looked down at the literal fire, which was warming his knees. "It all started with the railway. That I'm sure of, son. The railroad brought money to men who'd never had the smell of two dollars together in all their lives. The iron horse spoiled the land, and now financial collapse is going to spread like a stain over this whole country." And looked at Lewis with the clear shrewd eyes of Sears James.

"I promised her I'd bury her in the rose garden," Lewis said. "They'll be back with the car soon."

"The *car*." His father turned away in disgust. "You never listened to the important things I had to tell you. You have forsaken me, Lewis."

"You excite yourself too much," Lewis said. "You'll give yourself a stroke."

"His will be done."

Lewis looked at his father's rigid back. "I'll see to it now." His father made no answer. "Good-bye."

His father spoke without turning around. "You never listened. But mark me, son, it will come back to haunt you. You were seduced by yourself, Lewis. Nothing sadder can be said of any man. A handsome face and feathers for brains. You got your looks from your mother's Uncle Leo, and when he was twenty-five he stuck his hand into the woodstove and held it there until it was charred like a hickory log."

Lewis went through the dining-room door. Linda was peeling the sheet off her naked body in the vacant upper room. She smiled at him with bloody teeth. "After that," she said, "your mother's Uncle Leo was a godly man all his life long." Her eyes glowed, and she swung her legs down off the bed. Lewis backed away toward the bare wooden wall. "After that he saw Scripture in spider webs, Lewis." She moved slowly toward him, twisting on a broken hip. "You were going to put me in the pond. Did you see Scripture in the pond, Lewis? Or were you distracted by your pretty face?"

"Now it's over, isn't it?" Lewis asked.

"Yes." She was close enough for him to catch the dark brown smell of death.

Lewis straightened his body against the rough wall. "What did you see in that girl's bedroom?"

"I saw you, Lewis. What you were supposed to see. Like this."

9

As long as Peter was concealed by the underbrush he was safe. A wiry network of branches hid him from the road. On the other side, beginning ten or fifteen yards back, were trees like those before Lewis's house. Peter worked his way back into them to be further screened from the man in the car. The Jehovah's Witness had not moved off the shoulder of the highway: Peter could see the top of his car, a bright acrylic blue shield, over the top of the dry brambles. Peter ducked from the safety of one tree to another; then to another. The car inched forward. They continued in this way for some time, Peter moving slowly over the damp ground and the car clinging to his side like a shark to which he was the pilot fish. At times the Witness's car moved slightly ahead, at times it hung back, but never was it more than five or ten yards off in either direction—the only comfort available for Peter was that the driver's errors proved that he could not see him. He was just idling down the shoulder of the road waiting for a section of cleared ground.

Peter tried to visualize the landscape on his side of the highway, and remembered that only for a mile or so in the vicinity of Lewis's house was there heavy ground cover—most of the rest of the land, until an eruption of gas stations and drive-ins marked the edges of Milburn, was field. Unless he crawled in ditches for seven miles, the man in the car would be able to see him as soon as he left the stretch of woods.

Come out, son.

The Witness was aimlessly sending out messages, trying to coax him into the car. Peter shut his mind to the whispers as well as he could and plunged on through the woods. Maybe if he kept on running, the Witness would drive down the road far enough to let him think.

Come on, boy. Come out of there. Let me take you to her.

Still protected by the high brambles and the trees, Peter ran until he could see, strung between the massive trunks of oaks, double strands of silvery wire. Beyond the wire was a long curved vacancy of field— empty white ground. The Witness's car was nowhere in sight. Peter looked sideways, but here the trees were too thick and the brambles too high for him to see the section of highway nearest him. Peter reached the last of the trees and the wire and looked over the field, wondering if he could get across unseen. If the man saw him on the field, Peter knew he would be helpless. He could run, but eventually the man would get him as the thing back in the Montgomery Street house got Jim.

She's interested in you, Peter.

It was another aimless, haphazard dart with no real urgency in it.

She'll give you everything you want.

She'll give you anything you want.

She'll give you back your mother.

The blue car edged forward into his vision and stopped just past the point where the field began. Peter shuddered back a few feet deeper into the wood. The man in the car turned sideways, resting his arm along the top of the seat, and in this posture of patient waiting looked out at the field Peter would have to cross. *Come on out and we'll give you your mother.*

Yes. That was what they would do. They'd give him back his mother. She would be like Jim Hardie and Freddy Robinson, with empty eyes and amnesiac conversation and no more substance than a ray of moonlight.

Peter sat down on wet ground, trying to remember if any other roads were near. He would have to go through the woods or the man would find him when he crossed the field; was there another road, running parallel to the highway, going back to Milburn?

He remembered nights of driving around the countryside with Jim, all of the footloose journeying of high school weekends and summers: he would have said that he knew Broome County as well as he knew his own bedroom.

But the patient man in the blue car made it difficult to think. He could not remember what happened on the other side of this wood—a developer's suburb, a factory? For a moment his mind would not give him the information he knew it had, and instead offered images of vacant buildings where dark things moved behind drawn blinds. But whatever lay on the other side of the woods, the other side was where he had to go.

Peter stood up quietly and retreated a few yards farther into the woods before turning his back on the highway and running away from the car. Seconds later he remembered what he was running toward. There was an old two-lane macadam highway in this direction, in Milburn, called "the old Binghamton road" because once it had been the only highway between the two towns: pitted, obsolete and unsafe, it was avoided by nearly all traffic now. Once there had been small businesses dotted along it, fruit markets, a motel, a drugstore. Now most of these were empty, and some of them had been razed. The Bay Tree Market alone flourished: it was heavily patronized by the better-off people of Milburn. His mother had always bought fruit and vegetables there.

If he remembered the distance between the old and new highways correctly, it would take him less than twenty minutes to get to the Market. From there he could get a lift into town and make it safely to the hotel.

In fifteen minutes he had wet feet, a stitch in his side and a rip in his jacket from a snagged branch, but he knew he was getting near the old road. The trees had thinned out and the ground sloped gently down.

Now, seeing in the blank gray air ahead of him that the woods were ending, he went nearer the fence and crept slowly along it for the final thirty yards. He still was not sure if the fruit market was to the left or the right, or how far off it was. All he hoped was that it would be in sight, and show a busy parking lot.

He squelched forward, peering around the few remaining trees.

You're wasting your time, Peter. Don't you want to see your mother again?

He groaned, feeling the feathery touch of the Witness's mind. His stomach went cold. The blue car was parked on the road before him. On the front seat Peter saw a bulky shape he knew was the Witness, leaning back, waiting for him to show himself.

The Bay Tree Market was in sight about a quarter mile down the old highway to Peter's left—the car faced the other way. If he made a run for it, the man would have to turn his car around on the narrow old road.

That still would not give him enough time.

Peter looked again at the market: there were plenty of cars in the lot. At least one of them would belong to someone he knew. All he had to do was to get there.

For a moment he felt no more than five years old, a shivering boy helpless and with no weapons and with no hope of defeating the murderous creature waiting for him in the car. If he tore his windbreaker into pieces and then tied them together and then put one end in the gas tank—but that was just a bad idea from worse movies. He could never get to the car before the man saw him.

In fact, the only thing he could do, apart from rushing the man, was to go openly across the field to the market and see what happened. The man was looking the other way, and at least he would have some time before he was seen.

Peter separated the strands of wire clipped to the trees and climbed through. A quarter of a mile away, in a straight line, was the rear parking lot of the Bay Tree Market. He held his breath and started walking across the field.

The car did a three-point turn behind him and drew up alongside him, just visible in the periphery of his vision. *Nice brave boy. Nice boys shouldn't go hitch-hiking, should they?* Peter closed his eyes and went stumbling over the field.

Stupid brave boy. He wondered what the man would do to stop him.

He did not have to wait long to find out.

"Peter, I have to talk to you. Open your eyes, Peter." The voice was Lewis Benedikt's. Peter opened his eyes and saw Lewis standing twenty yards before him, dressed in baggy trousers, boots, an unfastened khaki army jacket.

"You're not here," Peter said.

"Talk sense, Peter," Lewis said, and began to come toward him. "You can see me, can't you? You can hear me? I'm here. Please listen to me. I want to tell you about your mother."

"She's dead." Peter stopped walking, unwilling to get closer to the Lewis-creature.

"No, she is not." Lewis stopped too, as if not wishing to frighten Peter. Off on the road to their side, the car also halted. "Nothing's that black or white. She wasn't dead when you saw her in my house, was she?"

"She was."

"You can't be sure, Pete. She passed out, just like you." Lewis opened his hands and smiled at Peter.

"No. They cut—they cut open her throat. They killed her. Just like those animals were killed." He closed his eyes again.

"Pete, you're wrong and I can prove it. That man in the car doesn't want to hurt you. Let's go to him. Let's go there now."

Peter opened his eyes. "Did you really sleep with my mother?"

"People our age sometimes make mistakes. They do things they're sorry about later. But it didn't mean anything, Pete. You'll see when you get home. All you have to do is come home with us, and she'll be there, just like she always is." Lewis was smiling toward him with intelligent concern. "Don't judge her badly because she made one mistake." He started coming forward again. "Trust me. I always hoped we'd be friends."

"I did too, but you can't be my friend because you're dead," Peter said. He bent over and picked up a double handful of wet snow. He squeezed it together in his hands.

"You're going to throw a snowball at me? Isn't that a little juvenile?"

"I feel sorry for you," Peter said, and threw the snowball and blew the thing that looked like Lewis into a shower of falling light.

As if shell-shocked, he trudged ahead, walking straight through the space where Lewis had stood. The air tingled on his face. He felt another feathery tickling in his mind, and braced himself.

But no words followed. Instead came a wave of bitterness and anger which nearly knocked him down with its force. It was the same blackness of feeling he had seen when the creature holding his mother had taken off its dark glasses, and the violence of the emotion made him stagger; but there was a wide current of defeat in it.

Peter snapped his head sideways in surprise; the blue car accelerated down the macadam road.

Relief buckled his knees. He did not know why, but he had won. Peter sat heavily, clumsily down in the snow and tried not to cry. After a while he stood up again and continued on toward the parking lot. He was too numb for feeling; he made himself concentrate on getting his legs to move. First one step, then another. His feet were very cold. Another step. Now he was not far from the lot.

Then an even greater sweetness flooded through him. His mother was flying through the parking lot, running toward him. "Pete!" she shouted, half-sobbing. "Thank God!"

She reached the cars at the edge of the lot and ran past them onto the field. He stood watching her run toward him, too crowded with feeling to speak, and then trudged forward. She had a large bruise on one cheek and her hair was as tangled as a gypsy's. A scarf tied around her neck showed a line of red at its center.

"You got away," he said, stupefied with relief.

"They took me out of the house—that man—" She stood a few yards away from him, and her hands went to her throat. "He cut my neck—I fainted—I thought they were going to kill you."

"I thought you were dead," he told her. "Oh, mom."

"Poor Pete." She hugged her arms around herself. "Let's get out of here. We'll have to get a ride back to town. I guess both of us can just about move that far."

That she could joke, however feebly, moved him again to the point of tears. He put a hand over his eyes.

"Cry later," she said. "I think I'll cry for a week after I sit down. Let's find a ride."

"How did you get away from them?" He walked beside her, about to hug her, but she stepped backward, leading him toward the lot. He fell into step with her.

"I guess they thought I was too frightened to move. And when they got me outside, the fresh air sort of revived me. That man relaxed his hold on my arm, and I swung around and belted him with my bag. Then I ran away into the woods. I heard them looking for me. I've never *never* been so scared in my life. After a while they just gave up. Were they looking for you?"

"No," he said. "No." And the tension melted in him. "There was someone else, but he left—he didn't get me."

"They'll leave us alone now," she said. "Now that we're away from there."

He looked into her face, and she glanced down. "I owe you a lot of explanations, Peter. But this isn't the time. I just want to get home and put a real bandage on my throat. We'll have to think of something to tell your father."

"You won't tell him what happened?"

"We'll just let it die, can't we?" she asked, and looked pleadingly at him. "I'll explain everything to you —in time. Let's just be thankful now that we're alive."

They stepped onto the surface of the parking lot.

"Okay," Peter said. "Mom, I'm so—" He struggled with his emotions, but they were too dense to be expressed. "We have to talk to someone, though. The same man that hurt you killed Jim Hardie."

She looked back at him, having walked forward toward the crowded middle of the lot. "I know."

"You know?"

"I mean I guessed. Hurry up, Pete. My neck hurts. I want to get home."

"You said you knew."

She made a gesture of exasperation. "Don't cross-examine me, Peter."

Peter looked wildly around the parking lot and saw the blue car just nosing past the side of the market. "Oh, mom," he said. "They did. They did. You didn't get away from them."

"*Peter*. Snap out of it. I see someone we can get a ride with."

As the blue car swung up the lane behind her, Peter walked toward his mother, staring at her. "Okay, I'm coming."

"Good. Peter, everything will be the way it was again, you will see. We both had a terrible fright, but a hot bath and a good sleep will work wonders."

"You'll need stitches in your neck," Peter said, coming closer.

"No, of course not." She smiled at him. "A bandage is all I need. It was just a scratch. Peter. What are you doing, Peter? Don't touch it, it hurts. You'll start the bleeding again."

The blue car was now at the top of their row. Peter reached out toward his mother.

"Don't, Pete, we'll get our ride in a minute . . ."

He clamped his eyes shut and swung his arm toward his mother's head. A second later his fingers were tingling. He yelled: a horn sounded, terrifyingly loud.

When he opened his eyes his mother was gone and the blue car was speeding toward him. Peter scrambled toward the protection of two parked cars and slipped between them just as the blue car raced by, scraping its side against them and making them rock.

He watched it squeeze down to the end of the aisle, and when it cut across to drive up the next aisle, he saw Irmengard Draeger, Penny's mother, walk out of the back door of the market carrying a sack of groceries. He ran toward her, cutting through the rows of parked cars.

Stories

10

Inside the hotel, Mrs. Hardie looked at him curiously but told him Don Wanderley's room number and then watched him as he climbed the steps at the end of the lobby. He knew that he should have turned around to say something, but he could not trust himself, after the strain of riding back to town with Mrs. Draeger, to make even the most perfunctory conversation with Jim's mother.

He found Don's door and knocked.

"Mr. Wanderley," he said when the writer opened the door.

For Don, the appearance of the shaken teenager outside his room meant the arrival of certainty. The period when the consequences of the final Chowder Society story—whatever that would turn out to be— were limited to its members and a few outlyers was over. The expression of shock and loss on Peter Barnes's face told Don that what he had been brooding about in his room was no longer the property of himself and four elderly men.

"Come in, Peter," he said. "I thought we'd be meeting again soon."

The boy moved like a zombie into the room and sat blindly in a chair. "I'm sorry," he began, and then closed his mouth. "I want—I have to—" He blinked, and was obviously unable to continue.

"Hang on," Don said, and went to his dresser and took out a bottle of whiskey. He poured an inch into a water glass and gave it to Peter. "Drink some of this and settle down. Then just tell me everything that happened. Don't waste time thinking that I might not believe you, because I will. And so will Mr. Hawthorne and Mr. James, when I tell them."

"'My older friends,'" Peter said. He swallowed some of the whiskey. "That's what he called them. He said you thought his name was Greg Benton."

Peter twitched, uttering the name, and Don felt the shock of a conviction hitting his nerves: whatever the danger to himself, he would destroy Greg Benton.

"You met him," he said.

"He killed my mother," Peter said flatly. "His brother held me and made me watch. I think—I think they drank her blood. Like they did to those animals. And he killed Jim Hardie. I saw him do it, but I got away."

"Go on," Don said.

"And he said someone—I can't remember his name —would call him a Manitou. Do you know what that is?"

"I've heard of it."

Peter nodded, as if this satisfied him. "And he turned into a wolf. I saw him. I saw him do it." Peter set the glass down on the floor, then looked at it again and picked it up and took another sip. His hands trembled badly enough nearly to splash the whiskey over the lip of the glass. "They *stink*—they're like rotten dead things—I had to scrub and scrub. Where Fenny touched me."

"You saw Benton turn into a wolf?"

"Yes. Well, no. Not exactly. He took off his glasses. They have yellow eyes. He let me *see* him. He was— he was nothing but hate and death. He was like a laser beam."

"I understand," Don said. "I've seen him. But I never saw him without his glasses."

"When he takes them off, he can make you do things. He can talk inside your head. Like ESP. And they can make you see dead people, ghosts, but when you touch them, they sort of blow up. But *they* don't blow up. They grab you and they kill you. But they're dead too. Somebody else owns them—their benefactor. They do what she wants."

"She?" Don asked, and remembered a lovely woman holding this handsome boy's chin at a dinner party.

"That Anna Mostyn," Peter said. "But she was here before."

"Yes, she was," Don said. "As an actress."

Peter looked at him with grateful surprise.

"I just figured out some of the story, Peter," Don said. "Just in the past few days." He looked at the shivering boy in the chair. "It looks like you figured out a lot more than I did and in a shorter time."

"He said he was *me,*" Peter said, his face distorting. *"He said he was me,* I want to *kill* him."

"Then we'll do it together," Don said.

"They're here because I'm here," Don told him. "Ricky Hawthorne said that when I joined him and Sears and Lewis Benedikt, that we brought these things —these beings—into focus. That we gathered them here. Maybe if I had stayed away, there'd just be a few dead sheep or cows or something, and that would be that. But that was never a possibility, Peter. I couldn't stay away—and they knew I would have to come. And now they can do anything they want."

Peter interrupted him. "Anything *she* wants them to do."

"That's right. But we're not helpless. We can fight back. And we'll do it. We'll get rid of them however we can. That's a promise."

"But they're already dead," Peter said. "How can we kill them? I *know* they're dead—they have that smell—"

He was beginning to slide into panic again, and Don reached over and took his hand. "I know because of the stories. These things aren't new. They've probably been around for centuries—for longer than that. They've certainly been talked about and written about for hundreds of years. I think they are what people used to call vampires and werewolves—they're probably behind a thousand ghost stories. Well, in the stories, and I think that means in the past, people found ways to make them die again. Stakes through the heart or silver bullets —remember? The point is that they can be destroyed. And if it takes silver bullets, that's what we'll use. But I don't think we'll need them. You want revenge and I do too, and we'll get it."

"But that's just them," Peter said, looking straight at Don. "What do we do about *her?*"

"That'll be harder. She's the general. But history is full of dead generals." It was a facile answer, but the boy seemed calmer. "Now I think you'd better tell me everything, Peter. Begin with how Jim died, if that's the beginning. The more you remember, the more you'll help us. So try to tell it all."

"Why didn't you tell anyone else about this?" he asked when Peter was done.

"Because I knew no one would believe me but you. You heard the music."

Don nodded.

"And nobody will, will they? They'll think it's like Mr. Scales and the Martians."

"Not quite. The Chowder Society will. I hope."

"You mean Mr. James and Mr. Hawthorne and . . ."

"Yes." He and the boy looked at each other, knowing that Lewis was dead. "We'll be enough, Peter. It's the four of us against her."

"When do we start? What do we do?"

"I'll meet with the others tonight. I think you ought to go home. You have to see your father."

"He won't believe me. I know he won't. Nobody would, unless they . . ." The boy's voice trailed off.

"Do you want me to come with you?"

Peter shook his head.

"I will if you want me to."

"No. I won't tell him. It wouldn't do any good. I'll have to tell him later."

"Maybe that's better. And if you want help when the times comes, I'll give it to you. Peter, I think you've been brave as hell. Most adults would have folded up like tissue paper. But you're going to have to be even braver from now on. You might have to protect your father as well as yourself. Don't open your door to anybody unless you know who they are."

Peter nodded. "I won't. You bet I won't. But why are they here, anyhow? Why is *she* here?"

"That's what I'm going to find out tonight."

Peter stood up and began to leave, but when he put his hands in his pockets, he touched a folded pamphlet. "I forgot. The man in the blue car gave me this after he took me to Mr. Benedikt's house." He brought out *The Watchtower* and smoothed it out on Don's desk. Beneath the name, in large black letters on the cheap pulpy paper, were the words DR. RABBITFOOT LED ME TO SIN.

Don ripped the pamphlet in half.

11

Harold Sims tramped into the upper woods, disgusted with both himself and Stella Hawthorne. His shoes and the bottoms of his trousers were soaked, the shoes probably ruined. But what was not? He had lost his job, and when he had finally asked Stella to leave with him, after weeks of thinking about it, he had lost her too. Damn it, did she think that he had just asked her on the spur of the moment? Didn't she know him better than that? He ground his teeth.

It's not like I forgot she was sixty, he told himself: I worried about that plenty. "I came to that bitch with clean hands," he said out loud, and saw the words vaporize before him. She had betrayed him. She had insulted him. She had never—he could see it now—really taken him seriously.

And what was she, anyhow? An old bag with no morals and a freakish bone structure. Intellectually, she hardly counted.

And she wasn't really adaptable. Look at her view of California—trailer parks and tacoburgers! She was shallow—Milburn was where she belonged. With that stuffy little husband, talking about old movies.

"Yes?" he said. He had heard a quick, gasping noise, very near.

"Do you need help?" No one answered, and he put his hands on his hips and looked around.

It had been a human noise, a sound of pain. "I'll help if you tell me where you are," he said. Then he shrugged, and walked toward the area where he thought the sound had come from.

He stopped as soon as he saw the body lying at the base of the fir trees.

It was a man—what was left of a man. Sims forced himself to look at him. That was a mistake, for he nearly vomited. Then he realized that he would have to look again. His ears were roaring. Sims bent over the battered head. It was, as he had feared, Lewis Benedikt. Near his head was the body of a dog. At first Sims had thought that the dog was a severed piece of Lewis.

Trembling, Sims straightened up. He wanted to run. Whatever kind of animal had done that to Lewis Benedikt was still nearby—it couldn't be more than a minute away.

Then he heard crashing in the bushes, and was too scared to move. He visualized some huge animal leaping out at him from behind the firs—a grizzly. Sims opened his mouth, but nothing came out.

A man with a face like a Halloween pumpkin emerged from around the fir trees. He was breathing hard, and he held a huge blunderbuss of a shotgun pointed at Sim's belly. "Hold it there," the man said. Sims was certain that the frightening-looking creature was going to blow him in half, and his bowels voided.

"I ought to kill you stone dead right now," the man said.

"Please . . ."

"But this is your lucky day, killer. I'm taking you to a telephone and gedding the police to come. Hey? Why did you do this to Lewis, hey?"

When Sims could not answer, understanding only that this horrible peasant would not kill him after all, Otto inched around behind him and prodded him in the back with the barrels of the shotgun. "So. Play soldier, *scheisskopf*. March. *Mach schnell.*"

Ancient History

12

Don waited in his car outside Edward Wanderley's house for Sears and Ricky to arrive. Waiting, he found in himself all the emotions he had seen in Peter Barnes that evening—but the boy was a rebuke to his fear. Over a few days, Peter Barnes had done and understood more than he and his uncle's friends had in more than a month.

Don lifted the two books he had taken from the Milburn library just before Peter had come. They supported the notion he'd had while talking to the three men in Sears's library: he thought he knew what they were fighting. Sears and Ricky would tell him why. Then, if their story fit his theory, he would do what they had asked him to Milburn for: he would give them their explanation. And if the explanation seemed lunatic, perhaps it was—perhaps it was even wrong; but Peter's story and the copy of *The Watchtower* proved that they had long since lurched into a time when madness offered a truer picture of events than sanity. If his mind and Peter Barnes's had shattered, Milburn had shattered to their pattern. And out of the cracks had crawled Gregory and Fenny and their benefactor, all of whom they must destroy.

Even if it kills us, Don thought. Because we are the only ones who have a chance of doing it.

The headlights of a car appeared in a swirl of falling snow. After a moment, Don saw the outline of a high dark car behind them, and the car swung to the curb on the other side of Haven Lane. The lights died. First Ricky, then Sears got out of the old black Buick. Don left his own car and trotted across the street to join them.

"And now Lewis," Ricky said to him. "Did you know?"

"Not definitely. But I thought so."

Sears, who had been listening to this, nodded impatiently. "You thought so. Ricky, give him the keys." As Don opened the door, Sears grumbled behind him, "I hope you'll tell us how you got your information. If Hardesty fancies himself as the town crier, I'll arrange to have him spitted."

The three men went into a black entryway; Sears found the light switch. "Peter Barnes came to me this afternoon," Don said. "He saw Gregory Bate kill his mother. And he saw what must have been Lewis's ghost."

"Oh, God," Ricky breathed. "Oh, my God. Oh poor Christina."

"Let's get the heat going before we say any more," Sears requested. "If everything's blowing up in our faces, I for one at least want to be warm." The three of them began wandering through the ground floor of the house, lifting dust sheets off the furniture. "I will miss Lewis very much," Sears said. "I used to malign him terribly, but I did love him. He gave us spirit. As your uncle did." He dropped a dust sheet on the floor. "And now he is in the Chenango County morgue, apparently the victim of a savage attack by some sort of animal. A friend of Lewis's accused Harold Sims of the crime.

Under different circumstances, that would be comic."
Sears's face sagged. "Let's take a look at your uncle's
office, and then take care of the heating. I don't know
if I can bear this anymore."

Sears led him into a large room at the rear of the
house while Ricky switched on the central heating
boiler. "This was the office." He flicked a switch, and
track lights on the ceiling shone on an old leather couch,
a desk with an electric typewriter, a file cabinet and a
Xerox machine; on a broad shelf jutting out below narrower shelves filled with white boxes sat a reel-to-reel
tape recorder and a cassette recorder.

"The boxes are the tapes he made for his books?"

"I guess so."

"And you and Ricky and the others never came here
after he died?"

"No," Sears said, gazing at the well-ordered office. It
evoked Don's uncle more wholly than any photograph
—it radiated the contentment of a man happy in what
he did. This impression helped to explain Sears's next
words. "I suppose that Stella told you we were afraid
to come in here. There might be some truth in that. But
I think that what really kept us away was guilt."

"And that was part of the reason you invited me to
Milburn."

"Yes. I think all of us except Ricky thought you
would—" He made a shooing-away gesture with his
hands. "Somehow magically dispel our guilt. John Jaffrey most of all. That is the wisdom of hindsight."

"Because it was Jaffrey's party."

Sears nodded curtly, and turned out of the office.
"There still must be most of a cord of wood out in
back. Why don't you bring some of it in so we can have
a fire?"

"This is the story we never thought we'd tell," Ricky
said ten minutes later. A bottle of Old Parr and their
glasses stood on the dusty table before Ricky's couch.
"That fire was a good idea. It'll give Sears and me
something to look at. Did I ever tell you that I started

everything by asking John about the worst thing he'd ever done? He said he wouldn't tell me, and he told me a ghost story instead. Well, I should have known better. I knew what the worst thing was. We all knew."

"Then why did you ask?"

Ricky sneezed violently, and Sears said, "It happened in 1929—October of 1929. That was a long time ago. When Ricky asked John about the worst thing he'd ever done, all that we could think about was your Uncle Edward—it was only a week after his death. Eva Galli was the last thing on our minds."

"Well, now we have truly crossed the Rubicon," said Ricky. "Up until you said the name, I still wasn't sure that we'd tell it. But now that we're here we'd better go on without stopping. Whatever Peter Barnes told you had better wait until we're done—if after that you still want to stay in the same room with us. And I suppose that somehow what happened to him must be related to the Eva Galli affair. Now; I've said it too."

"Ricky never wanted you to know about Eva Galli," said Sears. "Way back when I wrote to you, he thought it would be a mistake to rake it all up again. I guess we agreed with him. I certainly did."

"Thought it would muddy the waters," Ricky said through his cold. "Thought it couldn't possibly have anything to do with our problem. Spook stories. Nightmares. Premonitions. Just four old fools losing their marbles. Thought it was irrelevant. It was all so mixed up anyhow. Should have known better when that girl came looking for a job. And now with Lewis gone . . ."

"You know something?" Sears said. "We never even gave Lewis John's cufflinks."

"Slipped our minds," Ricky said, and drank some of his Old Parr. He and Sears were already deep in the well of their story, concentrated on it so wholly that Don, seated near them, felt invisible.

"Well, what happened to Eva Galli?" he asked.

Sears and Ricky glanced at each other; then Ricky's eyes went to his glass and Sears's to the fire. "Surely that's obvious," Sears said. "We killed her."

"The two of you?" Don asked, thrown off balance. It was not the answer he had expected.

"All of us," Ricky answered. "The Chowder Society. Your uncle, John Jaffrey, Lewis, and Sears and myself. In October, 1929. Three weeks after Black Monday, when the stock market collapsed. Even here in Milburn, you could see the beginnings of the panic. Lou Price's father, who was also a broker, shot himself in his office. And we killed a girl named Eva Galli. Not murder—not outright murder. We'd never have been convicted of anything—maybe not even of manslaughter. But there would have been a scandal."

"And we couldn't face that," Sears said. "Ricky and I had just started out as lawyers, working in his father's firm. John had qualified as a doctor only the year before. Lewis was the son of a clergyman. We were all in the same fix. We would have been ruined. Slowly, if not immediately."

"That was why we decided on what we tried to do," said Ricky.

"Yes," said Sears. "We did an obscene thing. If we'd been thirty-three instead of twenty-three, we would probably have gone to the police and taken our chances. But we were so young—Lewis wasn't even out of his teens. So we tried to conceal it. And then at the end—"

"At the end," Ricky said, "we were like characters in one of our stories. Or in your novel. I've been re-living the last ten minutes for two months now. I even hear our voices, the things we said when we put her in Warren Scales's car . . ."

"Let's start at the beginning," Sears said.

"Let's start at the beginning. Yes."

"All right," Ricky said. "It begins with Stringer Dedham. He was going to marry her. Eva Galli hadn't been in town two weeks when Stringer set his cap for her. He was older than Sears and myself, thirty-one or two, I imagine, and he was in a position to marry. He ran the Colonel's old farm and stables with the girls' help, and Stringer worked hard and had good ideas. In short, he was a prosperous, well-thought-of fellow, and made a good catch for any of the local girls. Good-looking fellow too. My wife says he was the handsomest man she'd ever seen. All the girls above school age were after him. But when Eva Galli came to town with all her money and her metropolitan manners and her good looks, Stringer was sandbagged. She knocked him off his pins. She bought that house on Montgomery Street—"

"Which house on Montgomery Street?" Don asked. "The one Freddy Robinson lived in?"

"Why yes. The one across the street from John's house. Miss Mostyn's house. She bought that house, and set it up with new furniture and a piano and a gramophone. And she smoked cigarettes and drank cocktails, and she wore her hair short—a real John Held girl."

"Not entirely," Sears said. "She was no bubble-headed flapper. The time for those had passed, anyhow. And she was educated. She read quite widely. She could speak intelligently. Eva Galli was an enchanting woman. How would you describe the way she looked, Ricky?"

"Like a nineteen-twenties Claire Bloom," Ricky said immediately.

"Typical Ricky Hawthorne. Ask him to describe someone, and he names a movie star. I guess you can take it as an accurate description. Eva Galli had all this exciting modernity about her, what was modernity for Milburn at any rate, but there was also a refinement about her—an air of grace."

"That's true," said Ricky. "And a certain mysteriousness we found terribly attractive. Like your Anna Mobley. We knew nothing about her but what she hinted—she had lived in New York, she had apparently spent some time in Hollywood as an actress in silents. She did a small part in a romance called *China Pearl*. A Richard Barthelmess movie."

Don took a piece of paper from his pocket and wrote down the name of the film.

"And she was obviously partly of Italian ancestry, but she told Stringer at one point that her maternal grandparents were English. Her father had been a man of considerable substance, one gathered, but she had been orphaned when just a child and was raised by relatives in California. That was all we knew about her. She said that she had come here for peace and seclusion."

"The women tried to take her under their wing," Sears said. "She was a catch for them too, remember. A wealthy girl who had turned her back on Hollywood, sophisticated and refined—every woman of position in Milburn sent her an invitation. The little societies women here had in those days all wanted her. I think that what they wanted was to tame her."

"To make her identifiable," Ricky said. "Yes. To tame her. Because with all her qualities, there was something else. Something fey. Lewis had a romantic imagination then, and he told me that Eva Galli was like an aristocrat, a princess or some such, who had turned her back on the court and gone off to the country to die."

"Yes, she affected us too," said Sears. "Of course, for us she was out of reach. We idealized her. We saw her from time to time—"

"We paid court," Ricky said.

"Absolutely. We paid court to her. She had politely refused all the ladies' invitations, but she had no objections to five gangling young men showing up on her doorstep on a Saturday or Sunday. Your uncle Edward was the first of us. He had more daring than we other four. By this time, everybody knew that Stringer Dedham had lost his head over her, so in a sense she was seen as under Stringer's patronage—as if she always had a ghostly duenna by her side. Edward slipped between the cracks of convention. He paid a call on her, she was dazzlingly charming to him, and soon we all got into the habit of calling on her. Stringer didn't seem to mind. He liked us, though he was in a different world."

"The adult world," Ricky said. "As Eva was. Even though she could only have been two or three years older than us, she might have been twenty. Nothing could have been more proper than our visits. Of course some of the elderly women thought they were scandalous. Lewis's father thought so too. But we had just enough social leeway to get away with it. We paid our visits in a group, after Edward had broken the ground, about once every two weeks. We were far too jealous to allow any one of us to go alone. Our visits were extraordinary. It was like slipping out of time altogether. Nothing exceptional happened, even the conversation was ordinary, but for those few hours we spent with her, we were in the realm of magic. She swept us off our feet. And that she was known to be Stringer's fiancée made it safe."

"People didn't grow up so fast in those days," Sears said. "All of this—young men in their early twenties mooning about a woman of twenty-five or -six as if she were an unattainable priestess—must seem risible to you. But it was the way we thought of her—beyond our reach. She was Stringer's, and we all thought that after they married we'd be as welcome at his house as at hers."

The two older men fell silent for a moment. They looked into the fire on Edward Wanderley's hearth and drank whiskey. Don did not prod them to speak, knowing that a crucial turn in the story had come and that they would finish telling it when they were able.

"We were in a sort of sexless, pre-Freudian paradise," Ricky finally said. "In an enchantment. Sometimes we even danced with her, but even holding her, watching her move, we never thought about sex. Not consciously. Not to admit. Well, paradise died in October, 1929, shortly after the stock market and Stringer Dedham."

"Paradise died," Sears echoed, "and we looked into the devil's face." He turned his head toward the window.

13

Sears said, "Look at the snow."

The other two followed his gaze and saw white flakes blizzarding against the window. "If his wife can find him, Omar Norris will have to be out plowing before morning."

Ricky drank more of his whiskey. "It was *tropically* hot," he said, melting the present storm in the unseasonal October of nearly fifty years before. "The threshing got done late that year. It seemed folks couldn't get down to work. People said money worries made Stringer absentminded. The Dedham girls said no, that wasn't it, he'd gone by Miss Galli's house that morning. He'd seen something."

"Stringer put his arms in the thresher," Sears said, "and his sisters blamed Eva. He said things while he was dying, wrapped up in blankets on their table. But you couldn't make head or tail of what they thought they heard him say. 'Bury her,' that was one thing, and 'cut her up,' as though he'd seen what was going to happen to himself."

"And," said Ricky, "one other thing. The Dedham girls said he screamed something else—but it was so mixed up with his other screams that they weren't sure about it. 'Bee-orchid.' 'Bee-orchid,' just that. He had been raving, obviously. Out of his head with shock and pain. Well, he died on that table, and got a good burial a few days later. Eva Galli didn't come to the funeral. Half the town was on Pleasant Hill, but not the dead man's fiancée. That fueled their tongues."

"The old women, the women she had ignored," Sears said. "They laid into her. Said she'd ruined Stringer. Of course half of them had unmarried daughters and they'd had their eyes on Stringer long before Eva Galli showed up. They said he made some discovery—an abandoned husband or an illegitimate child, something like that. They made her out to be a real Jezebel."

"We didn't know what to do," Ricky said. "We were afraid to visit her, after Stringer died. She might be grieving as much as a widow, you see, but she was un-attached. It was our parents' place to console her, not ours. If we had called on her, the female malice would have gone into high gear. So we stewed—just stewed. Everybody assumed that she'd pack up and move back to New York. But we couldn't forget those afternoons."

"If anything, they became more magical, more poignant," Sears said. "Now we knew what we had lost. An ideal—and a romantic friendship conducted in the light of an ideal."

"Sears is right," Ricky said. "But in the end, we idealized her even more. She became an emblem of grief—of a fractured heart. All we wanted to do was to visit her. We sent her a note of condolence, and we would have gone through fire to see her. What we couldn't go through was the iron-bound social convention that set her apart. There weren't any cracks to slip through."

"Instead she visited us," Sears said. "At the apartment your uncle lived in then. Edward was the only one who had his own place. We got together to talk and drink applejack. To talk about all the things we were going to do."

"And to talk about her," Ricky said. "Do you know that Ernest Dowson poem: 'I have been faithful to thee, Cynara! in my fashion'? Lewis found it and read it to us. That poem went through us like a knife. 'Thy pale lost lilies.' It certainly called for more applejack. 'Madder music and stronger wine.' What idiots we were. Anyhow, she turned up one night at Edward's apartment."

"And she was *wild*," Sears said. "She was frightening. She came in like a typhoon."

"She said she was lonely," Ricky said. "Said she was sick of this damned town and all the hypocrites in it. She wanted to drink and she wanted to dance, and she didn't care who was shocked. Said this dead little town and all its dead little people could go to hell as far as she was concerned. And if we were men and not little boys, we'd damn the town too."

"We were speechless," Sears said. "There was our unattainable goddess, cursing like a sailor and raging . . . acting like a whore. 'Madder music and stronger wine.' That's what we got, all right. Edward had a little gramophone and some records, and she made us crank it up and put on the loudest jazz he had. She was so vehement! It was crazy—we'd never seen any woman act that way, and for us she was, you know, sort of a cross between the Statue of Liberty and Mary Pickford. 'Dance with me, you little toad,' she said to John, and he was so frightened by her that he scarcely dared touch her. Her eyes were just blazing."

"I think what she felt was *hate,*" Ricky said. "For us, for the town, for Stringer. But it was hatred, and it was boiling. A cyclone of hate. She kissed Lewis while they were dancing, and he jumped back like she burned him. He dropped his arms, and she spun off to Edward and grabbed him and made him dance. Her face was terrible—rigid. Edward was always more worldly than the rest of us, but he too was shaken by Eva's wildness— our paradise was crumbling all around us, and she kicked it into powder with every step. With every glance. She *did* seem like a devil; like something possessed. You know how when a woman gets angry, really angry, she can reach way back into herself and find rage enough to blow any man to pieces—how all that feeling comes out and hits you like a truck? It was like that. 'Aren't you little sissies going to drink?' she said. So we drank."

"It was unspeakable," Sears said. "She seemed twice our size. I think I knew what was coming. There was only one thing that *could* be coming. We were simply too immature to know how to handle it."

"I don't know if I saw it coming, but it came anyhow," Ricky said. "She tried to seduce Lewis."

"He was the worst possible choice," Sears said. "Lewis was only a boy. He may have kissed a gal before that night, but he certainly had done no more than that. We all loved Eva, but Lewis probably loved her most—he was the one who found that Dowson poem, remember. And because he loved her most, her performance that evening and her hatred stunned him."

"And she knew it," Ricky said. "She was delighted. It pleased her, that Lewis was so shocked he could scarcely utter a word. And when she pushed Edward away and went after Lewis, Lewis was frozen stiff with horror. As if he had seen his mother begin to act that way."

"His mother?" Sears asked. "Well, I suppose. At least it tells you the depth of his fantasy about her— our fantasy, to be honest. And he was dumbstruck. Eva snaked her arms around him and kissed him. It looked like she was eating half his face. Imagine that—those hate-filled kisses pouring over you, all that fury biting into your mouth. It must have been like kissing a razor. When she drew back her head, Lewis's face was smeared with lipstick. Normally it would have been a funny sight, but it was somehow horrifying. As if he was smeared with blood."

"Edward went up to her and said, 'Cool down, Miss Galli,' or something of the sort. She whirled on him, and we felt that enormous pressure of hatred again. 'You want yours, do you, Edward?' she said. 'You can wait your turn. I want Lewis first. Because my little Lewis is so pretty."

"And then," Ricky said, "she turned to me. 'You'll get some too, Ricky. And you too, Sears. You all will. But I want Lewis first. I want to show him what that insufferable Stringer Dedham saw when he peeked through my windows.' And she started to take off her blouse."

"'*Please*, Miss Galli,' Edward said," Sears remembered, "but she told him to shut up and finished taking off her blouse. She wore no bra. Her breasts were in period. Small and tight, like little apples. She looked incredibly lascivious. 'Now, pretty little Lewis, why don't we see what you can do?' She began eating his face again."

Ricky said, "So we all thought we knew what Stringer

had seen through her window. Eva Galli making love with another man. That, as much as her nakedness and what she was doing to Lewis, was a moral shock. We were hideously embarrassed. Finally Sears and I took a shoulder apiece and pulled her away from Lewis. Then she really swore. It was incredibly ugly. 'Can't you wait for it, you little so and sos and et ceteras and et ceteras?' She began unbuttoning her skirt while she swore at us. Edward was nearly in tears. 'Eva,' he said, 'please don't.' She dropped her skirt and stepped out of it. 'What's wrong, you pansy, afraid to see what I look like?"

"We were miles out of our depth," Sears continued. "She pulled off her slip. She went dancing up to your uncle. 'I think I'll take a bite out of you, little Edward,' she said and leaned toward him—toward his neck. And he slapped her."

"Hard," Ricky said. "And she slapped him back even harder. She put all her weight behind it. It sounded as loud as a gun going off. John and Sears and I practically fainted. We were helpless. We couldn't move."

"If we could have, we might have stopped Lewis," Sears said. "But we stood like tin soldiers and watched him. He took off like an airplane—he just flew across the room and tackled her. He was sobbing and slobbering and wailing—he had snapped. He gave her a real football tackle. They went down like a bombed building. And they made a noise as loud as Black Monday's crash. Eva never got up."

"Her head hit the edge of the fireplace," Ricky said. "Lewis crawled up on her back and kneeled over her and raised his fists, but even he saw the blood coming out of her mouth."

Both old men were panting.

"So that was that," Sears said. "She was dead. Naked and dead, with the five of us standing around like zombies. Lewis vomited on the floor, and the rest of us were close to it. We could not believe what had happened—what we had done. It's no excuse, but we really were in shock. I think we just vibrated in the silence for a while."

"Because the silence seemed immense," Ricky said. "It closed in on us like—like the snow out there. Finally Lewis said, 'We'll have to get the police.' 'No,' Edward said. 'We'll all go to jail. For murder.'

"Sears and I tried to tell him that no one had committed murder, but Edward said 'How will you like being disbarred then? Because that'll happen.' John checked her for pulse and respiration, but of course there was none. '*I* think it's murder,' he said. 'We're sunk.' "

"Ricky asked what we were supposed to do," Sears said, "and John said, 'There's only one thing we can do. Hide her body. Hide it away where it won't be found.' We all looked at her body, and at her bloody face, and we all felt defeated by her—she had won. That's how it felt. Her hatred had provoked us to something very like murder, if not murder under the law. And now we were talking about concealing our act— both legally and morally, a damning step. And we agreed to it."

Don asked, "Where did you decide to hide her body?"

"There was an old pond five or six miles out of town. A deep pond. It's not there anymore. It was filled in and they built a shopping center on the land. Must have been twenty feet deep."

"Lewis's car had a flat tire," Sears said, "so we wrapped the body in a sheet and left him there with her and went off into town to find Warren Scales. He had come in to shop with his wife, we knew. He was a good soul, and he liked us. We were going to tell him that we ruined his car, and then buy him a better one— Ricky and I paying the lion's share."

"Warren Scales was the father of the farmer who talks about shooting Martians?" Don asked.

"Elmer was Warren's fourth child and first son. He wasn't even thought of then. We went along downtown and found Warren and promised to bring his car back in an hour or so. Then we went back to Edward's and carried the girl down the stairs and put her in the car. Tried to put her in the car."

Ricky said, "We were so nervous and afraid and numb and we still couldn't believe what had happened or what we were doing. And we had great difficulty in fitting her into the car. 'Put her feet in first,' someone said, and we slid the body along the back seat, and the sheet got all tangled up, and Lewis started to swear about her head being caught and we pulled her halfway out again and John screamed that she moved. Edward called him a damned fool and said he knew she couldn't move—wasn't he a doctor?"

"Yet finally we got her in—Ricky and John had to sit in back with the body. We had a nightmarish trip through town." Sears paused and looked into the fire. "My God. I was driving. I just remembered that. I was so rattled that I couldn't remember how to get to the pond. I just backtracked and drove around and went four or five miles out of our way. Finally someone told me how to get there. And we got onto that little dirt road which led down to the pond."

"Everything seemed so *sharp*," Ricky said. "Every *leaf*, every *pebble*—flat and sharp as a drawing in a book. We got out of that car and the world just hit us between the eyes. 'Do we have to do this?' Lewis asked. He was crying. Edward said, 'I wish to God we didn't.'"

"Then Edward got back behind the wheel," Sears said. "The car was ten-fifteen yards from the pond, which fell off almost immediately to its full depth. He switched on the ignition. I cranked it up. Edward retarded the spark, put it in first, popped the clutch and jumped out. The car crawled forward."

Both men fell silent again, and looked at each other. "Then—" Ricky said, and Sears nodded. "I don't know how to say this . . ."

"Then we saw something," Sears said. "We hallucinated. Or something."

"You saw her alive again," Don said. "I know."

Ricky looked at him with a tired astonishment. "I guess you do. We saw her face through the rear window. She was staring·at us—grinning at us. Jeering at us. We damn near dropped dead. The next second the car splashed into the pond and started to sink. We all ran forward and tried to look into the side windows. I was scared silly. I knew she was dead, back in the apartment—I *knew* it. John jumped into the water just as the car started to go down. When he came back up he said he had looked through the side window and . . ."

"And he didn't see anything on the back seat," Sears told Don. "He said."

"The car went down and never came back up. It must be still down there, under thirty thousand tons of fill," Ricky said.

"Did anything else happen?" Don asked. "Please try to remember. It's important."

"Two things did happen," Ricky said. "But I need another drink, after all that." He poured some of the whiskey into his glass and drank before resuming. "John Jaffrey saw a lynx on the other side of the pond. Then we all saw it. We jumped about a mile—it made us even guiltier, being seen. By even an animal. It switched its tail and disappeared back into the woods."

"Fifty years ago, were lynxes common around here?"

"Not at all. Maybe farther north. Well, that was one. The other was that Eva's house burned, caught on fire. When we walked back to town we saw the neighbors all standing around, watching the volunteers try to put it out."

"Did any of them see how it started?"

Sears shook his head, and Ricky continued the story. "Apparently it just started by itself. Seeing it made us feel worse, as if we had caused that too."

"One of the volunteers said something odd," Sears remembered. "All of us must have looked so haggard, standing around looking at the fire, and the firemen assumed we were worried about the other houses on the street. He said the other buildings were safe because

the fire was getting smaller. He said from what he had
seen, it looked like part of the house exploded *inward*—
he couldn't explain it, but that's the way it looked to
him. And the fire was only in that part of the house, up
on the second floor. I saw what he was talking about.
You could see some of the beams, and they were
buckled in toward the fire."

"And the windows!" Ricky said. "The windows were
broken, but there was no glass on the ground—they
burst inward."

"Imploded," Don said.

Ricky nodded. "Yes. I couldn't remember the word.
I saw a light bulb do it once. Anyhow, the fire ruined
the second floor, but the first floor wasn't touched by it.
A year or two later a family bought the place and had
it rebuilt. We were all back at work, and people had
stopped wondering what had happened to Eva Galli."

"Except for us," Sears said. "And we didn't talk
about it. We had a few nasty moments when the de-
velopers started filling in that pond fifteen-twenty years
ago, but they never found the car. They just buried it.
And whatever was inside it."

"Nothing was inside it," Don said. "Eva Galli is here
now. She's back. For the second time."

"Back?" Ricky said, jerking his head up.

"She is back as Anna Mostyn. And before, she came
here as Ann-Veronica Moore. As Alma Mobley, she
met me in California and killed my brother in Amsterdam."

"Miss *Mostyn?*" Sears asked incredulously.

"Is that what killed Edward?" Ricky asked.

"I'm sure it is. He probably saw whatever Stringer
saw—she let him see it."

"I will not believe that Miss Mostyn has anything
to do with Eva Galli, Edward or Stringer Dedham,"
Sears said. "The idea is ridiculous."

"What is 'it'?" Ricky asked. "What did she let him
see?"

"Herself changing shape," Don said. "And I think she

planned for him to see it, knowing it would literally scare him to death." He looked at the two old men. "Here's another. I think that in all probability she knows we are here tonight. Because we are unfinished business."

Do You Know What It Means
To Miss New Orleans?

14

"Changing shape," Ricky said.

"Changing shape indeed," Sears said, less charitably. "You're saying that Eva Galli and Edward's little actress and our secretary are all the same person?"

"Not a person. The same being. The lynx you saw on the other side of the pond was probably her too. Not a person at all, Sears. When you felt Eva Galli's hate that day she came to my uncle's apartment, I think you perceived the truest part of her. I think she came to provoke the five of you into some kind of destruction— to ruin your innocence. I think it backfired, and you injured her. At least that proves it can be done. Now she has come back to make you pay for it. Me, too. She took a detour from me to get my brother, but she knew that eventually I'd turn up here. And then she would be able to get us one by one."

"Was this the idea you said you'd tell us about?" Ricky asked.

Don nodded.

"What in the world makes you imagine that it is anything but a particularly bad idea?" Sears asked.

"Peter Barnes, for one," Don answered. "I think this will convince you too, Sears. And if it fails, I'll read you something from a book that should work. But Peter first. He went to Lewis's house today, as I told you before." He recounted everything that had happened to Peter Barnes—the trip to the abandoned station, the death of Freddy Robinson, the death of Jim Hardie in Anna Mostyn's house and the final, terrible events of the morning. "So I think it's inescapable that Anna Mostyn is the 'benefactor' Gregory Bate mentioned. She animates Gregory and Fenny—Peter says he knew intuitively that Gregory was owned by something, that he was like a savage dog obeying an evil master. Together, they want to destroy the whole town. Just like Dr. Rabbitfoot in the novel I was planning."

"They're trying to make that novel come true?" Ricky asked.

"I think so. They also called themselves night-watchers. They're playful. Think of those initials. Anna Mostyn, Alma Mobley, Ann-Veronica Moore. That was playfulness—she wanted us to notice the similarity. I'm sure she sent Gregory and Fenny because Sears had seen them before. Or years ago, they appeared to him because she knew she'd be able to use them now. And it's no accident that when I saw Gregory in California, I thought of him being like a werewolf."

"Why no accident, if that's what you're claiming he is?" Sears asked.

"I'm not claiming that. But creatures like Anna Mostyn or Eva Galli are behind every ghost story and supernatural tale ever written," Don said. "They are the originals of everything that frightens us in the supernatural. I think in stories we make them manageable. But the stories at least show that we can destroy them. Gregory Bate isn't a werewolf any more than Anna Mostyn is. He is what people have described as a werewolf. Or as a vampire. He feeds on living bodies. He sold himself to his benefactor for immortality."

Don took up one of the books he had brought with him. "This is a reference book, the *Standard Dictionary of Folklore, Mythology and Legend*. There's a long entry under 'Shapeshifting,' written by a professor named R. D. Jameson. Listen to this: 'Although no census of shapeshifters has been taken, the number of them found in all parts of the world is astronomical.' He says they appear in the folklore of all peoples. He goes on for three columns—it's one of the longest entries in the book. I'm afraid it isn't actually of much help to us, apart from showing that these beings have been talked about in folk history for thousands of years, because Jameson doesn't recount ways, if any, in which the legends say these creatures can be destroyed. But listen to the way he ends the entry: 'The studies made of shapeshifting foxes, otters, etc., are sound but miss the central problem of shapeshifting itself. Shapeshifting in folklore is clearly connected with hallucination in morbid psychology. Until the phenomena in both areas have been scrutinized with care, we are not able to go beyond the general observation that nothing is, in fact, what it seems to be.' "

"Amen," said Ricky.

"Precisely. Nothing is what it seems to be. These beings can convince you that you are losing your mind. That's happened to each of us—we've seen and felt things we argued ourselves out of later. It can't be true, we tell ourselves; such things do not happen. But they do happen, and we did see them. You did see them. You did see Eva Galli sit up on the car seat, and you saw her appear as a lynx a moment later."

"Just suppose," Sears said, "that one of us had a rifle along that day, and had shot the lynx. What would have happened?"

"I think you would have seen something extraordinary, but I can't imagine what it would have been. Maybe it would have died. Maybe it would have shifted to some preferred form—maybe, if it had been in great pain, it would have gone through a series of changes. And maybe it would have been helpless."

"A lot of maybes," Ricky said.

"That's all we have."

"If we accept your theory."

"If you have a better one I'll listen to it. But through Peter Barnes we know what happened to Freddy Robinson and Jim Hardie. Also, I checked with her agent and found out some things about Ann-Veronica Moore. She came literally from nowhere. There is no record at all of her in the town she said she was born in. Because there couldn't be—there never was an Ann-Veronica Moore until the day she enrolled in acting class. She just arrived, plausible and well documented, at the door of a theater, knowing it was a way to get to Edward Wanderley."

"Then these—these things you think exist—are even more dangerous. They have wit," Sears said.

"Yes, they do have wit. They love jokes, and they make long-term plans, and like the Indians' Manitou, they love to flaunt themselves. This second book gives a good example of that." He picked it up and showed the spine to the two men. *I Came This Way,* by Robert Mobley. He was the painter Alma claimed was her father. I made the mistake of never looking at his autobiography until today. Now I think that she wanted me to read it and discover that in calling herself Mobley she was making a pun on an earlier appearance. The fourth chapter is called 'Dark Clouds'—it's not a very well-written autobiography, but I want to read you a few paragraphs from that chapter."

Don opened the book to a marked page, and neither of the two old men stirred.

" 'Even in a life so apparently fortunate as mine has been, dark and troubling periods have intruded and marked months and years with indelible grief. The year 1958 was one such; only by hurling myself with the utmost concentration into my work, I believe, did I maintain my sanity during that year. Knowing the sunny watercolors and rigid formal experimentation in oils which had been characteristic of my work during the five years previous, people have often questioned me about the stylistic transformation which led to my so-called Supernatural Period. I can say now only that my mind was very likely unbalanced, and the violent disorder of my emotions found expression in the work I forced myself to do.

" 'The first painful event of the year was the death

of my mother, Jessica Osgood Mobley, whose affection and wise advice had . . .' I'll skip a page or two here." Don scanned the page, and turned it over. "Here we are. 'The second, even more shattering loss was the death by his own hand in his eighteenth year of my elder son, Shelby. I shall mention here only the circumstances surrounding Shelby's death which led directly to my work of the so-called Supernatural Period, for this book is chiefly an account of my life in painting: yet I must assert that my son's was a gay, innocent and vibrant spirit, and I am certain that only a great moral shock, the apprehension of a hitherto unsuspected evil, could have led him to take his life.

" 'Shortly after the death of my mother, a spacious house near our own was sold to an evidently prosperous, attractive woman in her mid-forties whose sole family consisted of a niece of fourteen who had become her ward after the death of the girl's parents. Mrs. Florence de Peyser was friendly and reserved, a woman with charming manners who wintered in Europe as my own parents had: in fact she seemed altogether more representative of another age than our own, and for a time I speculated about doing her portrait in watercolor. She collected paintings, as I saw when invited to her house, and was even knowledgeable about my own work— though my abstractions of the period would have fitted oddly with her French Symbolists! But for all Mrs. de Peyser's charm, the principle attraction of her household soon became her niece. Amy Monckton's beauty was almost ethereal, and I believe that she was the most feminine being I have ever seen. Every action she undertook, be it merely entering a room or pouring a cup of tea, spoke a volume of quiet grace. The child was an enchantment, entirely self-possessed and modest— as delicate as (but perhaps more intelligent than) Pansy Osmond, for whose sake Henry James's Isobel Archer sacrificed herself so willingly. Amy was a welcome guest in our home: both of my sons were drawn to her.'

"And there she is," Don said. "A fourteen-year-old Alma Mobley, under the guidance of Mrs. de Peyser.

Poor Mobley didn't know what he was letting into his house. He goes on: 'Though Amy was the same age as Whitney, my younger son, it was Shelby—sensitive Shelby—who became closer to her. At the time, I thought it was proof of Shelby's *politesse,* that he gave so much time to a girl four years younger than himself. And even when I picked up clear signs of affection (poor Shelby blushed when the girl's name was mentioned), I could never have imagined that they indulged in any behavior of a morbid, degrading or precocious kind. In truth, it was one of the delights of my life to observe my tall, handsome son walking through our garden with the pretty child. And I was not surprised, though perhaps a bit amused, when Shelby confided to me that when she was eighteen and he twenty-two, he would marry Amy Monckton.

" 'After several months I noticed that Shelby had become increasingly withdrawn. He was no longer interested in his friends, and in the last months of his life, he concentrated exclusively on the de Peyser household and Miss Monckton. They had lately been joined by a servant of sinister and Latin appearance named Gregorio. I distrusted Gregorio on sight, and attempted to warn Mrs. de Peyser about him, but was informed that she had known him and his family for many years, and that he was an excellent chauffeur. I felt I could say no more.

" 'In this short account I can say only that my son became haggard in appearance and secretive in manner during the last two weeks of his life. I played the heavy parent for the first time in my life and forbade him to communicate with the de Peyser household. His attitude led me to believe that under Gregorio's influence, he and the child were experimenting with drugs—perhaps also with illicit sensuality. That noxious and debasing weed, marijuana, was even then to be found in the lower sections of New Orleans. And I feared also that they experimented too with some gimcrack form of Creole mysticism. That sort of thing suits the drug milieu.

" 'Whatever Shelby had been drawn into, its results were tragic. He disobeyed my orders and continued clandestinely to frequent the de Peyser house; and on the last day of August he returned home, took the service revolver I kept in a drawer in my bedroom, and shot himself. It was I, painting in my studio, who heard the shot and discovered his body.

" 'What occurred next must have been the result of shock. I did not think to call the police or an ambulance: I wandered outside, imagining somehow that help would already have arrived. I found myself on the road outside our house. I was looking at Mrs. de Peyser's residence. What I saw there nearly made me lose consciousness.

" 'I imagined I saw the chauffeur Gregorio standing at an upper window, sneering down at me. Malevolence seemed to flow from him. He was exultant. I tried to scream and could not. I looked down and saw something worse. Amy Monckton stood by the side of the house, similarly staring at me, but with a calm, expressionless gaze and a grave face. *Her feet were not touching the ground!* Amy appeared to be floating nine or ten inches above the grass. Exposed to them, I felt an utter terror, and pressed my hands to my face. When I removed them and could see again, they were gone.

" 'Mrs. de Peyser and Amy sent flowers to Shelby's funeral, but by then had gone to California. Though I was and am now convinced that I had imagined my last sight of the child and the chauffeur, I burned the flowers rather than let them adorn Shelby's coffin. The paintings of my so-called Supernatural Period, which I propose now to discuss, flowed from this experience.' "

Don looked at the two old men. "I read that for the first time today. You see what I mean by flaunting themselves? They want their victims to know, or at least to suspect, what sort of things happened to them. Robert Mobley got a shock that nearly unhinged him, and he did the best paintings of his life; Alma wanted me to read about it and know that she had lived in

New Orleans with Florence de Peyser under another name and killed a boy as surely as she killed my brother."

"Why hasn't Anna Mostyn killed us already?" Sears asked. "She's had every opportunity. I can't even pretend not to be convinced by what you've told us, but why has she waited? Why aren't the three of us as dead as the others?"

Ricky cleared his throat. "Edward's actress told Stella that I'd be a good enemy. I think what she was waiting for was the moment when we knew exactly what we were up against."

"You mean now," Sears said.

"Do you have a plan?" Ricky asked.

"No, just a few ideas. I'm going to go back to the hotel and pick up my things and move back here. Maybe in the tapes she made with my uncle there'll be some information we can use. And I want to break into Anna Mostyn's home. I hope you will come with me. We might find something there."

"What you'll find in there is a long walk on a short pier," Sears said.

"No, I don't think they'll be there anymore. The three of them will know that we'll try the house first. They'll have found somewhere else already."

Don looked at Sears and Ricky. "There is just one thing left to say. As Sears asked, what would have happened if you'd shot the lynx? That's what we'll have to find out. This time we'll have to shoot the lynx, whatever that will mean."

He smiled at them. "It's going to be a hell of a winter."

Sears James rumbled something affirmative. Ricky asked, "What do you suppose the odds are that we three and Peter Barnes will ever see the end of it?"

"Rotten," Sears answered. "But you've certainly done what we asked you here to do."

"Do we tell anybody?" Ricky asked. "Should we try to convince Hardesty?"

"That's absurd," Sears snorted. "We'd end up in the booby hatch."

"Let them think they're fighting Martians," Don said. "Sears is right. But I'll give you a much better bet than the one you gave me."

"What's that?"

"I bet your perfect secretary won't come to work tomorrow."

When the old men left him in his uncle's house, Don built up the fire and sat in Ricky's warm place on the couch. While snow piled up on the roof and tried to wind its way around doors and window frames, he remembered a warm-chilly night, the smell of burning leaves, a sparrow lighting on a rail and a pale already loved face shining at him with luminous eyes from a doorway. And a naked girl looking out of a black window and pronouncing words he only now understood: "You are a ghost." You Donald. You. It was the unhappy perception at the center of every ghost story.

II

The Town Besieged

Narcissus, gazing at his image in the pool, wept.
When his friend, passing by, enquired the reason,
Narcissus replied, "I weep that I have lost my innocence."
   His friend answered, "You would
wiser weep that you ever had it."

1

December in Milburn; Milburn moving toward Christmas. The town's memory is long, and this month has always meant certain things, maple sugar candy and skating on the river and lights and trees in the stores and skiing on the hills just outside of town. In December, under several inches of snow, Milburn always took on a festive, almost magically pretty look. A tall tree always went up in the square, and Eleanor Hardie matched its lights by decorating the front of the Archer Hotel. Children lined up before Santa Claus in Young Brothers' department store and put in their nonnego-

tiable demands for Christmas—only the older ones
noticed that Santa looked and smelled a little bit like
Omar Norris. (December always reconciled Omar not
only with his wife, but also with himself—he cut his
drinking in half, and talked to the few cronies he had
about "moonlighting down at the store.") As his father
had done, Norbert Clyde always drove his old horse-
drawn sleigh through town and gave the kids rides so
they would know what real sleighbells sounded like—
and would know the feeling of skimming along through
pine-smelling air behind two good horses. And as *his*
father had done, Elmer Scales pulled open a gate in one
of his pasture fences and let the town people come out
to sled down a hill at the edge of his property: you always saw half a dozen station wagons pulled up alongside the fence, and half a dozen young fathers pulling
Flexible Flyers laden with excited children up Elmer's
hill. Some families pulled taffy in their kitchens; some
families roasted chestnuts in their fireplaces. Humphrey
Stalladge put up red and green lights over the bar, and
started making Tom and Jerries. Milburn wives swapped
recipes for Christmas cookies; the butchers took orders
for twenty-pound turkeys and gave away recipes for
turkey gravy. Eight-year-olds in the grade school cut
out trees from colored paper and pasted them to classroom windows. High school kids concentrated more on
hockey than English and history, and thought about the
records they'd buy with the holiday checks from aunts
and uncles. The Kiwanis and Rotary and the Kaycees
held a huge party in the ballroom of the Archer Hotel,
with three bartenders imported from Binghamton, and
cleared several thousand dollars for the Golden Agers
fund; from this evening, and from all the cocktail parties
the younger, newer residents of Milburn held—the
people who still did not look quite familiar to Sears and
Ricky, though they might have lived in Milburn for
years—people came to work with headaches and queasy
stomachs.

   This year there still were a few cocktail parties and
women still made Christmas cookies, but December in

Milburn was different. People who met in Young Brother's department store didn't say "Isn't it nice to have
a white Christmas?" but "I hope this snow doesn't keep
up"; Omar Norris had to stay on the municipal snowplow all day long, and junior clerks said they'd get into
his Santa suit only if someone fumigated it first; the
mayor and Hardesty's deputies set up an enormous
tree, but Eleanor Hardie didn't have the heart to deco-
rate the front of the hotel—indeed she began to look
so harried and lost that a tourist couple from New York
City took one glance at her and decided on the spot to
keep on going until they found a motel. And Norbert
Clyde, the first time ever, didn't take his sleigh out of
his barn and grease up the runners: ever since seeing
that "thing" on his land, he had gone into a funny
decline. You could hear him at Humphrey's or other
bars on the outskirts of town, saying that the County
Farm Agent didn't know his ass from his elbow, and
that if people had any sense they'd start paying a little
more attention to Elmer Scales, who didn't open up
his gate to let the sledders onto his hill, but skipped
dinners and scribbled crazy poetry and waited up nights
with his loaded twelve-gauge over his knees. His tribe
of children sledded on the hill by themselves, feeling
ostracized. Snow fell all day, all night; the drifts at
first covered fences, and then reached the eaves of the
houses. In the second two weeks of December, the
schools were closed for eight days: the high school's heating system failed, and the board shut it down until mid-
January, when a heating engineer from Binghamton
was finally able to get into town. The grade school closed
a few days later: the roads were treacherous, and after
the school bus went into a ditch twice in one morning,
the parents would have kept their kids home anyway.
People of the age of Ricky and Sears—those who were
the town's memory—looked back to the winters of
1947 and 1926, when no traffic had come in or out of
Milburn for weeks, and fuel had run out and old folks
(who were no older than the present ages of Sears and

Ricky) had, along with Viola Frederickson of the auburn hair and exotic face, frozen to death.

This December Milburn looked less like a village on a Christmas card than a village under siege. The Dedham girls' horses, forgotten even by Nettie, starved and died in their stables. This December, people stayed in their houses more than they were used to, and tempers wore thin—some broke. Philip Kneighler, one of the new Milburnites, went inside and beat up his wife after his snow blower broke down on his driveway. Ronnie Byrum, a nephew of Harlan Bautz's home on leave from the Marines, objected to the harmless remarks of a man standing beside him in a bar and broke his nose: he would have broken his jaw if two of Ronnie's old high school buddies had not pinned his arms back. Two sixteen-year-old boys named Billy Byrum (Ronnie's brother) and Anthony "Spacemaker" Ortega concussed a younger boy who insisted on talking through the eight-twenty-five showing of *Night of the Living Dead* at Clark Mulligan's Rialto Theater. All over Milburn couples locked together in their houses quarreled about their babies, their money, their television programs. A deacon of the Holy Ghost Presbyterian Church—the same church of which Lewis's father had once been pastor—locked himself in the unheated building one night two weeks before Christmas and wept and cursed and prayed all night because he thought he was going crazy: he thought he had seen the naked boy Jesus standing on a snowdrift outside the church windows, begging him to come out.

At the Bay Tree Market, Rhoda Flagler pulled a clump of blond hair out of the scalp of Bitsy Underwood because Bitsy had challenged her right to the last three cans of puréed pumpkin: with the trucks unable to make deliveries, all the stocks were getting low. In the Hollow, an unemployed bartender named Jim Blazek knifed and killed a mulatto short-order cook named Washington de Souza because a tall man with a shaven head who dressed like a sailor had told Blazek that de Souza was messing around with his wife.

During the sixty-two days from the first of December to the thirty-first of January, these ten citizens of Milburn died of natural causes: George Fleischner (62), heart attack; Whitey Rudd (70), malnutrition; Gabriel Fish (58), exposure; Omar Norris (61), exposure following concussion; Marion Le Sage (73), stroke; Ethel Birt (76), Hodgkin's Disease; Dylan Griffen (5 months), hypothermia; Harlan Bautz (55), heart attack; Nettie Dedham (81), stroke; Penny Draeger (18), shock. Most of these died during the worst of the snows, and their bodies, along with those of Washington de Souza and several others, had to be kept, stacked and covered with sheets in one of the unused utility cells in Walter Hardesty's tiny jail—the wagon from the morgue in the county seat couldn't make it into Milburn.

The town closed in on itself, and even the ice skating on the river died out. At first, the skating went as it always had: every hour of daylight saw twenty or thirty high school students, mixed in with kids from elementary school, dashing back and forth, playing crack the whip and skating backward: a print by Currier and Ives. But if the high school juniors and seniors who swept off the ice never noticed the death of three old women and four old men and did not much mourn the passing of their dentist, another loss hit them like a slap in the face as soon as they glided out onto the frozen river. Jim Hardie had been the best skater Milburn had ever seen, and he and Penny Draeger had worked out tandem routines which looked to their contemporaries as good as anything you saw in the Olympics. Peter Barnes had been nearly as good, but he refused to come skating this year; even when the weather paused, Peter stayed at home. But Jim was the one they missed: even when he showed up in the morning with bloodshot eyes and a stubble on his cheeks, he had enlivened them all—you couldn't watch him without trying to skate a little better yourself. Now even Penny did not show up. Like Peter Barnes, she had drifted away into privacy. Soon, most of the other skaters did the same: every day more snow had to be shoveled off the river, and some of the boys doing the shoveling thought that Jim Hardie was not in New York after all; they had a feeling that something had happened to Jim —something they didn't want to think about too much. Days before it was proven, they knew that Jim Hardie was dead.

One day during his afternoon break Bill Webb picked up his battered old hockey skates from his locker behind the restaurant and walked over to the river and looked dully at the two untouched feet of fresh snow blanketing it. For this winter, the skating was dead too.

Clark Mulligan never bothered to book the new Disney film he always brought in at Christmas, but ran horror movies all through the season. Some nights he had seven or eight customers, some nights only two or three; other nights he started up the first reel of *Night of the Living Dead* and knew he was showing it only to himself. Saturday's matinee usually brought out ten or fifteen kids who had already seen the movie but couldn't think of anything else to do. He began letting them in for free. Every day he lost a little more money, but at least the Rialto got him away from home; as long as the power lines stayed up, he could keep warm and busy, and that was all he wanted. One night he walked down from the booth to see if anybody had bothered to sneak in through the fire door, and saw Penny Draeger sitting beside a wolf-faced man wearing sunglasses: Clark hurried back up to his projection booth, but he was sure the man had grinned at him before he could turn away. He didn't know why, but that frightened him —badly.

For the first time in most of their lives, Milburn people saw the weather as malevolent, a hostile force that would kill them if they let it. Unless you got up on your roof and knocked off the snow, the rafter beams would crack and buckle under its weight, and in ten minutes your house would be a frigid ruined shell, uninhabitable until spring; the wind chill factor sometimes brought the temperature down to sixty below, and if you stayed outside for much longer than it took to run from your car to your house, you could hear the wind chuckling in your inner ear, knowing that it had you where it wanted you. That was one enemy, the worst they knew. But after Walt Hardesty and one of his deputies identified the bodies of Jim Hardie and Christina Barnes, and word got around about the condition of their bodies, Milburn people drew their drapes and switched on their television instead of going out to their neighbor's party and wondered if it was a bear after all that killed handsome Lewis Benedikt. And when, like Milly Sheehan, they saw that a line of snow had worked in around the storm window and lay like a taunt on the sill, they began to think about what else might get in. So they, like the town, closed in; shut down; thought about survival. A few remembered Elmer Scales standing in front of the statue, waving his shotgun and ranting about Martians. Only four people knew the identity of an enemy more hostile than the murderous weather.

Sentimental Journey

2

"I see on the news that it's worse in Buffalo," Ricky said, talking more for its own sake than because he thought the other two would be interested. Sears was driving his Lincoln in extremely Sears-like style: all the way to Edward's house where they had picked up Don, and now back to the west side of town, he had hunched over the wheel and proceeded at fifteen miles an hour. He blew his horn at every intersection, warning all comers that he did not intend to stop.

"Stop babbling, Ricky," he said, and blasted his horn and rolled across Wheat Row to the north end of the square.

"You didn't have to blow the horn, that was a green light," Ricky pointed out.

"Humpf. Everybody else is going too fast to stop."

Don, in the back seat, held his breath and prayed that the traffic lights on the other end of the square would turn green before Sears reached them. When they passed the steps to the hotel, he saw the lights facing Main Street flash to amber; the lights switched to green just as Sears put the entire palm of his hand down on the button and floated the long car like a galleon onto Main Street.

Even with the headlights on, the only objects truly visible were traffic lights and the red and green pinpoints of illumination on the Christmas tree. All else dissolved in swirling white. The few approaching cars appeared first as streamers of yellow light, then as shapeless forms like large animals: Don could see their colors only when they were immediately alongside, a proximity Sears acknowledged with another imperious blast of the Lincoln's horn.

"What do we do when we get there, if we ever do?" Sears asked.

"Just have a look around. It might help." Ricky looked at him in a way that was as good as speaking, and Don added, "No. I don't think she'll be there. Or Gregory."

"Did you bring a weapon?"

"I don't own a weapon. Did you?"

Ricky nodded; held up a kitchen knife. "Foolish, I know, but . . ."

Don did not think it was foolish; for a moment he wished that he too had a knife, if not a flamethrower and a grenade.

"Just out of curiosity, what are you thinking about at this moment?" Sears asked.

"Me?" Don asked. The car began to drift slowly sideways, and Sears turned the wheel very slightly to correct it.

"Yes."

"I was just remembering something that used to happen back when I was a prep school student in the Midwest. When we had to choose our colleges, the staff would give us talks about 'the East.' 'The East' was where they wanted us to go—it was simple snobbery, and my school was very old-fashioned in that way, but the school would look better if a big proportion of its seniors went on to Harvard or Princeton or Cornell— or even a state university on the East Coast. Everybody pronounced the word the way a Muslim must pronounce the word Mecca. And that's where we are now."

"Did you go East?" Ricky asked. "I don't know if Edward ever mentioned it."

"No. I went to California, where they believed in mysticism. They didn't drown witches, they gave them talk shows."

"Omar never got around to plowing Montgomery Street," Sears said; Don, surprised, turned to his window and saw that while he had talked they had reached the end of Anna Mostyn's street. Sears was right. On Maple, where they were, hard-packed snow about two inches deep showed the treads and deep grooves of Omar Norris's plow; it was like a white riverbed cut through high white banks. On Montgomery, the snow lay four feet deep. Already filling up with fresh snowfall, deep indentations down the middle of the road indicated where two or three people had fought through to Maple.

Sears turned off the ignition, leaving the parking lights on. "If we're going through with this, I see no point in waiting."

The three men stepped out onto the glassy surface of Maple Street. Sears turned up the fur collar of his coat and sighed. "To think I once balked at stepping into the two or three inches of snow on Our Vergil's field."

"I hate the thought of going into that house again," Ricky said.

All three could see the house through the swirls of falling snow. "I've never actually broken into a house before," Sears said. "How do you propose to do it?"

"Peter said that Jim Hardie broke a pane of glass in the back door. All we have to do is reach in and turn the knob.

"And if we see them? If they are waiting for us?"

"Then we try to put up a better fight than Sergeant York," Ricky said. "I suppose. Do you remember Sergeant York, Don?"

"No," Don said. "I don't even remember Audie Murphy. Let's go." He stepped into the drift left by the plow. His forehead was already so cold it felt like a metal plate grafted onto his skin. When he and Ricky were both on top of the drift they reached down to Sears, who stood with his arms extended like a small boy, and pulled him forward. Sears lumbered forward and up like a whale taking a reef, and then all three men stepped from the top of the drift into the deep snow on Montgomery Street.

The snow came up past their knees. Don realized that the two old men were waiting for him to begin, so he turned around and began to move up the street toward Anna Mostyn's house, doing his best to step in the deep depressions made by an earlier walker. Ricky followed, using the same prints. Sears, off to the side and stumping through unbroken snow, came last. The bottom of his black coat swept along after him like a train.

It took them twenty minutes to reach the house. When all three were standing in front of the building, Don again saw the two older men looking at him and knew that they would not move until he made them do it. "At least it'll be warmer inside," he said.

"I just hate the thought of going in there again," Ricky said, not very loudly.

"So you said," Sears reminded him. "Around the back, Don?"

"Around the back."

Once again he led the way. He could hear Ricky sneezing behind him as each of them plowed on through snow nearly waist-high. Like Jim Hardie and Peter Barnes, they stopped at the side window and looked in; saw only a dark empty chamber. "Deserted," Don said, and continued around to the rear of the house.

He found the window Jim Hardie had broken, and just as Ricky joined him on the back step, reached in and turned the handle of the kitchen door. Breathing heavily, Sears joined them.

"Let's get in out of the snow," Sears said. "I'm freezing." It was one of the bravest statements Don had ever heard, and he had to answer it with a similar courage. He pushed the door and stepped into the kitchen of Anna Mostyn's house. Sears and Ricky came in close behind him.

"Well, here we are," Ricky said. "To think it's been fifty years, or near enough. Should we split up?"

"Afraid to, Ricky?" Sears said, impatiently brushing snow off his coat. "I'll believe in these ghouls when I see them. You and Don can look at the rooms upstairs and on the landings. I'll do this floor and the basement."

And if the earlier statement had been an act of courage, this, Don knew, was a demonstration of friendship: none of them wanted to be alone in the house. "All right," he said. "I'll be surprised if we find anything too. We might as well start."

Sears led as they left the kitchen and went into the hall. "Go on," he said—commanded. "I'll be fine. This way will save time, and the sooner we get it over with, the better." Don was already on the stairs, but Ricky had turned questioningly back to Sears. "If you see anything, give a shout."

3

Don and Ricky Hawthorne were alone on the staircase. "It didn't used to be like this," Ricky said. "Not at all, you know. This place used to be so beautiful, then. The rooms downstairs—and her room, up there on the landing. Just beautiful."

"So were Alma's rooms," Don said. He and Ricky could hear Sears's footsteps on the boards of the lower room. The sound brought a new awareness flooding across Ricky's features. "What is it?"

"Nothing."

"Tell me. Your whole face changed."

Ricky blushed. "This is the house we dream about. Our nightmares are set here. Bare boards, empty rooms —the sound of something moving around, like Sears just now, down below. That's how the nightmare begins. When we dream it, we're in a bedroom—up there." He pointed up the staircase. "On the top floor." He went up a few steps. "I have to go up there. I have to see the room. It might help to—to stop the nightmare."

"I'll go with you," Don said.

When they reached the landing, Ricky stopped short. "Didn't Peter tell you this was where—?" He pointed to a dark smear down the side of the wall.

"Where Bate killed Jim Hardie." Don swallowed involuntarily. "Let's not stay here any longer than we have to."

"I don't mind splitting up," Ricky hastily said. "Why don't you take Eva's old bedroom and the rooms on the next landing, and I'll prowl around on the top floor? It'll go faster that way. If I find anything, I'll call for you. I want to get out of here too—I can't stand being here."

Don nodded, agreeing with him wholeheartedly. Ricky continued up the stairs, and Don climbed to a half-landing and swung open the door to Eva Galli's bedroom.

Bare, desolate; then the noises of an invisible crowd: hushing feet and whispers, rattling papers. Don hesitantly took a step deeper into the empty room, and the door crashed shut behind him.

"Ricky?" he said, and knew that his voice was no louder than the whispers behind him. The dim light guttered; and from the moment he could no longer see the walls, Don felt that he was in a much larger room —the walls and ceiling had flown out, expanded, leaving him in a psychic space he did not know how to leave. A cold mouth pressed against his ear and said or thought the word "Welcome." He swung around to the source of the sound, thinking belatedly that the mouth, like the greeting, had been only a thought. His fist met air.

As if playfully to punish him, someone tripped him, and he landed painfully on hands and knees. A carpet met his hands. This gradually took on color—dark blue —and he realized that he could see again. Don lifted his head and saw a white-haired man in a blazer the color of the carpet and gray slacks above mirror-polished black loafers standing before him: the blazer covered a prosperous little paunch. The man smiled down in a rueful fashion and offered him a hand; behind him other men moved. Don knew immediately who he was.

"Have a little accident, Don?" he asked. "Here. Take my hand." He pulled him upright. "Glad you could make it. We were waiting for you."

"I know who you are," Don said. "Your name is Robert Mobley."

"Why, of course. And you read my memoir. Though I wish you could have been more complimentary about the writing. No matter, my boy, no matter. No apologies necessary."

Don was looking around the room, which had a long, slightly pitched floor ending at a small stage. There were no doors he could see, and the pale walls rose almost to cathedral height: way up, tiny lights flashed and winked. Under this false sky, fifty or sixty people milled about, as if at a party. At the top end of the room, where a small bar had been set up, Don saw Lewis Benedikt, wearing a khaki jacket and carrying a bottle of beer. He was talking to a gray-suited old man with sunken cheeks and bright, tragic eyes who must have been Dr. John Jaffrey.

"Your son must be here," Don guessed.

"Shelby? Indeed he is. That's Shelby over there." He nodded in the direction of a boy in his late teens, who smiled back at them. "We're all here for the entertainment, which promises to be very exciting."

"And you were waiting for me."

"Well, Donald, without you none of this could have been arranged."

"I'm getting out of here."

"Leave? Why, my boy, you can't! You'll have to let the show roll on, I'm afraid—you've already noticed there are no doors here. And there's nothing to fear—nothing here can harm you. It's all entertainment, you see—mere shadows and pictures. Only that."

"Go to hell," Don said. "This is some kind of charade she set up."

"Amy Monckton, you mean? Why, she's only a child. You can't imagine—"

But Don was already walking away toward the side of the theater. "It's no good, dear boy," Mobley called after him. "You're going to have to stay with us until it's over." Don pressed his hands against the wall, aware that everybody in the room was looking at him. The wall was covered in a pale felt-like material, but beneath the fabric was something cold and hard as iron. He looked up to the winking dots of light. Then he pounded the wall with the flat of his hand—no depression, no hidden door, nothing but a flat sealed surface.

The invisible lights dimmed, as did the imitation stars. Two men took him, one holding an arm, the other a shoulder. They forcibly turned him to face the stage, on which a single spotlight shone. In the middle of the spot stood a placard board. The first placard read:

RABBITFOOT DE PEYSER PRODUCTIONS
TAKES PRIDE IN
PRESENTING

A hand dipped into the light and removed the sign.

A SHORT WORD FROM OUR SPONSOR

The curtain went up to reveal a television set. Don thought it was blank until he noticed details on the white screen—the red brick of a chimney, the "snow" which was real snow. Then the picture jumped into life for him.

It was a high-angled shot of Montgomery Street, taken from over the roof of Anna Mostyn's house. Immediately after he recognized the setting, the characters appeared. He, Sears James and Ricky Hawthorne struggled up the middle of Montgomery Street: he and Ricky looking at the house for as long as they were in frame, Sears looking down as if consciously to give contrast to the shot. There was no sound, and Don could not remember what they had said to each other before marching toward the house. Three faces in fast-cut closeups: their eyebrows crusted with white, they looked like soldiers conducting a mopping-up operation in some Arctic war. Ricky's tired face was obviously that of a man with a bad cold. He was suffering: it was much clearer to Don now than it had been outside the house.

Then a shot of his reaching in through the broken window. An exterior camera followed the three men into the house, tracking them through the kitchen and into the dark hallway. More unheard conversation; a third camera picked up Don and Ricky climbing the stairs, Ricky pointing to the bloodstain. On Ricky's civilized face was the expression of pain he had seen. They parted, and the camera left Don just as he pushed at the door to Anna Mostyn's bedroom.

Don uneasily watched the camera following Ricky up the stairs. A jump-cut to the end of an empty corridor: Ricky seen in silhouette pausing on a landing, then going up to the top floor. Another jump cut: Ricky entering the top floor, trying the first door and entering a room.

Inside the room now: Ricky came through the door with the camera watching him like a hidden assailant. Ricky breathing heavily, looking at the room with open mouth and widening eyes—the room of the nightmare, then, as he had guessed. The camera began to creep toward him. Then it, or the creature it represented, sprang.

Two hands gripped Ricky's neck, choking him. Ricky

fought, pushing at his murderer's wrists, but was too weak to break his grip. The hands tightened, and Ricky began to die: not cleanly, as on the television programs this "commercial" imitated, but messily, with streaming eyes and bleeding tongue. His back arched helplessly, fluids streamed from his eyes and nose, his face began to turn black.

Peter Barnes said they can make you see things, Don thought, *that's all they're doing now . . .*

Ricky Hawthorne died in front of him, in color on a twenty-six inch screen.

4

Ricky forced himself to open the door of the first bedroom on the top floor of the house. He wished he were home with Stella. She had been very shaken by Lewis's death, though she knew nothing of Peter Barnes's story.

Maybe this is where it ends, he thought, and went through into the bedroom.

And forced himself to stand still: even the breath in his body wanted to flee. It was the room of the dream, and every atom of it seemed pervaded with the Chowder Society's misery. Here they had each sweated and gone cold with fear; on this bed—now with a single gray blanket thrown over the bare mattress—each had struggled helplessly to move. In the prison of that wretched bed they had waited for life to end. The room stood only for death: it was an emblem of death, and its bare cold bleakness was its image.

He remembered that Sears was, or soon would be, in the cellar. But there was no cellar-beast: just as there was no sweating Ricky Hawthorne pinned to the bed. He turned around slowly, taking in all of the room.

On a side wall hung the only anomaly, a small mirror.

(*Mirror, mirror on the wall . . .* who's the scaredest of them all?)

(*Not I,* said the little hed hen.)

Ricky went around the bed to approach the mirror. Set opposite the window, it reflected a white section of sky. Tiny flakes of snow drifted across its surface and disappeared at the bottom of the frame.

When Ricky got closer to the mirror a whisper of breeze slid against his face. He bent forward and a sparse handful of snowflakes spun out to touch his cheek.

He made the mistake of looking directly into what he now confusedly thought must be a small window open directly to the weather.

A face appeared before him, a face he knew, wild and lost; then he glimpsed Elmer Scales moving clumsily through the snow; carrying a shotgun. Like the first apparition, the farmer was splashed with blood; the jug-eared face had starved down to skin-covered bone, but in Scales's fierce gauntness was something which forced Ricky to think *he saw something beautiful— Elmer always wanted to look at something beautiful:* this bubbled to the surface of Ricky's mind and broke. Elmer was screaming into the blaring storm, lifting his gun and shooting at a small form, flipping it over in a spray of blood . . .

Then Elmer and his target blew away and he was looking at Lewis's back. A naked woman stood in front of Lewis, soundlessly mouthing words. *Scripture,* he read, then *see Scripture in the pond, Lewis?* The woman was not living, nor was she beautiful, but Ricky saw the lineaments of returned desire in the dead face and knew he was looking at Lewis's wife. He tried to back away and escape the vision, but found he could not move.

Just when the woman closed on Lewis, both she and he melting into unrecognizable forms, Ricky saw Peter Barnes crouching in a corner of the storm. No—in a building, some building he knew but could not recognize. Some long-familiar corner, a worn carpet, a curved tan wall with a dim light in a sconce . . . a man like a wolf was bending over terrified Peter Barnes, grinning at him with white prominent teeth. This time there was no melting, merciful snowfall to hide the dreadful thing from Ricky Hawthorne: the creature leaned over cowering Peter Barnes, picked him up and like a lion killing a gazelle, broke his back. Lionlike, it bit into the boy's skin and began to eat.

5

Sears James had inspected the front rooms of the house and found nothing; and nothing, he thought, was what they were most likely to find in all the rest of the house. One empty suitcase scarcely justified going even a foot beyond one's door, in weather like this. He came back into the hall, heard Don walking aimlessly about in a bedroom at the top of the stairs, and made a quick check through the kitchen. Wet footprints, their own, dirtied the floor. A single bleary water glass sat on a dusty counter. An empty sink, empty shelves. Sears chafed his cold hands together and came back out into the dark hallway.

Now Don was banging the walls upstairs—looking for a secret panel, Sears imagined, and shook his head. That all three of them were still alive and prowling through the house proved to Sears that Eva had moved on and left nothing behind.

He opened the door to the cellar. Wooden steps led down into complete blackness. Sears flicked the switch, and a bulb at the top of the steps went on. Its light revealed the steps and concrete floor at their bottom, but seemed to extend only seven or eight feet from the bottom of the steps. Apparently it was the only light; which meant, Sears realized, that the cellar was unused. The Robinsons had never turned the basement into a den or family room.

He went down a few steps and peered into the murk. What he could see looked like any Milburn cellar: extending under the whole of the house, about seven feet high, with walls of painted concrete block. The old furnace sat near the wall at the far end, casting a deep many-armed shadow which met and melted smoothly into the gloom; on one side stood the tall tubular cylinder for hot water and two disconnected iron sinks.

Sears heard a thump from upstairs, and his heart leaped: he was vastly more nervous than he wished to acknowledge. Tilting his head back toward the top of the stairs, he listened for further noises or sounds of distress, but heard none: probably no more than a slamming door.

Come down and play in the dark, Sears.

Sears took a step further down and saw his gigantic shadow advance along the concrete floor. *Come on, Sears.*

He did not hear the words spoken in his mind, he saw no images or pictures: but he had been commanded, and he followed his bloated shadow down onto the concrete floor.

Come and see the toys I left for you.

He reached the concrete floor and experienced a sick thrill of pleasure that was not his own.

Sears spun around, afraid that something was coming for him from under the wooden staircase. Light banded the concrete in stripes, streaming between the wood: nothing was there. He would have to leave the protection of the light and look into the corners of the cellar.

He moved forward, wishing wholeheartedly that he too had brought a knife, and his shadow melted away into dark. Then all doubt left him. "Oh, my God," he said.

John Jaffrey was stepping out into the shadowy light beside the furnace. "Sears, old friend," he said. His voice was toneless. "Thank heavens you're here. They told me you would be, but I didn't know—I mean I—" He shook his head. "It's all been so *confused.*"

"Stay away from me," Sears said.

"I saw Milly," John said. "And do you know, Milly just won't let me in the house. But I warned her . . . I mean, I told her to warn you—and the others. About something. Can't remember now." He lifted his sunken face and twisted his mouth into a ghastly smile. "I went over. Isn't that what Fenny said to you? In your story? That's *right*. I went over, and now Milly won't—won't open—ah—" He raised his hand to his forehead. "Oh, it's just awful, Sears. Can't you help me?"

Sears was backing away from him, unable to speak.

"Please. Funny. Here in this place again. They made me come here—wait for you. Please help me, Sears. Thank heavens you're here."

Jaffrey lurched into the light, and Sears saw fine gray dust covering his face and outstretched hands, his bare feet. Jaffrey was moving in a painful, senile circle, his eyes too seemingly covered by a mixture of dust and drying tears—this spoke of more pain than his addled words and shuffling walk, and Sears, who remembered Peter Barnes's story about Lewis, at last felt more pity than fear.

"Yes, John," he said, and Dr. Jaffrey, apparently unable to see in the light from the naked bulb, turned toward his voice.

Sears went forward to touch Dr. Jaffrey's extended hand. At the last minute he closed his eyes. A tingling sensation passed through his fingers and traveled halfway up his arm. When he opened his eyes, John was no longer there.

He stumbled into the staircase, painfully bumping his ribs. *Toys*. Sears began mechanically to rub his hand against his coat: would he have to find more creatures shambling and dazed like John?

But no, that was not what he would have to do. Sears soon discovered the reason for the plural noun. He walked out of the light toward the furnace and saw a heap of clothing dumped by the far wall. A pile of discarded boots and rags: it was eerily like the scrubby bodies of the sheep on Elmer Scales's farm. He wanted to turn away: all the truly bad things had begun back there, with him and Ricky freezing on a cold white hill. Sears saw a flaccid hand, a swirl of blond hair. Then he recognized one of the rags as Christina Barnes's

coat; it lay flat, nearly empty, flung over a second flattened and emptied body, and it enveloped a gray de-
flated thing ending in blond hair which was Christina's
body.

Instinctively, the shout escaping him, he called for
the other two; then Sears forced control on himself
and went to the bottom of the stairs and began methodically, loudly, shamelessly to repeat their names.

6

"So you three found them," Hardesty said. "You look
pretty shook up, too." Sears and Ricky were seated on
a couch in John Jaffrey's house, Don in a chair immediately beside them. The sheriff, still wearing his coat
and hat, was leaning against the mantel, trying to disguise the fact that he was very angry. The wet traces of
his footprints on the carpet, a source of evident irrita-
tion to Milly Sheehan until Hardesty had sent her out
of the room, showed a circling path of firm heelprints
and squared-off toes.

"So do you," Sears said.

"Yeah. Suppose I do. I never saw bodies like those
two, exactly. Even Freddy Robinson wasn't that bad.
You ever seen bodies like that, Sears James? Hey?"

Sears shook his head.

"No. You're damn right. Nobody ever did. And I'm
gonna have to store 'em up in the jail until the meat
wagon can get in here. *And* I'm the poor son of a bitch
who has to take Mrs. Hardie and Mr. Barnes along to
see those goddamned things to identify them. Unless
you'd like to do that for me, Mr. James?"

"It's your job, Walt," Sears said.

"Shit. My job, is it? My job is finding out who did
what to those people—and you two old buzzards just
sit there, don't you? You found 'em by accident, I suppose. Just happened to break into that particular house,
just happened to be taking a walk on a goddamned
day like this, I suppose, and just thought you'd try a

little house-breaking—Jesus, I oughta lock all three of you in the same cell with them. Along with torn-up Lewis Benedikt and that nigger de Souza and the Griffen boy who froze to death because his hippy mommy and daddy were too cheap to put a heater in his room. God damn. That's what I ought to do, all right." Hardesty, now entirely unable to hide his anger, spat into the fireplace and kicked at the fender. "Jesus, I live in that fucking jail, I really oughta haul you three assholes along and see how you like it."

"Walt," Sears said. "Cool down."

"Sure. By God, if you two weren't nothin' but a couple of hundred-year-old lawyers with teeth in the palms of your hands, I'd do it."

"I mean, Walt," Sears calmly said, "if you will stop insulting us for a moment, that we'll tell you who killed Jim Hardie and Mrs. Barnes. And Lewis."

"You will. Hot damn. Guess I don't have to get out the rubber hoses after all."

Silence for a moment: then Hardesty said, "Well? I'm still here."

"It was the woman who calls herself Anna Mostyn."

"Swell. Just dandy. Okay. Anna Mostyn. Okay. It was her house, so she's the one. Good work. Now. What did she do, suck 'em dry, like a hound'll do to an egg? And who held 'em down, because I know no woman could have taken that crazy Hardie kid by herself. Huh?"

"She did have help," Sears said. "It was a man who calls himself Gregory Bate or Benton. Now hold on to yourself, Walt, because here comes the difficult part. Bate has been dead for almost fifty years. And Anna Mostyn—"

He stopped. Hardesty had clamped both eyes shut.

Ricky took it up. "Sheriff, in a way you were right about all this from the beginning. Remember when we looked at Elmer Scales's sheep? And you told us about other incidents, lots of them, that happened in the sixties?"

Hardesty's bloodshot eyes flew open.

"It's the same thing," Ricky said. "That is, we think it's probably the same thing. But here, they're out to kill people."

"So what's this Anna Mostyn?" Hardesty asked, his body rigid. "A ghost? A vampire?"

"Something like that," Sears said. "A shapeshifter, but those words will do."

"Where is she now?"

"That's why we went to her house. To see if we could find anything."

"And that's what you're gonna tell me. Nothing more."

"There is no more," Sears said.

"I wonder if anyone can lie like a hundred-year-old lawyer," Hardesty said, and spat once more into the fire. "Okay. Now let me tell you something. I'm going to put out a bulletin on this Anna Mostyn, and that's all she wrote. That's all I'm gonna do. You two old buzzards and this kid here can spend the rest of the winter ghost-hunting, for all I'm concerned. You're screwball—as far as I'm concerned, you're plumb outa your heads. And if I get some goddamned *killer* who drinks beer and eats hamburgers and takes his kid out for a drive on Sundays, then I'm gonna call you up and laugh in your faces. And I'll see that people around here never stop laughing when they hear your names. You understand me?"

"Don't shout at us, Walt," Sears said. "I'm sure we all understand what you said. And we understand one thing more."

"Just what the hell is that?"

"That you're frightened, Sheriff. But you have a lot of company."

Conversation with G

7

"Are you really a sailor, G?"

"Um."

"Did you go lots of places?"

"Yes."

"How come you can hang around Milburn so long? Don't you have a ship to get back to?"

"Shore leave."

"Why don't you ever want to do anything but go to the movies?"

"No reason."

"Well, I just like being with you."

"Um."

"But why don't you ever take off your shades?"

"No reason."

"Someday I'll take them off."

"Later."

"Promise?"

"Promise."

Conversation with Stella

8

"Ricky, what's happening to us? What's happening to Milburn?"

"A terrible thing. I don't want to tell you now. There'll be time when it's all over."

"You're frightening me."

"I'm frightened too."

"Well, I'm frightened because you're frightened." For a time, the Hawthornes simply held each other.

"You know what killed Lewis, don't you?"

"I think so."

"Well, I discovered an astonishing thing about myself. I can be a coward. So please don't tell me. I know I asked, but don't. I just want to know it'll end."

"Sears and I will make it end. With young Wanderley's help."

"He *can* help you?"

"He can. He has already."

"If only this terrible snow would stop."

"Yes. But it won't."

"Ricky, have I given you an awful time?" Stella propped herself up on an elbow to look into his eyes.

"A worse time than most women would," he said. "But I rarely wanted any other women."

"I am sorry that I ever had to cause you pain. Ricky, I've never cared for any man as much as I have cared for you. Despite my adventures. You know that's all over, don't you?"

"I guessed."

"He was an appalling man. He was in my car, and I just overwhelmingly realized how much better than he you were. So I made him get out." Stella smiled. "He shouted at me. It seems I am a bitch."

"At times you certainly are."

"At times. You know, he must have found Lewis's body right after that."

"Ah. I wondered what he was doing up there."

Silence: Ricky held his wife's shoulder, aware of her timeless profile beside him. If she had not looked like that, could he have endured it so long? Yet if she had not looked like that, she would not have been Stella— it was an impossible speculation.

"Tell me something, baby," she breathed. "Who was this other woman you used to want?"

Ricky laughed; then both of them, at least for a time, were laughing.

9

Motionless days: Milburn lay frozen under the accumu-
lating snow. Garage owners took their telephones off
their hooks, knowing they already had too much snowplow business with their regular customers; Omar Norris carried a bottle in each of his coat's deep pockets,
and rammed the city's plow into twice his usual quota
of parked cars—he was on triple time, often plowing
the same streets two or three times a day, and sometimes when he got back to the municipal garage, Omar
was so drunk that he simply rolled onto a cot in the
foreman's office instead of going home. Copies of *The
Urbanite* stood in wrapped bundles at the back of the
print room—the newsboys couldn't get to their collection points. Finally Ned Rowles shut the paper down
for a week and sent everybody home with a Christmas
bonus. "In this weather," he told his staff, "nothing's
going to happen except more of this weather. Have yourselves a merry little Christmas."

But even in an immobilized town, things happen.
Dozens of cars went off the roads and stayed nose down
for days, buried under fresh drifts. Walter Barnes sat
in his television room nursing a succession of drinks
and watched an endless round of giveaway shows with
the sound turned off. Peter cooked their meals. "I could
understand a lot of things," Barnes told his son, "but I
sure as hell can't understand *that*." And went back to
his quiet, nonstop drinking. One Friday night, Clark
Mulligan put the first reel of *Night of the Living Dead*
back in the projector for the Saturday-noon showing,
turned off all the lights, flipped the broken lock on the
fire door and decided once again not to bother with it
and went back out into the blizzard to find Penny
Draeger's body lying half-covered with snow beside an
abandoned car. He slapped her face and rubbed her

wrists, but nothing he could do would put breath back in her throat or change the expression on her face—G had finally allowed her to take off his dark glasses.

And Elmer Scales finally met the man from Mars.

10

It happened on the day before Christmas. The date meant nothing to Elmer. For weeks he had done his chores in a blind rage of impatience, cuffing his children if they came too close and leaving the Christmas arrangements to his wife—she had bought the presents and put up the tree, having given up on Elmer until he realized that what he was waiting up for every night didn't exist and never would wait around to get shot. On Christmas Eve Mrs. Scales and the children went to bed early, leaving Elmer sitting with the shotgun across his lap and his paper and pencil on the table to his right.

Elmer's chair faced his picture window, and with the lights off, he could see about as far as the barn— a big shape in the darkness. Except for where he had shoveled, the snow was waist-high: enough to slow down any sort of creature who was after more of his animals. Elmer did not need light to scribble down the random lines he thought of: by now he did not even have to look at the paper. He could write while staring out the window.

summers them old trees was high enough to glide from

and

Lord Lord farmings a ballbreaking business

and

somethings not a squirrel scratching under the eaves—

lines he knew would come to nothing, were not poetry, were nonsense, but which he had to write down anyhow because they came into his mind. At times they were joined by other lines, part of a conversation someone was having with his father, and these fragments too he wrote down: *Warren, can we borrow your automobile? We promise to bring it back real soon. Real soon. Got urgent business.*

Sometimes it seemed his father was there in the dark room with him, trying to explain something about the old plow horses he'd finally replaced with a John Deere, trying to say that those were good horses, you got to care for them boy, they done good by us, those five kids you got could get a lot of pleasure outa nice old horses like that—horses dead for twenty-five years! —trying to tell him something about the car. *Watch them two lawyer boys, sonny, banged up my car and lost it, drove it into a swamp or something, gave me cash dollars but nobody can trust boys like that, no matter how rich they daddies are*—creaky old voice getting at him just like when the old man was alive. Elmer wrote it all down, getting it mixed up with the poetry that wasn't poetry.

Then he saw a shape gliding toward the window, coming toward him through the snow and night with shining eyes. Elmer dropped the pencil and jerked up the shotgun, nearly firing both barrels through the picture window before he realized that the creature was not running away—that it knew he was there and was coming for him.

Elmer kicked away the chair and stood up. He patted his pockets to make sure he was carrying the extra shells, and then lifted the shotgun and sighted down the barrel, waiting for the thing to get close enough for him to see what it really was.

As it advanced, he began to doubt. If it knew he was there, waiting to blast it all the way back to the barn, why wasn't it running away? He cocked the hammers. The thing was coming up his walk, going between the two big drifts, and Elmer finally saw that it was much shorter than what he had seen before.

Then it left the walk and came over the snow to press its face against the window and he saw that it was a child.

Elmer lowered the gun, numb with confusion. He could not shoot a child. The face at the window peered in at him with a frantic, lost appeal—it was the face of misery, of every human wretchedness. With those yellow eyes, it begged him to come out, to give it rescue.

Elmer moved to the door, hearing his father's voice behind him. He paused with his hand on the doorknob, the shotgun dangling from his other hand, and then opened the door.

Freezing air, powdery snow blew in his face. The child was standing on the walk with its head averted. Someone said, "Thank you, Mr. Scales." Elmer jerked his head back and saw the tall man standing on the snowdrift to his left. Way up there, balancing on the snow like a feather, he was smiling gently down at the farmer. His face was ivory, and his eyes were vibrant accumulations of—it seemed to Elmer—a hundred shades of gold.

He was the most beautiful man Elmer had ever seen, and Elmer knew that he could not shoot him if he stood in front of him for a decade with a loaded and cocked shotgun.

"You—why—uh," Elmer managed to say.

"Precisely, Mr. Scales," the beautiful man said, and effortlessly stepped down from the snowbank onto the path. When he was facing Elmer, the golden eyes seemed to shimmer with wisdom.

"You're no Martian," Elmer said. He did not even feel the cold anymore.

"Why, of course not. I'm part of *you*, Elmer. You can see that, can't you?"

Elmer nodded dumbly.

The beautiful thing put a hand on Elmer's shoulder. "I'm here to talk to you about your family. You'd like to come with us, wouldn't you, Elmer?"

Elmer nodded again.

"Then there are a few details you have to take care of. At the moment you're slightly—encumbered? You cannot imagine the harm done to you by the people around you, Elmer. I am afraid there are things about them you have to know."

"Tell me," Elmer said.

"With pleasure. And then you will know what to do?"

Elmer blinked.

11

Some hours later on Christmas Eve, Walt Hardesty woke up in his office and noticed that the brim of his Stetson bore a new stain—he had knocked over a glass while sleeping at his desk, and the small amount of bourbon remaining in the glass had soaked into his hat. "Assholes," he pronounced, meaning the deputies, then remembered that the deputies had gone home hours before and would not return for two days. He uprighted the glass and blinked around him. The light in his untidy office hurt his eyes but seemed oddly pale—dim and somehow pinkish, as if on some early morning of a Kansas spring forty years before. Hardesty coughed and rubbed his eyes, feeling a little like that bozo in the old story who went to sleep one day and woke up with white hair and a long beard, about a hundred years older. "Rip van Shitstorm," he muttered, and worked for a while at clearing the phlegm from his throat. After that he tried to blot the hatbrim on his shirtsleeve, but the stain, though still damp, had set. He lifted the hat to his nose: County Fair. *Well, what the hell,* he thought, and sucked at the coffee-colored stain. Lint, dust, a faint trace of bourbon came into his mouth along with the disagreeable flavor of wet felt.

Hardesty went to the sink in his office, rinsed out his mouth, and bent down to look into the mirror. There was Rip van Shitstorm indeed, the famous hat-sucker, a sight which gave him no pleasure, and he was about to turn away when he finally recorded that behind him and to his left, just visible over his shoulder, the door to the utility cells was open wide.

And that was impossible. He unlocked that door only when Leon Churchill or some other deputy brought in another body waiting to be shipped up to the county morgue—the last time it had been Penny Draeger, her long silky black hair fouled and matted with dirt and snow. Hardesty had lost track of time since the discovery of Jim Hardie's and Mrs. Barnes's bodies and the beginning of the heavy snow, but he thought that Penny Draeger must have come in at least two days ago—that door had stayed locked ever since. But now it was open—open to its fullest extent—as if one of the bodies back there had strolled out, seen him sleeping with his head on his cheek, and turned around to go back to its cell and its sheet.

He walked past the file cabinets and his battered desk to the door, swung it back and forth reflectively for a moment, and then went through to the corridor which led to the cells. Here stood a tall metal door which he had not touched since leaving the Draeger girl's body; and it too was unlocked.

"Jesus H. *Christ*," Hardesty said, for while the deputies had keys to the first door, only he had the key to this, and he had not even looked at the metal door for two days. He took the big key from the ring which hung beside his holster, fit it into the slot, and heard the mechanism clicking shut, driving the bolt. He looked at the key for a second, as if trying to see if it would open the door by itself, and then experimented by unlocking it: difficult as ever, the key taking a lot of pressure before it would move. He began to pull the door open, almost afraid to look behind it to the cells.

He remembered the screwball story Sears James and Ricky Hawthorne had tried to tell him: something out of Clark Mulligan's horror movies. A smokescreen for whatever they really knew, a thing you'd have to be crazy to believe. If they had been younger, he would have swung on both of them. They were ridiculing him, hiding something. If they weren't lawyers . . .

He heard a noise from the cells.

Hardesty yanked at the door and stepped through onto the narrow concrete walkway between the utility cells. Even in the darkness, the air seemed full of some dirty pink light, hazy and very faint. The bodies lay beneath their sheets, mummies in a museum. He could not have heard a noise, not possibly; unless he had heard the jail itself creaking.

He realized that he was frightened, and detested himself for it. He couldn't even tell who most of them were any more, there were so many of them, so many sheet-covered bodies . . . but the corpses in the first cell on his right, he knew, were Jim Hardie and Mrs. Barnes, and those two were never going to make any more noise again ever.

He looked into their cell through the bars. Their bodies were on the hard floor beneath the cot against the far wall, two still white forms. Nothing wrong there. *Wait a second,* he thought, trying to remember the day he had put them in the cell. Didn't he put Mrs. Barnes on top of the bunk? He was almost certain . . . he peered in at them. *Now wait, now just hold it up a minute here,* he thought, and even in the cold of the unheated cells, began to sweat. A white-covered little parcel that could only be the Griffen baby—frozen to death in his own bed—lay on the cot. "Now just wait a goddamned second," he said, "that can't be." He'd put the Griffen baby with de Souza, in a cell on the other side of the corridor.

What he wanted to do was lock the doors behind him again and open a fresh bottle—*get out of this place right away*—but he pushed open the cell door and stepped in. There had to be some explanation: one of the deputies had come back here and rearranged the bodies, made a little more room . . . but that too couldn't be, they never came back here without him . . . he saw Christina Barnes's blond hair leaking out from beneath the edge of her sheet. Just a second before the sheet had been tucked securely around her head.

He backed away toward the cell door, now absolutely unable to stand so near the body of Christina Barnes, and when he had reached the threshold of the cell looked wildly around at the other bodies. They all seemed subtly different, as if they'd moved an inch or so, rolled over and crossed their legs while his back had been turned. He stood in the entrance to the cell, now unpleasantly conscious that his back was turned to all those other bodies, but unable to stop looking at Christina Barnes. He thought that even more of her hair was frothing out from beneath the sheet.

When he glanced at the little form on the cot, Hardesty's stomach slammed up into his throat. As if the dead child had wriggled forward in its sheet, the top of its bald round head protruded through an opening in the sheet—a grotesque parody of birth.

Hardesty jumped backward out of the cell into the dark corridor. Though he could not see them moving, he had a wild, panicky sense that all of the bodies in the cells were in motion—that if he stayed back here in the dark a second longer, they would point toward him like the needles of a dozen magnets.

From an end cell, one he knew was empty, came a dry rasping voiceless sound. A chuckle. This empty sound of mirth unfolded in his mind, more a thought than a sound. Hardesty backed nervelessly down the corridor until he thumped into the edge of the metal door, then whirled around it and slammed it shut.

Edward's Tapes

12

Don leaned against the window, looking anxiously toward Haven Lane—they should have arrived fifteen or twenty minutes earlier. Unless Sears was in charge. If

Sears had insisted on driving, Don had no idea how long the journey from Ricky's house would take. Crawling at five or ten miles an hour through the streets, risking collision at every intersection and stoplight: at least they could not be killed, going at Sears's speed. But they could be isolated, away from what they assumed was the safety of Ricky's and his uncle's houses. If they were out there alone in the snow, on foot, their car off the road, Gregory could close in, talking amiably, waiting until they moved or ran.

Don turned from the window and said to Peter Barnes, "Want some coffee?"

"I'm fine," the boy said. "Do you see them coming?"

"Not yet. They'll be here."

"It's a terrible night. The worst yet."

"Well, I'm sure they'll be here soon," Don said. "Your father didn't mind your leaving the house on Christmas Eve?"

"No," Peter said, and looked truly unhappy for the first time that night. "He's—I guess he's mourning. He didn't even ask me where I was going." Peter kept his intelligent face steady, not permitting his grief to demonstrate itself in the tears Don knew were close.

Don went back to the window and leaned forward, pressing his hands on the cold glass. "I see someone coming."

Peter stood up behind him.

"Yes. They're stopping. It's them."

"Mr. James is staying with Mr. Hawthorne now?"

"It was their idea. We all felt safer that way." He watched Sears and Ricky leave the car and begin to fight their way up the walk.

"I want to tell you something," Peter said behind him, and Don turned to look at the tall boy. "I'm really glad you're here."

"Peter," Don said, "if we get these things before they get us, it'll be mostly because of you."

"We will," Peter said quietly, and as Don went to

the door he knew that he and the boy were equally grateful for each other's company.

"Come in," he said to the two older men. "Peter is already here. How's your cold, Ricky?"

Ricky Hawthorne shook his head. "Stable. You have something you want us to listen to?"

"On my uncle's tapes. Let me help you with your coats."

A minute later he was leading them down the hall. "I had quite a struggle to find the right tapes," he said. "My uncle never marked the boxes he kept them in." He opened the door to the office. "That's why the place looks like this." Empty white boxes and spools of tape covered the floor. Other white boxes littered the desk.

Sears knocked a spool of tape off a chair and lowered himself into it; Ricky and Peter sat on camp chairs against a book-lined wall.

Don went behind the desk. "I guess Uncle Edward had some sort of filing system, but I never found out what it was. I had to go through everything before finding the Moore tapes." He sat down behind the desk. "If I were another kind of novelist, I'd never have to dream up a plot again. My uncle was told more dirt off the record than Woodward and Bernstein."

"At any rate," Sears said, extending his legs deliberately to push over a stack of white boxes, "you found them. And you want us to listen to something. Let's get to it."

"Drinks are on the table," Don said. "You'll need it. Help yourselves." While Ricky and Sears poured whiskey for themselves and Peter took a Coke, Don described his uncle's taping technique.

"He'd just let the recorder run—he wanted to get everything the subject said. During the formal taping sessions, of course, but also during meals, having drinks, watching television—to catch anything the subject came up with. So from time to time, the subject would be left alone in a room with a tape recorder running. We're going to listen to a couple of moments when that happened."

Don swiveled his chair around and pushed the "on" button of the recorder on the shelf behind him. "This is set just about on the right spot. I won't have to tell you what to listen for." He pushed the "play" button, and Edward Wanderley's voice filled the room, floating down from the big speakers perched up behind the desk.

"So he beat you because of the money you spent on acting lessons?"

A girlish voice answered. "No. He beat me because I existed."

"How do you feel about it now?"

Silence for a time: then the other voice said, "Could you get me a drink, please? It's difficult for me to talk about this."

"Sure, of course, I understand. Campari soda?"

"You remembered. Lovely."

"I'll be right back."

Noises of the desk chair squeaking, footsteps; the door closed.

In the few seconds of quiet which followed, Don kept his eyes on Sears and Ricky. They watched the spools of tape hissing through the heads.

"Are my old friends listening to me now?" It was another voice: older, brisker, drier. "I want to say hello to all of you."

"It's Eva," Sears said. "That's Eva Galli's voice." Instead of fear, his face showed anger. Ricky Hawthorne looked as if his cold had just grown much worse.

"We parted, the last time we all met, so ignominiously, that I wanted all of you to know that I remember you very well. You, dear Ricky; and you, Sears—what a dignified man you became! And you, handsome Lewis. How lucky you are to be listening today! Haven't you ever wondered what would have happened if you had gone into the girl's room instead of letting your wife answer her call? And poor ugly John—let me thank you in advance for having such a wonderful party. I am going to enjoy myself enormously at your party, John, and I am going to leave a present behind—a token of future presents to all of you."

Don took the reel off the recorder, said, "Don't say anything now. Listen to the next one first." He put on a second reel and advanced it to a number he had written on a pad. Then he pushed the "play" button again.

Edward Wanderley: "Do you want to take a break for a little while? I could make us some lunch."

"Please. Don't worry about me. I'll just stay here and look at your books until everything's ready."

After Edward left the room, Eva Galli's voice came again through the speakers.

"Hello, my old friends. And are you joined by a young friend?"

"Not you, Peter," Don said. "Me."

"Is Don Wanderley with you? Don, I look forward to seeing you again too. For I will, you know. I will visit each of you and thank you in person for the treatment you gave me some time ago. I hope you are looking forward to the extraordinary things in store for you." Then she paused, using the spacing of the sentences to form separate paragraphs.

"I will take you places where you have never been.

"And I will see the life run out of you.

"And I will see you die like insects. *Insects.*"

Don switched off the machine. "There's one more tape I want to play, but you can see why I thought you ought to hear them."

Ricky still looked shaken. "She *knew*. She knew we were all going to sit here . . . and listen to her. To her threats."

"But she spoke to Lewis and John," Sears said. "That's rather leading."

"Exactly. You see what that means. She can't predict things, she can just make good guesses. She thought one of you would go through these tapes shortly after my uncle's death. And stew over them for a year, until she celebrated the anniversary of Edward's death by killing John Jaffrey. Obviously she thought you would write to me, and that I would come out to take possession of the house. Of course putting my name on that tape meant that you would have to get in touch with me. It was always part of her plan that I come here."

Ricky said, "As it was we stewed pretty well on our own."

"I think she caused your nightmares. Anyhow, she wanted all of us here so that she could get us one by one. Now I want you to hear the last tape." He removed the spent reel from the machine and took up the third reel beside him and placed it on the recorder.

A lilting southern voice came through the big speakers.

"Don. Didn't we have a wonderful time together? Didn't we love each other, Don? I hated leaving you— really, I was heartbroken when I left Berkeley. Do you remember the smell of burning leaves when you walked me home, and the dog barking streets away? It was all so lovely, Don. And look at what a wonderful thing you made of it! I was so proud of you. You thought and thought about me, and you came so close. I *wanted* you to see, I wanted you to see everything and have your mind open up to all the possibilities we represent —right through the stories about Tasker Martin and the X.X.X.—"

He switched it off. "Alma Mobley," he said. "I don't think you have to hear the rest of it."

Peter Barnes stirred in his chair. "What's she trying to do?"

"To convince us of her omnipotence. To get us so scared that we'll give up." He leaned forward over the desk. "But these tapes prove that she's not omnipotent. She makes mistakes. So her ghouls can make mistakes. They can be defeated."

"Well, you're not Knute Rockne and this isn't the big game," Sears said. "I'm going home. To Ricky's home, that is. Unless there are other ghosts you want us to hear."

Surprisingly, Peter answered him. "Mr. James, pardon me, but I think you're wrong. This is the big game

—it's a stupid term and I know that's why you used it, but getting rid of these horrible *things* is the most important thing we'll ever do. And I'm glad we found out that they can make mistakes. I think it's wrong to be sarcastic about it. You wouldn't act like that if you ever saw them—if you ever saw them kill someone."

Don waited resignedly for Sears to crush the boy, but the lawyer merely drained his whiskey and leaned forward to speak quietly to Peter. "You forget. I have seen them. I knew Eva Galli, and I saw her sit up after she was dead. And I know the beast who killed your mother, and his pathetic little brother—the one who held you and made you watch—I knew him too. When he was merely a retarded schoolboy I tried to save him from Gregory, just as you must have tried to save your mother, and like you I failed. And like you I am morally offended to hear that creature's voice, in any of her guises—I am morally outraged to hear that preening voice. It is unspeakable, that she taunts us in this way, after what she has done. I suppose I meant only that I would be more comfortable with some specific action." He stood up. "I am an old man, and I am accustomed to expressing myself in whatever manner I please. Sometimes I fear I am rude." Sears smiled at the boy. "That too might be morally offensive. But I hope that you live long enough to enjoy the pleasure of it."

If I ever need a lawyer, Don thought, you're the one I want.

It seemed to have worked for the boy as well. "I don't know if I'd have your style," Peter said, returning the old man's smile.

And so, Don reflected after everyone had left, the voices on the tapes had failed: the tapes had drawn the four of them even closer together. Peter's comment to Sears had been expressed in an adolescent fashion, but it had been a tribute all the same; and Sears had shown his enjoyment of it.

Don went back to the tape recorder: Alma Mobley

lay within it, trapped on a few spools of coated amber stuff.

Frowning, he pushed the "play" button. Silky at first, sunny, her voice resumed.

"—and Alan McKechnie and all the other stories I used to hide the truth from you. It's true, I did want you to see: your intuition was better than anyone else's. Even Florence de Peyser became curious about you. But what good would it have done? Like your 'Rachel Varney,' I have lived since the times when your continent was lighted only by small fires in the forest, since Americans dressed in hides and feathers, and even then our kinds have abhorred each other. Your kind is so bland and smug and confident on the surface: and so neurotic and fearful and campfire-hugging within. In truth, we abhor you because we find you boring. We could have poisoned your civilization ages ago, but voluntarily lived on its edges, causing eruptions and feuds and local panics. We chose to live in your dreams and imaginations because only there are you interesting.

"Don, you make a grave mistake if you underestimate us. Could you defeat a cloud, a dream, a poem? You are at the mercy of your human imaginations, and when you look for us, you should always look in the places of your imagination. In the places of your dreams. But despite all this talk about imagination, we are implacably real, as real as bullets and knives—for aren't they too tools of the imagination?—and if we want to frighten you it is to frighten you to death. For you are going to die, Donald. First your uncle, then the doctor, then Lewis. Then Sears, and after Sears, Ricky. And then you and whomever you have enlisted to help you. In fact, Donald, you are dead already. You are finished. And Milburn is finished with you." Now the Louisiana accent had vanished; even femininity had gone from the voice. It was a voice with no human resonance at all. "I am going to shatter Milburn, Donald. My friends and I will tear the soul from this pathetic town and crush its bare bones between our teeth."

A hissing silence followed: Don yanked the tape

from the machine and tossed it into a cardboard box. In twenty minutes he had all his uncle's tapes in boxes. He carried the cartons into the living room and methodically fed all of the tapes into the wood fire, where they smoked and curled and stank and finally melted down to black bubbles on the burning logs. If Alma could see him, he knew, she'd be laughing.

You're dead already, Donald.

"Like hell I am," he said out loud. He remembered the haggard face of Eleanor Hardie, into which age had so suddenly burrowed; Alma had been laughing at him and the Chowder Society for decades, belittling their achievements and engineering their tragedies, hiding in the dark behind a false face, waiting for the moment to jump out and say boo.

And Milburn is finished with you.

"Not if we can get to you first," he said into the fire. "Not if this time we shoot the lynx."

III

The Last of the
Chowder Society

"Could you defeat a cloud, a dream, a poem?"
—Alma Mobley

"And what is innocence?" Narcissus enquired of his friend.
    "It is to imagine that your life is a secret," his
friend replied. "Most particularly, to imagine it a
secret between yourself and a mirror."
    "I see," Narcissus said. "It is the illness for
which mirror-gazing is the cure."

1

Near seven o'clock Ricky Hawthorne rolled over in bed
and groaned. Feelings of panic, of emergency, filled
him, making the darkness admonitory: he had to get
out of bed, get moving, to avert some terrible tragedy.
"Ricky?" Stella uttered beside him. "Fine, fine," he
answered, and sat up in bed. The window at the far end
of the room showed dark gray shot through with lazily

falling snow—flakes so big they looked like snowballs. Ricky's heartbeat sounded: *doom, doom*. Someone was in terrible danger; in the instant before shooting into wakefulness, he'd seen an image and known—rendingly —who it was. Now all he knew was that it was impossible for him to stay in bed. He raised the covers and put one leg over the side.

"Was it your nightmare again, baby?" Stella whispered hoarsely.

"No. No, not that. I'll be okay, Stella." He patted her shoulder and left the bed. The urgency clung. Ricky slid his feet into his slippers, pulled a robe over his pajamas, and padded to the window.

"Honey, you're upset, come back to bed."

"I can't." He rubbed his face: still that wild feeling, trapped in his chest like a bird, that someone he knew was in mortal danger. Snow transformed Ricky's back yard into a range of shifting and dimpled hills.

It was the snow which reminded him: the snow blowing through a mirror in Eva Galli's house, and a glimpse of Elmer Scales, his face distorted by an obligation to a commanding and cruel beauty, running raggedly through the drifts. Raising a shotgun: turning a small form into a spray of blood. Ricky's stomach savagely bent in on itself, shooting pain down into his bowels. He pressed a hand into the soft flesh below his navel and groaned again. Elmer Scales's farm. Where the last stage of the Chowder Society's agony had begun.

"Ricky, what's wrong?"

"Something I saw in a mirror," he said, straightening up now that the pain had dissolved, aware that his statement would be nonsense to Stella. "I mean, something about Elmer Scales. I have to get out to his farm."

"Ricky, it's seven o'clock on Christmas morning."

"Makes no difference."

"You can't. Call him up first."

"Yes," he said, already on his way out of the bedroom, going past Stella's white, startled face. "I'll try that."

He was on the landing outside the bedroom, still with that wakening emergency sounding along his veins *(doom, doom)* and was torn for a second between rushing into the wardrobe closet and throwing on some clothes so he'd be ready to leave and running downstairs to the telephone.

A noise from downstairs decided him. Ricky put his hand on the banister and descended.

Sears, fully dressed and with the fur-collared coat over his arm, was just coming out of the kitchen. The look of aggressive blandness which was Sears's lifelong expression was gone: his old friend's face was as taut as he knew his own to be.

"You, too," Sears said. "I'm sorry."

"I just woke up," Ricky said. "I know what you're feeling—I want to go with you."

"Don't interfere," Sears said. "All I'm going to do is get out there, have a look around and make sure everything's all right. I feel like a cat on a griddle."

"Stella had a good idea. Let's try to call him first. Then the two of us will go together."

Sears shook his head. "You'll slow me down, Ricky. I'll be safer alone."

"Come on." Ricky put a hand on Sears's elbow and steered him back to the couch. "Nobody's going anywhere until we try the telephone. After that we can talk about what to do."

"There's nothing to talk about," Sears said, but sat down anyhow. He twisted his body to watch Ricky lift the phone off its stand and place it on the coffee table. "You know his number?"

"Of course," Ricky said, and dialed. Elmer Scales's telephone rang; and rang again; and again. "I'll give him more time," Ricky said, and let it go for ten rings, then twelve. He heard it again: *doom, doom,* that frantic pulse.

"It's no good," Sears said, "I'd better go. Probably won't make it anyhow, on these roads."

"Sears, it's still early morning," Ricky said, putting down the phone. "Maybe nobody heard it ringing."

"At seven—" Sears looked at his watch. "At seven-ten on Christmas morning? In a house with five children? Does that sound likely to you? I know something is wrong out there, and if I can get there at all, I might be able to stop it from getting worse. I don't intend to wait for you to get dressed." Sears stood up and began putting on his coat.

"At least call Hardesty and let him go out there instead. You know what I saw, back in that house."

"That is a feeble joke, Ricky. Hardesty? Don't be foolish. Elmer won't shoot at me. We both know that."

"I know he won't," Ricky said miserably. "But I'm worried, Sears. This is something Eva's doing—like what she did to John. We should not let her split us up. If we go running in all directions she can get to us— destroy us. We ought to call Don and get him to come with us. Oh, I know something terrible is happening out there, I'm convinced of it, but you'll court something even worse if you try to go there by yourself."

Sears looked down at pleading Ricky Hawthorne, and the impatience on his face melted. "Stella would never forgive me if I let you take that wretched cold outside again. And it would take Don half an hour or more to get there. You can't make me wait, Ricky."

"I could never make you do anything you didn't want to do."

"Correct," Sears said, and buttoned his coat.

"You're not expendable, Sears."

"Who is? Can you name one person you think is expendable, Ricky? I've lost too much time already, so don't make me hang around while you try to justify naming Hitler or Albert de Salvo or Richard Speck or—"

"What in the world are you two talking about?" Stella was in the entrance of the living room, smoothing down her hair with the palms of her hands.

"Nail your husband to the couch and pour hot whiskey into him until I get back," Sears said.

"Don't let him go, Stella," Ricky said. "He can't go alone."

"Is it urgent?" she asked.

"For heaven's sake," Sears muttered, and Ricky nodded.

"Then he'd better go. I hope he can get the car started."

Sears moved toward the hallway, and Stella stepped aside to let him pass. But before he went into the hall, he turned back to look once more at Ricky and Stella. "I'll be back. Don't fret about me, Ricky."

"You realize it's probably too late already."

"It's probably been too late for fifty years," Sears said. Then he turned and was gone.

2

Sears put on his hat and went outside into the coldest morning he could remember. His ears and the tip of his nose immediately began to sting; a moment later the unprotected part of his forehead was also blazing with cold. He moved carefully down the slippery walk, noticing that the previous night's snow had been the lightest in three weeks—only five or six inches of fresh snow lay on the old, and that meant that he had a good chance of being able to take the big Lincoln out onto the highway.

The key stuck halfway into the lock: cursing with impatience, Sears yanked it out and removed a glove to search his pockets for his cigar lighter. The cold bit and tore at his fingers, but the lighter snapped out its flame; Sears played it back and forth over the key, and just when his fingers felt as though they were about to drop off, slotted the key neatly into the lock. He opened the door and slid himself onto the leather seat.

Then the interminable business of starting the engine: Sears ground his teeth and tried to get the engine to turn over by willing it. He saw Elmer Scales's face as he

had when coming awake, staring at him with dazed unfocused eyes and saying *You gotta get out here, Mr.
James, I don't know what I been doin', just get here for
Chrissake* . . . the engine gnashed and sputtered, then
mercifully caught. Sears fluttered the gas pedal, making
the engine roar and then rocked the car back and forth
to roll it out of its depression and through the snow
which had built up around it.

After he got the car pointed out onto the street,
Sears took the ice tool from the dashboard and pushed
the powder off the windshield: the big harmless fluffs of
snow swirled about him in a soundless dawn. He reversed the tool and used the bladed end to clear an
eight-inch hole in the ice directly in front of the steering
wheel. He'd let the heater do the rest.

"Things you're better off not knowing, Ricky," he
said to himself, thinking of the childish footprints he'd
seen in the drifts outside his window three mornings
running. The first morning he'd pulled his drapes shut
in case Stella came into the guest room to clean; a
day later he had realized that Stella had an extremely
haphazard approach to housekeeping, and that not even
bribery would induce her to enter the guest room—she
was waiting until the cleaning woman would be able to
come from the Hollow. For two mornings, those prints
of bare feet dotted the snow which relentlessly climbed
up to the window, even on Sears's protected side of the
house. This morning, after Elmer's drugged face had
pulled him unceremoniously from sleep, he had seen
the prints on the windowsill. How long would it be before Fenny appeared inside the Hawthorne house, trot-
ting gleefully up and down the stairs? One more night?
If Sears could lead him away, perhaps he could win
more time for Ricky and Stella.

In the meantime he had to see to Elmer Scales and
just get here for Chrissake . . . . . Ricky too had been
tuned into whatever kind of signal that was, but fortunately Stella had appeared to keep him at home.

The Lincoln rolled out onto the street and began
bulling through the snow. There's one comfort, Sears

thought: at this time of the morning on Christmas day the only other person on the road will be Omar Norris.

Sears pushed Elmer Scales's face and voice out of his consciousness and concentrated on driving. Omar had worked most of the night again, it seemed, because nearly all the streets in the center of Milburn were scraped down to the last four or five inches of hard-packed frozen snow. On these streets, the only danger was of skidding on the glassy cake beneath the wheels and going off into a spin to collide with a buried car . . . he thought of Fenny Bate on his windowsill, levering up the window, gliding into the house, snuffling for the scent of living things . . . but no, those windows had storms on them and he had made sure the inner windows were locked.

Maybe he was doing the wrong thing; maybe he ought to turn around and go back to Ricky's house.

But he couldn't do that, he realized. He swung the car through the red light at the top of the square and lifted his foot from the accelerator, letting the car coast into its own angle past the front of the hotel. He could not go back: Elmer's voice seemed almost to get stronger, sounding deep tones of pain, of confusion *(Jesus Sears, I can't get my head around what's happening out here)*. He twitched the wheel and straightened out the car: the only rough spot now would be the highway, those few miles of treacherous hills, cars stacked up in the ditches on both sides . . . he might be forced to walk.

Jesus Sears I can't figure out all this blood . . . seems like those trespassers got in finally and now I'm scared bad, Sears, scared real bad . . .

Sears nudged the accelerator down a fraction of an inch.

3

At the top of Underhill Road he paused: it was much worse than he expected. Through the snow and gloom of the morning he could see the red lights on Omar's plow, pushing maddeningly slowly toward the highway. A nine-foot drift shaped like a surfer's ideal wave curled over all the unplowed section of Underhill Road. If he tried to get around Omar's plow, he'd bury the Lincoln in the drift.

For a second he had a mad impulse to do just that, floor the accelerator and sail down the fifty yards to the bottom of the hill and then smash the Lincoln through the snow, crashing through it around Omar on his slow-motion throne and exploded out of the big drift onto the highway—it was as if Elmer were telling him to do it. *Get that car moving, Mr. James, I need you bad*—

Sears blew his horn, mashing his hand down on the button, Omar turned around to gape at him: when he saw the Lincoln, he jabbed one finger in the air, and through the glass behind the cab Sears saw him weave on the seat, his face covered with a snow-crusted ski mask, and knew two things at once. Omar was drunk and half-dead with exhaustion; and he was yelling at him, telling him to turn around and not come down the hill. The Lincoln's tires would never hold on the slope.

Elmer's dogged, wheedling voice had kept him from seeing it.

The Lincoln, idling, rolled a few inches down the long hill. Omar switched off the plow and stood up half-out of the cab, supporting himself on one of the struts to the blade. He held a hand out palm-forward like a traffic cop. Sears stamped on his brake pedal, and the Lincoln shuddered on the slippery plowed surface. Omar was making circular motions with his free hand, telling him to turn around or back up.

Sears's car lurched another six inches down the

slope and he grabbed for the handbrake, no longer thinking of how to handle the car but just trying to stop it. He heard Elmer saying *Sears—need—need—* that dogged, high-pitched voice urging the car forward.

And then saw Lewis Benedikt at the bottom of the hill running toward him, waving his arms to make him stop, a khaki jacket flapping out behind him, his hair blowing.

—need—need—

Sears released the handbrake and pushed his foot down on the accelerator. The Lincoln skidded forward, its rear tires whining, and plummeted down the long hill, fishtailing from side to side. Behind Lewis's running figure, Sears saw a blurry Omar Norris standing stock-still on the snowplow.

Traveling at seventy-five miles an hour, the Lincoln sliced through the figure of Lewis Benedikt; Sears opened his mouth and shouted, twisting the wheel savagely to the left. The Lincoln spun three fourths of the way around and jolted the snowplow with its right rear fender before plunging into the huge curling drift.

His eyes closed, Sears heard the mushy, sickening thud of a heavy object striking the windshield: a moment later he felt the atmosphere about him become thicker: in the next endless second the car crumped to a stop as if he'd hit a wall.

He opened his eyes and saw he was in darkness. Sears's head stung where he had struck it in the crash. He put one hand to a temple and felt blood; with the other he switched on the interior lights. Omar Norris's masked face, jammed against the windshield, peered with an empty eye in at the passenger seat. Five feet of snow held the car like cement.

"Now, little brother," said a deep voice from the back of the car.

A small hand, earth embedded under its nails, reached forward to brush against Sears's cheek.

The violence of his reaction took Sears by surprise: he rocketed sideways on the seat, getting his body out from under the wheel without planning or forethought, moved by a galvanic revulsion. His cheek felt scraped where the child touched it; and already, in the sealed-off car, he could smell their corruption. They sat forward in the back seat, glowing at him, their mouths open: he had startled them, too.

Disgust for these obscene beings kindled up in him. He would not die passively at their hands. Sears threw himself forward and grunted, aiming the only punch he had thrown in sixty years: it caught Gregory Bate's cheekbone and slid, tearing the flesh, into a damp, reeking softness. Glistening fluid slid over the torn cheek.

"So you can be hurt," Sears said. "By God, you can." Snarling, they flew at him.

Twelve Noon, Christmas Day

4

Ricky knew that Hardesty was drunk again the moment Walt had finished breathing two words into the telephone. By the time he had uttered as many sentences, he knew that Milburn was without a sheriff.

"You know where you can put this job," Hardesty said, and belched. "You can shove it. Hear me, Hawthorne?"

"I hear you, Walt." Ricky sat on the couch and glanced over at Stella, whose face was averted into her cupped hands. Mourning already, he thought, mourning because she let him go alone, because she sent him out of here without a blessing, without even thanks. Don Wanderley squatted on the floor beside Stella's chair and put an arm over her shoulders.

"Yeah, you hear me. Well, listen. I used to be a Marine, you know what, lawyer? Korea. Had three stripes, hear that?" A loud crash: Hardesty had fallen into a chair or knocked over a lamp. Ricky did not answer. "Three goddamned stripes. A leatherneck. You could call me a goddamned hero, I don't mind. Well, I didn't need you to tell me to go out to that farm. Neighbor went in there around eleven—found 'em all. Scales killed 'em all. Shot 'em. And afterward laid down under his goddamned tree and blew his head apart. State cops took all the bodies away in a helicopter. Now you tell me why he did it, lawyer. And you tell me how you knew something happened out there."

"Because I once borrowed his father's car," Ricky said. "I know it doesn't make sense, Walt."

Don looked up at him from beside Stella, but she merely pushed her face deeper into her hands.

"Doesn't make—shit. Beautiful. Well, you can find a new sheriff for this town. I'm clearin' out as soon as the county plows get in. I can go anywhere—record like mine. Anywhere? Not because of out there—not because of Scales's little massacre. You and your rich-bitch friends been sittin' on something all along—*all along*—and whatever it is *does* things—meaner'n a stirred-up hog. Right? It got into Scales's place, didn't it? Got into his *head*. Can go anywhere, can't it? And who called all this down on us, hey Mr. Lawyer? You. Hey?"

Ricky said nothing.

"You can call it Anna Mostyn, but that's just sheer plain lawyer's crap. Goddamn it, I always thought you were an asshole, Hawthorne. But I'm tellin' you now, anything shows up around here with ideas about moving me around, I'm gonna blow it in half. You and your buddies got all the fancy ideas, if you got any buddies left, you can take care of things around here. I'm stayin' in here until the roads get clear, sent the deputies home, anybody comes around here I shoot first. Questions later. Then I get out."

"What about Sears?" Ricky asked, knowing that Hardesty would not tell him until he asked. "Has anyone seen Sears?"

"Oh, Sears *James*. Yeah. Funny about that. State cops found him too. Saw his car half-buried in a drift,

bottom of Underhill Road, snowplow all fucked over
. . . you can bury him whenever the hell you want, little
buddy. If everybody in this goddamned freakshow town
doesn't end up cut to pieces or sucked out dry or blown
in half. Ooof." Another belch. "I'm pig-drunk, lawyer.
Gonna stay that way. Then I cut outa here. To hell with
you and everything about you." He hung up.

Ricky said, "Hardesty's lost his mind and Sears is
dead." Stella began to weep; soon he and she and Don
were in a circle, arms around each other for that prim-
itive consolation. "I'm the only one left," Ricky said into
his wife's shoulder. "My God, Stella. I'm the only one
left."

Late that night each of them—Ricky and Stella in
their bedroom, Don in the guestroom—heard the music
playing through the town, exclamatory trumpets and
breathy saxophones, the arcadian music of the soul's
night, the liquid music of America's underside, and they
heard in it an extra strain of release and abandonment.
Dr. Rabbitfoot's band was celebrating.

5

After Christmas even neighbors stopped seeing each
other, and the few optimists who still had plans for New
Year's Eve quietly forgot them. All the public buildings
stayed closed, Young Brothers and the library, the
drugstores and the churches and the offices: on Wheat
Row the drifts lapped up against the façades all the way
to the rain gutters. Even the bars stayed closed, and fat
Humphrey Stalladge stayed in his frame house out behind the tavern listening to the wind and playing pinochle with his wife, thinking that when the county
plows got in he'd start making more money than the
mint—nothing brought people into bars like bad times.
His wife said, "Don't talk like a gravedigger," and that
killed the conversation and the pinochle too for a while:
everybody knew about Sears James and Omar Norris

and, the worst of all, about what Elmer Scales had done. It seemed that if you listened to that snow hissing long enough, you wouldn't just hear it telling you that it was waiting for you, you'd hear some terrible secret —a secret to turn your life black. Some Milburn people snapped awake in the dog-hours of morning, three o'clock, four o'clock, and thought they saw one of those poor Scales kids standing at the foot of the bed, grinning at them: couldn't place which of the boys it was, but it had to be Davey or Butch or Mitchell. And took a pill to get back to sleep and forget the way little Davey or Butch or whoever-it-was looked, with his ribs shining underneath his skin and his skinny face shining too.

Eventually the town heard about Sheriff Hardesty: how he was holed up in his office with all those bodies waiting in the utility cells. Two of the Pegram boys had snowmobiles, and they coasted up the door of the sheriff's office to check him out—see if he was as nutty as the rumor said. A whiskery face jammed itself up against the window as they climbed off the snowmobiles: Hardesty lifted his pistol so the boys could see it and shouted through the glass that if they didn't pull off those damn ski masks and show their faces they wouldn't have any faces left. Most people knew someone who had a friend who'd had to go past the sheriff's office and swore that he heard Hardesty shouting in there, yelling at nothing or at himself—or at whatever it was that could move freely around Milburn in this weather, sliding in and out of their dreams, exulting in shadows whenever they'd just turned their heads: whatever it was that could account for that music some of them had heard around midnight on Christmas night— inexplicable music that should have sounded joyful but was instead wound full of the darkest emotions they knew. They pushed their heads into their pillows and told themselves it was a radio or a trick of the wind— they'd tell themselves anything rather than believe that something was out there that could make a noise so fearsome.

Peter Barnes got out of bed that night, having heard the music and imagining that this time the Bate brothers and Anna Mostyn and Don's Dr. Rabbitfoot were making a special trip to get him. (But there was another cause, he knew.) He locked his door and climbed back into bed and pushed his hands down on his ears; but the wild music got louder, coming down his street, and louder still.

It stopped directly in front of his house: sliced off in the middle of a bar, as if a button on a tape recorder had been pushed. The silence was more charged with possibilities than the music had been. Finally Peter could stand the tension no longer, and softly left his bed and looked out of his window onto the street.

Down there, down where he had once seen his father marching off to work looking dumpy and Russian, stood a line of people in bright moonlight. Nothing could stop him from recognizing the figures standing on the fresh snow where the road should have been. They stood gazing up at him with shadowed eyes and open mouths, the town's dead, and he would never know if they stood there only in his mind or if Gregory Bate and his benefactor had stirred these facsimiles and made them move: or if Hardesty's jail and a half-dozen graves had opened to let their inhabitants walk. He saw Jim Hardie staring up at his window, and the insurance salesman Freddy Robinson, and old Dr. Jaffrey and Lewis Benedikt, and Harlan Bautz—he had died while shoveling snow. Omar Norris and Sears James were beside the dentist. Peter's heart moved to see Sears— he'd known that was why the music had sounded again. A girl stepped out from behind Sears, and Peter blinked to see Penny Draeger, her once-exciting face as blank and dead as all the others. A small group of children stood mutely beside a tall scarecrow with a shotgun, and Peter nodded, mouthing the word "Scales" to himself: he had not known. Then the crowd divided to let his mother come forward.

She was not the lifelike ghost he had seen in the Bay Tree Market's parking lot: like the others, his mother was washed of life, too empty even for despair. She seemed animated only by need—need at a level beneath all feeling. Foreshortened by his angle of vision, Christina came forward over the snow to the boundary of their property; she extended her arms up to him and her mouth moved. He knew that no human words could have issued from that mouth, from that driven body—it must have been only a moan or a cry. She, they, all were asking him to come out: or were they pleading for surcease, for sleep? Peter began to cry. They were eerie, not frightening. Standing out there below his window, so pitiably drained, they were as if merely dreamed. The Bates and their benefactor had sent them, but it was him they needed. The tears cold on his cheeks, Peter turned away from the window; so many, so many, so many.

Face up, he lay back on his bed; stared with open eyes at the ceiling. He knew they would go: or would he look out in the morning to see them all still there, frozen into place like snowmen? But the music blared into life again, suddenly as present as a bright slash of red, and yes, they would be drifting away, following Dr. Rabbitfoot's bright tempo.

When the music had faded, Peter got up from his bed and checked the window. Yes. Gone. They had not even left marks on the snow.

He went downstairs in the dark; at the foot of the stairs saw a line of light beneath the television room door. Peter gently pushed it open.

The television showed a pattern of moving dots divided by a slowly upward-drifting black bar. The strong brown smell of whiskey filled the room. His father lay back in the chair with his mouth open, tie undone, the skin on his face and neck gray and parchmentlike: breathing with the soft rattling inhalations of an infant. A nearly empty bottle, a full glass in which the ice had melted, sat beside him on the table. Peter went to the television set and switched it off. Then he tenderly shook his father's arm.

"Mnn." His father's eyes opened cloudy and dazed. "Pete. Heard music."

"You were dreaming."

"What time?"

"Near one."

"I was thinking about your mother. You look like her, Pete. My hair, her face. Lucky—could've looked like me."

"I was thinking about her too."

His father got out of the chair, rubbed his cheeks, and gave Peter a look of unexpected clarity. "You're grown up, Pete. Funny. I saw it just now—you're a grown man."

Peter, embarrassed, said nothing.

"Didn't want to tell you earlier. Ed Venuti called me up this afternoon—heard it from the state cops. Elmer Scales, farmer a little way out of town? Had his mortgage with us. All those kids? Ed says he killed them all. Shot all the kids and then shot his wife and then killed himself. Pete, this town is going crazy. Just plain sick and crazy."

"Let's get upstairs," Peter said.

6

For some days Milburn stood as still as Humphrey Stalladge's card game after his wife had uttered a word which seemed obscene to both of them: gravediggers and graves were a taboo subject, when everybody in town knew well or was related to one of the sheet-covered bodies in the jail. People settled down in front of the television and ate pizzas from the freezer and prayed that the power lines would stay up; they avoided one another. If you looked outside and saw your next-door neighbor fighting up his lawn to get to his front door, he looked unearthly, transformed by stress into a wild ragged frontier version of himself: you knew he'd damage anyone who threatened to touch his dwindling store of food. He'd been touched by that savage music you had tried to escape, and if he looked through your Thermopane picture window and saw you his eyes were barely human.

And if good old Sam (assistant manager down at Horn's Tire Recapping Service and a shark at poker) or good old Ace (retired foreman from a shoe factory in Endicott and a terrible bore, but sent his son through medical school) were not outside, catching your eye with a starved glance which meant *take your eyes off me, you bastard,* then it was even worse: because what you saw looked not murderous but dead. The streets impassable except on foot, nine-foot, twelve-foot drifts, a constant swirl of white in the air, a glooming sky. The houses on Haven Lane and Melrose Avenue looked vacant, drapes drawn against the desolation outside. In town, snow drifted up to the roofs and sheeted across the streets; windows reflected chill emptiness. Milburn looked as though everyone in town were lying still under a sheet in one of Hardesty's cells; and when someone like Clark Mulligan or Rollo Draeger, who had lived all his life in Milburn, looked at it now a cold whisper of wind brushed across his heart.

That was in the daytime. Between Christmas and New Year's Day, ordinary people in Milburn, those who had never heard of Eva Galli or Stringer Dedham and thought of the Chowder Society (if they thought of it at all) as a collection of museum pieces, wound up going to bed earlier and earlier—at ten, then at nine-thirty—because the thought of all that black weather out there made them want to close their eyes and not open them again until dawn. If the days were threatening, the nights were ferocious. The wind tore around the corners of the houses, rattling shutters and storm windows, and two or three times a night a big gust flattened itself against the wall like an enormous wave—hard enough to make the lights sway. And it often seemed to ordinary people in Milburn that mixed up with all that banging and hissing outside were voices—voices that couldn't contain their glee. The Pegram boys heard something tapping at their bedroom window, and in the morning saw the prints of bare feet outside on a drift. Grieving Walter Barnes was not the only person in Milburn who thought the whole town was going crazy.

On the last day of the year the mayor finally got through to all three of the deputies and told them that they had to get Hardesty out of the office and into a hospital—the mayor was afraid that looting would begin soon if they couldn't get the streets plowed. He appointed Leon Churchill acting sheriff—the biggest and dumbest of the deputies, the one most likely to follow orders—and told Leon that if he didn't patch up Omar Norris's plow himself and start clearing the streets, he'd be out of a job permanently. So on New Year's Day Leon walked to the municipal garage and found that the plow wasn't as bad as it had looked. Sears James's big car had bent some of the plates, but everything still worked. He took the plow out that morning, and in the first hour developed more respect for Omar Norris than he'd ever had for the mayor.

But when the deputies got to the sheriff's office all they found was an empty room and a smelly cot. Walt Hardesty had disappeared sometime during the previous four days. He had left behind six empty bourbon bottles but no note or forwarding address—certainly nothing to tell of the gut-panic he'd felt one night when he lifted his head from his desk to pour himself another drink and heard more noises from back in the utility cells. At first it had sounded to Hardesty like conversation, and then like the sound a butcher makes when he slaps raw steak on the counter. He hadn't waited for whoever it was back there to start coming down the corridor, but had put on his hat and his jacket and slipped out into the blizzard. He made it as far as the high school before a hand closed over his elbow and a calm voice said in his ear, "Isn't it time we met, sheriff?" When Leon's plow uncovered him, Walt Hardesty looked like a piece of carved ivory: a life-size ivory statue of a ninety-year-old man.

7

Though the weather station predicted more snow all during the first week of January, it held off for two days. Humphrey Stalladge opened up again, working the entire long bar by himself—Annie and Anni, off in the country, were still snowed in—and found business as lively as he had predicted. He put in long days, working sixteen or seventeen hours, and when his wife came in to make hamburgers, he said to her, "Okay. The roads finally get plowed enough so guys can get their cars moving again, and the first place they head to is a bar. Where they stay all day long. Does that make sense to you?"

"You called it," was all she'd say.

"It's good drinking weather, anyhow," Humphrey said.

Good drinking weather? More than that: Don Wanderley, driving with Peter Barnes to the Hawthorne house, thought that this dark gray day, still punishingly cold, was like the weather inside a drunk's mind. It had none of the uncanny flashes of brightness he had seen in Milburn earlier in the winter: no doorposts or chimneys gleamed, no sudden colors jumped forward. There were none of these magician's tricks. Everything that was not white was blurry in the gray clinging weather; with no true shadows and a hidden sun, everything looked heavily shadowed.

He glanced over his shoulder at the rolled-up parcel on the back seat. His poor weapons, found in Edward's house. They were almost childishly crude. Now that he had a plan and the three of them were going to fight, even the depressive weather seemed to imply their defeat. He and a tense seventeen-year-old boy and an old man with a bad cold: for a moment it seemed comically hopeless. But without them, hope did not exist.

"The deputy doesn't plow as good as Omar," Peter

said beside him. It was merely to interrupt the silence, but Don nodded: the boy was right. The deputy had trouble holding the plow at a steady level, and when he was through with a street it had an oddly terraced look. The three-and four-inch variations in the road made the car jounce like a fairground trolley. On either side of the street they could see mailboxes tilted crazily into the snowbanks—Churchill had skittled them with the edge of the plow.

"This time we're going to do something," the boy said, making it half a question.

"We're going to try," Don said, glancing at the boy. Peter looked like a young soldier who'd seen a dozen firefights in two weeks—looking at him, you could taste the bitterness of spent adrenalin.

"I'm ready," he said, and while Don heard the firmness in it he also heard ragged nerves and wondered if the boy, who had done so much more than he and Ricky Hawthorne, could endure any more.

"Wait until you hear what I have in mind," Don said. "You might not want to go through with it. And that would be okay, Peter. I'd understand."

"I'm ready," the boy repeated, and Don could feel him shivering. "What are we going to do?"

"Go back into Anna Mostyn's house," he answered. "I'll explain it at Ricky's."

Peter slowly exhaled. "I'm still ready."

8

"It was part of the message on the Alma Mobley tape," Don said. Ricky Hawthorne was leaning forward on his couch, looking not at Don but at the box of Kleenex before him. Peter Barnes glanced at him momentarily, and then turned sideways again, resting his head against the back of the couch. Stella Hawthorne had disappeared upstairs, but not before giving Don a look of the clearest warning.

"It was a message for me, and I didn't want to subject anyone else to it," he explained. "Especially not you, Peter. You can both imagine the kind of thing it was."

"Psychological warfare," Ricky said.

"Yes. But I've been thinking about one thing she said. It . . . call it. It could explain where she is. I think she meant it as a clue, or a hint, or whatever you want to call it."

"Go on," said Ricky.

"She said that we—human beings—are at the mercy of our imaginations, and if we want to look for her, or for any of them, we should look in the places of our dreams. In the places of our imaginations."

" 'In the places of our dreams,' " Ricky repeated. "I see. She means Montgomery Street. Well. I should have known we weren't through with that house." Peter extended one arm along the top of the couch and rolled deeper into it: rejection. "We deliberately didn't bring you the first time we went there," Ricky said to the boy. "Of course now you have even more reason for not wanting to go. How do you feel about it?"

"I have to go," Peter said.

"It almost has to be what she means," Ricky continued, still gently probing the boy with his eyes. "Sears and Lewis and John and I all had dreams about that house. We dreamed about it almost every night for a year. And when Sears and Don and I went there, when we found your mother and Jim, she didn't attack us physically, but she attacked our imaginations. If it's any consolation, the thought of going back there scares the hell out of me too."

Peter nodded. "Sure it does." Finally, as if another's admission of fear gave him courage, he leaned forward. "What's in the package, Don?"

Don reached down and picked up the rolled blanket beside his chair. "Just two things I found in the house. We might be able to use them." He lay the bundle on the table and unrolled it. All three of them looked at the long-handled axe and the hunting knife which now lay uncovered on the blanket.

"I spent the morning sharpening and oiling them. The axe was rusty—Edward used it for his firewood. The knife was a gift from an actor—he used it in a film and gave it to my uncle when his book was published. It's a beautiful knife."

Peter leaned over and picked up the knife. "It's heavy." He turned it over in his hands: an eight-inch blade with a cruel dip along the top end and a groove from tip to base, fitted with a hand-carved handle, the knife was obviously designed for one purpose only. It was a machine for killing. But no, Don remembered; that was how it looked; not what it was. It had been made to fit an actor's hand: to photograph well. But beside it the axe was brutal and graceless. "Ricky has his own knife," Don said. "Peter, you can take the Bowie knife. I'll carry the axe."

"Are we going there right away?"

"Is there any point in waiting?"

Ricky said, "Hang on. I'll go upstairs and tell Stella that we're going out. I'll say that if we don't come back in an hour, she should call whoever is at the sheriff's office these days and have a car sent to the Robinson house." He left them and began going up the staircase.

Peter reached forward and touched the knife. "It won't take an hour," he said.

9

"We'll go in the back again," Don said to Ricky, bending forward to speak into his ear. They were just outside the house. Ricky nodded. "We'll have to be as quiet as we can."

"Don't worry about me," said Ricky. He sounded older and weaker than Don had ever heard him. "You know, I saw the movie that knife came from. Big scene—a long scene about it being forged. Man making it melted down a piece of asteroid or meteor he had— used it in the knife. Supposed to have—" Ricky stopped and breathed heavily for a moment, making sure that

Peter Barnes was listening to him. "Supposed to have special properties. Hardest substance anyone ever saw. Like magic. From space." Ricky smiled. "Typical movie foolishness. Looks like a dandy knife, though."

Peter pulled it from the pocket of his duffel coat and for a second each of them—almost embarrassed to be caught in such childishness—looked at it again. "Outer space worked wonders for Colonel Bowie," Ricky said. "In the movie."

"Bowie—" Peter started to say, remembering something from a grade-school history class, and then clamped his mouth shut on the rest of the sentence. *Bowie died at the Alamo.* He swallowed, shook his head, and turned toward the Galli house. It was what he should have learned from Jim Hardie: good magic lay only in human effort, but bad magic could come from around any corner.

"Let's go," Don said, and looked hard at Peter to make sure he knew enough to keep quiet.

Using their hands, they pushed snow away from the back door to open it; and then, moving quietly in single file, they entered. To Peter the house seemed nearly as dark as it had been on the night he and Jim Hardie had broken in. Until Don had led him through the kitchen, he had not been sure that he would be able to take the first step over the threshold. Even then, he feared for a moment that he would faint or scream—the gloom in the house whispered about him.

In the hallway, Don pointed to the cellar door. He and Ricky took their knives from their pockets, and Don pulled the door open. The writer led them soundlessly down the wooden steps to the basement.

Peter knew that this and the landing would be the worst places for him. He took a quick glance under the staircase and saw only a floating spider web. Then he and Don went slowly toward the octopus-armed furnace while Ricky Hawthorne moved down the other side of the basement. The big knife felt solid and good in his hands, and even when he knew that he would soon have to look at the place where Sears had found his mother and Jim Hardie, Peter also knew that he would not pass out or yell or do anything childish: the knife seemed to pass some of its competence into him.

They reached the deeply shadowed area beside the furnace. Don stepped behind the furnace with no hesitation, and Peter followed, gripping the handle of the knife. *You have to slash up,* he remembered from some old adventure story. *If you bring the blade down it's easier to take away from you.* He saw Ricky coming around from the other side, already shrugging.

Don lowered the axe; both men looked beneath the workbench across the near wall. Peter shivered. That was where they had been. Of course nothing was there now: he knew by the way Don and Ricky straightened up that no Gregory Bate had jumped out, ready to begin talking . . . there wouldn't even be bloodstains. Peter sensed that the men were waiting for him to move, and he bent quickly and took a second's glance beneath the workbench. Only shadowed cement wall, a gray cement floor. He straightened up.

"Top floor now," Don whispered, and Ricky nodded.

When they reached the brown stain on the landing Peter clutched the knife tightly and swallowed; looked quickly back over his shoulder to make sure Bate wasn't standing down there in a Harpo Marx wig and sunglasses, grinning up at them; and checked the next flight of stairs. Ricky Hawthorne turned to interrogate him with a kind look. He nodded—*okay*—and continued softly after the men.

Outside the first bedroom door at the top of the house Ricky paused and nodded. Peter hefted his knife: it might be the room the old men had dreamed about, whatever that meant, but it was also the room where he had met Freddy Robinson, the room where he might have died. Don stepped in front of Ricky and put his hand very firmly on the knob. Ricky glanced at him, set his mouth, nodded. Don turned the knob and pushed the door open. Peter saw an abrupt line of sweat run down the side of the writer's face, as sudden as a tapped spring, and everything in him went dry. Don moved rapidly through the door, bringing the axe up as he went. Peter's legs carried him into the room as if an invisible cord pulled him along.

He took in the bedroom in a series of snapshotlike tableaux: Don beside him, crouching, axe held up to one side; an empty bed; dusty floor; a bare wall; the window he had forced open centuries ago; Ricky Hawthorne planted beside him open-mouthed, holding out his knife as if he were trying to give it away; a wall with a small mirror. An empty bedroom.

Don lowered his axe, the tension cautiously leaving his face; Ricky Hawthorne began to prowl around the room as if he'd have to see every inch of it before he could believe that Anna Mostyn and the Bates weren't hiding there. Peter realized that he was holding the knife slackly at his side; he realized that he was relaxed. The room was safe. And if this room was safe, then the house was too. He looked at Don, who lifted the edges of his mouth in a closed smile.

Then he felt idiotic, standing inside the door smiling at Don, and he went forward, double-checking all the places Ricky Hawthorne had already examined. Nothing under the bed. An empty closet. He went up to the far wall; a muscle jumped in the small of his back, loosening with a snap like a rubber band. Peter brushed his fingers against the wall: cold. And dirty. Gray stuff came away on his fingers. He glanced into the mirror.

Shockingly loud, Ricky Hawthorne's voice shouted at him from across the room: "Not the mirror, Peter!"

But it was already too late. He'd been caught by a breeze from the depth of the mirror, and turned unthinkingly to look deeply into it. His own face was fading to a pale outline and beneath the outline, on the other side of it, swimming up, was the face of a woman. He did not know her, but he took her in as if he were in love: light freckles, softly brown-blond hair, soft shining eyes, the mouth bracketed by the most tender lines he'd ever seen. She touched all the tension in him, all the feeling he had, and he saw things in her face that he knew were beyond his understanding, promises and songs and betrayals he would not know for years. He felt all the shallowness and insularity of his relationships with the girls he had known and kissed and strained against, and saw that the areas in him which had gone out to women had never been enough, had never been complete. And, in a rush of tenderness, an enveloping nimbus of emotion, she was speaking to him. *Beautiful Peter. You want to be one of us. You already are one of us.* He did not move or speak, but he nodded and said yes. *And so are your friends, Peter. You can live through all time, singing the one song which is my song—you can be with me and them forever, moving like a song. Just use the knife, Peter, use your knife, you know how, do it beautifully, raise your knife, lift your knife, raise your knife and turn—*

He was bringing the knife up when the mirror went falling, still musically speaking, though he couldn't hear it so well for the sound of a blow and a voice near his head: the mirror hit the floor and split.

"It was a trick, Peter," Ricky Hawthorne was saying. "I should have warned you before, but I was afraid to speak," his face and experienced eyes so near to Peter's own face that Peter, looking down in shock, saw in surreal close-up the tight loops in the knot of Ricky's bow tie. "Just a trick." Peter trembled and embraced him.

When they separated, Peter bent down to the two halves of the mirror and held his palm over one of the pieces. A delicious wind *(the one song which is my song)* lilted up from it. He felt or sensed Ricky stiffening beside him: half of a tender mouth glimmered beneath his hand, just visible. He drove his heel into the broken mirror, then brought it down again and again, splitting the silvery glass into a scattered jigsaw puzzle.

10

Fifteen minutes later they were back in the car, traveling slowly toward the center of town, following the random, looping trail of plowed streets. "She wants to make us like Gregory and Fenny," Peter said. "That's what she meant. 'Live through all time.' She wants to turn us into those *things*."

"We don't have to let it happen," Don said.

"You talk so brave sometimes." Peter shook his head. "She said I already *was* one of them. Because when I saw Gregory turn into—you know—he said he was me. It was like Jim. Just keeping going. Never stopping. Never doubting."

"And you liked that in Jim Hardie," Don said, and Peter nodded, his face marked with tears. "I would too," Don said. "Energy is always likeable."

"But she knows I'm the weak link," Peter said, and put his hand to his face. "She tried to use me, and it almost worked. She could use me to get you and Ricky."

"The difference between you—between all of us— and Gregory Bate," Don said, "is that Gregory wanted to be used. He chose it. He sought it."

"But she almost made me choose it too," Peter said. "God, I hate them."

Ricky spoke from the back seat. "They've taken your mother, most of my friends and Don's brother, Peter. We all hate them. She could do to any of us what she did to you back there."

As Ricky continued to speak comfortingly from the back, Don drove on, no longer bothering to notice the desolation caused by the snow: there would be more of it in an hour, in a day or two at the most, and then Milburn would not only be sealed off from outside but a sprung trap. One more heavy snow would see a wave of death to take half the town.

"Stop the car," Peter said. "*Stop*." He laughed. "I know where they are. The place of dreams." His laughter was high-pitched and tremulous, spiraled out of the boy's hysteria. "The place of dreams, didn't she say? And what's the only place in town that stayed open all during the storms?"

"What in the world are you talking about?" Don asked, turning around on the seat to look at Peter's face, suddenly open and sure.

"There," Peter said, and Don followed the line of his pointing finger.

Across the street from them, in giant red neon letters:

RIALTO

And beneath that, in smaller black letters, one last proof of Anna Mostyn's wit:

NIGHT OF THE LIVING DEAD

11

Stella checked her watch for the sixtieth time, and then stood up to compare what it said with the clock on the mantel. The mantel clock was three minutes ahead, as it always was. Ricky and the other two had been gone somewhere between thirty and thirty-three minutes. She thought she knew how Ricky had felt on Christmas morning—that if he didn't get out of the house and start moving, something terrible would happen. And now Stella knew that if she did not get over to the Robinson house in one hell of a hurry that Ricky would be in awful danger. He had said to give them an hour, but that was surely too long. Whatever had frightened Ricky and the rest of the Chowder Society was in that house, waiting to strike again. Stella would never have described herself as a feminist, but she had long ago seen how men mistakenly assumed that they had to do everything themselves. The Milly Sheehans locked their doors and hallucinated—or whatever—when their men died or left them. If some inexplicable catastrophe took their men, they cowered behind female passivity and waited for the reading of the will.

Ricky had simply assumed that she was not fit to join them. Even a boy was of more use than she. She looked again at her watch. Another minute had gone by.

Stella went to the downstairs closet and put on her coat: then she took it off, thinking that, after all, maybe she would not be able to help Ricky. "Nuts," she said out loud, and pulled the coat on again and went out the door.

At least it was not snowing now: and Leon Churchill, who had gaped at her since he was a boy of twelve, had cleared some of the streets. Len Shaw from the service station, another remote-control conquest, had cleared their driveway as soon as his plow could make it to the Hawthorne house—in an unfair world, Stella had no compunctions about taking unfair advantage of her looks. She started her car easily (Len, denied Stella, had given almost erotic attention to the Volvo's engine) and rolled down the drive out into the street.

By now Stella, having decided to go there, was in an almost frantic hurry to get to Montgomery Street. Direct access was blocked by the unplowed roads, and she put her foot down on the accelerator and followed the maze of streets Leon had opened—she groaned when she realized that she was being taken all the way over to the high school. From there she'd have to cut down School Road to Harding Lane, and then over on Lone Pine Road back the way she had started and then on Candlemaker Street past the Rialto. Working out this circuitous map in her head, Stella let the car get nearly to her normal driving speed. The drops and elevations left by Churchill's handling of the plow jolted her against the wheel, but she took the corner into School Road quickly, not seeing in the woolly light that the level of the roadbed dropped seven inches. When the front end slammed down onto the packed snow, Stella floored the accelerator, still trying to think of the roads that could take her to Montgomery once she got off Candlemaker Street.

The rear end of the car spun out sideways, struck a metal fence and a mailbox, and then continued to revolve around so that Stella was traveling astraddle the road: in a cold panic, she wrenched at the wheel just as the car dropped into another of Churchill's terraces. The car rolled up on its side, wheels spinning, and then dropped down, still traveling, onto the metal fence.

"Damn," she said, and clenched her hands on the wheel and breathed deeply, forcing herself to stop trembling. She swung the door open and looked down. If she edged off the seat and let her legs dangle, she would be only three or four feet from the ground. The car could stay where it was—in any case, it had to. She'd need a tow-truck to pull it off the fence. Stella let her legs hang out of the open door, took another deep breath and pushed herself off the seat.

She landed hard, but stayed on her feet and began walking down School Road without once looking back at her car. Door open, key in the ignition, leaning against the fence like a stuffed toy—she had to get to Ricky. Ahead of her a quarter of a mile down the road, the high school was a fuzzy dark-brown cloud.

Stella had just realized that she would have to hitch-hike when a blue car appeared out of the gray blur behind her. For the first time in her life, Stella Hawthorne turned to face an oncoming car and stuck out her thumb.

The blue car rolled toward her and began to brake. Stella lowered her arm as the car drew up beside her. When she bent down and looked in she saw a pudgy man bending sideways and giving her a shy welcoming look. He leaned across the seat and opened the passenger door for her. "It's against my principles," he said, "but you look like you need a ride."

Stella got in and leaned back against the seat, forgetting for the moment that this helpful little man would not be able to read her mind. Then she and the car started forward and she said, "Oh, please excuse me, I just had an accident and I'm not thinking right. I must—"

"Please, Mrs. Hawthorne," the man said, turning his head to smile at her. "Don't waste your breath. I assume you were going to Montgomery Street. You needn't bother. That was all a mistake."

"You know me?" Stella asked. "But how did you know—"

The man silenced her by reaching out with a boxer's quickness and tightening his hand around her hair. "Soft," he said, and his voice, formerly as shyly ingratiating as the man's appearance, was the quietest she'd ever heard.

12

Don was the first of them to see Clark Mulligan's body. The theater owner lay huddled on the carpet behind the candy counter—another corpse bearing the signs of the Bate brothers' appetites. "Yes, Peter," he said, turning away from the body, "you're right. They're inside."

"Mr. Mulligan?" Peter asked quietly.

Ricky came up to the counter and looked over. "Oh, no." He drew his knife from his coat pocket. "We still don't know that what we're trying to do is possible, do we? For all we know, we need wooden stakes or silver bullets or a fire or . . ."

"No," Peter said. "We don't need any of those things. We have everything we need right here." The boy was very pale, and he avoided looking over the counter at Mulligan's body, but the determination set deeply in his face was unlike anything Don had ever seen: it was fear's negation. "That was just how they killed vampires and werewolves—what they thought were vampires and werewolves. They could have used anything." He challenged Don directly. "Isn't that what you think?"

"Yes," Don said, not adding that it was one thing to offer a theory in comfortable rooms, another to stake your life on it.

"I do too," Peter said. He held his knife, blade up, so rigidly that Don could sense the tautness of his

muscles all the way up his arm. "I know they're inside.
Let's go."

Then Ricky spoke and simply said what was obvious.
"We don't have a choice."

Don lifted his axe and held the head pressed flat
against his chest; went quietly to the doors to the stalls;
slipped inside. The other two followed him.

He flattened himself out against the wall in the dark
theater, realizing that he had never considered that
the movie might be running. Giant forms moved across
the screen, bellowing, rampaging. The Bates must have
killed Clark Mulligan less than an hour before the
three of them had arrived. Clark had set up the film,
started it as he had done every day during the storms,
and come down to find Gregory and Fenny waiting for
him in the lobby. Don inched sideways along the back
wall, looking for a movement in the seats ahead of him.

As his eyes adjusted, he saw only the rounded backs
of the seats stretching away. The heavy blade of the axe
pressed against his chest. The movie's soundtrack filled
his head with shouts and cries. It played to an empty
theater. And of all the spectacles to which their enemy
had treated him, Don thought that this was surely the
strangest—the horror on the screen, the turmoil of
voices and music washing out in darkness over all those
empty seats. He looked sideways toward Peter Barnes
and even in the dark saw the set of his face. He pointed
to the far aisle; then bent forward to see Ricky, who
was only a shadow against the wall, and motioned toward the wide middle aisle. Peter immediately moved
away toward the other side of the theater. Ricky went
more slowly to the center, and checked Peter and Don's
position before bending down to make sure Gregory or
Fenny was not hiding in the row. Then they advanced
forward, checking each row in turn.

And what if Ricky finds them? Don thought. *Could
we get to him in time to save him? He's exposed, way
out there in the open.*

But Ricky, holding his knife out to one side, moved

down the wide center aisle, looking calmly on either side of him as if he were looking for a lost ticket—he was being as thorough as he had been in Anna Mostyn's house.

Don moved in tandem with the others, straining to see into the darkness between the rows. Candy wrappers, torn paper, what looked like a winter's worth of dust, rows of seats, some torn, some taped together, a few in every row with broken arms—and in the middle of each row, a well of darkness that wanted to suck him toward it. Above him, ahead of him, the film paraded a succession of images Don caught as disconnected frames whenever he looked up from the floor of the theater. Corpses pushing themselves up from their graves, cars rolling dangerously fast around corners, a girl's stricken face ... Don glanced up at the screen and thought for a moment he was seeing a film of himself in Anna Mostyn's cellar.

But no, of course not, the scene was just part of the film, a man unlike him in a cellar unlike Anna's. The movie family had barricaded themselves in a basement, and the soundtrack boomed with the sounds of doors closing: *maybe that's how you fight them, you just hole up until they go away ... you bite down and close your eyes and hope they get your brother, your friend, anybody, before they get you* ... and that, he realized, was what the nightwatchers had done. He looked over the rows of seats, seeing them filled with Gregory's victims, and then saw Ricky and Peter looking curiously back at him. He was two rows behind. Don bent forward again, found himself staring stiffly with embarrassment at a flattened popcorn box, and moved hurriedly down the broad steps to catch up with the others.

When they reached the bottom row without finding anything, Don and Peter went toward the center aisle to join Ricky. "Nothing," Don said.

"They're here, though," Peter whispered. "They have to be."

"There's the projection booth," Don said. "The

toilets. And Mulligan must have had some sort of office."

On the screen a door slammed: noise of life walled in, and of death walled in with it.

"Maybe the balcony," Peter said, and glanced up at the screen. "And what's behind there? How do you get there?"

Again, a door slammed. Inhuman voices matching the scale of the people on the screen, inflated with assumed emotions, fell toward them from the speakers.

The door clicked open with a flat, ticking noise—the sound made when a metal bar, depressed, lifts a catch; then it slammed shut again.

"Of course," Ricky said, "that's where they'd"—but the other two were not paying attention. They had recognized the sound, and were staring at the entrance to a lighted cavernous tunnel to the right of the screen. Above the tunnel a white sign read EXIT.

The soundtrack blared down on them, to their side giant forms enacted a pantomime romantic enough for the music, but what they listened to was a light, dry noise coming down the exit corridor toward the light: a noise like clapping hands. It was the sound of bare feet.

A child appeared at the end of the corridor and paused at the edge of the light. He looked toward them—an apparition from a thirties' study of rural poverty, a small boy with shivering sides and prominent ribs and a smudgy, shadowy face that would never be invaded by thought. He stood in the last traces of the corridor's light, drool forming on his lower lip. The boy raised his arms, holding his bunched hands level before him, and made the gesture of pumping up and down on an iron bar. Then he tilted back his head and giggled; and again made the gesture of closing a heavy door.

"My brother is telling you that the doors are locked," said a voice from above them. They whirled around, Don hefting the axe in his arms, and saw Gregory Bate standing on the stage beside the red curtains flanking the screen. "But three such brave adventurers wouldn't have it otherwise, would they? You have come for this, haven't you? Especially *you*, Mr. Wanderley—all the way from California. Fenny and I were sorry not to have been properly introduced there." He moved easily to the center of the stage, and the movie broke and flowed over the surface of his body. "And you really think that you can harm us with those medieval objects you carry? Why, gentlemen . . ." He flung out his arms, his eyes glowing. Every part of him was printed with gigantic forms—an open hand, a falling lamp, a splintering door.

And beneath all that, Don saw what Bate had demonstrated to Peter Barnes—that the gentlemanly diction and theatrical manner were insubstantial clothing over a terrible concentration, a purpose as implacable as a machine's. Bate was standing on the stage, smiling down at them. *"Now,"* he said, his tone like a god's summoning light.

Don jumped sideways, hearing something rush past him, and saw Fenny's mad little body crashing into Peter Barnes. None of them had seen the child move; now he was already on top of Peter, forcing his arms to the floor of the theater, snarling, holding Peter's knife harmlessly away while he wriggled on top of him, making a squealing noise that got lost in the screams from the speakers.

Don raised his axe and felt a strong hand close over his wrist. (*Immortal* whispered up his arm, *don't you want to be?*)

"Wouldn't you like to live forever?" Gregory Bate said in his ear, blowing foulness toward his face. "Even if you must die first? It's a good Christian bargain, after all."

The hand spun him easily around, and Don felt his own strength draining out as if Bate's hand on his wrist drew it out of him like a magnet. Bate's other hand took his chin and tilted it up, forcing Don to look into his eyes. He remembered Peter telling him how Jim Hardie had died, how Bate had sucked him down into his eyes, but it was impossible not to look: and his feet seemed to be floating, his legs were water, at the bottom of the shining gold was a comprehensive wisdom and beneath that was total mindlessness, a rushing violence, pure cold, a killing winter wind through a forest.

"Watch this, you scum," he dimly heard Ricky saying. Then Bate's attention snapped away from him, and his legs seemed to be filled with sand, and the side of the werewolf's head moved past his face as slowly as a dream. Something was making an appalling racket, and Bate's profiled head slid past his own, marble skin and an ear as perfect as a statue's—Bate flung him away.

"Do you see this, you filth?" Ricky was shouting, and Don, lying all tumbled over his axe *(now what was that for?)*, half-wedged beneath one of the front-row seats, looked dreamily up and saw Ricky Hawthorne sawing into the back of Fenny's neck.

"Bad," he whispered, and "no," and no longer sure that it was not really just a part of the giant shadowy action blazing on above them all, saw Gregory slap the old man down onto Peter Barnes's motionless body.

13

"There's no need to make trouble, is there, Mrs. Hawthorne?" said the man gripping her hair. "You hear me, don't you?" He tugged at her hair, pulling it painfully.

Stella nodded.

"And you heard what I said? No need to go to Montgomery Street—no need at all. Your husband isn't there anymore. He didn't find what he was looking for, so he went elsewhere."

"Who are you?"

"A friend of a friend. A good friend's good friend." Still holding her hair, the man reached across the wheel to move the automatic shift, and drove slowly off. "And my friend is very eager to meet you."

"Let me go," Stella said.

He yanked her toward him. "Enough, Mrs. Hawthorne. You have a very exciting time ahead of you. So—enough. No fighting. Or I'll kill you here. And that would be a terrible waste. Now promise me you'll be quiet. We are just going into the Hollow. Okay? You'll be quiet?"

Stella, terrified and fearful that the handful of hair was about to be ripped from her head, said, "Yes."

"Very intelligent." He let her hair fall slack and pressed his hand against the side of her head. "You're such a pretty woman, Stella."

She recoiled from his touch.

"Quiet?"

"Quiet," she breathed, and the driver went on slowly toward the high school. She looked back through the rear window and saw no other cars: her own, tilted against the fence, grew smaller behind her.

"You're going to kill me," she said.

"Not unless you force me to do it, Mrs. Hawthorne. I am quite a religious person in my present life. I would hate to have to take a human life. We're pacifists, you know."

"We?"

He pursed his lips at her in an ironic little smile, and gestured toward the back seat. She looked down and saw dozens of copies of *The Watchtower* scattered there.

"Then your friend is going to kill me. Like Sears and Lewis and the others."

"Not quite like that, Mrs. Hawthorne. Well, perhaps just a little bit like Mr. Benedikt. That was the only one our friend conducted by herself. But I can promise you that Mr. Benedikt saw many unusual and interesting things before he passed away." They were going by the school now, and Stella heard a familiar grinding noise before recognizing it: she looked frantically out the window and saw the town snowplow chugging into a twelve-foot drift.

"In fact," the man continued, "you could say that he had the time of his life. And as for you, you will have an experience many would envy—you will see directly into a mystery, Mrs. Hawthorne, a mystery which has endured in your culture for centuries. Some would say that would be worth dying for. Especially since the alternative is dying quite messily right here."

Now even the snowplow was a block behind them. The next clear street, Harding Lane, was twenty feet ahead, and Stella saw herself being driven away from safety—from Leon on the plow—toward terrible danger, passive at the hands of this maniac Jehovah's Witness.

"In fact, Mrs. Hawthorne," the man said, "since you are cooperating so nicely—"

Stella kicked out as hard as she could and felt the toe of her boot connect solidly with his ankle. The man yelped with pain and twisted toward her. She threw herself at the wheel, getting her body between it and the man, who was clubbing her on the head, and forced the car toward the snowbank left by the plow.

Now if Leon would only look, she prayed: but the car thudded almost noiselessly into the bank.

The man tore her off the wheel and forced her back against the door, twisting her legs painfully beneath her. Stella raised her hands and struck his face, but the man put all his weight on her and batted her hands away. *Be still!* shouted in her mind, and Stella nearly lost consciousness. *Stupid, stupid woman.*

She opened her eyes wide and looked at the face above hers—pouchy with excess flesh, black open pores on the thick nose, sweat on the forehead, meek bloodshot eyes; the face of a prim little man who would tell hitchhikers that it was against his principles to pick them up. He was hitting her on the side of the head, and every blow released a spray of saliva over her. *Stupid woman!*

Grunting, he brought a knee up between her legs and leaned forward and put his hands on her throat.

Stella flailed at his sides and then managed to hook a hand under his chin: it was not enough. He continued to crush her throat, the voice in her mind repeating *stupid stupid stupid* . . .

She remembered.

Stella dropped her hands, pulled at her lapel with her right hand, found the pearl base of the hatpin. She used all the strength in her right arm to drive the long pin into his temple.

The meek eyes bulged and the monotonous word repeating in her mind became a babble of astonished voices. *What what (she) no this (sword) woman what—* the man's hands went limp on her throat, and he dropped onto her like a boulder.

Then she was able to scream.

Stella scrambled to open the door and fell backward out of the car. For a moment after she rolled over she lay panting on the ground, tasting the blood in her mouth mix with dirty snow and rock salt. She pushed herself up, saw his balding head lolling off the edge of the seat, whimpered and got to her feet.

Stella turned away from the car and ran down School Road toward Leon Churchill, who was now standing by the side of the plow, gazing at something dark he had evidently uncovered. She shouted his first name, slowed to a walk, and the deputy swiveled to watch her come toward him.

Leon glanced back at the dark thing in the snow and then trotted toward her: Stella was too distraught to see that the deputy was nearly as shocked as herself. When he caught her, he spun her halfway around and said, "Uh now Mrs. Hawthorne you don't want to look at that what's the matter anyhow you had an accident Mrs. Hawthorne?"

"I just killed a man," she said. "I hitchhiked in his car. He tried to hurt me. I stuck a hatpin in his head. I killed him."

"He tried to hurt you?" Leon asked. "Uh—" He glanced back at his plow, and then looked again at Stella Hawthorne's face. "Come on, let's have a look. It happened up there?" He pointed to the blue car. "You had an accident."

As he marched her along toward the car, she tried to explain. "I had an accident in my car, he stopped to give me a ride and then he tried to hurt me. He did hurt me. And I had a long hatpin . . ."

"Well, you didn't kill him, anyhow," Leon said, and looked at her almost indulgently.

"Don't patronize me."

"He ain't in the car," Leon said. He put his hands on her shoulders and turned her to face the open door, the empty front seat.

Stella nearly fainted.

Leon held her up and tried to explain. "See, what probably happened is you got shook up after the accident, this guy who gave you a lift went away to get help, and you maybe even passed out a little bit. You banged yourself up when the car went off the road. Why don't I take you home on the plow, Mrs. Hawthorne?"

"He's not there," Stella said.

A large white dog jumped on top of the snowbank from the front yard of one of the neighboring houses, walked along the top and jumped down to the road in a shower of snow.

"Yes, please take me home, Leon," Stella said.

Leon looked anxiously toward the school. "Yeah, I gotta get to the office anyhow. You stay right here and I'll come back with the plow in five seconds."

"Fine."

"Not much of a chariot," Leon said, and smiled at her.

14

"Now, Mr. Wanderley," Bate said, "back to the topic we were discussing." He began to move across the aisle toward Don.

Screams, moans, the sound of rushing wind filled the theater.

—*live forever*

—*live forever*

Don stretched out his legs, dazedly looking at the

pile of bodies lying beneath the risers to the stage. The old man's white face twisted toward him, lying across the body of a barefoot child. Peter Barnes was at the bottom of the heap, feebly moving his hands.

"We should have concluded matters two years ago," Bate purred. "So much trouble would have been saved if we had. You remember two years back, don't you?"

Don heard Alma Mobley saying *His name is Greg. We knew each other in New Orleans,* and remembered a moment so vividly that it was as if he were there again: he standing on a corner in Berkeley and looking in shock at a woman in the shadows beside a bar named The Last Reef. A leaden sense of betrayal made it impossible to move.

"So much trouble," Bate repeated. "But it makes this moment all the sweeter, don't you think?"

Peter Barnes, bleeding from a cheek, pushed himself halfway out of the tangle.

"Alma," Don managed to say.

Bate's ivory face flickered. "Yes. Your Alma. And your brother's Alma. Mustn't forget David. Not nearly as entertaining as you."

"Entertaining."

"Oh, yes. We enjoy entertainment. Only proper, since we have provided so much of it. Now look at me again, Donald." He reached down to pull Don up from the floor, smiling coldly.

Peter groaned: pulled himself clear. Don looked confusedly across at him and saw that Fenny also was moving, rolling over, his smudgy face a soundless screaming grimace.

"They hurt Fenny," Don said, blinking, and saw Bate's hand slowly reaching toward him. He shot his legs out and squirmed away from Bate, moving faster than he ever had in his life. Don rolled to his feet, halfway between Gregory and Peter, who was—

—live forever—

blinking at the squirming, grimacing form of Fenny Bate. "They *hurt* Fenny," Don said, the meaning of Fenny's agony going through him like an electric current. The giant sounds of the film opened up again in his ears.

"You don't," he said to Bate, and looked under the seats. His axe lay out of reach.

"Don't?"

"You don't live forever."

"We live much longer than you," Bate said, and the civilized veneer of his voice cracked open to reveal the violence beneath it. Don backed toward Peter, looking not at Bate's eyes but at his mouth.

"You won't live another minute," Bate said, and took a step forward.

"Peter—" Don said, and looked over his shoulder at the boy.

Peter was holding the Bowie knife above Fenny's writhing body.

"*Do* it," Don shouted, and Peter brought the knife down into Fenny's chest. Something white and foul exploded upward, a reeking geyser, from Fenny's ribcage.

Gregory Bate launched himself toward Peter, howling, and knocked Don savagely over the first row of seats.

Ricky Hawthorne at first thought he was dead, the pain in his back was so bad that he thought only death or dying could account for it, and then he saw the worn carpet under his face, the loops of thread seeming inches high and heard Don shouting: so he was alive. He moved his head: the last thing he could remember was cutting open the back of Fenny Bate's neck. Then a locomotive had run into him.

Something beside him moved. When he lifted his head to see what it was, Fenny's bare streaming chest leaped—seeming six feet long—a yard into the air. Small white worms swam across the white skin. Ricky recoiled, and though his back felt as though it were broken, forced himself to sit up.

To his side, Gregory Bate was lifting Peter Barnes off the floor, howling as if his chest were a cave of winds. A section of the beam from the projector caught Gregory's arms and Peter's body, and swarming blotches of black and white moved over them for a second. Still howling, Bate threw Peter into the screen.

Ricky could not see his knife, and went on his knees to scrabble for it. His fingers closed around a bone handle, and a long blade reflected a line of gray light. Fenny thrashed beside him, rolling over onto his hand, and uttered a thin *eee,* dead air rushing out. Ricky snatched the knife from under Fenny's back, feeling his hand come away wet, and made himself stand.

Gregory Bate was just scrambling up onto the stage to leap through the rip in the screen after Peter, and Ricky threw out his free hand and grasped the thick collar of his pea jacket. Bate suddenly went rigid, his reflexes as good as a cat's, and Ricky knew in terror that he would kill him, spinning around with pulverizing hands and slashing teeth, if he did not do the only possible thing.

Before Bate could move, Ricky slammed the Bowie knife into his back.

Now he could hear nothing, not the noises on the soundtrack, not the cry that must have come from Bate: he stood still gripping the bone handle, deafened by the enormity of what he had done. Bate fell back down and turned around and showed Ricky Hawthorne a face to carry with him all his life: eyes full of tearing wind and blizzard and a black mouth open as wide as a cavern.

"Filth," Ricky said, almost sobbing.

Bate fell toward him.

Don climbed over the seats carrying the axe, in a desperate hurry to get to Bate before he could tear open Ricky's throat; then he saw the muscular body slump and Ricky, gasping, pushing him off. Bate fell back into the front of the stage and went to his knees. Fluid dribbled from his mouth.

"Get away, Ricky," Don said, but the old lawyer was unable to move. Bate began to crawl toward him.

He stepped beside Ricky and Bate tilted back his head and looked straight into his eyes.

—live forever

Don hurriedly raised the axe over his head and brought the sharpened blade down into Bate's neck, cutting down deeply into the chest. With the next blow he severed the head.

Peter Barnes crawled back out through the screen, dazzled by pain and the beam from the projector. He made himself move across the few feet of bare wood to the edge of the stage, hearing a wild shrieking of voices, thinking that if he could get to the Bowie knife before Gregory Bate saw him, he might at least be able to save Don. Ricky had been killed by the first blow, he knew: he had seen its force. Then the beam of light slipped over his head and he saw what Don was doing. Gregory Bate, headless, squirmed under the blows of the axe; beside him Fenny rolled helplessly back and forth, covered in moving white pulp.

"Let me," he said, and both Ricky and Don stared up at him with white faces.

When Peter was down on the floor of the theater beside them, he took the axe from Don and brought it weakly, glancingly down, his hysteria and loathing spoiling the blow; then he felt suddenly stronger, as strong as a logger, felt as if he were glowing, filled with light, and raised it effortlessly, all the pain leaving him, and brought the axe down again; and again; and again; and then moved to Fenny.

When they were only shreds of skin and smashed bones a zero breeze lifted off their ruined bodies and swirled up into the beam from the projector, passing Peter with such force that it knocked him aside.

Peter bent down into the mess and picked up the Bowie knife.

"By God," Ricky said, and tottered into one of the seats.

When they left the theater, limping, their minds numb, they felt an impatient, hurrying wind even in the lobby—a wind that seemed to swirl through the empty space, rattling posters and the bag of potato chips on the candy counter, searching the way out— and when they broke open the doors, it streamed over them to join the worst blizzard of the season.

15

Don and Peter half-carried Ricky Hawthorne home through the storm; and now there were two convalescents in the Hawthorne home. Peter explained it to his father like this: "I'm staying with Mr. and Mrs. Hawthorne, dad—I'm stuck at their house. Don Wanderley and I had to practically bring Mr. Hawthorne home on a stretcher. He's in bed and so is she, because she feels bad after a little accident in her car—"

"There'll be a lot of accidents on the roads this afternoon," his father said.

"And we finally got a doctor to come give her a sedative, and Mr. Hawthorne has a terrible cold the doctor said could turn into pneumonia if he doesn't rest, so Don Wanderley and I are taking care of them both."

"Let me get this straight, Pete. You were *with* this Wanderley and Mr. Hawthorne?"

"That's right," Peter said.

"Well, I wish you'd thought of calling before this. I was worried half to death. You're all I have, you know."

"I'm sorry, Dad."

"Well, at least you're with good people. Try to get home when you can, but don't take any chances in the storm."

"Okay, Dad," Peter said and hung up, grateful that his father had sounded sober, and even more grateful that he had asked no more questions.

He and Don made soup for Ricky, and brought it up to the guest-room where the old man was resting while his wife slept undisturbed in their bedroom.

"Don't know what happened to me," Ricky said. "I just couldn't move another step. If I'd been alone, I would have frozen to death out there."

"If any of us had been alone," Don said, and did not have to finish the sentence.

"Or if there had been only two of us," Peter said. "We'd be dead. He could have killed us easily."

"Yes, well he didn't," Ricky said briskly. "Don was right about them. And now two-thirds of what we have to do is accomplished."

"You mean we have to find her," Peter said. "Do you think we can do it?"

"We'll do it," Don said. "Stella might be able to tell us something. She might have learned something—heard something. I don't think there's any doubt that the man in the blue car was the same man who was after you. We should be able to talk to her tonight."

"Will it do any good?" Peter asked. "We're snowed in again. We'll never be able to drive anywhere, even if Mrs. Hawthorne does know something."

"Then we'll walk," Don said.

"Yes," Ricky said. "If that's what it takes, we'll walk." And lay back against the pillows. "You know, *we're* the Chowder Society now. The three of us. After Sears was found dead I thought—I said I was the only one left. I felt terribly bereft. Sears was my best friend; he was like my brother. And I'll miss him as long as I live. But I know that when Gregory Bate cornered Sears, Sears put up a hell of a good scrap. He did his best to save Fenny once a long time ago, and I know he did his best against them when his time came. No, there's no need to feel bad about Sears—he probably did better than any of us could have done alone."

Ricky put his empty soup bowl down on the bedside table. "But now there's a new Chowder Society, and here we all are. And there's no whiskey and no cigars, and we're not dressed right—and good heavens, look at me! I'm not even wearing a bow tie." He plucked at the open collar of his pajama shirt and smiled at them. "And I'll tell you one other thing. No more awful stories and no nightmares either. Thank God."

"I'm not so sure about the nightmares," Peter said.

After Peter Barnes went off to his own room to lie down for an hour, Ricky sat up in bed and looked candidly at Don Wanderley through his glasses. "Don, when you first came here you saw that I didn't like you very much. I didn't like you being here, and until I saw that you were like your uncle in certain ways, I didn't much take to you personally. But I don't have to tell you that's all changed, do I? Good Lord, I'm chattering away like a magpie! What was in that shot the doctor gave me, anyhow?"

"A huge dose of vitamins."

"Well, I feel much better. All revved up. I still have that terrific cold, of course, but I've had that so long that it feels like a friend. But listen here, Don. After what we've been through, I couldn't feel closer to you. If Sears felt like my brother, you feel like my son. Closer than my son, in fact. My boy Robert can't talk to me—I can't talk to him. That's been true since he was about fourteen. So I think I'm going to adopt you spiritually, if you don't object."

"It makes me too proud of myself to object," Don said, and took Ricky's hand.

"You sure there were just vitamins in that shot?"

"Well."

"If this is how dope makes you feel, I can understand how John became an addict." He lay back and closed his eyes. "When all this is over, assuming we're still alive, let's stay in touch. I'll take Stella on a trip to Europe. I'll send you a barrage of postcards."

"Of course," Don said, and started to say something, but Ricky was already asleep.

Shortly after ten o'clock, Peter and Don, who had eaten downstairs, brought a grilled steak, a salad and a bottle of burgundy up to Ricky's room. Another plate on the tray held a second steak for Stella. Don knocked on the door, heard Ricky say "Come in," and entered, carrying the heavy tray.

Stella Hawthorne, her hair in a scarf, looked up at Don from beside her husband on the guest-room bed. "I woke up an hour or so ago," she said, "and I got lonely, so I came down here to Ricky. Is that food? Oh, you're lovely, both of you." She smiled at Peter, who was standing shyly in the door.

"While the two of you were eating us out of house and home I had a little talk with Stella," Ricky said. He took the tray and put it on Stella's lap, and then removed one of the plates. "What luxury this is! Stella, we should have had maids years ago."

"I think I mentioned that once," Stella said. Though still obviously shaken and exhausted by shock, Stella had improved enormously during the evening; she did not look like a woman in her forties now, and perhaps she never would again, but her eyes were clear.

Ricky poured wine for himself and Stella and cut off a piece of steak. "There's no doubt that the man who picked up Stella was the same one who followed you, Peter. He even told Stella that he was a Jehovah's Witness."

"But he was *dead*," Stella said, and for a moment the shock swept wholly back into her face. She snatched at Ricky's hand and held it. "He was."

"I know," Ricky said, and turned to the other two again. "But after she came back with help, the body was gone."

"Will you please tell me what is going on?" Stella said, now almost in tears.

"I will," said Ricky, "but not now. We're not finished yet. I'll explain everything to you this summer. When we get out of Milburn."

"Out of Milburn?"

"I'm going to take you to France. We'll go to Antibes and St. Tropez and Arles and anywhere else that looks good. We'll be a pair of funny-looking old tourists together. But first you have to help us. Is that all right with you?"

Stella's practicality saw her through. "It is if you're really promising, and not just bribing me."

"Did you see anything else around the car when you came back with Leon Churchill?" Don asked.

"No one else was there," Stella replied, calmer again.

"I don't mean another person. Any animals?"

"I don't remember. I felt so—sort of unreal. No, nothing."

"You're sure? Try to remember how it looked. The car, the open door, the snowbank you hit—"

"Oh," she said, and Ricky paused with the fork halfway to his mouth. "You're right. I saw a dog. Why is that important? It jumped on top of the snowbank from someone's yard, and then jumped down onto the street. I noticed it because it was so beautiful. White."

"That's it," Don said.

Peter Barnes looked back and forth from Don to Ricky, his mouth open.

"Wouldn't you like some wine, Peter? And you, Don?" Ricky asked.

Don shook his head, but Peter said, "Sure," and Ricky passed him his glass.

"Can you remember anything the man said?"

"It was all so horrible . . . I thought he was crazy. And then I thought he knew me because he called me by name, and he said I shouldn't go to Montgomery Street because you weren't there anymore—where were you?"

"I'll tell you all about it over a Pernod. This spring."

"Anything else you remember?" Don asked. "Did he say where he was taking you?"

"To a friend," Stella said, and shuddered. "He said I'd see a mystery. And he talked about Lewis."

"Nothing more about where his friend was?"

"No. Wait. No." She looked down at her plate, and pushed the tray down toward the foot of the bed. "Poor Lewis. That's enough questions. Please."

"You'd better leave us," Ricky said.

Peter and Don were at the door when Stella said, "I

remember. He said he was taking me to the Hollow. I'm sure he said that."

"That's enough for now," Ricky said. "See you in the morning, gentlemen."

And in the morning, Peter and Don were startled to find Ricky Hawthorne already in the kitchen when they came down. He was scrambling eggs, pausing now and then to blow his nose into Kleenex from a convenient box. "Good morning. Do you want to help me think about the Hollow?"

"You ought to be in bed," Don said.

"Like the dickens I ought to be in bed! Can't you smell how *close* we're getting?"

"I can only smell eggs," Don said. "Peter, get some plates out of the cupboard."

"How many houses are there in the Hollow? Fifty? Sixty? No more than that. And she's *in* one of them."

"In there waiting for us," Don said, and Peter, putting plates on the Hawthorne's kitchen table, paused and set the final plate down more slowly. "And we must have had two feet of snow last night. It's still snowing. You wouldn't call it a blizzard anymore, but we could easily have another blizzard by this afternoon. There's a snow emergency over most of the state. Do you want to hike over to the Hollow and knock on fifty or sixty doors?"

"No, I want us to think," Ricky said, and carried the pan of eggs to the table and spooned a portion onto each plate. "Let's get some bread in the toaster."

When everything was ready, toast and orange juice and coffee, the three of them ate breakfast, following Ricky's lead. He seemed vibrant, sitting at the table in his blue dressing gown; almost elated. And he had obviously been thinking a great deal about the Hollow and Anna Mostyn.

"It's the one part of town we don't know well," Ricky said. "And that's why she's there. She doesn't want us to find her yet. Presumably she knows that her creatures are dead. For the moment, her plans have been delayed. She'll want reinforcements, either more like the Bates or more like herself. Stella got rid of the only other one around with a hatpin."

"How do you know he was the only other one?" Peter asked.

"Because I think we would have encountered any others, if they were here."

They ate in silence for a moment.

"So I think she's just holed up—in a vacant building, most likely—until more of them arrive. She won't be expecting us. She'll think we won't be able to move, in this snow."

"And she'll be vengeful," Don said.

"She might also be afraid."

Peter snapped his head up. "Why do you say that?"

"Because I helped kill her once before. And I'll tell you something else. If we don't find her soon, everything we have done will be wasted. Stella and the three of us bought time for the whole town, but as soon as outside traffic gets in . . ." Ricky bit into a piece of toast. "Things will be even worse than before. She won't just be vengeful, she'll be rabid. Twice we've blocked her. So we'd better lay out everything we can come up with about the Hollow. And we'd better do it now."

"Wasn't it originally the place where the servants lived?" Peter asked. "Back when everybody had servants?"

"Yes," Ricky said, "but there has to be more. I'm thinking of what she said on Don's tape. 'In the places of your dreams.' We found one of those places, but I'm thinking that there must be another one, someplace where we could have been lured if we hadn't found Gregory and Fenny at the Rialto. But I just can't think . . ."

"Do you know anybody who lives there?" Don asked.

"Of course I do. I've lived here all my life. But I can't for the life of me see the connection . . ."

"What did the Hollow used to be like?" Peter asked. "In the old days."

"In the old days? Back when I was a boy, you mean?

Oh, much different—much nicer. It was a lot cleaner than it is now. A bit raffish. We used to think of it as the Bohemian section of town. There was a painter who lived in Milburn then—did magazine covers. He lived there, and he had a splendid white beard and wore a cape—he looked just the way we thought painters should look. Oh, we used to spend a lot of time down there. Used to be a bar with a jazz band. Lewis liked to go there—had a little dancehall. Like Humphrey's place, but smaller and nicer."

"A band?" Peter asked, and Don too lifted his head.

"Oh, yes," Ricky said, not noticing their excitement. "Only a little six-eight piece band, pretty good for anything you'd hear out here in the sticks . . ." He picked up the plates and took them to the sink; ran hot water over them. "Oh, Milburn was lovely in those days. We all used to walk for miles—down to the Hollow and back, hear some music, have a beer or two, take a hike out into the country . . ." His arms deep in soapy water, Ricky abruptly ceased all movement. "Good Lord. I know. I know." Still holding a soapy plate, he turned toward them. "It was Edward. It was Edward, you see. We used to go down to see Edward in the Hollow. That was where he moved when he wanted his own apartment. I was in YPSL, my father hated that—" Ricky dropped the plate, and stepped unseeing over the shattered pieces—"and the owner was one of our first black clients The building's still there! The town council condemned it last spring, and it's supposed to be demolished next year. We *got* Edward that apartment—Sears and I." He wiped his hands on his dressing gown. "That's it. I know that's it. Edward's apartment. *The place of your dreams.*"

"Because Edward's apartment . . ." Don began, knowing that the old man was right.

"Was where Eva Galli died and our dreams began," Ricky said. "By God, we've got her."

16

They dressed in all the warm clothing Ricky had, putting on several layers of underclothes and two shirts— Ricky's shirts couldn't be buttoned over the other two, but they meant two more layers of trapped air—and then sweaters. Two pairs of socks; even Don managed to slide his feet into an old pair of Ricky's lace-up boots. For once, Ricky had a reason to be grateful for his attachment to his clothes. "We have to live long enough to get there," he said, sorting through a box of old wool scarves. "We'll wrap some of these around our faces. It must be about three-fourths of a mile from here to the Hollow. Good thing this is a small town. When we were all in our twenties, we used to walk from this part of town down to Edward's apartment and back two or three times in one day."

"So you're sure you can find the place?" Peter asked.

"I'm reasonably sure," Ricky said. "Now, let's have a look at ourselves." They looked like three snowmen, padded out with so many layers of clothing. "Ah, hats. Well, I have a lot of hats." He fitted a high fur hat over Peter's head, put a red hunting cap that must have been half a century old on his own head, and told Don, "This one was always a little big on me." It was a soft green tweed, and it fitted Don perfectly. "Got it to go fishing with John Jaffrey. Wore it once. Hated fishing." He sneezed and wiped his nose with a peach tissue from his coat pocket. "In those days, I always preferred hunting."

At first Ricky's clothing kept them warm, and as they went through lightly falling snow in a hard bright light, they walked past a few men attacking their driveways with shovels and snow blowers. Children in bright snowsuits played on the drifts, active blots of color in the dazzle of light from the snow. It was five degrees above zero, and the cold attacked the exposed sections of their faces, but they might have been three normal men out on a conventional errand—hunting strayed children or an open store.

But even before the weather changed, walking was difficult for them. Their feet began to feel the cold first, and their legs tired from the effort of wading through the deep snow. They soon gave up the luxury of speech —it took too much energy. Their breath condensed on the heavy wool scarves, and the moisture turned cold and froze. Don knew that the temperature was dropping faster than he'd ever seen it: the snow came down harder, his fingers tingled in the gloves, even his legs began to feel the cold.

And sometimes, when they turned a corner and looked down a street hidden by a long wide drift peaked up fifteen feet high, he thought the three of them resembled photographs of polar explorers—doomed driven men with blackened lips and frozen skin, small figures in a rippling white landscape.

Halfway to the Hollow, Don was sure that the temperature had reached several degrees below zero. His scarf had become a stiff mask over his face, varnished by his breath. Cold bit at his hands and feet. He and Peter and Ricky were just straggling past the square; lifting their feet out of deep snow and leaning forward to get distance on the next step. The tree the mayor and the deputies had set up in the square was visible only as scattered green branches protruding through a mountain of white. Clearing Main Street and Wheat Row, Omar Norris had buried it.

By the time they reached the traffic lights, the brightness had left the air and the piled snow no longer sparkled: it seemed as gray as the air. Don looked up and saw thousands of flakes swirling between dense clouds. They were alone. Down Main Street, the tops of a few cars sat like inverted saucers on the drifts. All the buildings were closed. New snow spun around them: the air was darkening to black.

"Ricky?" he asked. He tasted frozen wool: his cheekbones, open to the air, burned.

"Not far," Ricky gasped. "Keep on going. I'll make it."

"How are you doing, Peter?"

The boy peered out at Don from under the snow-crusted fur cap. "You heard the boss. Keep on going."

The new snow at first fell harmlessly, no more an obstacle than the candy-floss snowfall at the start of their trip; but by the time they had gone three blocks more in a building wind, Don's feet now like two blocks of ice painfully welded to his ankles, the new snow was unequivocally a storm: not falling vertically or spinning prettily, but sleeting down diagonally, at intervals coming in waves like a surf. It stung where it hit. Whenever they reached the end of one of the high-curled drifts snow came straight at them, following the currents of the wind, blasting into their chests and faces.

Ricky fell down backward, and sat up chest high in the snow like a doll. Peter bent down to offer him an arm. Don turned around to see if he could help, and felt the snow-laden wind pound against his back. He called, "Ricky?"

"Just have to. Sit. For a little."

He breathed deeply, and Don know how the cold would be scraping against his throat, how it would chill his lungs.

"No more than two-three blocks," Ricky said. "God my *feet*."

"I just had a hell of a thought. What if she's not there?"

"She's there," Ricky said, and took Peter's hand and pulled himself up. "*It's* there. Few more blocks."

When Don turned back into the storm he could not see for a moment; then he saw thousands of fast-moving particles of white veering toward him, so close together they were like lines of force. Vast semitransparent sheets cut him off from Ricky and Peter. Only partially visible beside him, Ricky motioned him on.

Don was never sure when they crossed into the Hollow: in the storm, it was no different from the rest of

Milburn. Perhaps the buildings seemed marginally shabbier: perhaps fewer lights shone dimly in the depths of rooms, seeming thousands of feet away. Once he had written in his journal that the area had a "sepia '30's prettiness": that seemed unutterably remote now. All was dark gray dirty brick and taped windows. But for the few dim lights flickering behind curtains, it seemed ominous and deserted. Don remembered other facile words he had written in his journal: *if trouble ever comes to Milburn, it won't start in the Hollow*. Trouble had come to Milburn, and here in the Hollow, on a sunny day in mid-October fifty years before, it had started.

The three of them stood in the weak light of a street lamp, Ricky Hawthorne tottering, squinting across the street at three identical high brick buildings. Even in the noises of the storm Don could hear him breathing. "Over there," Ricky said harshly.

"Which one?"

"Can't tell," Ricky said, and shook his head, causing a shower of snow to whirl off the red hunting cap. "Just can't." He peered up into the storm: pointed his face like a dog. The building on the right. Then back to the building in the middle. He raised the hand which held his knife and used it to point at the windows on the third floor. They were curtainless, and one was half-open. "There. Edward's apartment. Just there."

The street lamp over them died, and light faded all about them.

Don stared at the windows high up on the desolate building, half expecting to see a face appear there, beckoning toward them; fear worse than the storm froze him.

"Finally happened," Ricky said. "Storm blew down the power lines. You afraid of the dark?"

The three of them floundered across the drifted street.

17

Don pushed open the building's front door, and the other two followed him into the vestibule. They pulled their scarves away from their faces, their breath steaming in the small cold space. Peter brushed snow from his fur hat and the front of his coat; none of them spoke. Ricky leaned against the wall, looking almost too weak to climb the stairs. A dead light bulb hung over their heads.

"Coats," Don whispered, thinking that the sodden garments would slow them down; he lay the axe down in the dark, unbuttoned his coat and dropped it on the floor. Then the scarf, stinking of wet wool; his chest and arms were still constricted by the tight sweaters, but at least the heaviest weight no longer pulled at his shoulders. Peter too removed his coat, and helped Ricky with his.

Don saw their white faces hovering before him, and wondered if this was the last act—they had the weapons which had destroyed the Bate brothers, but the three of them were limp as rags. Ricky Hawthorne's eyes were closed: thrown back, its muscles lax, his face was a death mask.

"Ricky?" Don whispered.

"A minute." Ricky's hand trembled as he raised it to blow on his fingers. He inhaled, held the air for a long moment, exhaled. "Okay. You'd better go first. I'll bring up the rear."

Don bent down and picked up the axe. Behind him Peter wiped the blade of the Bowie knife against his sleeve. Don found the bottom step with his numb toe and climbed onto it. He glanced back. Ricky stood behind Peter, propping himself against the staircase wall. His eyes were closed again.

"Mr. Hawthorne, do you want to stay down here?" Peter whispered.

"Not on your life."

With the other two following him, Don crept up the
first flight of steps. Once, three well-off young men just
beginning their practices in law and medicine and a
preacher's son of seventeen had gone up and down these
stairs: each of them close to twenty in the century's
twenties. And up these stairs had come the woman with
whom they were infatuated, as he had been infatuated
with Alma Mobley. He reached the second landing, and
peeked around the corner to the top of the last flight of
stairs. With part of his mind, he wished to see an open
door, an empty room, snow blowing unnoticed into an
empty apartment . . .

What he saw instead made him pull back. Peter
looked over his shoulder and nodded; and finally Ricky
appeared on the landing to look up at the door at the
top of the stairs.

A phosphorescent light spilled out from beneath the
door, illuminating the landing and the walls a soft
green.

Silently, they came up the final set of stairs into the
phosphorescent light.

"On three," Don whispered, and cradled his axe just
below the head. Peter and Ricky nodded.

"One. Two." Don gripped the top of the banister
with his free hand. *"Three."*

They hit the door together, and it broke open under
their weight.

Each of them heard a single distinct word; but the
voice delivering it was different for each of them. The
word was *Hello.*

18

Don Wanderley, caught in a huge dislocation, spun
around at the sound of his brother's voice. Warm light
fell around him, traffic noises attacked him. His hands
and feet were so cold they might have been frostbitten,
but it was summer. Summer: New York. He recognized
the corner almost immediately.

It was in the East Fifties, and it was so familiar to him because quite near—somewhere very near—was a cafe with outdoor tables where he had met David for lunch whenever he was in New York.

This was not a hallucination—not a mere hallucination. He *was* in New York, and it was summer. Don felt a weight in his left hand, and looking down, saw that he was carrying an axe. *An axe? Now what . . . ?* He dropped the axe as if it had jumped in his hand. His brother called, "Don! Over here!"

Yes, he had been carrying an axe . . . they had seen green light . . . he had been turning, moving fast . . .

"Don!"

He looked across the street and saw David, looking healthy and extremely prosperous, standing up at one of the outdoor tables, grinning at him and waving. David in a crisp lightweight blue suit, aviator glasses smoked over his eyes, their bows disappearing into David's sun-blond hair. "Wake up!" his brother called over the traffic.

Don rubbed his face with his freezing hands. It was important not to appear confused in front of David— David had asked him to lunch. David had something to tell him.

New York?

But yes, it was New York, and there was David, looking at him amusedly, happy to see him, full of something to say. Don looked down at the sidewalk. The axe was gone. He ran between the cars and embraced his brother and smelled cigars, good shampoo, Aramis cologne. He was here and David was alive.

"How do you feel?" David asked.

"I'm not here and you're dead," came out of his mouth.

David looked embarrassed, then disguised it behind another smile. "You'd better sit down, little brother. You're not supposed to be talking like that anymore." David held his elbow and led him to a chair beneath one of the sun umbrellas. A martini on the rocks chilled a sweating glass.

"I'm not supposed . . ." Don began. He sat heavily in the chair; Manhattan traffic went down the pleasant East Fifties street; on the other side, over the top of the traffic, he read the name of a French restaurant painted in gold on dark glass. Even his cold feet could tell that the pavement was hot.

"You bet you're not," David said. "I ordered a steak for you, all right? I didn't think you'd want anything too rich." He looked sympathetically across the table at Don. The modish glasses hid his eyes, but David's whole handsome face exuded warmth. "Is that suit okay, by the way? I found it in your closet. Now that you're out of the hospital, you'll have to shop for some new clothes. Use my account at Brooks, will you?" Don looked down at what he wore. A tan summer suit, a brown-and-green-striped tie, brown loafers. It all looked a little out of date and shabby beside David's elegance.

"Now look at me and tell me I'm dead," David said.

"You're not dead."

David sighed happily. "Okay. Good. You had me worried there, pal. Now—do you remember anything about what happened?"

"No. Hospital?"

"You had about the worst breakdown anyone's ever seen, brother. It was the next thing to a one-way ticket. Happened right after you finished that book."

"The Nightwatcher?"

"What else? You just blanked out—and when you'd say anything, it was just crazy stuff about me being dead and Alma being something awful and mysterious. You were in outer space. If you don't remember any of this, it's because of the shock treatments. Now we have to get you settled again. I talked to Professor Lieberman, and he says he'll give you another appointment in the fall—he really liked you, Don."

"Lieberman? No, he said I was . . ."

"That was before he knew how sick you were. Anyhow, I got you out of Mexico and put you in a private hospital in Riverdale. Paid all the bills until you got straightened out. The steak'll be here in a minute. Better get that martini down. The house red isn't bad here."

Don obediently sipped at his drink: that familiar cold potent taste. "Why am I so *cold?*" he asked David. "I'm frozen."

"Aftereffect of the drug therapy." David patted his hand. "They told me you'd feel like that for a day or two, cold, not too sure of yourself yet—it'll go away. I promise you."

A waitress came with their food. Don let her take away his martini glass.

"You had all these disturbed ideas," his brother was saying. "Now that you're well again, they'll shock you. You thought my wife was some kind of monster who had killed me in Amsterdam—you were convinced of it. The doctor said you couldn't face the fact that you'd lost her: that's why you never came out here to talk about it. You wound up thinking that what you wrote in your novel was real. After you mailed the book off to your agent, you just sat in a hotel room, not eating, not washing—you didn't even get up to shit. I had to go all the way down to Mexico City to bring you back."

"What was I doing an hour ago?" Don asked.

"You were getting a sedative shot. Then they put you in a cab and sent you down here. I thought you'd like to see the place again. Something familiar."

"I've been in a hospital for a year?"

"Nearly two years. For the past few months, you've been making great progress."

"Why can't I remember it?"

"Simple. Because you don't want to. As far as you're concerned, you were born five minutes ago. But it'll all come back slowly. You can recuperate in our place on the Island—lots of sun, sand, a few women. Like the sound of that?"

Don blinked and looked around. His entire body felt unreasonably cold. A tall woman was just now coming down the block toward them, pulled along by an enormous sheepdog on a leash—the woman was slender and tanned, she wore sunglasses pushed up into her hair, and for a moment she was the emblem of what was real: the epitome of all not hallucinated or imagined, of sanity. She was no one important, she was a stranger, but if what David was telling him was the truth, she meant health.

"You'll see plenty of women," David said, almost laughing. "Don't burn out your eyes on the first one who crosses your path."

"You're married to Alma now," Don said.

"Of course. She's dying to see you. And you know," David said, still smiling, holding a fork with a neatly speared section of meat, "she's kind of flattered about that book of yours. She feels she contributed to literature! But I want to tell you something," and David hitched his chair closer. "Think about the consequences of it, if what you said in that book was true. If creatures like that really existed—and you thought they did, you know."

"I know," Don said. "I thought—"

"Wait. Let me finish. Can't you see how puny we'd look to them? We live—what? A miserable sixty-seventy years, maybe. They'd live for centuries—for a century of centuries. Becoming anything they want to become. Our lives are made by accident, by coincidence, by a blind combination of genes—they make themselves by will. They would detest us. And they'd be right. Next to them, we would be detestable."

"No," Don said. "That's all wrong. They're savage and cruel, they live on death . . ." He felt as though he were about to be sick. "You can't say those things."

"Your problem is that you're still caught up in the story you were telling yourself—even though you're out of it, that story is still hanging around in your memory somewhere. You know, your doctor told me he never saw anything like it—when you flipped, you flipped into a *story*. You'd be walking down the hall in the hospital, and you'd be carrying on a conversation with people who weren't there. You were all wrapped up in some sort of plot. Impressed the hell out of the doctors. You'd be talking to them, and they'd talk back, but you answered back like you were talking to some guy named Sears or another guy named Ricky . . ." David smiled and shook his head.

"What happened at the end of the story?" Don asked.

"Huh?"

"What happened at the end of the story?" Don set down his fork and leaned forward, staring at his brother's bland face.

"They didn't let you get there," David said. "They were afraid to—looked like you were setting yourself up to get killed. See, that was part of your problem. You invented these fantastic beautiful creatures, and then you 'wrote' yourself into the story as their enemy. But nothing like that could ever be defeated. No matter how hard you tried, they'd always win in the end."

"No, that isn't . . ." Don said. That wasn't correct: he could only remember the vague outlines of the "story" David was talking about, but he was sure David was wrong.

"Your doctors said it was the most interesting way for a novelist to commit suicide they ever heard of. So they couldn't let you push it to the end, do you see? They had to bring you out of it."

Don sat as if in freezing wind.

"Hello and welcome back," Sears said. "We've all had that dream, but I imagine you must be the first to have it at one of our meetings."

"What?" said Ricky, snapping up his head and seeing before him Sears's beloved library: the glass-fronted bookcases, the leather chairs drawn into a circle, the dark windows. Immediately across from him, Sears drew on his cigar and gazed at him with what looked like mild annoyance. Lewis and John, holding their whiskey glasses and dressed like Sears in black tie, appeared to be more embarrassed than annoyed.

"What dream?" Ricky said, and shook his head. He too was in evening dress: by the cigar, by the quality of the darkness, by a thousand familiar details, he knew they were at the last stage of a Chowder Society meeting.

"You dozed off," John said. "Right after you finished your story."

"Story?"

"And then," Sears said, "you looked right at me and said, 'You're dead.' "

"Oh. The nightmare," Ricky said. "Oh, yes. Did I really? My goodness, I'm cold."

"At our age, we all have poor circulation," said Dr. Jaffrey.

"What's the date?"

"You really *were* out," Sears said, lifting his eyebrows. "It's the ninth of October."

"And is Don here? Where is Don?" Ricky looked frantically around the library, as if Edward's nephew might be hiding under a chair.

"Really, Ricky," Sears grumped. "We just voted on writing to him, if you remember. It is extremely unlikely that he should appear before the letter is written."

"We have to tell him about Eva Galli," Ricky said, remembering the vote. "It's imperative."

John smiled thinly, and Lewis leaned back in his chair, looking at Ricky as if he thought he'd lost his mind.

"You do make the most amazing reversals," Sears said. "Gentlemen, since our friend here evidently needs his sleep, perhaps we'd better call it a night."

"*Sears,*" Ricky said, suddenly galvanized by another memory.

"Yes, Ricky?"

"Next time we meet—when we meet at John's house—don't tell the story you have in mind. You cannot tell that story. It will have the most appalling consequences."

"Stay here a moment, Ricky," Sears ordered, and showed the other two men out of the room.

He came back carrying the freshly fired-up cigar and a bottle. "You seem to need a drink. It must have been quite a dream."

"Was I out long?" He could hear, down on the street, the sound of Lewis trying to start up the Morgan.

"Ten minutes. No longer. Now what was that about my story for next time?"

Ricky opened his mouth, tried to recapture what had been so important only minutes before, and realized that he must look very foolish. "I don't know any more. Something about Eva Galli."

"I can promise you I was not going to speak about that. I don't imagine any of us ever shall, and I think that really is for the best, don't you?"

"*No*. No. We have to—" Ricky realized he was going to mention Donald Wanderley again, and blushed. "I suppose it must have been part of my dream. Is my window open, Sears? I'm actually freezing. And I feel so tired. I can't imagine what . . ."

"Age. No more or less. We're coming to the end of our span, Ricky. All of us. We've lived long enough, haven't we?"

Ricky shook his head.

"John's dying already. You can see it in his face, can't you?"

"Yes, I thought I saw . . ." Ricky said, thinking back to a time at the start of the meeting—a plane of darkness sliding across John Jaffrey's forehead—which now seemed to have happened years before.

"Death. That's what you thought you saw. It's true, my old friend." Sears smiled benignly at him. "I've been giving this a lot of thought, and you mentioning Eva Galli—well, it stirs it all up. I'll tell you what I've been thinking." Sears drew on the cigar and leaned massively forward. "I think Edward did not die of natural causes. I think he was given a vision of such terrible and unearthly beauty that the shock to his poor mortal system killed him. I think we have been skirting the edges of that beauty in our stories for a year."

"No, not beauty," Ricky said. "Something obscene—something terrible."

"Hold it. I want you to consider the possibility of another race of beings—powerful, all-knowing, beautiful beings. If they existed, they would detest us. We would be cattle compared to them. They'd live for centuries—for a century of centuries, so that you and I would look like children to them. They would not be bound by accident, coincidence or a blind combination of genes. They'd be right to detest us: beside them, we would be detestable." Sears stood up, put down his glass, and began to pace. "Eva Galli. That was where we missed our chance. Ricky, we could have seen things worth our pathetic lives to see."

"They're even vainer than we are, Sears," Ricky said. "Oh. Now I remember. The *Bates*. That's the story you can't tell."

"Oh, that's all finished now," Sears said. "Everything is finished now." He walked to Ricky, and leaned on his chair looking down at him. "I fear that from now on all of us are—is it *hors commerce* or *de combat?*"

"In your case, I am sure it is *hors de combat,*" Ricky said, remembering his lines. He felt terribly ill, shivering, he felt the onslaught of the worst cold of his life: it lay like smoke in his lungs and weighted his arms like a winter's worth of snow.

Sears leaned toward him. "That's true for all of us, Ricky. But still, it was quite a journey, wasn't it?" Sears plugged the cigar in his mouth and reached out to palp Ricky's neck. "I *thought* I saw swollen glands. You'll be lucky not to die of pneumonia." Sears's massive hand circled Ricky's throat.

Helplessly, Ricky sneezed.

"Pay attention to me," David said. "Do you understand the importance of this? You put yourself in a position where the only logical end is your death. So although you consciously imagined these beings you invented as evil, unconsciously you saw that they were superior. That's why your 'story' was so dangerous. Unconsciously, according to your doctor, you saw that they were going to kill you. You invented something so superior to yourself that you wanted to give your life to them. That's dangerous stuff, kid."

Don shook his head.

David put down his knife and fork. "Let's try an experiment. I can prove to you that you want to live. Okay?"

"I know I want to live." He looked across the indisputably real street and saw the indisputably real woman walking up the other side, still tugged along by the sheepdog. No: not walking up the other side, he realized, but coming down it, as she had just come down his side. It was like a film in which the same extra is shown in different scenes, in different roles, jarring you with his presence, reminding you that this is only invention. Still, there she was, moving briskly behind the handsome dog, not an invention but part of the street.

"I'll prove it. I'm going to put my hands around your throat and choke you. When you want me to stop, just say stop."

"That's ridiculous."

David reached quickly across the table and gripped his throat. "Stop," he said. David tightened his muscles, and went up off his chair, knocking the table aside. The carafe toppled and bubbled wine over the tablecloth. None of the other diners appeared to notice, but went on eating and talking in their indisputably real way, indisputably forking food into their indisputably real mouths. "Stop," he tried to say, but now David's hands were bearing down too hard, and he could not form the word. David's face was that of a man writing a report or casting a fly: he knocked the table over with his hip.

Then David's face was not his, but the head of an antlered stag or the huge head of an owl or both of those.

Shockingly near, a man explosively sneezed.

"Hello, Peter. So you want to look behind the scenes." Clark Mulligan backed away from the door of the projection room, inviting him in. "Nice of you to bring him up, Mrs. Barnes. I don't get much company up here. What's the matter? You look sort of confused, Pete."

Peter opened his mouth, closed it again. "I—"

"You could thank him, Peter," his mother said dryly.

"That movie probably shook him up," Mulligan said. "It has that effect on people. I've seen it hundreds of times by now, but it still gets me. That's all it was, Pete. A movie."

"A movie?" Peter said. "No—we were coming up the stairs . . ." He held out his hand and saw the Bowie knife.

"That's where the reel ended. Your mother said you were interested in seeing how it all looks from up here. Since you're the only people in the theater, there's no harm in that, is there?"

"Peter, what in the world are you doing with that knife?" his mother asked. "Give it to me *immediately*."

"No, I have to—ah. I have to—" Peter stepped away from his mother and looked confusedly around at the little projection booth. A corduroy coat draped from a hook; a calendar, a mimeographed piece of paper had been tacked to the rear wall. It was as cold as if Mulligan were showing the movie in the street.

"You'd better settle down, Pete," Mulligan said. "Now here you can see our projectors, the last reel is all ready to go in this one, see, I get them all set up beforehand and when a little mark shows up in a couple of the frames I know I have so many seconds to start up the—"

"What happens at the end?" Peter asked. "I can't get straight in my head just what's—"

"Oh, they all die, of course," Mulligan said. "There's no other way for it to end, is there? When you compare them with what they're fighting, they really do seem sort of pathetic, don't they? They're just accidental little people, after all, and what they're fighting is—well, splendid, after all. You can watch the ending up here with me, if you'd like. Is that okay with you, Mrs. Barnes?"

"He'd better," Christina said, sidling toward him.

"He went into some kind of trance down there. Give me that knife, Peter."

Peter put the knife behind his back.

"Oh, he'll see it soon enough, Mrs. Barnes," Mulligan said, and flicked up a switch on the second projector.

"See what?" Peter asked. "I'm freezing to death."

"The heaters are broken. I'm liable to get chilblains up here. See what? Well, the two men are killed first, of course, and then . . . but watch it for yourself."

Peter bent forward to look through the slot in the wall, and there was the empty interior of the Rialto, there the hollow beam of light widening toward the screen . . .

Beside him, an unseen Ricky Hawthorne loudly sneezed, and he was aware of everything shifting again, the walls of the projection booth seemed to waver, he saw something recoil in disgust, something with the huge head of an animal recoiling as if Ricky had spat on it, and then Clark Mulligan locked back into place again, saying, "Film has a rough spot there, I guess, it's okay now," but his voice was trembling, and his mother was saying, "Give me the knife, Peter."

"It's all a trick," he said. "It's another slimy *trick*."

"Peter, don't be rude," his mother said.

Clark Mulligan looked toward him with concern and puzzlement on his face, and Peter, remembering the advice from some old adventure story, brought the Bowie knife up into Mulligan's bulging stomach. His mother screamed, already beginning to melt like everything around him, and Peter locked both hands on the bone handle and levered the knife up. He cried out in sorrow and misery, and Mulligan fell back into the projectors, knocking them off their stands.

19

"Oh, *Sears*," Ricky said—gasped. His throat blazed. "Oh, my poor friends." For a moment they had all been alive again, and their fragile world had been whole:

the double loss of his friends and their comfortable world reverberated through the whole of his being, and tears burned in his eyes.

"Look, Ricky," he heard Don saying, and the voice was compelling enough to make him turn his head. When he saw what was happening on the floor of the apartment, he sat up. "Peter did it," he heard Don say beside him.

The boy was standing six feet away from them, his eyes intent on the body of the woman lying some little way from them. Don was on his knees, rubbing his neck. Ricky met Don's eyes, saw both horror and pain there, and then both of them looked back down at Anna Mostyn.

For a moment she looked as she had when he had first seen her in the reception room at Wheat Row: a young woman with a lovely fox face and dark hair: even now the old man saw the real intelligence and false humanity in her oval face. Her hand clutched the bone handle protruding out just below her breastbone; dark blood already poured from the long wound. The woman thrashed on the floor, contorting her face; her eyes fluttered. Random flakes of snow whirled in through the open window and settled down on each of them.

Anna Mostyn's eyes flew open, and Ricky braced himself, thinking she would say something; but the lovely eyes drifted out of focus, not seeming to recognize any of the men. A wave of blood gushed from her wound; then another boiled out, sheeting across her body and touching the knees of the two men; she half-smiled, and a third wave rushed across her body and pooled on the floor.

For an instant only, as if the corpse of Anna Mostyn were a film, a photographic transparency over another substance, the three of them saw a writhing life through the dead woman's skin—no simple stag or owl, no human or animal body, but a mouth opened beneath Anna Mostyn's mouth and a body constrained within Anna Mostyn's bloody clothing moved with ferocious life: it was as swirling and varied as an oil slick, and it

angrily flashed out at them for the moment it was
visible; then it blackened and faded, and only the dead
woman lay on the floor.

In the next second, the color of her face died to
chalky white and her limbs curled inward, forced by a
wind the others could not feel. The dead woman drew
up like a sheet of paper tossed on a fire, drawing in,
her entire body curling inward like her arms and legs.
She fluttered and shrank before them, becoming half
her size, then a quarter of her size, no longer anything
human, merely a piece of tortured flesh curling and
shrinking before them, hurtled and buffeted by an un-
felt wind.

The tenement room itself seemed to exhale, releasing
a surprisingly human sigh through whatever was left of
her throat. A green light flashed about them, flaring like a
thousand matches: and the remainder of Anna Mostyn's
body fluttered once more and disappeared into itself.
Ricky, by now leaning forward on his hands and knees,
saw how the particles of snow falling where the body
had been spun around in a vortex and followed it into
oblivion.

Thirteen blocks away, the house across the street
from John Jaffrey's on Montgomery Street expoded into
itself. Milly Sheehan heard the crack of the explosion,
and when she rushed to her front window she was in
time to see the façade of Eva Galli's house fold inward
like cardboard, and then break up into separate bricks
flying inward to the fire already roaring up through the
center of the house.

"The lynx," Ricky breathed. Don took his eyes from
the spot on the floor where Anna Mostyn had dwindled
into vacant air, and saw a sparrow sitting on the sill of
the open window. The little bird cocked its head at the
three of them, Don and Ricky already beginning to
move across the floor toward it, Peter still gazing at the
empty floor, and then the sparrow lifted itself off the
sill and flew out through the window.

"That's it, isn't it?" Peter asked. "It's all over now. We did it all."

"Yes, Peter," Ricky said. "It's all over."

And for a moment the two men exchanged glances of agreement. Don stood up and walked as if idly to the window and saw only a slackening storm. He turned to the boy and embraced him.

20

"How do you feel?" Don asked.

"He asks how I feel," Ricky said, supported by pillows on his bed in the Binghamton hospital. "Pneumonia is no fun. It affects the system adversely. I advise you to refrain from getting it."

"I'll try," Don said. "You almost died. They just got the highway open in time for the ambulance to bring you up here. If you hadn't pulled through, I'd have had to take your wife to France this spring."

"Don't tell that to Stella. She'll run in here and pull my tubes out." He smiled wryly. "She's so eager to get to France she'd even go with a pup like you."

"How long will you have to stay in here?"

"Two more weeks. Apart from the way I feel, it's not too bad. Stella has managed to terrify all the nurses, so they take excellent care of me. Thank you for the flowers, by the way."

"I missed you," Don said. "Peter misses you too."

"Yes," Ricky said simply.

"It's a funny thing about this whole affair. I feel closer to you and Peter—and Sears, I guess I have to say—than anyone since Alma Mobley."

"Well, you know my thoughts about that. I blurted them all out when that young doctor doped me to the gills. The Chowder Society is dead, long live the Chowder Society. Sears once said to me that he wished he wasn't so old. I was a bit taken aback at the time, but I agree with him now. I wish I could see Peter Barnes grow up—I wish I could help him. You'll have to do that for me. We owe him our lives, you know."

"I know. Whatever we don't owe to your cold."

"I was completely befuddled, back in that room."

"So was I."

"Well, thank God for Peter. I'm glad you didn't tell him."

"Agreed. He's been through enough. But there is still a lynx to be shot."

Don nodded.

"Because," Ricky continued, "otherwise she'll just come back again. And keep on coming back until all of us and most of our relatives are dead. I've supported my children for too long to want to see them go that way. And as much as I hate to say it, it looks like it's your job."

"In every way," Don said. "It was really you who destroyed both Gregory and Fenny. And Peter killed their boss. I have to take care of the remaining business."

"I don't envy you the job. But I do have confidence in you. You have the knife?"

"I picked it up off the floor."

"Good. I'd hate to think of it being lost. You know, back in that terrible room I think I saw the answer to one of the puzzles Sears and I and the others used to talk about. I think we saw the reason for your uncle's heart attack."

"I think so too," Don said. "Just for a second. I didn't know that you saw it too."

"Poor Edward. He must have walked into John's spare bedroom, expecting at the worst to find his actress in bed with Freddy Robinson. And instead she—what? Threw off the mask."

Ricky was now very tired, and Don stood up to go. He put a stack of paperback books and a bag of oranges on the table beside Ricky's bed.

"Don?" Even the old man's voice was grainy with exhaustion.

"Yes?"

"Forget about pampering me. Just shoot me a lynx."

21

Three weeks later, when Ricky was at last released from the hospital, the storms had wholly vanished, and Milburn, no longer under siege, convalesced and healed as surely as the old lawyer. Supplies reached the grocery stores and supermarkets: Rhoda Flagler saw Bitsy Underwood at the Bay Tree Market, turned red as a radish and rushed over to apologize for pulling out her hair. "Oh, those were terrible days," Bitsy said. "I probably would have clobbered you if you'd got to that damned pumpkin first."

The schools reopened; businessmen and bankers went back to work, taking down their shutters and facing the mounds of paperwork that had accumulated on their desks; slowly, the joggers and walkers began to appear on Milburn's streets again. Annie and Anni, Humphrey Stalladge's two good-looking barmaids, grieved for Lewis Benedikt and married the men they were living with; they conceived within a week of one another. If they had boys, they'd name them Lewis.

Some businesses never did open up again: a few men had gone bankrupt—you have to pay rent and property taxes on a shop, even if it is buried under a snowdrift. Others closed for more somber reasons. Leota Mulligan thought about running the Rialto by herself, but sold the site to a franchise chain and married Clark's brother six months later: Larry was less a dreamer than Clark had been, but he was a dependable man and good company and he liked her cooking. Ricky Hawthorne quietly closed down the law office, but a young attorney in town persuaded him to sell him the firm's name and goodwill. The new man took back Florence Quast and had new nameplates made for the door and the front of the building. Hawthorne, James was now Hawthorne, James and Whittacker. "Pity his name isn't Poe," Ricky said, but Stella didn't think that was funny.

During all this time, Don waited. When he saw Ricky and Stella, they talked about the travel brochures that now covered the enormous coffee table; when he saw Peter Barnes, they talked about Cornell, about the writers the boy was reading, about how his father was adjusting to life without Christina. Twice Don and Ricky drove to Pleasant Hill and placed flowers on all the graves which had come into being since John Jaffrey's funeral. Buried together in a straight line were Lewis, Sears, Clark Mulligan, Freddy Robinson, Harlan Bautz, Penny Draeger, Jim Hardie—so many new graves, separate piles of earth, still lumpy. In time, when the earth had settled, they would have their headstones. Christina Barnes was buried farther off beneath another heap of raw earth, on half of the double plot Walter Barnes had bought. Elmer Scales's family had been buried closer to the top of the hill, in the Scales family plot first purchased by Elmer's grandfather: a weather-worn stone angel guarded over them. There too they put flowers.

"No sign of a lynx yet," Ricky said as they drove back to town.

"No lynx," Don answered. Both of them knew that when it came, it would not be a lynx; and that the waiting might take months, years.

Don read, looked forward to his dinners with Ricky and Stella, watched entire sequences of movies on television (Clark Gable in a bush jacket turning into Dan Duryea in a gangster's nipped-in suit turning into graceful, winning Fred Astaire in a Chowder Society tuxedo), found he could not write; waited. Often he woke himself up in the middle of the night, weeping. He too had to heal.

In mid-March on a black wintry day just like those he and the Chowder Society had endured, a mail truck delivered a heavy package from a film rental company in New York. It had taken them two months to find a copy of *China Pearl*.

He threaded his uncle's projector and set up the screen and discovered that his hands were trembling so badly that it would have taken him three tries to light a cigarette. Just the sequence of setting up Eva Galli's only movie brought back the apparition of Gregory Bate in the Rialto, where all of them could have died. And he found that he feared that Eva Galli would have Alma Mobley's face.

He had attached the speakers in case someone had added a musical sound track: made in 1925, *China Pearl* was a silent film. When he switched the projector on and sat back to watch, holding a drink to help his nerves, he discovered that the print had been altered by the distribution company. It was not just *China Pearl,* it was number thirty-eight in a series called "Classics of the Silent Screen"; besides a soundtrack, a commentary had been added. That meant, Don knew, that the film had been heavily edited.

"One of the greatest stars of the silent era was Richard Barthelmess," said the announcer's colorless voice, and the screen showed the actor walking down a mock-up of a street in Singapore. He was surrounded by Hollywood Filipinos and Japanese dressed as Malays—they were supposed to be Chinese. The announcer went on to describe Barthelmess's career, and then summarized a story about a will, a stolen pearl, a false accusation of murder: the first third of the film had been cut. Barthelmess was in Singapore looking for the true murderer, who had stolen "the famous Pearl of the Orient." He was aided by Vilma Banky, who owned a bar "frequented by waterfront scum" but "as a Boston girl, has a heart the size of Cape Cod . . ."

Don turned the speakers off. For ten minutes he watched the lipsticked little actor gaze soulfully at Vilma Banky, topple villainous "waterfront scum," run about on boats: he hoped that if Eva Galli would appear in this butchered version, he would recognize her. Vilma Banky's bar housed a number of women who draped themselves over the customers and languorously sipped tall drinks. Some of these prostitutes were plain, some of them were stunning: any of them, he supposed, could have been Eva Galli.

But then a girl appeared framed in the doorway of the bar, studio fog boiling behind her, and pouted at the camera. Don looked at her sensual, large-eyed face, and felt his heart freeze. He hurriedly switched on the soundtrack.

". . . the notorious Singapore Sal," crooned the announcer. "Will she get to our hero?" Of course she was not the notorious Singapore Sal, that was an invention of whoever had written the inane commentary; but he knew she was Eva Galli. She sauntered through the bar and approached Barthelmess; she stroked his cheek. When he brushed her hand away, she sat down on his lap and kicked one leg in the air. The actor dumped her on the floor. "So much for Singapore Sal," gloated the announcer.

Don yanked out the speaker leads, stopped the film and backed it up to Eva Galli's entrance, and watched the sequence again.

He had expected her to be beautiful, and she was not. Beneath the makeup, she was just a girl of ordinary good looks; she looked nothing like Alma Mobley. She had enjoyed the business of acting, he saw, playing the part of an ambitious girl playing a part had amused her—how she would have enjoyed stardom! As Ann-Veronica Moore, she had played at it again; even Alma Mobley had seemed fitted for the movies. She could have molded that passive beautiful face over a thousand characters. But in 1925, she had miscalculated, made a mistake: cameras exposed too much, and what you saw when you looked at Eva Galli on screen was a young woman who was not likable. Even Alma had not been likable; even Anna Mostyn, when truly seen—as at the Barnes's party—seemed coldly perverse, driven by willpower. They could for a time evoke human love, but nothing in them could return it. What you finally saw was their hollowness. They could disguise it for a time, but never finally, and that was their greatest mistake; a mistake in being. Don thought he could recognize it anywhere now, in any nightwatcher pretending to be man or woman.

22

At the beginning of April Peter Barnes came to visit him. The boy, who had seemed to be recovering from their terrible winter, slumped into a chair and ran his hands over his face. "I'm sorry to interrupt you. If you're busy I'll go away again."

"You can always come to see me," Don said. "You never have to think twice about it. I mean that, Peter. I'll never be anything but happy to see you. That's a guarantee."

"I was hoping you'd say something like that. Ricky's leaving in a week or two, isn't he?"

"Yes. I'm driving them to the airport next Friday. They're both very excited about their trip. But if you want to see Ricky now, all I have to do is call him up. He'll come."

"No, please don't," the boy said. "It's bad enough I'm bothering you . . ."

"For God's sake, Peter," Don said. "What's the matter?"

"Well, it's just that I've been having an awful time lately. That's why I wanted to see you."

"I'm glad you did. What's wrong?"

"I keep seeing my mother," Peter said. "I mean, I dream about her all the time. It's like I'm back in Lewis's house, and I'm seeing that Gregory Bate grab her again—and I keep dreaming about the way he looked on the floor of the Rialto. All those smashed-up pieces of him moving around. Refusing to die." He was close to tears.

"Have you talked to your father about it?"

Peter nodded. "I tried. I wanted to tell him everything, but he won't listen. Not really. He looks at me like I'm five years old and telling him some made-up nonsense. So I stopped before I really started."

"You can't blame him, Peter. Nobody who hadn't been with us could believe it. If he can listen to part of it and not tell you you're crazy, maybe that's enough. Part of him was listening. Maybe part of him believes it. You know, I think there's another problem too. I think you're afraid that if you give up the horror and fear, that you'll also be giving up your mother. Your mother loved you. And now she's dead, and she died in a terrible way, but she put her love into you for seventeen or eighteen years, and there's a lot of it left. The only thing you can do is carry on with it."

Peter nodded.

Don said, "I once knew a girl who spent all day in a library and said she had a friend who protected her from vileness. I don't know how her life turned out, but I do know that nobody can protect anybody else from vileness. Or from pain. All you can do is not let it break you in half and keep on going until you get to the other side."

"I know that's true," Peter said, "but it just seems so hard to do."

"You're doing it right now. Coming here and talking to me is part of getting to the other side. Going to Cornell will be another big part of it. You'll have so much work to do that you won't be able to brood about Milburn."

"Can I see you again? After I'm in college?"

"You can come to see me anytime at all. And if I'm not in Milburn, I'll write to let you know where I am."

"Good," Peter said.

23

Ricky sent him postcards from France; Peter continued to visit, and gradually Don saw that the boy was beginning to let the Bate brothers and Anna Mostyn fade into the background of his experience. In warm weather, with a new girlfriend who was also going to Cornell, Peter was beginning to relax.

But it was a false peace, and Don still waited. He never let Peter see his own tension, but it grew every week.

He had watched new arrivals to Milburn, had managed to look at all the tourists who checked into the Archer Hotel, but none of them had given him the thrill of fear Eva Galli had projected across fifty years. Several nights after drinking too much, Don dialed Florence de Peyser's telephone number and said, "This is Don Wanderley. Anna Mostyn is dead." The first time, the person at the other end simply replaced the phone in its cradle; the second time, a female voice said, "Isn't this Mr. Williams at the bank? I think your loan is about to be recalled, Mr. Williams." The third time, an operator's voice told him that the telephone had been switched to an unlisted number.

The other half of his anxiety was that he was running out of money. His bank account had no more than two or three hundred dollars in it—now that he was drinking again, enough for only a couple of months. After that he would have to find a job in Milburn, and any sort of job would keep him from patrolling the streets and shops, searching for the being whose arrival Florence de Peyser had promised.

He spent two or three hours every day, now that the weather was warm, sitting on a bench near the playground in Milburn's only park. You have to remember their time scale, he told himself: you have to remember that Eva Galli gave herself fifty years to catch up with the Chowder Society. A child growing up unobtrusively in Milburn could give Peter Barnes and himself fifteen or twenty years of apparent safety before beginning to play with them. And then it would be someone everybody knew; it would have a place in Milburn; it would not be as visible as a stranger. This time, the night-watcher would be more careful. The only limit on its time would be that it would want to act before Ricky died of natural causes—so perhaps it had to be ready in ten years.

How old would that make it now? Eight or nine. Ten, perhaps.

If.

24

And that was how he found her. At first, he was doubtful, watching the girl who had appeared at the playground one afternoon. She was not beautiful, not even attractive—she was dark and intense, and her clothes never seemed to be clean. The other children avoided her, but children often did that; and her air of separation from them, swinging herself in lonely arcs or bouncing up and down on an otherwise empty teeter-totter, could have been a resilient child's defense against rejection.

But perhaps children were quicker at seeing real difference than adults.

He knew he would have to make up his mind quickly: his account had shrunk to a hundred and twenty-five dollars. But if he took the girl away and he was wrong, what was he: a maniac?

He started wearing the Bowie knife strapped to his side beneath his shirt when he went to the playground.

Even if he was right and the girl Ricky's "lynx," she could stick to her role—if he took her away, she could damage him irreparably by not revealing anything and waiting for the police to find them. But the night-watcher wanted them dead: if he was right, he did not think she would let the police and the legal system punish him for her. She liked gaudier conclusions than that.

She seemed to take no notice of him, but the child began to appear in his dreams, sitting off to one side, observing him expressionlessly, and he imagined that even when she was sitting on a swing, seemingly absorbed, she peeked at him.

Don had only one real clue that she was not the ordinary child she appeared to be, and he clung to it with a fanatic's desperation. The first time he had seen her, he had gone cold.

He became a fixture in the park, a motionless man who never had his hair cut and seldom shaved, after some weeks as much to be expected at his place on the bench as the swings were in their places. Ned Rowles had done a short piece about him in *The Urbanite* in the early spring, so he was recognized, not molested or chased away by a deputy. He was a writer, presumably he was thinking about a book; he owned property in Milburn. If people thought he was odd, they liked having a well-known eccentric in their town; and he was known to be a friend of the Hawthornes.

Don closed out his account and took his remaining money away in cash; he could not sleep, even when he drank too much; he knew he was falling back into the patterns of his breakdown after David's death. Each morning, he taped the big knife to his side before walking to the park.

If he did not act, he knew, one day he would not be able to leave his bed: his indecision would spin back into every atom of his life. It would paralyze him. This time he would not be able to write his way out of it.

One morning he motioned to another of the children, and the little boy shyly came up to him.

"What's the name of that girl?" he asked, pointing.

The boy shuffled his feet, blinked and said, "Angie."

"Angie what?"

"Don't know."

"Why doesn't anybody ever play with her?"

The boy squinted at him, cocking his head; then, deciding that he could be trusted, leaned forward charmingly, cupping his hands beside his mouth to tell a dark secret. "Because she's *awful*." He scampered away, and the girl swung back and forth, back and forth, higher and higher, uncaring.

Angie. Sitting inside his sweaty clothes under a warm eleven o'clock sun, he froze.

That night, in the midst of some harried dream, Don

fell out of bed and staggered to his feet, holding a head which felt as though it had fractured like a dropped plate. He went into the kitchen for a glass of water and aspirin, and saw—imagined he saw—Sears James sitting at the dining-room table playing solitaire. The hallucination looked at him disgustedly, said, "It's about time you straightened out, isn't it?" and went back to its game.

He returned to the bedroom and began throwing clothes into a suitcase, taking the Bowie knife from the top of the dresser and rolling it up in a shirt.

At seven o'clock, unable to wait any longer, he drove to the park, went to his bench and waited.

The girl appeared, walking across the damp grass, at nine. She wore a shabby pink dress he had seen many times before, and she moved swiftly, wrapped as ever in her private isolation. They were alone for the first time since Don had thought of watching the playground. He coughed, and she looked directly at him.

And he thought he understood that all of these weeks, he sitting rooted to his bench and fearing for his sanity, she obliviously, concentratedly playing by herself, had been part of her game. Even the doubt (which still would not leave him) was part of the game. She had tired him, weakened him, tortured him as she had surely tortured John Jaffrey before persuading him to jump from the bridge into a freezing river. If he was right.

"You," he said.

The girl sat on a swing and looked across the playground to him.

"You."

"What do you want?"

"Come here."

She stood up off the swing and began to march toward him. He couldn't help it—he was afraid of her. The girl paused two feet in front of him and looked into his face with unreadable black eyes.

"What's your name?"

"Angie. Nobody ever talks to me."

"Angie what?"

"Angie Messina."

"Where do you live?"

"Here. In town."

"Where?"

She pointed vaguely east—the direction of the Hollow.

"You live with your parents?"

"My parents are dead."

"Then who do you live with?"

"Just people."

"Have you ever heard of a woman named Florence de Peyser?"

She shook her head: and maybe it was true, maybe she had not.

He looked up toward the sun, sweating, unable to speak.

"What do you want?" the girl demanded to know.

"I want you to come with me."

"Where?"

"For a ride."

"Okay," she said.

Trembling, he left the bench. As simple as that. *As simple as that.* No one saw them go.

What's the worst thing you've ever done? Did you kidnap a friendless girl and drive without sleeping, hardly eating, stealing money when your own melted away . . . did you point a knife toward her bony chest?

What was the worst thing? Not the act, but the ideas about the act: the garish film unreeling through your head.

Epilogue

Moth in a Killing Jar

"Put the knife away," said his brother's voice. "You hear me, don't you, Don? Put it away. It won't do you any good anymore."

Don opened his eyes and saw the open-air restaurant about him, the gilt lettering across the street. David sat across the table, still handsome, still radiating concern, but dressed in a moldering sack which once had been a suit; the lapels were gray with fine dust, the seams sprouted white threads. Mold grew up the sleeves.

His steak and a half-full wineglass were before him; in his right hand he held a fork, in his left a bone-handled Bowie knife.

Don freed a button on his shirt and slid the knife between his shirt and his skin. "I'm sick of these tricks," he said. "You're not my brother, and I'm not in New York. We're in a motel room in Florida."

"And you haven't had nearly enough sleep," his brother said. "You really look like you're in terrible shape." David propped one elbow on the table and lifted the smoky aviator glasses off his eyes. "But may-

be you're right. It doesn't unsettle you so much anymore, does it?"

Don shook his head. Even his brother's eyes were
right; that seemed indecent, that she should have copied
his eyes so exactly. "It proves I was right," he said.

"About the little girl in the park, you mean. Well, of
course you were right about her. You were supposed to
find her—haven't you worked that out yet?"

"Yes. I did."

"But in a few hours little Angie, the poor orphan
girl, will be back in the park. In ten or twelve years,
she'll be just about the age for Peter Barnes, wouldn't
you say? Of course, poor Ricky will have killed himself
long before that."

"Killed himself."

"Very easy to arrange, dear brother."

"Don't call me *brother*," Don said.

"Oh, we're brothers all right," David said, and smiled
as he snapped his fingers.

In the motel room, a weary-looking black man settled
back into the chair facing him and unclipped a tenor
saxophone from the strap around his neck. "Now me,
of course, you know," he said, putting the saxophone
down on a bedside table.

"Dr. Rabbitfoot."

"The celebrated."

The musician had a heavy, authoritative face, but
instead of the gaudy minstrel's getup Don had imagined
him wearing, he dressed in a rumpled brown suit shot
with iridescent threads of a paler, almost pinkish brown;
and he too looked rumpled, tired from a life spent on
the road. Dr. Rabbitfoot's eyes were as flat as the little
girl's, but their whites had turned the yellow of old
piano keys.

"I didn't imagine you very well."

"No matter. I don't take offense easy. You can't think
of everything. In fact, there's a lot you didn't think of."
The musician's breathy confidential voice had the timbre
of his saxophone. "A few easy victories don't mean you
won the war. Seems like I be reminding folks of that

a lot. I mean, you got me here, but where did you get *yourself?* That's an example of the kind of thing you gotta keep in mind, Don."

"I got face to face with you," Don said.

Dr. Rabbitfoot lifted his chin and laughed:

and in the middle of the laugh, which was hard and explosive, as regular as a stone skipping over water, Don was in Alma Mobley's apartment, all of the luxurious objects in their old places around him, and Alma was seated on a cushion before him.

"Well, that's hardly new, is it?" she asked, still laughing. "Face to face—that's a position we knew many times, as I remember it. Top to tail, too."

"You're despicable," he said. These transformations were starting to work: his stomach burned and his temples ached.

"I thought you got beyond that," she said in her glancing, sunshiny voice. "After all, you know more about us than nearly anyone on this planet. If you don't like our characters, at least you should respect our abilities."

"No more than I respect the sleazy tricks of a night-club magician."

"Then I'll have to teach you to respect them," she said and leaned forward and was David, half his skull flattened and his jaw broken and his skin broken and bleeding in a dozen places.

"Don? For God's sake, Don . . . can't you help me? Jesus, Don." David pitched sideways on the Bokhara rug and groaned with pain. *"Do* something—for God's sake . . ."

Don could not bear it. He ran around his brother's body, knowing if he bent over to help David they would kill him, and opened the door of Alma's apartment, shouted *"No!"* and saw that he was in a crowded, sweaty room, a nightclub of some sort (It's only because I said *nightclub,* he thought, she picked up the word and yanked me into it) where black and white people sat together at small round tables facing a bandstand.

Dr. Rabbitfoot was sitting on the edge of the bandstand, nodding at him. The saxophone was back on its chain, and he fingered the keys as he spoke.

"You see, boy, you *got* to respect us. We can take your brain and turn it to cornmeal mush." He pushed himself off the stand and came toward Don. "Pretty soon"—and now, shockingly, Alma's voice came from his wide mouth—"you don't know where you are or what you're doing, everything inside you is all mixed up, you don't know what's a lie and what isn't." He smiled. Then in the doctor's voice again, and lifting the saxophone toward Don, he said, "You take this horn here. I can tell little girls I love them through this horn, and that's probably a lie. Or I can say I'm hungry, and that sure as hell ain't no lie. Or I can say something beautiful, and who knows if that's a lie or not? It's a complicated business, see?"

"It's too hot in here," Don said. His legs were trembling and his head seemed to be spinning in wide arcs. The other musicians on the stand were tuning up, some of them hitting the A the piano player fed them, others running scales: he was afraid that when they started to play, the music would blow him to pieces. "Can we leave?"

"You got it," said Dr. Rabbitfoot. The yellow around his pupils shone.

The drummer splashed a cymbal, and a throbbing note from a bass vibrated through the humid air like a bird, taking his stomach with it, and all the musicians came in together, the sound hitting him like an enormous breaker,

And he was walking along a Pacific beach with David, both of them barefoot, a seagull gliding overhead, and he didn't want to look at David, who wore the dreadful moldering gravesuit, so he looked at the water and saw shimmering, iridescent layers of oil sliding through the pools around them. "They just got it all," David was saying, "they watched us so long they know us right down to the ground, you know? That's why we can't win—that's why I look this way. You can get a few lucky breaks like you did back in Milburn, but believe me, they won't let you get away now. And it's not so bad."

"No?" Don whispered, almost ready to believe it, and looked past David's terrible head and saw behind them, up on a bluff, the "cottage" he and Alma had stayed in, several thousand years before.

"It's like when I first went into practice," David explained, "I thought I was such hot stuff, Don—Jesus, I thought I'd turn the place upside down. But the old guys in that firm, Sears and Ricky, they knew so many tricks, they were smooth as grease, man. And I was the only thing that got turned upside down. So I just settled down to learn, brother, I apprenticed myself to them, and I decided that if I was ever going to go anywhere I had to learn to be just like they were. That's how I got ahead."

"Sears and Ricky?" Don asked.

"Sure. Hawthorne, James and Wanderley. Isn't that what it was?"

"In a way it was," Don said, blinking into a red sun.

"In a *big* way. And that's what you have to do now, Don. You have to learn to honor your betters. Humility. Respect, if you like. See, these guys, they live forever, and they know us inside out, when you think you got them pinned down they wiggle out and come up fresh as flowers—just like the old lawyers in my first firm. But I learned, see, and I got all this." David gestured encompassingly around, taking in the house, the ocean, the sun.

"All this," Alma said, beside him now in her white dress, "and me too. Like your saxophone player says, it's a complicated business."

The patterns of oil in the water deepened, and the sliding colors wrapped around his shins.

"What you need, boy," Dr. Rabbitfoot said beside him, "is a way out. You got an icicle in your belly and a spike through your head, and you're as tired as three weeks of a Georgia summer. You gotta get to the final bar. You need a door, son."

"A door," Don repeated, ready to drop, and found

himself looking at a tall wooden door upended in the
sand. A sheet of paper was pinned to it at eye level;
Don trudged forward and saw the typed letters on the
sheet.

Gulf View Motor Lodge

1. The Management requests that all guests depart
   by noon, or pay another night's cabin rental.

2. We respect your property, please respect ours.

3. No frying, grilling or boiling in the cabins.

4. The Management wishes you a hearty welcome,
   a happy stay and a purposeful departure.

The Management.

"See?" David said behind him. "A purposeful departure. You have to do what the Management tells
you to do. That's what I was talking about—open it,
Don."

Don opened the door and walked through. Broiling
Florida sun fell on him, lay across the shining asphalt
of the parking lot. Angie was standing before him, holding open the door of his car. Don staggered and leaned
on the baking red flank of a Chevrolet van; the man
who resembled Adolf Eichmann, immured in his concrete booth, turned his head to stare at him. Light
gleamed from his thin gold spectacles.

Don got in the car.

"Now just drive on out," Dr. Rabbitfoot said beside
him, leaning back into the car seat. "You found that
door you needed, didn't you? It's all gonna work out
fine."

Don pulled out into the exit lane. "Which way?"

"Which way, son?" The black man giggled, and then
gave his breathy, explosive laugh. "Why, *our* way. That's
the only way you got. We're just gonna get off by ourselves somewhere in the countryside, you see that?"

And of course, he did see it: turning out onto the

highway in the direction away from Panama City, he
saw not the road but a broad field, a checkered tablecloth on grass, a windmill turning in a scented breeze.
"Don't," he said. "Don't do that."

"Fine, son. You just drive."

Don peered ahead, saw the yellow line dividing the
highway, gasped for air. He was tired enough to fall
asleep driving.

"Boy, you stink like a goat. You need a shower."

As soon as the musical voice had ceased, a shattering
rain hit the windshield. He switched on the wipers, and
when the windows cleared for a moment, saw sheets of
rain bouncing off the highway, slicing down through
suddenly darkened air.

He screamed and, not knowing he was going to do
it, stamped on the accelerator.

The car squealed forward, rain pouring in through
the open window, and they shot over the edge of the
highway and plummeted down the bank.

His head struck the wheel and he knew the car was
rolling over, flipping once and bouncing him up on the
seat, then flipping again and righting itself, pointed
downward, rolling free toward the railroad tracks and
the Gulf.

Alma Mobley stood on the tracks, holding up her
hands as if that would stop them: she flickered out like
a light bulb as the car jounced over the tracks and went
on gathering speed toward the access road.

"You damned cracker," Dr. Rabbitfoot shouted, violently rocked into him and then rocked back against
the door.

Don felt a sudden pain in his shirt, clasped his hand
over it, and found the knife. He ripped open his shirt,
shouting something that was not words, and when the
black man lunged at him, met him with the blade.

"Damn . . . *cracker*," Dr. Rabbitfoot managed to
gasp. The knife bumped against a rib, the musician's
eyes widened and his hand closed around Don's wrist,

and Don pushed, *willing* it: the long blade scraped past the rib and found the heart.

Alma Mobley's face appeared across the windshield, wild and raddled as a hag's, screeching at him. Don's head was jammed into Dr. Rabbitfoot's neck; he felt blood pouring out over his hand.

The car lifted six inches off the ground, hoisted by an internal blast of wind that battered Don against the door and tore his shirt up into his face. They bounded off the access road and rode on the nightwatcher's death down into the Gulf.

The car mired itself in water and Don watched the man's body shriveling and shrinking as Anna Mostyn's had done. He felt warmth on his neck and knew that the rain had stopped before he saw the sunlight streaming across the whipping, tortured form blown back and forth on the car seat. Water poured in through the bottom of the doors; spouts of it whirled up to join Dr. Rabbitfoot's last dance. Pencils and maps on the dashboard lifted off and whirled too.

A thousand screaming voices surrounded him.

"Now, you bastard," he whispered, waiting for the moan from the spirit inhabiting that disappearing form.

A whirling pencil winked into invisibility: vibrant greenish light colored everything like a flash of green lightning. *Cracker,* hissed a voice from nowhere, and the car pitched violently, and shafts of color as violent as that, as if the car were a prism, burst out from the center of the pinwheeling water.

Don aimed at a spot inches above the vortex and shot out his hands, throwing himself forward just as his ear recorded that the last hissing of the voice had become an angry, enduring buzz.

His hands closed around a form so small that at first he thought he had missed it. His motion carried him forward, and his joined hands struck the edge of the window and he tumbled off the seat into the water.

The thing in his hands stung him.

LET ME GO!

It stung him again, and his hand felt the size of footballs. He scraped his palms together and rolled it into his left hand.

RELEASE ME!

He squeezed his fingers down into his palm, and was stung again before the enormous voice in his head dampened into a thin, wriggling shriek.

Crying now, partly from pain but far more from a savage sense of triumph that made him feel he was shining like the sun, streaming light from every pore, he used his right hand to take the knife from the sodden car seat and push the passenger door open against the lapping water of the Gulf.

Then the voice in his mind widened out like a hunting horn. The wasp stung him twice rapidly, hitting the base of two fingers.

Don crawled sobbing across the seat and dropped out into the waist-high water. *Time to see what happens when you shoot the lynx.* He stood up and saw a row of men standing seventy yards off outside the sheds, staring at him in the sun. An overweight man in a security guard's uniform was running down to the edge of the water.

Time to see what happens. Time to see. He waved the security guard away with his right hand, and dropped the left into the water to stun the wasp.

The guard saw the knife in his hand, and put his own hand on his holster. "You okay?" he shouted.

"Get away!"

"Look, buddy—"

RELEASE ME!

The guard lowered his hand, backed a few inches up the beach, bewilderment chasing the belligerence from his face.

YOU HAVE TO LET ME GO!

"Like hell I do," Don said, and came up onto the sand and went to his knees, cramping his left hand down again. "Time to shoot the lynx."

He raised the knife over his swollen, flaming left hand and curled back the fingers a fraction of an inch at a time. When a part of the wasp's body, struggling legs and a bloated hindquarters, was uncovered, he slashed down with the knife, laying open his hand.

NO! YOU CANNOT DO THIS!

He tilted his palm and dropped the severed section of the wasp onto the sand. Then he slashed down again and cut the remainder of the wasp in half.

NO! NO! NO! NO! CANNOT!

"Hey, mister . . ." said the security guard, coming nearer across the sand. "You cut your hand all to hell."

"Had to," Don said, and dropped the knife beside the pieces of the wasp. The enormous flaring voice had become a shrill piping scream. The guard, still red-faced and fuddled, looked down at the pieces of the wasp, twitching and rolling feverishly over the sand. "Wasp," he said. "Thought maybe that freak storm took you off the . . . uh . . ." He rubbed his mouth. "It prob'ly stung you right then, huh? Jeeze, I never knew those things live when they're . . . uh . . ."

Don was winding his shirt around his wounded hand, and he dropped it back into salt water to help it heal.

"Guess you wanted revenge on the l'il sonofabitch, huh?" the guard said.

"I did," Don said, and met the man's baffled eyes and laughed. "That's right, I did."

"Yeah, you got it too," the guard said. Both of them watched the severed pieces of wasp rolling in the wet sand. "That thing ain't *ever* gonna give up the ghost."

"Doesn't look like it." Don used his shoe to scrape sand over the wriggling sections of the wasp. Even then dimples and depressions in the sand showed that the thing continued to struggle.

"Tide'll come in and take it," the guard said. He motioned toward the sheds, the rank of curious men. "Can we do anything for you? We could get a truck out here, call from the plant to get your car hauled out."

"Let's do that. Thank you."

"You got somewhere you got to go in a hurry?"

"Not in a hurry," Don said, knowing all at once what he had to do next. "But there's a woman I have to meet in San Francisco." They began to go toward the sheds and the quiet men. Don stopped to look back; saw only sand. Now he could not even find the spot where he had buried it.

"Tide'll take that l'il bastard halfway to Bolivia," the fat guard said. "You don't want to worry about that anymore, friend. It'll be fishfood by five o'clock."

Don tucked the knife into his belt and experienced a wave of love for everything mortal, for everything with a brief definite life span—a tenderness for all that could give birth and would die, everything that could live, like these men, in sunshine. He knew it was only relief and adrenalin, but it was all the same a mystical, perhaps a sacred emotion. Dear Sears. Dear Lewis. Dear David. Dear John, unknown. And dear Ricky and Stella, and dear Peter too. Dear brothers, dear humankind.

"For a guy whose car is turning into salt rust, you look awful happy," the guard said.

"Yes," Don answered. "Yes, I am. Don't ask me to explain it."